Walter Besant

The Captain's Room etc.

Walter Besant

The Captain's Room etc.

ISBN/EAN: 9783337161194

Printed in Europe, USA, Canada, Australia, Japan

Cover: Foto ©Andreas Hilbeck / pixelio.de

More available books at **www.hansebooks.com**

THE CAPTAINS' ROOM

ETC.

BY

WALTER BESANT

AUTHOR OF 'ALL SORTS AND CONDITIONS OF MEN' ETC.

A NEW EDITION

WITH A FRONTISPIECE BY E. J. WHEELER

LONDON

CHATTO & WINDUS

1897

CONTENTS.

THE CAPTAINS' ROOM.

'LET NOTHING YOU DISMAY.'

THEY WERE MARRIED.

PART I.—MON DÉSIR.

PART II.—IN THE SEASON.

THE CAPTAINS' ROOM.

CHAPTER I.

THE MESSAGE OF THE MUTE.

PERHAPS the most eventful day in the story of which I have to tell, was that on which the veil of doubt and misery which had hung before the eyes of Lal Rydquist for three long years was partly lifted. It was so eventful, that I venture to relate what happened on that day first of all, even though it tells half the story at the very beginning. That we need not care much to consider, because, although it is the story of a great calamity long dreaded and happily averted, it is a story of sorrow borne bravely, of faith, loyalty, and courage. A story such as one loves to tell, because, in the world of fiction, at least, virtue should always triumph, and true hearts be rewarded. Wherefore, if there be any who love to read of the mockeries of fate, the wasting of good women's love, the success of craft and treachery, instances of which are not wanting in the world, let them go elsewhere, or make a Christmas tale for themselves ; and their joy bells, if they like it, shall be the funeral knell, and their noels a dirge beside the grave of ruined and despairing innocence, and for their feast they may have the bread and water of affliction.

The name of the girl of whom we are to speak was Alicia Rydquist, called by all her friends Lal ; the place of her birth and home was a certain little-known suburb of London, called Rotherhithe. She was not at all an aristocratic person, being nothing but the daughter of a Swedish sea-captain and an English wife. Her father was dead, and, after his death, the widow kept a captains' boarding-house, which of late, for reasons which will presently appear, had greatly risen in repute.

The day which opens my story, the day big with fate, the day from which everything that follows in Lal's life, whether that be short or long, will be dated, was the fourteenth of October, in the

B

grievous year of rain and ruin, one thousand eight hundred and seventy-nine. And though the summer was that year clean forgotten, so that there was no summer at all, but only the rain and cold of a continual and ungracious April, yet there were vouchsafed a few gracious days of consolation in the autumn, whereof this was one, in which the sun was as bright and warm as if he had been doing his duty like a British sailor all the summer long, and was proud of it, and meant to go on giving joy to mankind until fog and gloom time, cloud and snow time, black frost and white frost time, short days and long nights time, should put a stop to his benevolent intentions.

At eleven o'clock in the forenoon, both the door and the window belonging to the kitchen of the last house of the row called 'Seven Houses' were standing open for the air and the sunshine.

As to the window, which had a warm south aspect, it looked upon a churchyard. A grape vine grew upon the side of the house, and some of its branches trailed across the upper panes, making a green drapery which was pleasant to look upon, though none of its leaves this year were able to grow to their usual generous amplitude, by reason of the ungenerous season. The churchyard itself was planted with planes, lime-trees, and elms, whose foliage, for the like reason, was not yellow, as is generally the case with such trees in mid-October, but was still green and sweet to look upon. The burying-ground was not venerable for antiquity, because it was less than a hundred years old, church and all ; but yet it was pleasing and grateful—a churchyard which filled the mind with thoughts of rest and sleep, with pleasant dreams. Now, the new cemeteries must mostly be avoided, because one who considers them falls presently into grievous melancholy, which, unless diverted, produces insanity, suicide, or emigration. They lend a new and a horrid pang to death.

It is difficult to explain why this churchyard, more than others, is a pleasant spot : partly, perhaps, on account of the bright and cheerful look of the place in which it stands ; then, there are not many graves in it, and these are mostly covered or honoured by grey tombstones, partly moss-grown. On this day the sunshine fell upon them gently, with intervals of shifting shade, through the branches ; and though the place around was beset with noises, yet, as these were always the same, and never ceased except at night, they were not regarded by those who lived there, and so the churchyard seemed full of peace and quiet. The dead men who lie there are of that blameless race who venture themselves upon the unquiet ocean. The dead women are the wives of the men, their anxieties now over and done. When such men are gone, they are, for the most part, spoken of with good will, because they have never harmed any others but themselves, and have been kind-hearted to the weak. And so, from all these causes together, from the trees and the sunshine, and the memory of the dead sailors, it is a churchyard which suggested peaceful thoughts.

At all events it did not sadden the children when they came out from the school, built in one corner of it, nor did its presence ever disturb or sadden the mind of the girl who was making a pudding in the kitchen. There were sparrows in the branches, and in one tree sat a blackbird, now and then, late as it was, delivering himself of one note, just to remind himself of the past, and to keep his voice in practice against next spring.

The girl was fair to look upon, and, while she made her pudding, with sleeves turned back and flecks of white flour upon her white arms, and a white apron tied round her waist, stretching from chin to feet like a child's pinafore or a long bib, she sang snatches of songs, yet finished none of them ; and when you come to look closer into her face you saw that her cheeks were thin and her eyes sorrowful, and that her lips trembled from time to time. Yet she was not thinking out her sad thoughts to their full capabilities of bitterness, as some women are wont to do—as, in fact, her own mother had done for close upon twenty years, and was still doing, having a like cause for plaint and lamentation ; only the sad thoughts came and went across her mind, as birds fly across a garden, while she continued deftly and swiftly to carry on her work.

At this house, which was none other than the well-known Captains' boarding-house, sometimes called 'Rydquist's, of Rotherhithe,' the puddings and pastry were her special and daily charge. The making of puddings is the poetry of simple cookery. One is born, not made, for puddings. To make a pudding worthy of the name requires not only that special gift of nature, a light and cool hand, but also a clear intelligence and the power of concentrated attention, a gift in itself, as many lament when the sermon is over and they remember none of it. If the thoughts wander, even for a minute, the work is ruined. The instinctive feeling of right proportion in the matter of flour, lemon-peel, currants, sugar, allspice, eggs, butter, breadcrumbs : the natural eye for colour, form, and symmetry, which are required before one can ever begin even to think of becoming a maker of puddings, are all lost and thrown away, unless the attention is fixed resolutely upon the progress of the work. Now, there was one pudding, a certain kind of plum-duff, made by these hands, the recollection of which was wont to fill the hearts of those Captains who were privileged to eat of it with tender yearnings whenever they thought upon it, whether far away on southern seas, or on the broad Pacific, or in the shallow Baltic ; and it nerved their hearts when battling with the gales, while yet a thousand knots at least lay between their plunging bows and the Commercial Docks, to think that they were homeward bound, and that Lal would greet them with that pudding.

As the girl rolled her dough upon the white board and looked thoughtfully upon the little heaps of ingredients, she sang, as I have said, scraps of songs ; but this was just as a man at work, as a carpenter at his bench or a cobbler over his boot, will whistle scraps of tunes, not because his mind is touched with the beauty of the melody, but because this little action relieves the tension of the brain for a moment, without diverting the attention or disturbing the current of thought. She was dressed—behind the big apron—in a cotton print, made up by her own hands, which were as clever with the needle as with the rolling-pin. It was a dress made of a sympathetic stuff—there are many such tissues in every draper's shop—which, on being cut out, sewn up, and converted into a feminine garment, immediately proceeds, of its own accord, to interpret and illustrate the character of its owner ; so that for a shrew it becomes draggle-tailed, and for a lady careless of her figure, or conscious that it is no longer any use pretending to have a figure, it rolls itself up in unlovely folds, or becomes a miracle of flatness ; and for a lady of prim temperament it arranges itself into stiff vertical lines ; and for an old lady, if she is a nice old lady, it wrinkles itself into ten thousand lines, which cross and recross each other like the lines upon her dear old face, and all to bring her more respect and greater consideration ; but for a girl whose figure is tall and well-formed, this accommodating material becomes as clinging as the ivy, and its lines are every one of them an exact copy of Hogarth's line of beauty, due allowance being made for the radius of curvature.

I do not think I can give a better or clearer account of this maiden's dress, even if I were to say how-much-and-eleven-pence-three-farthings it was a yard and where it was bought. As for that, however, I am certain it came from Bjornsen's shop, where English is spoken, and where they have got in the window, not to be sold at any price, the greatest curiosity in the whole world (except the Golden Butterfly from Sacramento), namely, a beautiful model of a steamer, with everything complete—rigging, ropes, sails, funnel, and gear—the whole in a glass bottle. And if a man can tell how that steamer got into that bottle, which is a common glass bottle with a narrow neck, he is wiser than any of the scientific gentlemen who have tackled the problems of Stonehenge, the Pyramids, the Yucatan inscriptions, or the Etruscan language.

That is what she had on. As for herself, she was a tall girl ; her figure was slight and graceful, yet she was strong ; her waist measured just exactly the same number of inches as that of her grandmother Eve, whom she greatly resembled in beauty. Eve, as we cannot but believe, was the most lovely of women ever known, even including Rachel, Esther, Helen of Troy, Ayesha, and fair Bertha-with-the-big-feet. The colour of her hair depended a good deal upon the weather : when it was cloudy it was dark brown ; when the sunlight fell upon it her hair was golden. There was quite enough of it to tie about her waist for a girdle, if she was so minded ; and she was so little of a fine lady, that she would rather have had it brown in all weathers, and was half ashamed of its golden tint.

It soothes the heart to speak of a beautiful woman ; the contemplation of one respectfully is, in itself, to all rightly constituted masculine minds, a splendid moral lesson.

'Here,' says the moralist to himself, 'is the greatest prize that the earth has to offer to the sons of Adam. One must make oneself worthy of such a prize ; no one should possess a goddess who is not himself godlike.'

Having drawn his moral, the philosopher leaves off gazing, and returns, with a sigh, to his work. If you look too long, the moral is apt to evaporate and vanish away.

The door of the kitchen opened upon the garden, which was not broad, being only a few feet broader than the width of the house, but was long. It was planted with all manner of herbs, such as thyme, which is good for stuffing of veal ; mint, for seasoning of that delicious compound, and as sauce for the roasted lamb ; borage, which profligates and topers employ for claret-cup, though what it was here used for I know not ; parsley, good for garnish, which may also be chopped up small and fried ; cucumber, chiefly known at the West End in connection with salmon, but not disdained in the latitude of Rotherhithe for breakfast, dinner, tea, or supper, in combination with vinegar or anything else, for cucumber readily adapts itself to all palates save those set on edge with picksomeness. Then there were vegetables, such as onions, which make a noble return for the small space they occupy, and are universally admitted to be the most delightful of all roots that grow ; lettuces, crisp and green : the long lettuce and the round lettuce all the summer ; the scarlet-runner, which runneth in brave apparel, and eats short in the autumn, going well with leg of mutton ; and, at the end of the strip of ground, a small forest of Jerusalem artichoke, fit for the garden of the Queen. As for flowers, they were nearly over for the year, but there were trailing nasturtiums, long sprigs of faint mignonette, and one great bully hollyhock ; there were also, in boxes, painted green, creeping-jenny, bachelors'-button, thrift, ragged-robin, stocks, and candy-tuft, but all over for the season. There was a cherry-tree trained against the wall, and beside it a peach ; there were also a Siberian crab, a medlar, and a mulberry-tree. A few raspberry-canes were standing for show, because among them all there had not been that year enough fruit to fill a plate. The garden was separated from the churchyard by wooden palings, painted green ; this made it look larger than if there had been a wall. It was, in fact, a garden in which not one inch of ground was wasted ; the paths were only six inches wide, and wherever a plant could be coaxed to grow, there it stood in its allotted space. The wall fruit was so carefully trained that there was not a stalk or shoot out of place ; the flower borders were so carefully trimmed that there was not a weed or a dead flower ; while as for grass, snails, slugs, bindweed, dandelion, broken flower-pot, brickbat, and other such things, which do too frequently disfigure the gardens of the more careless, it is delightful to record that there was not in this little slice of Eden so much as the appearance or

suspicion of such a thing. The reason why it was so neat and so
well watched was that it was the delight and paradise of the
captains, who, by their united efforts, made it as neat, snug, and
orderly as one of their own cabins. There were live creatures in
the garden, too. On half a dozen crossbars, painted green, were
just so many parrots. They were all trained parrots, who could
talk and did talk, not altogether as is the use of parrots, who too
often give way to the selfishness of the old Adam, but one at a time,
and deliberately, as if they were instructing mankind in some new
and great truth, or delighting them with some fresh and striking
poetical ejaculation. One would cough slowly, and then dash his
buttons. If ladies were not in hearing he would remember other
expressions savouring of fo'k'sle rather than of quarter-deck.
Another would box the compass as if for an exercise in the art of
navigation. Another seldom spoke except when his mistress came
and stroked his feathers with her soft and dainty finger. The bird
was growing old now, and his feathers were dropping out, and
what this bird said you shall presently hear.

Next there was a great kangaroo hound, something under six
feet high when he walked. Now he was lying asleep. Beside him
was a little Maltese dog, white and curly; and in a corner—the
warmest corner—there was an old and toothless bulldog. Other
things there were—some in boxes, some in partial confinement, or
by a string tied to one leg, some running about—such as tortoises,
hedgehogs, Persian cats, Angola cats, lemurs, ferrets, Madagascar
cats. But they were not all in the garden, some of them, including
a mongoose and a flying-fox, having their abode on the roof, where
they were tended faithfully by Captain Zachariasen. In the
kitchen, also, which was warm, there resided a chameleon.

Now, all these things—the parrots, the dogs, the cats, the
lemurs, and the rest of them—were gifts and presents brought
across the seas by amorous captains to be laid at the shrine of one
Venus—of course I know that there never can be more than one
Venus at a time to any well-regulated male mind—whom all wooed
and none could win. There were many other gifts, but these were
within doors, safely bestowed. It may also be remarked that
Venus never refuses to accept offerings which are laid upon her
altar with becoming reverence. Thus there were the fragile coral
fingers, named after the goddess, from the Philippine Islands ; there
were chests of the rich and fragrant tea which China grows for
Russia. You cannot buy it at all here, and in Hong-Kong only as
a favour, and at unheard-of prices. There were cups and saucers
from Japan ; fans of the *coco de mer* from the Scychelles ; carved
ivory boxes and sandal-wood boxes from China and India ; weapons
of strange aspect from Malay islands ; idols from Ceylon ; praying
tackle brought down to Calcutta by some wandering Thibetan ;
with fans, glasses, mats, carpets, pictures, chairs, desks, tables, and
even beds, from lands *d'outre mer*, insomuch that the house looked
like a great museum or curiosity-shop. And everything, if you

please, brought across the sea and presented by the original im-
porters to the beautiful Alicia Rydquist, commonly called Lal by
those who were her friends, and Miss Lal by those who wished to
be, but were not, and had to remain outside, so to speak, and
all going, in consequence, green with envy.

On this morning there were also in the garden two men. One
of them was a very old man—so old that there was nothing left of
him but was puckered and creased, and his face was like one of
those too faithful maps which want to give every detail of the
country, even the smallest. This was Captain Zachariasen, a Dane
by birth, but since the age of eight on an English ship, so that he
had clean forgotten his native language. He had been for very
many years in the timber trade between the ports of Bergen and
London. He was now, in the protracted evening of his days,
enjoying an annuity purchased out of his savings. He resided
constantly in the house, and was the dean, or oldest member among
the boarders. He said himself sometimes that he was eighty-five,
and sometimes he said he was ninety, but old age is apt to boast.
One would not baulk him of a single year, and certainly he was
very, very old.

This morning, he sat on a green box half-way down the garden
—all the boxes, cages, railings, shutters, and doors of the house
were painted a bright navy-green—with a hammer and nails in his
hand, and sometimes he drove in a nail, but slowly and with consideration, as if noise and haste would confuse that nail's head, and
make it go loose, like a screw. Between each tap he gazed around
and smiled with pleased benevolence. The younger man, who was
about thirty years of age, was weeding. That is, he said so. He
had a spud with which to conduct that operation, but there were
no weeds. He also had a pair of scissors, with which he cut off
dead leaves. This was Captain Holstius, also of the mercantile
marine, and a Norwegian. He was a smartly-dressed sailor—wore
a blue cloth jacket, with trousers of the same ; a red silk handkerchief was round his waist ; his cap had a gold band round it, and a
heavy steel chain guarded his watch. His face was kind to look
upon. One noticed, especially, a greyish bloom upon a ruddy
cheek. It was an oval face, such as you may see in far-off Bamborough, or on Holy Island, with blue eyes ; and he had a gentle
voice. One wonders whether the Normans, who so astonished the
world a thousand years ago, were soft of speech, mild of eye, kind
of heart, like their descendants. Were Bohemond, Robert the
Devil, great Canute, like unto this gentle Captain Holstius ? And
if so, why were they so greatly feared ? And if not, how is it that
their sons have so greatly changed ? They were sailors—the men
of old. But sailors acquire an expression of unworldliness not found
among us who have to battle with worldly and crafty men. They
are not tempted to meet craft with craft, and treachery with deceit.
They do not cheat ; they are not tempted to cheat. Therefore,
although the Vikings were ferocious and bloodthirsty pirates,

thinking it but a small thing to land and spit a dozen Saxons or so, burn their homesteads, and carry away their pigs, yet, no doubt, in the domestic circle, they were mild and gentle, easily ruled by their wives, and obedient even to taking charge of the baby, which was the reason why they were called, in the pronunciation of the day, the hardy Nursemen.

A remarkable thing about that garden was that if you looked to the north, over the garden walls of the Seven Houses, you obtained, through a kind of narrow lane, a glimpse of a narrow breadth of water, with houses on either side to make a frame. It was like a little strip of some panorama which never stops, because up and down the water there moved perpetually steamers, sailing-ships, barges, boats, and craft of all kinds. Then, if you turned completely round, and looked south, you saw, beyond the trees in the churchyard, a great assemblage of yard-arms, masts, ropes, hanging sails, and rigging. And from this quarter there was heard continually the noise of labour that ceaseth not—the labour of hammers, saws, and hatchets ; the labour of lifting heavy burdens, with the encouraging ' Yo-ho ' ; the labour of men who load ships and unload them ; the labour of those who repair ships ; the ringing of bells which call to labour ; the agitation which is caused in the air when men are gathered together to work. Yet the place, as has been already stated, was peaceful. The calm of the garden was equalled by the repose of the open place on which the windows of the house looked, and by the peace of the churchyard. The noise was without ; it affected no one's nerves ; it was continuous, and, therefore, was not felt any more than the ticking of a watch or the beating of the pulse.

The old man presently laid down his hammer, and spoke, saying, softly :

' Nor—wee—gee.'

' Ay, ay, Captain Zachariasen,' replied the other, pronouncing the name with a foreign accent, and speaking a pure English, something like a Welshman's English. They both whispered, because the kitchen door was open, and Lal might hear. But they were too far down the garden for her to overhear their talk.

' Any luck this spell, lad ? '

The old man spoke in a meaning way, with a piping voice, and he winked both his eyes hard, as if he was trying to stretch the wrinkles out of his face.

Captain Holstius replied, evasively, that he had not sought for luck, and, therefore, had no reason to complain of unsuccess.

' I mean, lad,' whispered the old man, ' have you spoke the barque which once we called the Saucy Lal ? And if not '—because here the young man shook his head, while his rosy cheek showed a deeper red—' if not, why not ? '

' Because,' said Captain Holstius, speaking slowly—' because I spoke her six months ago, and she told me—— '

Here he sighed heavily.

'What did she tell you, my lad ? Did she say that she wanted
to be carried off and married, whether she liked it or not ?'

'No, she did not.'

'That was my way, when I was young. I always carried 'em
off. I married 'em first and axed 'em afterwards. Sixty year ago,
that was. Ay, nigh upon seventy, which makes it the more comfortable a thing for a man in his old age to remember.'

'Lal tells me that she will wait five years more before she
gives him up, and even then she will marry no one, but put on
mourning, and go in widow's weeds—being not even a wife.'

'Five years !' said Captain Zachariasen. ''Tis a long time for
a woman to wait for a man. Five years will take the bloom off of
her pretty cheeks, and the plumpness off of her lines, which is
now in the height of their curliness. Five years to wait ! Why,
there won't be a smile left on her rosy lips. Whereas, if you'd
the heart of a loblolly boy, Cap'en Holstius, you'd ha' run her
round to the church long ago, spoke to the clerk, whistled for the
parson, while she was still occupied with the pudding and had her
thoughts far away, and—well, there, in five years' time she'd be
playin' with a four-year-old, or, may be, twins, as happy as if there
hadn't never been no Cap'en Armiger at all.'

'Five years,' Captain Holstius echoed, 'is a long time to wait.
But any man would wait longer than that for Lal, even if he did
not get her, after all.'

'Five years ! It will be eight, counting the three she has
already waited for her dead sweetheart. No woman, in the old
days, was ever expected to cry more than one. Not in my day.
No woman ever waited for me, nor dropped one tear, for more
than one twelvemonth, sixty years ago, when I was dr——.' Here
he recollected that he could never have been drowned, so far back
as his memory served. That experience had been denied him.
He stopped short.

'She thinks of him,' Captain Holstius went on, seating himself
on another box, face to face with the old man, 'all day ; she
dreams of him all night ; there is no moment that he is not in her
thought—I know because I have watched her ; she does not speak
of him : even if she sings at her work, her heart is always sad.'

'Poor Rex Armiger ! Poor Rex Armiger !' This was the
voice of the old parrot, who lifted his beak, repeated his cry, and
then subsided.

Captain Holstius's eyes grew soft and humid, for he was a
tender-hearted Norwegian, and he pitied as well as loved the
girl.

'Poor Rex Armiger !' he echoed : 'his parrot remembers
him.'

'She is wrong,' said the old man, 'very wrong. I always tell
her so. Fretting has been known to make the pastry heavy :
tears spoil gravy.' He stated this great truth as if it was a well-
known maxim, taken from the Book of Proverbs.

'That was the third time that I spoke to her; the third time that she gave me the same reply. Shall I teaze her more? No, Captain Zachariasen, I have had my answer, and I know my duty.'

'It's hard, my lad, for a sailor to bear. Why, you may be dead in two years, let alone five. Most likely you will. You look as if you will. What with rocks at sea and sharks on land, most sailors, even skippers, by thirty years of age, is nummore. And though some'—here he tried to recollect the words of Scripture, and only succeeded in part—'by good seamanship escape, and live to seventy and eighty, or even, as in my case, by a judgmatic course and fair winds, come to eighty-five and three months last Sunday, yet in their latter days there is but little headway, the craft lying always in the doldrums, and the rations, too, often short. Five years is long for Lal to wait in suspense, poor girl! Take and go and find another girl, therefore,' the old man advised.

'No'—the Norwegian shook his head sadly—'there is only one woman in all the world for me.'

'Why, there, there,' the old Captain cried, 'what are young fellows coming to? To cry after one woman! I've given you my advice, my lad, which is good advice; likely to be beneficial to the boarders, especially them which are permanent, because the sooner the trouble is over, the better it'll be for meals. I did hear there was a bad egg, yesterday. To think of Rydquist's coming to bad eggs! But if a gal will go on fretting after young fellows that is long since food for crabs, what are we to expect but bad eggs? Marry her, my lad, or sheer off, and marry some one else. P'raps, when you are out of the way, never to come back again, she will take on with some other chap.'

Captain Holstius shook his head again.

'If Lal, after three years of waiting, says she cannot get him out of her heart—why, why there will be nothing to do, no help, because she knows best what is in her heart, and I would not that she married me out of pity.'

'Come to pity!' said Captain Zachariasen, 'she can't marry you all out of pity. There's Cap'en Borlinder and Cap'en Wattles, good mariners both, also after her. Should you like her to marry them out of pity?'

'I need not think of marriage at all,' said the Norwegian. 'I think of Lal's happiness. If it will be happier for her to marry me, or Captain Borlinder, or Captain Wattles, or any other man, I hope that she will marry that man; and if she will be happier in remembering her dead lover, I hope that she will remain without a husband. All should be as she may most desire.'

Then the girl herself suddenly appeared in the doorway, shading her eyes from the sunshine, a pretty picture, with the flour still upon her arms, and her white bib still tied round her.

'It is time for your morning beer, Captain Zachariasen,' she said. 'Will you have it in the kitchen, or shall I bring it to you in the garden?'

'I will take my beer, Lal,' replied the old man, getting up from the box, 'by the kitchen fire.'

He slowly rose and walked, being much bent and bowed by the weight of his years, to the kitchen door.

Captain Holstius followed him.

There was a wooden armchair beside the fire, which was brigh' and large, for the accommodation of a great piece of veal already hung before it. The old man sat down in it, and took the glass of ale, cool, sparkling, and foaming, from Lal's hand.

'Thoughtful child,' he said, holding it up to the light, 'she forgets nothing—except what she ought most to forget.'

'You are pale to-day, Lal,' said the Norwegian, gently. 'Will you come with me upon the river this afternoon?'

She shook her head sadly.

'Have you forgotten what day this is, of all days in the year?' she asked.

Captain Holstius made no reply.

'This day, three years ago, I got his last letter. It was four months since he sailed away. Ah me! I stood upon the steps of Lavender Dock and saw his ship slowly coming down the river. Can I ever forget it? Then I jumped into the boat and pulled out mid-stream, and he saw me and waved his handkerchief. And that was the last I saw of Rex. This day, three years and four months ago, and at this very time, in the forenoon.'

The old man, who had drained his glass and was feeling just a little evanescent headiness, began to prattle in his armchair, not having listened to their talk.

'I am eighty-five and three months, last Sunday; and this is beautiful beer, Lal, my dear. 'Twill be hard upon a man to leave such a tap. With the Cap'ens' room; and you, my Lal.'

'Don't think of such things, Captain Zachariasen,' cried Lal, wiping away the tear which had risen in sympathy for her own sorrows, not for his.

''Tis best not,' he replied, cheerfully. 'Veal, I see. Roast veal! Be large-handed with the seasonin', Lal. And beans? Ah! and apple-dumplings. The credit of Rydquist's must be kept up. Remember that, Lal. Wherefore, awake, my soul, and with the sun. Things there are that should be forgotten. I am eighty-five and a quarter last Sunday, like Abraham, Isaac, and Jacob—even Methusalem was eighty-five once, when he was little more than a boy, and never a grey hair—and, like the patriarchs at their best and oldest, I have gotten wisdom. Then, listen. Do I, being of this great age, remember the gals that I have loved, and the gals who have loved me? No. Yet are they all gone like that young man of yourn, gone away and past like gales across the sea. They are gone, and I am hearty. I shall never see them nummore; yet I sit down regular to meals, and still play a steady knife and fork.

And what I say is this : "Lal, my dear, wipe them pretty eyes with your best silk pockethandkercher, put on your best frock, and go to church in it for to be married."'

'Thank you, Captain Zachariasen,' said the girl, not pertly, but with a quiet dignity.

'Do not,' the old man went on—his eyes kept dropping, and his words rambled a little—'do not listen to Nick Borlinder. He sings a good song, and he shakes a good leg. Yet he is a rover. I was once myself a rover.'

She made no reply. He yawned slowly and went on :

'He thinks, he does, as no woman can resist him. I used to have the same persuasion, and I found it sustaining in a friendly port.'

'I do not suppose,' said Lal, softly, 'that I shall listen to Captain Borlinder.'

'Next,' the old man continued, 'there is Cap'en Wattles. Don't listen to Wattles, my dear. It is not that he is a Yankee, because a Cap'en is a Cap'en, no matter what his country, and I was, myself, once a Dane, when a boy, nigh upon eighty years ago, and drank corn brandy, very likely, though I have forgotten that time, and cannot now away with it. Wattles is a smart seaman ; but Wattles, my dear, wouldn't make you happy. You want a cheerful lad, but no drinker and toper like Borlinder ; nor so quiet and grave as Wattles, which isn't natural, afloat nor ashore, and means the devil.'

Here he yawned again and his eyes closed.

'Very good, sir,' said Lal.

'Yes, my dear—yes—and this is a very—comfortable—chair.'

His head fell back. The old man was asleep.

Then Captain Holstius drew a chair to the kitchen door, and sat down, saying nothing, not looking at Lal, yet with the air of one who was watching over and protecting her.

And Lal sat beside the row of freshly-made dumplings, and rested her head upon her hands, and gazed out into the churchyard.

Presently her eyes filled with tears, and one of them in each eye overflowed and rolled down her cheeks. And the same phenomenon might have been witnessed directly afterwards in the eyes of the sympathetic Norweegee.

It was very quiet, except, of course, for the screaming of the steam-engines on the river, and the hammering, yo-ho-ing, and bell-ringing of the Commercial Docks ; and these, which never ceased, were never regarded. Therefore, the calm was as the calm of a Sabbath in some Galilean village, and broken only in the kitchen by the ticking of the roasting-jack, and an occasional remark made, in a low tone, by a parrot.

Captain Holstius said nothing. He stayed there because he felt, in his considerate way, that his presence soothed and, in some sort, comforted the girl. It cost him little to sit there doing nothing at all.

Of all men that get their bread by labour it is the sailor alone who can be perfectly happy doing nothing for long hours together. He does not even want to whittle a stick.

As for us restless landsmen, we must be continually talking, reading, walking, fishing, shooting, rowing, smoking tobacco, or in some other way wearing out brain and muscle.

The sailor, for his part, sits down and lets time run on, unaided. He is accustomed to the roll of his ship and the gentle swish of the waves through which she sails. At sea he sits so for hours, while the breeze blows steady and the sails want no alteration.

So passed half an hour.

While they were thus sitting in silence, Lal suddenly lifted her head, and held up her finger, saying, softly,

' Hush ! I hear a step.'

The duller ears of her companion heard nothing but the usual sounds, which included the trampling of many feet afar off.

' What step ? ' he asked.

Her cheeks were gone suddenly quite white and a strange look was in her eyes.

' Not his,' she said. ' Oh, not the step of my Rex ; but I know it well for all that. The step of one who —— Ah ! listen ! '

Then, indeed, Captain Holstius became aware of a light hesitating step. It halted at the open door (which always stood open for the convenience of the Captains), and entered the narrow hall. It was a light step, for it was the step of a barefooted man.

Then the kitchen door was opened softly, and Lal sprang forward, crying madly :

' Where is he ? Where is he ? Oh, he is not dead ! '

At the sound of the girl's cry the whole sleepy place sprang into life ; the dogs woke up and ran about, barking with an immense show of alertness, exactly as if the enemy was in force without the walls ; the Persian cat, which ought to have known better, made one leap to the palings, on which she stood with arched back and upright tail, looking unutterable rage ; and the parrots all screamed together.

When the noise subsided, the new comer stood in the doorway. Lal was holding both his hands, crying and sobbing.

Outside, the old parrot repeated :

' Poor Rex Armiger ! Poor Rex Armiger ! '

Captain Zachariasen, roused from his morning nap, was looking about him, wondering what had happened.

Captain Holstius stood waiting to see what was going to happen.

The man, who was short in stature, not more than five feet three, wore a rough cloth sailor's cap, and was barefoot. He was dressed in a jacket, below which he wore a kind of petticoat, called, I believe, by his countrymen, who ought to know their own language, a 'sarong.' His skin was a copper colour ; his eyes dark brown ; his face was square, with high cheek-bones ; his eyes were soft, full, and black ; his mouth was large with thick lips ; his nose.

was short and small, with flat nostrils; his hair was black and coarse—all these characteristics stamped him as a Malay.

Captain Zachariasen rubbed his eyes.

'Ghosts ashore!' he murmured. 'Ghost of Deaf-and-Dumb Dick!'

'Who is Dick?' answered Captain Holstius.

'Captain Armiger's steward—same as was drowned aboard the *Philippine* three years ago along with his master and all hands. Never, nevermore heard of, and he's come back.'

The Malay man shook his head slowly. He kept on shaking it, to show them that he quite understood what was meant, although he heard no word.

'Where is he? Oh, where is he!' cried the girl again.

Then the dumb man looked in her face and smiled. He smiled and nodded, and smiled again.

'Like a Chinaman in an image,' said Captain Zachariasen. 'He can't be a ghost at the stroke of noon. That's not Christian ways nor Malay manners.'

But the smile, to Lal, was like the first cool draught of water to the thirsty tongue of a wanderer in the desert. Could he have smiled were Rex lying in his grave?

A Malay who is deaf and dumb is, I suppose, as ignorant of his native language as of English; but there is an atmosphere of Malayan abroad in his native village out of which this poor fellow picked a language of his own. That is to say, he was such a master of gesture as in this cold land of self-restraint would be impossible.

He nodded and smiled again. Then he laughed aloud, meaning his most cheerful note; but the laughter of those who can neither hear nor speak is a gruesome thing.

Then Lal, with shaking fingers, took from her bosom a locket, which she opened and showed the man. It contained, of course, the portrait of her lover.

He took it, recognised it, caught her by one hand, and then, smiling still, pointed with eyes that looked afar towards the east.

'Lies buried in the Indian Ocean,' murmured the old man; 'I always said it.'

Lal heard him not. She fell upon the man's neck and embraced and kissed him.

'He is not dead,' she cried. 'You hear, Captain Holstius? Oh, my friend, Rex is not dead. I knew he could not be dead—I have felt that he was alive all this weary time. Oh, faithful Dick!' She patted the man's cheek and head as if he was a child. 'Oh, good and faithful Dick! what shall we give him as the reward for the glad tidings! We can give him nothing—nothing—only our gratitude and our love.'

'And dinner, may be,' said Captain Zachariasen. 'No, not the veal, my dear;' for the girl, in her hurry to do something for this messenger of good tidings, made as if she would sacrifice the joint. 'First, because underdone veal is unwholesome, even for deaf and dumb Malays ; second, roast veal is not for the likes of him, but for Cap'ens. That knuckle of cold pork now——'

Lal brought him food quickly, and he ate, being clearly hungry.

'Does he understand English?' asked Captain Holstius.

'He is deaf and dumb ; he understands nothing.'

When he had broken bread, Dick stood again, and touched the girl's arm, which was equivalent to saying, 'Listen, all of you!'

The man stood before them in the middle of the room with the open kitchen door behind him, and the sunlight shining upon him through the kitchen window. And then he began to act, after the fashion of that Roman mime, who was able to convey a whole story with by-play, under-plot, comic talk, epigrams, tears, and joyful surprises, without one word of speech. The gestures of this Malay were, as I have said, a language by themselves. Some of them, however, like hieroglyphics before the Rosetta Stone, wanted a key.

The man's face was exceedingly mobile and full of quickness. He kept his eyes upon the girl, regarding the two men not at all.

And this, in substance, was what he did. It was not all, because there were hundreds of little things, every one of which had its meaning in his own mind, but which were unintelligible, save by Lal, who followed him with feverish eagerness and attention. Words are feeble things at their best, and cannot describe these swift changes of face and attitude.

First, he retreated to the door, then leaped with a bound into the room. Arrived there he looked about him a little, folded his arms, and began to walk backwards and forwards, over a length of six feet.

'Come aboard, sir,' said Captain Zachariasen, greatly interested and interpreting for the benefit of all. 'This is good mummicking, this is.'

Then he began to jerk his hand over his shoulder each time he stopped. And he stood half-way between the extremities of his six-foot walk and lifted his head as one who watches the sky. At the same time Lal remarked how by some trick of the facial muscles, he had changed his own face. His features became regular, his eyes intent and thoughtful, and in his attitude he was no longer himself, but—in appearance—Rex Armiger.

'They're clever at mummicking and conjuring,' said Captain Zachariasen ; 'I've seen them long ago, in Calcutta, when I was in——'

'Hush!' cried Lal imperatively. 'Do not speak! Do not interrupt.'

The Malay changed his face and attitude, and was no more Rex Armiger, but himself ; then he held out his two hands, side by side, horizontally, and moved them gently from left to right, and right to left, with an easy wave-like motion, and at the same time he swung himself slowly backwards and forwards. It seemed to the girl to imitate the motion of a ship with a steady breeze in smooth water.

'Go on,' she cried ; 'I understand what you mean.'

The man heard nothing, but he saw that she followed him, and he smiled and nodded his head.

He became once more Rex Armiger. He walked with folded arms, he looked about him as one who commands and who has the responsibility of the ship upon his mind.

Presently he lay down upon the floor, stretched out his legs straight, and with his head upon his hands went to sleep.

'Even the skipper's bunk is but a narrow one,' observed Captain Zachariasen, to show that he was following the story, and proposed to be the principal interpreter.

The dumb actor's slumber lasted but a few moments. Then he sprang to his feet and began to stagger about. He stamped, he groaned, he put his hand to his head, he ran backwards and forwards ; he presented the appearance of a man startled by some accident ; he waved his arms, gesticulated wildly, put his hands to his mouth as one who shouts.

Then he became a man who fought, who was dragged, who threatened, who was struck, tramping all the while with his feet so as to produce the impression of a crowd.

Then he sat down and appeared to be waiting, and he rocked to and fro continually.

Next he went through a series of pantomimic exercises which were extremely perplexing, for he strove with his hands as one who strives with a rope, and he made as one who is going hand over hand, now up, now down a rope ; and he ran to and fro, but within narrow limits, and presently he sat down again, and nodded his head and made signs as if he were communicating with a companion.

'Dinner-time,' said Captain Zachariasen, 'or, may be, supper.'

After awhile, still sitting, he made as if he held something in his hand which he agitated with a regular motion.

'Rocking the baby,' said Captain Zachariasen, now feeling his way surely.

Lal, gazing intently, paid no heed to this interruption.

Then he waved a handkerchief.

'Aha?' cried Captain Zachariasen ; 'I always did that myself.'

Then he lay down and rested his head again upon his arm ; but Lal noticed that now he curled up his legs, and the tears came into her eyes, because she saw that he, personating her Rex, seemed for a moment to despair.

But he sat up again, and renewed that movement, as if with a stick, which had made the old skipper think of babies.

Then he stopped again, and let both arms drop to his side, still sitting.

'Tired,' said Captain Zachariasen.   'Pipe smoke time.'

The Malay did not, however, make any show of smoking a pipe. He sat a long time without moving, arms and head hanging.

Then he started, as if he recollected something suddenly, and taking paper from his pocket, began to write. Then he went through the motion of drinking, rolled up the paper very small, and did something with it difficult to understand.

'Sends her a letter,' said the Patriarch, nodding his head sagaciously. 'I always wrote them one letter after I'd gone away, so's to let 'em down easy.'

This done, the Malay seated himself again, and remained sitting some time. At intervals he lay down, his head upon his hands as before, and his legs curled.

The last time he did this he lay for a long time—fully five minutes—clearly intending to convey the idea of a considerable duration of time.

When he sat up, he rubbed his eyes and looked about him. He made motions of surprise and joy, and, as before, communicated something to a companion. Then he seemed to grasp something, and began again the same regular movement, but with feverish haste, and painfully, as if exhausted.

'Baby again !' said the wise man. 'Rum thing to bring the baby with him.'

Then the Malay stopped suddenly, sprang to his feet, and made as if he jumped from one place to another.

Instantly he began again to rush about, shake and be shaken by shoulders, arms, and hands, to stagger, to wave his hands, finally to run along with his hands straight down his sides.

'Now I'm sorry to see this,' said Captain Zachariasen, mournfully. 'What's he done? Has that baby brought him into trouble? Character gone for life, no doubt.'

Lal gazed with burning eyes.

Then the Malay stood still, and made signs as if he were speaking, but still with his arms straight to his sides. While he spoke, one arm was freed, and then the other. He stretched them out as if for relief. After this, he sat down, and ate and drank eagerly.

'Skilly and cold water,' said Captain Zachariasen. 'Poor young man !'

Then he walked about, going through a variety of motions, but all of a cheerful and active character. Then he suddenly dropped the personation of Rex Armiger and became himself again. Once more he went through that very remarkable performance of stamping, fighting, and dragging.

Then he suddenly stopped and smiled at Lal. The pantomime was finished.

The three spectators looked at each other inquiringly, but Lal's face was full of joy.

'I read this mummicking,' said Captain Zachariasen, 'very clearly, and if, my dear, without prejudice to the dumplings, which I perceive to be already finished, and if I may have a pipe, which

c

is, I know, against the rules in the kitchen—but so is a mouthing mummicking Malay—I think I can reel you off the whole story, just as he meant to tell it, as easy as I could read a ship's signals. Not that every man could do it, mind you ; but being, as one may say, at my oldest and best——'

Lal nodded. Her eyes were so bright, her cheeks so rosy, that you would have thought her another woman.

'Go, fetch him his pipe, Captain Holstius,' she said. Then, seized by a sudden impulse, she caught him by both hands. 'It could never have been,' she said, 'even—even—if—— You will rejoice with me ? '

'If it is as you think,' he said, 'I both rejoice and thank the Father humbly.'

Fortified with his pipe, the old man spoke slowly in full enjoy- ment of his amazing and patriarchal wisdom.

'Before Cap'en Armiger left Calcutta,' he began, 'he did a thing which many sailors do, and when I was a young man, now between seventy and eighty years ago, which is a long time to look back upon, they always did. Pecker up, Lal, my beauty. You saw how the mummicker rolled his eyes, smacked his lips, and clucked his tongue. Not having my experience, prob'ly you didn't quite understand what he was wishful for to convey. That meant love, Lal, my dear. Those were the signs of courting, ccmmon among sailors. Your sweetheart fell in love with you in the Port of London, and presently afterwards with another pretty woman in the Port of Calcutta, which is generally the way with poor Tom Bowling. She was a snuff-and-butter, because at Calcutta they are as plenty as blackberries ; and when young, snuff-and-butter is not to be despised, having bright eyes ; and there was another thing about her which I guess you missed, if you got so far as a right understanding of the beginning. She was a widow. How do I know she was a widow ? This way. The mummicking Malay, whose antics can only be truly read, like the signs of the weather, by the wisdom of eighty and odd, put his two hands together. You both saw that—second husband that meant. Then he waved his hands up and down. If I rightly make out that signal it's a signal of distress. She led the poor lad, after he married her, a devil of a life. Temper, my girl, goes with snuff-and-butter, though when they're young I can't say but there's handsome ones among them. A devil of a life it was, while the stormy winds did blow, and naturally Cap'en Armiger began to cast about for to cut adrift.'

'Go on, Captain Zachariasen,' said Lal, who only laughed at this charge of infidelity.

The Malay looked on gravely, understanding no word, but nod- ding his head as if it was all right.

'He marries this artful widow then, and, in due course, he has a baby. You might ha' seen if you'd got my eyes, which can't be 'ooked for at your age, that the mummicking mouther kept rocking that baby. Very well, then ; time passes on, he has a row with the mother ; she, as you may have seen, shies the furniture at his head, which he dodges, being too much of a man and a sailor to heave the tables back. Twice she shies the furniture. Then he ups and off to sea, taking—which I confess I cannot understand, for no sailor to my knowledge ever did such a thing before— actually taking—the—baby—with him !' The sagacious old man stopped, and smoked a few moments in meditation. 'As to the next course in this voyage,' he said, 'I am a little in doubt. For whether there was a mutiny on board, or whether his last wife followed him and carried on shameful before the crew, whereby the authority of the skipper was despised and his dignity lowered, I cannot tell. Then came chucking overboards, and whether it was Cap'en Armiger chucking his wife and baby, or whether he chucked the crew, or whether the crew chucked him, is not apparent, because the mummicker mixed up Jonah and the crew, and no man, not even Solomon himself, in his cedar-palace, could tell from his actions which was crew and which was Jonah. However, the end is easy to understand. The Cap'en, in fact, was run in when he got to shore—you all saw him jump ashore—for this chucking over-board, likely. He made a fight for it, but what is one man against fifty. So they took him off, with his arms tied to his sides, being a determined young fellow, and he was tried for bigamy, or chuck-ing overboard, or some such lawful and statutable crime. And he was then sentenced to penal servitude for twenty years or it may be less. At Brisbane, Queensland, it was perhaps, or Sydney, New South Wales, or Singapore, or perhaps Hong-Kong, I can't say which, because the mummicker at this point grew confused. But it must be one of these places where there's a prison. There he is still, comfortably working it out. Wherefore, Lal, my dear, you may go about and boast that you always knew he was alive, because right you are and proud you may be. At the same time, you may now give up all thoughts of that young chap, and turn your at-tentions, my dear, to '—here he pointed with his pipe—' to the Norweegee.'

Captain Holstius, who had shaken his head a great deal during the Seer's interpretation, shook his head again, deprecatingly.

'Thank you, Captain Zachariasen,' said Lal, laughing. What a thing joy is ! She laughed, who had not laughed for three years. The dimples came back to her cheek, the light to her eyes. 'Thank you. Your story is a very likely one, and does your wisdom great credit. Shall I read you my interpretation of this acting ? '

The Captain nodded.

'Rex set sail from Calcutta with a fair wind, leaving no wife behind, and taking with him no baby. How long he was at sea I know not ; then there came a sudden storm, or perhaps the strik-ing on a rock, or some disaster. Then he is in an open boat alone with Dick here, though what became of the crew I do not know ; then he writes me a letter, but I do not understand what he did

with it when he had written it ; then they sit together expectant
of death ; they row aimlessly from time to time ; they have no
provisions ; they suffer greatly ; they see land, and they row as
hard as they can ; they are seized by savages and threatened, and
he is there still among them.   He is there, my Rex, he is there,
waiting for us to rescue him.   And God has sent us this poor dumb
fellow to tell us of his safety.'

The old man shook his head.

'Poor thing !' he said compassionately.   'Better inquire at
every British port, where there's a prison, in the East, after an
English officer working out his time, and ask what he done, and
why he done it ?'

'Let be, let be,' said Captain Holstius.   'Lal is always right.
Captain Armiger is among the savages, somewhere.   We will bring
him back.   Lal, courage, my dear ; we will bring him back to you
alive and well !'

CHAPTER II.

THE PRIDE OF ROTHERHITHE.

THE terrace or row called Seven Houses is situated, as I have
stated above, in a riverside township, which, although within sight
of London Bridge, is now as much forgotten and little known as any
of the dead cities on the Zuyder-Zee or the Gulf of Lyons.   In all
respects it is as quiet as primitive, and as little visited, except by
those who come and go in the matter of daily business.

The natives of Rotherhithe are by their natural position, aided
by the artificial help of science, entirely secluded and cut off from
the outer world.   They know almost as little of London as a High-
lander or a Cornish fisherman.   And as they know not its
pleasures, they are not tempted to seek them ; as their occupations keep them for the most part close to their own homes,
they seldom wander afield ; and as they are a people contented
and complete in themselves, dwelling as securely and with as
much satisfaction as the men of Laish, they do not desire the
society of strangers.   Therefore great London, with its noises
and mighty business, its press and hurry, is a place which
they care not often to encounter ; and as for the excitement and
amusements of the West, they know them not.   Few there are in
Rotherhithe who have been farther west than London Bridge,
fewer still who know the country and the people who dwell west of
Temple Bar.

It is a place protected and defended, so to speak, by a narrow
pass, or entrance, uninviting and unpromising, bounded by river

on one side and docks on the other. This Thermopylæ passed, one finds oneself in a strange and curious street with water on the left and water on the right, and ships everywhere in sight.

It possesses no railway, no cabstand, no omnibus runs thither; there is no tram. The nearest station is for one end, Thames Tunnel, and for the other, Deptford. All the local arrangements for getting from one place to the other seem based on the good old principle that nobody wants to get from one place to the other; one would not be astonished to meet a string of pack-horses laden with the produce of the town, so quiet, so still, so far removed from London, so old-world in its aspect is the High Street of Rotherhithe.

If, however, they are little interested in the great city near which they live, they know a great deal about foreign countries and strange climates; if they have no politics, they read and talk much about the prospects of trade across the sea; they do not take in 'Telegraph,' 'Standard,' or 'Daily News,' but they read from end to end that admirable paper the 'Shipping and Mercantile Gazette.' For all their prospects and all their interests are bound up in the mercantile marine. No one lives here who is not interested in the Commercial Docks, or the ships which use them, or the boats, or in the repairs of ships, or in the supply of ships, or in the manners, customs, and requirements of skippers, mates, and mercantile sailors of all countries. Their greatest man is the Superintendent of the Docks, and after him, in point of importance, are the dock-masters and their assistants.

Rotherhithe consists, for the most part, of one long street, which runs along the narrow strip of ground left between the river and the docks when they were built. The part of the river thus overlooked is Limehouse Reach; the street begins at the new Thames Tunnel Station, which is close beside the old Rotherhithe Parish Church, and it ends where Deptford begins. There are many beautiful, and many wonderful, and many curious streets in London 'and her daughters;' but this is, perhaps, the most curious. It is, to begin with, a street which seems to have been laid down so as to get as much as possible out of the way of the ships which press upon it to north and south. Ships stick their bows almost across the road, the figure-heads staring impertinently into first-floor windows. If you pass a small court or wynd, of which there are many, with little green-shuttered houses, you see ships at the end of it, with sails hanging loosely from the yard-arms.

On the left hand you pass a row of dry docks. They are all exactly alike; they are built to accommodate one vessel, but rarely more; if you look in, no one questions your right of entrance; and if you see one you have seen them all.

Look, for instance, into this dry dock. Within her is a two-masted sailing vessel; most likely she hails from Norway or from Canada, and is engaged in the timber trade. Her planks show signs of age, and she is shored up by great round timbers like bits of a mast. Her repairs are probably being executed by one man, who is seated on a hanging board leisurely brandishing a paint-brush. Two more men are seated on the wharf, looking on with intelligent curiosity. One man—perhaps the owner of the ship, or some other person in authority—stands at the far end of the dock and surveys the craft with interest, but no appearance of hurry, because the timber trade, in all in its branches, is a leisurely business. No one is on board the ship except a dog, who sits on the quarter-deck sound asleep, with his nose in his paws.

The wharf is littered all about with round shores, old masts, and logs of ship timber ; it is never tidied up, chips and shavings lie about rotting in the rain—the remains of old repairs, long since done and paid for, upon ships long since gone to the bottom ; there is a furnace for boiling pitch, and barrels for the reception of that useful article ; there is a winch with rusty chains ; there is a crane, but the wheels are rusty. The litter and leisure of the place are picturesque. One wonders who is its proprietor ; probably some old gentleman with a Ramillies wig, laced ruffles, gold buckles on his shoes, silk stockings, a flowered satin waistcoat down to his knees, sober brown coat, and a gold-headed stick.

At the entrance to the dock there is a little house with green shutters, a pretence of green railings which enclose three feet of ground, and green boxes furnished with creeping jenny and mignonette. But this cannot be the residence of the master.

Beyond the dock, kept out by great gates which seem not to have been opened for generations, so rusty are the wheels and so green are their planks with weed and water-moss, run the waters of the Thames. There go before us the steamers, the great ocean steamers, coming out of the St. Katherine's, London, and West India Docks ; there go the sailing ships, dropping easily down with the tide, or slowly making way with a favourable breeze up to the Pool ; there creep the lighters and barges, heavily laden, with tall mast and piled-up cargo, the delight of painters ; there toil continually the noisy steam-tug and the river packet steamer ; there play before us unceasingly the life, the movement, the bustle of the Port of London.

But all this movement, this bustle, seems to us, standing in the quiet dock, like a play, a procession of painted ships upon a painted river, with the background of Limehouse church and town all most beautifully represented ; for the contrast is so strange.

Here we are back in the last century ; this old ship, whose battered sides the one man is tinkering, is a hundred years old ; the Swedish skipper, who stands and looks at her all day long, in no hurry to get her finished and ready for sea, flourished before the French Revolution ; the same leisurely dock, the same leisurely carpenter, the same leisurely spectators, the same green palings, the same little lodge with its green door and green flower-box, were all here a hundred years ago and more ; and we, who look

about us, find ourselves presently fumbling about our heads to see
whether, haply, we wear tye-wigs and three-cornered hats.

On the doors of this dock we observe an announcement warning
marine-store dealers not to enter. What have they done—the
marine-store dealers?

A little farther on there is another dry dock. We look in. The
same ship, apparently; the same leisurely contemplation of the
ship by the same man; the same dog; the same contrast between
the press and hurry of the river and the leisure of the dock; the
same warning to marine-dealers. Again we ask, what have they
done—the marine-store dealers?

Some of the docks have got suggestive and appropriate names.
The 'Lavender' leads the poet to think of the tender care bestowed upon ships laid up in that dock (the name is not an advertisement, but a truthful and modest statement); the 'Pageant' is
magnificent; the 'Globe' suggests geographical possibilities which
cannot but fire the imagination of Rotherhithe boys; and what
could be more comfortable for a heart of oak than 'Acorn'
Wharf?

One observes presently a strange sweet fragrance in the air,
which, at first, is unaccountable. The smell means timber. For
behind the street lie the great timber docks. Here is timber
stacked in piles; here are ships unloading timber; here is timber
lying in the water. It is timber from Canada and from Norway;
timber from Honduras; timber from Singapore; timber from
every country where there are trees to cut and hands to cut
them.

It is amid these stocks of timber, among these ships, among
these docks, that the houses and gardens of Rotherhithe lie
embowered.

Some of the houses were built in the time of great George Ter-
tius. One recognises the paucity of windows, the flat façade, the
carved, painted, and varnished woodwork over the doors. More,
however, belong to his illustrious grandfather's period, or even
earlier, and some, which want painting badly, are built of wood
and have red-tiled roofs.

Wherever they can they stick up wooden palings painted green.
They plant scarlet-runners wherever they can find so much as a
spare yard of earth. They are fond of convolvulus, mignonette,
and candy-tuft in boxes. They all hammer on their walls tin
plates, which show to those who can understand that the house is
insured in the 'Beacon.' And some of the houses—namely, the
oldest and smallest—have their floors below the level of the
street.

There is one great house—only one—in Rotherhithe. It was
built somewhere in the last century, before the Commercial Docks
were excavated. It was then the home of a rich merchant living
among the dry docks—probably he was the proprietor of Lavender
and Acorn Docks. There is a courtyard before it; the door, with

a porch, stands at the top of broad stairs; there is ornamental
stone-work half-way up the front of the house, and there is a gate
of hammered iron, as fine as any in South Kensington.

The shops have strange names over the doors. They are chiefly
kept by Norwegians, Dutchmen, Swedes, and Danes, with a sprink-
ling of Rotherhithe natives. The things exhibited for sale look
foreign. Yet we observe with satisfaction that the public-houses
are kept by Englishmen, and that the Scandinavian taste in liquor
is catholic. They can drink—these Northmen—and do, anything
which ' bites.'

Quite at the end of this long street you come to a kind of open
place, in which stands the terrace called ' Seven Houses.' They
occupy the east side. On the west is, first, a timber-yard, open to
the river; next a row of houses, white, neat, and clean; beyond
the terrace is the church, with its churchyard and schools. Then
there is another short street, with shops, the fashionable shopping-
place of Rotherhithe. And here the town, properly so called, ends,
for beyond is the entrance to the Commercial Docks, and all around
spread great sheets of water, in which lie the timber-ships from
Norway, Sweden, Canada, Archangel, Stettin, Memel, Dantzic, St.
Petersburg, Savannah, and the East.

Hither, too, come ships from New Zealand, bringing grain and
wool, and here put in ships, but in smaller number, bound for
almost every port upon the globe.

And what with the green trees in the churchyard, the clean
houses, the bright open space, the ships in the dock, and the
glimpses of the river, one might fancy oneself not in London at all,
but across the North Sea and in Amsterdam.

It was in Rotherhithe that Lal Rydquist was born, and in
Rotherhithe she was educated. Nor for eighteen years and more
did the girl ever go outside her native place, but continued as
ignorant of the great city near her as if it did not exist. On the
other hand, from the conversation of those around her, she became
perfectly familiar with the greater part of the globe; namely, its
oceans, seas, ports, harbours, gulfs, bays, currents, tides, prevalent
winds, and occasional storms. Most people are brought up to know
nothing but the land: it is shameful favouritism to devote geo-
graphy books exclusively to the land upon this round globe; Lal
knew nothing about the land, but a good deal about the water.
Such other knowledge as she had acquired pertained to ships, harbours, cargoes, Custom dues, harbour dues, bills of lading, insurance, wet and dry docks, and the current price of timber, grain,
rice, and so forth. A very varied and curious collection of facts
lay stored in her brain; but as for the accomplishments and ac-
quirements of ordinary English girls, she knew none of them.

Her Christian name was Alicia. When she was but a toddler,
the sailor folk with whom she played, and who gave her dolls,
called her Lal. As she grew up, these honest people remained her
friends, and therefore her name remained. Girls grow up, by

Nature's provision, gradually, so that there never comes a time when a pet name ceases of its own accord. Therefore, to the captains who used the boarding-house, being all personal friends —none but friends, in fact, were admitted to the privileges of that little family hotel—she continued to be Lal.

The boarding-house was carried on by Mrs. Rydquist, Lal's mother, who had been a notable woman in her day. The older inhabitants of Rotherhithe testified to that effect. But her misfortunes greatly affected and changed her for the worse. One need only touch upon the drowning of her father, which happened many years before, and was regarded by the burgesses of Rotherhithe as a special mercy bestowed upon his family, so wasteful was he and fond of drink when ashore. He was chief officer of an East Indiaman which went down with all hands in a cyclone, as was generally believed, somewhere north of the Andaman Islands, outward bound. He had spent all his pay in ardent drinks, and there was nothing left for his daughter. But she married a stout fellow, a Swede by nation, and Rydquist by name, who sailed to and fro between the ports of Bjorneborg and London, captain and part owner of a brig in the timber trade. Alas ! that brig dropped down stream one morning as usual, having the captain on board, and leaving the captain's wife ashore with the baby, and she was never afterwards heard of. Also there was some trouble about the insurance, and so the captain's widow got nothing for her husband's share in the ship.

Mrs. Rydquist, then a young woman and comely still, who might have married again, took to crying, and continued to cry, which was bad for the boarding-house which her husband's friends started for her. In most cases time cures the deadliest wounds, but in this poor lady's case the years went on and she continued to bewail her misfortunes, sitting, always with a teapot before her, upon a sofa as hard as a bed of penitence, and plenty of pocket handkerchiefs in her lap.

There could not have been a happier child, a brighter, merrier child, a more sunshiny child, a more affectionate child, a more contented child than Lal, during her childhood, but for two things : her mother was always crying, and the house went on anyhow. When she grew to understand things a little, she ventured to point out to her mother that men who go to sea do often get drowned, and among the changes and chances of this mortal life this accident must be seriously considered by the woman who marries a sailor. But no use. She remonstrated again, but with small effect, that the house was not kept with the neatness desired by captains ; that it was in all respects ill-found ; that the quality of the provisions was far from what it ought to be, and that meals were not punctual. The aggravation of these things, and the knowledge that they were received with muttered grumblings by the good fellows who put up with them chiefly for her own sake, sank deep into her heart, and shortened—not her life, but her schooling.

When she was fourteen, being as tall and shapely as many a girl of eighteen, she would go to school no more. She announced her intention of staying at home; she took over the basket of keys—that emblem of authority—from her mother's keeping into her own; she began to order things; she became the mistress of the house, while the widow contentedly sat in the front parlour and wept, or else, which made her deservedly popular among the captains, prophesied, to any one who would listen, shipwreck, death, and ruin, like Cassandra, Nostradamus, and Old Mother Shipton, to these friends.

Immediately upon this assumption of authority the house began to look clean, the windows bright, the bedrooms neat; immediately the enemies of the house, who were the butcher, the baker, the bacon-man, the butterman, and every other man who had shot expensive rubbish into the place, began, to use the dignified language of the historian, to 'roll back sullenly across the frontier.' Immediately meals became punctual; immediately rules began to be laid down and enforced. Captains must henceforth only smoke in the evening; captains must pay up every Saturday; captains must not bring friends to drink away the rosy hours with them; captains must moderate their language—words beginning with a D were to be overhauled, so to speak, before use; captains must complain to Lal if they wanted anything, not go about grumbling with each other in a mean and a mutinous spirit. These rules were not written, but announced by Lal herself in peremptory tones, so that those who heard knew that there was no choice but to obey.

She was the best and kindest of managers; she made such a boarding-house for her captains as was never dreamed of by any of them. Such dinners, such beer, spirits of such purity and strength, tobacco of the finest; no trouble, no disturbance, the wheels always running smoothly. Captains' bills made out to a penny, with no surcharge or extortion. And, withal the girl was thoughtful for each man, mindful of what he liked the best, and with a mother's eye to buttons.

It was indeed a boarding-house fit for the gods. So startling were the 'effects' in cleanliness that honest Dutchmen rubbed their eyes, and seeing the ships all round them, thought of the Boompjes of Rotterdam; not a plank in the house but was like a tablecloth for cleanliness.

Then, as to punctuality: at the stroke of eight, breakfast on the table, and Lal, neat as a band-box, pouring out tea and coffee, made as they should be; while toast, dry and buttered, muffins, chops and steaks, ham and eggs, bacon, and fish just out of the frying-pan, were on the table.

On the stroke of one, the dinner, devised, planned, and personally conducted by Lal herself, more diligently than any cook of modern or ancient history, was borne from the kitchen to the Captains' room.

The nautical appetite is large, both on shore and afloat; but on shore it is critical as well. The skipper aboard his ship may contentedly eat his way through barrels of salt junk, yet ashore he craves variety, and is as particular about his vegetables as a hippopotamus who has studied the art of dining.

And this is the reason, not generally understood, why the market-gardens in the neighbourhood of Deptford are so extensive, and why every available square inch of Rotherhithe grows a cabbage or a scarlet-runner.

There were no complaints here, however, about vegetables.

Tea was served at five, for those who wanted any.

Supper appeared at eight; and after supper, grog and pipes. Yet, as at dinner the supply of beer was generous yet not wasteful, so at night, every captain knew that if he wanted more than his ration, or double ration, he must get up and slink out of the house like a truant school-boy, to seek it at the nearest public-house.

The mercantile skipper in every nation is much the same. He is a responsible person, somewhat grave; ashore he does not condescend to high jinks, and leaves sprees to the youngsters. Yet among his fellows in such a house as Rydquist's, he is not above a song or even a cheerful hornpipe. He is generally a married man with a large family of whom he is fond and proud. He reads little, but has generally some book to talk of; and he is brimful of stories, mostly, it must be owned, of a professional and pointless kind, and some old, old Joe Millers, which he brings out with an air as if they were new and sparkling from the mint of fancy.

These men were the girl's friends, all the friends she had. They were fond of her and kind to her. When, as often happened, she found herself in the Captains' room in the evening and sat on the arm of Captain Zachariasen's chair, the stories went on with the songs and the laughing, just as if she was not present, for they were an innocent-minded race, and whether they hailed from Russia, Sweden, Norway, Denmark, Holland, or America, they were chivalrous and respected innocence.

The house accommodated no more than half a dozen, but it was always full, and the captains were of the better sort. Captain Hansen from Christiania dropped in after his ship was in dock; if the house was full he went back to his ship; if he could have a room he stayed there. The same with Captain Bebbington of Quebec, Captain Griggs of Edinburgh, Captain Rosenlund of Hamburg, Captain Eriksen of Copenhagen, Captain Vidovich of Archangel, Captain Ling of Stockholm, and Captain Tilly of New Brunswick, and a dozen more.

They rallied round Rydquist's; they thought it a proud thing to be able to put up there; and they swore by Lal.

Then who but Lal overhauled the linen, gave out some to be mended and some to be condemned, and rigged them out for the next voyage? And as for confidences, the girl was not fifteen years old before she knew all the secrets of all the men who went there, with their love stories, their disappointments, their money matters, their hopes, and their ambitions. And she was already capable, at that early age, of giving sensible advice, especially in matters of the heart. Those who followed that advice subsequently rejoiced ; those who did not, repented.

When she was seventeen, they all began, with one consent, to fall in love with her. She remarked nothing unusual for awhile, having her mind greatly occupied in considering the price of vegetables, which during that year remained like runagates for scarceness. Presently, however, the altered carriage of the boarders was impossible to be otherwise than remarkable.

Love, we know, shows itself by many external symptoms. Some went careless of attire ; some went in great bravery with waistcoats and neckties difficult to describe and impossible to match ; some laughed, some heaved sighs, some sang songs ; one or two made verses ; those who were getting grey tried to look as if they were five-and-twenty, and made as if they still could shake a rollicking leg ; those who were already turned of sixty persuaded themselves that a master mariner's heart is always young, and that no time of life is too far advanced for him to be a desirable husband.

Lal laughed and went on making the puddings ; she knew very well what they wanted, but she felt no fancy, yet, for any of them.

When, which speedily happened, one after the other came to lay themselves, their ships, and their fortunes at her feet, she sent them all away, not with scorn or unkindness, but with a cheerful laugh, bidding them go seek prettier, richer, and better girls to marry ; because, for her own part, she had got her work to do, and had no time to think about such things, and if she had ever so much time she most certainly would not marry that particular suitor.

They went away, and for a while looked gloomy and ashamed, fearing that the girl would tell of them. But she did not, and they presently recovered, and when their time came and their ships were ready, they dropped down the river with a show of cheerfulness, and so away to distant lands, round that headland known as the Isle of Dogs, with no bitterness in their hearts, but only a little disappointment, and the most friendly feelings towards the girl who said them nay.

When those were gone, the house, which was never empty, received another batch of captains, old and young. Presently similar symptoms were developed with them ; all were ardent, all confident. They had been away a year or two. They found the little Lal, whom they left a handy maiden, a mere well-grown girl of fourteen or so, developed into a tall and beautiful young woman. Upon her shoulders, invisible to all, sat Love, discharging arrows right and left into the hearts of the most inflammable of men. This batch—excepting two, who had wives in other ports, and openly lamented the fact—behaved in the same surprising manner as their predecessors. They were presently treated with the same dismissal, but with less courtesy, because to the girl this behaviour was becoming monotonous, and it sometimes seemed as if the whole of mankind had taken leave of their senses. They retired in their turn, and when their ships were laden, they, too, sailed away a little discomfited, but not revengeful or bearing malice. Then came a third batch, and so on. But of sea-captains there is an end : Lal's friends one after the other, came, disappeared after a while, and then came back again. Those who used the house at Rotherhithe were like comets rather than planets, because they had no fixed periods, but returned at intervals which could only be approximately guessed. When, however, the cycle was fulfilled, and there was no more to fall in love with her (strangers, as has been stated, not being admitted), there was a lull, and the rejected, when they came back again and found the girl yet heart free, rejoiced, because every man immediately became confident that sooner or later Lal's fancy would fall upon him ; and every man cherished in his own mind the most delightful anticipations of a magnificent wedding feast, with the joy of Rotherhithe for the bride, and himself for bridegroom.

CHAPTER III.

THE SAILOR LAD FROM OVER THE SEA.

A WOMAN's fate comes to her, like most good or bad things, unexpectedly. Nothing is sure, says the French proverb, but the unforeseen. Nothing could have been more unexpected, for instance, than that the falling overboard of a Malay steward from an Indian liner should have led to the sorrow and the happiness of Lal Rydquist. That this was so you will presently read, and the fact suggests a fine peg for meditation on causes and effects. Had it not been for that event, this story, which it is a great joy to write, would never have been written, and mankind would have been losers to so great an extent ; whereas, that temporary immersion in the cold waters of the river in Limehouse Reach produced so many things one after the other that they have now left Lal in the possession of the most necessary ingredient of happiness quintessential. We all know what that is, and in so simple a matter a lifting of the eye is as good as a printer's sheet of words.

And could one, had it not been so, have had the heart to write this tale ? Why, instead of a Christmas story, it would have been a mere winter's tale, a Middle-of-March story, a searching, biting, cast-wind story, fit only to be cut up and gummed upon doors and windows to keep out the cold.

When the dinner was off her mind, served, commended, and eaten, and when her mother was deposited for the day upon the sofa, with teapot and the kettle ready, the pocket-handkerchiefs for weeping, the book which she never read in, and, perhaps, one of the younger captains who had not yet heard the story of her misfortunes more than a dozen times or so; or with some of her friends among the widows and matrons of Rotherhithe, with whom she would exchange prophecies of disasters, general and particular; Lal would hasten to enjoy herself after her free and independent fashion. One of the captains had given her a little dingy, and taught her how to row it, and her pleasure was to paddle about the river in Limehouse Reach, dodging the steamers, and watching the craft as they went up and down.

This is a pursuit full of peril, because steamers in ballast sometimes come down the river at a reckless speed, their pilots being drunk, cutting down whatever falls in their way; yet to a girl who is handy with her sculls, and has a quick eye, the danger is part of the delight. On the Thames in Limehouse Reach one may be easily run over and one's boat cut in two. There then follows a bad time for a few moments, while the victim of the collision is getting drowned or saved; still, if one thinks of danger, half the fun of the world is gone. Lal thought of the change, the amusement, the excitement: on the Thames there is continual life, movement, and activity; on the Thames, there may be found by girls, sometimes worried by perpetual housekeeping, rest and soothing. As for Lal, the daily press of work was practically finished with the dinner, because the 'service' might be trusted with the rest. And after dinner, on the river she breathed fresh air. Here was not only mental rest, but also exercise for her young muscles; here was all the amusement and variety she ever desired; here she could even let her imagination wander abroad, to the pinnacles and spires of the city of which she knew so little even by hearsay, or to the foreign lands of which she heard so much. Above all, she was alone. This is so rare, so unattainable a thing to most girls, even to those who do not make puddings for sea-captains, that one quite understands how Lal valued the privilege. Her life was all before her. Like other maidens she loved to sit by herself and take a Pisgah-like view of her future. It might lie among the steeples and streets—she had never heard of any West End splendours—of London; it might be in those far-off lands where some of her captains had wives; say, in New Brunswick, or beside the beauty of the Great St. Lawrence, or even in Calcutta, or in Dantzic, or in Norway; or it might lie always in simple and secluded Rotherhithe, among the timber piles of the Commercial Docks. Not a girl given to self-communings, tearing her religion up by the roots to see how it was getting on, or the doubts which nowadays seem to assail most fiercely those who have the least power or knowledge to help them to a solution, a quiet, simple, cheerful, hopeful girl, with a smile for everyone and a laugh for all her friends, yet a girl so hard-worked and so full of responsibilities that there were days when she had what the French ladies call an attack of nerves, and must fain get away from all and float at rest, thinking of other things than the wickedness of butchers, upon the bosom of the great river.

Sometimes, if the weather was too rough for her little boat, she would paddle along the bank till she came to the mouth of the Commercial Docks, and there would row about among the timber ships, watching the men at work, and the great planks being shot from the port-holes in the stern of the vessels, or the dockmen piling the timbers, or the foreign sailors idling about upon the wharves. But mostly she loved the river.

Now it came to pass, one Saturday afternoon, late in the month of May, and the year eighteen hundred and seventy-six, that Lal happened to be out in her boat upon the river. It was a delightful afternoon, quite an old-fashioned May day, without a breath of east wind, a sky covered with light flying clouds, so that the sunshine dropped about in changing breaths, now here and now there, throwing a bright patch upon the water, gilding a steeple, flashing from a window, making even a stumpy little tug glorious for a moment. She sang to herself as she sat in her boat, not a loud song like a Siren or a Lurlei person, but a gentle happy melody—I think it was some hymn—and she sat with her face to the bows, keeping the boat's head well to the waves raised by the swell of the passing ships. She was quite safe herself, being near the shore and between two heavily-laden lighters, waiting for tide to go up stream ; the river was rising, and was covered with all kinds of craft.

Presently she became aware of a vast great ship, one of the big Indian liners, slowly rounding the Isle of Dogs. A great ship always attracted her imagination ; it is a thing so vast, so easily moved, and so life-like. As the tall hull drew nearer, her eyes were fixed upon it, and she paddled a little beyond her protecting lighters, so as to get a better view of the vessel as she passed.

The ship moved up stream slowly here, because the river was so full. First Lal saw from her place the lofty bows, straight cut like a razor, rounding the Isle of Dogs and steadily growing nearer. Then her pilot put her a point more to starboard, and Lal saw the long and lofty side of her, her port-holes open wide, high out of the water. Along the bulwarks were ranged a line of faces, mostly pale with Indian summers, but not all ; they were the faces of the passengers who leaned over and watched the crowded river and talked together. Lal wondered whether they were glad to come home again, and what they were telling each other, and she hoped they would think their country improved since they saw it last ; and then ventured in mute wish to congratulate their mothers, daughters, and sisters, wives, sweethearts, and all female cousins, relatives. and friends, that the ship had not gone to Davy's Locker

on her homeward voyage, with s) many brave fellows on board.
The ship belonged to the great Indian Peninsular Line, and was
called the 'Aryan.' She was so great a ship, and she moved so
slowly, that Lal had time for a great many observations as she passed
her. Also when her little boat was about midships, still kept bows-
on to meet the coming waves, one of the passengers, a young fellow,
took off his hat to her with a loud 'Hurrah !' He meant a respectful salutation to the first pretty girl they had met in the good old
country, which is full of the prettiest girls in the world. Lal
wondered what it felt like, this coming home. All her life long
she had been among men who went out of port and presently put
into port again ; one or two, in her own experience, never came
back, having met with the fate reserved for many sailors ; but that
was not a home-coming like that of these exiles from India. There
would be joy in their homes, no doubt, but what would the poor
fellows themselves feel after these years of separation ? The
feminine mind, everybody knows very well, reserves nearly all its
sympathies for the sufferings of the men ; while it is an honourable
trait in the male character, that it is roused to fury by the sufferings of women.

Just before the ship passed her, the great wave which rolled
upwards from her keel came curling six feet high, like the Bore of
the Severn and the Parrott, towards Lal's little boat. The lighters
reeled and rolled, she seized her sculls and held her bows straight,
steady to meet the swell, so that the little vessel gallantly rode over
the wave ; and this passed swiftly on trying to swamp everything
in its way, and presently capsized a boat with two promising and
ambitious young thieves, who had gone down the river gaily, hoping
to pick up plunder by the way. They got no plunder on that occasion, but a wet skin and a very near escape from the habitual
criminal life for which they were preparing themselves. In this
they are now, in fact, actively engaged ; insomuch that one has
been in prison during three of the five years since that event, and
the other two and a half years. When they are out they enjoy
themselves very much and drink bad gin. Then the wave caught a
Greenwich steamboat and knocked the land-lubber passengers off
their legs ; and then it filled and sunk a barge full of hay. The
hay went down the river with the next tide and littered the shore
of Greenwich, where people who went down to dine gazed upon it
from the windows of the Ship. There was also a sister or a brother
wave on the north bank, proceeding from the starboard bow, but I
do not know what mischief that wave succeeded in accomplishing.

While Lal was considering the ways of this swell, and looking
to see what a pother, with a rolling and a rocking and a staggering
to and fro it caused, she heard a sudden splash, and right in front
of her she was aware of a man in the water. Immediately afterwards another man leaped gallantly from the ship after the first
man, and a moment afterwards came up to the surface holding
him.

Then, without waiting to think, because at such moments the reasoning faculty only brings people to grief and discredit, Lal shot her boat ahead to help, for certainly the two appeared to want immediate assistance, and that so badly, that if it came not at once, they would very soon want it no longer. Their arms were interlocked; they beat, or one of them beat, the water helplessly; their heads kept disappearing and coming up again. On the ship there was a crowd of faces, terror-stricken. The girl caught one hand as her boat came to the spot. The hand belonged to one of the two men, that was clear, but whether the first or the second she could not tell; in fact, only that one hand and a little piece of coat cuff were at the moment visible above water, and probably the next moment there would have been nothing at all. The fingers clutched hers like a vice. Lal threw herself down in the boat to prevent being drawn over, and caught the wrist with her other hand.

Then the group, so to speak, emerged again from the water, and the hand the girl had seized caught the gunwale of the boat, and the eyes in the head which belonged to the hand opened, and the mouth in the head gasped something inarticulate. As for the man's other hand and the whole of the rest of him, that was locked tight in the embrace of the first man who had fallen overboard. It is, anybody knows, the general custom and the base ingratitude of persons who are drowning, to try and drown their rescuers.

'Row us ashore quickly,' cried the one who clung to the gunwale; 'I can hold on for a spell. He won't let go, even to be helped into the boat.'

The ship was brought to now, and there was a vast crowd of passengers, and the officers shouting and gesticulating.

They saw the action of the girl in the boat, and then they saw her seize the sculls and pull vigorously to shore. As for Lal, all she saw was a pale and dripping face, fingers which clutched the gunwale and nearly pulled it under, and an indiscriminate something in the water.

'Oh, can you hold on?' she cried. 'It is but a moment—twenty strokes—see, we are close to the steps.'

'Quick!' he replied; 'it is a heavy weight. Row as hard as you can, please.'

Presently, when the captain of the ship saw the boat landed at the steps, and was sure of the safety of the two men, he made a sign to the pilot, and the ship went on her way, for time is precious.

'Lucky escape,' he said. 'Armiger will come over presently, none the worse for a ducking.'

But the passengers with one accord raised a mighty cheer as the boat touched the shore, and the men on the lighters cheered lustily, and even the two young capsized thieves, who were wet and dripping, cheered. And there were some who said the case must be forwarded to the Royal Humane Society; and some who talked about Grace Darling, and made comparisons; and some who said it

D

was their sacred duty to write to the papers, and tell the story of
this wonderful presence of mind. But they did not, because shortly
afterwards they reached the docks, and there was kissing of relations, packing of wraps, counting of boxes, and afterwards so much
to see and talk about, and so many things to tell, that the rescue of
the second officer in the Thames became only an incident in the
history of the voyage, and the voyage itself only an incident in the
history of their sojourn abroad.

The distance to be rowed was more, indeed, than twenty
strokes, but not much more. Still, there are times when twenty
strokes of the oar take more time, to the imagination, than many
hours of ordinary work. Lal rowed with beating heart; in two
minutes the boat lay alongside the steps.

When her passenger's feet touched the stones he let go, and,
being a strong young fellow and none the worse for his cold bath,
he carried his burden, an apparently inanimate body, up the stairs
to the top. Here he laid him while he ran down again to help his
preserver.

'These are my steps,' she said; 'my boat is always moored
here. Thank you, but if you don't give her the whole length of
her painter she will be hung up by the bows when the tide runs
out.'

She jumped out and ran lightly up the stone steps. At the top
the man who had given them all this trouble sat up, looking about
him with wondering eyes. Then Lal saw that he was of some
foreign country, partly by his dress and partly from his face. The
other, who did indeed present a rueful appearance in his dripping
clothes, was, she perceived, an officer of the steamer. Then Lal
began to laugh.

'It is all very well to laugh,' he said, grimly, and shaking himself
like Tommy Trout, medallist of the Humane Society, after rescuing
that Tom, 'but here's half my kit ruined. And, I say, you've
saved my life and I haven't even thanked you. But I do not
know how to thank you.'

'It was all by chance,' replied Lal, 'and I am very glad.'

'And what are we to do next?' he asked.

He made a sign to the other man, who sprang to his feet,
shivered, and nodded.

'I am very glad you saved his life, at any rate,' the young man
went on; 'he is the steward of the officers' mess, and he cannot
thank you himself, because he is deaf and dumb; we call him
Dick.'

'Come, both of you,' said the girl, recovering her wits, which
were a little scattered by this singular event. 'Come, both, and
dry your clothes.'

She led the way, and they all three set off running—a remarkable procession of one dry girl and two wet men, which drew all
eyes upon them, and a small following of boys, in the direction of
the Captains' house.

'I thought we should have dragged the gunwale under water,' gasped the young fellow.

'So did I,' said Lal, simply. 'Can you swim ?'

'No,' he replied.

'Yet you jumped overboard to rescue your steward. What a splendid thing to do.'

'I forgot I couldn't swim till I was in the water. Never mind. I mean to learn.'

The young fellow was a tall, slight-built lad of twenty-one or twenty-two. Lal pushed him into a bedroom, and pointed to a bundle of clothes. It was not her fault that they belonged to Captain Jansen, who was five feet nothing high, and about the same round the waist. So that when the lad was dressed in them he felt a certain amount of embarrassment, as anyone might who was sent forth into an unknown house with trousers no longer than his knees, and of breadth phenomenal.

'Where can I hide,' he said to himself, 'till the things are dry ?'

He found a room set with a long table and a good many chairs. This was the Captains' room, where they took their meals by day and smoked pipes at night. Just then no one was in it. He wanted to find the girl who had saved his life and rescued him ; so, after a look round, he went on his cruise of discovery.

Next, he opened another door. It was Lal's housekeeping-room, in which sat an old, old man in an armchair, sound asleep. This was Captain Zachariasen.

He shut the door quietly and opened another. This was the front parlour, and in it sat Mrs. Rydquist alone, also fast asleep ; but the opening of the door awakened her, and she sat up and put on her spectacles.

'Come in, captain,' she said, thinking it was one of her friends, but uncertain which of them looked so young and wore clothes of such an amplitude. 'Come in, captain. It is a long time since we have had a talk.'

'Thank you, ma'am,' he replied. 'It is my first visit here. We always, you know, put into East India Docks.'

'Ah !' She shook her head. 'Very wrong—very wrong ! Many have been robbed at Shadwell. But come in, and I will tell you some of my troubles. Do take a chair.'

She drew out a handkerchief, and wiped a rising tear.

'Dear me, what a delightful thing to see a young fellow like you—not drowned yet !'

'I might have been,' he replied, 'but for ——'

'Ah, and you may be yet.' This seemed a very cheerful person. 'Many no older than yourself are lying at the bottom of the sea this minute.'

'That is very true,' he said, ' but——'

'Oh, I know what you would say. And Captain Zachariasen eighty-six years of age if a day.'

The young man began to feel as if he had got into an enchanted palace.

When Lal found him there, he was sitting bolt upright, while Mrs. Rydquist was discoursing at large on perils and disasters at sea.

'You yourself,' she was saying, 'look like one who will go early and find your end——'

'Gracious, mother!' cried Lal, in her quick, sharp way, 'how can you say such things? Time enough when he does go to find it out. Besides —— Your clothes are quite dry now, and—oh! oh! oh!'

Then she laughed again, seeing the delightful incongruity of trousers, sleeves, arms, and legs, so that he retired in confusion.

When he came to put on his own things, he discovered that the girl of the boat—this girl so remarkably handy with her sculls—had actually taken the opportunity to restore a button to the back of his neck. The loss of this button had troubled him for two voyages and a half. So delicate and unusual an attention naturally went straight to his heart, which was already softened by the consideration of the girl's bravery and beauty.

He thought she looked prettier than ever, with her large eyes and the sweet innocence of her face, when he came down again in his uniform.

'Your steward is dry, too,' she said, 'and warming himself before the kitchen fire. Will you have some tea with the captains? It is their tea-time.'

'I would rather have some tea with you,' he replied, 'if I might.'

'Would you? Then of course you shall.'

She spoke as if it were a mere nothing, a trifle of no value at all, this invitation to take tea with her.

She took him into her own room, where the young man had seen the old fellow asleep, and presently brewed him a cup of tea, the like of which, he thought, he had never tasted, and set before him a plate of hot toast.

'That is better for you,' she said, as wisely as any doctor, 'than hot brandy and water.'

At last he rose, after drinking as much tea as he could and staying as long as he dared. The ship would be in dock by this time. He must get across.

'May I come over, when I can get away, to see you again!' he asked, bashfully.

She replied, without any bashfulness at all and with straightforward friendliness, that she would be very glad to see him whenever he could call upon her, and that the best time would be in the afternoon, or, as the evenings were now long, in the evening; but not in the morning, when she was busy with all sorts of things, and especially in superintending the captains' dinner.

'I will come,' he said, and this time he blushed. 'What is your name?'

'I am Lal Rydquist,' she replied, as if everybody ought to know her. But that was not at all what she meant.

'Lal! What a pretty name.' It suits——' And here he stopped and blushed again.

'And what is your name?'

'Rex Armiger,' he said. 'And I am second officer on board the "Aryan," of the Indian Peninsular line, homeward bound from Calcutta.'

This was the beginning of Lal's love-story. A young fellow, gallant and handsome, pulled dripping out of the river—a sailor, too—how could Lal fall in love with anybody but a sailor?

Every love-story has its dawn, its first faint glimmering, which grows into a glorious rose of day. There are generally, as we know, clouds about the east at the dawn of day. Clubmen about Pall Mall frequently remark this in the month of June on leaving the whist-table; policemen have told me the same thing; milkmen, in spring and autumn, report the phenomenon; old-fashioned poets observed it. There can be no real doubt or question about it. After the dawn and the morning comes the noon, when the story becomes uninteresting to outsiders, yet is a very delightful story to the actors themselves. There are different kinds of clouds, and you already know pretty well what was the cloud which for a long time made poor Lal's story a sad one.

When, however, the first streaks of dawn appeared the sky was cloudless. You must not suppose that this young lady beheld the man and straightway fell in love with him. Not at all. Love is a plant which takes time to grow. In her case it kept on growing long after Rex had left her; long, indeed, after everybody said he was dead. But it cannot be denied that she thought about him.

The captains congratulated her on having pulled the young fellow out of the river. Captain Zachariasen, with a gallantry beyond his years, even went so far as to wish he had himself been the subject of the immersion and the rescue. He also related several stories of his own daring, fifty, sixty, or seventy years before, in various parts of the ocean. All this was pleasing.

Lal laughed at the compliments and sang the more about the house, nor did it disturb her in the least when her mother lifted up her voice in prophecy.

'My dear,' she said, 'mark my words. If ever I saw shipwreck and drowning—I mean quite young drowning—on any man's face, it is marked on the face of that young man. The heedless and the giddy may laugh; but we know better, my dear—we who have gone through it.'

When a ship comes home and has but three weeks in which to discharge her cargo and take in her new lading, the officers have by no means an easy time. It is not holiday with them, but quite the reverse; and it was not often that Rex could get even an evening free. In fact, the whole of his wooing was accomplished in five visits to Rotherhithe.

On his first visit he was disappointed. Lal was on the river in her boat, and so he sat with her mother and waited. Mrs. Rydquist took the opportunity, which might never occur again, of solemnly warning him against falling in love with her daughter. This, she said, was a very possible thing to happen, especially for a sailor, because her girl was well set-up, not to say handsome. Therefore, it was her duty to warn him—as she had already warned a good many, including Captain Skantlebury, afterwards cast away in Torres Straits—that it was an unlucky thing to marry into a family whose husbands and male relations generally found a grave at the bottom of the sea. Further, it was well known among sailors that if you rescued a person from drowning, that person would, at some time or other, repay your offices by injuring your earthly prospects. So that there were two excellent reasons why Rex should avoid the Rock of Love.

They were doubtless valid ; but they were not strong enough to repress in the young man a look of joy and admiration when the girl came home fresh and bright as an ocean nymph. He took supper with her, and between them the two managed to repress the gloom even of the prophetess who sat with them, as cheerful as Cassandra at a Trojan supper. Did ever anyone consider how much that good old man King Priam had to put up with ?

Another time was on a Sunday evening. They went to church together and sang out of the same hymn-book. Captain Zachariasen was in the pew also, and he went to sleep three times—viz., during the first lesson, the second lesson, and the sermon, without counting the prayers, during which he probably dropped off as well. After the service, as the evening was fine and the air warm, they sat awhile in the churchyard, and the young fellow, seated on a tombstone, unconscious of the moral he was illustrating, had a very good time indeed talking with Lal. When they were tired of the churchyard they walked away to the bridge over the entrance to the docks, and leaned over the rail talking still. Lal was quite used to the confidences of her friends, but somehow this one's confidences were different. He sought no advice, he confessed no love-affair ; he did not begin to look at her as if he was struck silly, and then ask her to marry him—which so many of the captains had done ; he asked her about herself, and seemed eager to know all she would tell him, as if there was anything about herself that so gallant a sailor would care to know, with such stupid particulars about her daily life, and how she never left Rotherhithe at all, and had seen no other place.

'What a strange life ! ' he said, after many questions. 'What a dull life ! Are you not tired of it ? '

'No,' she answered. 'Why should I be ? Do they not bring a constant change into the house, my captains ? I know all their adventures, and I could tell you, oh ! such stories. You should hear Captain Zachariasen when he begins to recollect.'

'Ay, ay, we can all spin yarns. But never to leave this place !'
He paused, with a sigh.

'I am happy,' said Lal. 'Tell me about yourself.·

It was her turn now, and she began to question him until he
told all he had to tell ; but I suppose he kept back something, as
one is told to leave something on the dish, for good manners. But
if he did not tell all, it was because he was modest, not because he
had things to hide of which he was ashamed.

He was, he said, the son of a Lincolnshire clergyman, and he
was destined to the Church ; solemnly set apart, he was, by his
parents and consecrated in early infancy. This made his subse-
quent conduct the more disgraceful, although, as he pleaded, his
own consent was not asked nor his inclinations consulted. The
road to the Church is grievously beset by wearisome boulders, pits,
ditches, briars, and it may be fallen trunks, which some get over
without the least difficulty, whereas to others they are grievous
hindrances. These things are an allegory, and I mean books.
Now unlucky Rex, a masterly youth in all games, schoolboy feats,
fights, freaks, and fanteegs, regarded a book, from his earliest
infancy, unless it was a romance of the sea or story of adventure,
with a dislike and suspicion amounting almost to mania. In his
recital to Lal, he avoided mention of the many floggings he received, the battles he fought, and the insubordination of which he
was guilty, and the countless lessons which he had not learned. He
simply said that he ran away from school and got to Liverpool,
where, after swopping clothes with a real sailor boy, he got on
board a Canadian brig as loblolly boy, and was kicked and cuffed
all the way to Quebec and all the way back again. The skipper
cuffed him ; the mate cuffed him ; the cook cuffed him ; the crew
cuffed him ; he got rough treatment and bad grub. His faculties
were stimulated, no doubt, and a good foundation laid for smart-
ness in after life as a sailor. Also, his frame was hardened by
the fresh breeze of the Windy Fifties. On his return, he wrote
to his father, to say that he was about to return to school. He did
return ; was the hero of the school for two months, and then again
ran away and tried the sea once more, from Glasgow to New York, in
a cargo steamer. Finally, his father had to renounce his ambitious
schemes, in spite of the early consecration and setting apart,
and got him entered as a middy in the service of a great line of
steamers. Now, at the age of twenty-two, he was second officer.

Such was the modesty of the young man that he omitted to
state many remarkable facts in his own life, though these redounded
greatly to his credit ; nor was it till afterwards that Lal discovered
how good a character he bore for steady seamanship and pluck,
how well he stood for promotion. Also, he did not tell her that he
was the softest-hearted fellow in the world, though his knuckles
were so hard ; that he was the easiest man in the world to lead,
although the hardest to drive ; that on board he was always ready,
when off duty, to act as nursemaid, protector, and playfellow for

any number of children ; that he was also at such times as good as
a son or a brother to all ladies on board ; that on shore he was ever
ready to give away all his money to the first who asked for it ; that
he thought no evil of his neighbour ; that he considered all women
as angels, but Lal as an archangel ; and that he was modest,
thinking himself a person of the very smallest importance on
account of these difficulties over books, and a shameful apostate
in the matter of the falling off from the early dedication.

When a young woman begins to take a real interest in the adventures of a young man, and, like Desdemona, to ask questions,
she generally lays a solid foundation for much more than mere
interest. Dido, though she was no longer in her *première jeunesse*,
is a case in point, as well as Desdemona. And every married person recollects the flattering interest taken in each other by *fiancé*
and *fiancée* during the early days, the sweet sunshiny days of their
engagement.

That Sunday night, after the talk in the churchyard, they went
back to the house, and Rex had supper with the captains, winning
golden opinions by his great and well-sustained powers over cold
beef and pickles. After this they smoked pipes and told yarns,
and Lal sat among them by the side of Rex, which was a joy to
him, though she was sitting on the arm of Captain Zachariasen's
wooden chair, and not his own.

On another occasion during that happy and never-to-be-for-
gotten three weeks, Rex carried the girl across the river and showed
her his own ship lying in the East India Docks, which, she was fain
to confess, are finer than the Commercial Docks. He took her all
over the great and splendid vessel, showed her the saloon with its
velvet couches, hanging lamps, gilt ornaments, and long tables in
the officers' quarters ; and midships, and the sailors' for'ard ; took
her down to the engine-room by a steep ladder of polished iron bars,
showed her the bridge, the steering tackle, and the captain's cabin,
in which he lowered his voice from reverence as one does in a
church. When she had seen everything, he invited her to return
to the saloon, where she found a noble repast spread, and the chief
officer, the third mate, the purser, and the doctor waiting to be
introduced to her. They paid her so much attention and deference ;
they said so many kind things about her courage and presence of
mind ; they waited on her so jealously ; they were so kind to her,
that the girl was ashamed. She was so very ignorant, you see, of
the power of beauty. Then a bottle of champagne, a drink which
Lal had heard of but never seen, was produced, and they all drank
to her health, bowing and smiling, first to her and then to Rex,
who blushed and hung his head. Then it appeared that every man
had something which he ardently desired her to accept, and when
Lal came away Rex had his arms full of pretty Indian things,
smelling of sandal-wood, presents to her from his brother-officers.
This, she thought, was very kind of them, especially as they had
never seen her before. And then Dick, the officers' steward, the

deaf and dumb Malay whom she had helped to pull out of the
water, came and kissed her hand humbly, in token of gratitude.
A beautiful and wonderful day. Yet what did the doctor mean
when they came away? For while the purser stood at one end of
the gangway, and the chief officer at the other, and the third mate
in the middle, all to see her safe across, the doctor, left behind
on board, slapped Rex loudly upon the shoulder and laughed,
saying :—

'Gad! Rex, you're a lucky fellow!'

How was he lucky? she asked him in the boat, and said she
should be glad to hear of good luck for him. But he only blushed
and made no reply.

One of the things which she brought home after this visit was a
certain grey parrot. He had no particular value as a parrot.
There were many more valuable parrots already about the house,
alive or stuffed. But this bird had accomplishments, and among
other things, he knew his master's name, and would cry, to everybody's admiration : 'Poor Rex Armiger! Poor Rex Armiger!'

When Lal graciously accepted this gift, the young man took it
as a favourable sign. She had already, he knew, sent away a dozen
captains at least, and he was only second mate. Yet still, when a
girl takes such a present she means—she surely means to make
some difference.

Then there was one day more—the last day but one before the
ship sailed—the last opportunity that Rex could find before they
sailed. He had leave for a whole day : the lading was completed,
the passengers were sending on their boxes and trunks ; the purser
and the stewards were taking in provisions—mountains of provisions, with bleating sheep, milch cows, cocks and hens—for the
voyage.

All was bustle and stir at the Docks, but there was no work for
the second officer. He presented himself at Seven Houses at ten
o'clock in the morning, without any previous notice, and proposed,
if you please, nothing short of a whole day out. A whole day,
mind you, from that moment until ten o'clock at night. Never
was proposal more revolutionary.

'All day long?' she cried, her great eyes full of surprise and
joy.

'All day,' he said, 'if you will trust yourself with me. Where
shall we go?'

'Where?' she repeated.

I suppose that now and then some echoes reach Rotherhithe of
the outer world and its amusements. Presumably there are natives
who have seen the Crystal Palace and other places ; here and there
might be found one or two who have seen a theatre. Most of
them, however, know nothing of any place of amusement whatever. It is a city without any shows. Punch and Judy go not
near it ; Cheap Jack passes it by ; the wandering feet of circus
horses never pass that way ; gipsies' tents have never been seen

there ; the boys of Rotherhithe do not know even the travelling
caravan with the fire-eater. To conjurers, men with entertainments, and lecturers it is an untrodden field. When Lal came, in
a paper, upon the account of festive doings she passed them over,
and turned to the condition of the markets in South Africa or
Quebec as being a subject more likely to interest the captains.
Out of England there were plenty of things to interest her. She
knew something about the whole round world, or, at least, its
harbours ; but of London she was ignorant.

'Where ?' she asked, gasping.

'There's the Crystal Palace and Epping Forest ; there's the
National Gallery and Highgate Hill ; there's the top of St. Paul's
and the Aquarium ; there's Kew Gardens and the Tower ; there's
South Kensington and Windsor Castle '—Rex bracketed the places
according to some obscure arrangement in his own mind—'lots of
places. The only thing is where ?'

'I have seen none of them,' she replied. 'Will you choose
for me ?'

'Oh !' he groaned. 'Here is a house full of great hulking
skippers, and she works herself to death for them, and not one
among them all has ever had the grace to take her to go and see
something !'

'Don't call them names,' she replied, gently ; 'our people
never go anywhere, except to Poplar and Limehouse. One of
them went one evening to Woolwich Gardens, but he did not like
it. He said the manners of the people were forward, and he was
cheated out of half a crown.'

'Then, Lal,' he jumped up and made a great show of preparing
for immediate departure with his cap ; 'then, Lal, let us waste no
more time in talking, but be off at once.'

'Oh, I can't !'

Her face fell, and the tears came into her eyes as she suddenly
recollected a reason why she could not go.

'Why can't you ?'

'Because—oh, because of the pudding. I can trust her with
the potatoes, and she will boil the greens to a turn. But the pudding I always make, and no one else can make it but me.'

The lady referred to was not her mother, but the assistant—the
'service.'

'Can't they go without pudding for once ?'

Lal shook her head.

'They always expect pudding, and they are very particular
about the currants. You can't think what a quantity of currants
they want in their pudding.'

'Do you always give them plum-duff, then ?'

'Except when they have roly-poly or apple dumplings. Sometimes it is baked plum-duff, sometimes it is boiled, sometimes with
sauce, and sometimes with brandy. But I think they would never
forgive me if there was no pudding.'

Rex nodded his head, put on his cap—this conversation took place in the kitchen—and marched resolutely straight into the Captains' room, where three of them were at that moment sitting in conversation. One was Captain Zachariasen.

'Gentlemen,' he said, politely saluting ; 'Lal wants a whole holiday. But she says she can't take it unless you will kindly go without your pudding to-day.'

They looked at each other. No one for a time spoke. The gravity of the proposal was such that no one liked to take the responsibility of accepting it. A dinner at Rydquist's without pudding was a thing hitherto unheard of.

'Why,' asked Captain Zachariasen, severely—'why, if you please, Mr. Armiger, does Lal want a holiday to-day? And why cannot she be content with a half-holiday ? Do I ever take a whole day ? '

' Because she wants to go somewhere with me,' replied Rex, stoutly ; 'and if she doesn't go to-day she won't go at all, because we sail the day after to-morrow.'

' Under these circumstances, gentlemen,' said Captain Zacharia- sen, softening, and feeling that he had said enough for the asser- tion of private rights, ' seeing that Lal is, for the most part, an obliging girl, and does her duty with a willing spirit, I think— you are agreed with me, gentlemen ? '

The other two nodded their heads, but with some sadness.

' Then, sir,' said Captain Zachariasen, as if he were addressing his chief officer at high noon, ' make it so.'

' Now,' said Rex, as they passed Rotherhithe parish church and drew near unto Thames Tunnel Station, ' I've made up my mind where to take you to. As for the British Museum, it's sticks and stones, and South Kensington is painted pots ; the National Gallery is saints and sign-boards ; the Crystal Palace is buns and boards and ginger-beer, with an organ ; the Monument of London is no better than the crosstrees. Where we will go, Lal—where we will go for our day out—is to Hampton Court, and we will have such a day as you shall remember.'

There had been, as yet, no word of love ; but he called her Lal, and she called him Rex, which is an excellent beginning.

They did have that day ; they did go to Hampton Court. First they drove in a hansom—Lal thought nothing could be more delightful than this method of conveyance—to Waterloo Station, where they were so lucky as to catch a train going to start in three- quarters of an hour, and by that they went to Hampton Court.

It was in the early days of the month of June, which in England has two moods. One is the dejected, make-yourself-as- miserable-as-you-can mood, when the rain falls dripping all the day, and the leaves, which have hardly yet fully formed on the trees, begin to get rotten before their time, and think of falling off. That mood of June is not delightful. The other, which is far preferable, is that in which the month comes with a gracious smile, bearing in her hands lilac, roses, laburnum, her face all glorious with sunshine, soft airs, and warmth. Then the young year springs swiftly into vigorous manhood, with fragrance and sweet perfumes, and the country hedges are splendid with their wealth of a thousand wild flowers, and the birds sing above their nests. Men grow young men again, lapped and wrapped in early summer ; the blood of the oldest is warmed ; their fancies run riot ; they begin to babble of holidays, to talk of walks in country places, of rest on hill-sides, of wanderings, rod in hand, beside the streams, of shady woods, and the wavelets of a tranquil sea ; they feel once more—one must feel it every year again or die—the old simple love for earth, fair mother-earth, generous earth, mother, nurse, and fosterer—as well as grave ; they enjoy the sunshine. Sad autumn is as yet far off, and seems much farther ; they are not yet near unto the days when they shall say, one to the other :

'Lo! the evil days are come when we may say, "I have no pleasure in them."'

The train sped forth from the crowded houses, and presently passed into the fields and woods of Surrey. Rex and Lal were alone in a second-class carriage, and she looked out of the window while he looked at her. And so to Hampton, where the Mole joins the silver Thames, and the palace stands beside the river bank.

I have always thought that to possess Hampton Court is a rare and precious privilege which Londoners cannot regard with sufficient gratitude, for, with the exception of Fontainebleau, which is too big, there is nothing like it—except, perhaps, in Holland—anywhere. It is delightful to wander in the cool cloisters, about the bare chambers hung with pictures, and in the great empty hall, where the Queen might dine every day if she chose, her crown upon her head, with braying of trumpets, scraping of fiddles, and pomp of scarlet retainers. But she does not please. Then one may walk over elastic turf, round beds of flowers, or down long avenues of shady trees, which make one think of William the Third ; or one may look over a wooden garden gate into what was the garden in the times before Cardinal Wolsey found out this old country grange and made it into a palace. Young people—especially young people in love—may also seek the windings of the maze.

This boy Rex, with the girl who seemed to him the most delightful creature ever formed by a benevolent Providence, enjoyed all these delights, the girl lost in what seemed to her a dream of wonder. Why had she never seen any of these beautiful places? For the first time in her life, Rotherhithe, and the docks and ships became small to her. She had never before known the splendour of stately halls, pictures, or great gardens. She felt humiliated by her strangeness, and to this day, though now she has seen a great many splendid places, she regards Hampton Court as the most wonderful and the most romantic of all buildings ever erected, and I do not think she is far wrong.

One thing only puzzled her. She had read, somewhere, of the elevating influences of art. This is a great gallery of art. Yet somehow she did not feel elevated at all. Especially did a collection of portraits of women—all with drooping eyes and false smiles and strange looks, the meaning of which she knew not—make her long to hurry out of the room and into the fair gardens, on whose lawns she could forget these pictures. How could they elevate or improve the people? Art, you see, only elevates those who understand a little of the technique, and ordinary people go to the picture-galleries for the story told by each picture. This is the reason why the contemplation of a vast number of pictures has hitherto failed to improve our culture or to elevate our standards. But these two, like most visitors, took all for granted, and it must be owned that there are many excellent stories, especially those of the old sea-fight pictures, in the Hampton Court galleries.

Then they had dinner together in a room whose windows looked right down the long avenue of Bushey, where the chestnuts were in all their glory ; and after dinner Rex took her on the river. It was the same river as that of Rotherhithe. But who would have thought that twenty miles would make so great a change? No ships, no steamers, no docks, no noise, no shouting, no hammering. And what a difference in the boats ! They drifted slowly down with the silent current. The warm sun of the summer afternoon lay lovingly on the meadows. It was not a Saturday. No one was on the river but themselves. The very swans sat sleepily on the water ; there was a gentle swish and slow murmur of the current along the reeds and grasses of the bank ; crimson and golden leaves hung over the river ; the flowers of the lilies were lying open on the water.

Lal held the ropes and Rex the sculls ; but he let them lie idle and looked at the fair face before him, while she gazed dreamily about, thinking how she should remember, and by what things, this wonderful day, this beautiful river, this palace, and this gentle rowing in the light skiff. As she looked, the smile faded out of her face and her eyes filled with tears.

' Why, Lal ? ' he asked.

She made no reply for a minute or two, thinking what reason she might truthfully allege for her tears, which had risen unbidden at the touch of some secret chord.

' I do not know,' she said. ' Except that everything is so new and strange, and I am quite happy, and it is all so beautiful.'

Rex reflected on the superior nature of women who can shed tears as a sign of happiness.

' I am so happy,' he said, ' that I should like to dance and sing, except that I am afraid of capsizing the craft, when to Davy's locker we should go for want of your dingy, Lal.'

But they could not stay on the river all the evening. The sun began to descend ; clouds came up from the south-west ; the wind freshened ; a mist arose, and the river became sad and mysterious.

Then Rex turned the bows and rowed back.

The girl shuddered as she stepped upon the shore.

'I shall never forget it,' she said ; 'never. And now it is all over.'

'Will you remember, with this day, your companion of the day ?' asked Rex.

'Yes,' she replied, with the frank and truthful gaze which went straight to the young man's heart ; 'I shall never forget the day or my companion.'

They went back to the palace, and while the shadows grew deeper, walked in the old-fashioned garden of King William, beneath its arch of branches, old now and knotty and gnarled.

Rex was to sail in two days' time. He would have no other chance. Yet he feared to break the charm.

'We must go,' he said. 'Yes, it is all over.' He heaved a mighty sigh. 'What a day we have had. And now it is gone, it is growing dark, and we must go. And this is the last time I shall see you, Lal.'

'Yes,' she murmured ; 'the last time.'

Years afterwards she remembered those words and the thought of ill omens and what they may mean.

'The last time,' she repeated.

'I suppose you know, Lal, that I love you ?' said Rex, quite simply. 'You must know that. But, of course, everybody loves you.'

'Oh !' she laid her hand upon his arm. 'Are you sure, quite sure, that you love me ? You might be mistaken, Rex.'

'Sure, Lal ?'

'Can you really love me ?'

'My darling, have not other men told you the same thing ? Have you not listened and sent them away ? Do not send me away, too, Lal.'

'They said they—— Oh, it was nonsense. They could not really have loved me, because I did not love them at all.'

'And—and—me ?' asked Rex, with fine disregard of grammar.

'Oh, no, Rex. I do not want to send you away—not if you really love me ;——and, Rex, Rex, you have kissed me enough.'

They could not go away quite then ; they stayed there till they were found by the custodian of the vine, who ignominiously led them to the palace-gates and dismissed them with severity. Then Rex must needs have supper, in order to keep his sweetheart with him a little longer. And it was not till the ten o'clock train that they returned to town : Lal quiet and a little tearful, her hand in her lover's ; Rex full of hope and faith and charity, and as happy as if he were, indeed, 'rex orbis totius,' the king of the whole world.

At half-past eleven he brought her home. It was very late for Rotherhithe ; the captains were mostly in bed by ten, and all the lights out, but to-night Mrs. Rydquist sat waiting for her daughter.

'Mrs. Rydquist,' said the young man, beaming like a sun-god between the pair of candles over which the good lady sat reading, 'she has promised to be my wife—Lal is going to marry me. The day after to-morrow we drop down the river, but I shall be home again soon—home again. Come Lal, my darling, my sweet, my queen,' he took her in his arms and kissed her again—this shameless young sailor—'and as soon as I get my ship—why—why—why——' he kissed her once more, and yet once more.

'I wish you, young man,' said Lal's mother, in funereal tones, 'a better fate than has befallen all the men who fell in love with us. I have already given you my most solemn warning. You rush upon your fate, but I wash my hands of it. My mother's lost husband, and my husband, lie dead at the bottom of the sea. Also two of my first cousins' husbands, and a second cousin's once-removed husband. We are an unlucky family ; but, perhaps, my daughter's husband may be more fortunate.'

'Oh, mother,' cried poor Lal, 'don't make us down-hearted !'

'I said, my dear,' she replied, folding her hands with a kind of resignation to the inevitable, 'I said that I hope he may be more fortunate. I cannot say more ; if I could say more I would say it. If I think he may not be more fortunate, I will not say it ; nor will I give you pain, Mr. Armiger, by prophesying that you will add to our list.'

'Never mind,' said Rex ; 'we sailors are mostly as safe at sea as the landlubbers on shore, only people won't think so. Heart up, Lal ! Heart up, my sweet ! Come outside and say good-bye.'

'Look !' said Mrs. Rydquist, pointing cheerfully to the candle-stick, when her daughter returned with tears in her eyes and Rex's last kiss burning on her lips ; 'there is a winding-sheet, my dear, in the candle. To-night a coffin popped out of the kitchen-fire. I took it up in hopes it might have been a purse. No, my dear, a coffin. Captain Zachariasen crossed knives at dinner to-day. I have had shudders all the evening, which is as sure a sign of graves as any I know. Before you came home the furniture cracked three times. No doubt, my dear, these warnings are for me, who am a poor, weak creature, and ready and willing and hopeful, I am sure, to be called away ; or for Captain Zachariasen, who is, to be sure, a great age, and should expect his call every day instead of going on with his talk and his rum and his pipe as if he was forgotten ; or for any one of the captains, afloat or ashore ; these signs, my dear, may be meant for anybody, and I would not be so presumptuous in a house full of sailors as to name the man for whom they have come ; but, if I read signs right, then they mean that young man. And oh ! my poor girl——' she clasped her hands as if now, indeed, there could be no hope.

'What is it, mother ?'

'My dear, it is a Friday, of all the days in the week !'

She rose, took a candle and went to bed, with her handkerchief to her eyes.

CHAPTER IV.

OVERDUE AND POSTED.

THIS day of days, this queen of all days, too swiftly sped over the first and last of the young sailor's wooing. Lal's sweetheart was lost to her almost as soon as he was found. But he left her so happy in spite of her mother's gloomy forebodings, that she wondered—not knowing that all the past years had been nothing but a long preparation for the time of love—how could she ever have been happy before? And she was only eighteen, and her lover as handsome as Apollo, and as well-mannered. Next morning at about twelve o'clock she jumped into her boat and rowed out upon the river to see the 'Aryan' start upon her voyage. The tide was on the turn and the river full when the great steamer came out of dock and slowly made her way upon the crowded water a miracle of human skill, a great and wonderful living thing, which, though even a clumsy lighter might sink and destroy it, yet could live through the wildest storm ever known in the Sea of Cyclones, through which she was to sail. As the 'Aryan' passed the little boat Lal saw her lover. He had sprung upon the bulwark and was waving his hat in farewell. Oh, gallant Rex, so brave and so loving! To think that this glorious creature, this god-like man, this young prince among sailors, should fall in love with her! And then the doctor, and the purser, and the chief officers, and even the captain, came to the side and took off their caps to her, and some of the passengers, informed by the doctor who she was, and how brave she was, waved their hands and cheered.

Then the ship forged ahead, and in a few minutes Rex jumped down with a final kiss of his fingers. The screw turned more quickly ; the ship forged ahead. Lal lay to in mid-stream, careless what might run into her, gazing after her with straining eyes. When she had rounded the point and was lost to view, the girl, for the first time in her life since she was a child, burst into tears and sobbing.

It was but a shower. Lal belonged to a sailor family. Was she to weep and go in sadness because her lover was away doing his duty upon the blue water? Not so. She shook her head, dried her eyes, and rowed homewards, grave yet cheerful.

' Is his ship gone ?' asked her mother. ' Well, he is a fine lad to look at, Lal, and if he is as true as he is strong and well-favoured, I could wish you nothing better. Let us forget the signs and warnings, my dear'—this was kindly meant, but had an unpleasant and gruesome sound—'and let us hope that he will come back again. Indeed, I do not see any reason why he should not come back more than once.'

Everything went on, then, as if nothing had happened. What a strange thing it is that people can go on as if nothing had happened, after the most tremendous events! Life so changed for her, yet Captain Zachariasen taking up the thread of her discourse just as before, and the same interest expected to be shown in the timber trade! Yet what a very different thing is interest in timber trade compared with interest in a man! Then she discovered with some surprise that her old admiration of captains as a class had been a good deal modified during the last three weeks. There were persons in the world, it was now quite certain, of culture superior even to that of a skipper in the Canadian trade. And she clearly discovered, for the first time, that a whole life devoted to making captains comfortable, providing them with pudding, looking after their linen, and hearing their confidences, might, without the gracious influences of love, become a very arid and barren kind of life. Perhaps, also, the recollection of that holiday at Hampton Court helped to modify her views on the subject of Rotherhithe and its people. The place was only, after all, a small part of a great city ; the people were humble. One may discover as much certainly about one's own people without becoming ashamed of them. It is only when one reaches a grade higher in the social scale that folk become ashamed of themselves. An assured position in the world, as the chimney-sweep remarked, gives one confidence. Lal plainly saw that her sweetheart was of gentler birth and better breeding than she had been accustomed to. She therefore resolved to do her best never to make him on that account repent his choice, and there was an abundance of fine sympathy—the assumption or pretence of which is the foundation of good manners—in this girl's character.

It was an intelligent parrot which Rex had given her, and at this juncture proved a remarkably sympathetic creature, for at the sight of his mistress he would shake his head, plume his wings, and presently, as if necessary to console her, would cry :

'Poor Rex Armiger ! Poor Rex Armiger !'

But she was never dull, nor did she betray to anyone, least of all to her old friend Captain Zachariasen, that her manner of regarding things had in the least degree changed, while the secret joy that was in her heart showed itself in a thousand merry ways : with songs and laughter, and little jokes with her captains, so that they marvelled that the existence of a sweetheart at sea should produce so beneficial an effect upon maidens. Perhaps, too, in some mysterious way, her happiness affected the puddings. I say not this at random, because certainly the fame of Rydquist's as a house where comforts, elsewhere unknown, and at Limehouse and Poplar quite unsuspected, could be found, spread far and wide, even to Deptford on the east, and Stepney on the north, and the house might have been full over and over again, but they would take in no strangers, being in this respect as exclusive as Boodle's.

This attitude of cheerfulness was greatly commended by Captain

E

Zachariasen. 'Some girls,' he said, 'would have let their thoughts
run upon their lover instead of their duty, whereby houses are
brought to ruin and captains seek comfort elsewhere. Once the
sweetheart is gone, he ought never more to be thought upon till he
comes home again, save in bed or in church, while there is an egg to
be boiled or an onion to be peeled.'

The first letter which Rex sent her was the first that Lal had
ever received in all her life. And such a letter! It came from the
Suez Canal ; the next came from Aden ; the next from Point de
Galle ; the next from Calcutta. So far all was well. Be sure that Lal
read them over and over again, every one, and carried them about
in her bosom, and knew them all word for word, and was, after the
way of a good and honest girl, touched to the very heart that a man
should love her so very, very much, and should think so highly of
her, and should talk as if she was all goodness—a thing which no
woman can understand. It makes silly girls despise men, and good
girls respect and fear them.

The next letter was much more important than the first four,
which were, in truth, mere rhapsodies of passion, although on that
very account more interesting than letters which combine matter-
of-fact business with love, for, on arriving at Calcutta, Rex found a
proposal waiting for his acceptance. This offer came from the
Directors of the Company, and showed in what good esteem he was
held, being nothing less than the command of one of their smaller
steamers, engaged in what is called the country trade.

'It will separate us for three years at least,' he wrote, 'and
perhaps for five, but I cannot afford to refuse the chance. Perhaps,
if I did, I might never get another offer, and everybody is congratulating me, and thinking me extremely fortunate to get a ship so
early. So, though it keeps me from the girl of my heart, I have
accepted, and I sail at once. My ship is named the "Philippine."
She is a thousand-ton boat, and classed 100 A1, newly built. She
is not like the "Aryan," fitted with splendid mirrors and gold and
paint and a great saloon, being built chiefly for cargo. The crew
are all Lascars, and I am the only Englishman aboard except the
mate and the chief engineer. We are under orders to take in rice
from Hong-Kong ; bound for Brisbane, first of all ; if that answers
we shall continue in the country grain trade ; if not, we shall, I
suppose, go seeking, when I shall have a commission on the cargo.
As for pay, I am to have twenty pounds a month, with rations and
allowances, and liberty to trade—so many tons every voyage—if I
like. These are good terms, and at the end of every year there
should be something put by in the locker. Poor Lal! Oh, my dear
sweet eyes! Oh, my dear brown hair! Oh, my dear sweet lips! I
shall not kiss them for three years more. What are three years?
Soon gone, my pretty. Think of that, and heart up! As soon as I
can I will try for a Port-of-London ship. Then we will be married
and have a house at Gravesend, where you shall see me come up
stream, homeward bound.' With much more to the same effect.

Three years—or it might be five! Lal put down the letter, and tried to make out what it would mean to her. She would be in three years, when Rex came home, one and twenty, and he would be five and twenty. Five and twenty seems to eighteen what forty seems to thirty, fifty to forty, and sixty to fifty. One has a feeling that the ascent of life must then be quite accomplished, and the descent fairly begun ; the leaves on the trees by the wayside must be ever so little browned and dusty, if not yellow ; the heart must be full of experience, the head must be full of wisdom, the crown of glory, if any is to be worn at all, already on the brows. The ascent of life is like the climbing of some steep hill, because the summit seems continually to recede, and so long as one is young in heart it is never reached. Rex five and twenty ! Three years to wait !

It is, indeed, a long time for the young to look forward to. Such a quantity of things get accomplished in three years ! Why, in three years a lad gets through his whole undergraduate course, and makes a spoon or spoils a horn. Three years make up one hundred and fifty-six weeks, with the same number of Sundays, in every one of which a girl may sit in the quiet church and wonder on what wild seas or in what peaceful haven her lover may be floating. Three years are four summers in the course of three years, with as many other seasons ; in three years there is time for many a hope to spring up, flourish for a while, and die ; for friendship to turn into hate ; for strength to decay ; and for youth to grow old. The experience of the long succession of human generations has developed this sad thing among mankind that we cannot look forward with joy to the coming years, and in everything unknown which will happen to us we expect a thing of evil. Three years ! Yet it must be borne, as the lady said to the school-boy concerning the fat beef, 'It is helped, and must be finished.'

When Mrs. Rydquist heard the news she first held up her hands, and spread them slowly outwards, shaking and wagging her head—a most dreadful sign, worse than any of those with which Panurge discomfited Thaumast. Then she sighed heavily. Then she said aloud :

'Oh, dear, dear, dear ! So soon ! I had begun to hope that the bad luck would not show yet ! Dear, dear ! Yet what could be expected after such certain signs ?'

'Why,' said Captain Zachariasen, 'as for signs, they may mean anything or anybody, and as for fixing them on Cap'en Armiger, no reason that I can see. Don't be downed, Lal. The narrow seas are as safe as the Mediterranean. In my time there were the pirates, who are now shot, hanged, and drowned, every man Jack. No more stinkpots in crawling boats, pretending to be friendly traders. You might row your dingy about the islands as safe as Lime'us Reach. Lord ! I'd rather go cruising with your sweetheart in them waters than take a twopenny omnibus along the Old Kent Road. Your signs, ma'am,' he said to Mrs. Rydquist,

E 2

politely, 'must be read other ways. There's Cap'en Biddiman; perhaps they're meant for him.'

Then came another letter from Singapore. Rex was pleased with the ship and his crew. All was going well.

After six weeks there came another letter. It was from Hong-Kong. The ' Philippine' had taken on board her cargo of rice and was to sail next day.

Rex wrote in his usual confident, happy vein—full of love, of hope, and happiness.

After that—no more letters at all. Silence.

Lal went on in cheerfulness for a long time. Rex could not write from Brisbane. He would write when the ship got back to Hong-Kong.

The weeks went on, but still there was silence. It was whispered in the Captains' room that the ' Philippine ' was long over-due at Moreton Bay. Then the whispers became questions whether there was any news of her : then one went across to the office of the company, and brought back the dreadful news that the owners had given her up ; and they began to hide away the ' Shipping and Mercantile Gazette.' Then everybody became extremely kind to Lal, studying little surprises for her, and assuming an appearance of light-heartedness so as to deceive the poor girl. She went about with cheerful face, albeit with sinking heart. Ships are often over-due ; letters get lost on the way. For a while she still carolled and sang about her work, though at times her song would suddenly stop like the song of a bullfinch, who remembers something, and must needs stay his singing while he thinks about it.

Then there came a time when the poor child stopped singing altogether, and would look with anxious eyes from one captain to the other, seeking comfort. But no one had any comfort to give her.

Captain Zachariasen told her at last. He was an old man ; he had seen so many shipwrecks that they thought he would tell her best ; also it was considered his duty, as the father or the oldest inhabitant of Rydquist's, to undertake this task ; and as a wise and discreet person he would tell the story, as it should be told, in few words, and to get it over without beatings on and off. He accepted the duty, and discharged himself of it as soon as he could. He told her the story, in fact, the next morning in the kitchen.

He said, quietly :

' Lal, my dear, the "Philippine" has gone to the bottom, and —and don't take on, my pretty. But Cap'en Armiger he is gone, too ; with all hands he went down.'

' How do you know ?' she asked. The news was sudden, but she felt it coming ; that is, she had felt some of it—not all.

' The insurances have been all paid up : the ship is posted at Lloyd's. My dear, I went to the underwriter's a month ago and more, and axed about her. Axed what they would underwrite her for, and they said a hundred per cent. ; and then they wouldn't do

It. Not an atom of hope—gone she is, and that young fellow aboard her. Well, my dear, that's done with. Shall I leave you here alone to get through a spell o' crying ?'

'The ship,' said Lal, with dry eyes, 'may be at the bottom of the sea, and the insurances may be paid for her. But Rex is not drowned.'

That was what she said : ' Rex is not drowned.'

Her mother brought out her cherished crape—she was a woman whom this nasty, crinkling, black stuff comforted in a way—and offered to divide it with her daughter.

Lal refused ; she bought herself gay ribbons and she decked herself with them. She tried, in order to show the strength of her faith, to sing about the house.

' Rex,' she said, stoutly, ' is not drowned.'

This was the most unexpected way of receiving the news. The captains looked for a burst of tears and lamentation, after which things would brighten up, and some other fellow might have a chance. No tears at all ! No chance for anybody else !

' Ribbons !' moaned Mrs. Rydquist. ' Oh, Captain Zachariasen, my daughter wears ribbons—blue ribbons and red ribbons—while her sweetheart, lying at the bottom of the sea, cries aloud, poor lad, for a single yard of crape !'

''Twould be more natural,' said Captain Zachariasen, ' to cry and adone with it. But gals, ma'am, are not what gals was in my young days, when so many were there as was taken off by wars, privateers, storms, and the hand of the Lord, that there was no time to cry over them, not for more than a month or so. And as for flying in the face of Providence, and saying that a drowned man is not drowned—a man whose ship's insurances have been paid, and his ship actually posted at Lloyd's—why it's beyond anything.'

' Rex is not dead,' said the girl, to herself, again and again. ' He is not dead. I should know if he were dead. He would, somehow or other, come and tell me. He is sitting somewhere—I know not where it is—waiting for deliverance, and thinking—oh, my Rex ! my Rex !—thinking about the girl he loves.'

This was what she said. Her words were brave, yet it is hard to keep one's faith up to so high a level as these words demanded. For no one else thought there was, or could be, any chance. For nearly three years she struggled to keep alive this poor ray of hope, based upon nothing at all : and for all that time no news came from the far East about her lover's ship, nor did anyone know where she was cast away or how.

Sometimes this faith would break down, and she would ask in tears and with sobbings what so many women bereft of their lovers have asked in vain—an answer to her prayers. Ah ! helpless ones, if her prayers were mockeries and her lover were dead in very truth !

CHAPTER V.

THE PATIENCE OF PENELOPE.

THE longer Ulysses stayed away from the rocky Ithaca the more numerous became the suitors for the hand of the lovely Penelope, who possessed the art, revived much later by Ninon de l'Enclos, of remaining beautiful although she grew old. That was because Penelope wickedly encouraged her lovers—to their destruction—and held out false hopes connected with a simple bit of embroidery. Why the foolish fellows, whose wits should have been sharpened by the vehemence of their passion, did not discover the trick, is not apparent. Perhaps, however, the climate of Ithaca was bracing and the wine good, so that they winked one upon the other, and pretended not to see, or whispered : 'He will never come, let us wait.'

The contrary proved the case with the lass of Rotherhithe. When, after two years or so, some of her old suitors ventured with as much delicacy as in them lay to reopen the subject of courtship, they were met with a reception so unmistakable, that they immediately retired, baffled and in confusion ; some among them—those of coarser mind—to scoff and sneer at a constancy so unusual. Others, those of greater sympathies—to reflect with all humility on the great superiority of the feminine nature over their own, since it permitted a fidelity which they could not contemplate as possible for themselves, and were fain to admire, while they regretted it.

Gradually it became evident to most of them that the case was hopeless, and those captains who had once looked confidently to make Lal their own, returned to their former habits of friendly communications, and asked her advice and opinion in the matter of honourable proposals for the hands of other young ladies.

Three suitors still remained, and, each in his own way, refused to be sent away.

The first of these was Captain Holstius, whose acquaintance we have already made. He was, of course, in the Norway trade.

Perhaps it is not altogether fair to call Captain Holstius a suitor. He was a lover, but he had ceased to hope for anything except permission to go on in a friendly way, doing such offices as lay in his power to please and help the girl whom he regarded—being a simple sort of fellow of a religious turn—as Dante regarded Beatrice. She was to him a mere angel of beauty and goodness ; in happier times she had been that rare and wonderful creature, a merry, laughing, happy angel, always occupied in good works, such as making plum-duff for poor humanity ; now, unhappily, an angel who endured suspense and the agony of long waiting for news which would never come.

For the good Norwegian, like all the rest, believed that Rex was dead long ago. Captain Holstius was not a man accustomed to put his thoughts into words ; nor did he, like a good many people, feel for thoughts through a multitude of phrases and thousands of words. But had he been able to set forth in plain language the things he intended and meant, he would certainly have said something to this effect. I think he would have said it more simply, and therefore with the greater force.

' If I could make her forget him ; if I could substitute my own image entirely for the image of that dead man, so that she should be happy, just as she used to be when I first saw her, and if all could be as if he had never known her. I should think myself in heaven itself ; or, if by taking another man to husband, and not me at all, she would recover her happiness, I should be contented, for I love her so much that all I ask is for her to be happy.'

It is a form of disinterested love which is so rare that at this moment I cannot remember any other single instance of it. Most people, when they love a girl, vehemently desire to keep her for themselves. Yet in the case of Captain Holstius, as for marrying her, that seemed a thing so remote from the region of probability, that he never now, whatever he had done formerly, allowed his thoughts to rest upon it, and contented himself with thinking what he could do for the girl ; how he could soften the bitterness of her misfortune ; how he could in small ways relieve the burden of her life, and make her a little happier.

Lal accepted all he gave : all his devotion and care. Little by little, because she saw Captain Holstius often, it became a pleasure to her to have him in the house. He became a sort of brother to her, who had never had that often unsatisfactory relative a brother, or, at all events, a true and unselfish friend, much better than the majority of brothers, who gave her everything and asked nothing for himself. She liked to be with him. They walked together about the wharves of the Commercial Docks in the quiet evenings ; they rowed out together on the river in the little dingy, she sitting in the stern gazing upon the waters in silent thought, while the Norwegian dipped the sculls gently, looking with an ever increasing sorrow in the face which had once been so full of sunshine, and now grew daily more overcast with cloud. They spoke little at such times to each other, or at any time ; but it seemed to her that she thought best, most hopefully, about Rex when she was with Captain Holstius. He was always a silent man, thinking that when he had a thing to say there would be no difficulty in saying it, and that if anyone had a thing to say unto him they could say it without any stimulus of talk from himself. Further, in the case of this poor Lal, what earthly good would it do to interrupt the girl in her meditations over a dead lover by his idle chatter.

When they got home again she would thank him gently and return to her household duties, refreshed in spirit by this companionship in silence.

It is a maxim not sufficiently understood that the most refreshing thing in the world, when one is tired and sorry, disappointed or vexed, is to sit, walk, or remain for awhile silent with a silent friend whom you can trust not to chatter, or ask questions, or tease with idle observations. Pythagoras taught the same great truth, but obscurely and by an allegory. He enjoined silence among all his disciples for a term of years. This meant a companionship of silence, so as to forget the old friction and worry of the world.

The Norway ships come and go at quickly-recurring periods. Therefore Captain Holstius was much at the Commercial Docks, and had greater chances, if he had been the man to take advantage of them, than any of the other men. He was also favoured with the good opinion and the advocacy of Captain Zachariasen, who lost no opportunity of recommending Lal to consider her ways and at the same time the ways of the Norweegee. His admonition, we have seen, produced no effect. Nor did Holstius ask for his mediation any longer, being satisfied that he had got from the girl all the friendship which she had to offer.

The other two suitors, who would not be denied, but returned continually, were of coarser mould. They belonged to the very extensive class of men who, because they desire a thing vehemently, think themselves ill-used if they do not get it, fly into rages, accuse Providence, curse the hour of their birth, and go distraught. Sometimes, as in the case of the young Frenchman whose story is treated by Robert Browning, they throw themselves into the Seine, and so an end, because the joys of this world are denied to the poor. At other times they go about glaring with envious and malignant eyes. At all times they are the enemies of honest Christian folk.

One of these men was Captain Nicolas Borlinder, whose ship sailed to and fro from Calais to the Port of London, carrying casks of sherry for the thirsty British aristocracy. It is not a highly-paid service, and culture of the best kind is not often found among the captains in that trade. Yet Nick Borlinder was a happy man, because his standard was of a kind easily attainable. Like his friends of the same service, he loved beer, rum, and tobacco ; like them he loved these things in large quantities ; like them he delighted to sit and tell yarns. He could also sing a good song in a coarse baritone ; he could dance a hornpipe—only among brother captains, of course—as well as any fo'k'sle hand ; and he had the reputation of being a smart sailor. This reputation, however, belonged to all.

It was an unlucky day for Lal when this man was allowed a right of entry to Rydquist's. For he immediately fell in love with her and resolved to make her his own—Mrs. Borlinder—which would have been fine promotion for her.

He was a red-faced, jolly-looking man of five and thirty, or thereabouts. He had a bluff and hearty way ashore ; aboard ship he was handy with a marlingspike, a rope's-end, a fist, a kick, or a round, stimulating oath, or anything else strong and rough and good for knocking down the mutinous or quickening the indolent. Behind his hearty manner there lay—one can hardly say concealed—a nature of the most profound selfishness ; and it might have been remarked, had any of the captains been students of human nature—which is not a possible study, save on a very limited scale, for sailors—that among them all Nick Borlinder was about the only one who had no friends.

He came and went. When he appeared no one rejoiced ; while he stayed he sang and laughed and told yarns ; when he went away nobody cared.

Now, a skipper can go on very well as a bachelor up to the age of thirty-five or even forty. He is supported by the dignity and authority of his position ; he is sustained by a sense of his responsibilities ; perhaps, also, he still looks forward to another fling in port, for youthful follies are cherished and linger long in the breasts of sailors, and are sometimes dear even to the gravity of the captain. When a man reaches somewhere about thirty-five years of age, however, there generally comes to him a sense of loneliness. It seems hard that there should be no one glad to see him when he puts into port ; visions arise of a cottage with green palings and scarlet-runners, and, in most cases, that man is doomed when those visions arise.

Captain Borlinder was thirty-one or so when he first saw Lal. She was in her housekeeper's room making up accounts, and he brought her a letter from a ' Rydquist's man,' introducing him and requesting for him admission. She read the letter, asked him what his ship was, and where she traded, and showed him a room in her girlish, business-like manner. This was in the year eighteen hundred and seventy-six, shortly before she met Rex Armiger.

Captain Borlinder instantly, in her own room, at the very first interview, fell in love with her, and, like many men of his class, concluded that she was equally ready to fall in love with him.

All the next voyage out he thought about her. His experience of women was small, and of such a woman as Lal Rydquist, such a dainty maiden, he had no experience at all, because he had never known any such, or even distantly resembling her. The talk of such a girl, who could be friendly and laugh with a roomful of captains, and yet not one of them would dare so much as to chuck her under the chin—a delicate attention he had always heretofore allowed himself to consider proper—was a thing he had never before experienced. Then her figure, her face, her quickness, her cleverness—all these things excited his admiration and his envy. Should he allow such a treasure to be won by another man ?

Then he thought of her business capacity and that snug and comfortable business at Rydquist's. What a retreat, what a charming retreat for himself, after his twenty years of bucketing about the sea ! He pictured himself a partner in that business—

sleeping partner, smoking partner, drinking partner, the partner told off to narrate the yarns and shove the bottle round. What a place for a bluff, hearty, genuine old salt! How richly had he deserved it!

He resolved, during that voyage, upon making Lal Rydquist his own as soon as he returned. They met with nasty weather in the Bay, and a night or two on deck, which he had alway previously regarded as part of his profession and all in the day's work, became a peg for discontent as he thought of the snug lying he might have beside—not in—the churchyard in the Seven Houses.

The more he thought of the thing the more clearly he saw, in his own mind, its manifest advantages. And then, because the seclusion of the cabin and the solitude of the captain's position afford unrivalled opportunities for reflection, he began to build up a castle of Spain, and pictured to himself how he would reign as king-consort of Rydquist's.

'The old woman,' he said, 'shall be the first to go. No useless hands allowed aboard that craft. Her room shall be mine, where I will receive my own friends and count the money. As for old Zachariasen, he may go too, if he likes. We shall get more by a succession of captains than by feeding him all the year round. And as for the feeding, it's too good for the money; they don't want such good grub. And the charges are too low; and the drinks ridiculous for cheapness. And as for Lal, she'd make any house go, with her pretty ways.'

About this point a certain anxiety crossed his mind, because the girl herself rather frightened him. In what terms should he convey his intentions? And how would she receive them?

When he got back to London he hastened to propose to Lal. He adopted the plain and hearty manner, with a gallant nautical attitude, indicating candour and loyalty. This manner he had studied and made his own. It was not unlike the British tar of the stage, except that the good old ' Shiver my timbers ! ' with the hitch-up of the trousers, went out before Nick Borlinder's time. Now it must be remembered that this was very shortly after young Armiger's departure.

'What you want, my hearty,' said Captain Borlinder, ' is a jolly husband, that's what you want; and the best husband you can have is a sailor.'

Lal was accustomed to propositions of this kind, though not always conveyed in language so downright, having already refused four and twenty captains, and laughed at half a dozen more, who lamented their previous marriages for her sake, and would have even seen themselves widowers with resignation.

' Why a sailor, Captain Borlinder ? '

' Because a sailor is not always running after your heels like a tame cat and a puppy-dog. He goes to sea, and is out of sight; he leaves you the house to yourself; and when he comes home again he is always in a good temper. A sailor ashore is easy, contented, and happy-go-lucky.'

'It certainly would be something,' said Lal, 'always to have a good-tempered husband.'

'A sailor for me, says you,' continued the Captain, warming to his work. 'That's right ; and if a sailor, quartermaster is better than able seaman ; mate is better than quartermaster. Wherefore, skipper is better than mate ; and if skipper, why not Nick Borlinder ? Eh ! Why not Nick Borlinder ?'

And he stuck his thumbs in his waistcoat-pockets, and looked irresistible tenderness, so that he was greatly shocked when Lal laughed in his face, and informed him that she could not possibly become Mrs. Borlinder.

He went away in great indignation, and presently hearing about Rex Armiger and his successful courtship, first declared that he would break the neck of that young man as soon as he could get a chance, and then found fault with his own eyes because he had not struck at once and proposed when the idea first came into his head. Lost ! and all for want of a little pluck. Lost ! because the moment his back was turned, this young jackanapes, no better than a second mate in a steamer, cut in, saw his chance, and snapped her up.

For two voyages he reflected on the nature of women. He said to himself that out of sight, out of mind, and she would very likely forget all about the boy. He therefore resolved on trying the effect of bribery, and came offering rare gifts, consisting principally of an octave of sherry.

Lal accepted it graciously, and set it up in the Captains' room, where everybody fell to lapping it up until it was all gone.

Then Lal refused the donor a second time. So the sherry was clean thrown away and wasted. Much better had made it rum for his own consumption.

We know what happened next, and none rejoiced more cordially than Captain Borlinder over his rival's death.

When a reasonable time, as he thought, had elapsed, he renewed his offer with effusion, and was indignantly, even scornfully, refused. He concluded that he had another rival, probably some fellow with more money, and he looked about him and made more guarded inquiries. He could find no one likely to be a rival except Captain Holstius, who appeared to be a poor religious creature, not worth the jealousy of a lusty English sailor ; and later on, he discovered that a certain American captain called Barnabas B. Wattles, who came and went, having no ship of his own, and yet always full of business, was certainly a rival.

Captain Wattles puzzled him, because, so far as he could see, Lal was no kinder to him than to himself. Always there was present to his mind that vision of himself the landlord or proprietor of Rydquist's, counting out the money in the front parlour over a pipe and a cool glass of rum and water, while Lal looked after the dinners and made out the bills.

'Bills !' he thought. 'Yes ; they should be bills with a profit in them, too, when he was proprietor !'

Rage possessed his soul as the time went on and he got no nearer the attainment of his object. He could not converse with the girl, partly because she avoided him, and partly because he had nothing to say. Worst of all, she told him when he ventured once more to remark that a jolly sailor—namely, Nick Borlinder—would restore her to happiness, that if he ever dare to propose such a thing again he would no longer be admitted to Rydquist's, but might stay aboard his own ship in the London Docks, or find a house at Poplar. Fear of being sent to Poplar kept him quiet.

There remained the third suitor, Captain Barnabas B. Wattles.

When he made the acquaintance of Lal, a skipper without a ship, it was in the year eighteen hundred and seventy-seven. He was an American by birth, hailing, in fact, from the town of Portsmouth, New Hampshire, and he was always full of business, the nature of which no man knew. He was quite unlike the jovial Nick Borlinder, and indeed, resembled the typical British tar in no respect whatever. For he was a slight, spare man, with sharp features and hairless cheek. He was not, certainly, admitted to the privileges of Rydquist's, but he visited when his business brought him to London, and sat of an evening in the Captains' room drinking with anyone who would offer gratuitous grog; at other times he was fond of saying that he was a temperance man, and went away without grog rather than pay for it himself.

He first came when Lal was waiting for that letter from Rex which never came. He learned the whole story; and either did not immediately fall in love, like the more inflammable Borlinder, being a man of prudence and forethought, else he refrained from speech, even from the good words of courtship. But he came often; by speaking gently, and without mention of love and marriage, he established friendly relations with Lal; he even ventured to speak of her loss, and, with honeyed sympathy, told the tales of like disasters, which always ended fatally, to American sailors. When she declared that Rex could not be drowned, he only shook his head with pity. And, in speaking of those early deaths at sea which had come under his own observation, he assumed as a matter of course, that the bereaved woman mourned for no more than a certain term, after which time she took unto herself another sweetheart, and enjoyed perfect happiness ever afterwards. He thought that in this way he would familiarise her mind with the idea of giving up her grief.

'When she reflected,' he would conclude his narrative, 'that cryin' would not bring back any man to life again, she gave over cryin' and looked about for consolation. She found it, Miss Lal, in the usual quarter. As for myself, my own name is Barnabas, which means, as perhaps you have never heard, the Son of Consolation.'

With such words did he essay to sap the fidelity of the mourner, but in vain, for though there were times when poor Lal would doubt, despite the fervent ardour of her faith, whether Rex might not be really dead and gone, there was no time at all when she ever wavered for a moment in constancy to his memory. Though neither Borlinder or Barnabas Wattles could understand the thing, it was impossible for Lal ever to think of a second lover.

He would talk of other things, but always came back to the subject of consolation.

Thus one evening he began to look about him, being then in her own room.

'This,' he said, 'is a prosperous concern which you are running, Miss Lal. I guess it pays?'

Yes; Lal said that it paid its expenses, and more.

'And you've made your little pile already out of it?'

Yes, said Lal, carelessly, there was money saved.

His eyes twinkled at the thought of handling her savings, for Captain Wattles was by no means rich. He forgot, however, that the money belonged to her mother.

'Now,' he went on, with an insinuating smile, 'do you never think the time will come when you will tire of running this ho—tel?'

Lal said she was too busy to think of what might happen, and that, as regards the future, she said, sadly, she would rather not think about it at all, the past was already too much for her to think about.

'Yes,' he said, 'that time will come. It has not come yet, Miss Lal, and, therefore, I do not say, as I am ready to say, Take me and let me console you. My name is Barnabas, which means, as perhaps you do not know, the Son of Consolation.'

'It would be no use at all,' said Lal; 'and if we are to remain friends, Captain Wattles, you will never speak of this again.'

'I will not,' he replied, 'until the right moment. Then, with your little savings and mine, we will go back to the States. I know what we will do when we get there. There's an old ship-building yard at Portsmouth which only wants a few thousand dollars put into it. We will put our dollars into that yard, and we will build ships.'

'You had better give up thinking of such nonsense,' said Lal.

'Thought is free, Miss Lal. The time will come. Is it in nature to go on crying all your life for a man as dead as Abraham Lincoln? The time will come.'

'Enough said, Captain Wattles,' Lal said. It was in her own room, and she was busy with her accounts. 'You can go now, and you need not come back any more unless you have something else to say. I thought you were a sensible man. Most American captains I know are as sensible as Englishmen and Norwegians.'

Captain Wattles rose slowly.

'Wal,' he said, 'you say so now. I expected you would. But the time will come. I'm not afraid of the other men. As for Cap'en Borlinder, he is not fit company for a sweet young thing like you. He would beat his wife after a while, that man would. He drinks

nobblers all day, and swaps lies with any riff-raff who will stand in
a bar and listen to him. You will not lower yourself to Cap'en
Borlinder. As for the Norweegee, he is but a poor soft shell; you
might as well marry a gell. I shan't ask you yet, so don't be
afraid. When your old friends drop away one by one, and you
feel a bit lonesome with no one to talk to, and these bills always on
your mind, and the house over your head like a cage and a prison, I
shall look in again, and you will hold out your pretty hand, and
you will sweetly say: "Cap'en Wattles, you air a sailor and a
temperance man; you subscribe to a missionary society and have
once been teacher in a Sunday-school; you have traded Bibles
with natives for coral and ivory and gold-dust; you air smart; you
air likewise a kind-hearted man, who will give his wife her head in
everything, with Paris bonnets and New York frocks; your name
is Barnabas, the Son of Consolation." . . . Don't run away, Miss
Lal. I've said all I wanted to say, and now I am going. Business
takes me to Liverpool to-night, and on Thursday I sail again for
Baltimore.'

CHAPTER VI.

THE MESSAGE FROM THE SEA.

It was, then, in October, eighteen hundred and seventy-nine, that
Dick, the Malay, made his appearance and told his tale. Having
told it he remained in the house, attaching himself as by right to
Lal, whose steward he became as he had been steward to Rex.

The thing produced, naturally, a profound sensation in the
Captains' room, whither Dick was invited to repeat his performance,
not once, but several times.

It was observed that, though substantially the same, the action
always differed in the addition or the withdrawal of certain small
details, the interpretation of which was obscure. One or two facts
remained certain, and were agreed upon by all: an open boat, a
long waiting, a rescue, either by being picked up or by finding
land, and then one or two fights, but why, and with whom, was a
matter of speculation.

Captain Zachariasen remained obstinate to his theory. There
was a widow, there was a marriage, there was a baby, there were
conjugal rows, and finally a prison in which Rex Armiger still
remained. How to fit the pantomime into these wonderful details
was a matter of difficulty which he was always endeavouring to
overcome by the help of the more obscure gestures in the mummicking.

The general cheerfulness of the house was naturally much
elevated by this event. It was, indeed, felt not only that hope
had returned, but also that honour was conferred upon Rydquist's
by so mysterious and exciting a revelation.

This distinction became more generally recognised when the Secretary and one of the Directors of the Indian Peninsular Line came over to see the Malay, hoping to get some light thrown upon the loss of their ship.

Captain Zachariasen took the chair for the performance, so to speak, and expounded the principal parts, taking credit for such mummicking as no other house could offer.

The Director learned nothing definite from the pantomime, but came away profoundly impressed with the belief that their officer, Captain Armiger, was living.

The Malay, now domesticated at Seven Houses, was frequently invited of an evening to the Captains' room, where he went through his performance—Captain Zachariasen always in the chair—for every new comer, and was a continual subject of discussion. Also there were great studyings of charts, and mappings out of routes, with calculations as to days and probable number of knots. And those who had been in Chinese and Polynesian waters were called upon to narrate their experiences.

The route of a steamer from Hong-Kong to Moreton Bay is well known, and easily followed. Unfortunately, the Malay's pantomime left it doubtful of what nature was the disaster. It might have been a piratical attack, though that was very un'ikely, or a fire on board, or the striking on a reef.

'Her course,' said Captain Holstius, laying it down with Lal for the fiftieth time, 'would be—so—E.S.E. from Hong-Kong, north of Luçon here ; then due S.E. between the Pelews and Carolines, through Dampier Straits, having New Guinea to the starboard. Look at these seas, Lal. Who knows what may have happened ? And how can we search for him over three thousand miles of sea, among so many islands ?'

How, indeed ! And yet the idea was growing up strong in both their minds that a search of some kind must be made.

And then came help, that sort of help which our pious ancestors called Providential. What can we call it ? Blind chance ? That seems rather a long drop from benevolent Providence, but it seems to suit a good many people nowadays almost as well—more's the pity.

Two months after the Malay's appearance, while winter was upon us and Christmas not far off, when the churchyard trees were stripped of leaf, and the vine about the window was trimmed, the garden swept up for the season, and the parrots brought indoors, and Rydquist's made snug for bad weather, another person called at the house, bringing with him a message of another kind. It was no other than the Doctor of the 'Aryan,' Rex's old ship. He bore something round, wrapped in tissue paper. He carried it with great care, as if it was something very precious.

The time was evening, and Lal was in her room making up accounts. In the Captains' room was a full assemblage, numbering Captain Zachariasen, Captain Borlinder, who purposed to spend his

Christmas at Rydquist's and to consume much grog, Captain Holstius, Captain Barnabas B. Wattles, whose business had again brought him to London, and two or three captains who have nothing to do with this history except to fill up the group in the room where presently an important Function was to be held.

At present they were unsuspicious of what was coming, and they sat in solemn circle, the Patriarch at the head of the table, getting through the evening, all too quickly, in the usual way.

'This was picked up,' the Doctor said, still holding his treasure in his hands as if it was a baby, 'in the Bay of Bengal, by a country ship sailing from Calcutta to Moulmein; it must have drifted with the currents and the wind, two thousand miles and more. How it contrived never to get driven ashore or broken against some boat, or wreck, or rock, or washed up some creek among the thousands of islands by which it floated, is a truly wonderful thing.'

'Oh, what is it?' she cried.

He took off the handkerchief and showed a common wide-mouthed bottle, such as chemists use for effervescing things.

'It contains,' he said, solemnly, 'poor Rex Armiger's last letter to you. The skipper who picked it up pulled out the cork and read it. He brought it to our office at Calcutta, where, though it was written to you, we were obliged to read it, because it told how the "Philippine" was cast away; for the same reason our officers read it.'

'His last letter?'

'Yes; his last letter. It is dated three years ago. We cannot hope—no, it is impossible to hope—that he is still alive. We should have heard long ago if he had been picked up.'

'We have heard,' said Lal. She went in search of the Malay, with whom she presently returned. 'We have heard, Doctor. Here is Rex's steward, who came to us two months ago.'

'Good heavens! it is the dumb Malay steward, who was with him in the boat.'

'Yes. Now look, and tell me what you read.'

She made a sign to Dick, who went through, for the Doctor's instruction, the now familiar pantomime.

'What do you think, Doctor?'

'Think? There is only one thing to think, Miss Rydquist. He has escaped. He is alive, somewhere, or was when Dick last saw him, though how this fellow got away from him, and where he is ——'

'Now give me his letter.'

It was tied round with a green ribbon—a slender roll of paper, looking as if sea-water had discoloured it.

The Doctor took it out of the bottle and gave it her.

'I will read Rex's letter,' she said, quietly, 'alone. Will you wait a little for me, Doctor?'

She came back in a quarter of an hour. Her eyes were heavy with tears, but she was calm and assured.

'I thank God, Doctor,' she said ; 'I thank God most humbly for preserving this precious bottle and this letter of my dear Rex--my poor Rex—and I thank you, too, and your brother-officers, whom he loved, and who were always good to him, for bringing it home to me. For now I know where he is, and where to look for him, and now I understand it all.'

'If he is living we will find him,' said the Doctor. 'Be sure that we will find him.'

'We will find him,' she echoed. 'Yes, we will find him. Now, Doctor, consider. You remember how they got into the boat ?'

'Yes—off the wreck. The letter tells us that.'

'Dick told us that two months ago, but we could not altogether understand it. How long were they in the boat ?'

'Why, no one knows.'

'Yes, Dick knows, and he has told us. Consider. They were left, when this bottle was sent forth like the raven out of the ark, with no food. They sat in the boat, waiting for death. But they did not die. They drifted—you saw that they made no attempt to row—for awhile ; they grew hungry and thirsty ; they passed two or three days with nothing to eat. It could not have been more, because they were not so far exhausted but that, when land appeared in sight, they still had strength to row.'

'Go on,' cried the Doctor. 'You are cleverer than all of us.'

'It is because I love him,' she replied, 'and because I have thought day and night where he can be. You know the latitude and longitude of the wreck ; you must allow for currents and wind ; you know how many days elapsed between the wreck and the writing of the letter. Now let us look at the chart and work it all out.'

She brought the chart to the table, and pointed with her finger.

'They were wrecked,' she said, 'there. Now allow five days for drifting. Where would they land ? Remember he says that the wind was S.W.'

'Why,' said the Doctor, 'they may have landed on one of the most westerly of the Caroline Islands, unless the current carried them to the Pelews. There are islands enough in those seas.'

'Yes,' she replied ; 'it is here that we shall look for him. Now come with me to the Captains' room.'

She walked in, head erect and paper in hand, followed by the Doctor, and stood at Captain Zachariasen's right—her usual place when she visited the captains in the evening.

'You, who are my friends,' said Lal, bearing in one hand the chart and in the other the precious letter, 'will rejoice with me, for I have had a letter from Rex.'

'When was it wrote and where from ?' asked Captain Zachariasen.

'It is nearly three years old. It has been tossing on the sea, driven hither and thither, and preserved by kind .Heaven to show that Rex is living still, and where he is.'

Captain Wattles whistled gently. It sounded like an involuntary note of incredulity.

F

Lal spread the chart before Captain Zachariasen.

'You can follow the voyage,' she said, 'while I read you this letter. It is on the back of one from me. It is written with a lead pencil, very small, because he had a great deal to say and not much space to say it in—my Rex !'

Her voice broke down for a moment, but she steadied herself and went on reading the message from the sea.

'"Anyone who picks this up," it begins, "will oblige me by sending it to Miss Rydquist, Seven Houses, Rotherhithe, because it tells her of the shipwreck and perhaps the death "—But you know, all of you,' Lal interposed, 'that he survived and got to land, else how was Dick able to get to England?—"of her sweetheart, the undersigned Rex Armiger, Captain of the steamer 'Philippine,' now lying a wreck on a reef in latitude 5·30 N. and longitude 133·25, as near as I could calculate."

' "MY DEAREST LAL,—I write this in the captain's gig, where I am floating about in or about the above-named latitude and longitude, after the most unfortunate voyage that ever started with good promise. First, I send you my last words, dear love, solemnly, because a man in a boat on the open seas, with no provisions and no sail, cannot look for anything but death from starvation, if not by drowning. God help you, my dear, and bless you, and make you forget me soon, and find a better husband than I should ever have made. You will take another man——"'

'Hear, hear!' said Captain Borlinder, softly.

'Hush!' said Captain Wattles, reproachfully. 'Captain Armiger was a good man and a prophet.'

'"You will take another man,"' Lal repeated. 'Never!' she cried, after the repetition, looking from one to the other, 'Never! Not if he were dead, instead of being alive, as he is, and wondering why we do not come to rescue him.'

'The boy had his points,' said Captain Zachariasen, 'and a good husband he would have made. Just such as I was sixty years ago, or thereabouts. Get on to the shipwreck, Lal, my dear.'

'"It was on December the First that we set sail from Calcutta. The crew were all Lascars, except Dick my Malay steward, the chief officer, who was an Englishman, and the engineer. We made a good passage under canvas, with auxiliary screw, to Singapore, and from thence, in ballast, except for a few bales of goods, to Hong-Kong. Here we took in our cargo of rice, and started, all well, on January the Fourteenth, eighteen hundred and seventy-seven. The mate was a good sailor as ever stepped on a bridge, and the ship well found, new, and good in all respects.

'"We had fair weather across the China Sea and in the straits north of Luçon until we came to the open seas. Here a gale, which blew us off our course to N.E., but not far, and still in clear and open sailing, with never a reef or an island on the chart. We kept steam up, running in the teeth of the wind, all sails furled. When the wind moderated, veering from S.E. to S.W. (within a point or two), we made the Pelew Islands to the starboard bow, and came well in the track of the Sydney steamers. If you look at the chart you will find that here the sea is open and clear ; not a shoal nor an island laid down for a good thousand miles. Wherefore, I make no doubt that after inquiry I should have my certificate returned to me, in spite of having lost so good a ship.

' " On Sunday, at noon, the wind having moderated, we found we had made two hundred and twenty-seven knots in four and twenty hours.

' " We were, as I made it, in latitude 5·30 N. and longitude 133·25, as near as I could calculate. At sunset, which was at six twenty-five, we must have made some sixty miles more to the S.W., so that you can lay down the spot on the map. The wind was fresh, and the sea a little choppy, but nothing of any consequence in open water. At eight I turned in, going watch and watch about with the mate, and at five minutes past eight I suppose I was fast asleep.

' " It was, I think, a little after six bells, that I was awakened by the ship striking. I ran on deck at once. We were on a reef, and by the grating and the grinding of her bottom I guessed that it was all over. I'm sorry to say that in the shock the mate seems to have been knocked overboard and drowned, because I saw him no more. The ship rolled from side to side, grinding and tearing her bottom upon the reef. The men ran backwards and forwards crying to each other. There was no discipline with them, nor could I get them to obey orders. The engineer went below and reported water gaining fast. He and I did our best to keep the crew in hand, but it was no use. They lowered the boats and pushed off, leaving behind only the engineer, and Dick the steward, and myself. They were in too great a hurry to put provisions on board, so that I greatly fear they must have perished, unless they have been picked up by some steamer.

' " All that night we stayed on deck, we three, expecting every moment that she would break her back. The cargo of grain was loose now, and rolled with the ship like water. Her bows were high upon the rocks, and I believe we were only saved because she was lodged upon the reef as far aft as the engine-room. In the darkness the engineer must have slipped his hold and fallen overboard, I don't know how. Then there was only Dick and me.

' " In the morning, at daybreak, the look-out was pretty bad. The reef is a shoal, with nothing but a fringe of white water round it to mark where it lies. It is now, I reckon, about seventeen feet below the surface of the water, but I take it to be a rising reef, so that every year will make it less, and I hope it will be set down at once on the chart. My mate was gone and my engineer, the boats and their crews were out of sight, or, may be, capsized, not a sail upon the sea. But there was the captain's gig.

' " When we got afloat, my purpose was to keep alongside the poor wreck until we had got enough victuals to last a week or two, and some running tackle whereby we could hoist some sort of a sail. But, my dear, we hadn't time, because no sooner had we lowered the boat and put in a few tins, with a bottle half full of brandy and a keg of water, than she parted amidships, and we had no more than time to jump into the boat and shove off.

' "There we were then, with no oars, no mast, no sail, no rudder even, and provisions for two or three days.

' " We have now been floating a week. We drifted first of all in a nor'-westerly direction, so near as I could make out, so long as the poor wreck remained in sight. Since then I know not what our course has been. There is a strong current here, I suspect, from the short time we took to lose sight of her, and there has been a good breeze blowing from the S.W. for three days.

' " We have now got to the end of our provisions ; the last drop of water has been drunk ; the last biscuit eaten. Poor Dick sits opposite to me all day and all night, he cannot speak, but he refused his share of the last ration for my sake.'

Here Lal broke down again, and Captain Zachariasen said something strong, which showed that his admiration for a generous action was greater than his religious restraint.

' " We spend the day in looking for a sail ; at night we take watch about. There remains only a little brandy in the heel of the bottle. We husband that for a last resource. We have fashioned a couple of rough oars out of two planks of the boat.

' " I have kept this a day longer. No sail in sight. We have had two or three drops of brandy each. They are the last. Now I must commit this letter to the sea in the bottle. Oh, my dear Lal, my pretty tender darling ! I shall never, never see you any more. Long before you get this letter I shall be drifting about in this boat a dead man. I pray Heaven to bless you——" '

Here Lal stopped and burst into tears.

' Read no more,' said Captain Holstius, ' the rest concerns yourself alone.'

Lal kissed her letter, folded it tenderly, and laid it in her bosom.

' The rest only concerns me,' she repeated, and was silent awhile.

Captain Zachariasen, meantime, was at work upon the chart.

' I read this story somewhat different,' he said. ' You can't always follow a mummicker in his antics, and I now perceive that I was wrong about the baby. The widow I stick to. Nothing could be plainer than the widow, though, of course, it was not to be expected that he'd make a clean breast of it in that letter, which otherwise does him credit. Lal, my dear, you are right. If Dick is alive, then his master is alive. Question is, where would he get to, and where is he now ? '

They were all silent, waiting the conclusion of the Patriarch before any other ventured to speak. He was bending over the chart, his right thumb as the position of the reef, and his forefinger acting as a compass.

'I calculate from the position of the reef, which is here, and the run of the currents, and the direction of the wind, that they drifted towards the most westerly of the Caroline Islands.'

It hardly required patriarchal wisdom to surmise this fact, seeing that these islands are the nearest places north-west of the reef.

'And next?' asked Lal.

'Next, my pretty, they were taken off of that island, but I do not know by whom, and were shipped away to some prison, but I don't know where, and there Cap'en Armiger is still lying, though what for, as there was seemingly no baby and no chucking overboard, we mortals, who are but purblind, cannot say.'

Then Captain Holstius spoke again.

'I think we might have in the Malay and go through the play acting again. May be, with this letter before us, we may get more light.'

The Doctor now showed Dick the bottle. He seized it, grinned a recognition, and, on a sign from the girl, began the story again at that point.

First, leaning over the imaginary side of the boat, he laid it gently on the floor.

'Thereby,' said Captain Zachariasen, solemnly, 'committing the letter to the watery deep, to be carried here and driven there while the stormy winds do blow, do blow. Amen!'

Then Dick became pensive. He sat huddled up, with his elbows on his knees and his head in his hands, looking straight before him. For the time, as always in this performance, of which he never tired, he was Rex himself; the same poise of the head, the same look of the eyes; he had put off the Malayan type, and sat there, before them all, pure Caucasian.

'Creditable, my lad,' said Captain Zachariasen. 'I think you can, all of you, understand so far, without my telling.'

They certainly could.

Then the Malay sprang to his feet and pointed to some object in the distance.

'Sail ho!' cried Captain Borlinder.

Then he sat down again and began the regular motion of his arm, which the Patriarch had mistaken for rocking the baby.

'This,' said the Venerable, 'is plain and easy. Land it is. not a sail—why? Because, if the latter, they would wave their pocket-handkerchiefs; if the former, they would h'ist sail or out sculls. If the mummicker had been as plain and easy to understand the first time, we shouldn't have gone astray and sailed on that wrong tack about the baby.'

With the help of the letter the pantomime became perfectly intelligible. The whole scene stood out plainly before the eyes of all. They were no longer in the Captains' room at Seven Houses, Rotherhithe; they were somewhere far away, east of New Guinea, watching two men in a little boat on a sea where there was no sail nor any smoke from passing steamers. Low down on the horizon was a thin streak, which a landsman would have taken for a cloud. The two men with straining faces were rowing with feverish eagerness, encouraging each other, and ceasing not, though the paddles nearly fell from their hands with fatigue.

'Oh! Rex, Rex!' cried Lal, carried away by the acting. 'Rest awhile; oh, rest!'

But still they paddled on.

Then came the scene of the struggle and the binding of the arms, and the march up country. Next the release and the quiet going up and down; and then the second struggle, with another capture, and a second binding of arms.

'See, Lal,' said Captain Holstius, pointing triumphantly to the actor; 'who is bound this time?'

Why, there could be no doubt whatever. It was not Rex, but the Malay.

'This is the worst o' mummicking now,' said the Patriarch, as if pantomime was a recognised instrument in the teaching and illustration of history. 'You're never quite sure. We've had to give up the baby with the chucking overboard. I was sorry for that, because it was so plain and easy to read. And now it seems as if it was the poor devil himself that got took off to gaol. Was his hair cut short, do you remember, Lal, when he came here two months ago? I can't quite give up the prison, neither, so beautiful as it reeled itself out first time we did the mummicking. You're a stranger, sir,' he addressed the Doctor, 'and you knew Cap'en Armiger. What do you think? For my own part—well, let's hear you, sir.'

'There cannot be a doubt,' said the Doctor, 'that the man personated Armiger, and no other, until the last scene, and that there he became himself intentionally. He exaggerated himself. He walked differently; he carried his head differently. There was a fight of some kind, and the Malay, not Armiger at all, was taken prisoner.'

'What is your opinion, Captain Borlinder?' asked Lal, anxious to know what each man thought.

'My opinion,' said Captain Borlinder, with emphasis, 'is this. They got ashore; no one can doubt that. Very well, then. Where? Not many degrees of longitude from the place where they were wrecked. Who were the people they fell among? The natives. That's what I read so far. Now we go on to the fight at the end. A better fight I never saw on the stage, not even at the Pavilion Theatre, though but one man in it. As for Captain Armiger, he was knocked on the head. That is to me quite certain. Knocked on the head with a stick, or stuck with a knife, according to the religion and customs of them natives, among whom I never sailed, and therefore do not know their ways. It's a melancholy comfort, at all events, to know the manner of his end. Next to looking forward to a decent burial, people when they are going to be knocked on the head die more comfortable if they know that other people will hear how they came to be knocked on the head—whether a club, or a boat-hook, or a bo'sn's cutlash.'

'I think, sir,' said the Doctor, 'that you are perfectly wrong. There is nothing whatever to show that Armiger was killed.'

But then he did not know that Captain Borlinder spoke according to the desire of his own heart.

Then Lal turned to the only man who had not yet spoken :

'And what is your opinion, Captain Wattles ?'

'I think,' replied Barnabas the Consoler, 'that Cap'en Armiger landed on some island, and worried through the first scrimmage. I know them lands, and I know that their ways to strangers may be rough. If you get through the first hearty welcome, which means clubs and knives and spears mostly, there's no reason why you shouldn't settle down among 'em. There's many an English and American sailor living there contented and happy. P'raps Cap'en Armiger is one of them.'

'Not contented,' said Lal, ' nor yet happy.'

Captain Wattles went on :

'On the other hand, there's fights among themselves and drunken bouts, and many a brave fellow knocked on the head thereby.'

'Do you speak from your own knowledge ?' asked the Doctor.

'I was once,' he replied, unblushingly, 'a missionary in the Kusaie station. Yes, we disseminated amongst us the seeds of civilisation and religion among those poor cannibals. I also traded in shirts and trousers, after they had been taught how to put them on. They are a treacherous race : they treasure up the recollection of wrongs and take revenge ; they are insensible to kindness and handy with their arrows. I fear that Cap'en Armiger has long since been killed and eaten. They probably spared the Malay on account of his brown skin, as likely to disagree.'

Then Captain Holstius rose and spoke.

'Friends all,' he said, 'and especially Captain Borlinder and Captain Wattles, here is a message come straight from Captain Armiger himself, though now nigh upon three years old. And it comes close upon the heels of that other message brought us by this poor fellow, who gave it as he knew best ; though a difficult message to read in parts. Now we know, partly from Dick and partly from the letter, what happened and how it happened, and we are pretty certain 'that they must have landed, as Captain Zachariasen has told us, in one of the islands lying to the nor'-west of the spot where she struck.' Here he paused. Captain Borlinder blew great clouds of tobacco and looked straight before him. Captain Wattles listened with impatience. Then the Norwegian went on : 'I think, friends all, that here we have our duty plain before us. Here are three men in this room, Captain Borlinder, Captain Wattles, and myself, who have been in love with Lal, who is Captain Armiger's sweetheart, and therefore has no right to listen to us so long as there is any

hope that he is alive. If no hope, why, I do not say myself that
she has no right——'

'No right, Captain Holstius,' said Lal ; 'no right to listen to
any other man, whatever happens.'

'Very well, then. But for us who love her in a respectful way,
and desire nothing but her happiness, there is only one duty, and
that is——'

Here Captain Wattles sprang to his feet.

'To go in search of him. That is what I was going to propose.
Miss Rydquist, I promise to go in search of Cap'en Armiger. If
he is alive I will bring him home to you. If he is dead, I will bring
you news of how and when he died. I ask no reward. I leave
that to you. But I will bring you news.'

This was honestly and even nobly spoken. But the effect of
the speech was a little marred by the allusion to reward. What
reward had Lal to offer, except one ? and she had just declared that
to be impossible.

Then Captain Borlinder rose, ponderously, and slapped his
chest.

'Nick Borlinder, Lal, is at your service. Yours truly to command. He hasn't been a missionary, nor a dealer in reach-me-down
shirts, like some skippers, having walked the deck since a boy.
And he doesn't know the Caroline Islands. But he can navigate a
ship, or he can take a passage aboard a ship. Where there's missionaries there's ships. He will get aboard one of them ships, and
he will visit those cannibals and find out the truth. Lal, if Cap'en
Armiger is alive, he shall be rescued by Nick Borlinder, and shall
come home with me arm-in-arm to the Pride of Rotherhithe. If
he isn't alive, why—then——'

He sat down again, nodding his head.

Lal turned to Captain Holstius.

'Yes,' he said ; 'I thought this brave Englishman and this
brave American would see their duty plain before them. I will
go in search of him, too, Lal. I know not yet how ; but I shall
find a way.'

'Gentlemen,' said Lal, 'I have nothing to give you except my
gratitude. Nothing at all. Oh ! who in the world has ever had
kinder and nobler friends than I ?'

She held out her two hands. Captain Wattles seized the right
and kissed it with effusion, murmuring something about Barnabas,
the Son of Consolation. Captain Borlinder followed his example
with the left, though he had never before regarded a woman's hand
as a proper object for a manly kiss. He took the opportunity to
whisper that, in all her troubles, Nick Borlinder was the man to
trust.

'Now,' said Captain Holstius, 'there is no time to be lost ; we
all have things to arrange, and money to raise. Shall we all go
together, or shall we go separate ?'

'Separate,' said the Son of Consolation.

'Separate,' cried Borlinder, firmly. 'If the job is to be done, let ME do the job single-handed.'

'Very well,' said Captain Holstius ; 'then how shall we go ? '

'We will go,' said Captain Wattles, 'in order. First one, and then another, to give every man a fair chance and no favour. And to get that fair chance we will draw straws. Longest straw first, shortest last.'

He retired and returned with three straws in his hand.

'Now, Borlinder,' he said, 'you shall draw first.'

Borlinder took a straw, but with hesitation.

The Doctor, who was rather short-sighted, thought he detected a little sleight-of-hand on the part of Captain Wattles at this moment. But he said nothing. Captain Holstius then drew. Again the Doctor thought he observed what seemed to be tampering with the oracle of the straw.

On the display of the straws it was found that the longest straw was Captain Borlinder's ; the shortest, that of Captain Holstius. The order of search was therefore, first, Captain Borlinder. He heaved a great breath, struck his hands together, and smote his chest with great violence and heartiness. You would have thought he had drawn a great prize instead of the right to go first on an extremely expensive voyage of search. The next was to be Captain Wattles. The third and last, Captain Holstius.

Captain Zachariasen called for glasses round to drink health and success to the gallant fellows going out on this brave and honourable quest.

Outside the house, presently, two of the gallant seekers stood in discourse.

'You don't think, Wattles,' asked Borlinder, 'that he's really alive ? '

'I can't say,' replied the ex-missionary. 'I shouldn't like, myself, to be wrecked on one of those islands. You see, there's been a little labour traffic in those parts, and the ungrateful people, who don't know what's good for them, are afraid of being kid— I mean recruited. And they bear malice. But I suppose he's one of the sort that don't easily get killed. I shall be going Sydney-way about my own business next year, or thereabouts, I expect, so it's all in my day's work to make enquiries. As for you——'

'As to me, now, brother ? ' Captain Borlinder spoke in his most insinuating way. 'As to me, now ? Come, let's have a drink.'

'As to you,' said the Consoler, after a drink at his friend's expense, 'I'm sorry for you, because you've got to go at once, and you've got no experience. Among cannibals, a man of your flesh is like a prize ox at Christmas.'

Captain Borlinder turned pale.

'Yes—that is so. They would put you in a shallow pit, with a few onions and some pepper, cover all up snug with stones, and make a fire on top till you were done to a turn ! '

Captain Borlinder shuddered.

It always comes to this, that he, Nick Borlinder, was to go out first, got devoured by the cannibals, and never get back again.

Then the Yankee, himself out of the way, would try another way.

'I shan't go at all,' he murmured. 'Yah! for cheating and dishonesty give me a Yankee! I shall pretend to have been there!'

'As for finding him,' he went on with his meditations, 'it's a thousand to one that you don't light on the island where he put foot ashore; and if you do find him, a million to one at least that he's dead—and all the journey, with the expense of it, for nothing.

'To say nothing of risk and danger. Shipwreck: I suppose that goes for nothing. Fever: I suppose we needn't reckon that. Oh, no, certainly not. Sunstroke: that never kills in tropical climates, does it? Oh, no; don't reckon that. Natives: they are a mild and dovelike race, ain't they? Everybody knows that! Don't reckon natives.'

It was, after all, very well to propose a pretended voyage, but what would the Yankee do? And what did he really mean about the cat and the india-rubber ball?

This doubt puzzled him not a little. The plan he proposed to himself was simple—beautiful in its simplicity. But he could not help feeling that his American cousin had some other and some deeper plan, by means of which he would himself be circumvented and anticipated.

Nothing more disturbs the crafty and subtle serpent, or more fills him with virtuous indignation, than the suspicion that his brother serpent is more crafty and more subtle than himself.

Everybody knows how the two burglars, friends in private but strangers in profession, met one night in the same house, proposing independent research.

His plan involved no expense, no danger, no possible privations. It was nothing more nor less than to wait awhile, and then to present himself with the report of a pretended voyage.

At first he thought he would so far give in to the outward seeming of things as to get a substitute to take command of his ship for a certain space, spending that time on shore in some secluded spot. This plan, however, involved a considerable amount of expense, with the necessity of much explanation to his employers. It therefore seemed to him best to go on just the same—to take his ship from the London Docks to Cadiz as usual, and back again, to give Rotherhithe a wide berth, and then, after a certain decent interval, to present himself at Seven Houses with a narrative.

Seven weeks to Hong-Kong, seven weeks back, eight weeks for the search—say six months in all.

Having roughly drawn out his plan of action, and considered in broad outlines the leading features of the narrative, Captain Borlinder purchased a few sheets of paper, on which to set down the account of his voyage, which he intended should be a masterly

performance. He then, without waiting for the Christmas festivi-
ties, though nigh at hand—and no such pudding anywhere as at
Rydquist's — presented himself at Rotherhithe to take farewell
before he started on his long and dangerous journey.

This haste to redeem his promise could not fail, he thought, of
producing a favourable impression.

He carried a red pocket-handkerchief, as if that contained all
the luggage required for a hardy mariner even with such a journey
before him. He had tied a string, with a jack-knife at the end of
it, round his waist, like a common sailor. He had a profoundly
shiny hat, and his face was set to an expression of as deep sympathy
as he could command.

'I know,' he said, in his lowest tones, 'that to look for Cap'en
Armiger in the Eastern Seas will very likely be a mighty tough
job ; but I've passèd my word to tackle that job, and when Nick
Borlinder's word is passed to do a thing, that thing has got to be
done, or the reason why is asked, pretty quick. Same as if I was
in command of my own ship. For, sezi to myself, before ever the
Norweegee up and spoke, or the Yankee pretended to have meant
it—but I am slow to speak, though amazing quick to think—I sez,
" What we three men have got to do in this business is to look
after Lal's happiness." That I sez after you read that most
affecting letter, before the talk begun, and speaking in a whisper,
as a man might say, down his baccy-pipe. " Nothing else consarns
us now. It is that which we have to look after. The way to look
after it is to make quite sure that Cap'en Armiger is gone, and the
way he went, and where his remains remain ; or else, if he is not -
gone, but he still alive-and-kicks, wherever that may be, then to
bring him home." '

'Thank you, Captain Borlinder,' said Lal, thinking that the
Patriarch's dislike to this good and disinterested man was founded
on prejudice ; and, indeed, the meaning was quite plain, though
the language was a little mixed.

'There's a many islands in the Eastern Seas,' continued
Nicholas the Brave. 'I've been looking at them in the charts.
There's thousands of islands—say ten thousand, little and big.
Say every one of those islands has to be searched. If we give a
month to each island all round, counting little and big, that will
make close upon nine hundred years. If it's only a fortnight, four
hundred years. What's four hundred years to a determined man ?
I shall search among them islands, if it's four hundred or nine
hundred years, till I find him.'

'But this will cost a great deal, Captain Borlinder, I am afraid.'
'Never mind about the cost,' he replied, grandly. 'If it was
ten times as much I'd never grudge it. We will say good-bye now.
Perhaps I shall come home, with news, in a year, or even less.
Perhaps it may be forty years before I come home again. Perhaps
I shall bring him home in a few months, well and hearty ; perhaps
in about fifty years, with never a tooth to his head. But never

you fear. Pluck up. Say to yourself : " Nick Borlinder, as never puts his hand to nothing but he carries that thing through, has got this job in hand." Perhaps I may come with news that you don't want. But there—we will not talk of that. If I never come home at all, but get, maybe, devoured by sharks, cannibals, and alligators, besides being struck with sunstroke, fever, rheumatics, and other illnesses, and knocked on the head with clubs, and shot with poisoned arrows, so that there's an end, then, Lal, you will perhaps begin to think kind of a man who loved you so dear, that he went all that way alone to look for Cap'en Armiger, also with the Lord. For women never know the value of a man until he's gone.'

This said, he shook hands, wagging his head mournfully, but smiting his chest as if to repress the gloomy forebodings of his soul, and the manly sobs that choked further utterance.

Captain Holstius also went away, and Captain Wattles, who made no further allusion to the letter or the pledge he had made, also returned to Liverpool, whither, he said, business called him.

Then Lal was left alone with the letter of Rex to read and read again, and she never doubted that Captain Borlinder, true to his word, was on his way to the far East, to begin the search for her lost lover.

One man, however, doubted very much, but in a vague way. It was the Patriarch.

'Lal, my pretty,' he said, 'I mistrust two of them three chaps— the Yankee first, and Nick Borlinder next. As to Cap'en Wattles, he's told me over and over again that he wants to get back to the Pacific. It isn't hunting for Cap'en Armiger will take him back there. And as for Cap'en Borlinder, it's my opinion, my dear, that he means to make a voyage there and a voyage back, whereby to clear the cobwebs from his brain and the wrinkles from his eyes, and to gain experience. What then ? Will either of them bring him back ? Do they want him back ? Think, my dear. No ; they want him dead. The more dead he is the better they will be pleased. And if I was Cap'en Armiger, my pretty, and I was to see either of them brave master-mariners sailing up a creek with no one else in sight, I would sit snug, or I would prepare for a fight. My dear, they may talk, but they don't want him back ! The only man who means honest is the Norweegee. As for him, he loves the very ground you tread upon, and I think he'd rather be your father than your husband, which, to be sure, was never a sailor's way when I was young ; and that, my dear, is seventy, and soon will be eighty, years ago : which proves the Fifth Command- ment and shows how much I honoured my father and my mother— all the more because I never saw neither of them since ten years old.'

Captain Borlinder, dropping down the river on his next voyage, passed the Commercial Docks with a light and jocund heart. He was about to earn the gratitude of the girl he loved at a cheap rate—namely, at the cost of remaining out of her sight on the next occasion of his return to the Port of London. His love was not of that ardent and absorbing kind which prevents a man from feeling happy unless he is in the presence of the object of his affections. Quite the contrary. Captain Borlinder was happier away from the young lady, because conversation with her was carried on under considerable constraint. Once safely married, that constraint, he felt, would be removed, and expressions, now carefully guarded, might be again freely used. If a married man's house is not his own quarter-deck, what is it? thought the Captain, who, despite the culture of many centuries and the religion of his ancestors, retained the ideas of marital authority common among primitive men. He is now married, however, though not to Lal, and has learned to think quite otherwise.

The weather was favourable across the Bay, and with all sail set, a rolling sea, and a fresh breeze, the Captain stood aft and began to consider the shaping of his narrative.

He was a good hand at a yarn. But then to write a yarn is, if you please, much more difficult than to spin one. The pen is a slow, tedious instrument. We want, in fact, something more rapid with which to interpret our thoughts. While we are painfully setting down one thing, the next, equally important, escapes us and is forgotten.

Captain Borlinder felt this, and therefore, very wisely, resolved upon not writing anything until he had thoroughly mastered the whole story and told it to himself half a dozen times over. Thus great novelists, I believe, get the whole of their situations clearly in their mind, with the grouping of the characters, before writing a word. And it would be an admirable plan if certain lady novelists would also follow the Captain's method, and write nothing before they are almost word-perfect with their story.

His crew were amazed at the behaviour of their skipper, both outward and homeward bound. For he paced the quarter-deck all day long, gazing at sky and sea. He struck strange attitudes ; he shook his head ; he swore at himself sometimes ; he left the navigation of the ship to the mate ; he seemed to be perpetually repeating words.

These things were strange. He was not drunk. He even seemed to drink less than usual ; and, if he had got a touch of ' horrors,' as sometimes happens to sailors after a spell ashore, they were manifested in a most unusual manner.

On the voyage to Cadiz and back the Captain restricted himself to mental composition. We all know how difficult it is to describe a place which you have never seen. One would like to see a competitive young man's description, say of Rotherhithe, which nobody but myself has ever visited. That difficulty is, of course, lessened when your readers are equally ignorant, but immensely increased by the consideration that perhaps they know the place.

Now, certainly Lal had not seen any of the islands of Micro-nesia, or Polynesia. The contemplation of the chart whereon the countless islands of the Pacific lie dotted among the coral-reefs, the shoals and atolls of that great sea, only filled her mind with vague thoughts of palm-trees, soft winds, and brown natives. In those seas sailed the ships she had heard of, the whalers, the schooners trading from island to island. On those dots of dry land lived men, of whom she had heard, who had grown grey in these lati-tudes, who cared no more to return to England, who had learned native ways and native customs. Though Lal had never travelled, she knew a great deal more than Captain Borlinder, and it might be embarrassing for him to be asked questions arising out of her superior knowledge.

Again, there was Captain Zachariasen. Nobody knew where that old man had not been in his long life of sixty years' sailing upon the sea. In his garrulous way, he laid claim to a knowledge of every port under the sun. Now, supposing he had actually visited the place fixed on by himself for the scene of Captain Armiger's exile and death. This, too, would be embarrassing.

It is true that Nick Borlinder was not one of those who place truth among the highest duties of mankind, but rather considered the search for enjoyment, in all its branches, as a duty immensely superior and, indeed, a duty to be ranked foremost among those imposed on suffering humanity. Yet the worst of lying is that you have got to be consistent in order to be believed. Random lying helps no man. It is a mere amusement, a display of cleverness, intellectual fireworks, the indulgence of imagination. The story, therefore, must be constructed in accordance, somehow, with pos-sible facts.

The romancer had provided himself, not only with a few sheets of paper, but with a map, and over this he pored continually, seeking a likely spot for the scene of his Fabulous History. But it was not till his second return voyage that he found himself so far advanced with the story as to begin committing it to writing.

It is interesting to record further that the Captain on returning to London sought a bookseller's shop, and enquired after any work which treated of the Eastern Seas. He obtained a second-hand copy of an old book—I think by Captain Mundy—and then learned that the island of New Guinea, which he easily found on the map, was entirely unknown, and had hardly ever been visited. He therefore resolved to make New Guinea the scene of Rex Armiger's landing. At all events, Captain Zachariasen would be unable to put him to shame in the matter of New Guinea.

He made three voyages to and from Cadiz, bringing home a vast quantity of sherry, Portugal plums, raisins, oranges, and other things, and taking out I know not what, except that what he took out was not worth so much as what he brought home. And as this appears to be the case with every ship which leaves a British port, we must be working our way gaily through the national savings, and shall all very shortly take refuge in the national workhouse, so that the dreams of the Socialist will be realised, and all shall be on the same level. This is a very delightful prospect to contemplate, and the position of things reflects the highest credit on both sides of the House.

It was on October 14, 1879, that Dick, the Malay, came back and told his tale. It was in December following that the Doctor of the 'Aryan' brought the message from the sea. On January 2, Captain Borlinder took his farewell, and sallied forth on that desperate quest to the Eastern Seas, the description of which was written between Cadiz and London.

No news came to Rotherhithe all the winter. The 'Aryan' returned, and the Doctor came to say that the Company were making enquiries among the ships trading with the islands for news of a white man cast away upon one of them. No news had yet been received.

It was on June 8, 1880, that Captain Borlinder returned from the East.

He bore in his hand the same red silk pocket-handkerchief with which he had started, he wore the same blue clothes, in the same state of preservation, because they were his best ; the same shiny hat.

He presented himself in the kitchen because it was in the forenoon, and Lal was engaged in her usual occupation—namely, the daily pudding. The Patriarch, as usual, sat in the armchair sound asleep.

She dropped her work and turned pale, seeing that he was alone.

' Alone ! ' she cried.

' Alone,' he answered, in the deepest and most sepulchral notes which his voice contained. 'Alone,' he repeated. 'I have been a long voyage, and have come back—alone. But not empty-handed. No ; I have brought you news. Yes ; bad news, I grieve to say.'

She sat down and folded her hands, prepared for the worst.

' Go on,' she said ; ' tell me what you have to tell.'

At this juncture Captain Zachariasen awoke and rubbed his eyes

' Ho ! ho ! ' he said ; ' here's one of them come back. Well, 1 thought he would be the first. What cheer, mate ?' .

' Bad,' replied the traveller.

' Where's Cap'en Armiger ?'

Captain Borlinder pointed upwards, following the direction of his finger with one eye, as if that eye of faith could readily discern Rex among the angels.

' I thought he'd say that ; I told you so, Lal, my dear. Keep your pluck up, and go tell Cap'en Holstius and Cap'en Wattles. They must hear the news too.'

' They here ?'

Captain Borlinder changed colour. He had not thought of this possibility.

'Never mind the chart, my lad,' said Captain Zachariasen; 'go on.'

'Nobody, before me and Cap'en Armiger, had ever landed on that desolate coast. They set me ashore with six foot or so of baccy, a pipe, a box of lucifers, a bottle of rum, a gun, and a small fishing-net. That, I thought, would be enough to carry me along for a spell, while I made my enquiries.

'I found the natives black but friendly. They appeared not to be cannibals. They greatly admired my appearance and manners. They invited me to stay among them with the gun and be their king. And, although I was obliged to refuse, they were civil, and answered all my questions to the best of their capacities, which are naturally limited.'

Another grunt.

'After a bit I discovered that I had not been mistaken in my conclusions. Three years before, or thereabouts—because you cannot expect naked savages to be as accurate as us truth-telling Christians—a white man and a Malay had been washed ashore in an open boat.

'Directly I heard that I pricked up my ears. There might have been two different white men come ashore in an open boat, but not two pairs of white man and Malay man. That seemed impossible. So I up and enquired at once where they were.

'They told me that at landing there was a fight, but that they were taken up-country after the fight with their arms bound to their sides.' Here Captain Borlinder stopped. 'You remember, Venerable,' he said, 'how you interpreted that scrimmage shown by the dumb man? You were quite right.'

The Venerable grunted again.

'Of course,' the discoverer resumed, 'I made haste to find out which way they were taken, and it was not long before I started following their track, led by a native boy who knew the country well, having been born and brought up there.'

'Where were the rest of the natives born and brought up?' asked Captain Zachariasen. 'Go on, brother. Reel it out.'

'The first day——' Captain Borlinder turned suddenly pale, as if a weak point had been discovered in his armour, and went on reading rapidly. 'The first day we made five-and-twenty miles, as near as I could reckon, going in a bee-line across country, over hills and valleys where lions, bears, tigers, hyænas, leopards, elephants, and hippopotamuses roamed free, seeking whom they may devour; cross rivers where crocodiles sat with open jaws snapping at the people as they passed by.'

'It is hot, I suppose, in these latitudes?' said Captain Zachariasen.

'Hottish,' replied the traveller. 'I was given to understand that it was their summer. Hottish walking. Made a man relish his rum and water. And I found a pint of cold water with a jack-towel refreshing on a Saturday night. The next day we made

thirty knots of sandy desert, where there were camels and os-
triches, and never a drop of water to make a cup of tea with. The
third day we crossed a mountain, twenty-five thousand feet high,
on the sides of which were bears, wolves, and pemmican. From
the summit we obtained a splendid view right across the China
Seas, and with my glass I could easily make out Hong-Kong.

'On the fourth day, after doing thirty miles good, and living
for a week on the bark of trees and wild roots, we passed through
a thick forest inhabited solely by monkeys and snakes, after which
we emerged upon a town, the like of which I had never expected
to find in the heart of New Guinea. It appeared to consist of a
million and a half of people, as near as I could learn. They go
dressed in white cotton knee-breeches and turbans; they smoke
cigarettes and drink Jamaica rum; their manners are pleasant and
their ways hospitable.

'As soon as they saw that a white man had arrived, they
flocked round me and began to ask questions. These I satisfied to
the best of my power and requested to be taken to the king.
They led me, or rather carried me, shouting along the streets, to
the Royal Palace, which is a trifle bigger than the Crystal Palace,
and all made of solid gold.

'The king is a young man, who wears his crown both day and
night. He is always surrounded by his guards, and has to be
approached on bended knees.

'After the usual compliments, he invited me to tell him what
I came for.

'I replied that I was sent by the most beautiful girl in Rotherhithe—at this he seemed pleased, and said he wished she had come
herself—in order to discover what had become of her sweetheart,
named Rex Armiger, wrecked upon his majesty's coast in the
year 1876.

'I confess that I felt sorry, when I had put the question, but
then I had come all the way on purpose to put it. For the king
and all his courtiers immediately burst into tears.

'I then learned the whole story.

'Cap'en Armiger had, in fact, landed on this shore, as I expected and calculated. He had been separated from his steward
Dick in a scrimmage on the coast, and had been brought inland to
be presented as a captive to the king. At the court he made himself at once a great favourite, being a good shot, which pleased his
majesty, and a good dancer which pleased the ladies. He lived
three years with them in great favour with everybody, and at the
end, though this you will hardly credit, engaged to be married to
the king's sister, being by that time in despair of ever getting
away.

'Unfortunately, only the week before I arrived, he was killed
and devoured by a lion, and the princess was gone off her royal
chump.

'I am truly sorry to be the bearer of such bad news, Lal. You
will own that I done my best.

'The rest of my log, how I got away, and how I came here again, would not interest you now. You will, perhaps, like to hear them yarns in the long winter evenings when we have got nothing else to do.

'As for poor Cap'en Armiger, I brought away with me one relic of him—the last cap he ever wore. The king sent it to you by my hands. He said a great many civil things about my courage in coming all that way to find my friend, and I had to promise to go back again. However, that is nothing. Here, then, is Cap'en Armiger's cap—the cap of the Company.'

He untied the handkerchief and took out a cap with a gold band and a couple of anchors in silver embroidery upon the front. It was a uniform cap, that of the Indian Peninsular Company.

Lal received it, and turned it over in her hand, but with some doubt, stimulated by Captain Zachariasen's grunts.

The old man reached out his hand for the cap, examined it carefully, tried it on his own head, and grunted again.

'What are you grunting for now?' asked Captain Borlinder in great uneasiness.

'Gentlemen,' said Captain Zachariasen to the other two, 'tell me what you think?'

Captain Holstius made answer, like the country gentleman who read Gulliver's Travels, that he did not believe a word of it. And why? Because no one who had read accounts of those latitudes could reconcile Captain Borlinder's narrative with the tales of other travellers.

Captain Wattles shook his head.

'Coarse work,' he said. 'Very common, and coarse work.'

Upon this Captain Borlinder lost his temper, and behaved like an officer of his rank when in a rage upon his own quarter-deck.

'You shouldn't ha' thought, brother,' said the old man, holding out the cap and examining it with contempt, 'that a man of four-score and odd could be taken in by such a clumsy jemmy as yourn. I'd ha' spun a better yarn myself, by chalks. Two things shall set you right. First, my lad, this cap, which I suppose, you bought on your way in Houndsditch, is the cap of a boy of thirteen, a midshipmite. Now, Cap'en Armiger, like me, had a big head. We may toss the cap into the fire, Lal, my pretty, because it isn't your sweetheart's cap, and never was.' He did toss it into the fire, where it was immediately consumed, all except the gold lace which twisted into all shapes. 'Look at him!' he added. 'Sails in gaily with a boy's cap in one hand and a yard and half of lies, made up Lord knows where, in the other. Another thing.' Captain Borlinder at this juncture, because he had, in fact, bought that cap in Houndsditch, presented every appearance of discomfiture. 'When he landed among the blacks, all alone, what language did he talk with them? English? He knows no other. What do you say, Cap'en Wattles?'

'Coarse work. Coarse and clumsy work.'

Captain Borlinder replied in general terms, and endeavouring to bluster it out, that this was hard for a man to bear, this was, after going through all he had gone through.

But here Captain Wattles gave him the *coup de grâce.*

'I can tell all of you where that precious narrative was written. For I made it my business to enquire at the London Docks. He has been all the time aboard his own ship, and he has made three voyages to Cadiz and back since January. If you doubt, go and ask his people.'

This was an unexpected one. Captain Borlinder reeled. Then Lal rose in her wrath.

'Go!' she cried. 'You are not fit to be under the same roof with honest people. Go, impudent liar! Oh, that mon can be so wicked! He has kept my Rex for six long months more in his captivity. Go! let us never see your face again.'

She clenched her hands and pointed to the door with as threatening a gesture as Medea might have employed.

Captain Borlinder hastened to obey. He crammed the Narrative in his pocket, and his shiny hat upon his head, and walked forth, saying never a word. And although he has never since set foot upon the southern shores of the Port of London, I think he still sometimes feels over again the humiliation of that moment.

'And now,' said Captain Wattles, 'it is my turn. We have lost more than six months, it is true. I have settled all my business, and I have got command of a ship which trades among the islands, a Sydney schooner. I meant to tell you this to-day, not expecting to find this—this lying lubber here. Why, there ain't a lad of ten in the States that wouldn't put together a better story than that. Coarse and clumsy work.'

CHAPTER VIII.

THE QUEST OF CAPTAIN WATTLES.

THE next turn, therefore, fell to Captain Wattles. He, for his part, took leave in a quiet and business-like manner, making no protestations.

'I shall be,' he said, 'off and on about the Carolines, where we expect to find him. He is not in the regular track of the traders, else you would have heard from him. He is on none of the islands touched for pearl and *bêche de mer*—that we may be quite certain of; therefore, I shall try at those places which are seldom visited. If I find him, good; if not, I will let you know. I don't pretend to waste my time in looking for a man and nothing else; I am going to trade on my own account, and look about me the while. News runs from island to island in an astonishing way, and we shall likely hear about him. That's all I have to say, Miss Lal, and here's my hand upon it. Barnabas, the Son of Consolation, will act up to his name.' So he, too, disappeared.

Then, for a while, the house resumed its usual aspect, and things went on as before. A letter came in due course from Captain Wattles. He had arrived at Sydney and was preparing for departure. Then no more letters.

The time passed slowly. Captain Holstius was away with his ship. The life and light seemed to have gone from the girl. Only the old man was left to cheer her continually, and Dick to raise her courage.

'I shall live, Lal, my dear,' he said, 'to see Cap'en Armiger come home again. I have no doubt of that; and, pretty, I've been thinking about the mummicker and the end of his story. Somehow, I doubt whether it wasn't him, and not the Cap'en, they took off to prison. I wish I could trust that Yankee chap; he's worse than the other. Now if the Norweegee could go——'

As for Barnabas, there was something in his cold and quiet way which impressed those who made his acquaintance. Such men, when they are on the right side, make good generals; when they are on the wrong, they provide the picturesque element of history. Thus in the sixteenth century he would have been invaluable as a buccaneer, being full of courage and as cool as a melon; also, under favourable conditions, he might have developed a fine religious fanaticism, under the influence of which he would have hated a Spaniard and a Papist more than even Sir Walter Raleigh hated him. In the seventeenth century he would have found scope as a pirate, with Madagascar, the West-Indian and Floridan Keys, the harbours of Eastern Africa, and nearly all the ports of South America for refuge; and the navies of the world, with the rich galleons of Spain, and the East-Indiamen of England for his booty; and all the rogues and murderers afloat, actual or possible, longing to become part of his crew. In the eighteenth century the trade of pirate fell into disrepute, by reason of the singularly disagreeable end which happened to many of its followers. Happily, that of privateer took its place. In the present century, men like Barnabas B. Wattles have gone filibustering; have carried black cargoes from the West Coast across the Atlantic; and have gone blockade-running to Charleston and Galveston. All these exciting pursuits have come to an end; and there would seem, at first sight, little for a sailor to find ready for a willing hand to do, except perfectly legal pursuits.

There is not much. Still, there is always something. A man may carry Chinese coolies to Trinidad, Peru, or Cuba. Under what pretences he inveigles them aboard, what promises he makes them, and how much he gets for each, no one, outside the trade, which is a limited company, knows or can discover. You might sooner hope to learn the secrets of the Royal Arch. Again, you may ship coolies for Réunion. They are British subjects, but they are taken on board at Pondicherry, which is a French settlement. And the like mystery surrounds each transaction in Hindoo flesh. Lastly, there is a delightful pastime still carried on in Polynesia, known as the Labour Traffic. Opinions differ as to the beneficial results of a few years of cooliedom in Queensland. For whereas some authorities say that the Polynesian learns the blessings of second-hand reach-me-downs, with a smattering of Christianity, with which to astonish his relatives, the Browns, on his return ; others declare that the extra garments are discarded as soon as he lands, the rudiments of the Christian faith forgotten, and only the taste for rum remains. I know not which is right, because in order to decide the point, one ought to live along with native Poly-nesians, or with Australian colonists, in order to hear both sides of the question, and no controversialist has as yet done that. One thing, however, is quite certain, that the coolies embark for various reasons, among which no one has as yet pretended to find a desire to toil on the Queensland cotton and sugar estates. Toil of any kind is, indeed, the last thing which these children of the Equatorial Pacific desire. Rest is what they love, or, if any exercise, then a languid swim in tepid waters, a dance in the evening, and the joyous cup. Now to ship these innocents and to bring them to the market where they may be hired is a profitable, albeit a dangerous, pursuit.

It is never a fault of the American adventurer that he too care-fully considers the danger. Where there are dollars to be picked up there is generally danger. The round earth may be mapped out in different belts of fertility, so far as dollars are concerned. Where they most abound and may most readily be gathered there is such a crowd, with so much fighting and struggling, or there are so many perils from climate, crocodiles, settlers, snakes, na-tives, and sharks, that it is only the brave man who ventures thither, and only the strong man who comes home in safety, bringing with him the treasures he has fought for. Barnabas B. Wattles was brave and strong, and he knew the islands of old, where he had sojourned, though certainly not, as we have once heard him state, as a missionary. He now saw his way to a neat stroke of business combined with love. He would prove, not clumsily, as did his rival, but prove beyond a doubt, the death of Rex Armiger. Then he would return, carry off the girl with the money, which he supposed belonged to her, forgetting the existence of Mrs. Rydquist, and get back to America, where he knew of a certain dry dock, to possess which was the dream of his soul. It may be also stated that he firmly believed that the man was dead, and to find Rex Armiger alive was the last thing which he expected.

Yet this, as you will see, was exactly what he did find.

He took command of his trading schooner, loaded her with the things which Polynesians love, such as gaudy cottons, powder, tobacco, rum, and strong perfumes, and set sail.

It is not my purpose to follow the voyage of the 'Fair Maria'

across the Pacific Ocean, nor to toll of the various adventures which befel her captain, and the trade he did. Wherever he touched he made enquiries, but he could hear nothing of a young white man cast ashore in an open boat. No one knew or had heard of any such jetsam.

At last he began to think his search would lead to nothing, and that all trace of the man was lost. This he regretted, because he was unfeignedly anxious to send home or bring home proofs of his death; so anxious that he had grown perfectly certain that Rex was dead.

It came to pass, however, after many days that he sighted an island, an outlying member of a group at which he knew that traders never touch, because it was too small a place and lay out of the usual track.

It is very well known that a large number of the Caroline Islands are composed of certain coral formations called atolls. These consist of a round ring of rock just appearing above the surface, enclosing a shallow lagoon, whose diameter varies from a few yards to a hundred miles, in which lie islands, some of them large islands with hills, streams, and splendid woods of cocoa-palm, bread-fruit, durian, and pandang; whose islanders lead, or would lead if they knew how, delightful lives in fishing in their smooth waters, eating the fruits which Heaven sends, and doing no kind of work. Others there are, small atolls with small lagoons, whose islets are mere rocks on which grow nothing but the universal pandang, the screw palm, which serves the people for everything. Such was this. It was too insignificant even to have a name; it was distant about two hundred miles from the group of which it might be supposed to be a member; it was simply laid down on the chart as a 'shoal,' and had, perhaps, never been visited by any ship since its first discovery.

Moved by some impulse, perhaps a mere curiosity as to the capabilities of trade and the possibility of pearls, Captain Wattles steered towards this low-lying land.

When his boat lay upon the shallow waters within the reef he found a group of the inhabitants of the principal islet gathered upon the beach. They were of the brown Polynesian race, and were apparently preparing for a hostile reception.

Among them stood, passive, a man almost as brown as themselves, but with fair hair and blue eyes. He was a white man; he was a young white man; he was evidently no common beach-comber; and Captain Wattles immediately recognised, without any doubt, the man of whom he was in search. He was dressed in rags; the sleeves were torn from his jacket and his bare arms were tattooed; his trousers had lost most of their legs; he wore some kind of sandals made of the pandang leaf; his beard was long, his hair was hanging in an unkempt mass; his head was protected from the sun by an ingenious arrangement of another leaf of the same tree. It could be no other than Rex Armiger.

A strange feeling, akin to pity, seized on Captain Wattles. He repressed it, as unworthy of himself. But he did at first feel pity for him.

The white man stood among the natives afraid to excite their suspicion by running before them to meet the boat : yet his eagerness was visible in his attitude, in the trembling of his lips, in the way in which he looked upon the boat.

He carried a short lance in his hand like all the rest.

Captain Wattles rowed within hailing distance of the shore. Then he stood up.

' White man, ahoy ! '

The white man said something to his companions, and stepped forward, but in a leisurely manner, as if he was not at all anxious to speak the boat.

He came to the water's edge and sat down.

' I am an Englishman,' he said, speaking slowly, because he was speaking a language he had not used for three years. ' I am an Englishman. My name is Armiger. I was the captain of the Indian Peninsular ship "Philippine," wrecked on a shoal three years or so ago. I have been living since among these people.'

' Do you know their lingo ? '

' Yes.'

' Then tell them I am harmless and I want to row nearer land.'

Rex turned to the men and addressed them in their own language.

They all sat down and waited.

' You may come nearer,' he said ; ' but make no movement that may alarm them, and do not attempt to land. They are suspicious since two years ago a ship came down from the Ladrone Islands and kidnapped twenty of them, including a Malay, cast away with me.'

Here then was the interpretation of Dick's second pantomimic flight. He did not escape, he was kidnapped. How he got away from the Ladrone Islands, how he found his way to England, remains a matter hitherto undiscovered.

Captain Wattles brought up his boat within a few yards of the beach, but in deep water, holding his men in readiness to give way.

Sitting in the stern he was able to talk freely with Rex, who stood at the very edge of the water waiting for an opportunity to leap on board.

' So,' said Captain Wattles, ' you are Cap'en Armiger, are you ? '

Rex was astonished at the salutation.

' Why ? Do you know me ? '

' You see I know your name, stranger. I confess I am sorry to find you. I thought you were dead. I hardly calculated that I'd find you, though I certainly did promise to keep one eye open for you.'

' What promise ? ' asked Rex.

'I promised—— We'll come to that directly. Now, what are those black devils dancing about for?'

The natives had jumped to their feet, and were now shaking clubs and spears in a threatening way.

'They want my assurance,' Rex said, 'that you are not a black-birder.'

'Honest trading schooner,' replied Captain Wattles. 'Tell them they may come aboard and see for themselves. What have they got to sell?'

'What should we have on this little island? We live on kabobo. Do you want to buy any? What is your name?'

'Barnabas B. Wattles, cap'en of the "Fair Maria," lying yonder. Guess you'd like to be aboard her. Well, business first. Let's trade something. Got no turtle?'

'No.'

'No *bêche de mer*? No copra?'

'We have nothing.'

'Very well, then,' said Captain Wattles. 'After business, pleasure. Mate, I guess you are tired of this gem of the sea—eh?'

'So tired,' replied Rex Armiger, 'that if you had not turned up I believe I should have made a raft out of the pandang leaves and tried my luck.'

'Then I'm devilish glad we came,' said Captain Wattles. 'The more so as I have a little bargain to propose before you come aboard my craft.'

'Any bargain that's fair.'

'I guess this is quite fair and honourable,' the Captain went on. 'You have been a beach-comber upon this island for nigh upon three years. Three years is a long time. The gell you were in love with has likely got tired of waiting. Your name is wrote off the books; your ship is long since posted; your friends have put on mourning for you——'

'What's the good of so much talk?' interrupted Rex. 'I want to be taken off this island. What's your bargain?'

'Fair and easy, lad. Let me have my talk out.' Captain Wattles looked at him with a curious expression. 'Why, you are as good as dead already.'

'What do you mean?'

'I mean this. There's one or two men who would like you to be dead. I'm one of those. What's more, I ain't goin', for my part, to be the means of restoring you to life. No, sir. I don't exactly wish you dead, and yet I don't want to see you alive in England.'

This was said with great decision.

Rex listened with amazement.

'What harm have I ever done to you, man?' he cried. 'You wish me dead?'

'There's no use keeping secrets between us two,' continued the strange trader. 'Look here, three years ago, before you got command of the "Philippine," you were in love with a certain young lady who lives at Rotherhithe.'

' Go on. For God's sake, go on.'

' That sweet young thing, sir, whom it's a privilege to know and a pride to fall in love with, peaked and pined more than a bit, thinkin' about you and wonderin' where you were.'

' Poor Lal ! dear Lal !'

' Yes, she was real faithful and kindhearted, that gell. Her friends, and especially her mother, who takes a kind of pleasure in reckoning up the dead men she knows located at the bottom of the briny, gave you up. But she never gave you up. No, never.'

' Poor Lal ! dear Lal !'

The tears stood in the castaway's eyes as he sat and listened. Behind him the men of the island stood like wild beasts on the alert, waiting for the moment of flight or attack. And also like wild beasts, they were never certain whether to fly or to fight.

' No one like that gell, sir, no one,' continued Captain Wattles ; ' which is all the more reason why other fellows want to cut in.'

Rex began to understand.

' Among other fellows is myself, Barnabas B. Wattles. Very good. Now you see why I would rather hear that you were dead than alive, and why I'm darned disappointed to meet you here. However, you are on about as desolate a place as I know of, that's one comfort.'

The fact brought no comfort to Rex, but quite the reverse.

' Mate, I want to tell you the whole story fair and above board. I will tell you no lies. Therefore, you may trust what I say. And first let me know how you came here, and all about it.'

Rex told his story. It was all as Lal had divined from Dick's action. They sighted the island, being then half dead with hunger, and with difficulty managed to paddle themselves ashore. They were seized by the natives, and a consultation was held whether they should be killed. They were spared.

Life on that island is necessarily simple. The people live entirely on kabobo, which is a sort of rough bread made of the pandang nut. They have no choice, because there is nothing else to live upon. It is the only tree that grows upon this lonely land. Kabobo is said to be wholesome, but it is monotonous.

Rex explained briefly that he had learned to talk with them, and won by slow degrees their confidence ; that he had taught them a few simple things, and he was regarded by them with some sort of affection ; that, after a year's residence on the island, a ship came in sight, but did not anchor. That a boat put off, manned by an armed crew, who, when the people came down to meet them, half disposed to be friendly, attacked them, killed some, and carried off others, among whom was the Malay. This made them extremely suspicious. Since that event nothing had happened ; nothing but the slow surge of the wave upon the reef and the sigh of the wind in the pandang trees.

'Now that you have come,' Rex concluded, 'you who know—her,' he added cheerfully, though his heart was heavy in thinking of the bargain, 'you will take me off this island—for her sake.'

'For her sake?' echoed Captain Wattles. 'Man alive! It is for her sake that I won't do no such silly thing. No, sir. You understand that she thinks you're alive. Very good then. Bein' a faithful gell, she keeps her word with you. Once she knows you are dead, why there will be a chance for another chap. And who so likely as the man who came all the way out here to discover that interestin' fact? See, pard?'

'Good God!' cried Rex. 'Do you mean that you will leave me here and say I am dead?'

'That is exactly what I am coming to, Cap'en Armiger. I take it, sir, that you air a sensible man, and I have been told that you know better than most which way that head of yours is screwed on. You can understand what it is to be in love with that most beautiful creature. What you've got to do is to buy your freedom.'

'How am I to buy my freedom?'

'I've thought of this meeting, sir,'—this was a happy invention of the moment—'and I considered within myself what would be best. The easiest way out of it, the way most men would choose, would be to get up a little shindy with those brown devils there and to take that opportunity of dropping a bead into your vitals. That way, I confess, did seem to me, at first sight, the best. But why kill a man when you needn't? I know it's foolish, but I should like to go back to that young creature without thinking that she'd disapprove if she knew.'

Rex sprang to his feet. The man who lay there in the stern of the boat, six feet from the shore, his head upon his hands, calmly explaining why he did not murder him, was going back to England to marry Lal—his Lal. To marry her! He threw up his arms and was speechless with rage and horror.

Behind him the savages stood grouped, waiting for any sign from him to fly or rush upon the strangers with their spears.

The day was perfectly calm, the sea was motionless in the land-locked water, and, in the calm and peace of the hot noonday, the words fell upon his brain like words one hears in a ghastly dream of the night.

'Yes,' the man went on, 'I want to do what is right, and this is my proposal, Cap'en Armiger. I know you can be trusted, because I've made enquiries. Some Englishmen can lie like Rooshans, but some can't. You, I am told, are one of that sort who can't. Promise me to drop your own name, not to go back to England for twenty years at least, never to let out that you are Rex Armiger, to stay in these seas, and I'll take you aboard my schooner and land you at Levuka or Honolulu, or wherever you please. Come, you may even go to Australia if you like. As for names, I'll lend you mine. You shall have the name of my brother, Jacob B. Wattles, now in

Abraham's bosom. He won't mind, and if he does, it don't matter. As for work, there's plenty to get and plenty to do among these islands. There's the labour traffic; there's pearl-fishing; there's trading. You may live among them, marry among them; turn beach-comber for life; you may get to Fiji and run a plantation. Cap'en Armiger, if I were you, I would rather not go back.

'As for this place, now, I don't suppose a man grows to get a yearning for kabobo for a permanence, and on this darned one-horse island there doesn't seem much choice outside the pandang tree. Likewise, those young gentlemen with their toothpicks are not quite the company you were brought up to, I reckon. Whereas, except for the missionaries, who spoil everything, I don't suppose there's better company to be got anywhere in this world than you'll find in this ocean when I land you on an island worth the name. At Honolulu, for instance, there's nobblers and champagne, and——. Wal, I'd rather live there, or in one or two other islands that I know, than anywhere in Europe or the States. And so would you, come to look at things rightly.'

Rex still kept silence, pacing on the narrow beach.

'As for being dead, you've been dead for three years, so that can't be any objection. Why, man, I give you life; I resurrect you. Think of that!

'As for being altered, you are so changed that your own mother would not know you again. No fear of any old friends recognising you. And, so far as a few dollars go to start with, say the word and you shall have them, with a new rig-out.'

Still Rex made no reply.

'There is my offer, plain and open. I'm sorry for you, Cap'en Armiger, I re'lly am, because she's out an' out the best set-up gell that walks. But two men can't both have her. And I mean to be the man that does—not you. And all is fair in love.'

'And if I refuse your offer?'

'Then, Cap'en Armiger, you stay just where you now happen to be. And a most oncomfortable location. Now, sir, make no error. Since the day that you landed on this island, have you seen ary a sail on the sea? No. Ships don't come here. Even the Germans at Yap know that it's no manner of good coming here. You are out of the reach of hurricanes, so you can't expect so much as a wreck. You are hundreds of miles from any land; you have got no tools to make a raft, and no provisions to put aboard her if you could make one; you are altogether lonely, and hopeless, and destitute. Robinson Crusoe hadn't a more miserable look-out. As for that young lady, you have no chance, not the least mite of a chance, sir, of seeing her ever again. You have lost her. Why, then, give her another chance, and let me say you are dead. Cap'en, you can write—that's another of my conditions —a last dying will and testament on a bit o' paper, which I will send her. Come, be reasonable.'

Rex stood still, staring blankly before him. On the one hand, liberty and life—for to stay upon the island was death ; on the other, perhaps a hopeless prison.

Yet—Lal Rydquist ! If she mourned him as one dead, would it hurt to let her mourn until she forgot him ? He shuddered as he thought of her marrying the cold-blooded villain before him. Perhaps she would never marry anyone, but go on in sadness all her days.

I am happy to say that the third course open to him—to give his parole and then to break it—did not occur to him as possible. He decided according to the nobler way.

'Go without me,' he said. And then, without a word of reproach or further entreaty, he left the beach and walked away, and was lost among the palm-trees standing thickly upon the thin and sandy soil.

Captain Wattles gazed after him in admiration.

'There goes,' he said, 'one of the real old sort. Bully for the British bulldog yet ! '

The group of savages stood still, looking on and wondering. They suspected many things : that their white prisoner would run away with the boat ; that the crew might fire upon them or try to kidnap them. They also hoped a few things, such as that the white captain would give them things, fine beads, fine coloured stuffs, or rum to get drunk with. Yet nothing happened. Then Captain Wattles, seeing that Rex Armiger had disappeared, bethought him of something. And he began to make signs to the black fellows and to show them from the stern of his boat things wonderful and greatly to be desired, and at the same time he gave certain directions to his crew.

Thereupon the savages, moved with the envy and desire of those things, did with one accord advance a few yards nearer.

Captain Wattles spread out more things, holding them up in the sun for their admiration, and making signs of invitation.

They then divided into two groups, of whom one retreated and the other advanced.

Captain Wattles next displayed a couple of most beautiful knives, the blades of which, when he opened them, flashed in the sun in a most surprising manner. And he pointed to two of the islanders, young and stalwart fellows, and invited them by gestures to come into the water and take these knives.

The crew meantime remained perfectly motionless, hands on oars. Only those experienced in rowing might have observed that their oars were well forward ready for the stroke.

The advanced group again separated into two more groups, of which one consisting of a dozen of the younger men, including the two invited, advanced still nearer, until they were close to the water's edge, and the others retreated further back. All of them, both those behind and those in front, remained watchful and suspicious, like a herd of deer.

Presently the two singled out plunged into the water and swam out to the boat. At first they swam round it, while Captain Wattles continued to smile pleasantly at them and to exhibit the knives. Also the crew dipped their oars without the least noise, and with a half stroke, short and sharp, not moving their bodies, got a little way upon the boat. The swimmers, with their eyes upon the knives, did not seem to notice this manœuvre. Nor did they suspect though the oars were dipped again and the boat fairly moving.

For just then they made up their minds that Captain Wattles was a kind and benevolent person, and they swam close to the stern of the vessel and held up their hands for the knives.

It is very well known that the Polynesian natives have long and thick black hair, which they tie up in a knot at the top of their heads.

What, then, was the surprise of these two poor fellows to find their top-knots grasped, one by Captain Wattles, and the other by his interpreter, and their own heads held under water till they were half drowned, while the crew gave way and the boat shot out to sea.

There was a wild yell of the natives on shore, and a rush to the water. But the boat was too far out for missiles to reach or shouts to terrify.

'Now,' said Captain Wattles, when the half-drowned fellows were hauled up the ship's side, 'we didn't exactly want this kind o' cargo, and I had hoped to have stuck to legitimate trade. Wal! this will make it very awkward for the next ship which touches here, and I don't think it will add to Captain Armiger's popularity. After all,' he added, 'I doubt I was a fool not to finish this job and have done with it. Who knows but some blundering ship may find out the place by mistake and pick him up?'

When the 'Fair Maria' returned to Sydney, some months later, the very first thing Captain Wattles did was to put into the post a bulky letter.

Like Captain Borlinder he had written a Narrative. Unlike that worthy's story, this had all the outward appearance of *vraisemblance*. I would fain enrich this history with it at length, but forbear. Yet it was a production of remarkable merit, combining so much that was true with so much that was false.

As a basis we may recall the history, briefly touched upon, of the kidnapping by the ship from the Ladrones.

This story put Captain Wattles upon the track of as good a tale of adventure, ending with the death of Rex Armiger, as was ever told. Some day, perhaps, with changed names, it may see the light as a tale for boys.

The local colouring was excellent, and the writer's knowledge of the natives made every detail absolutely correct. It ended by an appeal, earnest, religious, to Lal's duties as a Christian. No

H

woman, said Captain Barnabas, was allowed to mourn beyond a
term ; nor was any woman (by the Levitical law) allowed to consider herself as belonging to one man, should that man die.
Wherefore, he taught her, it was her bounden duty to accept the
past as a thing to be put away and done with.

'We forget,' he concluded, 'the sorrows of childhood ; the
hopes and disappointments of early youth are remembered no more
by healthy minds. So let it be with the memory of the brave and
good man who loved you, doubtless faithfully as you loved him.
Do not hide it, or stifle it. Let it die away into a recollection of
sadness endured with resignation. I would to Heaven that it had
been my lot to touch upon this island, where he lived so long,
before the fatal event which carried him off. I would that it had been
my privilege to bring him home with me to your arms. I cannot
do this now. But when I return to England, and call at Seven
Houses, may it be my happiness to administer that consolation
which becomes one who bears my Christian-name.'

This was very sweet and beautiful. Indeed, Captain Wattles
had a poetical spirit, and would doubtless have written most sweet
verses had he turned his attention to that trade.

After the letter was posted, he was sitting in a verandah, his
feet up, reading the latest San Francisco paper. Suddenly he
dropped it, and turned white with some sudden shock.

His friends thought he would faint, and made haste with a
nobbler which he drank. Then he sat up in his chair and said
solemnly :

'I have lost the sweetest gell in all the world, through the
darndest folly ! Don't let any man ask me what it was. I had
the game in my own hands, and I threw it away. Mates ! I shan't
never—no, never—be able to hold my head up again. A nobbler ?
Ten nobblers !'

The letter reached England in due course, and, for reasons
which will immediately appear, was opened by Captain Zachariasen.
He read it aloud right through twice. Then he put it down, and
the skin of his face wrinkled itself in a thousand additional crow's
feet, and a ray of profound wisdom beamed from his sagacious
eyes, and he said slowly :

'Mrs. Rydquist, ma'am, I said at first go off that I didn't trust
that Yankee any more than the Borlinder lubber. Blame me if
they ain't both in the same tale. You and me, ma'am, will live
to see !'

'I hope we may, Captain Zachariasen ; I hope we may. Last
night I lay awake three hours, and I heard voices. We have yet
to learn what these voices mean. Winding-sheets in candles I
never knew to fail, but voices are uncertain.'

CHAPTER IX.

THE GREAT GOOD LUCK OF CAPTAIN HOLSTIUS.

THE clumsy cheat of Captain Borlinder brought home to Lal the sad truth that nobody, except herself and perhaps Captain Holstius, believed Rex could still be living, Even the Doctor of the 'Aryan,' who called every time the ship came home, frankly told her that he could not think it possible for him to be anywhere near the track of ships without being heard of. The Company had sent to every port touched by Pacific traders, and to every missionary station, asking that enquiry should be made, but nothing had been heard. All the world had given him up. There came a time when anxiety became intolerable, with results to nerve and brain which might have been expected had Lal's friends possessed any acquaintance with the diseases of the imagination.

'I must do something,' she said one day to Captain Holstius, who remonstrated with her for doing too much. 'I must be working; I cannot sit still. All day I think of Rex—all night I see Rex—waiting on the shore of some far-off land, looking at me with reproachful eyes, which ask why I do not send someone to take him away. In my dreams I try to make him understand—alas! he will not hear me, and only shakes his head when I tell him that one man is looking for him now, and another will follow after.'

Captain Holstius, slowly coming to the conclusion that the girl was falling into a low condition, began to cast about, in his thoughtful way, for a remedy. He took a voyage to Norway to think about it.

Very much to Lal's astonishment, he re-appeared a month later, without his ship. He told her, looking a little ashamed of himself, that he had come by steamer, and that he had made a little plan which, with her permission, he would unfold to her.

'I drew the shortest straw,' he said ; 'otherwise I should have gone long ago. Now, without waiting for Captain Wattles, who may be an honest man or he may not be——'

'Not be,' echoed the Patriarch.

'I mean to go at once.'

Lal clasped her hands.

'But there is another thing,' he went on. 'Lal, my dear, it isn't good for you to sit here waiting ; it isn't good for you to be looking upon that image all day long as well as all night.'

'It never leaves me now,' she cried, the tears in her eyes. 'Why, I see him now, as I see him always while you are talking—while we are all sitting here.'

Indeed, to the girl's eyes, the figure stood out clear and distinct.

'See !' she said, 'a low beach with palm-trees, such as you read

H 2

to me about last year. He is on the sands, gazing out to sea. His eyes meet mine. Oh, Rex—Rex! how can I help you? What can I do for you?'

Captain Holstius shuddered. It seemed as if he, too, saw this vision.

Captain Zachariasen said that mummicking was apt to spread in a family like measles.

'Then, Lal dear,' said Captain Holstius, 'hear my plan. I have sold my share in the ship. I got a good price for it—three hundred pounds. I am ready to start to-morrow. But I fear that when I am gone you will sit here and grieve worse because I shall not be here to comfort you. It is the waiting that is bad. So,'— he hesitated here, but his blue eyes met Lal's with an honest and loyal look—'so, my dear, you must trust yourself to me, and we will go together and look for him.'

'Go with you?'

'Yes; go with me. With my three hundred pounds we can get put from port to port, or pay the captain of a trader to sail among the Carolines with us on board. I daresay it will be rough, but ship captains of all kinds are men to be trusted, you know, and I shall be with you. You will call me your brother, and I shall call you my sister, if you like.'

To go with him! Actually to sail away across the sea in quest of her lover! To feel that the distance between them was daily growing less! This seemed at first sight an impossible thing, more unreal than the vision of poor Rex.

To be sure such a plan would not be settled in a day. It was necessary to get permission from Mrs. Rydquist, whose imagination would not at first rise to the Platonic height of a supposed brotherhood.

She began by saying that it was an insult to the memory of her husband, and that a daughter of hers should go off in broad daylight was not what she had expected or hoped. She also said that if Lal was like other girls she would long since have gone into decent crapes and shown resignation to the will of Heaven. That fair warning with unmistakable signs had been given her; that, after all, she was no worse off than her mother; with more to the same effect. Finally, if Lal chose to go away on a wild goose chase, she would not, for her part, throw any obstacle in the way, but she supposed that her daughter intended to marry Captain Holstius whether she picked up Rex or not.

'He ought, my dear,' said Captain Zachariasen, meaning the Norweegee, 'to have been a naval chaplain, such is his goodness of heart. And as gentle as a lamb, and of such are the kingdom of heaven. You may trust yourself to him as it were unto a bishop's apron. And if 'twill do you any good, my pretty, to sail the salt seas o'er in search of him, who may be for aught we know, but we hope he isn't, lying snug at the bottom, why take and up and go. As for the Captains, I'll keep 'em in order, and with authority to give a month's warning, I'll sit in the kitchen every morning and keep 'em at it. Your mother can go on goin' on just the same with her teapot and her clean handkerchiefs.'

This was very good of the old man, and in the end he showed himself equal to the task, so that Rydquist's fell off but little in reputation while Lal was away.

As for what people might say, it was very well known in Rother hithe who and of what sort was Lal Rydquist, and why she was going away. If unkind things were spoken, those who spoke them might go to regions of ill repute, said the Captains in discussion.

How the good fellows passed round the hat to buy Lal a kit complete; how Captain Zachariasen discovered that he had a whole bag full of golden sovereigns which he did not want, and would never want; how it was unanimously resolved that Dick must go with them; how the officers of the 'Aryan' for their share provided the passage-money to San Francisco and back for this poor fellow; how the Director of the Company, who had come with the Secretary to see the 'mummicking,' heard of it, and sneaked to Rotherhithe unknown to anybody with a purse full of bank-notes and a word of good wishes for the girl; how everybody grew amazingly kind and thoughtful, not allowing Lal to be put upon or worried, so that servants did what they ought to do without being looked after, and meals went on being served at proper times, and the Captains left off bringing things that wanted buttons; how Mrs. Rydquist for the first time in her life received supernatural signs of encouragement; and how they went on board at last, accompanied by all the Captains—these things belong to the great volumes of the things unwritten.

All was done at last, and they were in the Channel steaming against a head wind and a chopping sea. They were second-class passengers, of course; money must not be wasted. But what mattered rough accommodation?

All the way across to New York on the 'Rolling Forties' they had head winds and rough seas. Yet what mattered bad weather? It began with a gale from the south-west in the Irish Sea, which bucketed the ship about all the way from the Mersey to Queenstown. The sailors stamped about the deck all night, and there was a never-ending yo-ho-ing with the dashing and splashing of the waves over the deck. The engines groaned aloud at the work they were called upon to do; the ship rolled and pitched without ceasing; the passengers were mostly groaning in their cabins, and those who could get out could get no fresh air except on the companion, for it was impossible to go on deck; everything was cold, wet, and uncomfortable. Yet there was one glad heart on board who minded nothing of the weather. It was the heart of the girl who was going in quest of her lover; so that every moment brought them nearer to him, what mattered for rough weather? Besides, Lal was not sea-sick, nor was her companion, as by profession forbidden that weakness.

When they left Queenstown the gale, which had been south-west, became north-west, which was rather worse for them, because it was colder. And this gale was kept up for their benefit the whole way across, so that they had no easy moment, nor did the ship once cease her plunging through angry waters, nor did the sun shine upon them at all, nor did the fiddles leave the tables, nor were the decks dry for a moment. Yet what mattered wind and rain and foul weather? For every moment brought the girl nearer to her lost lover.

When Lal stood on the rolling deck, clinging to the arm of Captain Holstius, and looked across the grey waters leaden and dull beneath the cloudy sky, it was with a joy in her heart which lent them sunshine.

'I see Rex no longer in my dreams,' she said; 'what does that mean?'

'It means, Lal,' replied Captain Holstius, who believed profoundly that the vision was sent direct by Providence, 'that he is satisfied, because he knows that you are coming.'

Some of the passengers perceiving that here was an extremely pretty girl, accompanied by a brother—brothers are not generally loth to transfer their sisters to the care of those who can appreciate them more highly—endeavoured to make acquaintance, but in vain. It was not in order to talk with young fellows that Lal was crossing the ocean.

Then, the voyage having passed through like a dream, they landed at New York, and another dream began in the long journey across the continent among people whose ways and speech were strange.

This is a journey made over land, and there was no more endurance other than that of patience. But it is a long and tedious journey which even the ordinary traveller finds weary, while to Lal, longing to begin the voyage of search, it was well-nigh intolerable. Some of the passengers began to remark this beautiful girl with eyes that looked always westward as the train ploughed on its westward way. She spoke little with her companion, who was not her husband and did not seem to be her brother. But from time to time he unrolled a chart for her, and they followed a route upon the ocean, talking in undertones. Then these passengers became curious, and one or two of them, ladies, broke through the American reserve towards strangers and spoke to the English girl, and discovered that she was a girl with a story of surpassing interest. She made friends with these ladies, and after a while she told them her story, and how the man with whom she travelled was not her brother at all, and not even her cousin, but her very true and faithful friend, her lover, more loyal than Amadis de Gaul, who had sold all that he had and brought the money to her that she might go herself to seek her sweetheart. And then she told what reason she had to believe that Rex was living, and pointed to the Malay who had brought the message from the sea, and was as faithful to her as any bull-dog.

They pressed her hands and kissed her ; they wished her God-
speed upon her errand, and they wondered what hero this lover of
hers could be, since for his sake, she could accept without offer of
reward the service, the work, the very fortune of so good and unselfish a man.

He was no hero, in truth, poor Rex ! nor was he, I think, so
good a man as Captain Holstius ; but he was her sweetheart, and
she had given him her word.

Yet, although she talked, although the journey was shortened
by the sympathy of these kind friends, it was like the voyage, a
strange and unreal dream ; it was a dream to be standing in the
sunshine of California ; a dream to look upon the broad Pacific ; a
dream that her brother stood beside her with thoughtful eyes and
parted lips, looking across the ocean on which their quest was to be
made.

'Yes, Lal,' he murmured, pointing where westward lie the
lands we call Far East, 'yonder over the water, are the Coral Islands.
They are scattered across the sea for thousands of miles, and on
one of them sits Captain Anniger. Doubt not, my dear, that we
shall find him.'

Now it came to pass that the thing for which a certain English
girl, accompanied by a Norwegian sea-captain, had come to San
Francisco became noised abroad in the city, and even got into the
papers, and interviewers called upon Captain Holstius begging for
particulars, which he supplied, saying nought of his own sacrifices,
nor of the money, and how it was obtained.

The story, dressed up in newspaper fashion, made a very pretty
column of news. It was copied, with fresh dressing up, into the
New York papers, and accounts of it, with many additional details,
all highly dramatic, were transmitted by the various New York
correspondents—all of whom are eminent novelists—to the London
papers. The story was copied from them by all the country and
colonial papers, whence it came that the story of Lal's voyage, and
the reason of it became known, in garbled form, all over the
English-speaking world. But, as a great quantity of most interesting and exciting things, including the Irish discussion, have happened during this year, public interest in the voyage was not
sustained, and it was presently forgotten, and nobody enquired
into the sequel.

This, indeed, is the fate of most interesting stories as told by
the papers. An excellent opening leads to nothing.

But the report of her doings was of great service to Lal in San
Francisco. In this wise. Among those who came to see the beautiful
English girl in search of her sweetheart was a lady with whom she had
travelled from New York, and to whom she had told her story. This
lady brought her husband. He was a rich man just then, although
he had recently spent a winter and spring in Europe. A financial
operation, which was to have been a Bonanza boom, has since then
smashed him up ; but he is beginning again in excellent heart,

none the worse for the check, and is so generous a man that he deserves to make another pile. He is, besides, so full of courage, resource, quickness, and ingenuity that he is quite certain to make it. Also, he is so extravagant that he will most assuredly lose it again.

'Miss Rydquist,' he said, 'my wife has told me your story. Believe me, young lady, you have everybody's profound sympathy, and I am here, not out of curiosity, because I am not a press man, but to tell you that perhaps I can be of some help to you if you will let me.'

'My dear,' said his wife, interrupting, 'we do not know yet whether you will let us help you, and we are rather afraid of offering. May we ask whether—whether you are sure you are rich enough for what may turn out a long and expensive voyage?'

'Indeed,' said Lal, 'I do not know. Captain Holstius sold his share in a ship, and that brought in a good deal of money, and other friends helped us, and I think we have about five hundred pounds left.'

'That is a good sum to begin with,' said the American. 'Now, young lady, is your—your brother what is reckoned a smart sailor?'

'Oh yes.' Lal was quite sure about this. 'Everybody in the Commercial Docks always said he was one of the best seamen afloat.'

'So I should think. Now then. A week or two ago—so that it seems providential—I had to take over a trading schooner as she stands, cargo and all. She's in the bay, and you can look at her. But—she has no skipper.'

'Now,' said his wife, 'you see how we might help you, my dear. My husband does not care where his ship is taken to, nor where she trades. If it had not been for this accident of your arrival, he would have sold her. If Captain Holstius pleases, he can take the command, and sail wherever he pleases.'

This was a piece of most astonishing good fortune, because it made them perfectly independent. And, on the other hand, it was not quite like accepting a benefit and giving nothing in return, because there was the trading which might be done.

In the end, there was little profit from this source, as will be seen.

Therefore they accepted the offer with grateful hearts.

A few days later they were sailing across the blue waters in a ship well manned, well found, and seaworthy. With them was a mate who was able to interpret.

Then began the time which will for ever seem to Lal the longest and yet the shortest in her life, for every morning she sighed and said, 'Would that the evening were here!' and every evening she longed for the next morning. The days were tedious and the nights were long. Now that they are all over, and a memory of the past, she recalls them one by one, each with its little tiny incident to mark and separate it from the rest, and remembers all, with every hour saying, 'This was the fortieth day before we found him,' and 'Thirty days after this day we came to the island of my Rex.'

The voyage, after two or three days of breeze, was across a smooth sea, with a fair wind. Lal remembers the hot sun, the awning rigged up aft for her, the pleasant seat that Captain Holstius arranged for her, where she lay listening to the plash of the water against the ship's side, rolling easily with the long waves of the Pacific, watching the white sails filled out, while the morning passed slowly on, marked by the striking of the bells.

It seemed, day after day, as her eye lay upon the broad stretch of waters, that they were quite alone in the world ; all the rest was a dream ; the creation meant nothing but a boundless ocean, and a single ship sailing slowly across it.

In the evening, after sunset, the stars came out—stars she had never seen before. They are no brighter, these stars of the equator, than those of the North. They are not so bright ; but, seen in the cloudless sky from the deck of the ship, they seemed brighter, clearer, nearer. Under their light, in the silence of the night, the girl's heart was lifted, while her companion stood beside her and spoke, out of his own fulness, noble thoughts about great deeds. She felt humbled, yet not lowered. She had never known this man before ; she never suspected, while he sat grave and silent among the other Captains, how his brain was like a well undefiled, a spring of sweet water, charged with thoughts that only come to the best among us, and then only in times of meditation and solitude.

Thinking of those nights, she would now, but for the sake of Rex, fain be once more leaning over the taffrail, listening to the slow and measured words of this gentle Norweegee.

As for Dick, he knew perfectly what they left England for, and why they came aboard this ship. At night, when they got into warm latitudes, he lay coiled up on deck, for'ard ; all day long he stood in the bows, and gazed out to sea, looking for the land where they were cast ashore.

It matters little about the details of the voyage. The first land they made was Oahu, one of the Sandwich Islands. They put in at Honolulu and took in fresh provisions. Then they sailed again across a lonely stretch of ocean, where there are no islands, where they hailed no vessel, and where the ocean soundings are deepest.

Then they came into seas studded with groups of islands most beautiful to look upon. But they stayed not at any, and still Dick stood in the bows and kept his watch. Sometimes his face would light up as he saw, far away, low down in the horizon, a bank of land, which might have been a cloud. He would point to it, gaze patiently till he could make it out, and then, as if disappointed, would turn away and take no more interest in it.

If you look at a map you will perceive that there lies, north of New Guinea, a broad open sea, some two thousand miles long, and five or six hundred in breadth. The sea is shut in by a group of

Islands, great and small, on the south, and another group, all small, on the north. There are thousands of these islands. No one ever goes to them except missionaries, ships in the *bêche de mer* trade, and 'blackbirders.' On some of them are found beach-combers, men who make their way, no one knows how, from isle to isle, who are white by birth, but Polynesian in habits and customs, as ignorant as Pagans, as destitute of morals and culture as the savages among whom they live. They have long since imparted their own vices to the people, and, as a matter of course, learned the native vices. They are the men who have relapsed into barbarism. All over the world there are found such men ; they live among the lands where civilised men have been, but where they do not live. On some of these islands are missionary stations with missionary ships.

It was among these islands that they expected to find their castaway, or at least to hear something of him. And first Captain Holstius put his helm up for Kusaie, where there is a station of the American mission.

Kusaie, besides being a missionary station, occupies a central situation among the Carolines ; if you look at the map you will see that it is comparatively easy of access for the surrounding islands. Unfortunately, however, communication between is limited. In the harbour there lay the missionary schooner, and a brig trading in *bêche de mer*. She had returned from a cruise among the western islands. However, she had heard nothing of any such white man living among the natives. Nor could the missionaries help. They knew of none who answered at all to the description of Rex. But there were many places where they were not permitted to land, the people being suspicious and jealous ; and there were other places where traders had set the people against them so, that they were sullen and would give no information. There was a white man, more than one white man, living among the islands in the great atoll of Hogoleu. There was a white man who had lived for thirty years on Lugunor, and had a grown-up family of dusky sons and daughters. There were one or two more, but they were all old sailors, deserters at first, who had run away from their ships, and settled down to a life of ignoble ease under the warm tropical sun, doing nothing among the people who were contented to do nothing but to breathe the air and live their years and then die.

One of them, an old beach-comber of Kusaie, who knew as much as any man can know of this great archipelago, gave them advice. He said that it was very unlikely a castaway would be killed even by jealous or revengeful islanders. No doubt he was living with the natives, but the difficulty might be to get him away ; that the temper of the people had been greatly altered for the worse by the piratical kidnapping of English, Chilian, and Spanish ships ; and he warned them, wherever they landed, to go with the utmost show of confidence, and to conceal their arms, which they must, however, carry.

From Kusaie they sailed to Ponapé, where the American missionaries have another station. Here they stayed a day or two on shore, and were hospitably entertained by the good people of the station, their wives making much of Lal, and presenting her with all manner of strange fruit and flowers. Here the girl, for the first time, partly comprehended what beautiful places lie about this world of ours, and how one can never rightly comprehend the fulness of this earth which declareth everywhere the glory of its Maker. There are old mysterious buildings at Ponapé, the builders of which belong to a race long since extinct, their meaning as long since forgotten as the people who designed them. They stand among the woods, like the deserted cities and temples of Central America, a riddle insoluble. As Lal stood beside those mysterious buildings with an old missionary, he told her how, thousands of years before, there was a race of people among these islands who built great temples to their unknown gods, carved idols, and hewed the rock into massive shapes, and who then passed away into silence and oblivion, leaving a mystery behind them, whose secret no one will ever discover. Lal thought the man who told her this, the man who had spent contentedly fifty years in the endeavour to teach the savages, who now dwelt here, more marvellous and more to be admired than these mysterious remains, but then she was no archæologist.

Then with more good wishes, again they put out to sea.

They were now in the very heart of the Caroline Archipelago. Nearly every day brought them in sight of some island. Dick, the Malay, in the bows, would spring to his feet and gaze intently while the land slowly grew before them and assumed definite proportions. Then he would sit down again as if disappointed, and shake his head, taking no more interest in the place. But, indeed, they could not possibly have reached the island they sought. That must be much farther to the west, somewhere near the Pelew Islands.

'See, Lal,' said Captain Holstius for the hundredth time over the chart, 'if Rex was right as to the current and the wind, he may have landed at any one of the Uliea Islands, or on the Swedes, or perhaps the Philip Islands, but I cannot think that he drifted farther east. If he was wrong about the currents, which is not likely, he may be on one of the Pelews, or on one of the islands south of Yap. If he had landed on Yap itself, he would have been sent home in one of the Hamburg ships, long ago. Let us try them all.'

For many weeks they sailed upon those smooth and sunny waters, sending ashore at every islet, and learning nothing. Lapped in the soft airs of the Pacific, the ship sailed slowly, making from one island to another. Lal lay idly on the deck, saying to herself, as each land came in sight, 'Haply we may find him here.' But they did not find him, and so they sailed away, to make a fresh attempt.

Does it help to name the places where they touched? You may find them on the map.

They examined every islet of the little groups. They ventured within the great lagoon of Hogoleu, a hundred miles across, where an archipelago of islets lies in the shallow land-locked sea, clothed with forest. The people came off to visit them, paddling in canoes of sandal-wood ; there were two or three ships put in for pearls and *bêche de mer*. Then they touched at the Enderby Islands, the Royalist Islands, the Swede Islands, and the Uliea Islands.

'Perhaps,' said Captain Holstius, as they sighted every one, ' he may have drifted here.'

But he had not.

To these far-off islands few ships ever come. Yet from time to time there appears the white sail of a trader or a missionary schooner, or the smoke of an English war-vessel. The people are mostly gentle and obliging, when they recognise that the ship does not come to carry them off as coolies. But to all enquiries there was but one answer—that they had no white man among them, unless it was some poor beach-comber living among them and one of themselves. They knew nothing of any boat. Worse than all, Dick shook his head at every place, and showed no interest in the enquiries they prosecuted.

A voyage in these seas is not without danger. They are shallow seas, where new reefs, new coral islands, and new shoals are continually being formed, so that where a hundred years ago was safe sailing, there are now rocks above the surface, and even islands. There are earthquakes too, and volcanic eruptions. There are islands where plantations and villages have been swallowed up in a moment, and their places taken by boiling lather ; in the seas lurk great sharks, and by the shores are poisonous fish. The people are not everywhere gentle and trustful ; they have learned the vices of Europe and the treacheries of white men. They have been known to surround a becalmed ship and massacre all on board. Yet Captain Holstius went among them undaunted and without fear. They did not offer him any injury, letting him come and go unmolested. Trust begets trust.

So they sailed from end to end of this great archipelago and heard no news of Rex.

Then their hearts began to fail them.

But always in the bows sat Dick, searching the distant horizon, and in his face there was the look of one who knows that he is near the place which he would find.

And one day, after many days' sailing—I think they had been out of San Francisco seventy-five days, they observed a strange thing.

Dick began to grow restless. He borrowed the captain's glasses and looked through them, though his own eyes were almost as good. He rambled up and down the deck continually, scanning the horizon.

'See,' cried Lal, ' he knows the air of this place ; he has been here before. Is there no land in sight ?'

'None,' He gave her the glass. 'I see the line of sea and the blue sky. There is no land in sight.'

Yet what was the meaning of that restlessness ? By some sense unknown to those who have the usual five, the man who could neither hear or speak knew very well that he was near the place they had come so far to find.

Captain Holstius showed his companion their position upon the chart.

'We are upon the open sea,' he said. 'Here are the Uliea Isles two hundred miles and more from anywhere. A little more and we shall be outside the shallow seas, and in the deep water again. Lal, we have searched so far in vain. He is not in the Carolines, then where can he be ? Nothing is between us and the Pelews excepting this little shoal.

The charts are not always perfect. The little shoal, since the chart was laid down, had become an atoll, with its reef and its lagoon.

It was early morning, not long after sunrise.

While they were looking upon the chart, which they knew by heart, the Malay burst into the cabin and seized Lal by the hand. He dragged her upon the deck, his eyes flashing, his lips parted, and pointed with both hands to the horizon. Then he nodded his head and sat down on deck once more, imitating the action of one who paddles.

Lal saw nothing.

The captain followed with his glasses.

'Land ahead,' he said slowly, 'off the starboard bow.'

He gave her the glasses. She looked, made out the land, and then offered the glass to Dick, who shook his head, pointed, and nodded again.

'We have found the place,' cried Lal ; 'I know it is—I feel it is—Oh, Rex, Rex, if we should find you there ! '

As the ship drew nearer, the excitement of the Malay increased. It became certain now that he had recognised the place, of which nothing could be seen except a low line of rock with white water breaking over it.

The day was nearly calm, a breath of air gently floating the vessel forward ; presently the rock became clearly defined ; a low reef, of a horseshoe shape, surrounded, save for a narrow entrance, a large lagoon of perfectly smooth water ; within the lagoon were visible two, or perhaps three islands, low, and apparently with little other vegetation than the universal pandang, that beneficent palm of the rocks which wants nothing but a little coral sand to grow in, and provides the islanders with food, clothing, roofs for their huts, and sails for their canoes.

As soon as Dick saw the entrance to the lagoon he ran to the boats and made signs that they should lower and row to the land.

'Let him have his way,' said the captain ; 'he shall be our leader now. Let us not be too confident, Lal, my dear, but I verily believe that we have found the place, and, perhaps, the man.'

They lowered the boat. The first to jump into her was the Malay, who seated himself in the bows and seized an oar. Then he made signs to his mistress that she should come too.

They lowered her, and she sat in the stern. Then the captain got in, and they pushed off.

'What do you say, Lal?' asked Holstius, looking at her anxiously.

'I am praying,' she replied, with tears in her eyes. 'And I am thinking, brother,' she laid her hand in his, 'how good a man you are, and what reward we can give you, and what Rex will say to you.'

'I need no reward,' he said, 'but to know and to feel that you are happy. You will tell Rex, my dear, that I have been your brother since he was lost. Nothing more, Lal, never anything else. That has been enough.'

She burst into tears.

'Oh! what shall I tell him about you? what shall I not tell him? Shall I in very truth be able to tell him anything—to speak to him again? Kiss me, before all these men, that they may know how much I love my brother, and how grateful I am, and how I pray that God will reward you out of His infinite love.'

She laid her hand on his while he stooped his head and kissed her forehead.

'Enough of me,' he said; 'think now of Rex.'

By this time they were in the mouth of the lagoon. The boat passed over a bar of coral, some eight feet deep, and then the water grew deeper. In this beautiful and remote spot Lal was to find her lover. All the while the Malay looked first to the islands and then back at his mistress, his face wreathed with smiles, and his eyes flashing with excitement.

The sea in this lagoon was perfectly, wonderfully transparent. The flowers of the seaweeds, the fish, the great sea slugs—the *bêches de mer*—collected by so many trading vessels; the sharks moving lazily about the shallow water were as easily visible as if they were on land. This small land-locked sea was, apparently, about three miles in diameter, bounded on all sides by the ring of narrow rocks, and entered by one narrow mouth. The islets, which had been visible from the ship, were four in number. The largest one, of irregular shape, appeared to be about a mile and a half long, and perhaps a mile broad; it was a low island, thinly set with the pandang, the screw palm, which will grow when nothing else can find moisture in the sandy soil; there were no signs of habitation visible. The other three islands, separated from the larger one, and from each other, by narrow straits, were quite small, the largest not more than two or three acres in extent.

The place was perfectly quiet; no sign of life was seen or heard.

Dick pointed to the large island, which ran out a low bend of cape towards the entrance of the lagoon. His face was terribly in earnest, he laughed no longer; he kept looking from the island to his mistress and back again. As they drew nearer, he held up his finger to command silence.

The men took short strokes, dipping their oars silently, so that nothing was heard but the grating of the oars in the rowlocks.

On rounding the cape they found a narrow level beach of sand stretching back about a hundred feet. . This was the same place where, five months before, Captain Wattles held his conference with the prisoner.

'Easy !' cried the captain.

The boat with her way on slowly moved on towards the shore.

There seemed on the placid bosom of the lagoon to be no current and no tide, nor any motion of the waters. For no fringe of hanging seaweed lay upon the rocks, nor was there any belt of the flotsam which lies round the vexed shores where waves beat and winds roar. Strange, there was not even the gentle murmur of the washing wavelet, which is never still elewhere on the calmest day.

All held their breaths and listened. The air was so still that Lal heard the breathing of the boat's crew ; the boat slowly moved on towards the shore. The Malay in the bows had shipped his oar and now sat like a wild creature waiting for the moment to spring.

'Hush !' It was Lal who held up her finger.

There was a sound of distant voices. The place was not, then, uninhabited.

The boat neared the shore. When it was but two feet or so from the shelving bank, the Malay leaped out of the bows, alighting on hands and knees, and ran, waving his arms, towards the wood.

It was now five months since the offer of freedom was brought to Rex and refused on conditions so hard. So far the prediction of Captain Wattles was fulfilled ; no sail had crossed the sea within sight of the lonely island, no ship had touched there. It was likely, indeed, that the castaway would live and die there abandoned and forgotten. Rex kept the probability before his mind ; he remembered Robinson Crusoe's famous list of things for which he might be grateful ; he was well ; the place was healthy ; there was food in sufficiency though rough; and he was not alone, though perhaps that fact was not altogether a subject for gratitude.

The sun was yet in the forenoon, and Rex, inventor-general of the island, while perfecting a method of improving the fishing by means of nets made of the pandang fibre, was startled by the rush of twenty or thirty of the people, seizing clubs and spears, and shouting to each other.

The rush and the shout could mean but one thing—a ship in sight.

He sprang to his feet, hesitated, and then went with them.

He saw, at first, nothing but a boat close to land, and a figure running swiftly across the sandy beach.

What they saw from the boat, was a group of very ferocious

natives, yelling to one another and brandishing weapons, intent, no doubt, to slay and destroy every mother's son. They were darker of hue than most Polynesians ; they were tattooed all over ; their noses and ears were pierced and stuck with bits of tortoise-shell for ornament ; their abundant and raven-black hair was twisted in knots on the top of their heads.

And among them stood one with a long brown beard ; he wore a hat made out of a palm-leaf ; his feet were bare ; his clothes were shreds and rags ; his bare arms were tattooed like the islanders' arms ; his hair was long and matted ; his cheeks, his hands, arms, and feet were bronzed ; he might have passed for a native but for his face and hair.

It was exactly what Captain Wattles had seen, but that the men were fiercer.

When they saw from the boat the white man, they grasped each other's hands.

'Courage, Lal,' said Captain Holstius.   'Courage and caution.'

When Rex, among the natives, saw and recognised Dick, his faithful servant, running to greet him and kissing his hand ; when he saw the people suddenly stop their shouts, and gather curiously about their old friend, who had been kidnapped long before with their own brother, he stared about him as if in a dream.

Then Dick seized his master's hand and pointed.

A ship was standing off the mouth of the lagoon ; a boat was on the beach; and in the boat—— But just then Captain Holstius leaped ashore, and a girl after him.   And then—then—the girl followed the Malay and ran towards him with arms outstretched, crying :

'Rex ! Rex !'

This must be a dream.   Yet no dream would throw upon his breast the girl of whom he thought day and night, his love, his promised wife.

'Rex ! Rex !   Do you not know me ?   Have you forgotten ?'

For a while, indeed, he could not speak.   The thing stunned him.

In a single moment he remembered all the past ; the long despair of the weary time, especially of the last three months ; the dreadful prospect before him ; the thought of the long years creeping slowly on, unmarked even by spring or autumn ; the loneliness of his life ; the gradual sinking deeper and deeper, unto the level of the poor fellows around him ; living or dead no one would know about him ; perhaps the girl he loved being deceived into marrying the liar and villain who had sat in the boat and offered him conditions of freedom—he remembered all these things.   He remembered, too, how of late he had thought that there might come a time when it would be well to end everything by a plunge in the transparent waters of the lagoon.   Two minutes of struggle and all would be over.   Death seemed a long and conscious sleep. To sleep unconscious and without a waking, is nothing.   To sleep conscious of repose, knowing that there will be no more trouble, is the imaginary haven of the suicide.

Then he roused himself and clasped her to his heart, crying : ' My da ling ! You have come to find me ! '

But how to get away !

First, he took the ribbons from Lal's hat and from her neck, and presented them to the chief, saying a few words of friendship and greeting.

The finery pleased the man, and he tied it round his neck, saying that it was good. The Malay he knew, and Rex he knew, but this phenomenon in bright-coloured ribbons he did not understand. Could she, too, mean kidnapping.

Meantime the boat was lying close to the beach, and beside the bow stood Captain Holstius, motionless, waiting.

' Lal,' said Rex. ' Go quietly back to the boat and get in. Take Dick and make him get into the boat with you. I will follow. Do nothing hurriedly. Show no signs of fear.'

She obeyed ; the people made no attempt to oppose her return ; Captain Holstius helped her into the boat. Unfortunately Dick did not obey. He stood on the beach waiting.

Then Rex began, still talking to the people, to walk slowly towards the boat. He was promising to bring them presents from the ship ; he begged them to stay where they were, and not to crowd round the boat ; he bade them remember the bad man who stole two of their brothers, and he promised them to find out where they were and bring them back. They listened, nodded, and answered that what he said was good.

When he neared the boat they stood irresolute, grasping the idea that they were going to lose the white man who had been among them so long.

I believe that he would have got off quietly but for the zeal of Dick, who could not restrain his impatience, but sprang forward and caught his old master in his strong arms, and tried to carry him into the boat.

Then the islanders yelled and made for the beach all together.

No one but Lal could tell, afterwards, exactly what happened at this moment.

It was this. Two of the islanders, who were in advance of the rest, arrived at the beach just as Dick had dragged his master into the boat. Captain Holstius had pushed her off and was standing by the bows, up to his knees in water, on the point of leaping in. In a moment more they would have been in deep water.

The black fellows, seeing that they were too late, stayed their feet, and poised their spears, aiming them, in the blind rage of the moment, at the man they had received amongst themselves and treated hospitably—at Rex. But as the weapons left their hands, Captain Holstius sprang into the boat, and standing upright, with outstretched arms, received in his own breast the two spears which would have pierced the heart of Rex. The action, though so swift

1

as to take but a moment, was as deliberate as if it had been determined upon all along.

Then all was over. Rex was safely seated in the stern beside his sweetheart ; Dick was crouching at his feet ; the boat was in deep water ; the men were rowing their hardest ; the savages were yelling on the beach ; and at Lal's feet lay, pale and bleeding, the man who had saved the life of her lover at the price of his own.

She laid his pale face in her lap ; she took his cold hands in her own ; she kissed his cold forehead, while from his breast there flowed the red blood of his life, given, like his labour and his substance, to her.

He was not yet quite dead, and presently he opened his eyes— those soft blue eyes which had so often rested upon her as if they were guarding and sheltering her in tenderness and pity. They were full of love now, and even of joy, for Lal had got back her lover.

'We have found him, Lal,' he murmured—'we have found him. You will be happy again—now—you have got your heart's desire.'

What could she say ? How could she reply ?

'Do not cry, Lal dear. What matters for me—if—only—you— are happy ?'

They were his last words.

Presently he pressed her fingers ; his head, upon her lap, fell over on one side ; his breath ceased.

So Captain Holstius, alone among the three, redeemed his pledge. If Lal was happy, what more had he to pray for upon this earth. What mattered, as he said, for him ?

At sundown that evening, when the ship was under way again and the reef of the lonely unknown atoll low on the horizon, they buried the Captain in the deep, while Rex read the Service of the Dead.

The blood of Captain Holstius must be laid to the charge of his rival ; the blood of all the white men murdered on Polynesian shores must be laid to the charge of those who have visited the island in order to kidnap the people, and those who have gone among them only to teach them some of the civilisation out of which they have extracted nothing but its vices.

As regards this little islet, the people know, in some vague way, that they have had living among them a man who was superior to themselves, who taught them things, and showed them certain small arts, by which he improved their mode of life ; if ever, which we hope may not be their fate, they fall in with the beach-combers of Fiji, Samoa, or Hawaii, they will easily perceive that Rex Armiger was not one of them. They will remember that he was a person of such great importance that two chiefs came to see him ; one of them carried off two of their people, the other, with whom was a great princess, carried off their prisoner himself.

In a few years' time the story will become a myth. Some of the missionaries are great hands at collecting folk-lore. They will land here and will presently enquire among the people for legends and traditions of the past. They will hear how, long, long ago (many years ago), they had living among them a white person, whose proper sphere—by birth—was the broad heaven ; how he stayed with them a long time (many moons) ; how one after the other white persons came to see him, both bad and good ; for some kidnapped their people and took them away to be eaten alive ; how at last a goddess, all in crimson, blue, and gold, came with a male deity and took away their guest, who had, meantime, taught them how to make clothes, roofs, and bread, out of the beneficent pandang ; how the companion was killed in an unlucky scrimmage ; and how they look forward for their return—some day.

The missionaries will write down this story and send it home ; wise men will get hold of it, and discuss its meaning. They will be divided into two classes ; those who see in it a legend of the sun-god, the princess being nothing but the moon, and her companion the morning star ; the other class will see in the story a corruption of the history of Moses. Others, more learned, will compare this legend with others exactly like it in almost all lands. It is, for instance, the same as the tale of Guinevere returning for Arthur, and will quote examples from Afghanistan, Alaska, Tierra del Fuego, Borneo, the valleys of the Lebanon, Socotra, Central America, and the Faroe Isles.

Five weeks later Lal was married at San Francisco. The merchant who lent her the schooner gave her a country house for her honeymoon.

'She ought,' said Rex, 'to have married the man who gave her himself, all his fortune, and his very life. I am ashamed that so good a man has been sacrificed for my sake.'

'No, sir,' said the Californian ; 'not for your sake at all, but for hers. We may remember some words about laying down your life for your friends. Perhaps it is worth the sacrifice of a life to have done so good and great a thing. If there were many more such men in the world, we might shortly expect to see the gates of Eden open again.'

'Unfortunately,' said Rex, 'there are more like Captain Wattles.'

'Yes, sir ; I am sorry he is an American. But you can boast your Borlinder, who is, I believe, an Englishman.'

The account of Lal's return and the death of Captain Holstius duly appeared in the San Francisco papers. It was accompanied by strictures of some severity upon the conduct of Captain Barnabas B. Wattles, who was compared to the skunk of his native country.

It was this account, with these strictures, which the Son of Consolation found in the paper after posting his packet of lies.

Further, a Sydney paper asked if the Captain Barnabas B.

Wattles, of the 'Fair Maria,' was the same Captain Wattles who behaved in the wonderful manner described in the Californian papers.

He wrote to say he was not.

From further information received, it presently appeared to everybody that he was that person.

He has now lost his ship, and I know not where he is nor what occupation he is at present following.

It remains only to suggest, rather than to describe, the joyful return to Seven Houses. We may not linger to relate how Mrs. Rydquist, who still found comfort in wearing additional crape to her widow's weeds for Rex, now kept it on for Captain Holstius, calling everybody's attention to the wonderful accuracy of her predictions : how Captain Zachariasen first sang a Nunc dimittis, loudly proclaiming his willingness to go since Lal was happy again ; and then explained, lest he might be taken at his word, that perhaps it would be well to remain in order to experience the fulness of wisdom which comes with ninety years. He also takes great credit to himself for the able reading he had given of the mummicking.

The morning after their arrival, Rex, looking for his wife, found her in the kitchen, making the pudding with her old bib on, and her white arms flecked with flour, just as he remembered her three years before. Beside her, the Patriarch slept in the wooden chair.

'It is all exactly the same,' he said ; 'yet with what a difference ? And I have had three years of the kabobo. Lal, you are going to begin again the old housekeeping ? '

She shook her head and laughed. Then the tears came into her eyes.

'The Captains like this pudding,' she said. 'Let me please them once more, Rex, while I stand here looking through the window, at the trees in the churchyard and through the open door into the garden, and when I listen to the noise of the docks and the river, and for the white sails beyond the church, and watch the dear old man asleep there beside the fire, I cannot believe but that I shall hear another step, and turn round and see beside me, with his grave smile and tender eyes, Captain Holstius, standing as he used to stand in the doorway, watching me without a word.'

Rex kissed her. He could hear this talk without jealousy or pain. Yet it will always seem to him somehow, as if his wife has missed a better husband than himself, a feeling which may be useful in keeping down pride, vain conceit, and over masterfulness ; vices which mar the conjugal happiness of many.

'He could never have been my husband,' the young wife went on in her happiness, thinking she spoke the whole truth ; 'not even if I had never known you. But I loved him, Rex.'

'LET NOTHING YOU DISMAY.'

CHAPTER I.

ALL THE PEOPLE STANDING.

WHEN the sun rose over northern England on a certain Sunday
early in May—year of grace 1764—it was exactly four o'clock in
the morning. As regards the coast of Northumberland, he sprang
with a leap out of a perfectly smooth sea into a perfectly cloudless
sky, and if there were, as generally happens, certain fogs, mists,
clouds, and vapours lying about the moors and fells among the
Cheviots, they were too far from the town of Warkworth for its
people to see them. The long cold spring was over at last; the
wallflower on the castle wall was in blossom; the pale primroses
had not yet all gone; the lilac was preparing to throw out its
blossoms; the cuckoo was abroad; the swallows were returning
with tumultuous rush, as if they had had quite enough of the sunny
south, and longed again for the battlements of the castle and the
banks of Coquet; the woods were full of song; the nests were full
of young birds, chirping together, partly because they were always
hungry, partly because they were rejoicing in the sunshine, and all
the living creatures in wood and field and river were hurrying,
flying, creeping, crawling, swimming, running, with intent to eat
each other out of house and home.

The eye of the sun fell upon empty streets and closed houses—
not even a poacher, much less a thief or burglar, visible in the
whole of Northumberland; and if there might be here and there a
gipsies' tent, the virtuous toes of the occupants peeped out from
beneath the canvas, with never a thought of snaring hares or
stealing poultry. Even in Newcastle, which, if you come to think
of it, is pretty well for wickedness, the night-watchmen slept in
their boxes, lanterns long since extinguished, and the wretches
who had no beds, no money, and slender hopes for the next
day's food, slept on the bunks and stalls about the market.
Nothing stirred except the hands of the church clocks; and
these moved steadily; the quarters and the hour were struck.
But for the clocks, the towns might have been so many cities

of the dead, each house a tomb, each bed a silent grave. The Northumbrian folk began to get up—a little later than usual because it was Sunday—first in the villages and farmhouses, next in the small towns ; last and latest, in Newcastle, which was ever a lie-abed city.

Warkworth is quite a small town, and a great way from New-castle. Therefore the people began to get up and dress about five. There were several reasons which justified them in being so early. Even on Sunday morning pigs and poultry have to be fed, cows to be milked, and horses to be groomed. Then there is the delightful feeling, peculiar to Sunday morning, that the earlier you get up, the longer you may lean with your shoulder against the door-post. Some men, on Sundays and holy-days, like to lie at full-length upon the grass, and gaze into the depths of the sky, till thirst impels them to rise and seek solace of beer. Some love to turn them in their beds as a door turneth upon its hinges ; some delight to sit upon a rail ; but the true Northumbrian loveth to stand with his shoulder hitched against a door-post. The attitude is one which brings repose to brain and body.

There is only one street in Warkworth. At one end of it is the church, and at the other end is the castle. The street runs uphill from church to castle. In the year 1764, the castle was more ruinous than it showed in later years, because the keep itself stood roofless, its stairs broken, and its floors fallen in—a great shell, echoing thunderously with all the winds. As for the walls, the ruined gateways, the foundations of the chapel, the yawning vaults, and the gutted towers, they have always been the same since the destruction of the place. The wallflowers and long grasses grew upon the broken battlements ; blackberries and elder-bushes occupied the moat ; the boys climbed up to perilous places by fragments of broken steps ; the swallows flew about the lofty keep ; the green woods hung upon the slopes above the river, and the winding Coquet rolled around the hill on which the castle stood— a solitary and deserted place. Yet in the evening there was one corner in which the light of a fire could always be seen. It came from a chamber beside the great gateway—that which looks upon the meadows to the south. Here lived the Fugleman. He had fitted a small window in the wall, constructed a door, built up the broken stones, and constituted himself, without asking leave of my Lord of Northumberland, sole tenant of Warkworth Castle.

I think there has always been about the same number of people and houses in Warkworth. If you reflect for a moment you will perceive that this must be so, partly because there is no room for any more on the river-washed peninsula upon which the town is built, and partly because while the same trades are practised for the same portion of country there must be the same number of craftsmen, and no more. You may expect, for instance, in every town, a shop where you can buy all the things which you must have yet cannot make for yourself, such as sugar, treacle, tape, cotton stuffs, flannel, needles, and thread. In country towns the

number of things which can be made at home—and well made too
—is more than dwellers where there are shops for everything would
understand. In Warkworth, for example, there is a blacksmith—
a man of substance, because everybody wants him and would pay
him well ; there is a carpenter and wheelwright, also a man to be
respected, not only for his honourable craft, but also for the fields
and meadows which he has bought ; a tailor—but he is a starveling,
because most people in Northumberland repair, if they do not
make, at home ; a cobbler, who has two apprentices and keeps both
at work, because nobody but a cobbler can get inside a boot, to
make or mend it ; and a barber, who also has two apprentices.
There is no baker, because all the bread is baked at home, which is
one, among many reasons, why country life in this eighteenth
century is so delightful ; there is no brewer, because everybody,
down to the cottager, brews his own beer—the old stingo, the
humming October, and the small beer for the maids and children.
Yet, for the sake of companionship, conversation, song, and the
arrangement of matches, there must be an ale-house, with a settle
round three sides of the room and another outside ; and for the
quality there must be an inn. There need be no place for the
buying and selling of butter, eggs, milk, or cream, because people
who have no cows are fain to go without these luxuries, or else to
beg and borrow. There need be no butcher, because the farmers
kill and send word to the gentry when beef or mutton may be had.
There is no apothecary, because every woman in the parish knows
what are the best simples for any complaint and where to find them.
There is no bookseller, because nobody at Warkworth ever wanted
to read at all, and very few know how ; one excepts the Vicar—
who may read the Fathers in Greek and Latin—and his Worship
Mr. Cuthbert Carnaby, Justice of the Peace, who reads 'The
Gentleman's Magazine,' to which he once contributed a description
of Warkworth. There is, in fact, a singular contempt for literature
in the town, and it is, I believe, a remarkable Northumbrian
characteristic. There are no undertakers, because in this county
people have grown out of the habit of dying, so that except in
Newcastle, where people fight and kill each other, the trade can
only be carried on at a loss ; and there are no lawyers, because the
townsfolk of Warkworth desire to have nothing to do with law, and
are only concerned with one of the many laws by which good order
is maintained in this realm of England—that, namely, which
forbids the landing of Geneva and brandy on the banks of the
Coquet without vexatious and tedious ceremonies, including
payment of hard money. If you, who live in great towns, consider
the trades, crafts, and mysteries by which men get a living in these
latter days, you will presently understand that most of them are
unnecessary for the simple life.

When the first comers had looked up the street and down the
street, straight through and across each other, and examined the
sky and inspected the horizon, and obtained all possible informa-

tion about the weather; they gave each other the good-morning, and asked for opinions on the subject of hay. Then one by one they went back to their houses—which are of stone, having very small windows with bull's-eye glass in leaden casements, and red-tiled roofs—and presently came out bearing with them their break-fast, such as two or three kned-cakes, or a chunk of three weeks' old bread, or a slice of bread-and-dripping, or bread and fat pork, or a pewter platter of bread and beef even, with a great pewter mug of small ale. They consumed their breakfast side by side in good fellowship, standing on the cobble-stones or leaning against the door-posts, taking time over it: first a mouthful and then a drink, then a period of reflection, then a remark, and then another mouthful. They mostly had the Northumbrian face, which I am told is the Norwegian face—an oval shape, with soft blue eyes; with the face goeth a gentle voice and a slow manner of speech. They are a folk born by nature with so deep a love of life that they desire nothing better than to stretch out and prolong the present. Time, who is an inexorable tyrant, will not allow so much as a single moment to be stretched. Yet, by dint of slow motion, slow speech, a steady clinging to old customs, never doing to-day anything different from what you did yesterday and the day before, always talking the same talk at the same times, so that every duty of each season has its formula, wearing the same clothes, eating the same food, sitting in the same place, and avoid-ing all temptation to change, it is quite astonishing how the sem-blance of sameness may be given to time so that the whole of life shall seem, at the end of it, nothing but one delightful moment stretched out and prolonged for three-score years and ten.

After breakfast, for two hours by the clock they fell to stroking of stubbly chins and to wondering when the barber would be ready. This could not be until stroke of nine at least, because he had to comb, dress, and powder first the Vicar's wig for Sunday. Heaven forbid that the Church should be put off with anything short of a wig newly combed and newly curled! And next the wig of his Worship Cuthbert Carnaby, Esquire, Justice of the Peace and second cousin to his lordship the Earl of Northumberland, newly succeeded to the title. When this was done the barber addressed himself to the chins and cheeks of the townsfolk, and this with such dexterity and despatch that before the church-bell began he had them all despatched and turned off. And then their counte-nances were glorious, and shone in the sun like unto the face of a mirror, and felt as smooth to the enamoured finger as the chin and cheek of a maid. Thus does Art improve and correct Nature. The savage who weareth beard knows not this delight.

It was a day on which something out of the common was to happen; a day on which expectation was on tiptoe; and when at ten o'clock the first stroke of the church-bell began, all the boys with one and the same design turned their steps—slowly at first, and as if the business did not greatly matter, yet should be seen

Into—towards the church-yard. They were all in Sunday best; their hair smooth, their hands white, their shoes brushed and their stockings clean ; they moved as if drawn by invisible ropes ; as if they could not choose but go ; and whereas on ordinary Sundays not a lad among them all entered the church till the very last toll of the bell, on this day they made straight for the porch at the first, and this, although they knew that if they once set foot within it, they must pass straight on without lingering, into the church, and so take their seats, and have half an hour longer to wait in silence and good-behaviour, with liability to discipline. For a rod is ever ready in church as well as at home, for the back of him who shows himself void of understanding. The Fugleman, who wielded that rod, was strong of arm ; and no boy could call himself fortunate, or boast that he had escaped the scourge of folly till the service was fairly done.

As regards the girls, who were still in the houses, at the first stroke of the bell they, too, hastened to put the finishing touch, with a ribbon and a white handkerchief, to the Sunday frock. And then, a good half an hour before the time, which was truly wonderful, they, like the boys, hastened to the church. At the first stroke of the bell the men, too, proceeded to equip them with the Sunday church-going clothes, which were very nearly the same in all weathers, to wit, every man wore his wide horseman's coat, his long waistcoat with sleeves, his thick woollen stockings, and his shoes, with steel buckles or without, according to their station. Thus attired they turned their faces all to the same point of the compass, and heavily, yet with resolution and set purpose, rolled down the hill into the church-yard.

Out in the fields, and in the fair meadows, and down the river-side, and along the quiet country paths, and among the woods which hang above the winding of the Coquet, the sound of the bell quickened the steps of those who were leisurely making their way to church, so that every man put best foot for'ard, with a 'Hurry up, lad ! Lose not this morning's sight ! Be in time ! Quick, laggard !' and so forth, each to the other ; those who were on horseback broke into a trot, and laughed at those who were afoot ; the old women cried, alas ! for their age, by reason of which limbs are stiff and folks can go no faster than they may, and so they might be too late for the best part of the show ; the old men cursed the rheumatism which stiffened their knees, and bent their hips, and took the spring out of feet which would fain be elastic still, wherefore they must perhaps lose the first or opening scene. And the boys and girls who were with them took hands, and instead of walking with the respectful slow step which should mark the Sabbath, broke away from the elders, and raced, with a whoop and a holla, across the grass, a scandal to the mild-eyed kine, who love the day to be hallowed and kept holy.

At Morwick Mill, Mistress Barbara Humble would not go to church, though her brother did. Nor would she let any other of the household go, neither her man nor her maid, nor the stranger, if any, that was within her gates; but at half-past ten of the clock she called them together, and read aloud the Penitential Psalms and the Commination Service.

The show, meantime, had begun. At the first stroke of the bell there walked forth from the vestry-room a little procession of two. First came a tall spare man of sixty or so, bearing before him a pike. He was himself as straight and erect as the pike he carried; he wore his best suit, very magnificent, for it was his old uniform kept for Sundays and holidays : that of a sergeant in the Fourteenth, or Berkshire, Regiment of Foot, namely, a black three-cornered hat, a scarlet coat, faced with yellow and with yellow cuffs, scarlet waistcoat and breeches, white gaiters and white cravat. On the hat was in silver the White Horse of his regiment, and the motto 'Nec aspera terrent.' He walked slowly down the aisle with the precision of a machine, and his face was remarkable, because he was on duty, for having no expression whatever. You cannot draw a face or in any way present the effigy of a human face which shall say nothing ; that is beyond the power of the rudest or the most skilled artist ; but some men have acquired this power over their own faces—diplomatists or soldiers they are by trade. This man was a soldier. He was so good a soldier that he had been promoted, first to be corporal, then to be sergeant, and lastly to be Fugleman, whose place was in the front before the whole regiment, and whose duty it was to lead the exercises at the word of command with his pike. In his age and retirement he acted as the executive officer in all matters connected with the ecclesiastical and civic functions of the town, whether to lead the responses, to conduct a baptism, a funeral, or a wedding, to set a man in the stocks and to stand over him, to cane a boy for laughing in church, to put a vagrant in pillory and stand beside him ; to tie up an offender to the cart-tail and give him five dozen ; or, as in the present case, to wrap a lad in a white sheet, and remain with him while he did public penance for his fault. He was constable, clerk, and guardian of the peace.

The boy who followed him was a tall and lusty youth, past sixteen, who might very well have passed for eighteen : a boy with rosy cheeks, blue eyes, and brown hair ; but his eyes were downcast, his cheek was flushed with shame because he was clad from head to foot in a long white sheet, and he was placed so clothed, for the space of half an hour, while the bells rang for service in the church porch, and then to stand up before all the congregation to ask pardon of the people, and to repeat the Lord's Prayer aloud in token of repentance.

The porch of Warkworth Church is large and square, fifteen feet across, with a stone bench on either side. The boy was stationed within the porch on the eastern side, and close to the church door, so that all those who passed in must needs behold him. At his left hand stood the Fugleman, pike grounded and head erect, looking straight before him, and saying nothing except at the beginning, when discipline for a moment gave way to friendship, and he murmured : ' Heart up, Master Ralph ! What odds is a white sheet ? '

Then he became rigid, and neither spake nor moved. As for the penitent, he tried to imitate the rigidity of his companion, but with poor success, for his mouth trembled, and his eyes sank, and his colour came and went as the people, all of whom he knew, passed him with reproachful or pitying gaze. The church and the porch and the churchyard were all eyes ; he was himself a gigantic monument of shame.

When the boys walked—as slowly as they possibly could—through the porch, they grinned and nudged each other. But for the stern aspect of the Fugleman they would have laughed aloud and danced with joy. They had, however, to move on and take their places in the church, and those were few indeed who were so privileged as to command a view through the open doors of the porch and its occupants.

When the men of the village ranged themselves as in a small amphitheatre round the porch, the younger ones, in a hoarse whisper said each to his neighbour : ' Oho ! ha ! yah !' After which they remained gazing with mouth agape.

The three interjections are capable of many meanings, and may indicate a great variety of feeling. Here was a lad found out and convicted on the clearest evidence and confession : he had made fools of the whole town ; here he was before all, undergoing the sentence pronounced upon him by his Worship, Mr. Carnaby ; and a sentence so seldom pronounced as to make it an occasion for wonder ; and the offender was not a gipsy or a vagrom man, or one of themselves, but young Ralph Embleton of Morwick Mill ; and the offence was not robbing, or pilfering, or cheating, or smuggling, or beating and striking, but quite an unusual and even a romantic kind of offence, for which there was no name even ; and an offence not falling within any law. Therefore their faces were fixed in an immovable gaze, and their mouths remained wide-open—some twenty or thirty mouths in all—like unto fly-traps.

When the girls, for their part, walked through the porch they looked at the offender with eyes of pity, and one or two shed tears, because it seemed dreadful that this tall and handsome lad should be compelled to stand up before all in guise so shameful. Yet he had caused many to tremble in their beds. But the elder women stopped as they passed and wagged their heads with frowns, and said : ' Oh, dear, dear ! . . . . Alack and alas ! . . . . Tut, tut ! . . . . Fye for shame ! . . . . This is the end of wickedness. . . . Ah, hinneys ! . . . . Oh ! oh ! . . . . Look you now. . . . Heigh, laddie ! did a body ever hear the like ?' and so forth, with grateful rustle of skirts, and so virtuously into the church. A noble example, indeed, for their own boys. Better one such illustration of the punishment which overtakes offenders than fifty patterns of the peace and tranquillity in which the good man begins and ends his days. Yet we humans are so foolish and perverse that we sometimes find vice attractive and the ways of virtue monotonous, and give no heed even to the most dreadful examples.

Towards the close of the ringing there entered the church, walking majestically through the lane formed by the rustics, Mr. Cuthbert Carnaby, Justice of the Peace, with Madam his good lady. He was attired in a full wig and a purple coat with laced ruffles, laced cravat, a flowered silk waistcoat, and gold buckles in his shoes; in his hand he carried a heavy gold-headed stick, and under his arm he bore his laced hat ; his ample cheeks were red, and red was his double chin. Though his bearing was full of authority, his eyes were kind, and when he saw the boy standing in the porch, he felt inclined to remit the remainder of the punishment.

‘So, Ralph,’ he said, stopping to admonish him, ‘thy father was a worthy man ; he hath not lived to see this. But courage, boy, and do the like no more. Shame attends folly. Thou art young ; let this be a lesson. After punishment and repentance cometh forgiveness ; so cheer up, my lad.’

‘Ralph,’ said his wife, with a smile in her eyes and a frown on her brow, ‘I could find it in my heart to flog thee soundly, but thou art punished enough. Ghosts indeed ! and not a maid would go past the castle after dark for fear of this boy ! Let us hear no more about ghosts.’

She shook her finger—they both shook their fingers—she adjusted her hoop, and entered the church. The boy’s heart felt lighter ; Mr. Carnaby and Madam would forgive him. His Worship went on, bearing before him his gold-headed stick, and walked up the aisle to his pew, a large room within the chancel, provided with chairs and cushions, curtains to keep off the draught, and a fireplace for winter.

After Mr. Carnaby there walked into the porch a man dressed in good broadcloth with white stockings, and shoes with silver buckles. And his coat had silver buttons, which marked him for a man of substance. His cheeks were full and his face fiery, as if he was one who, although young, lived well, and his eyes were small and too close together, which made him look like a pig. It was Mathew Humble, Ralph’s cousin and guardian.

At sight of him the boy’s face flushed and his lips parted ; but he restrained himself and said nothing, while the Fugleman gave him an admonitory nudge with his elbow.

The man looked at Ralph from top to toe, as if examining into the arrangements, and anxious to see that all was properly and scientifically carried out.

‘Ta-ta-ta !’ he said with an air of dissatisfaction. ‘What is this ? Call you this penance ? Where is the candle ? Did his Worship say nothing about the candle ?’

‘Nothing,’ replied the Fugleman with shortness,

'He ought to have carried a candle. Dear me ! this is irregular. This spoils all. But—— Ah !—bareheaded '—he stood as far back as the breadth of the porch would allow, so as to get the full effect and to observe the picture from the best point of view—' in a long white sheet ! Ah ! bareheaded and in a long white sheet ! Oh, what a disgraceful day ! These are things, Fugleman, which end in the gallows. For an Embleton, too ! If the old man can see it what will he think of the boy to whom he left the mill ? And to beg pardon '—he smacked his lips with satisfaction—' to beg pardon of the people ! Ah, and to repeat the Lord's Prayer in the church— the Lord's Prayer—in the church aloud ! the Lord's Prayer—in the church—aloud—before all the people ! Ah ! Dear me—dear me !'

He wagged his head, as if he could not tear himself away from the spectacle of so much degradation. Then he added with a smile of perfect satisfaction a detail which he had forgotten :

'Standing, too ! The Lord's Prayer—in the church—aloud— before all the people—standing ! This is a pretty beginning, Fugleman, for sixteen years.'

If the Lord's Prayer in itself were something to be ashamed of he could not have spoken with greater contempt. The boy, how- ever, looking straight up into the roof of the porch, made no answer nor seemed to hear.

The speaker held up both hands, shook his head, sighed, and slowly withdrew into the church.

Then there came down the street an old lady in a white cap, a white apron, a shawl, and black mittens, an old lady with a face lined all over, with kind soft eyes and white hair, but her face was troubled. Beside her walked a girl of twelve or thereabouts, dressed in white frock and straw hat trimmed with white ribbon, and white cotton mittens, and she was crying and sobbing.

'Thou mayest stand up in the church,' said the old lady, 'when he repeats the Lord's Prayer, but not beside him in the porch.'

'But I helped him,' she cried. 'Oh, I am as bad as he ! I am worse, because I laughed at him and encouraged him.'

'But thou hast not been sentenced,' said the old lady. 'It is thy punishment, child—and a heavy one—to feel that Ralph bears thy shame and his own too.'

'I was on one side of the hedge when Dame Ridley dropped her basket,' the child went on, crying more bitterly. 'I was on one side and he was on the other. Oh ! oh ! oh ! She said there were two ghosts—I was one.'

When they reached the porch the girl, at sight of the boy in the sheet, ran and threw her arms about his neck and kissed him, and cried loud enough for all within to hear :

'Oh, Ralph, Ralph, it is wicked of them !'

These words were heard all over the church, and Mathew Humble sprang to his feet, as if demanding that the speaker should be carried off to instant execution for contempt of court. All eyes were turned upon his Worship's pew, and I know not what would have happened, because his periwig was seen to be agitated and the gold head of his stick appeared above the pew; but luckily just then the bells clashed all together, frightening the swallows about the tower so that they flew straight to the castle and stayed there, and the Vicar came out of the vestry and sat down in the reading-desk, and, as was his custom, surveyed his church and congregation for a few minutes before the service began.

It is an old church of Norman work, in parts patched up and rebuilt from time to time by the Percies, but there are no monuments of them. The Vicar's eyes fell upon a plain whitewashed building, provided with rows of ancient and worm-eaten benches, worn black by many generations of worshippers. The choir and the music sat at the west end. In front of the chancel was a square space in which was set a long stool. While the Vicar waited the Fugleman marched up the aisle, followed by the boy in the sheet, and both sat on this stool of repentance. Then the Vicar rose—he was a benignant old man, with white hair—and began to read in a full and musical voice how sinners may repent and find forgiveness. But the people thought he meant his words to apply this morning especially and only to the boy in the sheet. This made them feel surprisingly virtuous and inclined to sing praises with a glad heart. So, too, with the lessons, one of which dealt with the fate of a wicked king. All the people looked at the boy in the sheet, and felt that under another name, it was his own story told beforehand, prophetically; and when they stood up to sing in thanksgiving, their gratitude took the form of being glad that they were not upon the stool. When the Psalms were read the people paid unusual attention, letting the boy have the benefit of all the penitential utterances, but taking the joyous verses to themselves. And the Litany they regarded as composed, as well as read, exclusively for this convicted sinner. Among the elder ladies there was hope that the offended ghosts might—some at least—be present in the church and see this humiliation, which would not fail to dispose their ghostliness to a benevolent attitude, and even influence the weather.

It seemed to the boy as if that service never would end. To the congregation it seemed, on account of this unusual episode, as if there never had been a service so short and so exciting.

When the Commandments had been recited, Ralph almost expected to hear an additional one, 'Thou shalt not pretend to be a ghost,' and be called on to pray, all by himself, for an inclination of the heart to keep that injunction. But the Vicar threw away the opportunity and ended as usual with the tenth commandment.

He gave out the psalm, and retired to put on his black gown. The music—consisting of a violin, a violoncello, and a clarionet—struck up the tune, and the choir, among whom Ralph ought to have been, hemmed and cleared their voices. The Northumbrians,

as is well known, have good voices and good ears. The tune was
' Warwick,' and the psalm was that which began :

> Lord, in the morning thou shalt hear
> My voice ascend to thee.

The boy trembled because the words seemed to refer to the part
he was about to play. His own voice would, immediately, be ascend-
ing high, but all by itself. He saw the face of his cousin, Mathew
Humble, fixed upon him with ill-concealed and malignant joy.
Why did Mathew hate him with such a bitter hatred? Also he saw
the face of the girl who had been his partner; her eyes were full
of tears; and at sight of her grief his own eyes became humid.

He did not take any part at all in the hymn.

When it was finished the Vicar stood in his pulpit waiting; his
Worship stood up in his pew, his face turned towards the culprit ;
in his hand his great gold-headed cane. All the people stared at
the culprit with curious eyes, as boys stare at one of their companions when he is about to be flogged. Just then the girl left her
seat and stepped deliberately up the aisle, and stood beside the boy
in the sheet. And the congregation murmured wonder.

The Fugleman touched the boy's shoulder and brought his pike
to 'tention.

' Say after me,' he said aloud. Then to the congregation he
added : ' And all the people standing.'

' I confess my fault,' he began.

' I confess my fault,' repeated boy and girl together.

' And am heartily sorry, and do beg forgiveness.'

And then the Lord's Prayer.

The boy spoke out the words clearly and boldly, and with his
was heard the girl's voice as well, but both were nearly drowned by
the loud voice of the Fugleman.

It was over then. All sat down ; the girl beside Ralph on the
stool of repentance, and the sermon began.

The sermon which the Vicar read had nothing to do with the
penance just performed ; it was a learned discourse, which would
be afterwards published, showing the Divine origin of the Hier-
archy ; it was stuffed full of references to the Fathers, and conviction was conveyed to hearers' hearts (in case the arguments were
difficult to follow) by quotations of Greek in the original. His
Worship fell fast asleep ; all the men in the church followed his
example ; the boys pinched and kicked each other, safe from the
Fugleman for once : the women and the girls alone kept their eyes
open, because they had on their best things, and with fine clothes
go good manners, and the feminine sex loveth above all things to
feel well dressed and therefore compelled to be well behaved. Even
the Fugleman allowed his eyelids to drop, but never relinquished
his pike ; and the girl, holding Ralph fast by the hand, wondered
if they would ever, as long as they lived, these two, recover from
the dreadful disgrace of that morning.

When the Vicar had drubbed the pulpit to the very end of his manuscript, and the service was over, the three stood up again and remained standing till the people were all gone.

'Come, lass,' said the Fugleman when the church was empty, 'we can all go now. Off with that rag, Master Ralph.'

He unbent; his face assumed a human expression; he laid down the pike.

'What odds, I say, is a white sheet? Why, think 'twas a show for the lads which they haven't had for many a year. And May nigh gone already, and never a man in the stocks yet, and the pillory rotting for want of custom, and never a thief flogged nor a bear-baiting. If it 'twasnt for the cocks of a Sunday afternoon and the wrestling, there would have been nothing for the poor fellows but your ghosts to keep 'em out of mischief. And, lad,' he pointed in the direction of the mill, 'your cousin means more mischief. It was him that laid the information before his Worship.'

'Oh !' said Ralph, clenching his fists.

'Aye, him it was, and his Worship thought it mean, but he was bound to take notice, for why, says his Worship, "he can't let this boy frighten all the maids out of their silly senses. Yet, for his own cousin and his guardian——" that's what his Worship said.'

'Oh !' Again Ralph clenched his fists.

'Should I, an old soldier, preach mutiny ? Never. But seeing that your cousin is no rightful officer of yourn, nor yet commissioned to carry pike in your company, why I, for one——'

'What, Fugleman ?'

'I, for one, if I was a well-grown boy, nigh upon seventeen, the next time he gave orders for another six dozen, or even three dozen, I would ask him if he was strong enough to tie up a mutineer.'

The boy nodded his head.

'Cousin thof he be,' continued the Fugleman, 'captain or lieutenant is he not.'

The boy had by this time divested himself of his sheet, and stood dressed in a long brown coat and plainly-cut waistcoat ; he, too, wore silver buckles to his shoes, like his cousin, but not silver buttons ; his hair was tied with a black ribbon, and his hat was plain, without lace or ornament.

When his adviser had finished, he walked slowly down the empty church, hand-in-hand with the girl.

In the porch he stopped, threw his arm round her neck, and kissed her twice.

'No one but you, Drusy,' he said, 'would have done it. I'll never forget it, never, as long as I live. Go home to Granny, my dear, and have your dinner.'

'And will you go home, too, Ralph ?'

'Yes, I am going home. I've got to have a talk with Mathew Humble.'

Left alone in the church, the Fugleman sat down irreverently on the steps of the pulpit, and laughed aloud.

'Mathew Humble,' he said, 'is going to be astonished.'

CHAPTER II.

THE ASTONISHMENT OF MATHEW HUMBLE.

BY this time the people had dispersed quadrivious—that is to say, north, south, east, and west ; and were making their way homewards, their appetites for dinner keener than usual. Penance, considered as a Sunday show, hath no fellow ; it is even superior to the stocks, which is a week-day show. You may not pelt a man in a white sheet with rotten eggs, it is true ; but the same objection applies to the stocks. Of course, it cannot compare with a good pillory, which is rare, especially when eggs are plentiful and rotten apples lying under every tree ; or with a really heartfelt whipping of a vagabond or gipsy at the cart-tail, which is, unfortunately, rarer still. Among simple people there is a feeling that the greater the pain endured by the subject, the greater is the pleasure of the onlooker. Just in the same way did the Roman ladies discuss among themselves before the play whether it was more desirable to see Hercules—represented by the young Herr Hermann newly arrived from the Rhine—burning to death in a shirt of pitch ; or Scævola—done to the life by that gallant captive, Owen ap Rice, from Britain—thrusting his bare arm into a clear fire and keeping it there till the hand was burnt off ; or Actæon—played with spirit by Joseph Ben Eleazar, the swift-footed Syrian—pursued and torn to pieces by the hounds of Dian.

Ralph walked quickly past some of these groups, who fell back to right and left, and looked at him curiously. On ordinary Sundays he would have a pleasant word with all, a kiss for the children, and a challenge for the boys. To-day he passed them without a word, with head erect, eyes flashing, and clenched fist. He was not thinking of salutations ; he was thinking what he should do : how he should begin his mutiny : what would be the issue of the fight. Whatever the result, there would be joy in bringing, if only for once, hand, fist, or stick into contact with the face or figure of his cousin. It was he, was it, who informed against him to his Worship ? It was no other than his cousin who had compassed this most disagreeable of mornings. And now, doubtless, he waited, with a great cane, his arrival at home, in order to administer another of those 'corrections' of which he was so fond. Hitherto, Ralph had submitted quietly ; but he had been growing ; he was within a month of seventeen ; was it to be endured that he should be beaten and flogged like a child of ten, because his cousin hated him ?

The girls, as he strode past them regardless, looked at him with great pity, because they knew—everybody knew—what awaited him. And Mathew Humble such a hard man ! Poor lad ! Yet

K

those who mock spirits and fairies never fail to have cause for repentance in the long run ; and punishment had fallen swiftly upon Ralph. Perhaps, after this, he would respect the things which belong to the other world.

Heavens ! one might as well sit among the ruins of Dunstanburgh after dark and pretend to be the Seeker ; or within the chapel of Dilston at midnight and pretend to be Lady Derwentwater's troubled spirit ; and then hope to escape scot-free. Yet, poor lad ! and Mathew so hard a man !

What Ralph said to himself—justifying rebellion, because he was a conscientious lad—was this : ' His Worship said that the penance would be enough ; who was Mathew, then, to override the decision of the court ? Also, he was past the age of flogging, being now able to hold his own against most—whether at quarterstaff, singlestick, or wrestling—young men older than himself ; lastly, since Mathew had played this trick, he wanted revenge. But Mathew was his guardian ; very well, then let him learn—— But here he broke down, because he could not, for the moment, think of any lesson which his own rebellion would be likely to teach his cousin.

When Ralph left the fields and turned into the lane leading down to the river, he began to look about among the trees and underwood as if searching for something. Presently he espied a long pliant alder-branch in its second year of growth which seemed promising. He cut it to a length of about three feet, trimmed off leaves and twigs, and balanced it critically with a tentative flourish or two in the air.

' As thick as my thumb,' he said, ' and as heavy as his cane. Blow for blow, Cousin Mathew. This will curl round his shoulders and leave its marks upon his legs.'

Morwick Mill stands upon the River Coquet, about two miles from Warkworth. You can easily get to it by following the banks of the river, which is perhaps the best way, though sometimes you must off shoes and stockings, and wade across knee-deep to the other side.

The mill consists of a square house upon the edge of the river, with a great wheel on one side ; and almost all the water of the river is here diverted so as to form a sufficient power for the mill-wheel. At the back of the mill, which is also a substantial dwelling-house, is a great careless garden, with pigsties and linneys for cattle, and vegetables, and fruit-trees ; and at the side are two or three cottages, where live the people employed at the mill. All the fields which lie sloping up from the river-side belong, as well, to the owner of the mill. The owner at this moment was no other than the scapegrace Ralph ; and his cousin, Mathew Humble, was his guardian, who had nothing at all in the world but a little farm of thirty acres. The thought of this great inheritance, compared with his own meagre holding, filled the good guardian's heart with bitterness, and his arm, when it came to correction, ·

with a superhuman strength. He would be guardian for four years more ; then he would have to give a strict account of his guardianship ; and the burden of this obligation, though he had only held the post for two years, filled him with such wrath and anxiety that he was fain, when he did think upon it, which was often, to pull the cork out of a certain stone jar and allay his anxieties with a dram of strong waters. He was very anxious, because already the accounts were confused ; the stone jar was always handy ; therefore, he had become swollen about the neck and coarse of nose, which was a full and prominent feature, and flabby, as well as fiery, about the cheeks. In these times of much drinking many men become pendulous of cheek and ruddy of nose at forty or so, but few at six-and-twenty. Mathew was not, at this time, much more than six-and-twenty ; say ten years older than Ralph.

The kitchen, dining-room, and sitting-room of Morwick Mill was a large low room, with one long window. At the sides of the room, and between the great joists, were hanging sides of bacon and hams, besides pewter-pots and pewter-dishes, brightly polished wooden platters, china cups, brass vessels, whips, bridles, a loaded blunderbuss, cudgels, strings of onions, dried herbs of every kind, and all the thousand things wanted for the conduct of a household. At one end was a noble fire of logs burning in an ample chimney, and before the fire a great piece of beef roasting, and now, to outward scrutiny and the sense of smell, ready to be dished. A middle-aged woman, full, comely, and good-natured of aspect, was engaged in preparation for that critical operation. This was Prudence, who had lived at the mill all her life.

She looked up as Ralph appeared in the doorway, and shook her head, but more in pity than in reproach. And she looked sideways, by way of friendly warning, in the direction of the table, at which sat another woman of different appearance. She was, perhaps, five or six and thirty, with thin features and sour expression, not improved by a cast in her eye. This was Barbara, sister of Mathew Humble, and now acting in the capacity of mistress of Morwick Mill, for her brother was not married. She had open before her the Bible, and she had found a most beautiful collection of texts appropriate to the case of Fools in the Book of Proverbs. The table was laid for dinner, with pewter plates and black-handled knives and steel forks. The beer had been drawn, and stood in a great brown jug, foaming with a venerably silver head. Ralph observed without astonishment that the plate set for him contained a piece of dry bread, ostentatiously displayed. It was to be his dinner.

This pleasing maiden, Barbara, who regarded the boy with an affection almost as great as her brother's, that is to say, with a malignity quite uncommon, first pointed with her lean and skinny forefinger to the page before her, and read aloud, shaking her head reproachfully :

'"As a man who casteth firebrands, arrows, and death, so is

the man that deceiveth his neighbour, and saith, Am I not in
sport ?" '

Solomon must surely have had Ralph in his mind.

Then she pointed with the same finger to a door opposite, and
said, a smile of satisfaction stealing over her countenance :

'Go to your guardian. Go to receive the wages of sin.'

'Those,' said Ralph, with a little laugh, feeling confidence in
his alder-branch, 'are not a flogging, on this occasion, but a
fight.'

Before she heard his words, or had begun to ask herself what
they might mean, because she was so full of satisfaction with her
texts, he had flung his hat upon a chair, and gone to the next
room. If Barbara had been observant, she might have remarked,
besides these extraordinary words, a certain brightness of the eyes
and setting of the mouth which betokened the spirit of resistance.

The inner room was one occupied and used by Mathew alone.
It contained all the papers, account-books, and documents connected with the property and business of the mill. Here, too, was
the stone jar already referred to. The decks had been, so to speak,
cleared for action, that is to say, the table was thrust into the
corner, and upon it lay the sacred instrument with which Mathew
loved to correct his ward. This promoter of virtue, or dispenser of
consequences, was a strong and supple cane, than which few instruments are more highly gifted with the power of inflicting torture.
Ralph knew it well, and had experienced on many occasions the
full force of this wholesome quality. He saw it lying ready for use,
and he reflected cheerfully that the alder-branch, partly up his left
sleeve and partly in his coat-pocket, would be more supple, equally
heavy, and perhaps more efficacious regarded simply as a pain
producer.

When the boy appeared, Mathew rose and removed his wig and
coat, because the work before him was likely to make him warm.
He then assumed the rod, and ordered Ralph to take off his coat
and waistcoat.

'This day,' he said, 'you have disgraced your family. I design
that you shall have such a flogging as you will not readily forget.'
He then remembered that he would be more free for action without
his waistcoat. A man can throw more heart into his work. 'Such
a flogging,' he repeated as he removed it, 'as you will remember
all your life.'

'Well, cousin,' said Ralph, 'Mr. Carnaby said that the penance
was the punishment. I have done the penance.'

'Silence, sir ! Do you dare to argue with your guardian ? ' He
now began to roll up his shirt-sleeves so as to have his arms quite
bare, which is an additional advantage when one wants to put out
all one's strength. 'I shall flog the flesh off your bones, you young
villain !'

But he paused, and for a moment his jaws stuck, and he was
speechless, for his cousin, instead of meekly placing himself in po-

sition to receive the stupendous flogging intended for him, was facing him, resolution in his eyes, and a weapon in his hands.

'Flogging for flogging, Cousin Mathew,' said Ralph ; ' flesh for flesh. Strip my bones, I strip yours.'

Mathew now observed for the first time—it was a most unfortunate moment for making the discovery—that Ralph was a good two inches taller than himself, that his arm was as stout, and that his weapon was of a thickness, length, and pliability which might make the stoutest quail ; also he remarked that his shoulders were surprisingly broad, and his legs of length and size quite out of the common. And it even occurred to him that he might have to endure hardness.

'Flesh for flesh,' said Ralph, poising the alder-branch.

'Villain ! Would you break the Fifth Commandment?'

Ralph shook his weapon, making it sing merrily and even thirstily through the air, but made no reply.

'Lay down the switch.'

Ralph raised it above his head as one who is preparing to strike.

'Down on your knees, viper, and beg for pardon.'

'Flesh for flesh, Mathew,' said Ralph.

'You will have it then, young devil. I will kill you !'

Mathew rushed upon his cousin, raining blows as thick as hail upon him. For the moment his weight told and the boy was beaten back. Swish. 'Viper !' Swish—swish—'twas a terrible cane. 'I will teach you to rebel.' Swish—swish—'twas a cane of a suppleness beyond nature. 'I will give you a lesson.' Swish—swish. 'I will break every bone in your body.' Swish—the end of the cane found out every soft place—there were not many—upon Ralph's body.

But then the tables were turned, for the boy, recovering from the first confusion, leaped suddenly aside, and with a dexterous movement of the left foot caused his cousin to stumble and fall heavily. He struggled, struck, kicked, and lashed out—but he did not get up again. A very important element in the fight was strangely overlooked by Mathew before he began to attack. It was this, that whereas he was himself out of condition, the boy was in splendid fettle, sound of wind as well as limb. So furious was Mathew's first assault that, brief as was its duration, no sooner was he tripped up than he perceived that his wind was gone, and though he could kick and struggle, yet if he half got up he was quickly knocked down again. And while he kicked and struggled, this young viper, this monster of ingratitude, was administering such a punishment as even he, Mathew, had never contemplated for Ralph.

'Have you had enough?' cried the boy at last, out of breath.

'I will murder you, I will—— Oh, Lord !' For the punishment began again.

'Stripping of flesh,' said Ralph. 'This you will remember, cousin, all your life.'

The alder-branch was like a flail in the lad's strong arm. The rapidity, the precision, the delicate perception of tender places, took away the sufferer's breath.   There was no sound place left in the whole of Mathew's body.

'Have you had enough?' cried Ralph.

'I will flay you alive for this—I will. Oh, oh! I have had enough.'

'Then,' said Ralph, with one final effort, the effect of which would be, by itself, felt for a week and more, 'get up.'

Mathew rose, groaning.

'We have had the last of punishments,' said the boy. 'I will fight you any day you please, but I will take no more punishments from you.' He threw down his stick, and put on his coat and waistcoat, with some tenderness, however, for the first part of the battle had left its marks.

Now outside, the two women were listening, one with complacency, and the other with pity.   And the first was ready with the Bible still open at the Book of Proverbs, which contains quite an armoury of texts good to hurl at a young transgressor.   The second, with one ear turned to the door of Mathew's room, went on dishing the beef, which she presently placed upon the table.

There was unusual delay in the sound which generally followed Ralph's visits to that room.   No doubt Mathew was commencing with a short Commination Service.   Presently, however, there was a great trampling of feet, with the swish, swish of the cane—Mathew's first charge.

'Lord ha' mercy!' cried Prudence.

'"The rod and reproof give wisdom,"' read her mistress from the Book.

Then they heard a heavy fall, followed by a heavier, faster, more determined swishing, hissing, and whistling of the instrument, till the air was resonant with its music, and it was as if all the boys in Northumberland were being caned at once.

'Lord ha' mercy!' repeated Prudence. 'He'll murder the boy.'

'"A reproof,"' read the other from her place, '"entereth more into a wise man than a hundred stripes into a fool."'

There was a pause, and then a sound of voices, and then another terrific hailstorm of blows.

Both women looked aghast.   Was the punishment never to end?

Then Prudence rushed to the door.

'Mistress,' she cried, 'you may look on while the boy is cut to pieces—I can't and won't.'

She opened the door.   Heavens! what a sight was that which met her astonished eyes.   The boy, cut and bruised about the face, was standing in the middle of the room, smiling.   The man was on his hands and knees, slowly rising; his shirt was torn off his back: his shoulders were cut to pieces; he was covered with weals and bruises; his face, scarred and seamed with Ralph's cruel alder-branch, was dreadful to look upon. He seemed to see nothing; he groaned as he lifted himself up; he staggered where he stood.

Presently he put on his coat with many groans and muttered curses, and Prudence observed that all the while he regarded the lad with looks of the most extreme terror and rage. Presently she began to understand the situation.

'Are you hurt, Master Ralph?' she asked.

'No; but Mathew is,' said Ralph.

'Mathew,' cried his sister, as the victim of the rebellion staggered into the room, 'what is this?'

He sank into his armchair with a long deep groan, and made no reply.

'Why, what in the world, Master Ralph?' asked the servant.

But the lad had gone. He went upstairs to his own room; made up a little bundle of things which he wrapped in a handkerchief, picked out the thickest and heaviest of his cudgels, and then returned to the kitchen.

'Give me my dinner,' he said.

Barbara had brought out her brother's wig and put it on now, but he still sat silent and motionless. He was in such an agony of pain all over, and his nervous system had sustained so terrible a shock that he could not speak.

'Give me my dinner,' Ralph repeated.

Barbara pointed to the crust of bread. She was appalled by this mutiny, but she preserved some presence of mind, and she remembered the bread. Then she sat down again before the Bible and began to read, like a clergyman while the plate goes round.

' "It is as sport to the Fool to do mischief." '

Prudence, the beef being already served, laid a knife and fork for each.

' "A Fool's mouth," ' Barbara said, as if she was quoting Solomon, ' "calleth for roasted beef and a stalled ox. Bread and water until submission and repentance." '

The young mutineer made no verbal reply. But he dragged the dish before his own plate, and began to carve for himself, largely and generously.

'Mathew!' cried Barbara, springing to her feet.

'Let be—let be,' said Mathew; 'let the young devil alone. I will be even with him somehow. Let be.'

'Not the old way, cousin,' replied Ralph with a nod. He then helped himself to about a pint or so of the good old October, and began, his appetite sharpened by exercise, to make the beef disappear in large quantities. Mathew looked on, saying nothing. The silence terrified his sister. What did it mean? And she perceived, for the first time, that their ward had ceased to be a boy and must henceforth be treated as a man. It was a fearful thought. She shut her Bible and sat back with folded hands, waiting the issue.

In course of time even a hungry boy of seventeen has had enough. Ralph lifted his head at last, took another prolonged pull at the beer, and told Barbara, politely, that he had enjoyed a good dinner.

Then he turned to his cousin and addressed him with a certain solemnity.

'Cousin,' he said, 'you have always hated me, because my uncle left the mill to me instead of to yourself. Yet you knew from the beginning that his design was for me to have it. I have done you no wrong. You have never lost any opportunity of abusing me before my face and behind my back. You became, unhappily for me, my guardian. You have never neglected any chance of flogging and beating me, if you could find a cause. As regards the ghost business, I was wrong. I deserved punishment, but was it the province of a cousin and a guardian to go and lay information before the Justice of the Peace? I shall be seventeen come next month. In four years this mill and the farm will be my own. But if I remain with you here I can expect nothing but hatred and ill-treatment as far as you dare. You have given me ploughboy's work without a ploughboy's wage, and often without a ploughboy's food. As for flogging, that is finished, because I think you have no more stomach for another fight.'

Mathew made no reply whatever, but sat with his head upon his hands, breathing heavily.

'I am tired of ill-treatment,' Ralph went on, 'and I shall go away.'

'Whither, boy?' asked Barbara.

'I know not yet. I go to seek my fortune.'

'Go, if you will,' said Mathew; 'go, in the devil's name; go, whither you are bound to go: long before four years are over you will be hanging in chains.'

Ralph laughed and took up his bundle.

'Farewell, Prudence,' he said; 'thou wast ever kind to me.'

The woman threw her arms about his neck and kissed him with tears, and prayed that the Lord might bless him. And, as he walked forth from the house, the voice of Barbara followed him, saying:

'"A whip for the horse, a bridle for the ass, and a rod for the Fool's back."'

The Fugleman was sitting in the sun before his door in the castle, smoking a pipe and inclined to be drowsy, when Ralph appeared with his startling news.

As regards the flogging, the old soldier made light of it. Nothing can be done in the army without the cat. Had not he himself once received three hundred all by a mistake, because they were meant for another man, who escaped. Did he, therefore, bear malice against his commanding officer? No. But the villainy of Mathew, first to lay information and then to make an excuse for a flogging just for pleasure, and to gratify his own selfish desire to be continually flogging, why, that justified the mutiny. As for the details of the fight, he blamed severely the inexperience in strategy shown by first knocking down the enemy. He should have expected better things of Ralph, whose true policy would have been to harass an annoy his adversary by feints, dodges, and unexpected skirmishes. This would not only have fatigued him, but, considering his short-ness of breath, would have worn him out so that he would in the end have fallen an easy prey, and been cudgelled without resistance till there was not a sound place left. Besides, it would have made the fight more interesting, considered as a work of art.

However, doubtless the next time—but then he remembered that the boy was going away.

'To seek my fortune, Fugleman,' Ralph said gaily. 'Look after Drusy for me, while I am away.'

'Aye—aye,' the Fugleman replied ; ' she shall come to no harm. And as for money, Master Ralph?'

'I've got a guinea,' he replied, ' which my uncle gave me three years ago.'

'A guinea won't go far. Stay, Master Ralph.' He went into his room and came back with a stocking in his hand. 'Here's all l've got, boy. It is twenty guineas. Take it all. I shall do very well. Lord ! what with the rabbits and the pheasants——'

'Nay,' said Ralph, ' I will not take your savings neither.'

But, presently, being pressed, he consented to take ten guineas on the understanding that when he came back (his fortune made) the Fugleman was to receive twenty. And then they parted with a mighty hand-shake.

Half-way down the street Ralph passed Sailor Nan, who was sitting on a great stone beside her door, smoking her short black pipe.

' Whither bound, my lad ?' she asked.

'I am bound to London,' he replied. 'I am off to seek my fortune.'

' Come here, I will read thy fortune.'

Like most old women, Nan could read a lad's fortune in the lines of his hand, or by the cards, or by the peeling of an apple.

' A good cruise,' she said, ' with fair wind aft and good weather for the most part. But storms belike on leaving port. There's a villain, and fighting and foreign parts, and gold, and a good wife. Go thy ways, lad. Art no poor puss-faced swab to fear fair fighting. Go thy ways. Take and give. Trust not too many. And stand by all old shipmets. Go thy ways.'

He laughed and left her. Yet he was cheered by her kindly prophecy.

He crossed the old bridge and presently found himself outside the green palings of Dame Hetherington's house. The girl who had joined him in church was in the garden. He whistled, and she came running.

'I am come to say good-bye, Drusy,' he said ; 'I am running away.'

'Oh, Ralph, whither? And you have a cruel blow upon your face.'

'I have fought Mathew,' he said, 'and I have beaten him. This scar upon my face is nothing compared with the scars over his. I believe he is one large bruise. But I can no longer endure his ill-treatment and Barbara's continual reproaches. Therefore I am resolved to remain no longer, but shall go to London, there to seek my fortune as thy father did, Drusy.'

They talked for half an hour, she trying to persuade him to stay, and he resolved to go. Then he went with her into the house, where he must needs tell all the story to Dame Hetherington, who scolded him, and bade him get home again and make submission, but he would not.

Then Drusilla remembered that her father would gladly aid any lad from Northumberland, and sat down and wrote a letter very quickly, being dexterous with her pen, and gave it to Ralph to carry.

'You will find him,' she said, 'at the sign of the Leg and Star in Cheapside. Forget not that address. Stay, I will write it outside the letter. Give it him with my respect and obedience. Oh, Ralph, shall you be long before you have found your fortune and are back to us?'

'Nay,' said Ralph, 'I know not what may be my fortune. I go to find it, like many a lad of old.'

Then, after many fond farewells, Ralph kissed her and trudged away manfully, while Drusy leaned her head over the garden-gate and wept and sobbed, and could not be consoled.

CHAPTER III.

HOW RALPH SOUGHT FORTUNE.

A YOUNG man's walk from Warkworth all the way to London cannot fail to be full of interest and adventure. There is, however, no space here to tell of the many adventures which befell this lad upon his journey. As for bad roads, he might have expected them, except that he was young and ignorant and expected nothing, so that each moment brought him some surprise, and each day taught him some new experience. As for the people to be met upon the roads, probably, had he known what to expect, he would have stopped short and sought fortune at Newcastle, Durham, or York, rather than have pressed on to London. But he was brave and full of hope. As to the roadside inns and the bedroom companions, he was astonished afterwards that he managed to get through all without having his weasand cut for the sake of his scanty stock of guineas, so desperate were some of the villains whom he encountered. Nevertheless, even among the most desperate of rogues, there is hesitation about murder, and even about robbing lads and persons of tender years.

He stowed away his money within his waistcoat, keeping in his pocket nothing but two or three shillings for the daily wants ; yet it seemed as if every man that he met had sinister designs upon him. If it was a solitary gipsy lying on the grass by the wayside, he rose to meet the boy as he went by, and looked highway robbery with resolution, yet refrained when he met equal resolution in the eyes of the wayfarer, and a stout stick in strong hands, and broad shoulders. If it was a pair of soldiers on the way to join their regiment, they stopped him, being two brave and gallant dare-devil heroes, and recommended the turning out of pockets, or else——. They swore terribly, these brave fellows, but a back-hander right and left with the cudgel, and then a light pair of heels, relieved the wayfarer of this danger, and left the heroes swearing more terribly than before, and lamenting the waste of good front teeth.

When he got near Durham he fell upon a party of pitmen out of work, and therefore parading the road, which is the manner of pitmen, one knows not what for except for mischief. These gentlemen of the underground, who have neither religion nor education, and are, in fact, more savage and heartless than North-American savages, began to set upon the boy out of pure sport, as if they felt that somebody must be damaged in order to keep up their own spirits. They handled him roughly, not for the sake of robbing him, but because he was young and unprotected, just as on Sundays they throw at cocks ; and it would have gone badly with him but for one among them who seemed to be a leader, and with many frightful imprecations bade his fellows let the boy alone. So they went on their godless way, and he went his, not much the worse for a roll in the dust.

As for the mounted highwaymen, they passed him or met him, riding in splendour, and scorned to fly at such small game as a country boy walking along the road. Substantial farmers riding home from market and tradesmen with money in their pockets were their prey. But Ralph met them in the evenings at the country inns, where they hardly pretended to disguise their profession, and bragged and swaggered among the admiring rustics over their punch, as if there were no such things as gallows and rope.

Worse than the highwayman was the common foot-pad, the cowardly and sneaking villain who would rob a little child of a sixpence—aye, and murder it afterwards to prevent discovery, and feel no remorse. When these road vagabonds accosted the boy it was with intent to rob him, even of the coat upon his back ; whereupon he either fought or else ran away. He fought so bravely with so stout a heart and so handy a cudgel, and he ran so fast, that he came to no harm ; more than that, he left behind him on the road half-a-score desperadoes at least, who bore upon their gloomy countenances for life the marks of his cudgel, and swore to have his blood whenever they might meet with him again.

The road was not, however, a long field of battle for the lad, like his Progress to Christian the Pilgrim, nor did he meet with Apollyon anywhere. There were waggoners to talk with, friendly hawkers, whom the people call muggers, and faws, or tinkers, who are too often robbers and pilferers; also farmers, their wives and daughters, cattle-drovers, carriers, honest sailors, who would scorn to rob upon the highway, on their way to join ship, and pleasant little country towns every eight or ten miles, where one could rest and talk, and drink a tankard of cool small beer. Then, as it was early summer, when there are fairs going on in many places, the roads in some parts were full of the caravans and the show people, whom Ralph found not only a curious and interesting folk, but also friendly, and inclined to conversation with a stranger who was not a rival; who was ready to offer a tankard; who admired without stint or envy the precious things they had to show, and who watched with delight unbounded and belief profound, the curious tricks, arts, artifices, and accomplishments by which they secured a precarious livelihood. In this way Ralph was so fortunate as to make personal acquaintance with the Pig-faced Lady, the Two-headed Calf, the Bous Potamos of Amphibious Beef (stuffed, but a most prodigious monster), and the Italian who played the pipe with his hands, the cymbals with his elbow, the triangle with his knees, and the bells with his head, while he made a most ingenious set of fantoccini dance with his right foot. All this the wonderful Italian would do, and he was not proud. Then there was the accomplished Posture Master, who had no joints at all in any of his limbs, but only flexible hinges turning every way, and could put arms, legs, head, fingers, and toes in any position he pleased. He had a monkey who had been taught to imitate him, but with stiffness. Ralph also was presented to an Albino or Nyctalope, a most illustrious lady, with hair a silvery white, and skin of incomparable clearness, but uncertain of temper; there were the wrestlers, boxers, and quarterstaff players, honest fellows and staunch drinkers, who went round from fair to fair to display their skill, fight with each other like Roman gladiators, and pick up the prizes; there were the conjurers and magicians, who palmed things wherever they pleased as if they were helped by a devil or two; the seventh son, who read the future for all comers, and whose boast was that he was never wrong; the bear-leaders and badger-baiters; the flyer through the air, who made nothing of descending from a steeple-top on a rope with fireworks on his hands and feet; the dancers on the tight or slack rope; the thrower of somersaults; the itinerant cock-fighter, who would fight his cock against all comers for a guinea a side; the horse-dealer; the quack doctor, and his Merry-Andrew; the pedlar with his pack; the cheap book-seller, and the ballad-crier, with many more of the great tribe of wanderers. Ralph walked with them along the road, and heard their stories. He also learned some of the strange language in which they talked to each other when minded not to be understood by the bystanders.

When they came to their destination, and set up their canvas booths, he stayed too, and enjoyed the fun of the fair. At seventeen there is plenty of time to make your fortune, and why grudge a few days spent in watching the humours of a country fair? To be sure it cost some money, but he had still a good many of his guineas left, and no one could think a shilling or two ill-spent if one could see Pizarro acted in the most enthralling manner, or hear the most charming singer in the whole world, dainty with ribbons, and a saucy straw hat, sing, ''Twas a Pretty Little Heart,' or 'Ben Bowsprit,' or 'Ned, You've no Call to Me.' Besides, there were the sports. Ralph played the cudgels one day and got a broken head, and won a 'plain hat, worth sixteen shillings,' but no one would give him more than four shillings and twopence for it; also he tried a fall, but was thrown by one mightier than himself in the Cumberland back-stroke; and he bowled for a cheese but did not win; and he longed to run in a sack but thought it beneath the dignity of a full-grown man. Also, there were lotteries; you could put in and draw everywhere all day long; there were prizes of sixpence, and prizes of ten pounds: he put in: sometimes he won, but oftener he lost, which is generally the way with sportsmen and those who wait upon the Goddess of Chance. At this Capua, or Paradise of Pleasures, which was then, and is still, called Grantham, Ralph had well-nigh taken a step which would have made his story much less interesting to us, though perhaps fuller of incident. For he made acquaintance—being a youth of innocent heart, and apt to believe in the honesty and virtue of everybody—with the company of players. Now it happened, first, that the troop were sadly in want of a young actor, if only to play up to the manager's daughter; and secondly, that this young lady, who was as beautiful as the day and as vivacious as Mrs. Bracegirdle (she afterwards became a most famous London actress, and married an aged earl), cast eyes of favour on the handsome lad, longed very much for him to play Romeo to her Juliet, or Othello to her Desdemona, or any other part in which the beauty of a handsome woman is set off by the beauty of a handsome fellow, a thing which very few actresses can understand: they think, which is a great mistake, that it is better for them to be the only well-favoured creature on the stage. Wherefore the manager took Ralph aside privately, and offered him refreshment, either ale, or rumbo, or Barbadoes water, with tobacco if he chose, and had serious conversation with him, providing all his victuals and those as abundant as the treasury would allow, and a salary—say five shillings a week, to begin in a few months, as soon as he had learned to act, and to teach him the rudiments; and the honour and glory of playing principal parts; and his own daughter to play up to; and a possible prospect of appearing at Drury Lane.

It was a tempting offer ; the stage—even the stage in a barn—
seemed splendid to the lad ; the voice and manner of the manager
were seductive ; more seductive still was the voice of his daughter.
When she lifted her great eyes and met his he trembled and could
not say her nay ; when she laid her pretty hand upon his, and
begged him to stay with them and be her Romeo, what could he
reply ? Yet he remembered in time that he was on his way to seek
his fortune ; that the troop were obviously out at elbows, all
horribly poor, and apparently badly fed ; that to fall in love with
an actress was not the beginning he had contemplated ; and that
Drusy, for her part, would certainly not consider a strolling actor's
life as the most honourable in the world. He took a resolution :
he would think no more upon those limpid eyes ; he hardened his
heart ; he would fly. He did fly ; but not before the young
actress, who was already beyond his own age, and ought to have
known better, had laid her arms round his neck, and kissed farewell, with many tears, to her first love who would not love her in
return. But her father was not displeased, and said, speaking more
from a business point of view than out of paternal tenderness, that she
would act the better for the little disappointment, and that it does
them good, when they are young, to feel something of what they
are always pretending. Said it put backbone into their attitudes,
and real tears in their eyes. Nothing on the stage so difficult
as real tears, except a blush, which cannot be had for love or
money.

Thus it happened that it was four or five weeks before Ralph
got to London.

He arrived by way of Highgate. He reached the top of
Highgate Hill at four in the afternoon. Here he sat down to rest,
and to look upon the city he had come so far to see. There had
been rain, but the clouds had blown over, leaving a blue sky, and
a bright sun, and a clear air. He saw in the distance the towers
and steeples of London ; his long journey was done ; the fortune he
came to seek was—where was it ? All the long way from Warkworth
it seemed to him that when he reached London he would immediately find that thing known as fortune in some visible and tangible
form, waiting to be seized by his strong young hands. Yet now
that he saw before him the City of the Golden Pavement it seemed
as if, perhaps—it was a chilling thought—he might not know or
recognise, or be able to seize this fortune when he actually saw it.
What is it like—Good Fortune ? In other words, he began for the
first time to experience the coldness of doubt which sometimes falls
upon the stoutest of us. His cheek was by this time burned a
deeper brown ; his hands were dyed and tanned by the June sun ;
his coat and waistcoat were stained with travel and with rain ; his
shoes were worn through the soles ; in his pocket jingled the last
two of his eleven guineas. When they were gone, he reflected with
dismay, what would have to be done ? But it was not a time to sit
and think. Every fortune must have its beginning ; every young

adventurer must make a start; every Dick Whittington must enter the City of London. He rose, seized his bundle, and set off down the hill, singing to keep up his spirits, with as much alacrity as if he were only just starting on his way from Warkworth, and as if his heart was still warmed by the recollection of his cousin's bruises.

The way from Highgate to London lies along a pleasant road between tall hedges. On either side are fields and woods, and here and there a gentleman's seat or the country box of a successful citizen. Presently the boy reached Highbury, where the road bends south, and he passed Islington, with its old church and its narrow shady lanes thick with trees. On his right he saw a great crowd in a garden, and there was music. This was Sadler's Wells. Soon after this he arrived at Clerkenwell Green, and so by a maze of streets, not knowing whither he went, to Smithfield, where he found himself in the midst of the crowd which fills all the streets of the city from dawn till night. Such a crowd, men so rough, he had never seen before. They seemed to take pleasure in jostling and hustling each other as they went along. It gave occasion for profane oaths, strange threats, the exhibition of courage, and the provocation of fear. If they carried loads they went straight ahead, caring nothing who was in the way. Some were fighting, some were swearing, some were walking leisurely, some were hastening along as if there was not a moment to be lost. There were open shops along one side; on another side was a great building, but what it was Ralph knew not. The broad open space was covered with pens and hurdles for cattle, and at the corners were booths and carts from which all kinds of things were sold. A man in a long black gown, with a tall hat and a venerable white beard, stood upon a platform in one place, a clown beside him, holding something in his hand and bawling lustily. When he was silent the clown turned somersaults. Ralph drew nearer and listened. He was selling a magic balsam which cured wounds as well as diseases. 'Only yesterday, gentlemen,' the quack was saying, 'at four in the afternoon, a young nobleman was brought to me run through the body. He bought the balsam, gentlemen, and is already recovered, though weak from loss of blood.' 'Buy! buy! buy!' shouted the clown. The people looked on, laughed, and went their way. Yet some stayed and bought a box of the precious ointment. Then there was a woman selling gin from a firkin or small cask on a cart. Her customers sat upon a stool and drank this dreadful stuff, which, as the ingenious Hogarth has shown, makes their cheeks pale and their eyes dull. And there was a stall in which well-dressed city ladies sat eating sweetmeats, march pane, and China oranges, while outside stood a cow, and a woman beside her crying, 'A can of milk, ladies! A can of red cow's milk!' The boy looked about here a while, and passed on, wondering what great holiday was going. He knew not where he was, but that he was in London town. He was to find the sign of the 'Leg and Star' in Cheapside. Perhaps he would see it as he walked along. If not,

he would ask. Meantime the novelty of the crowd and the noise
of the streets pleased him, and he walked slowly with the rest.
He would wait until there passed some gentleman of grave
appearance of whom he could ask the way. But he was in no
hurry. He went on, and although he knew not where he was, he
walked through Giltspur Street, past Cock Lane (where afterwards
appeared the ghost). On his left he saw Newgate, and so through
Great Old Bailey to Ludgate Hill, where, indeed, for the magnifi-
cence of the people and the splendour of the shops he was indeed
astonished. There were few of the rude jostling people here.
Most were gentlemen in powdered wigs, ruffles, and gold-headed
canes, being the better class of citizens taking the air in the
evening before supper, or ladies in hoops and silks, with gold
chains, fans, and gloves, walking with their husbands or their lovers,
very beautiful to behold. The shops, not yet shut for the day, had
all sorts of signs swinging from the wall. There were the 'Frying
Pan and Drum,' the 'Hog in Armour,' the 'Bible and Swan,' the
'Whale and Crow,' the 'Shovel and Boot,' the 'Razor and Strop,' the
'Axe and Bottle,' the 'Spanish Galleon,' the 'Catherine Wheel,' and
a hundred others. But he saw not the sign of the 'Leg and Star.'
   It was growing late. The boy was hungry and tired. He
looked in at a coffee-house, but the company within, the crowds of
fine gentlemen—some drinking coffee, wine, and brandy, and some
smoking pipes—and the gaily-dressed young women who stood
behind the counter, frightened him. He did not dare go in and
call for a cup of coffee ; besides, he had never tasted coffee. Then
he passed a barber's shop, and thought he might ask of the barber,
because at Warkworth the barber was everybody's friend, and
perhaps this city barber might take after so good an example. He
looked in at the open door, but quickly retreated. For within the
shop were two or three gentlemen in the hands of the apprentices ;
and one, whose bald head was wrapped in a handkerchief, was
singing some song which began, 'Happy is the child whose father
has gone to the devil,' while the barber himself, with an apron on
and a white nightcap, sat in a chair playing an accompaniment on
a kind of guitar. So Ralph went on his way, wondering what next
he should see in London, and where this fortune of his might be
found. Presently there came slowly along the street a venerable
gentleman in an ample wig and a full black gown. He seemed to
have a benevolent countenance. Ralph stopped him, and, pulling
off his hat, ventured to ask this reverend divine if he would condescend to tell him the shortest way to the sign of the 'Leg and
Star' in Cheapside.
   'Stay, young man,' said the clergyman ; 'I am somewhat hard
of hearing.'
   He pulled out and adjusted very slowly an ear-trumpet, into
which Ralph bellowed his question. His reverence then removed
the instrument, replaced it in his pocket, and shook his finger at
the boy.

'So young,' he said, 'yet already corrupted ! Boy, bethink thee that Newgate is but in the next street.'

With these words he went on his way, and left the lad greatly perplexed and humbled, and wondering what it was that he was supposed to have said.

It was, in short, seven of the clock when he found himself at the place whither he was bound. He had been wandering for an hour and a half, looking about him, and at last ventured to ask the way of a servant-girl, who seemed astonished that he should not know so simple a thing as the most expeditious road to Cheapside, seeing that it was only the other side of Paul's. But she told him, and he presently found himself in the broad and wealthy street called Cheapside.

The ' Leg and Star ' was on the south side, between Bread Street and Bow Church. It was a glover's shop, and because it was growing late, the boxes of gloves were now taken from the window, and the apprentices were putting all away. Ralph stopped and looked at the sign, then at the letter—which was not a little crumpled and travel-stained—and again at the sign. Yes, it must be the house, the sign of the 'Leg and Star,' in Cheapside.

At the door of the shop stood a tall and portly man, between fifty and sixty years of age, with large red cheeks and double chin. He was dressed in plain broadcloth and tye-wig, but he wore ruffles and neckcloth of fine white linen laced, as became a substantial citizen. Ralph knew it could be none other than Mr. Hetherington, wherefore he took off his hat and bowed low.

' What is thy business, young man ? ' asked the master glover.

' Sir, I bear a letter from your honour's daughter, now staying at Warkworth, in Northumberland.'

' My daughter ! Then, prithee, boy, who are you ? '

' My name is Ralph Embleton, and ——'

' Thou art the son, then, of my old friend, Jack Embleton ? Come in, lad, come in.' He seized the boy by the arm and dragged him into the house and across the shop to the sitting-room at the back. ' Wife ! wife !' he cried. ' Here is a messenger from Drusy with a letter. Give me the letter, boy. And this is young Ralph Embleton, son of my old friend and gossip, Jack Embleton, with whom I have had many a fight in the old days. Poor Jack ! poor Jack ! Well, we live. Let us be thankful. Make the boy welcome ; give him supper. Make him a bed somewhere. What art thou doing in this great place, lad ? So the letter—aye ! the letter.'

He read the superscription, and slowly opened it and began to read :

' Dear and Hon'd Parents—The bairer of this is Rafe, who has run away from cruell treetment, and wants to make his fortune in London. He will tell you that I am well, and that I pray for your helthe, and that you will be kind to Rafe.—Your loving and dutiful d'ter,   ' DRUSILLA.'

L

‘So,’ went on the merchant, ‘cruel treatment. Who hath cruelly ill-treated thee, boy?’

‘I have run away, sir,’ he said, ‘from my cousin Mathew Humble, because he seeks every opportunity to do me a mischief. And, since he is my guardian, there is no remedy but to endure or to run away.’

‘Ah, Mathew Humble, who bought my farm. Sam Embleton married his father’s sister. Did your Uncle Sam leave Morwick Mill to Mathew?’

‘No, sir; he left it to me.’

‘And Mathew is your guardian? Yet the mill is your own, and you have run away from your own property? Morwick Mill is a pretty estate. It likes me not. Yet you would fain seek your fortune in London. That is well. Fortune, my lad, is only to be made by men of resolute hearts, like me.’ He expanded as he spoke, and seemed to grow two feet higher and broad in proportion. ‘And strong arms, like mine’—he hammered his chest as if it had been an anvil,—‘and keen eyes, like mine. Weak men fail and get trampled on in London. Cowardly men get set on one side, while the strong and the brave march on. I shall be, without doubt, next year, a Common Councilman. Strong men, clever men, brave men, boy, march, I say, from honour to greater honour. I shall become Alderman in two or three years, if Providence so disposes. There is no limit to the exalted ambitions of the London citizen. You would climb like me. You would be, some day, my Lord Mayor. It is well. It does you credit. It is a noble ambition.’

Meantime a maid had been spreading the table with supper, and, to say the truth, the eyes of the boy were turned upon the cold meats with so visible a longing, that the merchant could not choose but observe his hunger. So he bade him sit and eat. Now, while Ralph devoured his supper, being at the moment one of the hungriest lads in all England, the honest glover went on talking in grand, if not boastful language, about himself and his great doings. Yet, inexperienced as he was, Ralph could not but wonder, because, although the merchant was certainly past fifty years of age, the great things were all in the future. He would become one of the richest merchants in London; he would be Lord Mayor; he would make his daughter a great heiress; he designed that she should marry a lord at least. At this announcement Ralph blushed and his heart sank. One of the reasons, said the merchant, why he kept her still in Northumberland was that he did not wish her to return home until they were removed to a certain great house which he had in his mind, but had not yet purchased. She should go in silk and satin; he would give such great entertainments that even the king should hear of them; London was ever the city for noble feasting. And so he talked, until the lad’s brain reeled for thinking of all these splendours, and he grew sad in thinking how far off Drusilla would be as, one by one, all these grandeurs became achieved.

Another thing he observed : that while the husband talked in his confident and braggart way, the wife, who was a thin woman, sat silent and sometimes sighed. Why did she sigh ? Did she want to live on in obscurity ? Had she no ambition ?

Then the merchant filled and lit a pipe of tobacco, and proceeded to tell Ralph how he would have to begin upon this ambitious career in search of fortune. First, he would have to be an apprentice. 'I was myself,' said Mr. Hetherington, 'an apprentice, though who would think it now ?' As an apprentice, he would sweep and clean out the shop, open it in the morning, and shut it at night, wait upon the customers all day, run errands, obey dutifully his master, learn the business, watch his master's interests, behave with respect to his betters, show zeal in the despatch of work, get no holidays or playtime, never see the green fields except on Good Fridays, take for meals what might be given him, which would certainly not be slices off the sirloin, and sleep under the counter at night. In short, the shop would be his work-room, his parlour, his eating-room, and his bed-room.

The boy listened to his instructions with dismay. Was this the road to fortune ? Was he to become a slave for some years ? But—after ? His apprenticeship finished, it appeared that he might, if he could find money, open a shop, and become a master. But most young men, he learned, found it necessary to remain in the employment of their masters for some years, and in some cases for the whole term of their natural lives.

He did not consider that he had already such a fortune as would, if laid out with judgment, enable him to open a shop or to buy a partnership. He forgot at the time that he was the owner of Morwick Mill. It seemed to him, being so young and inexperienced, that he had run away from his inheritance, and abandoned it to Mathew. He, too, might therefore have to remain in a master's employment. This was fine fortune, truly, to be a servant all your days. And the boy began already even to regret his Cousin Mathew's blows and Barbara's cruel tongue.

His pipe finished, the merchant remembered that at eight his club would meet, and therefore left the lad with his wife.

'Boy,' she leaned over the table and whispered eagerly as soon as her husband was gone, 'have you come up to London without money to become a merchant ? '

'Indeed, madam,' he replied, 'I know not what I may become.'

'Then fly,' she said ; 'go home again. Follow the plough, become a tinker, a tailor, a cobbler—anything that is honest. Trade is uncertain. For one who succeeds a dozen are broke ; you know not, any moment, but that you also may break. Your fortune hangs upon a hundred chances. Alas ! if one of these fail, there is the Fleet, or may be Newgate, or Marshalsea, or Whitecross Street, or the King's Bench, or the Clink—there are plenty of places for the bestowal of poor debtors—for yourself, and for your wife and innocent children ruin and starvation.'

L 3

'Yet,' said Ralph, 'Mr. Hetherington is not anxious.'

'He leaves anxiety,' she replied bitterly, 'to his wife.'

Then she became silent, and spoke no more to the boy, but sat with her lips working as one who conversed with herself. And from time to time she sighed as if her heart was breaking.

In the morning the merchant was up betimes, and began again upon the glories of the city.

'Art still of the same mind?' he asked. 'Wilt thou be like Whittington and Gresham, and me, also one of those who climb the tree?'

Then Ralph confessed with a blush—which mattered nothing, so deep was the ruddy brown upon his cheek—that he found city honours dearly bought at the price of so much labour and confinement.

'Then,' said his adviser in less friendly tones, 'what will you do?'

Ralph asked if there was nothing that a young man may do besides work at a trade or sit in a shop.

'Why, truly, yes,' Mr. Hetherington replied with severity; 'he may become a highwayman, and rob upon the road, taking their money from honest tradesmen and poor farmers—a gallant life indeed, and so he will presently hang in chains, or be anatomised and set up in Surgeons' Hall. There is the end of your fresh air for you.'

'But, with respect, sir,' Ralph persisted, 'I mean in an honest way.'

'If he is rich enough he may be a scholar of Cambridge, and so take orders, or he may become a physician, or a lawyer, or a schoolmaster, or a surgeon, and go to sea in His Majesty's ships and lead a dog's life, or a soldier and go a fighting——'

'Let me be a soldier,' cried the boy.

'Why, why? But you must first get His Majesty's commission, and to get this you must beg for letters to my Lord This and my Lord That, and dangle about great houses, praying for their influence, and bribe the lacqueys, and then perhaps never get your commission after all.'

This was discouraging.

'Rolling stones, lad,' said the great merchant, 'gather no moss. Better stand quiet behind the counter, sweep out the shop, serve customers, and keep accounts, and perhaps some day be partner and grow rich.'

But Ralph hung his head.

'Then how can I help thee, foolish boy? Yet, because I knew thy father, and for Drusy's sake—— Stay, would you go to India?'

To India! Little, indeed, of the great doings in India reached the town of Warkworth. Yet Ralph had heard the Vicar talking with Mr. Carnaby of Colonel Clive and the famous battle of Plassy. To India! His eye flashed.

'Yes, sir ; I would willingly go to India.'

'My worthy friend, Mr. Nathaniel Silvertop, is in the service of the Company. Come, let us seek his counsel.'

They walked, the boy being much astonished at the crowd, the noise, and the never-ceasing business of the streets, down Cheapside, through the Poultry, past the new Mansion House and the Royal Exchange, into Cornhill, where stands the Honourable East India Company's House, a plain solid building, adorned with pillars of the Doric order. Mr. Hetherington led the way into a great hall, where was already assembled a crowd of men who had favours to ask of the directors, and finding a servant he sent his name to Mr. Silvertop.

Presently, for nothing was done in undignified haste in this house, Mr. Silvertop himself—a gentleman of three score, and of grave appearance—descended the stairs. To him Mr. Hetherington unfolded his business.

Here, he said, was a young fellow from Northumberland, heir to a small and pretty estate, but encumbered for three or four years to come with a guardian, whose affection he appeared to have unfortunately lost, so that it would be well for both to remain apart; but he was a young gentleman of roving tastes, who would fain see a little of the world, and—but this he whispered—a brave and bold fellow.

Mr. Silvertop regarded the lad attentively.

'Our writers,' he said solemnly, 'go out on small salaries. They seldom rise above four hundred or five hundred pounds a year at the most. Yet—mark this, young gentleman—so great are their chances in India that they sometimes come home at forty, or even less, with a hundred—aye, two hundred thousand pounds. Think upon that, boy ! So great a thing it is to serve this Honourable Company.'

The boy's eyes showed no emotion. A dull dog, indeed, he seemed to Mr. Silvertop, not to tremble at the mere mention of so vast a sum.

'Leave him here, my good friend,' said Mr. Silvertop. ' I have business, but I will return and speak with him again. He can walk in the hall and wait.'

Mr. Hetherington went his way, and Ralph waited.

After an hour or so, he saw Mr. Silvertop coming down the stairs again. He was escorting, or leading to the door, or in some way behaving in respectful and deferential fashion to a tall and splendid gentleman, brave in scarlet, wearing a sash and a sword and a gold-laced hat. At the foot of the stairs, Mr. Silvertop bowed low to this gentleman, who joined a little group of gentlemen, some of them also in scarlet. He seemed to be the chief among them, for they all behaved to him with the greatest respect. Then Mr. Silvertop looked about in the crowd, and spying Ralph, beckoned him to draw near and speak with him.

'So,' said Mr. Silvertop, 'you are the lad. Yes, I remember.'

Ralph thought it strange that he should not remember, seeing that
it was but an hour or so since Mr. Silvertop had spoken last with
him. 'You are recommended by my friend Mr. Hetherington.
Well, I know not—we are pestered with applications for our writer-
ships. Every runaway'—Ralph blushed—'every out-at-elbows
younger son'—the great gentleman in scarlet, who was close at
hand, here turned his head and looked at the lad with a little interest—'every poor curate's brat who can read and cypher wants
to be sent to India.'

'You cannot, sir,' said the gentleman in scarlet, 'send too many
Englishmen to India. I would that the whole country was ruled
by Englishmen—yet not by quill-drivers.'

He added the last words in a lower voice, yet Ralph heard
them.

Mr. Silvertop bowed low, and turned again to the boy.

'A writership,' he continued, 'is the greatest gift that can be
bestowed upon a deserving lad. Remember that, and if—but I
cannot promise. I would oblige my friend if I could—but I will
not undertake anything. With my influence—yet I do not say for
certain ; a writership is a greater matter than you seem to think—
I might bring thy case before the directors. Is thy handwriting
fair, and thy knowledge of figures absolute ?'

Ralph blushed, because his handwriting was short of the clerkly
standard.

'I thank you, sir,' he said, 'but I love not writing. I would
rather carry a sword than a pen.'

'Ta-ta-ta,' replied Mr. Silvertop, whose influence lay wholly in
the mercantile department of the company. 'We waste our time.
A sword ! I know naught of swords. Go thy ways, boy—go thy
ways. Is London City, think you, a place for the carriage of
swords ! Go, take the king's shilling, and join a marching regiment. I warrant you enough of swords and bayonets.'

Ralph bowed and turned away sadly. The gentleman in scarlet,
who had apparently been listening to the conversation, followed
him to the doors with thoughtful eyes.

'A lad who would rather handle a sword than a pen,' he said.
'Are there many such lads left in this city of trade and greed ?'

They looked, at the 'Leg and Star,' that day, for the return of
the young Northumbrian in time for dinner. But he came not ;
nor did he come at night ; nor did he ever come. No one knew
whither he had gone or what had become of him, and much Mr.
Hetherington feared that in this wicked town he had been enticed
by some designing wretch to his destruction.

CHAPTER IV.

DRUSILLA'S STORY.

I WAS born in Cheapside, almost beneath the bells of Bow, on October 5, in the year of grace 1753, being the fifth and youngest child of Solomon Hetherington and Prudence his wife. My father was a citizen and glover, a Member of the Honourable Company of Glovers, his ambition being always to be elected, before becoming Lord Mayor, Master of his Company. These ambitions are laudable in a city merchant, yet, alas! they are not always attained, and in my unhappy father's case they were very far from being reached, as you shall presently hear.

There is, I am told, some quality in the London air which causeth the city, in spite of much that is foolish as regards cleanliness, to be a healthy place, and favourable to children. So that, for my own part, though I was brought up in the very centre and heart of the city, with no green fields to run in, nor any gardens save those belonging to the Drapers' Company, I, as well as my brothers and sisters, was a healthy and well-faring child up to the age of eight, when I, with all my brothers and sisters, was afflicted with that scourge of mankind, small-pox. This dreadful disease, to the unspeakable grief of my parents, killed their four eldest children, and spared none but myself, the youngest, and a girl. To lose three strong and promising boys, the hope of the house, as well as a girl of fourteen, already beginning to be useful, was a most dreadful thing, and I wonder that my mother, who passionately loved her boys, ever recovered cheerfulness. Indeed, until her dying day she kept the annual recurrence of this day, which robbed her of her children—for they all died on the same day—in prayer and fasting and tears. Yet I was left, and, by further blessing of Heaven, I recovered so far that, although I was weakly and ailing for a long time, I was not marked by a single spot or any of those ugly pits, which sometimes ruin many a woman's beauty and thereby rob her of that choicest blessing, the love of a husband. So different, however, was I from the stout and hearty girl before the small-pox, that my parents were advised that the best chance to save my life—this being for the time their chief and even their only hope—was to send me into the country, there to live in fresh pure air, running in the sun, and fed on oatmeal porridge, good milk, fat bacon, and new-laid eggs.

Then my father bethought him of his own mother who lived far away indeed from London, namely at Warkworth, in Northumberland. And he proposed to my mother that they should take this long journey, carrying me with them, and leave me for a while in charge of my grandmother; which being done, and my health show-

ing signs of amendment, they were constrained to go back to their
own business, leaving me in good hands, yet with sorrowful hearts,
because they were going home without me.   And for six or seven
years I saw them no more.

No girl, to be sure, had kinder treatment or more indulgent
governess than myself.   My grandmother, Dame Hetherington—
though not a lady by birth, but only a farmer's daughter—lived in
the house which stands outside the town, beyond the bridge, among
the trees.   You may know it by its garden and green railings.   It
is a small house, yet large enough for the uses and wants of an old
lady and a single serving-maid.   She was then about seventy years
of age, but this is considered young in Northumberland, and I have
seen many ladies from London and the south country, or even out
of Scotland, who at fifty were not so active.   She lived upon an
annuity, forty pounds a year, which her son bought for her when
he sold his father's farm of thirty acres ; it was bought by Mathew
Humble.   As for the cottage, it was also my father's, and the Dame
lived in it, rent free.

It was the Dame, my grandmother, who taught me all household
things, such as to spin, to sew, to darn, to hem, to knit, to em-
broider, to bake and brew, to make puddings, cakes, jellies, and
conserves, to compound skilfully cowslip, ginger, and gooseberry
wine ; to clean, sweep, dust, and keep in order my own and all the
other rooms in the house.   It was the Vicar's wife who undertook
—there being no school in the town, save a humble Dame's school—
to teach me reading, writing, cyphering, together with my Catechism
and the Great Scheme of Christian Redemption, of which, being
the daughter of pious parents, I already possessed the rudiments.
There were not many books to read in the house, because my grandmother did not read ; but there were the Bible, the Apocrypha, the
Pilgrim's Progress, a book of Hymns and Pious Songs, and a
bundle of the cheap books which tell of Valentine and Orson, Dick
Whittington, the last Appearance of the Devil, and the latest
Examples of Divine Wrath against fools and profligates.

But because the Dame, my grandmother, was a wise woman,
and reflected that I was sent away from London in order to recover
my health and grow strong, I was allowed and encouraged to run
about in the open air as much as possible, so that, as this part of
England is quite safe, and there are here few gipsies (who mostly
stay on the other side of Cheviot) nor any robbers on the road—
nor, indeed, any road at all to signify—I very soon grew to know
the whole country within the reach of a hearty girl's feet.

There is plenty to see, though this part of Northumberland is
flat, while the rest is wild and mountainous.   Firstly, there are the
ruins of the old castle, about which it is always pleasant for a child
to run and climb, or for a grown person to meditate on the vanity
of earthly things, seeing that this pile of ruins was once a great and
stately castle, and this green sward was once hidden beneath the
feet of fierce soldiers, who now are dust and ashes in the grave-yard.

From the castle one looks down upon the Coquet, which would
ever continue in my eyes the sweetest of rivers, even were I to see
the far-famed Tiber, or the silver Thames, or the great Ganges, or
the mysterious Nile, or even the sacred Jordan. It winds round
the foot of the hill on which the castle is built. There is one spot
upon its banks where I have often stood to watch the castle rising
proudly—albeit, in ruins—above the hill, and wholly reflected in
the tranquil waters below. It was my delight to scramble down
the banks and to wander fearless along the windings of the tortuous
stream, watching the brightness of its waters, now deep, now broad,
now silent, now bubbling with the fish leaping up and disappearing,
and the woods hanging on the rising bank. If you sat quite quiet,
moving not so much as a finger, you might, if you were lucky,
presently see a great otter swimming along in the shadow of the
bank, and you would certainly see a water-rat sitting in the sun.
But if you move so much as an eyelid the rat drops into the water
like a stone. Or if you crossed the river, which you can very easily
do in some parts by taking off your shoes and stockings and wading,
you could go visit the Hermitage. There is the little chapel in
which the hapless solitary prayed, and the figure which he rudely
sculptured, and even the stone bed on which he lay and the steps
of the altar worn by his knees. But children think little of these
things, and to me it was only a place where one could rest in cool
shade when the sun was hot, or seek shelter from the cold blast of
the winter wind.

Higher up the river was Morwick Mill, where Ralph Embleton
lived with his uncle.

Or, again, if instead of crossing the bridge and going up to the
castle, you walked across the fields which lay at the back of the
garden—wild and barren fields covered with tufts of coarse grass—
you came, after half a mile or so of rough walking, to the sea-shore,
fringed with low sand-hills. It was an endless joy to run over these
hills and explore their tiny valleys and peaks of twenty feet high at
least. Or one could wander on the sands, looking at the waves, an
occupation which never tires, or watching sea-gulls sailing with
long white wings in the breeze, or the little oxbirds on the sands.
If you walked down instead of up the river, you came, after three
miles, to its mouth and the little town of Amble, where every man
is a fisherman.

Beyond the town, half a mile out to sea, lies the little island of
Coquet. Ralph once rowed me across the narrow channel, and we
explored the desert island and thought of Robinson Crusoe, which
he had read and told me. But this was before the time when we
took to pretending at ghosts.

In those days, which seem to have been so happy, and I dare
say were, Ralph was free, and could come and go as pleased
him best, save that he went every morning to the Vicar, who
taught him Latin and Greek, and sometimes remembered—but in
kindly moderation—the advice of Solomon. The reason of this

freedom was that his uncle, with whom he lived, loved the lad greatly, and intended great things for him, even designing that he should become a great scholar and go to Cambridge. For once there was a member of his family who took to learning and rose from being a poor scholar in that university, which has ever been a kindly nurse or foster-mother of poor scholars, to be a Doctor of Divinity and a Bishop. But my Ralph was never to be a Bishop, nor even a Doctor of Divinity. And a sad change was to happen at the mill.

Everybody was our friend in those days, from Mr. Cuthbert Carnaby, Justice of the Peace, and the Vicar, down to Sailor Nan and her lodger, Dan Gedge, the Strong Man. Everybody had a kind word for Ralph, and nobody told me then how wicked it was to run about with a boy of such unnatural depravity. This, as you will see, was to come. He was a tall boy for his years, and he was six years older than myself, which proves how good-natured he must have been, for few boys of fifteen or sixteen care for the companionship of a girl of nine or ten. As for his face, it has always been the dearest face in the world to me, and always will be, so that I know not whether other people would call it a handsome face. His eyes were eager, as if—which was the case—he always wanted to be up and doing. They were blue eyes, because he was a Northumberland lad, yet not soft and dreamy eyes, as is too often the case with the people of the north. His face was oval and his features regular. He carried his head thrown back, and walked erect with both hands ready, as if there was generally a fight to be expected, and it was well to be prepared. To be sure, Ralph was one of those who love a fight and do not sulk if they are beaten, but bide a bit and then on again.

On Sunday afternoons, who so ready as he at quarterstaff or wrestling, or any of the manly sports? As regards the cock-fighting, bull-baiting, and dog-fighting, with which our common people so love to inflame their passions and to destroy their sensibility, Ralph would none of it, because he loved dogs, and, indeed, all animals. But at an otter-hunt he was always to the front. He was not fond of books and school-learning, yet he loved to read of foreign lands and of adventures. The Vicar lent him such books, and he told me, long before I thought that he too would become such an one himself, of Pizarro, Cortes, Raleigh, and Francis Drake (not to speak of Robinson Crusoe and Captain Gulliver), and of what great things they did and what fine places they visited. A brave boy always, whose heart leaped up when he heard of brave things.

All the town, I have said, were our friends. But of course we had some who were more with us than others. For instance, what should we have been without the Fugleman? To those who do not know him he was the chief terror of the town, being so stern and lean in appearance, so stiff and upright, and, besides, officially connected with such things as stocks, whipping-post, pound, and pillory; names of rebuke. To Ralph and to me he was a trusted and thoughtful friend, almost a playfellow. His room at the gateway of the castle, to which he had fitted a door and a window of glass in a wooden frame, was full of things curious and delightful. He had eggs strung in long festoons round the walls, and could tell us where to look for the nests in spring; he had a ferret in a box; he had fishing-rods and nets; he had traps for wild fowl, and for rabbits; he had a fowling-piece, and he could tell us stories without end of his campaigns. Why, this brave fellow, who was for thirty years and more in the Fourteenth Berkshire Regiment, could tell us of the great review held on Salisbury Plain by his Majesty King George the First, of pious memory. He could tell us of the famous Siege of Gibraltar, when the regiment was commanded by Colonel Clayton, and of the battle of Dettingen, where that gallant officer was killed; of Culloden and the Young Pretender. A brave regiment always and strong in Protestant faith, though much given to drink, and only kept in paths of virtue by strict discipline and daily floggings.

Had it not been for the Fugleman—and Sailor Nan, of whom more anon—I for one should never have learned about foreign places at all, any more than the rest of us in Warkworth. Now, indeed, having heard him talk about them so often, I seem to know the phlegmatic Dutch and the slow German, and the Frenchmen with their love of glory, and the Spaniards with their Papistical superstitions, and the cruel ways of the Moors, because the Fourteenth were once at Tangiers.

Ralph, of course, knew much more than I, because he was more curious, being a boy, and asked many more questions, being always, as I have said already, thirsty for information concerning other people. No one else in Warkworth had been abroad, not even Mr. Carnaby, though gentlemen of good birth, like himself, sometimes made the grand tour in their youth, accompanied by tutors. Yet Mr. Carnaby said that they often learned more wickedness than good, and would have been better at home. No one else talked about foreigners or knew anything of them, finding sufficient subject for conversation in the weather and the events of the day in town and country side. I do not except Sailor Nan, although she had sailed over many seas, because a person who only goes to sea remains always, it seems to me, in one spot.

Northumberland is enough, indeed, for the Northumbrians. To begin with, there is no part of England where there is so much left to be told by the old women, who are ever the collectors and treasurers of things gone by and old stories. Why, men are as wasteful of their recollections as of their money, and were it not for the women, the past would perish. It seems to me as if the Dame could never come to an end with the tales she told me, the songs she sang me (in a pretty voice still, though a little cracked with age), the proverbs she had for every occasion, and the adventures of many people with ghosts and fairies. There was the story of the Loathly Worm of Bamborough, to begin with, and the terrible tale of Sir Guy the Seeker. I have stood amid the ruins of Dunstanburgh and

wondered where might be the door through which he entered
when he found the beautiful lady. Then there was the story of
the farmer who found King Arthur and all his knights in an en·
chanted sleep, under Sewing Shields Castle. He saw waiting for
the first comer a sword and a horn. He drew the sword, indeed,
but was too terrified to blow the horn.

> Oh, woe betide that evil day
> On which the witless wight was born,
> Who drew the sword, the garter cut,
> But never blew the bugle-horn.

There was the story of the simple man of Ravensworth who
died, and was dead for twenty-four hours, during which he was
permitted to see both Heaven and Hell, and was sent back to earth
to tell the Bishop that he must prepare for death. There was the
story of the other simple countryman who had a dream of treasure.
In his dream he saw the place where the treasure lay. It was
in a triangular space made by three great stones beneath the
ground. That simple man was so foolish as to tell his dream.
Again the dream came to him. This time he got up early in the
morning and went out, spade in hand, to dig. Alas! he was too
late. Someone else had been there before him, guided by the
first dream, and all that was left was the triangular space made
by the three great stones. There was the other treasure-story connected with the name of Nelly the Knocker. Nelly the Knocker
was the ghost of an old woman. She came every evening at dusk,
and she stationed herself before a great stone standing by the
road-side near a farm. Here she knocked with a hammer. Everybody had seen her—no one was afraid of her; the rustics were so
used to her that they passed her without a shudder, though, of
course, no one ventured quite close to her; her tapping was heard
a long way off. One day two men thought they would dig under
the stone, to see if anything was there. They dug, and they found
a great pot full of gold coins. So that Nelly the Knocker was
justified of her knocking. But she came no more. There was still
another story of treasure: how it lay buried under a great stone,
and how those who would dig for it were frightened away by a
figure in white which seemed to fly from under it, no one having
courage to remain after the appearance of that figure. There were,
lastly, the stories of the fairies who were brought into the country
by the Crusaders, never having been heard of before. I have since
wondered how they were brought: whether in boxes, or in cages,
or in what other way. Those of Northumberland have yellow hair;
they live in chambers under green hills; they have a great day of
meeting every year—namely, on the eve of Roodsmass, called by
some Hallowe'en. The chief mischief they do—it is, to be sure, a
very great mischief—is to steal the babies (wherefore at reaping-
time it is most dangerous to leave their little children under the
hedges) and to substitute changelings.

' My dear,' said the Dame, gravely, ' I have known such a changeling. His name was Little Hobbie o' the Castleton ; he was a dwarf, and wrathful by disposition, insomuch that he would draw his gully upon any of the boys who offended him. But his legs were short, whereby he was prevented from the wickedness of murder, or at least striking and wounding.'

There was also the Brown Man of the Moors, but one feared him not at Warkworth, where there are no moors. And there was the fearful Ghost of Black Heddon, known as Silky, because she always appeared dressed in silk ; a stately dame, the sight of whom terrified the stoutest.

These are only a few of the tales with which my childish head was filled, and though I know that scoffers may laugh, in an age which affects with incredible boldness to disbelieve even the most sacred things, we of the country know very well that these things are too well authenticated not to be true. As regards Silky, for instance, the man was still living and could be spoken with when I was a girl, who, being then a youth of tender years, proposed to personate the figure in white which sometimes stood or sat by the bridge on the road to Edlingham from Alnwick. He put on a sheet and sat upon the bridge, expecting to frighten passengers. Lo ! beside him he saw, suddenly, the real ghost, saying never a word. And at sight of her he fell backwards over the bridge into the water and broke his leg, so that he went halt to his dying day. This ought to have been a warning both to Ralph and myself : but, alas ! it was not.

Sailor Nan, who lived in a cottage up the street between the church and the castle, had seen many ghosts, but hers were sea-ghosts, because, though she had sailed in a great many seas, she had never been ashore—I do not count an hour's run among grog-shops going ashore—in foreign parts, except at Portobello, when that place was taken in the year 1739, when she was with Admiral Burford, being also captain of the foretop, and at the time about thirty-six years of age ; here, by reason of a wound, her sex was discovered, so that they disrated her and sent her home. Her memory being good and her recollections being copious, her house was much frequented by young people who loved to hear how she boarded the ' Santa Isabella ' when aboard the ' Dorsetshire,' under Admiral Delaval, or how she was present at the famous cutting out of the pirate, with the hangings at the yard-arm of the pirate captain and all his crew, and how the ghost of the carpenter (unjustly hanged) haunted the main deck. She was at this time— I mean at the time when Ralph did penance—about sixty years of age. She wore a sailor's three-cornered hat, cocked, a thick woollen wrapper round her neck, and petticoats almost as short as a sailor's. She wore also thick worsted stockings and men's shoes, so that it was difficult to understand that she was a woman and not a man. Her voice could be either rough and coarse like a sailor's, or thin like a woman's, as she pleased ; round her waist she tied a

cord, which had a knife at the end of it. She smoked tobacco
continually, and drank as much rum as ever she could get. She
lived chiefly by selling tansy cakes. After she was dismissed from
the navy she married twice. Her first husband was hanged for
selling a stolen pig at Morpeth Fair, and her second hanged himself
—some said on account of his wife's cudgel. 'Hinneys,' she would
say, ' it's a fine thing to dee your own fair death.' Her conversation was full of strange sea oaths, and she was still as strong as
most men are at thirty, with thick brawny arms and sturdy feet, a
woman who feared no man. Besides her tansy cakes she told
fortunes to those who would give her silver, and she grew in her
garden, and sold, marsh and marigold. A tough, hardened old
woman, her face beaten and battered by all kinds of weather, who
sat outside her door on a big stone all day long, winter and summer,
rain, snow, frost, hail, east wind, south wind, sunshine, cloud, or
clear, smoking a black pipe of tobacco, and carrying in her hand
a stick with which she threatened the children when they ran after
her, crying, 'Sailor Nan, Sailor Nan ; half a woman, half a man !'
But I do not think that she ever harmed any of them. People
came to see her from all the country-side, partly to talk with her,
because she was so full of stories, and partly to look at a woman
who had actually carried a cutlass, handled pike and marlinspike,
been captain of the foretop, brandished a petty officer's rope's-end,
manned a boat, fought ashore side by side with the redcoats, and
valiantly boarded an enemy. In the end she lived to be a hundred
and eight, but she never altered or looked any older, or lost her
faculties, or drank less rum, or smoked less tobacco.

When Ralph was nearly fifteen a great and terrible misfortune
befell him. His uncle, Mr. Samuel Embleton, though not an old
man, died suddenly. After he was buried it was found that he had
left by will Morwick Mill and the farm, his household furniture,
his books, which were not many, and all the money he had in the
world, to Ralph as his sole heir. This inheritance proved at first
the cause of great unhappiness to the boy. For, unfortunately, the
will named Mathew Humble as the guardian and executor, to whom
the testator devised his best wig and his best coat with his second-
best bed and a gold-headed stick. Now it angered Mathew to
think that he, being also nephew and sister's son of Samuel
Embleton, of Morwick Mill, was left no part or portion of this
goodly heritage. It would seem that knowing his uncle's design to
send Ralph to Cambridge, and his hope that he would become a
credit to the family and a pillar of the Church, he had hoped and
even grown to believe firmly and to expect it as a right, that the
mill at least, if not the farm, or a portion of it, would be left to
him. It was, therefore, a bitter blow for him to find that he was
left nothing at all except what he could make or save as guardian
of the heir and administrator of the estate, with free quarters at
the mill, for six years. Surely for a man of probity and common
sense that would have been considered a great deal.

He came, with his sister, who was as much disappointed as himself, in a spirit of rancour, malice, and envy. He regarded the innocent boy as a supplanter. The first thing he did was to inform him that he should have no skulking or idleness. He therefore put a stop to the Latin and Greek lessons from the Vicar, and employed the boy about the work of the place, giving him the hardest and the most disagreeable tasks on the farm. For freedom was substituted servitude ; for liberty, restraint ; for affection and kindness, harsh language and continual floggings ; while Barbara with her tongue, that ill-governed weapon of women, made him feel, for the first time in his life, how idle, how useless, how greedy a creature he was. The boy bore with all, as meekly as was his duty, for quite two years. But he often came to me, or to the Fugleman, with fists clenched, declaring that he would endure this ill-usage no longer, and asking in wonder what he had done to deserve it. And at such times he would swear to leave the mill and run away and seek his fortune anywhere—somewhere in the world. It was always in his mind, from the first, when Mathew began his ill-treatment, that he would run away and seek his fortune. In this design he was strengthened by the example of my father, who left the village when a boy of fourteen to seek his fortune, and found—you shall hear presently what he found. I dissuaded him, as much as I could, because it was dreadful for me to think of being left without him, or of his running about the country helpless and friendless. The Fugleman, who knew the world and had travelled far, pointed out to him very sensibly that he would have to endure this hardness for a very short time longer, that he was already sixteen and as tall as most men, and could not for very shame be flogged much more ; while, as for Barbara's tongue, he declared that a brave man ought not to value what a woman said— let her tongue run as free as the serjeant at drill of recruits—no more than the price of a rope's end : and, again, that in five years' time, as soon as Ralph was twenty-one, he would have the right to turn his cousin out of the mill, which would then become his own property, and a very pretty property too, where an old friend would expect to find a pipe and a glass of Hollands or rum. And he promised himself to assist at the ducking in the river which he supposed that Ralph would give his cousin when that happy day should arrive, as well as at the great feast and rejoicing which he supposed would follow. The result of these exhortations, to which were added those of my grandmother, was that he remained at home, and when Mathew Humble cruelly belaboured him, he showed no anger or desire for revenge, and when Barbara smote him with harsh words and found texts out of the Bible to taunt him with, he made no reply. Nor did he rebel even though they treated him as if he were a common plough-boy and farm drudge, instead of the heir to all.

I confess, and have long felt sincerely, the wickedness of the thing which at length brought open disgrace upon poor Ralph and drove him away from us. Yet, deserving of blame and punishments as our actions were, I cannot but think that the conduct of Mathew in bringing the chief culprit—he knew nothing of my share or of the Fugleman's—before his Worship, Mr. Justice Carnaby, was actuated more by malice than by an honest desire to bring criminals to punishment. Besides, he had for some months before this been spreading abroad wicked rumours about Ralph, saying, among other false and malicious things, that the boy was idle, gluttonous, lying, and even thieving, insomuch that the Vicar, who knew the contrary, and that the boy was as good a lad as ever walked, though fond of merriment and a little headstrong, openly rebuked him for malice and evil-thinking, saying plainly that these things were not so, and that, if they were so, Mathew was much to blame in blabbing them about the country, rather than trying to correct the lad's faults, and doing his best to hide them from the general knowledge. Yet there are some who always believe what is spoken to one's dispraise, and sour looks and unfriendly faces were bestowed upon the boy, while my grandmother was warned not to allow me to run wild with a lad of so notorious a bad character. This is all that I meant when I said just now that at first all were our friends.

When Ralph was gone I took little joy in anything until I got my first letter from him, which was not for a very long time afterwards.

Now, one day, as I was walking sorrowfully home, having sat all the afternoon with the Fugleman, I saw Sailor Nan beckoning to me from her stone outside the door.

'Child,' she said, 'where's your sweetheart?'

'Alack,' I replied, 'I know not, Sailor Nan.'

'Young maids,' she went on, 'must not puke and pine because they hear nothing for awhile of the lads they love. Be of good cheer. Why, I read him his fortune myself in his own left hand. Did my fortunes ever turn out wrong? As good a tale of luck and fair weather as I ever read. Come, child, give me thy hand; let me read your lines too.'

It is strange how in the lines of one's hand are depicted beforehand all the circumstances of life, easy to be read by those who are wise. Yet have I been told that it is not enough to learn the rules unless you have the gift.

'He will come back,' she repeated, after long looking into the hand. 'Now, your own hand. Here is a long line of life—yet not as long as my own. Here is the line of marriage—a good line; a happy marriage; a fortunate girl—yet there will be trouble. Is it an old man? I cannot rightly read. Something is in the way. Trouble, and even grievous trouble. But all to come right in the end.'

'Is my fortune,' I asked, 'connected with the fortune of Ralph?'

She laughed her rough, hoarse sea-laugh.

'If it is an old man, or if it is a young man, say him nay.
Bide your old love. If he press or if he threaten, say him nay.
Bide your old sweetheart.

> 'There was an old man came over the lea,
> Heigho! but I won't have 'un;
> Came over the lea,
> A courtin' to me,
> Wi' his old gray beard just newly shaven.'

She crooned out the words in a cracked and rusty voice, and
pushed my hand away roughly. Then she replaced her pipe in
her mouth and went on smoking the tobacco which was her chief
food and her chief solace, and took no further heed of me.

CHAPTER V.

A SECOND WHITTINGTON.

It becomes not a young girl to pronounce judgment openly (whatever she may think) upon the conduct of her elders, or to show
resentment, whatever they may think fit to do ; so that when
Mathew Humble came to see my grandmother on certain small
affairs which passed between them—concerning the sale of a pig,
or I know not what—it was my duty, though my heart was aflame,
to sit, hands in lap, quiet and mum, when I would rather, Heaven
knows, have been boxing his ears and railing him in such language
as I could command, for I certainly could never forget, while this
man, with the fat red cheeks and pig's eyes, was drinking my
grandmother's best cowslip wine, as if he had been the most virtuous of men, that it was through him—though this my grandmother
knew not, for I never told her—that Ralph had been betrayed to
his Worship, and so been brought to public shame ; that it was
this man who had beaten the boy without a cause, and that it was
his sister who daily sought out hard words and cruel texts, as well
as coarse crusts, with which to torture my Ralph. I remembered,
as well, that it was this man who had been soundly cudgelled and
flogged by the boy he had abused so shamefully.

'You have heard nothing, I dare say, Mr. Mathew,' asked the
Dame, for it was now two months after the poor lad's flight, ' of
our young runaway, whom we in this house greatly lament and
wish him well ?'

'Nothing as yet,' replied Mathew. Then he drank off the rest
of his glass, and went on with much satisfaction : 'I fear'—yet he
looked as if he hoped—'that we shall hear nothing until we hear
the worst, as provided by the righteous laws of this country.
What, madam, can be expected of one so dead and hardened unto

M

conscience as to offer violence and to turn upon his guardian, and take him while off his guard and unawares with bludgeons and cudgels ? '

The whole town had heard by this time and knew very well how Ralph, before his flight, refused to be flogged, and fought his guardian and vanquished him, insomuch that grievous weals were raised and bruises sad to tell of. It was Mathew's version that he was taken by surprise. Otherwise, he said, it was nothing but Heaven's mercy prevented him from grievously wounding and hurting the boy, who ran away for fear and dared not come back. Opinion was divided : for some called shame on Mathew for flogging so tall and strong a lad—almost a man—and others declared that stripes, and those abundant and well laid on, alone could meet the deserts of one guilty of bringing ghostly visitors into discredit, because, should such practices continue, no ghost, even one who came to tell of buried treasure, would be sure of his— or her—reception, and might be scoffed at as an impostor, instead of being received with terror and the fearful knocking together of knees.

But mostly the general opinion was in favour of the boy and his flight ; the folk rejoiced that Mathew had met his match ; and our ignorance of Ralph's fate made the people remember once more his many good qualities, his merry friendliness, his honest face, and his blithe brown eyes, in spite of the ghost pretences and the stories spread abroad by his cousins.

'That,' said my grandmother, in answer to Mathew, ' was wrong, indeed. I had hoped that the lad would have returned, made submission, received punishment, and been pardoned. He was ever a boy of good disposition, and his uncle loved him, Mathew—a thing which did, without doubt, prepossess you in his favour.'

Mathew slowly put down his empty glass, and held up both hands to show astonishment.

' Good disposition ? This, madam, springs from your own goodness of heart. Who in Warkworth doth not know that the boy was already, so to speak, a man grown, so far as wickedness is concerned ? He of a good disposition ? Alas, madam, your heart is truly too full of kindness ! For the sake of Missy here—who grows a tall lass—I am glad that he is gone, because he would have taught her some of his own wickedness. Alas !' here he spread his hands, ' the things that I could tell you if I would. But one must spare one's cousin. Greediness, laziness, profligacy, luxury. Ha ! but I speak not of these matters, because he was my cousin. For his own sake, and because at his age an evil-disposed boy cannot but feel the want of those paternal corrections which I never spared, I grieve that he is no longer with us.'

' Nevertheless, Mr. Mathew,' said my grandmother, smiling, ' I cannot believe, even though you assure us, that Ralph was so wicked as all this, and I hope, for the credit of your family, that you will diligently spread abroad a better opinion. No one is hardened at sixteen.'

'Except Ralph,' said Mathew, shaking his head.

'And I for one shall continue to hope the best. He will return to us, Mr. Mathew, before long, penitent, and desirous of pleasing his guardian, and you will then be able to correct your judgment.'

'I do not think he will ever return,' said his cousin. 'As for being penitent, he must first take the punishment which awaits him. As for desiring to please——' He stopped short, doubtless remembering that alder-branch.

'If he does not return,' my grandmother continued, 'till after he becomes of age, it will be your great happiness to hand over his property, well husbanded and with careful stewardship.' Here Mathew shut both his eyes and shook his head, but I know not why. 'You will feel the pleasure of doing good to one who undutifully offered you violence. He will be the opposite to the man in the parable, for he will have left his talent tied up in a napkin, and he will return and find it multiplied.'

'Such as Ralph,' said Mathew, grimly, 'do not repent, nor desire to please, nor return. He began with penance—public penance—think upon that—and saying the Lord's Prayer aloud. He will be advanced next—which is the regular course of such as him—to pillory. After penance, pillory. It is the regular thing. After pillory, stocks ; after stocks, whipping-post or cart-tail ; after cart-tail, burning in the hand. Lastly, he will be promoted to the gallows.' He positively rubbed his hands together, and laughed at this delightful prospect. Why did he wish his cousin hanged, I wonder, unless that he would then get the mill ?

'I trust not,' said the Dame. 'Meantime, you will guard his property.'

'His property !' his face grew quite black. 'His property ! Why, if he comes back there will be something said about that as well. Ha ! His property ! Ha !'

'But, surely, Mr. Mathew, his uncle bequeathed Morwick Mill to Ralph ? '

'That, madam, has been the belief of the world. Nevertheless—— But I say nothing This is not the time for serious talk.'

When he was gone, my grandmother, who seldom discussed such high matters with me, said :

'Drusilla, I like it not. Doth Mathew Humble desire the death of his cousin ? It would seem so. Pillory, stocks, whipping-post, gallows ? All for our Ralph ? Why this passeth understanding ! And wherefore this talk of the world's belief ? I like it not, child.'

'But you do not think, grandmother, that Ralph will——'

'I think, child, that Ralph is a good lad, but headstrong, perhaps, and impatient of control. Wherever he is I will warrant him honest. Such boys get on, as your father got on. Some day, I

M 2

make no doubt that he will return. But as for Mathew Humble, I like not his manner of speech.'

The same day she put on her bonnet and best shawl and went to the house of Mr. Cuthbert Carnaby, from which I gathered— my little wits jumping as fast as bigger ones—that she went to lay the case before his Worship, which perhaps was the reason why, when Mr. Carnaby next met Mathew (it was after church on Sunday), he informed him that it should be his own business to watch that the mill and farm were properly managed in the interests of the heir, and that a strict account would be required when Ralph returned and came of age. Whereat Mathew became confused, and stammered words incoherent about proving who was the rightful heir. Yet, for the moment, nothing more was said upon that subject.

The summer and the autumn passed, but no sign or letter came from Ralph. The people in the town ceased, after the manner of mankind, to think of the boy. He was gone and forgotten, yet there were two or three of us who spoke and thought of him continually. First there was the Fugleman, who found his life dull without the boy to talk with. He promised to make a collection of birds' eggs in the spring as a present for him when he should return. Then there was the old woman, Sailor Nan, who kept his memory green. Lastly, there were my grandmother and myself. We knew not, however, where he was, or anything about him, nor could we guess what he was doing, or whither he had gone.

Twice in the year—namely, at Christmas or the New Year, and at Midsummer—I had letters from my parents, to which I duly replied. It was in May when Ralph ran away, so that they had three letters from me that year. When my Christmas letters arrived there was mention of our boy, but so strange a tale that we could not understand what to believe or what the thing might mean.

The letter told us that Ralph reached London safely in four or five weeks after leaving us, having walked all the way, save for such trifling lifts and helps as might be had for nothing on the road ; he found out my father's shop ; he gave him the letter ; he slept in the house, and was hospitably entertained. In the morning he was taken by my father to the East India Company's great house in Cornhill, and left there by him to talk with a gentleman about the obtaining of a post in their service ; that, the conversation finished, being dismissed by the gentleman with whom he had taken counsel, Ralph left the office. Then he disappeared, and was seen no more. Nor to the inquiries made was there any answer given or any news of him ascertained. 'So wicked is this unhappy town,' wrote my mother, 'that men are capable of murdering even an innocent lad from the country for the sake of the silver buckles, or the very coat upon his back. Yet there are other ways in which he may have been drawn away. He loved not the thought of city life ; he may have taken the recruiting sergeant's shilling, or he may have been pressed for a sailor and sent to sea; or, which Heaven forbid, he may have been decoyed into bad company, and now be in the company of rogues. Whatever the cause, he hath disappeared and made no sign. Yet he seemed a good and honest lad.'

So perplexed were we with the strange and unintelligible intelligence that, after turning it about in talk for a week, it was resolved that we would consult Mr. Carnaby in the matter. It would perhaps have been better if we had kept the thing to ourselves. For this gentleman, though he kindly considered the case, could do nothing to remove the dreadful doubt under which we lay, except that he recommended us to patience and resignation, virtues which, Heaven knows! we women who stay at home must needs continually practise. We should, I say, have done better had we held our tongues, because Mr. Carnaby told the barber, who told the townsfolk one by one, and then it was whispered about that Ralph had joined the gipsies, according to some; or been pressed and sent to sea, according to others; or had enlisted, according to others; with wild stories told in addition, born of imagination, idle or malignant, as that he had joined a company of common rogues and robbers; or—but I scorn to repeat these things. Everybody, however, at this juncture, remembered the wicked things said of the boy by his cousin. As for Mathew himself, overjoyed at the welcome news, which he received open-mouthed, so to speak, he went about calling all his acquaintance to witness that he had long since prophesied ruin and disaster to the boy, which, indeed, to the fullest extent, a lad so depraved as to horsewhip his own guardian richly deserved. As for coming back, he said, that was not likely, and indeed impossible, because he was already knocked on the head—Mathew was quite convinced of this—in some midnight brawl, or at least fallen so low that he would never dare to return among respectable people. These things we could not believe, yet they sank into our hearts and made us uneasy. For where could the boy be, and why did he not send us one letter, at least, to tell us what he had done, and how he had fared?

'Child,' said my grandmother, 'it is certain that Mathew does not wish his cousin to return. He bears malice in his heart against the boy, and he remembers that should he never come back the mill will be his own.' Already he began to give himself the airs of the master, and to talk of selling a field here and a field there, and of improving the property, as if all was his.

'He will come back,' said the Fugleman. 'Brave hearts and lusty legs do not get killed. Maybe, he hath enlisted. Then he may have gone a soldiering to America, or somewhere in the world, and no doubt will get promotion—aye, corporal first, sergeant next, and perhaps be made Fugleman. Or, maybe, as your lady mother says, he hath been pressed, and is now at sea, so that he cannot write. But, wherever he is, be sure he is doing well. Wherefore, heart up!'

Well, to shorten the story, we got no news at all, and could never discover for many years what had become of the boy. When four years had passed by without a word or line from him, Mathew grew horribly afraid because Ralph's one-and-twentieth birthday drew near, and he thought the time was come when the heir would appear and claim his own. What preparations he made to receive him I know not. Perhaps a blunderbuss and a cup of poison. But the day passed, and there was no sign of Ralph. Then, indeed, Mathew became quite certain that he would no more be disturbed and that the mill was his own.

As for myself, I sat at home chiefly with my grandmother, who was now beginning to grow old, yet brisk and notable still. There was a great deal to be done, and the days passed swiftly to industrious hands ; yet not one so busy and not one so swift but I could find time to think and to pray for Ralph. As for diversions, for those who want them, there are plenty. Do not think that in our little north-country town we have any cause to envy the pleasures of town. Why, to begin with, there are the mummers at Christmas ; all through the dark evenings the lads gamble at candle creel for the stable-lanterns ; on New Year's Eve we sit up all night long and keep the fire burning—it is dreadful bad luck to borrow fire on a New Year's morning ; in the summer there comes the fair ; on Sunday afternoons, for the young men there is wrestling, with quarter-staff and cock-fighting. At harvest-time there is the March of the Kirn baby—

> The master's corn is ripe and shorn,
> We bless the day that he was born ;
> Shouting a kirn—a kirn—ahoa !

with the feast afterwards and the cushion-dance, at which the old song of 'Prinkham Prankham' is always sung, and the girls are kissed, a proceeding which seems never to fail in causing the liveliest satisfaction to the men, though why they should wish to kiss young persons for whom they do not feel any affection, and perhaps, even any respect, passes my poor comprehension. I have seen, on these occasions, a gentleman kiss a dairymaid, and dissemble so well that one might say he liked it. Besides these amusements, the men had the excitement of the smuggling, whereof you will hear more presently.

To look back upon, in spite of these amusements, it was a long and dreary time of waiting. Yet still the Fugleman kept up my heart, and Sailor Nan swore, as if she was still captain of the foretop, that he would come home safe. I was young, happily, and youth is the time for hope. And about the end of the sixth year I had cause to think about other things, because my own misfortunes began.

I had long observed in the letters of my dear parents a certain difference, which constantly caused doubt and questioning ; for my mother exhorted me continually in every letter to the practice of frugality, thrift, simple living, and the acquisition of housewifely knowledge, and, in short, all those virtues which especially adorn the condition of poverty. She also never failed to bid me reflect upon the uncertainty of human affairs and the instability of fortune ; and every letter furnished examples of rich men becoming poor, and great ladies reduced to beg their bread. My grandmother bade me lay these things to heart, and I perceived that she was disturbed, and she would have written to my father to ask if things were going ill, but for two reasons. The first was that she could neither read nor write, those arts not having been taught her in her childhood ; and I testify that she was none the worse for want of them, but her natural shrewdness even increased, because she had to depend upon herself, and could not still be running to a book for guidance. The second reason was that the letters of my father, both to her and to myself, were full of glorious anticipation and confidence. Yes ; while my mother wrote in sadness, he wrote in triumph ; when she bade me learn to scour pots, he commanded me to study the fashions ; when she prophesied disaster, he proclaimed good fortune. Thus, he ordered that I was to be taught whatever could be learned in so remote a town as Warkworth, and that especial care was to be taken in my carriage and demeanour, begging my grandmother to observe the deportment of Mistress Carnaby, and to bid me copy her as an example ; for, he said, a city heiress not uncommonly married with a gentleman of good family, though impoverished fortunes ; that some city heiresses had of late married noblemen ; that as he had no son, nor any other child but myself, I would inherit the whole of his vast fortune (I thought how I could give it all to Ralph), and, therefore, I must study how to maintain myself in the position which I should shortly occupy ; that he was already of the Common Council, and looked before long to be made Alderman, after which it was but a step to Sheriff first and Lord Mayor afterwards ; that he intended to build or buy a great house worthy of his wealth ; and that he did not wish me to return home until such time as this house was in readiness, because, as one might truly say, his present dwelling in Cheapside, though convenient for his business and the place where his fortune was made, was but a poor place, quite unworthy of an heiress, and he wished that I should be seen nowhere until he had prepared a fitting place for my reception ; that, in point of beauty, he hoped and doubted not that I should be able to set off and adorn the jewels and fine dresses which he designed presently to give me ; and that he desired me especially to pay very particular attention not to seem quite rustical and country-bred, and to remember that the common speech of Northumberland would raise a laugh in London. With much more to the same effect.

I say not that my father wrote all this in a single letter, but in several, so that all these things became implanted in my mind, and both my grandmother and myself were, in spite of my mother's letters, firmly persuaded that we were already very rich and considerable people, and that my father was a merchant of the greatest renown—already a Common Councilman, and shortly to be Alderman, Sheriff, and Lord Mayor—in the City of London. This belief was also held by our neighbours and friends, and it gave my grandmother, who was, besides, a lady of dignified manners, more consideration than she would otherwise have obtained, with the title of Madam, which was surely due to the mother of so great and successful a man.

Now the truth was this : my father was the most sanguine of men, and the most ready to deceive himself. He lived continually (if I may presume to say so without breaking the fifth commandment) in a fool's paradise. When he was a boy nothing would do for him but he must go to London, refusing to till the acres which would afterwards be his own, because he was ambitious, and ardently desired to be another Whittington. See the dangers of the common chap books, in which he had read the story of this great Lord Mayor ! He so far resembled Whittington that he went up to London (by waggon from Newcastle) with little in his pocket, except a letter of recommendation from the then Vicar of Warkworth to his brother, at the time a glover in Cheapside. How he became apprentice—like Whittington—to this glover, how he fell in love—like Whittington—with his master's daughter, how he married her—like Whittington—and inherited the business, stock, capital, goodwill, and all, may here only be thus briefly told ; but by the death of his master he became actual and sole owner of a London shop, whereupon my poor father's brain being always full of visions, he was inflamed with the confidence that now, indeed, he had nothing to look for but the making of an immense fortune. Worse than this, he thought that the fortune would come of its own accord. How a man living in the city of London could make so prodigious a mistake I know not. Therefore he left the whole care of the business to his wife and his apprentices, and for his own part spent the day in coffee-houses or on 'Change, or wherever merchants and traders meet together. This made him full of great talk, and he presently proceeded to imagine that he himself was concerned in the great ventures and enterprises of which he heard so much ; or, perhaps, because he could not actually have thought himself a merchant adventurer, he believed that before long he also should be embarking cargoes to the East and West Indies, running under convoy of frigates safe through the enemy's privateers. It was out of the profits of these imaginary cargoes that he was to obtain that vast wealth of which he continually thought and talked until, in the end, he believed that he possessed it. Meantime his poor wife, my mother, left in charge of the shop, and with her household cares as well, found, to her dismay, that the respectable business which her father had made was quickly falling from them, as their old friends died, one by one, or retired from trade, and no new ones coming in their places ; for, as I have been credibly informed, the business of a tradesman or merchant in London is so precarious and uncertain, that, unless it be constantly watched, pushed, nursed, encouraged, coaxed, fed and flattered, it presently withers away and perishes.

For want of the master's presence, for lack of pushing and encouragement, the yearly returns of the shop grew less and less. No one knew this except my mother. It was useless to tell my father. If she begged his attention to the fact, he only said that business was, in the nature of things, fluctuating ; that a bad year would be succeeded by a good year ; that large profits had recently been made by traders to Calicut and Surinam, where he had designs of employing his own capital, and that ventures to Canton had of late proved extremely successful. Alas, poor man ! he had no capital left, for now all was gone--capital, credit, and custom. Yet he still continued to believe that his shop, the shop which came to him with his wife, was bringing him, every year, a great and steady return, and that he was amassing a fortune.

One day—it was a Saturday evening in May—in the year seventeen hundred and seventy, six years after the flight of Ralph Embleton, when I was in my seventeenth year, and almost grown to my full height, I saw coming slowly along the narrow road which leads from the highway to Warkworth a country cart, and in it two persons, the driver walking at the horse's head. I stood at the garden-gate watching this cart idly, and the setting sun behind it, without so much as wondering who these persons might be, until presently it came slowly down the road, which here slopes gently to the river and the bridge, and pulled up in front of our gate. When the cart stopped a lady got quickly down and seized my hands.

' You are my Drusilla ?' she asked, and without waiting for a reply, because she was my mother and knew I could be no other than her own daughter, she fell upon my neck in a passion of weeping and sobbing, saying that she knew I was her daughter dear, and that she was my most unhappy ruined mother. It was my father who descended after her. He advanced with dignified step and the carriage of one in authority. I observed that his linen and the lace of his ruffles were of the very finest, and his coat, though dusty, of the finest broadcloth. He seemed not to perceive my mother's tears ; he kissed me and gave me his blessing. He bade the carter, with majestic air, lead the ' coach '—he called the country cart a coach—and take great care of the horse, which he said was worth forty guineas if a penny ; but the horse was a ten-year-old cart-horse, worth at most four guineas, as I knew very well, because I knew the carrier.

Amazed at this extraordinary behaviour, I led my parents to my grandmother, and then we presently learned the truth. My father, if you please, was ruined ; he was a bankrupt ; his schemes of greatness had come to nothing ; his vast fortune lay in his imagination only ; he had lost his wife's money and his own. He had returned to his native county, his old friends having clubbed together and made a little purse for him, and his creditors having

consented to accept what they could get and to give him a quittance
in full, because he was known to be a man of integrity ; otherwise
he might have been lodged in gaol, where many an unfortunate,
yet honest, man lieth in misery.

. The disaster was more than my father's brain could bear.
Nothing more dreadful can happen to a merchant and one in trade
than to become a bankrupt. To lose his money is bad, but many
a man loses his all, yet does not become bankrupt, and so saves his
credit. A merchant's credit is for him what his honour is to a
soldier, his piety to a divine, her virtue to a woman, his skill to a
craftsman. My father, I say, could not bear it. First, as soon as
he fairly understood what had happened, he fell into a lethargy,
sitting in a chair all day in silence, and desiring nothing but to be
left alone. After a while the lethargy changed into a restlessness,
and he must needs be up and doing something—it mattered not
what. Then the restlessness disappeared and he became again his
old self, as cheerful, as sanguine, as confident, with no other
change than a more settled dignity of bearing, caused by the belief,
the complete delusion, that now his fortune was indeed made ; that
he possessed boundless wealth, and that he was going to leave
London and to retire into the country, as many great merchants
used to do, in order to enjoy it.

He was perfectly reasonable on all other points ; he could talk
on politics or on religion, on London matters, on the affairs of
Warkworth, or on the interests of the farmers ; but always on the
assumption of his own wealth. The broad fields everywhere he
believed to be his own. If he came with me, as he often did, when
I milked the cow, fed the pigs and the chickens, made the bread,
brewed the beer, or turned the churn, he laughed at what he was
pleased to call the condescension of his heiress in doing this menial
work, and called me his pretty shepherdess. And sometimes he
entertained me with stories of how his fortune was made. Chiefly
I found his imagination ran upon Canton, with trade in tea and silk.

' It is very well known,' he would say, ' that those who venture
in the Greek seas and the Levant run very heavy risks ; they are
more dangerous, my dear child, than many places much farther
away. I considered the Levant trade carefully, before embarking
my money in foreign ventures. I was always prudent, perhaps too
prudent. Yet the end hath justified me. Eh, Drusilla, hath not
the end justified me ? Why, I have known a man on 'Change
worth this day a plum—a round plum, child—and to-morrow not
half that sum, by reason of losses in the treacherous Levant. But,
alas ! there are perils in every sea. Tempests and hurricanes
arise ; there are hidden rocks ; there are fires at sea ; ships are
becalmed—all these things we call the Hand of God ; there are
also pirates everywhere ; they lurk in the Mahometan ports of
Morocco, Algiers, Tripoli, and Tunis ; they hide in the fever-
smitten harbours of Madagascar—but men born to be hanged
laugh at fever ; they abound in the West Indies and in the Narrow

Seas. We are always at war with some great power, and therefore
we have privateers to dread ; these, my dear, are more desperate
and blood-thirsty villains even than your murderous pirates. And
there is danger from mutiny aboard, whereby friends of my own—
substantial men, mark you, on 'Change—have lost many a noble
ship and precious cargo. We on 'Change think nothing of these
chances ; we are on the mountains one day and in the depths the
next. Yet, like the good old country to which we belong, we
weather the storm, and in the end grow rich. Rich ? Drusilla, my
child, we grow enormously rich. The Earl of Northumberland
himself, with all his acres, is not so rich as your father.'

My mother spoke of him, when he was not present, with a
bitterness which grieved me sore. But I knew not the trouble she
had had, and the long anticipation of this trouble. It appeared,
indeed, as if a sound, though modest, business, with the certainty
of a competence, had been thrown away and wasted for want of a
little—only a little forethought and care. My father, at the best,
was only a simple glover with a small shop and two apprentices.
What could a poor lad from Northumberland expect more ? All
that a woman can do my mother had done. But in trade a woman
can do but little. She can serve, but she cannot go about and
make trade—she cannot persuade Merchant Adventurers to load
their ships with her wares. Yet, even with the memory of her
wrongs, and her ruined hopes, she was always gentle and forbearing
in the presence of her afflicted husband, careful to keep him happy
in his delusion, and tender with him, so that he should never feel
the mischief he had done.

As for our means, I dared not ask. But presently I learned
that all we had was the annuity of forty pounds a year, which
would terminate with my grandmother's death, the cottage in
which we lived, and a slender stock of money, I knew not how
much, in my mother's hands.

Alas ! this was the end of my splendid hopes—of my father's
triumphant letters ! I was indeed an heiress !

CHAPTER VI.

THE LETTER AT LAST.

ONE must accept without murmuring the ordinances of Providence.
Murmuring avails nothing, and cannot restore things lost. The
hand which gives also takes away. The loss of that fortune, which
I knew only by hearsay, and expected without eagerness, affected
me but little in comparison with the burden of two more to keep
upon our forty pounds a year. I saw clearly that I must henceforth rise early and work late, and no more eat any bread of idleness.
We had a servant, but we now sent her away, my mother and I

doing all the house-work. In addition, I fed the poultry and milked the cow.

The good old Fugleman came every day as soon as he heard of our misfortunes and understood that I could no more go to the castle of an afternoon, and became of very great service indeed, for he kept the garden for us, and talked with my father, who, to be sure, was best out of the house, where he was only in our way. He also—which was kind of him—took the management of the pigs. And I must also confess my great obligations to Mrs. Carnaby, who, understanding the straits into which we were fallen, was so good as to send me and persuade other ladies of this part of the county to send me fine work to do, by means of which I earned a little money, which went into the common purse and was useful. My mother wept to think that I must rise at five, and, after doing the house-work and the out-door work, making butter and sending it away to be sold with eggs and cream-cheese and other little things—it was not much we got, but something—to be compelled to sit down in the afternoon to my needle, and work till nine at night. But I was a tall strong girl ; work did me no harm. I should have been happy but that I saw my grandmother grow daily weaker. She sickened and began to fail when she saw her son, of whom she was so proud, return a beggar to his native county, and when she heard his poor deluded talk. A grievous sight it was to see the poor old lady, once so strong and active, sit feeble in her chair by the fireside, while her sad eyes followed her son as he proudly walked to and fro in the room and told the tale of his investments and his wealth. Sometimes I noted how my mother looked wistfully upon this spectacle of age and decay, and saw how her mouth worked and her lips moved, and knew well that she was saying to herself, ' When she dies, what next ? ' And then I was fain to go away into the garden, where they could not hear me, and cry over troubles of the present and fears of the future which seemed hard to be borne.

' Don't cry, Miss Drusy '—yet the good old Fugleman, looked as if he, too, would willingly shed a tear—' don't cry ; think to yourself that when the boy comes home all will go well again. Merry as a wedding-bell shall we be then.'

' Ah, when—when ? '

We had two visitors who came often. One of them was his Worship Mr. Cuthbert Carnaby. He came, he said, in order to profit by the experience and conversation of my father.

' I know, child,' he said, ' and greatly commiserate, the disorder of his brain, yet I cannot but marvel at the extent of his knowledge, the justice of his remarks, and the weight of his opinion. It is indeed a marvel to me that one so richly endowed by Providence with understanding should have so conspicuously failed in the business of his life, which was to grow rich.'

I take pleasure in quoting the testimony of so eminent an authority to the great qualities possessed by my unfortunate father,

and it did one good to see them walking in the garden, my father
bearing himself with the deference due to a gentleman of good old
family, yet expecting equal deference to himself as a man of great
success and wealth, and both arguing on the politics and the
conduct of affairs with as much gravity as two plenipotentiaries or
ambassadors extraordinary.

Strange it was, indeed, to think that one was mad who could
converse so rationally, with such just estimate of things, with so
true a knowledge of their proportion, so vast a fund of information
as to the state of trade all over the world, the value of gold, the
balance of profit, the growth of industries ; yea, and even the
power and prospects of foreign states, with their wants and their
dangers. Or that one could be mad who could set forth with such
lucidity the foundation of our Christian faith, and the arguments
for the doctrines taught in our churches. He was not only sane,
but he was a man worth listening to on all subjects—save one.
For he was fully possessed with the idea that he was as wealthy as
he had ever desired to be. His poor brain was turned, indeed, on
this point, and after a while I thought little of it, because we
became accustomed to it, and because it seemed a harmless craze.
Yet it was not harmless, as you will hear. Indeed, even an
innocent babe in arms may be made the instrument of mischief in
the hands of a wicked man.

Our second visitor was Mathew Humble. He came first, he
said, to pay his respects to my father. Then he began to come
with great regularity. But I perceived soon, for I was no longer a
child, but already a woman, that he had quite another object in
view, for he cast his eyes upon me in such a way as no woman can
mistake. Even to look upon those eyes of his made me turn sick
with loathing. Why, if this man had been another Apollo for
beauty I would not have regarded him ; and so far was he from an
Apollo that a fat and loathsome Satyr more nearly resembled him.

He was already three or four and thirty, which I, being seventeen, regarded as a very great age indeed ; and most Northumbrian
folk are certainly married and the fathers of children already tall
before that time.

He was a man who made no friends, and lived alone with his
sister Barbara. No girl at all, so far as I know, could boast of
having received any attention from him ; he was supposed to care
for nothing except money and strong drink. Every evening
he sat by himself in the room which overlooks the river, with
account-books before him, and drank usquebaugh. But he loved
brandy as well, or Hollands, or rum, or indeed anything which was
strong. And being naturally short of stature he was grown fat and
gross, with red hanging cheeks, which made his small eyes look
smaller and more pig-like, a double chin, and a nose which already
told a tale of deep potations, so red and swollen was it. What girl
of seventeen could regard with favour—even if there were no image
of a brave and comely boy already impressed upon her heart—such

a man as this, a mere tosspot and a drinker? And, worst of all, a
secret and solitary drinker—a gloomy drinker.

It was strange that, about the time when Ralph's disappearance
was first heard of, rumours ran about the town that perhaps the
mill would turn out, after all, to be the property of Mathew
Humble; that these rumours were revived at the approach of
Ralph's twenty-first birthday; and that again, when Mathew first
began his approaches to me, the rumour was again circulated. By
the help of the Fugleman I traced these rumours to the barber;
and, still with his help—because every man must be shaved, and,
while being shaved, must talk—I traced these to none other than
Mathew himself. He had, then, some object to gain; I knew not
what at the time. Later on I discovered that his design was to
make it appear—should Ralph ever return—that I had taken him
for a husband when I thought he was the actual master and owner
of all; for I believe he allowed himself no doubt as to the result
of his offers. Doth it not seem as if the uglier, the older, the less
attractive a man is, whether in person or in mind, the more certain
he becomes of conquering a woman's heart?

The rumour on this occasion was more certain and distinct than
before. It was now stated that Mr. Embleton was discovered
to have made a later will, which had been proved, and was ready
to be produced, if necessary; that in this will the testator, after
deploring the badness of heart manifested by his nephew Ralph,
devised the whole of his property to his nephew Mathew. The
barber, for his part, had no doubt of the truth of this report; but
those who asked Mathew whether it was true, received mysterious
answers, as that time would show; that in this world no one should
be certain of anything; that many is the slip between cup and
lip; that should an occasion arise the truth of the story would be
tested; such oracles as incline the hearers to believe all that has
been said—and more. Barbara, his sister, for her own part, showed
great willingness to answer any questions which might be put to
her. But she knew little; her brother, she said, was a close man,
who sat much alone and spoke little.

And then the Fugleman told me a very strange story indeed,
and one which seemed to bode no good to any of us. By this time
I so regarded Mathew that I could not believe he could do or design
aught but evil. This was wrong, but he was most certainly a man
of very evil disposition.

His own private business, the Fugleman told me—this was
nothing in the world, as I very well knew, but the snaring of
rabbits, hares, partridges, and other game on the banks of the river
—led him sometimes past Morwick Mill, in the evening or late at
night. There was a room in the mill—the same room in which
Mathew was vanquished and beaten—the window of which looked
out upon the river, which is here a broad and shallow brook. The
bank rises steep on the other side, and is clothed with thick hanging
woods in which no one ever walked except the Fugleman, and he,

for those purposes I have just mentioned, always alone and after sundown. Now his eyes were like unto the eyes of a hawk ; they knew not distance ; they could see, quite far off, little things as well as great things ; and the Fugleman saw, night after night, that Mathew Humble was sitting locked up in his room, engaged in writing or copying something. I believe that if the Fugleman had known how to read, he would have read the writing even across the river. Unhappily, he had never learned that art. Mathew was making a copy, the Fugleman said, of some other document. But what that document was he could not tell. It was something on large sheets of paper, and in big handwriting. He wrote very slowly, comparing word for word with the papers which he seemed copying. Once when there was a noise as of someone at the door, he huddled all the papers together, and bundled them away in a corner quickly and with an affrighted air. He was therefore doing something secret, which means something wicked. What could it be ?

'Little he thinks,' said the Fugleman, 'that Master Ralph is sure to come home and confound his knavish tricks, and trip up his heels for him. Ah, I think I see him now, in lace ruffles and good broadcloth, walking up the street with a fine City Madam on his arm.'

I should have been very well contented with the lace ruffles and good broadcloth—indeed, I asked for nothing better—but I wanted no fine City Madam at the mill.

Later on I learned what this thing was which he took so long to copy, and which gave him so much anxiety. But it was like a fire-ship driven back by the wind among the vessels of those who sent it forth.

One morning when I was busy in the kitchen with household work, and my mother was engaged upon the family sewing, Mathew came and begged to have some conversation with her. He said that, first of all, he was fully acquainted with her circumstances, and the unhappy outlook before her, when my grandmother should die and leave us all without any income at all ; that, being of a compassionate heart, he was strongly minded to help them ; and that the best way, as well as he could judge, would be to make her daughter Drusilla his wife. This done, he would then see that their later years would be attended with comfort and the relief of all anxiety.

At first my mother did not reply. She had no reason to love Mathew, whose unkindness to his ward was well known to her. Again, she had still some remains of family pride left—you do not destroy a woman's pride by taking away her money. She thought, being the daughter of a well-to-do London citizen, that her child should look higher than a man who had nothing in the world of his own but thirty acres of land, although he lived at the mill and pretended to be its owner. And she very truly thought that the man was not in person likely to attract so young a girl as myself.

But she spoke him fair. She told him that I was young as yet, too young to know my own mind, and that perhaps he had better wait. He replied that he was not young, for his own part, and that he would not wait. Then she told him that she should not, certainly, force the inclinations of her daughter, but that she would speak to me about him.

She opened the subject to me in the evening. No sooner did I understand that Mathew had spoken for me than I threw myself upon my knees to my mother, and implored her with many tears and protestations not to urge me to accept his suit. I declared with vehemence, that if there were no other man in the world, I could not accept Mathew Humble. I reminded her of his behaviour towards Ralph. I assured her that I believed him to be one who sat drinking by himself, and a plotter of evil, a man with a hardened heart and a dead conscience.

Well, my mother shed tears with me, and said that I should not be married against my will ; that Mathew was not a good man, and that she would bid him, not uncourteously, go look elsewhere. This she did, thanking him for the honour he had proposed.

For some reason, perhaps because he did not really wish to marry me, perhaps because he had not thoroughly laid out the scheme of marrying me to revenge himself upon Ralph, Mathew gave me a respite for the time, though I went in great terror lest he might pester my mother or myself. Perhaps, which I think more likely, he trusted to the influence of poverty and privation, and was contented to wait till these should make me submissive to his will.

However that may be, he said nothing more concerning love, and continued his visits to my father, in whose conversation he took so great a pleasure. Oh, villain !

Things were in this posture, I being in the greatest anxiety and fear that something terrible was going before long to happen to us, when a most joyful and unexpected event happened.

It was in the month of May, seven years since Ralph's flight— like the followers of Mohammed, I reckoned the years from the Flight—that this event happened.

The event was this, that the Fugleman had a letter sent to him —the first letter he ever received in his life.

I saw the post-boy riding down the road early in the afternoon ; he passed by the house of Mr. Carnaby, where he sometimes stopped, past our cottage, where he never stopped because there was nobody who wrote letters to us, and over the bridge, his horse's hoofs clattering under the old gateway. I thought he was going to the vicarage, but he left that on his right and rode straight up the street, blowing his horn as he went. I wondered, but had no time to waste in wonder, who was going to get a letter in that part of the town. The letter, in fact, was for no other than the Fugleman.

Half an hour later the Fugleman, who had been at work in the

garden all the morning, came down the town again, and asked me—
with respect to her ladyship, my mother—if I would give him five
minutes' talk. With him was Sailor Nan, because the thing was
altogether so strange that he could not avoid telling her about it,
and she came with him, curious as a woman, though bold and brave
as becomes an old salt.

''Tis a strange thing,' said the Fugleman, turning the unopened
letter over and over in his hand ; ''tis a strange thing ; here is a
letter which tells me I know not what—comes from I know not
where. I have paid 3s. 8d. for it. A great sum. I doubt I was a
fool. It may mean money, and it may mean loss.'

'Burn it, and ha' done,' said Sailor Nan. ''Tis from some land
shark. Burn the letter.'

'I am sixty, or mayhap seventy years of age. Sixty, I must a-
be. Yes ; sure and certain, sixty. Yet never a letter in all my
days before.'

Now, which is very singular, not the least suspicion in our minds
as to the writer of the letter.

'Is it,' I asked, 'from a cousin or a brother ?'

'Cousin ?' he repeated, with the shadow of a smile across his
stiff lips. 'Why, I never had a father or a mother, to say nothing of
a brother or a cousin. When I first remember anything, I was
running in the streets with other boys. We stole our breakfast,
we stole our dinner, and we stole our supper. Where are they all
now, those little rogues and pickpockets, my companions ? Hanged,
I doubt not. What but hanging can have come to them ? But as
for me, by the blessing of the Lord, I was enlisted in the 14th
Line, and after a few hundreds taken mostly by three dozen doses,
which now are neither here nor there, and are the making of a lad,
I was flogged into a good soldier, and so rose as was due to merit.
A hearty three dozen, now and then, laid on with a will in the cool
of the morning, works miracles. Not such a regiment in the service as the 14th. And why ? Because the colonel knew his duty
and did it without fear or favour, and the men were properly
trounced. Good comrades all, and brave boys. And where are
they ? Dead, I take it ; beggars, some ; fallen in action, some ;
broke, some ; in comfortable berths, like me, some. If all were
living, who would there be to send me a letter, seeing there wasn't
a man in all the regiment who could write ?'

Strange that not one of us even then guessed the truth.

It was a great letter, thick and carefully sealed, addressed to
'Fugleman Furlong, At his room in the Castle of Warkworth,
Northumberland, England.' It came from foreign parts, and the
paper was not only stained, but had a curious fragrance.

I broke the seal and tore open the covering of the letter. Within was another packet. Oh, Heavens ! It was addressed to
'Drusilla Hetherington, care of the Fugleman, to be forwarded
without delay. Haste—post haste !'

And then I knew without waiting to open the letter that it would

N

be from none other than Ralph. It must be from Ralph. After all these years, we were to hear once more from Ralph. I stood pale and trembling, nor could I for some moments even speak. At last I said:

'Fugleman—Nan—this letter is addressed to me. It is, I verily believe, from Ralph Embleton. Wait a little, while I read it.'

'Read it—read it!' cried the old man.

Could I—ah! merciful Heaven—could I ever forget the rapture, the satisfied yearning, the blissful content, the gratitude, with which I read that sweet and precious letter? They waited patiently; even the rude and coarse old woman refrained from speech while I read page after page. They said nothing though they saw the tears falling down my face, because they knew that they were tears of happiness.

After seven long years, my Ralph was talking to me as he used to talk. I knew his voice, I recognised his old imperious way, I saw that he had not changed. As if he would ever change!

When I had finished and dried my tears they begged me to read his letter to them.

'My dear, dear Girl'—I told them that I could not indeed, read all, but that I would read them what I could; and this was the beautiful beginning, in order that I should know at the outset, so thoughtful he was, and for fear of my being anxious on the point, that he loved me still, and had never forgotten me. 'My dear, dear Girl,—It is now six years since I bade you farewell at your garden-gate and started upon my journey to London. Your father has doubtless told you how I presented myself and with what kindness he received me. I am very sure that you have not forgotten me, and I hope that you will rejoice to hear of my good fortune'—Hope, indeed! Could he not be sure?—'I have no doubt also that he hath informed you of the strange good fortune which befell me after he left me at the East India Company's House, of which I told him by letter and special messenger, to whom I gave, to ensure speed and safe delivery, one shilling.' (But it would appear that this wicked messenger broke his word, and took the shilling, but did nothing for it—a common thief, who deserved to be hanged, like many another no more wicked than himself. Oh! what punishment too great for this breach of trust, small as it seemed! See, now, what a world of trouble was caused by that little theft.) 'It was truly by special Providence that, while Mr. Silvertop talked with me, the great Captain who won the battle of Plassy should have been standing near and should have overheard what passed. When I was bidden go my ways for a foolish boy (because I did not wish to be a writer) and waste his time no longer, I was much cast down, for now I began to fear that I must, like the most of mankind, take what was assigned to me by Providence rather than what I would like. And I could plainly see that there remained only one choice for me; namely, I must return to the hated rule of my cousin who would keep me as a plough-boy as long as he could, or I must betake me to the task of sweeping out and serving a shop. And yet, what shop? But who would employ me? Therefore, I hung my head and stood irresolute without the Company's house. Now, presently, the gentleman whom I had seen within came forth with another officer, brave in scarlet. He saw me standing sadly beside the posts, and inspired by that noble generosity which has always distinguished this great man, he clapped his hand upon my shoulder.

' "So," he said, "you are the lad who loves a sword better than a pen?"

' "If it please your honour," I replied.

' "A sword means peril to life and limb," he said sternly; "he who goes a fighting in India must expect hard fare, rough sleeping, rude knocks. He must ever be on the watch against treachery. He must meet duplicity with equal cunning. He must obey blindly; he must never ask why; if he is sent to die like a rat in a hole, he must go without murmur or question. What! you think—do you?—that to carry a sword is to flaunt a scarlet coat before the ladies of St. James's?"

' "Nay, sir, with respect. I have read the lives of soldiers. I would willingly take the danger for the sake of the honour. But alas! I must stay at home and sweep a shop."

' "What is thy birth, boy?"

' I told him that, and satisfied him on other points, including the reason of my flight, in which I trust that I was no more than truthful. Then he said:

' "I am Lord Clive," and paused as if to know whether I had heard of him.

' You may be sure I was astonished, but I quickly doffed my hat and made him my best country-bred bow.

' "My lord," I said, "we have heard, even in Northumberland, of Plassy."

' "Good! I went to India as a writer—a miserable quill-driving writer. Think of that. What one man has done another may do. Now, boy, I sail this day for India. There will be more fighting, a great deal more fighting. If you please you shall go as a cadet with me. But there is no time to hesitate: I sail this day. Choose between the shop-sweeping and the musket. You will fight in the ranks at first, but if you behave well the sword will come after. Choose—peace and money-scraping at home like these smug-faced fat citizens," he swept his hand with lordly contempt, "or fighting and poverty, and perhaps death abroad. Choose."

' "I humbly thank your lordship," I said, "I will follow you if you will condescend to take me."

' Then he bade me go straight to Limehouse Pool, where I should find the ship at anchor. I was to take a note to the purser who would give me an outfit.

' Thus, my dear Drusilla, did I find my fortune and sail to
N 2

foreign parts under as brave and great a captain as this country
will ever see.

'Our voyage lasted eleven months. There were three hundred
raw recruits on board, mostly kidnapped or inveigled under false
pretences by crimps and the scoundrels of Wapping. When they were
first paraded, they were as beggarly-looking a lot as you would
wish to see, ragged, dirty, mutinous, and foul-mouthed. Yet in a
couple of months, by daily drill, by good food and sea air, by
moderate rations of rum, by sound flogging, by the continual discipline of the boatswain's rope's end and the sergeant's rattan, the
regimental supple-jack, and the ship's cat-o'-nine tails, they became
as promising soldiers as one would wish. As for me, I stood with
them in the drill and did my best. Of course I could not expect
his lordship to notice so humble a cadet as myself, but one evening,
when we were near the end of our voyage, he sent for me and
gave me a glass of wine, and kindly bade me be patient and of
good cheer, because, he said, young gentlemen of merit and courage
would be sure to find opportunities for distinction.'

Ralph then went on to describe the life of a soldier in India,
and to tell me—but this I leave out for fear of being tedious—how
he received his commission and how he got promotion. It is
sufficient to say that at the time he wrote, after six years of service,
he held the commission of a captain. Nor was that all. He had
been able to render such signal service to a certain Rajah, that this
prince, who was not ungrateful, and hoped, besides, for more such
services, took him one day into his treasure-house and bade him
help himself to all if he pleased.

'My dear,' he continued, 'I knew not that the world contained
so much treasure. Yet this Rajah is but a petty prince, and his
wealth is as nothing compared with that of many others. There
were diamonds in bags, uncut, whose worth I know not, and
diamonds in rings, sword-handles, and women's gauds ; there were
rubies, emeralds, sapphires, turquoises, opals, and all kinds of
precious stones strung rudely on common string as if they were but
pebbles. There were also gold and silver vessels of all kinds, and
there were casks full of gold coins. As I took out a handful I saw
that many of them were ancient, with Greek characters, perhaps
left in this country by that great soldier Alexander. When I had
surveyed these wonders I thanked him, and said that I should not
presume to take so much as a single gold coin from his treasure,
but that if it should please his Highness to offer me a present, I
should accept it with gratitude, provided it was not too costly. He
laughed at these words, and when we came away I was so loaded
with gold that I fancied myself already a rich man.

'Since this event it hath pleased Lord Clive to issue an order
which prohibits officers from accepting henceforth any presents at
all from the native princes. I cannot but feel grateful that the
order was not issued before my own good fortune. Doubtless his
Excellency hath good reasons for this order, which places the

military service at a disadvantage compared with the writers, who have great opportunities of making fortunes ; and I cannot but think that it is a more noble thing to win a fortune at the point of the sword, than by such arts as are daily practised by the writers and civil servants of the Company. There are many Englishmen, and many Frenchmen as well—but we are driving them out of the country—who have become rich in the military service of the Indian princes ; yet I shall not exchange my present masters so long as the merchants—who think nothing of glory or of this country, yet a great deal of their dividends—perceive that it is for their safety, as well as for their credit, to extend their power ; and I have a reasonable hope that the good fortune which hath hitherto attended me may continue, so that I may return to my native country, if only in my old age, amply provided. As regards the climate, I have as yet experienced no great inconvenience from the heat. The natives have learned to fear an Englishman rather than to love him, which is, methinks, the thing we should most desire when we have to rule over people as ignorant of the Christian virtues, although not barbarous, like the naked blacks, but a most ingenious, dexterous, and skilful people, and of subtle intellect, yet slothful of body, lovers of rest, deceivers, regardless of truth, for ever scheming plots and contriving subtleties, and more cruel to prisoners than the Spanish Inquisition. The best amongst them are followers of Mahomet, who make faithful servants and good soldiers. It is a country where the ambition and jealousy of princes are continually causing fresh wars to be undertaken, and where a European may lead a life of adventure to his heart's content.'

I was reading, as I have said, this letter aloud in presence of my two faithful friends. Now when I spoke of the drill on board, and the sergeant's rattan and the regimental supple-jack, the Fugleman drew himself upright and shouldered the garden-spade, because there was no pike at hand ; and when I read of the bos'n's rope's end and the ship's cat-o'-nine tails, Sailor Nan cocked her hat and stood with feet apart and hands upon her hips, and began, but in a whisper, to murmur strange sea-oaths ; and when I read the account of the fight in which Ralph's courage saved this grateful Rajah—it was a most dreadful battle, in which hundreds of brave fellows and treacherous Hindoos were killed, so that to read it made one's heart cease to beat—the Fugleman, carried beyond himself, executed capers with the spade which signified little to my ignorant eyes, but which were, I believe, the movements with which the trained soldier attacks with the bayonet, and the old sailor with a mop-stick cut down her thousands, mighty curses rolling softly from her lips like distant thunder.

If the beginning of the letter was delightful, judge how beautiful was the end:

'I have now, my dear, told you all that concerns myself. I suppose you have long since left Warkworth and gone to live with your parents, to whom I beg to convey my respects and best wishes. If, among your rich friends and the gaieties of the fashion '—the ' gaieties ! '—' you have found lovers (as, to be sure, you must) and a husband, or one whom you have distinguished with your favour and regard, you will remember that I shall ever be to you as a brother ; for, lover or brother, I can never cease to love——'

'A good lad !' said the Fugleman.

'As ever trod the deck !' said the sailor.   'Go on, Miss Drusy.'

'And I am sure that you have grown up as tall and as beautiful as an angel.'

'She has,' said the Fugleman.

'Taller, ye lubber,' said the sailor, 'and more beautiful an angel than ever I clapped eyes on, nor never a Peg nor a Poll at Sheerness or Deptford or the Common Hard to show a candle alongside her.   What's even a frigate in full sail compared with a lovely woman ?'

This enthusiasm for the loveliness of her own sex (unusual among old women), I put down to her naval experiences and familiarity with sailor talk, and went on quickly ; because, if Ralph loved to flatter me, I ought not to let these poor people follow his example.   An angel ! But men are so. They cannot give enough ; they lavish their praises, as they lavish the very fruits of their labours, upon the women they love. We women measure our gifts —except to our boys. I pass over, therefore, the fond words of a lover about blue eyes and curling hair, and Nymphs in cool grots, and soft smiles and other imaginary gifts and graces, all of which my listeners applauded, nodding their heads. Oh ! he could say what he pleased, he could imagine all the perfections, so that he continued to tell me, as he did in this letter, how he thought upon me daily, and loved me always more and more.

'As for the address of this letter,' he said, 'I know not where in London or elsewhere your father may now reside ; therefore I forward it to the care of the Fugleman, with request that he will send it to you at the earliest opportunity, and by a safe hand. Will you, in return, inform him of my continued esteem and friend-ship ?'

'"Esteem and friendship !"' repeated the Fugleman. 'This from a Captain ! Was ever such a boy ?'

'And if you find an opportunity, tell Sailor Nan that half her fortune has come true.'

She replied that at her time of life it was odd if she couldn't tell the fortune of a boy, and as for the present cruise, it was bound to be a fairweather voyage.

Finally, my brave lover begged me to write to him and tell him all that had happened since his departure, and subscribed himself, with much love, Ralph Embleton.

When we had read the letter twice, which took us all the after-noon, and cost me three hours' sewing, we took counsel together.

First they were both for telling it about the town, and having a bonfire, with the ringing of the church bells in a triple bob major, but I was of opinion that it would be best to keep our own counsel for awhile. Therefore I bound them both to secresy and silence. I would let Mathew alone, and watch him. He should not know anything, not even that Ralph was alive and prosperous ; and had I kept this resolution, because my two friends were loyal and secret as the grave, it would have been better in the end for all of us, and much better for Mathew. But, as the wise man said, 'Death and life are in the power of the tongue.'

CHAPTER VII.

MATHEW'S FRIENDLY OFFER.

THIS letter made me, from one of the most unhappy of girls, the most joyous. The immediate prospect of poverty—for the Dame declined daily—the hard work which began at daylight and ended at bed-time, the certain knowledge that Mathew was not satisfied with a simple refusal—these things, which had before filled my mind with terror, now appeared like the imaginary spectres of the night, which cease to alarm when the day has dawned. To me it was more than the dawn of day ; it was the uprising of a glorious sun of love and hope. Ralph loved me ; Ralph was well, prosperous and in high esteem ; Ralph was already wealthy ; Ralph would come home, and all things would be well, whatever might happen at the moment. Yet this I could not tell to any. Mathew was not to know ; my poor old grandmother was too old now, and too failing of mind and body, to care for earthly things ; my father had clean forgotten the boy ; my mother would not greatly care to know ; nor would it soothe her anxieties to feel that we had a protector separated from us by the rolling seas and by a voyage of ten months or more. What good would be his far-off treasures to us, she would have asked, when what we want is beef for the pot and bread for the board ? As for my father's madness, it increased every day, so that now our cottage was a palace indeed, every meal was a banquet, and the small beer of my brewing was champagne, port, Malaga, or Imperial Tokay. But Mathew was too much with him, and it made me uneasy to observe how he complimented my father on his wisdom, his resolution, and his wonderful success.

'In all respects, madam,' he said to my mother, 'I find your husband most sensible and full of sound judgment. I have taken his counsel, of late, in many private matters of importance.'

'Then the Lord help you !' said my mother, sharply.

'What if he does exaggerate his private fortune ?' Mathew went on. 'It is a failing with many persons concerned in trade.'

'If you mean this in kindness, sir,' said my mother, 'I thank

you humbly for your good opinion of my poor distraught husband.
If you mean it in mockery, you are a most cruel man.'

'Indeed, madam,' he replied, bowing, 'pray believe that I
mean it in kindness.'

He had no kindness at all in his nature. He designed these
words to cover his iniquitous purpose.

So he continued to come and go, and to walk with my father in
the garden, and whatever wild things my father said he would
accept gravely as if they were indeed words of wisdom. No one,
except myself, suspected him of sinister designs, and my father
disclosed to him the whole prodigious extent of his madness, so
that I could have cried with shame and humiliation, Mathew
knowing well, as all the world knew by this time, that we were
little better than the poorest in the parish.

'The world, sir,' the poor gentleman would say, with a lofty
air, 'has yet to learn how great a benefactor a simple London
citizen may be. There have been many benefactors. I acknowledge their greatness. But wait, sir, until my will is opened and
read. To you, friend Mathew, I have bequeathed a poor ten
thousand pounds -no more.'

'Oh, sir!' He bowed and spread his hands. 'This is indeed
goodness.'

'It is the duty of a rich citizen to discover merit and to reward
it—the plain duty. I am a London citizen, and am perhaps more
proud of this position than becomes a Christian. The bulk of my
fortune I have left to my daughter, whom I design in marriage for
some great nobleman. But I have not forgotten the poor of my
native parish, Mathew—no, no ; and you will find, when my will
is read, that schools, a hospital, marriage-portions for the girls,
and apprentice-money for the boys, will attest my remembrance of
this place.'

'Sir,' said Mathew, with a grin of contempt, 'you will be a
benefactor indeed.'

Now, before I answered Ralph's letter, which I kept for more
than a month in my bosom, reading it every day when I could
snatch a moment, Mathew came to me, and after a little preamble,
of which I am going to tell you, re-opened the distasteful subject
of his courtship. I was in the garden, gathering herbs for a mint-
julep, when I saw him standing at the garden-gate. He looked so
jocund, he smiled so pleasantly, and he wore so self-satisfied an
air, that I was quite certain some evil thing had happened.

'Drusilla,' he said, 'I have heard certain intelligence. You
may depend upon its truth, which is confirmed in every particular.
I think that you should be the first to hear it, sad though it be,
yet what I could not but expect.'

'I suppose,' I said with a laugh, because I knew that he was
about to invent some wicked falsehood, 'I suppose you have got
something to tell me about Ralph, whom your cruel conduct drove
out into the world ?'

'Nay,' he replied, looking darkly, yet with a smile, 'you may say what you please; you cannot offend me. I have just come from Alnwick, where I sold four fat beasts. At the inn I fell in with a strolling player, and talked with him over a glass about his wandering life. Presently I asked him whether he had seen, anywhere upon his travels, especially in places where actors like himself, with profligates and thieves resort, such a lad as Ralph. It is wonderful to relate that he remembered seeing the boy at a place called Grantham. It was about six or seven years ago. The reprobate lad was making love—actually making love—to a young actress. When my informant came across the party again, Ralph had left them.'

At first I concluded that this was sheer fabrication, but afterwards gleaned that it was to a certain extent true; that is, that Ralph had made the acquaintance of the actress and her family on his way to London; but there was no love-making. How could there be, when he was already in love with me? And what follows was pure and clumsy invention.

'He wandered about with them playing and acting,' Mathew went on, 'for four or five years. Then he deserted them, or was turned out in disgrace—it matters not which—and, I am ashamed to say'—but he looked delighted—'took to the road, where he is now known everywhere as Black Ralph, or Bloody Ralph.'

'Are you quite sure of what you say?'

'As sure as I am that he will be hanged as soon as he is caught.'

I know not by what means Mathew persuaded himself, if indeed he did persuade himself, that Black Ralph, who was a notorious highwayman about this time, and practised his wicked calling upon the York Road, was Ralph Embleton. Yet he made so certain of it that he told—under strict promise of secrecy—the barber, who told everybody, also under promise of secrecy, and it was noised abroad that the distinction of giving birth to the most bloodthirsty villain in England belonged to Warkworth, and many people advised Mathew to go armed, and to provide his house with a loaded blunderbuss, a bull-dog, and a few man-traps, because his cousin would probably visit him with intent to murder as well as to rob.

'I suppose,' Mathew went on to me, 'that you will now give up thinking of that young vagabond. A pretty girl like you should throw your thoughts higher. Why, though your father's a beggar, as one may say——'

'He is not a beggar, so long as my grandmother lives.'

'Perhaps that will not be much longer,' he replied with an ugly grin. 'Now, Drusilla, listen to me. You know that I've set my fancy upon you. I've been waiting just till you grew up, and then for—for one or two little things to ripen which have now ripened and turned out pretty well. Now that everything is ready, there is no reason to wait any longer. Ralph being a highwayman and certain to be hanged——'

'Then, Mathew,' I replied, 'I will wait until he is hanged, and then you can talk to me again if you like. Now, go away, and leave me to my work.'

He went away for that time, and next morning his sister Barbara came. She was at first mysterious about sudden changes of fortune, unexpected reverses, and the judgments of angered Heaven. These things I did not then consider as pertaining to myself, because I knew not how I had especially angered Heaven, more, that is, than thoughtless youth may do at any time, and yet obtain forgiveness by daily prayer. She also added a certain exhortation to kiss the rod, which I pass over. Then she launched into praises of her brother. He was most industrious, she said ; up early and to work before daybreak ; he was full of religion, which surprised me very much to hear ; he was thrifty and had already saved a large sum of money—this, I found afterwards, was false ; he could provide a comfortable home, and happy, indeed, she added, would be the woman on whom his choice should fall. Added to this that he was no longer young and scatter-brained, but arrived at the sober age of three or four and thirty ; and that Mathew's wife would have the advantage of her own society, help, example, and admonition.

I told her that Mathew had got his answer, and that I thought it hard that a woman could not be supposed to know her own mind in so important a matter.

'What is your answer, then ?' she asked.

'I will talk to Mathew on the subject again,' I replied, 'when Ralph is hanged, since this is a thing which both you and he desire so vehemently.'

Two days afterwards Mathew himself met me as I was on my way to the castle. He begged me to give him another hearing, and, as I could not refuse so simple a thing, I led him by the path below the castle to the bank of the river, where he could talk at his ease and unheard.

First it was the same story. Would I forget the young villain and marry him ? He was so much in love with me, that he would not say as some men—not so rich, mind you, as himself—would say, that I might go hang myself in my garters for aught he cared. He would forgive my disrespect and impudence ; he would forget the past altogether ; people should see that he was of a truly noble and forgiving disposition ; he would give me another chance, so great was his generosity. Very well, then, would I marry him ?

I replied very gravely, that he had already received his answer. When Ralph was hanged, and not before, I would listen to him. Then I asked him seriously why he thought so meanly of me as to try this trumped-up story about playactors and highwaymen upon me, and reminded him of what a truly wicked disposition he must be, thus to glory and delight in the supposed wickedness of his cousin, whose guardian he had been, and whose lands he now occupied.

He grew angry at this plain-speaking, and began to swear, as is the wont of such men. If kindness would not move me, he said, something else should be tried. I thought I was free and independent of him, did I? I should see what power was in his hands, and what mischief he could do me. I was young and imprudent. It chafed me to hear that he, and such a man as he, could do me harm—as if the meanest wretch who ever lived cannot do harm—and I told him what I ought to have kept a secret, that so long as Ralph lived, I should not want a protector; and that so far from his being a highwayman, I knew certainly that he was a prosperous gentleman, already held in great honour, and respected by all.

He was so staggered by this intelligence that I thought he was going to have some kind of fit. Consider how much it meant to him : he would certainly have to give up the mill, and to render a strict account of all his doings; he would be reduced to the station of a poor small farmer; he would be robbed of his revenge; and he would be convicted as a slanderer and calumnious person, if that mattered aught.

First he blustered and threatened. I dared, did I, to reproach him : very good, I should see what things he could do ; I should laugh the other side of my mouth. Did I refuse his offer? Very well then. I should find out what his displeasure meant. And, perhaps, before long, I should be sorry for the insult I had offered him, and the proposal I had refused. He then flung away, becoming at this point speechless, and indeed he looked so angry that I was afraid he would have thrown me into the stream.

I went home, and said nothing to anybody about the business ; but I was troubled in my mind, and greatly afraid that the man would do some dreadful mischief if he could.

Well, he came again a third time to me. It was three days later. If I was disquieted, I could see that he was more so. His red cheeks were become pale, and his eyes were red. He was quiet in his manner, and held out his hand.

'Drusilla,' he said, 'I was wrong the other day. You won't marry me? Very well then. Never mind ; someone else will if I want. What matters one woman more than another, if you come to think about it? What hurt me most wasn't your refusal, which I don't care for not one brass farthing, but your saying that I wanted Ralph to go bad. That was cruel to such a cousin and guardian as I was to that boy.'

'Well, Mathew,' I said, 'if I was wrong, I pray you to forgive me.'

'I should like to know, on the contrary, that he was becoming a credit to his family. I say,' he added, 'I should like to know it, if you can assure me of the fact.'

'Then you may depend upon the truth of my statement, Mathew,' I said. 'He is already a credit to your family.'

'How joyful a thing this is!' He folded his hands and raised his eyes hypocritically to heaven. 'It shows that the many correc-

tions I gave him produced their effect. I was a throwing of the
bread upon the waters. After many days, as one may say, it hath
come back to me.'

He spoke with a sweetness which did not deceive me.

'And this prosperity, Drusilla. Who told you of it ?'

'That 1 must not say.'

'Where, in what place, is the boy ?'

'That I shall not tell you.'

'How is he employed, then ?'

'I must say nothing, Mathew. Do not ask me. It is very
certain that Ralph is alive, and that he is prospering. I shall
answer no more questions.'

'I will ask other people, then.'

'It is of no use,' I said hurriedly. 'There is no one knows
except me.' This was not true, but at the moment I was thinking
of my mother, who certainly did not know.

'No one knows except you ?' he repeated. 'That is strange
indeed.'

'It is very strange.'

'And how long,' he went on, 'is the mystery to be kept up ?'

'As long,' I replied, 'as your cousin pleases.'

Then his sweetness left him, and he fell again into a madness
of wrath. He went away, however, when he found that I would
tell him nothing.

All this time I had not written my answer to Ralph's sweet
letter. The reason was that I feared my words would prove so
poor and weak compared with his noble language ; and I was afraid
besides that what I might say would offend or disappoint him.
What maiden but would have been ashamed ? Yet this business
with Mathew made me resolve to lose no time, and I began
seriously to consider what I should say in reply to the long letter
which I carried in my bosom and read daily. In order to be undis-
turbed I carried paper and pen to the Fugleman's room at the
castle, and wrote my letter in the afternoons, whenever I could
snatch an hour from my work. What was I to say in answer to
the many tender protestations of Ralph ? And how was I to speak
of Mathew ?

'Tell him,' said the Fugleman, 'that Mathew is a villain. Last
Tuesday week there was a run to Coldstream—lace and brandy—
Mathew stood in and found the ponies. Yet he is a villain.'

'And what about yourself ?' I asked.

'As for me,' he said, 'I always said that once the boy got his
foot on the lowest rung, it would not be long before he was on the
top of the ladder. Half-way up and more he is, I reckon by now.
So that I am not surprised to hear of his good fortune, and only
wish I was young enough to be his Fugleman. Tell him that first
of all. But Mathew is a villain. Next you may say that I'm well
and hearty, and likely to continue in the way of grace, such being
my constitution and my habits. Mathew, his cousin, is a desperate

villain. Tell him that. You may tell him next, that if he still
regardeth eggs, I have got such a collection for him as can't be
matched. As for Mathew, he is a rogue and a villain. Fish, tell
him, are plentiful this year, and otters there be in plenty. Yesterday I trapped a badger, and I know of a marten opposite the
Hermitage. The birds are wild, but I had good sport with his
Worship last winter, and hope to do something by myself when the
nights draw out. Say next, that I send him my faithful respects
and humble good wishes; and Mathew is a villain. And as for
your own pretty self, you sit down and tell him that there isn't a
straighter maid, nor one more beautiful, on the banks of Coquet;
while, as for eyes and shape and rosy lips——'

'Indeed,' I cried, 'I shall tell him no such nonsense. No, I
will not tell him such nonsense.'

'Why, he loves thee, sweetheart. Say it, child, to please him,
so lonely he is, and so far away from us. I wish he had thy picture
just now, with the pretty blushes on the cheeks and all. A girl
ought to be proud for such as him to fall in love with her.'

'Is he truly in love with me?' I said, with tears coming into
my eyes, because now that the words were spoken, I knew very
well how much I longed for that very thing, 'Why, he says he
wishes me happiness with my husband. As if I could take any
husband but Ralph.'

'There—there,' he cried, 'tell him that. Tell him that, and it
will make him happy and bring him home.'

'You think such a little thing as that would bring him home?'

'There's one thing,' said the old man, 'which women can never
understand, and that's the strength and power of love. There was
a man in Lord Falkland's regiment—but I cannot tell thee all the
story. There was a young gentleman in the Fourteenth, when we
were stationed at Gibraltar, in love with a Spanish lady—but of
that another time. What did the soldier care that he got three
hundred the next day? And as for the young gentleman, he would
have done the same—and always said so—if another dozen of duels
was to come after it, and him to be pinked in every one. Cheerfully he would have done the same for such another charmer. Ah!
he would, and more; but women never understand.'

With these mysterious words did he encourage me as to the
force and vehemence among men, of the passion called love.

If Ralph was only home again, we should have a protector. I
thought of this and hesitated no longer. Yet it was an unmaidenly
thing which I did, and to this day I am uncertain as to whether I
was justified by all the circumstances. It was, besides, a dangerous
thing to do, because I am convinced that nothing more effectually
turns aside the fancy of a man for a woman—which is a delicate
and tender plant, even at its strongest—than the thought that she
is lacking in the modesty and reserve which are the choicest virtues
of a maiden. Yet I ran that danger, though I imperilled the most
precious thing to me in all the world, the heart of my Ralph. But

there is a time to speak, as well as a time to keep silence. What I said was this :—

'DEAR RALPH,—I have now received your letter, and I thank you for it with all my heart. My father hath lost all in London, and is now returned to his native place ; we are, therefore, poor indeed, and have nothing to live upon except the annuity which he long ago bought for my grandmother, who fails daily ; when she dies we shall have nothing. Also my father is afflicted with a strange belief that he is rich. This makes us unhappy. Mathew hath spread abroad a report that the mill is his, and not yours at all, by reason of a second will, which nobody has seen except him-self. I fear that you will have trouble with your cousin. The Fugleman is well and hearty, and bids me tell you——.' Here I set forth as many of the messages as I could remember. 'As re-gards myself, he bade me say many things, out of his kind heart, for he loves me ; but I must not write them down. My dear Ralph, do not say again that you want me to have a husband. I shall never marry any husband, nor love any man, except yourself, if you still continue to love me. Indeed, there is no moment of the day—if you will not think me unmaidenly to confess this thing—when you are out of my thoughts, and I pray night and morning for your safety and speedy return. Mathew has asked me to marry him, and is angered because I refused. He has spread abroad reports that you are now a highwayman. Will you come back to us, dear Ralph ? I am in great sadness, and I am afraid that Mathew means some mischief. Yet I would not mar your fortune by calling you away from the work you have in hand. Mathew threatens me with revenge, and Barbara, his sister, bids me read passages in the Holy Scriptures which threaten woe to sinners. I am afraid what they may do, though I cannot think that they can do us any evil. It makes me unhappy to think that any can believe here that you have become a highwayman. Yet I keep your letter secret, and no one knows where you are. The Fugleman says that a villain must have rope enough to hang himself. Ah, Ralph, if you could come back to us. But the quiet country would be tedious to you after your splendours and the pleasure of an active life. But whether you come home or whether you stay, you must always believe that I am your loving   ' DRUSILLA.

' P.S.—I forgot to beg that you may not take it ill that I have written these words. For, indeed, you may be married, or at least in love, with one more worthy than myself. And if that is so, I wish both her and you many years of happiness and love, and shall only ask her to let me love you still as my brother. How can Mathew presume to court a girl who has known Ralph ?'

CHAPTER VIII.

IS IT TRUE?

Now was Mathew pulled asunder with a grievous doubt and anxiety. For not only might his enemy, as he considered him, appear at any moment to demand a strict account, but he knew very well that if he pushed on his suit or attempted any devilry with us, I might send for Ralph and ask his protection. Yet could my story be true? How could I know, and I alone, of his welfare and the place of his dwelling? Was it possible, he thought, that such a secret, if there was any secret, should be entrusted to the keeping of a mere girl? If the boy was really doing well, why did he not return on his twenty-first birth-day and claim his inheritance? So that the more he thought about it, the more he tried to persuade himself that the thing was false. And yet he was afraid; I could see that he was continually haunted by the fear of what might happen. He sought me often and begged for information concerning his cousin. Next, he tried my father, but his memory as regards the lad was quite gone; and my mother, but she took no interest in the subject, and said she knew nothing about the boy for her part.

'Yet,' said Mathew, 'your daughter pretends to know where he is and what he is doing.'

'Then,' replied my mother sharply, 'Lord help the man! go and ask my daughter.'

'But she will not tell me.'

'Then how can I? Hark ye, Master Mathew, you come here too often. My daughter hath given you her answer. She bears no love to you; she will have none of you. Go, then, and leave us alone. We are poor enough, God knows, but not so poor as to thrust husbands on our girl against her will. Leave us to ourselves, good man, and find another wife.'

My dear and sacred letter arrived in May. It was in July that I sent off my answer. I might look for a reply in sixteen, eighteen, or twenty months—some time in the winter of the next year, seventeen hundred and seventy-three. It seems a long time to an anxious heart when one has to wait three weeks for an answer to a letter sent to London. What, then, must be the patience of those who have to wait nearly two years? Had I reflected further on the perils of my lover's life, the daily risks of battle, wild creatures, treacherous foes, and deadly fevers, I must have been a miserable wretch indeed during those months of waiting. Yet I was sustained by hope, which belongs to the time of youth, and looked for nothing but such a reply from Ralph as would, I thought, remove every care from my mind.

What a fond and foolish girl was I to think that a mere love-letter--which was all I looked for—would be able to give us our daily bread !

After this, Mathew remained quiet again for three or four months. That is to say, he came no more to the house. And so we went on in our thrifty way—I engaged with my needle for such ladies as would employ me, my mother watching my father, and my grandmother sitting in her armchair beside the fire, for the most part silent. Indeed, we were all silent except my poor deluded father, who now added a new craze, for he announced one morning very proudly that he had received a despatch from the King himself, by which he learned that His Majesty had been graciously pleased to confer upon him the honour of knighthood, a distinction which in the present day seems reserved for eminent citizens of London rather than for soldiers, as of old. He was now, therefore, Sir Solomon, and his wife was my lady. He also terrified us greatly by saying that the new dignity would oblige him to assume greater state and a more sumptuous manner of living. Our banquets were sumptuous, truly, and worthy of a knight and his lady. However, in the matter of diet and lodging he was easily satisfied, having been accustomed to plain fare and so entirely carried away by his strange craze as to be persuaded in his own mind that a herring was a turbot ; mutton-broth, turtle-soup ; and a piece of roast mutton a haunch of venison. But now it was impossible to disguise from our neighbours what, indeed, they had long known, that my father was incurably mad. He expected when he took the air of an afternoon to be saluted with the respect due to Sir Solomon, and hats off from everybody, and was pleased with obeisances which were meant in pity, if not in ridicule. And in his presence my mother must be addressed as my lady and spoken of as her ladyship, which made her hang her head at first and look foolish until she became accustomed to the vanity of the thing and found that it pleased him. For it is a strange thing that if you humour a crazy person in his craze, although you strengthen and confirm him in his belief, you make him happy and satisfied with himself, whereas, if you argue or contest it, or if you pass it over in contempt, you are apt to make him uncomfortable and uneasy without convincing him at all of his error.

So great, and reasonably great, was my suspicion of Mathew, that I was certain he would do something to revenge himself upon me, or to get me in his power. Yet I knew not—I could not guess—what he would do, or in what way he could injure me, as if the machinations of wicked men can ever be suspected and guarded against ; as if the head of him who is desperately wicked may not conceive, yea, and execute, things which an innocent girl would believe incredible. The first alarm was caused by a visit from Barbara, who came to see my mother and myself, together or separately. She said she was a messenger from her brother, who, whatever I might say or think, was the most forgiving and the most long-suffering of men ; that he was perfectly prepared, if I would make submission, ask pardon for the injurious things I had said, and reveal what I knew of Ralph, viz. : where he was living, what he was doing, and what were his intentions ; to pass over all, and to take me once more into favour.

'Good Lord !' said my mother. 'Does the man think he is the Great Bashaw ? Favour, indeed !'

- 'Beggars,' said Barbara, 'must not be choosers.'

At these words my mother flamed up, and asked Mistress Barbara many questions relating to her birth, parentage, wealth, religious professions, personal beauty, and so forth, leaving her no time to answer any. This is, with respect to the memory of a kind parent, a manner of speech common among women—even well-bred City Madams when they are angry. Finally, she said that there had been quite enough said about Mathew's proposals, and that he was to understand again, and once for all, that they were distasteful ; upon which Barbara coughed, and said that she had delivered her message, that she had no desire, for her own part, for the alliance, which would certainly be as distasteful to herself as it was to Mrs. Hetherington, and more so, for her brother had a right to look for fortune, which would be of much more use to him than a baby-face ; that she was surprised, being a messenger of peace, and sent by a man of substantial estate, as all the world knew, to be thus treated by folk who were expected shortly to come upon the parish, and the daughter to be glad of honest service and a crust. But enough said.

'Hoity-toity !' cried my mother. 'This is brave talking, indeed, from plain millers and simple farmers. Is the world going upside down ?'

Barbara went away, but returned again a little before Christmas. Mathew, she repeated, was of so Christian a disposition that he was still waiting for submission and to know where the boy was to be found. She also held up her skinny finger in warning, and when I laughed and refused either to make submission or tell where Ralph was living, she bade me tremble and read the first chapter of the book of the Prophet Joel, applying verses four to twelve to my own case, especially the last clause, which on investigation proved to be a prophecy that joy should wither away from the sons of men. I laughed again, but I confess that I was disquieted. What consequences ? I was soon to discover that the woman used no idle threat, though I believe that she did not herself know anything of the abominable plot which Mathew was contriving for our destruction.

This, I say, was just before Christmas. We passed the season of festivity in comfort, thanks to a gift from Mr. Carnaby of a noble sirloin and some bottles of good wine for my father ; but on Twelfth Night my grandmother, who had become very feeble of late, suddenly showed signs of impending change. This was a truly dreadful thing for us, not only for the loss of a good and affectionate parent, which those who have faith ought not to lament, but because at her death we should lose even the small income which we had, and there would be nothing but the house. It was with despairing looks that my mother and I sat by her bedside all that night. In the morning she died, having been speechless for some hours ; but, as happens often with the dying, she rallied just before the end, and recovered for a moment the power of speech.

'Child,' she whispered to me with her last breath, 'thou hast been a good child. The Lord will reward thee. Be of good hope, and never doubt that the boy will return to be thy protector and thy guide.'

After her funeral I asked my mother if she had any money at all. She told me that on leaving London some of their old friends made up between them a purse of a hundred guineas in memory of old times, but after payment of their small debts and the cost of the journey from London, she had the sum of fifty-five guineas put by for unforeseen wants—that we must live on this money as long as it lasted, after which she supposed we must starve.

Fifty-five guineas ! Why, it would last us a year and a quarter at least with prudence. Fifty-five guineas ! It was a little fortune to us. It would keep us until I got a letter from Ralph. Whereupon I told my mother to be of good cheer and to wait patiently and hope for the best. She sighed, being never a woman of sanguine disposition, and ignorant of those secret springs of happiness within me which made me think lightly of present poverty.

And now you shall hear a plot of diabolical wickedness, which for the time was successful. We all know that for a season sinners are sometimes permitted to compass their own designs, but for their surer undoing in the end.

Two days after the burial of the Dame, at a time when we might be supposed to be overwhelmed by the calamity of being left destitute, Mathew came to the cottage. He looked ill at ease, and his eyes met mine shiftily, but he spoke out with boldness, while he produced a leather pocket-book and turned over certain papers within it.

'I have come, madam,' he said, addressing my mother, but looking at me, 'to inform you or your husband—it matters not which—that I can no longer wait for the interest or the principal of my money, and that you must be prepared to pay, or take the consequences.'

'What interest ? What money ?' asked my mother.

'Why,' he affected great surprise, 'is it possible that you are going to deny the debt ?'

'What means the man ?' my mother said impatiently.

'Nay,' said Mathew, smiling, but looking like a hangdog villain the while, 'this passes patience. I mean, madam, my loan to your husband.'

'What loan ?' she repeated ; 'and when ?'

'Why,' said Mathew, 'if you pretend not to know, I am not

obliged to tell you; but since—— Well, I will tell you. I mean this, madam: the sum of two hundred pounds advanced by me to your husband, for which, and for security, he hath assigned me a mortgage on this house.'

My mother was quite wise enough to know what was meant by a mortgage. She asked, but with pale face, where was his mortgage.

Mathew unrolled a paper and laid it on the table. My mother read it through hurriedly. Then she sank back in her chair and covered her face with her hands, saying:

'It is true, my child. Here is thy father's signature. This is the last blow.'

Mathew rolled up the paper again and put it in his pocket.

'Can you, madam,' he asked, 'pay me my money?'

'Go ask of the poor demented creature to whom you lent it,' she replied.

'Then,' said Mathew, 'if the money be not forthcoming, I must sell the house. Yet there is a way——'

'What way?' I asked.

'You know the way. You have only to tell me where the boy is, and to marry me.'

I shook my head.

'And you, sir,' cried my mother, 'you who lend money to poor madmen for the ruin of their house, you—a villain if ever there was one—you think that I would give my daughter to such as you?'

'Very well, madam, very well,' said Mathew, unmoved. 'Very likely the cottage will sell for as much as the mortgage. Perhaps, if not, your husband may carry his extravagances to a gaol, as provided by a righteous law.'

Here he lied, because, I believe, my father could be called upon for nothing more than the house which was his security.

My mother pointed to the door, and Mathew went away, leaving us bewildered indeed. Two hundred pounds! Now, indeed, we were ruined. But what had he done with the money?

'Mother,' I cried, 'it is a black and base conspiracy. My father has never, since he came from London, possessed a single sixpence. Think of it. If he had a penny we should have known it. Try to remember if ever you saw the least sign of his having money.'

No, there was none. He wrote no letters and received none; he bought nothing. His clothes, which were now old and worn, were the same as those he wore when he returned home. On the other hand, because he was of a generous heart, he was for ever giving away what he called money in large sums by means of drafts upon London bankers, which he would sign and press upon the recipient with kind words. For instance, on my birthday he always gave me an order for a hundred pounds on a piece of paper, signed by his own hand, 'Sol. Hetherington,' bidding me, because I was a good girl, go buy myself some finery and fallals. At Christmas,

the New Year, Easter, Roodsmass, fair-time, and other times of
rejoicing, he would fill his pockets with these valuable gifts, and
sally forth—first to the Vicar, with an offering for the poor, saying
that it was little merit to give out of abundance, that the Lord
loveth a cheerful giver, that the poor we have always with us, that
a rich man must remember the fate of Dives, and that, for his part,
he would that the Church had all charities in her own hand, so
that schismatics, profligates, and persons without religion should
starve, with other pithy and seasonable remarks.   Having received
the Vicar's thanks, and a glass of usquebaugh to keep out the raw
air of the morning, he would proceed up the village street, the
boys and girls touching their caps and making curtsies to him,
while the barber and blacksmith would offer the compliments of
the season, with a hope that her ladyship was well.   Then he
would pass the cottage of Sailor Nan, and would call her out and
press into her hand a folded paper, saying it was for Christmas
cheer ;   that she must rejoice, with a dish of good roast beef and
plum-porridge, and a great coal fire, and bidding her God speed,
would go on his charitable way, while some laughed and some
looked grave, and tears would fall from the eyes of the women to
think that one so good and generous should also be so poor.
     Alas ! my father was one of those who could never become rich.
     Even while we spoke of this, we heard outside the voice of my
father, as if to confirm our words :
     'It ill becomes men of substance, Mr. Carnaby, to allow poorer
parishioners to bear the burden of such things.   I will myself
repair the roof of the church at my own charges.   Nay, sir, permit
me to take no refusal in this matter.   If it stand me in a thousand
pounds I will do it.   Why, it is a lending unto the Lord ; it is a
good work.'
     It happened that in some way I had more influence over my
father than anyone.   That is to say, he would unfold his mind—
such as it was, poor man !—to me with greater freedom than to my
mother, who could never make any show of interest or belief in his
magnificent designs and charitable schemes.   I therefore tried to
learn from him, if I could, the truth of this business.   After listening to a long story of his intentions as regards the church and the
endowment of the living of Warkworth, I turned the conversation
upon Mathew Humble, and asked my father if he had of late seen
and spoken with him.   He said that Mathew now avoided rather
than sought his company, for which he knew no reason, except that
when you have obliged a man, it frequently happens that he keeps
out of your way—a thing, he said, of common experience in the
City, where young men, incautious men, and unlucky men often
obtain assistance in the prolongation of bills and in loans.
     'Since I have been of such great service,' he said, ' to Mathew
Humble, he seems to think that he must not come so often as he
did.   A worthy man, however, and, perhaps, he is moved by the
shame of taking assistance.'

'Very likely, sir,' I said, wondering what thing, short of the pillory, with the Fugleman and his pike beside it, would move Mathew to shame. 'It is strange that men should thus court the appearance of ingratitude. Did you ever, sir, borrow money, sums of money, of Mathew Humble?'

'Lend, you mean, Drusilla,' he replied, turning red with sudden anger.

'No, sir, I said borrow. Pray pardon me, sir, I had no intention to offend.'

'But you have offended, child.' He puffed his cheeks, and became scarlet with sudden passion. 'You have offended, I say. Not offended? Do you know what you have said? Have words meaning for you? Should I, Solomon Hetherington, Knight, known and venerated for my wealth, from Tower Hill to Temple Bar, and from London Bridge to Westminster, stoop to borrow—to borrow, I say, paltry sums—for he could lend none but paltry sums—of a petty farmer? Not mean to offend! Zounds! the girl is mad.'

'Pray, sir, forgive me. I am so ignorant that I knew not——'

'To be sure, my dear, to be sure.' He became as quickly appeased as he had been easily offended. 'She does not know the difference between lending and borrowing. How should she?'

'And have you lent Mathew much, sir?'

'As for lending, I have, it is true, placed in his hands, from time to time, sums of money for which I have no security and have demanded no interest. But let that pass. I am so rich that I can afford to lose. Let it pass. And whether he pays them back or not, I do not greatly care.'

'You gave this money to him,' I said, 'by drafts upon your bankers, I suppose?'

'Why, certainly. You do not suppose that we London merchants, however rich we are, carry our money about with us. That would indeed be a return to barbarous times.'

'Then there was the paper that you signed in the presence of an attesting attorney and of Barbara. What was that, father?'

He laughed and made as if he were annoyed, though he appeared pleased.

'Tut, tut,' he said. 'A trifle—a mere trifle; let an old man have his little whims sometimes, Drusilla.'

'But what was it, sir?' I persisted.

'Mathew would have me call it a mortgage,' my father went on. 'A mortgage, indeed! Because he wished his sister not to know. It was—ho, ho!—a deed of gift, child. That is all. It was when I assigned certain lands to him. A deed of gift. We called it a mortgage, but I could not prevent showing Barbara by laughing —ha, ha!—that it was something very different. In addition to the money, I have bestowed upon him a field or so for the improvement of his farm. The gain to him is great; the loss is small to me. A mortgage, we agreed to call it. Ha! ha! Duly signed and witnessed. Your father, Drusilla, is not one to do things irregularly. Duly signed and witnessed.'

This conversation made it quite clear to me that Mathew had contrived an abominable plot for our ruin. For the supposed deed of gift which my father wished to sign, he substituted a real deed of mortgage, in which my father was to acknowledge that he had received two hundred pounds, for which he assigned his house for security, and without, as afterwards appeared, any clause as to time allowed after notice should be given of foreclosing. How far the lawyer was concerned in this conspiracy I know not. Perhaps he was innocent. Indeed, I am now inclined to believe that he was innocent of any complicity. How far Barbara—perhaps she, too, was ignorant of this wickedness.

All that night I lay awake turning the thing over in my mind. I planned a thousand mad schemes : I would break into Mathew's room and steal the papers. I would go round the town and pro-claim his wickedness ; I would inveigle him into surrendering the papers by a false promise of marriage ; I would seek the protection of Mr. Carnaby. All these things I considered, but none of them approved themselves on consideration, because a forger and a cheat will always be ready, if he escapes punishment for the first offence, to repeat his wickedness. Lastly, I resolved upon seeking Matthew at the mill, where I could talk to him at greater freedom.

I went there in the afternoon about two of the clock. When I lifted the latch I saw Barbara sitting on the settle near the window working. Before her, as usual, lay an open Bible. Strange ! that one who was so hard and severe could draw no comfortable things from a book which should be full of comfort.

She shook her long lean forefinger at me.

'I have known,' she said, ' for a long time the ruin that hangs over your house. I saw your father sign the mortgage. He laughed and called it a deed of gift, I remember. Ah ! good money after bad. But my brother, who was foolish enough to lend the money, was not so foolish as to let it go without security. A deed of gift ! He is cunning, your father, and would deceive me if he could, I doubt not.' She turned over the leaves and found something that seemed to suit the occasion and my demerits. ' "He hath made thy vine bare." My brother is full of compas-sion. "He hath made it clean bare." Thy punishment hath begun.'

'I wish to see your brother alone.'

'Do you come in peace or in enmity ? If in peace, you must first make submission, and confess your deceits as regards the boy, who is surely dead. Nothing else will satisfy him. You can begin with me. Where is the boy ? '

'What I have to say is with your brother, not with you.'

'Go, then ; but remember, when you are married, look not to be mistress here. I shall continue to be the mistress as I have always been. If you come in enmity, then you have me to battle with and not my brother alone. Two hundred pounds is not a sum to be given away for nought. Men are soft where a woman is concerned ; Mathew may be a fool for your sake ; you may look to wheedle him out of his papers. Ah, but you shall not. He may be a fool, but I am behind. I am not soft ; your eyes will not make a fool of me, Mistress Drusilla.'

She then bade me go within, where I should find her brother.

It was a cloudy afternoon, and, so early in the season, already growing dusk : Mathew was seated before the fire, and on the table a stone jar containing Hollands which he had already begun to drink.

'Pretty Drusilla !' he cried, astonished. 'Have you brought the money ?'

'No,' I said. 'I come to learn if you are in earnest or in jest.'

'In jest ?' Then he swore a loud oath. 'See you, my lass ; if that money is not paid next week, your house will be sold. Make your account of that. But if you comply with my conditions, the papers shall be torn up.'

'Then I am come to tell you, Mathew, that although I shall not comply with your conditions, the cottage will not be sold.'

'Why not ?'

'Because, first of all, that mortgage is false. I know now what you did. You caused my father to sign one paper believing it to be another. That is a fraud, and a hanging matter, Master Mathew.'

He laughed, but uneasily, and he turned pale. Also, which is hardly worth the noting, he swore a great oath.

'It's a lie !' he cried. 'Prove it !'

'I can prove it, when the time comes. Meantime, reflect on what I have said. It is a wicked and detestable plot. Reflect upon this and tremble.'

He laughed again, but uneasily.

'There is another reason,' I said, 'why you will not sell the cottage. It is this. You are afraid that Ralph may come home and demand an account. Well, I can tell you this : that he will not come home just yet. But, if you do this thing, as sure as I am alive, Mathew, I will write to him and tell him all. I shall tell him how you have persecuted me to marry you, not because you want me for your wife, and though you have had your answer a dozen times over, but because you want to plague and spite your cousin. I will tell him, next, how you have spread false reports about another will, and how you have whispered that he is turned highwayman. And lastly, I will tell him how you have practised upon the kind heart of a poor demented man, and made him sign his name in testimony of your own foul plot and falsehood. I will not spare you. I will tell him all. I will beg him to return post haste, and to bring with him officers of justice. Then, indeed, you may look for no mercy, nor for anything short of the assizes and Newcastle Gaol.'

I spoke so resolutely, though, perhaps, through ignorance, I spoke foolishly, that I moved him and he trembled.

Yet he blustered. He said that all women are liars, as is very well known; that the boy was long since dead and buried; else why did he not return to claim the property? That, as for my story, he did not value it one farthing; while, as regards my accusation, he would laugh. In fact, he did laugh, but not mirthfully.

'Come, Drusilla,' he said; 'your father is welcome to the money, for aught I care. I do not desire to sell the cottage. Sit down and be friendly. Tell me all about the boy; and look, my lass'—his eyes were cunning indeed—'look you. Write to the boy; tell him, if you will, about the money. Tell him that I am willing not to press it if he will give reasonable assurance or security of his own in exchange. Let him, for instance, give me a mortgage on the mill, and let him, since he is so prosperous, pay the interest himself.'

This was a trap into which I nearly fell. But I saw in time that he designed to find out in this way what he had to fear.

'I have told you,' I said, 'what I shall do.'

'Ah! your story, I doubt, is but made up by woman's wit. Drusilla, you are a cunning baggage. Come, now, give over; stay here and be my wife; thou shalt be mistress in everything. As for Barbara, I am tired of her sour looks. She scolds all day. She may pack; she makes the meals uncomfortable; she may vanish; she stints the beer. We will keep house without her. She finds fault from morning to night. She is a——'

'You called me, Mathew?' Barbara suddenly opened the door and stood before us. Her eyes followed me as I went away with malignity difficult to describe, and Mathew, sinking back into his chair, feebly reached out his hand for the jar of Hollands.

CHAPTER IX.

THE WISDOM OF THE STRONG MAN.

WHEN I went home I told my mother that for the present, at least, we need not fear anything from Matthew. Of this I was quite certain. My assurance that I would appeal to his cousin, the doubt where 'the boy' might be—there was no reason, for instance, why he should not be at Newcastle, or at Rothbury, or at Hexham, or at Carlisle—to say nothing of my charge of fraud, went home to his guilty conscience. These things were sure, I thought, to deter a man not naturally courageous, although his conscience might be hardened, from tempting the vengeance of his injured cousin.

So far was I right; that for the whole of the spring and summer we had no further molestation from him, but continued in our quiet course, spending as little money as we could, yet looking forward to the time, now growing very near, when there would be no more left to spend. As for myself, I may truly declare that my faith was strong—I mean not the faith of a Christian, such as I ought to have held—but faith in my lover, so far away. He would send me an answer. The answer, whatever it might be, would surely set all right.

Mathew not only ceased to persecute us; but he ceased to desire the conversation and company of my father. He came no more even to church, as if conscious of his wickedness, and ashamed to face honest people. He was rarely seen even in the town, and he left me quite alone ; so that I began to think that repentance had perhaps seized upon his soul. Alas ! Repentance knocks in vain at the heart of such as Mathew.

Though, however, we saw him not, I heard, through my faithful Fugleman, certain intelligence about him. Thus, he drank harder; he neglected his business ; he quarrelled daily with his sister, who reproached him for his drunken ways, and the neglect of his worldly affairs ; also, she continually urged him to recover the two hundred pounds owed to him, as she thought, by my father. She hungered and thirsted after this money, which, it seemed, she did not know that her brother possessed. Why had he concealed from her, she asked him with anger, that he had so much as two hundred pounds, when he would not give her even money to buy things for the house ? Let him get the money back. Was he mad to let interest and all go ? She let him have no peace ; she longed to have this money ; perhaps she longed for our ruin as well. Then she constantly threw in her brother's teeth the fact that if the boy was not dead and should return, if, in fact, my story was true, he would find the books and accounts in such confusion as might lead to their ruin. She wanted to know what truth there was in the reports, once so industriously spread, about a second will. In fact, she led the wretched man a dog's life, having a tongue sharper than a sword and more dreadful than a fiery serpent. But, as concerning the things she said of Ralph, I could have desired nothing better, because it kept alive in Mathew's breast the wholesome fear of his cousin's return. So long as that lasted, we were safe. We should have continued in safety, because that fear did not die away, but rather increased day by day, save for the instigation, as I cannot but believe, of the Evil One, and the concoction of a design even more wicked than that of the mortgage. I suppose the plot was conceived in the spring or summer, but it was not until the late autumn that it was attempted. The way of it was as follows (I do no harm, I trust, by speaking openly of a traffic which, as everybody knows, is conducted almost openly all over the northern counties of England and the southern counties of Scotland).

I have mentioned one Daniel, or Dan, Gedge, always called the

Strong Man, because he was like Hercules, the fabled Greek, for
bodily strength, who lodged with Sailor Nan. He professed to
make a living out of his strong arms and legs. He went to fairs, and
was seen on market-days in all the towns of Northumberland,
Durham, and Carlisle performing great feats for wagers, or for
money laid down. He would tie heavy weights to his nose and
bear them so suspended round the market ; he would lift and carry
a pony or a cow ; he would crush—but this was nothing to him—
pewter pots with his hands, break iron bars and great pokers over
his left arm—as many as they might bring to him ; he would twist
gold and silver pieces of money, if gentlemen gave them to him,
with his fingers ; carry a dozen men upon his shoulders and in his
arms ; run round a table on his thumbs ; pull a cart against a yoke
of oxen, and perform many other surprising feats, the memory of
which still survives though the poor man is dead, having been
surprised by a snow-storm when in liquor, so that he sat down and
fell asleep in the drift, his mighty thews availing him naught,
never to wake again. By these performances he made great gain,
which he spent, for the most part, on the spot where he was paid,
and in drink, having a thirsty spirit, and, besides, being ready
when he had the means to oblige other thirsty souls who had not.
He was a man standing over six feet, with legs and arms of surprising stoutness, a square red face, and a kindly eye. Despite his
strength he was peaceful, and the softest-hearted of mankind.
Now, though he pretended to live by the exhibition of his strength,
which I believe was the reason why the Vicar called him Milo, it
was very well known everywhere that he had another and a more
important source of profit. This was in the running of 'stuff'
across the Border, a business which demands, as everybody knows,
much caution, with knowledge of the country and powers of endurance. The 'stuff' consists generally of brandy, lace, silk, and
Geneva. Salt is also smuggled across, but a better profit is made
out of the former articles, which are less in bulk and more easily
concealed. There are many reasons why Warkworth should be a
convenient spot for the illicit trade. First, it lies two miles up the
river, and has many safe hiding-places, so that a cargo once landed
at the mouth of the Coquet may be safely and speedily carried up
the river, and bestowed where it is judged safe ; for all along the
steep banks there are spots clearly designed by Nature for the convenient storage of valuable packages. Not to speak of the thick
hanging woods beside the banks, where enough Geneva and Hollands may be stored to supply London for a year, there is the
Hermitage, whose double chamber I have myself seen packed full
of silk in bales waiting for an opportunity, while in the Castle
itself there are vaults, dungeons, passages, and secret chambers,
known only to the Fugleman. Here, little suspected by my Lord
of Northumberland, enough brandy might be stored to supply the
county (which is a thirsty one) for a dozen years. The Border is
not, to be sure, so near as it is higher up the coast, but on the other

hand, the look-out and watch kept by the gaugers cannot be by any means so vigilant and close as where the county narrows to the north; while more than half the run takes place over the wild moors and pathless slopes of the Cheviots, a place in which the Excise people find it difficult indeed to discover or to stop a run made by men who know the country. They have a service of ponies for the work, little, hardy, sure-footed creatures, who carry the ankers, kegs, and bales slung across their backs, and can be trusted to make the whole thirty-five miles from Warkworth to the Border in a single night; that is, in seven or eight hours, the drivers walking or riding beside them.

Most of the farmers and craftsmen of Warkworth take a share in these risks and profits; one or two of them—of whom Mathew was one—often accompany and lead the expedition. Everybody knows beforehand when a run is arranged; many in the town know the very night when it will take place, the road chosen, and the value of the stuff. There is so much sympathy with this work, on both sides of the Border, and so many partners in the venture, that information is never given to the Excise, and hiding-places are found everywhere, with the help and connivance of the most innocent-looking plough-boy and the most demure country lass.

Now one morning—it was in November, when the days have already become short, and the nights are long and dark—Dan Gedge got up from his sleeping-bench or cupboard in the wall, about eight or a little after, calling lustily for small beer, of which he drank a quart or so as a stay to his stomach before breakfast. Then he dressed and came forth to the door with the mug in his hand.

Sailor Nan was already seated on her stone, pipe in mouth, and three-cornered hat on her head. She had taken her breakfast, and now sat, regardless of the raw cold air—for all the winds that blow were the same to her—looking up and down the street, in which nothing as yet was moving, though the blacksmith's apprentice across the road had lit the fire, and the cheerful breath of the bellows made one feel warm.

'Fugleman and me,' said Dan, yawning, 'Fugleman and me, we was rowing up and down from Amble most all night.'

'What is the run?' asked Nan, who needed no other explanation; 'and who's in it?'

'Mathew Humble is in it for one,' said Dan. 'Going with it himself, he is, this journey. Ho! ho! Folks will talk of this run when they come to hear of it. The Fugleman thinks he knows. But he don't; no, he don't know. He's not to be trusted. I'm the only one who knows. Aye, a rare run it will be, too—out of the common this run will be. Folks will lift up their heads when they hear of this night's work.'

'What is it, Dan? Lace belike?'

He shook his stupid head and laughed.

How could Mathew have been such a fool as to trust him?

'Belike there's lace in it, and silk in it, and brandy in it. There's always them things. But there's more, Nan—there's more.'

'What more, Dan?'

'Fugleman, he'll laugh when he hears the news. He's helping in the job, and he don't know nothing about it; only Mathew and me knows what that job is. Mathew and me—and one other.'

'Who is the other, Dan? And what is the job?'

He shook his head and buried it for safety in the pewter-pot.

'Mathew Humble,' he said, 'is a masterful man.'

'What is the job?' asked Nan, feeling curiosity slowly awaken.

'It is a job,' replied Dan, 'which can't be told unto women.'

'Why, ye lubber,' she sprang to her feet and shook her fist in the Strong Man's face, so that he started back; 'lubber and landlubber, you dare to call me a woman—Captain of the Foretop. Now, let me hear what this job is that I am not to be told. Out with it, or ——' I omit the garnish of her discourse, which consisted of sea-oaths.

'Mathew Humble did say ——' the Strong Man began. But strong men are always like babies in the hands of a woman.

''Vast there, Dan,' said Nan; 'd'ye think I value your job nor want to know what it is—a rope's end? But that you should refuse to tell it to me, your shipmet—that's what galls. And after yester'-forenoon's salmagundi!'

This accusation of ingratitude cut poor Dan to the quick. In the matter of sea-pie, lobscouse, and salmagundi (which is a mess of salt beef, onions, potatoes, pepper, oil, and vinegar, the whole fried to make a toothsome compound) Sailor Nan was more than a mother to him.

'Twenty years afloat,' continued Nan, in deep disgust; 'from boy to Captain of the Foretop, and from Cape Horn to the Narrow Seas and Copenhagen, and to be told by a land-swab, who never so much as smelt blue water, that I'm a woman!'

'O' course,' said Dan feebly, 'I didn't really mean it.'

'Didn't mean it! Why—there! What is it, then! Is it piracy, or murder?'

He shook his head.

'Look ye, Nan. It won't signify, not a button, telling you. I said to myself at the beginning, "Nan won't spoil sport;" and it's only a girl.'

Only a girl! Nan pricked up her ears. 'As if I cared about girls,' she said carelessly.

'Only a girl. It's Miss Drusy—that's all. You see she's been longing to run away with Mathew, and marry him, for months. Longing she has, having took a fancy for Mathew, which is a strange thing, come to think of it, and she so young. But women are——. Ay, ay, Nan, I know. You see I always thought she was saving up for Ralph Embleton. But Mathew, he says that's nonsense. Well—she all this time longing to marry him, and her

mother won't hear it—no chance till now. So it's fixed for to-night. What a run! Lace, and brandy, and Geneva, and a girl.'
' Oh—well ; I don't care. Go on, Dan, if you like.'
He then proceeded to explain that Mathew had arranged for a pony to be saddled in readiness ; that the signal agreed upon between the girl and Mathew was a message from the castle carried by a certain boy named Cuddy, pretending to come from the Fugleman, who was to be kept out of the way, employed at the Hermitage, where the stuff was bestowed ; the boy was to say that the Fugleman was ill. On receiving this message the girl would make an excuse to run up to the castle, where she would mount the pony, and so ride off with Mathew and be married over the Border. To keep up appearances, he went on—this soft-headed giant—it had been arranged that the young woman was to scream and struggle at the first, and that Dan should lift her into the saddle, and, if necessary, hold her on. Once across the Border they would be married without so much as a jump over the broomstick.

Nan slowly rose.
' I'll get you some more beer, Dan,' she said.
She went indoors, and poured about three-fourths of a pint of gin into a tankard which she filled up with strong ale, and brought it out to her lodger with tender care.
' Drink that, Dan,' she said ; ' it's good old stingo—none of your small beer. Drink it up ; then you can put on your coat and go about your work.'
He drank it off at a gulp, with every outward sign of satisfaction. Then he suddenly reeled, and caught at the doorpost.
' Go and put on your coat, Dan,' she said, looking at him with a little anxiety.
He disappeared. Nan heard one—two—heavy falls, and nodded her head. Then she followed into the room and found the Strong Man lying upon the floor, on his back with his mouth open and his eyes shut. She dragged a blanket over him, and went out again to sit on her stone with as much patience as a spider in October. She sat there all the morning as quiet as if she was on watch. About half-past two in the afternoon there came slowly down the street no other than Mathew Humble himself.
' Where is Daniel ?' he asked.
Nan pointed to the door.
' He's within, fast asleep. He came home late last night. I dare say he'll sleep on now, if you let him alone, till evening.'
' Have you—has he—talked with you this morning ?' Mathew's eyes were restless, and his cheek twitched, a sign of prolonged anxiety or much drink.
' Nay ; what should he say to me, seeing that he came home in the middle of the night as drunk as a pig ? Let him bide, Master Mathew. What do you want him for ? Is there a run ?'
He nodded.
She held out her hand. ' I'll drink luck to the venture,' she

said, taking the shilling which he gave her for luck. 'Thank you, this is sure to bring you luck. You'll say so to-morrow morning. Remember that you crossed old Nan's palm with a shilling. A lucky run! Such a run as you never had before. A run that will surprise the people.'

'Ha! ha!' said Mathew, pleased with the prophecy. 'It shall surprise them.'

'And how do you get on with Miss Drusy, now? So she said nay. She will and she won't—ay, ay—I know their tricks. Yes, a fine girl, and spoiling, as one may say, for a husband. Take care, Master Mathew. Better men than you have lost by shilly-shally.'

'Why, what would you have me do, Nan?'

'Do? A man o' mettle shouldn't ask. Capture the prize; pipe all hands and alongside; then off with her; show a clean pair of heels; clap all sails.'

'I believe, Nan,' Mathew said, 'that you are a witch.'

'I believe,' she replied, 'that after your run you'll be sure I am. Go in and wake Dan.'

The fellow, roused rudely, sat up and rubbed his heavy eyes.

'You can't be drunk still, man,' said Mathew, 'seeing it's half-past two in the afternoon.'

'My head,' said Dan, banging it with his great fist, 'is like the church bell before the service—goeth ding-dong. And my tongue, it is as dry as a bone. Last night—last night—— Where the devil was I last night?'

'Get up, fool, and put on your coat and come out. We have work to do.'

The fellow made no reply. He was stupidly wondering why his head was so heavy and his legs like lead.

'Come,' Mathew repeated, 'there is no time to lose. Up, man.'

They left the house and walked up the street.

When they were gone, Nan took the pipe out of her mouth, and considered the position of things with a cheerful smile.

'As for Mathew,' she said with a grin, 'he will get salt eel for his supper. Salt eel—nothing short.'

She doubted for awhile whether to impart the plot to the Fugle-man. But she remembered that though he was no older than her-self he would take the thing differently, and a fight between him and Dan, not to speak of Mathew as well, could have only one termination. Had she been twenty years younger, she would not have hesitated to engage the man herself, as she had led many a gallant boarding-party against any odds. But her fighting days were over.

What she at last resolved upon marked her as at once the bravest and the most sensible of women. But her resolution took time for the working out. She sat on her stone seat and smoked her pipe as usual. When any boys passed her door she shook her stick at them, and used her strange sea phrases, just as if nothing was on her mind.

It grows dark in the short November days soon after four, which is the hour when folks who can afford the luxury of candles light them, sweep the hearth, and prepare the dish of cheerful tea. There was no tea for us that year, but small ale of our own brewing or butter-milk. And my mother sat in great sadness for the most part, not knowing what would be the end, yet fearful of the worst, and being of feeble faith. Certainly, there was little to give her cause for hope.

It was at half-past six or seven that I heard footsteps outside, and presently a knock at the door. I saw, to my amazement, no other than old Nan. It was a cold and rainy evening, but she had on nothing more than her usual jacket and hat. A hard and tough old woman.

'Child,' she said earnestly, 'do you think that I would lead thee wrong, or tell thee a lie ?'

'Why, no, Nan.'

'Then, mark me, go not forth to-night.'

'Why should I go forth? It is past six o'clock, and already dark.'

'If messengers should come—— Look ! who is that ? '

She slipped behind the door as a boy came running to the door. I recognised him for a lad, half-gipsy, who was well known to all runners, and often took part in driving the ponies. A bare-headed boy with thick coarse hair and bright black eyes, who was afterwards sentenced to be hanged, but reprieved, I know not for what reason, and I forget now what he had done to bring upon him this sentence.

'The Fugleman says,' he began at once, seemingly in breathless haste, 'that he has fallen down and is like to have broken his back. He wants to see you at once.'

'Oh,' I cried, 'what dreadful thing is this ? Tell him I'll come at once. Run, boy, run. I will put on a hat and——'

The boy turned and ran clattering up the road and across the bridge.

Then Nan came out from behind the door.

'It's true, then. The kidnapping villains ! It's true. But I never had a doubt. Go indoors, hinney. Stay at home. As for the Fugleman, I'll warrant his back to be as sound as my own. Wait, wait, I say, till you see Mathew's face to-morrow ? A villain, indeed !'

'But, Nan, what do you mean ? My dear old Fugleman a villain ! What has he to do with Mathew ?'

'No, child, not he. There's only one villain in Warkworth, though many fools. The villain is Mathew Humble. The biggest fool is Dan Gedge. He is such a fool that he ought to be keelhauled or flogged through the Fleet, at least. Stay at home. This is a plot. The Fugleman is in the Hermitage at work among the stuff. There's to be a run to-night. And they think——

Avast a bit, brother. Aye, aye, they shall have what they want. There's a hock of salt pork and a pease-pudding for supper. I looked forward to that hock. Never mind it. The villain—he to run this rig upon a girl! But old Nan knows a mast from a manger yet, and values not his anger a rope's end.' Here she became incoherent, and one heard only an occasional phrase, such as—'from the sprit-sail yard to the mizen top-sail halyards'; 'a mealy-mouthed swab'; a 'fresh-water wishy-washy fair-weather sailor'; 'thinks to get athwart my hawse,' and so forth. To all of which I listened in blank wonder. Thus having in this nautical manner collected her thoughts—strange it is that a sailor can never mature his plans or resolve upon a plan of action without the use of strong words—she begged me to lend her my cardinal, which was provided with a thick and warm hood, of which we women of Northumberland stand in need for winter days and cold spring winds. She said that she should keep her own cloth jacket, because the work she should do that night was cold work, but she borrowed a woollen wrapper which she tied over her head and round her neck, leaving her three-cornered sailor's hat in my keeping. Lastly, she borrowed and put on a pair of warm leather gloves, remarking that all would be found out if once they saw or felt her hand. This, to be sure, was a great deal larger than is commonly found among women. When all these arrangements were complete, she put on the cardinal and pulled the hood over her head. 'Now,' she asked, 'who am I?'

Of course, having my clothes upon her, and being about the same height, with her face hidden beneath the hood, she seemed to be no other than myself. Then with a last reference to swabs, lubbers, and land pirates, she once more bade me keep within doors all night if I valued my life and my honour, and trudged away, telling me nothing but that a piratical craft should that night be laid on beam ends, that her own decks were cleared, her guns double-shotted, the surgeon in the cock-pit, and the chaplain with him, and, in short, that she was ready for action.

I saw no more of her that night, which I spent in great anxiety, wondering what this thing might mean. But in the morning, fearing some mischief, I walked up the street to the castle. The Fugleman was in his room; he had sent me, he said, no message at all; nor had he fallen; nor had he broken his back. The boy Cuddy, it appeared, had been helping him, and running about backwards and forwards all day. When the ponies were loaded he had returned to the Hermitage to set all snug and tidy. When he came back to the castle they were gone. But no breaking of backs and no sending of the boy. This was strange indeed.

'Then, Fugleman,' I said, 'Mathew Humble sent a lying message, meaning mischief.'

What he designed I understood in two or three days. But for the time I could only think that he wished to open again the question of his suit. Yet, why had Nan borrowed my cardinal and my gloves?

On the way back I looked into Nan's cottage. The door was open, but there was no one in the house.

I went home, little thinking what a narrow escape was mine. Had I known—but had I known, I should have been divided between gratitude to Heaven, and admiration of brave old Nan, and detestation of the greatest villain in England.

CHAPTER X.

SAILOR NAN'S RIDE.

THE night was cold and raw, with a north-east wind, which brought occasional showers of sleet. There was no moon. The street, as the old woman walked up to the castle, was quite deserted, all the women and girls being seated at home about bright coal-fires, knitting, sewing, and spinning, while all the men were at the ale-house, telling stories or listening to them, an occupation of which the male sex is never wearied, especially when beer or rumbo, with tobacco, accompanies the stories.

Nan climbed up the castle hill, and passing through the ruined gate, began to pick her way slowly among the stones and heaps of rubbish lying about in the castle-yard. The light of the fire in the Fugleman's chamber was her guide, and she knew very well that just beside the door of that room would be lurking Strong Dan, with intent to seize her by the waist and carry her off. Perhaps he designed to carry her in his arms all the way to the Border. This thought pleased her very much. Dan was quite able to do it, and the distance is only thirty-five miles or so. It pleased her to think of such a ride in the Strong Man's arms, and how tired he would be at the end.

Accordingly, when she drew near the door she went very slowly, and was not in the least surprised when, as she stood in the fire-light, the man stepped from some hiding-place at hand, caught her by the waist, and tossed her lightly over his shoulder, making no more account of her weight than if she had been a mere bag of meal.

'Now, mistress,' he said, 'struggle and kick as much as you like. It don't hurt me.'

She cheerfully acceded to this request, and began so vigorous a drumming upon his ribs that had they not been tougher than the hoops of the stoutest cask, they must have been broken every one. As it was, he was surprised, and perhaps bruised a little, but not hurt. He had not thought that a young girl like myself had such power in her heels.

'Go on,' he said ; 'you're a strong 'un, and I like you the better for it. Kick away, but don't try screaming, because if you do I shall have to tie your pretty head in a bag. Master Mathew's

P

orders, not my wish. Besides, what's the use of pretending, when there's nobody here but you and me, bless your pretty eyes! I know all about it, and here's a honour for you to be carried off, nothing less, by your own man. Why, there isn't another woman in Warkworth that he'd take so much trouble for. Think upon that! Now then, miss, another kick, or a dozen, if you like. Ah, you can kick, you can. You're a wife worth having. A happy man he'll be. Lord, it would take the breath out o' most that last kick would. Why, I'll swear there's not a woman in all Northumberland with such a kick as yours. Keep it up.'

Thus talking, while she drummed with her heels, he slowly carried her through the dark gateway, picking his feet among the stones.

Outside the castle, beyond the great gate, another man was waiting for them, wrapped in a great cloak. It was Mathew Humble. He had been drinking, and his speech was thick.

'Now,' he said, seizing the prisoner by the arm, 'you are in my power. Escape is impossible. If you cry out—but I am your master now, and for the rest of your life I mean to be. You have got to be an obedient wife. Do you hear? I've had enough of your contempts and your sneers. You'll write to the boy, will you, mistress? Ha! Fine opportunities you will have on the way to Scotland to-night. Ho! The boy will be pleased when he hears of this night's job, won't he?'

'Come, mistress,' said Dan, setting her down gently, 'here's the place and here's the ponies, and if you like, just for the look of the thing and out of kindness, as a body may say, to rax me a cuff or a clout, why—don't think I mind it. Oh, Lord!'

It was a kind and thoughtful invitation, and it was followed by so vigorous, direct, and well-planted a blow that he reeled.

'Lord!' he cried again, 'I believe she's knocked half my teeth down my throat. Who the devil would ha' thought a slip of a girl—— Why, even Nan herself——'

He asked for no more clouts, but kept at a respectful distance.

There were half-a-dozen ponies, all loaded in readiness for the road. Mathew, Dan, and the boy they called Cuddy were to conduct the expedition, the two latter on foot, the first on ponyback. There was also a pony with a saddle, designed, I suppose, for me.

'Now, Drusilla,' said Mathew, 'get up; there is a long journey before us and no time to spare. Remember—silence, whether we meet friend or stranger. Silence, I say, or——' He shook a pistol in her face.

She drew the hood more closely down, and pretended to shrink in alarm. Then, without any more resistance, she climbed into the saddle, and took the reins from Mathew's hands.

'That's a good beginning,' he said. 'Maybe you have come to your senses and know what is best for yourself. And hark ye, my lass, if you behave pretty, we'll send Barbara to the devil. If you

don't, you shall have a mistress at the mill as well as a master.
Think upon that, now.'

Then the procession started.. First Cuddy ; then the ponies,
two by two, who followed the boy as the sheep follow their
shepherd ; lastly, Mathew, upon his pony ; Nan upon hers; and
on the other side of her Dan Gedge, still wondering at the unexpected strength displayed in those kicks and that clout.

In addition to the advantages already spoken of possessed by
Warkworth for the convenience of a run, should be mentioned the
happy circumstance that it lies close to the wild lands, the waste
moors and hills which occupy so large a part of Northumberland.
These moors are crossed by bridle-paths, it is true, but they are
mere tracks, not to be distinguished from sheep-runs except by the
people who use them, and those are few indeed. If you lose the
track, even in broad daylight, you run the risk of deep quagmires,
besides that of wandering about with nothing to guide the inexperienced eye, and perhaps perishing miserably among the wild and
awful hills. As for the boy Cuddy, he possessed a gift which is
sometimes granted even to blind men, of always knowing where he
was and of keeping in the right path. It is with some an instinct.
He was invaluable on these winter runs, because, however dark the
night, whether the moors were covered with thick fog or impene-
trable blackness, or even if they were three feet deep in snow, he
never failed to find his way direct to the point whither they desired
to go. In general, however, the wildest road, though the shortest,
was avoided, and the ponies were driven through the country which
lies north, or north-east of the Cheviots. But on this occasion, so
great was Mathew's desire to ensure the safety of a run in which
his ponies carried something more precious even than lace or rum,
that he resolved upon trying the more difficult way across Chill
Moor, south of Cheviot. Even on a summer day the way across
this moor is difficult to find. On a winter's night it would seem
impossible. Yet Cuddy declared that he could find it blindfold.
They were to cross the Border by way of Windgate Fell and to
carry their stuff to the little village of Yetholm on the Scottish
side.

If you draw a straight line on a county map almost due west
from Warkworth, you will find that it passes near very few villages
indeed all the way to the Scottish Border. The ground begins to
rise a mile or so west of the town, and though up to the edge of the
moors the country is mostly cultivated, the only villages passed the
whole way for thirty miles, are Edlingham, Whittingham, and
Alnham, and it is very easy for safety's sake to avoid these. First,
then, they rode slowly and in silence for six or seven miles as straight
across the country as hedges and gates would allow. Presently
striking the bed of the Hampeth Burn, they followed it up, rough
as the way was, as far as the Black Tarn, which lies among the hills
east of Edlingham. Here they turned to the right, keeping still
upon the high ridge, and crossed Alnwick Moor, whence they

presently descended till they found themselves in the little valley down which the river Aln flows at this point. Here the going was as bad as could be, the ponies feeling their feet at every step, and the progress slow. Yet they never stopped for an instant, nor did the boy hesitate. Mathew kept silence, riding with hanging head, full of gloomy thoughts.

It was past midnight, and they had been in the saddle five hours and more, when they reached the place, close to the village of Alnham, where they were to leave the guidance of the winding burn and trust themselves to the knowledge of the boy upon the pathless moors. Here, under the shelter of a linney, Mathew called a halt. Dan produced a lantern and a tinder-box, and presently got a light. Then he found some provisions in one of the packs, and they ate and drank.

'You are so far from your friends now,' said Mathew to his prisoner, 'that you can talk and scream and do just exactly what you please, except run away. Now you guess what I am going to do. Once over the Scottish Border you will be my wife by Scottish law, if I call you wife. So that now, you know, you had better make up your mind and be cheerful.'

She made no reply.

'Well, then, have you got nothing to say?'

She had nothing.

'Sulk, then,' he said roughly. 'Fall a sulking till you are tired. You may think, if you please, what your young devil of a sweetheart will say when he finds the nest empty! Alive and prospering, is he?'

He proceeded to express his earnest hope that the boy would shortly be beyond the reach of hope. This done, he informed Nan that the worst part of her journey had yet to be accomplished, and that she had better take some meat and drink, unless she wished to fall off her saddle with fatigue, in which case Dan would have to carry her. She accepted without speaking, and, under cover of her hood, made an excellent supper, being, in fact, already pretty well exhausted with fatigue and hunger. When she had finished, Mathew offered her a bottle which contained brandy. He was amazed to find when she returned it to him that she had taken at one draught about half-a-pint of the spirit, so that he looked to see her reel and fall off the pony. That she did not do so he attributed to the effect of the cold night air and the long ride, being unsuspicious how strong and seasoned a head was hidden beneath that hood.

Supper finished, Mathew examined the boy concerning the road. He would tell nothing at all about it, yet he said he knew where to find it, and how to follow it, and, in short, undertook to guide the party without danger by as short a way as could be found across the moor. He was certain that he could do this, but he would not explain how he knew the way nor in what direction it wound among the hills. In fact, how was a boy to describe a road who knew not north from south, or east from west, nor had any but the most simple English at his command in which to speak of valley or hill, ascent or descent ?

The moor over which they crossed that dark night in as perfect safety as if a broad highway had been laid down for them, and was lit with oil lanterns like some of the streets of London, is the wildest, I suppose, in all England. I have heard of that great moor which covers half Devonshire, though I have never been in the south country. I have read about that other great and wild moorland which lies round the Peak in Derbyshire. I have ridden over the broad heath which stretches from Hexham to Teesdale, a place as wild as the people who live upon its borders, yet have I never seen, nor can I conceive, of any place or country so wild, so desolate, and so forsaken, save by hawks, vipers, and other evil things, as the land which lies by Cheviot, Hedgehope, and Windgate Fell.

The boy, as before, led the way, walking without hesitation, though the night was so dark. What he saw to indicate the road no one can tell. Nan, for her own part, could see nothing at all before her for the pitchy darkness of the night and the continual pattering of the rain.

Here is the very head of the Cheviots, the middle of the moors and fells, across which so many parties of plunderers, cattle-lifters, and smugglers have made their way. There is not a valley among these wild hills which has not witnessed many a gallant fight. There is not a hill-side which has not run with streams of blood. There is not a mountain among them all which has not its ghosts of slain men. The heath and ling have been trampled under the feet of thousands of soldiers, for in the old days there was no peace upon the border, and every man was a soldier all his life. But, since the invasion of the Young Pretender, there has been no fighting on the border. Smugglers have taken the place of the cattle-lifters, and peaceful ponies laden with forbidden goods go across the moor in place of horses ridden by men in iron. For those who love to be awed by the wildness of Nature, a place admirable and wonderful, but full of terror at all times to the heart of sensibility. I do not say, however, that the moors were terrible to any of those who crossed them on this cold and dark night, save for the darkness and the rain, and the fear that at any moment they might all go head first into a quag. The boy, to begin with, was quite insensible to any impressions which can be produced by natural objects ; rocks, precipices, wild stretches of land, dark woods—all were alike to him. As for Dan, I suppose he never thought of anything at all. Mathew was too full of the gloomy forebodings which always precede the punishment of wickedness, to regard the things around him, and Nan, as insensible as the boy, was wishing only that the journey was over, because she was horribly cold and getting tired.

The boy led them, by that wonderful instinct, up the slope of the hill to a high level, where the wind was keener and the rain

colder. He kept as nearly as possible to the same level, leading
them round the middle heights upon the slopes of the great Fells
and above the dales. The direct distance is not more than eight
miles, but by reason of the winding of the way I suppose they must
have doubled that distance. It was one o'clock when they left
Alnham behind them, and it was already five before they came
down the hill on the north side of Wind-Gate.

'Master,' said the boy at last, pointing at something invisible,
'yonder's Yetholm, and you are in Scotland.'

Mathew started and sat upright in the saddle, throwing back
his cloak. He was in Scotland. Why, then, his work was done.
He laughed and laid his hand upon his prisoner's arm.

'My wife!' he cried. 'Bear witness, Dan ; my wife, I say.'

'Aye, aye, master. Give ye joy, miss. Master, another dram
to drink the leddy's health.'

Mathew gave him his bottle. Dan took a deep draught, and
then wiping the mouth of the vessel, handed it to the lady.

'Take a drop,' he said, 'it'll warm your blood after that long
ride.'

Then followed so prolonged a draught of the brandy, that Dan
too, as Mathew had done five hours ago, looked to see the girl, unaccustomed to strong drink, fall from her saddle. But she did not.
And honest Dan marvelled, remembering, besides, the vigour of
her heels and the unexpected reality of that clout. A wife so gifted
with manly strength of heel and hand, who could also drink so fair,
seemed to this simple fellow a thing to be envied indeed.

As regards the run, let me say at once, so as to have done with
it, that it was quite successful, and proved a profitable venture to
all concerned, though Mathew, for his part, never showed any joy
when the work of the night was spoken of. It was a bold thing to
venture across the moors on so dark a night ; no one in office looked
for such a venture in the little village of Yetholm ; and the stuff,
taken in the farmers' carts to Kelso, was all sold off at once, therefore
Mathew might have been proud of his exploit. But he was not. And
when the old woman, accompanied by the boy, came home two days
later and brought the news of what had happened, the success of
the venture lost all its interest in the presence of the wonderful tale
they had to tell.

They rode into Yetholm a good while before daybreak, and the
people of the inn—little more than a little village ale-house—were
still in their beds. It was now raining again, with a cold wind,
while they waited for the house to be roused and the fire to be
laid. Nan began now, indeed, though she had borne bravely the
rough journey of the night, to feel the keen morning air and the
fatigue of the long ride. Her limbs were numbed, and when, at
last, the door was opened and the fire lit, Dan had to lift her off the
pony and to carry her in. They placed her in a chair before the
fire, where she sat huddled up in her cardinal and hood, refusing
to take them off.

When all was safely bestowed, Mathew thought him of his bride, and came into the parlour, now bright with a cheerful fire and a candle. He threw off hat and cloak with a sigh of relief.

'Come,' he said, 'let us be friends, Drusilla, since we are married. Yes, child, married. You would have me no other way. Let us have no more sulking.'

She answered nothing.

'Well, it matters not.' Here the landlord and his wife, with Dan and a servant wench, came in together. 'Something to eat,' Mathew ordered. 'Anything that you have. My wife is tired with her ride over the moors.'

'Over the moors?' This was the landlady. 'You haven't, surely, brought a leddy over the moors on sic a night as this?'

'Indeed, but I have,' he replied. 'Come, madam.' He seized her by the arm and dragged her off the chair—oh, the gentle wooer!—so that she stood before him. 'Bear witness, all of you,' he said, taking her gloved hand. 'This is my wife, my lawful wife, by Scottish law.'

Now whether such is the Scottish law I know not at all, but in Northumberland it was always believed that, across the Border, such a form of words, before witnesses, constituted the whole of marriage required by law, although by way of adding some grace of ceremony, the pair sometimes jumped over a broomstick, or wrote their names in a book, or gave a blacksmith a guinea.

'My lawful wife,' Mathew repeated.

The bride, who had been standing with bent shoulders and bowed head, straightened herself and stood upright. Then the witnesses observed a very curious and remarkable thing. The face of the bridegroom, which should surely on such an occasion show a lively sense of happiness, expressed first astonishment, then uneasiness, and finally terror.

The cause of these successive emotions was simple. When Mathew had repeated his form of words he would have dropped his bride's hand, but she now held his, first with a gentle pressure, next with a determination, and finally with a vice-like tenacity which amazed and filled him with strange fears.

Presently, still holding his hand, she spoke:

'I acknowledge Mathew Humble as my true and lawful husband!'

The voice was hoarse and rough. Mathew, with his left hand, tore off the hood. Before him stood, her mouth opening gradually to make room for the hoarse laugh which followed, no other than Sailor Nan herself, in her short petticoats and her cloth jacket, with a woollen wrapper tied about her head.

'My husband!' she repeated; 'my loving husband! Would ye believe it'—she addressed the company generally—'he's so fond of me that he couldn't wait to have the banns put up, but must needs carry me off! Saw ye ever such a braw lover?'

They were all astounded; and when she laughed, still holding the astonished bridegroom by the hand, some of them trembled, because they knew not whether she was man or woman, her voice was so rough, her hair was so short, her jacket was so sailor-like.

'Ah, hinneys!' she laughed again hoarsely, because the air had touched her throat. 'The bonny, bonny bride and the happy groom! Kiss your wife, my husband dear.'

She threw herself upon his neck, and began to kiss his lips.

'You? You?' He tore away his hand from her grasp, tried to push her from him with violence, but she clung fast to him, and retreated step by step to the corner of the room. 'You?'

'Yes, it's me, dearie—it's me. Did ye ever hear the like? To fall in love with an old woman of seventy, like me, and to run away with her! I never looked to get another husband. There's a spirit for you! There's a bold spirit! Mathew dear, when shall we go back? Oh, the wedding-feast that we will have! Well, we women love a lad of mettle. Is there a boy in Warkworth, except my man here, who would carry his wife all the way across the moors when he might have had me asked in church?'

Dan, one of those who are naturally slow to understand things unless they fall out exactly as is expected, had by this time succeeded in comprehending the whole. He had, he now perceived, carried off the wrong woman, which fully accounted for the vigour of the kicks, the amazing strength of the clout, and the capacity for strong drink.

'Nan!' he cried. 'It's our Nan!'

'It is, ye lubber,' she replied; 'and no one else.'

He then began to laugh too. He laughed so loud and so long, being a man who seldom sees a joke, and then cannot make enough of it, that the landlord, the landlady, and the servant-girl caught the infection, and they all laughed too. Mathew raged and swore. This made Dan laugh the louder and the longer. Mathew ceased to swear; he threw himself into a chair, with his hands in his pockets, and sat, cheeks red and eyes flashing, until the storm of mirth subsided. Then his dainty and delicate bride banged her great fist upon the table.

'No sheering off now,' she cried. 'You're my man, and a merry and a happy life you shall lead. Mates and jolly sailors all, this is my third husband. The first, he was hanged; the second, he hanged himself; better luck to the third. What a wife he's got!—what a wife! Now then, rum for this honourable company, and a fiddle for the wedding; and more rum and tobacco, and more rum. Stir about, I say.' She produced a bo's'n's whistle, and blew a long shrill call. 'Stir about, or I'll rope's-end the whole crew. Rum, I say; more rum for this honourable company!'

With these words she sprang into the middle of the room, and began to dance a hornpipe with the most surprising skill and agility.

CHAPTER XI.

THE SALE OF THE COTTAGE.

WHEN the old woman came home with the boy, the story which she had to tell surpassed all her yarns of salt-sea experience. She told her tale nightly, in exchange for glasses of strong drink. And even Cuddy, the boy, was in request, and sold his information for mugs of beer. The men laughed at Mathew's discomfiture. To most men, indeed, the punishment of wickedness is always an occasion for mirth rather than for solemn reflection. They laugh at suffering, especially when it is unexpected; and if their dearest friend experiences a misfortune when he most expects a stroke of luck, they laugh. When a vagabond is flogged at the cart-tail; when a shrew is ducked; when a miserable starving wretch is clapped into stocks or pillory, they laugh. That is the way of men. But I have observed that they do not laugh at their own afflictions. Everybody, therefore, including the Vicar and his Worship, laughed at Mathew's discomfiture. They went so far as to say that Mr. Carnaby told the story to my Lord of Northumberland, who was entertaining my Lord Bishop of Durham, and that both prelate and peer laughed until the valets had to unloose their cravats. Yet I cannot see why one should laugh because a young man is mated to an old wife, expecting to have carried off a young one. To me, it seems as if we should first condemn the crime of abduction, and next, bow to the rod.

After the first laughter, which was like an explosion, or a great thunder-storm, one of those during which the rain-water rattles and slates fall off the roof : a universal burst of laughter when all the men ran together laughing their loudest, holding each other up, loosing neck-ties, pumping on the apoplectic, and encouraging each other to fresh hilarity by pointing to Nan the bride : the question naturally arose if anything should be done to mark their sense of the attempted crime by those in authority. A most grievous and intolerable thing it was, indeed, that a young woman should be violently kidnapped and carried away like a sailor by a press-gang ; forced to ride thirty miles and more on a winter's night, across the cold and rainy Fells; married willy nilly in the morning without church or parson ; and this when she had not once, but many times, refused so much as to listen to proposals of marriage from the man. All were agreed that this was a thing not to be permitted. Yet, what could be done ? To run away with a girl of her own free will and accord, and when she would marry the man but for wickedness of guardians, is a different thing ; many a maiden has fled across the Border with her lover, amidst the sympathy of her friends. But in this case it was like the carrying away of the

Sabine women, and no words could be found by the moralist too strong to condemn the act.

While everybody talked about it, that is to say, for a whole week, there was so much indignation that if Mathew had appeared it would have gone hard with him among the men, to say nothing of the women, who would think of no punishment too bad for him. The townsfolk talked of ducking in the river, of pillory and stocks, and I confess that the thought of Mathew in the pillory was not disagreeable to me. Yet, considering the way of the world, perhaps, if he had been young, handsome, and of pleasant speech, he might have been forgiven the attempted abduction, on the plea of love inordinate. One man, we know, may steal a horse—but then he must be comely and generous—while another, if he is churlish and harsh, is clapped into gaol for looking over a hedge. While, however, they talked, Mathew kept away, nor did he return for three or four weeks, leaving his private affairs neglected ; and no one knew where he was in hiding.

We had, however, a visit from Barbara. She came, she said, not out of any love to me or my mother, who had used words so injurious as regards herself, but to express her abhorrence of the crime which her unhappy brother had attempted, and her thankfulness that this madness of his was defeated. She said that she knew nothing whatever of him ; where he was or what he was doing ; but she hoped that when he returned he would be in a better frame of mind, and feel the remorse which ought to follow such an action. As for the pretended marriage with the old woman, she said that was a thing not to be considered seriously. My mother received her excuses coldly, and she presently went away, after another attempt to discover whether I knew anything fresh about ' the boy.' She desired to know, she said, not out of curiosity, because she was not a curious person, as everybody knew, but because she feared that I might, by representing the late affair in its worst light, bring about a hostile feeling and even a conflict between her brother and the boy, which could not fail of being disastrous to the latter. My mother reassured her on this point, because, she said, Mathew was already well acquainted with Ralph's cane, and, having shown so much bravery in the late affair, which took two men to carry off one woman, would now most certainly have the courage to turn a submissive back to the chastiser when he should appear. Barbara thereupon went away. Though I loved her not, I could not but feel pity for a woman who had done and suffered so much on behalf of this thankless brother. She was grown much older to look at during the last year or two ; her face was pinched, and wrinkles had multiplied round her eyes with her constant cares. This is an age when gentlemen of exalted rank think it no sin to be put to bed helpless after a debauch of wine or punch ; I hope that more sober customs may shortly prevail ; else, one knows not what will become of us all. Yet, though drunkenness is in fashion, I think nothing can be more miserable for a woman than to sit, as Barbara sat daily, knowing that the only man in the world she cares for is slowly getting drunk by himself in another room, which is what Mathew did. As to the idle talk about the other will and the rightful heir, I know not what she believed in her heart, or how far she joined in the wicked designs of her brother, which were about to be frustrated.

Then Mr. Carnaby, accompanied by his lady and by the Vicar, came in person to express his horror of the crime, and his satisfaction that it was providentially prevented.

'We have discussed,' said his Worship, 'the action which we should take in the matter. At present all we have to go upon is the evidence of Nan, who is, she says, Mathew's wife, so that if such be veritably the case she cannot give evidence in the matter at all, and that of the boy Cuddy, an ignorant, half-wild lad, who knows not the nature of an oath. Abduction is a great crime ; but then Mathew, whatever were his intentions, my child, did actually only run away with an old woman, and she makes no complaint, but rather rejoices, while he is rendered ridiculous. To kidnap a young girl is a hanging matter ; but then, my dear, you were not kidnapped. In short, we feel that to bring Mathew to justice would be difficult and perhaps impossible.'

To be sure, one would not wish to hang any man for the worst of crimes, and we had no desire to bring Mathew before any court of law or justice, being quite contented that the offender should feel certain of sharp and speedy justice if he made another such attempt.

'Can we not see him, at least,' asked my mother, 'placed in pillory ?'

'I would place him in pillory,' his Worship went on, 'if the old woman who now calls herself his wife—Heaven knows with what right—would lodge a complaint. But she will not. He deserves pillory at the least. And as for rotten eggs, I would myself bring even a basket of new-laid eggs, so that he should want for nothing. And I would condescend to throw them. But she will not complain. She even laughs and boasts that she has gotten a young husband. And then, which is a difficult point in this doubtful case' —his Worship blushed and looked confused, while the Vicar hemmed and Mistress Carnaby coughed—' he was running a venture across the Border, and no one knows—I say that no one can tell— who may be compromised in this affair as to what he took across or what he brought back, for though Mathew had great faults, there is no one more skilled—more skilled, I say.'

'No one,' said the Vicar, which completed the sentence for his Worship.

'Wherefore, my dear girl,' continued his Worship, 'I propose waiting until the man returns, when I will reprimand him with such severity as will serve to deter him—and any others of a like mind with himself—from a renewal of his wickedness.'

Mathew did come back, three weeks later ; but, although his Worship sent the Fugleman, carrying his pike, to the mill with a command that Mathew should instantly repair to him for admo-

nition, and although the Vicar also repaired to Mr. Carnahy's house
in his best gown in order to receive the offender, and to give
greater authority to the discipline, Mathew came not. He positively and discourteously refused to obey.

There, it would seem, was a direct breaking of the law, or, at
least, contempt for authority, upon which imprisonment, I dare
say, might have followed. But whether from leniency, or on account of that difficulty connected with the late venture, his Worship
refrained from severity, and ordered instead that Mathew, for
violence and contumacy, should do penance in the church. Here,
indeed, was righteous retribution! He would stand, I thought, in
the very place where he had caused Ralph to stand nine years
before; he would be made to rise up before all the people, and, in
a loud voice, to ask their pardon, and to recite the Lord's prayer.
I hope I am not a vindictive woman, yet I confess that I rejoiced on
learning from the Fugleman that this punishment had been meted
out to the evil-doer. We both rejoiced, and we congratulated each
other, because we thought that Ralph would also rejoice. Little
did we know of that great and lofty mind, when we foolishly
imagined that he would ever rejoice over the fall of his enemy.

There was great excitement in the town when it became pub-
licly known by means of the barber, who had it direct from his
Worship, that this godly discipline was to be enforced on the
person of Mathew Humble—a substantial man, a statesman, a
miller, a man supposed (but erroneously) to be wealthy, and a man
already thirty-four years of age or thereabouts. Why, for a school-
boy, or a lad of sixteen, or a plain rustic to stand up in this white
sheet was joy enough, but for such a show of such a man, this, if
you please, was rapture indeed for the simple people. I confess
that I for one looked forward with pleasure to the spectacle.

Alas! who would believe that man could be found so daring?
Mathew refused contumaciously to perform the penance! This
was a great blow and heavy disappointment to all of us! and we
looked to see the Vicar excommunicate him. But he did not, saying that disobedience to the Church brought of itself excommunication without need of any form of words. Let Mathew look to his
own soul. And as there seemed no means of enforcing the punishment if the offender refused to undergo it, there was nothing more
to be said.

The behaviour of Nan at this time was worthy of admiration.
On Mathew's return, but not until then, she walked to the mill
and informed Barbara that, as her brother's wife, she was herself
the mistress, but that, being accustomed to her own cottage, she
should not for the present molest her in her occupation.

Then she sought her husband.

It was really terrible to mark how the ravages of drink and disappointment together had made havoc with the appearance of this
unfortunate man. Unfortunate, I call him, though his punishment
was but the just reward of his iniquities. The failure of his plot; the

consciousness of the ridicule which overwhelmed him; his shame
and discomfiture; the thought of the old woman whom he had
called his wife; the messages which he had received from his
Worship and the Vicar—his disobedience being connected in some
way with partnership in the recent venture; a dreadful vague
looking forward to the future, and the constant terror lest Ralph
should return, filled his mind with agitation, and gave him no peace
night or day. He neglected the work of mill and farm; he would
take no meals save by himself, and he drank continually.

He looked up from his half-drunken torpor when Nan came in.
'I expected you before,' he said. 'What are you going to do?'
She poured out a dram and tossed it off.

'I came to see my bonny husband,' she said, 'before I am a
widow once more. Eh, man, it's an unlucky wife ye have gotten.'

'Wife!' he repeated; 'wife! Yes, I supposed you would
pretend——'

'Hark ye, brother,' cried Nan, bringing down her cudgel on
the table with an emphasis which reminded Mathew uneasily of the
second husband's lot; 'hark ye! Sail on another tack, or you'll
have a broadside that'll rake you fore an aft from stem to stern.
Wife I am; husband you are; wherefore all that is yours is mine.'
She hitched a rope into the handle of the stone jar containing the
brandy and jerked it over her shoulder. 'The mill is mine, so
long as it is yours, which won't be long, shipmet. Last night I
read your fortune, my lad. By all I can discover, you and me
shall part company before long. But whether you will hang
yourself, like my second man, or be hanged, like my first; or
whether you will be knocked o' the head—which is too good for
such as you; or whether you will die by reason of takin' too much
rum aboard, which is fatal to many an honest Jack; or whether you
will die by hand of doctors, whereby the landlubbers do perish by
multitudes—I know not. Short will be our company; so, as long
as we sail together, let us share and share alike, and be merry and
drink about. Money—now, I want money.'

He refused absolutely to let her have any money. Without any
more words, this terrible woman prepared for action. That is to
say, she took off her rough sailor's jacket, rolled up her sleeves,
and seized the cudgel with a gesture and look so menacing that
Mathew hauled down his colours.

'How much do you want?' he asked.
'Short will be the voyage,' she said. 'Give me ten guineas.
Yes, I will take ten guineas to begin with. But don't think it's
pay-day. I'm not paid off, nor shall be so long as—— Pity 'tis
that I can't read those cards plainer. Well, my dearie, I'm going.
If I think I should like the mill better than my own cottage, I'll
come and stay here. You shall see, off and on, plenty of your
wife. Ho! ho! The bonny bride! and the happy groom!'

She left him for that time. But she went often, during the
brief space which remained of Mathew's reign at the mill. Each

time she came she demanded money, and rum or usquebaugh; each time she threatened to live with her husband; each time she terrified Barbara with the prospect of staying there. And the man sat still in his room, brooding over the past, and thinking, not of repentance, but of more wickedness.

One day, he rode away without telling his sister whither he was going or what he designed. He did not return that night, but two days later he rode into the town, accompanied by a grave and elderly gentleman, and after leaving the horses at the inn, he walked to our cottage. I saw them at the garden-gate, and my heart felt like lead, because I saw very clearly what was going to happen.

In fine, I felt certain that the money would be demanded and our house sold. Mathew, goaded by his sister, who clamoured without ceasing for the money supposed to have been lent to us, and unable any longer to endure his suspense and anxiety regarding their cousin, resolved to bring matters to an issue. Fortunate indeed was it for us he had delayed so long.

They came in, therefore; and the grave old gentleman opened the business. He said that he was an attorney from Morpeth; that the mortgage, of which mention had already been made to Mistress Hetherington, had been drawn up by him at the request of Mr. Mathew Humble; that he had witnessed the signature of my father, and that the business, in short, was regularly conducted in accordance with the custom and the requirements of the law.

I asked him if he had seen the money paid to my father. He replied that he had not, but that it was unnecessary. I informed him thereupon that the money never had been paid at all, but that my father, a demented person, as was very well known, yet not so dangerous or so mad that he must be locked up, was persuaded by Mathew that he was signing an imaginary deed of gift conveying lands which existed only in his own mind, because he had no land.

The lawyer made no reply to this at all.

'Now, mistress,' said Mathew roughly, 'is the time to show the proofs you talked about.'

'My proofs, sir,' I addressed the lawyer, 'are, first, that my father believes himself prodigiously rich, and would scorn to borrow money of such as Mathew Humble; next, that he perfectly well remembers signing this document, which he thought a deed of gift; thirdly, that we know positively that he has had no money at all in his possession; fourthly, that he denies with indignation having borrowed money; fifthly, that Mathew, like everybody else, knew of his delusions, and would certainly never have lent the money; sixthly, that two hundred pounds is a vast sum, and could not have been received and spent without our knowledge. Lastly, that Mathew was known to be a base and wicked wretch who even tried to kidnap and carry off a girl whom he wished to marry.'

'Every one of these proofs,' said my mother, 'is by itself enough for any reasonable person.'

The lawyer replied very earnestly that he had nothing to do with proving the debt ; that he came to carry out the instructions of his client, and to give us a week's notice—which was an act of mercy, because no clause of notice had been inserted in the mortgage ; that the house would be sold unless the money lent was paid ; that it was not his duty nor his business to advise us, but his own client ; that the law of England provides a remedy for everything by the help of attorneys, and that, by the blessing of Heaven, attorneys abound, and may be obtained in any town. Finally, he exceeded his duty by his client in counselling us to put our affairs in the hands of some skilled and properly qualified adviser.

This said, he bowed low and went away, followed by Mathew.

But Mathew returned half an hour later and found me alone.

'You told me,' he said, 'six months ago and more, that should I attempt any harm to you and yours, you would write to the boy. I waited. If your story was true, you would have written to him at once, out of fear. But your story was not true. Ah, women are all liars. I ought to have known that. Barbara says so, and she ought to know.'

'Go on, Mathew,' I said.

'I waited. If your story had been true, the boy would have hastened home. Well, I thought I would give you another chance. I would carry you off. That would make him wince, if he was living. Yet he has not come.'

Did one ever hear the like ? To bring his own terrors to an end, or to an issue, he would have made me his unwilling and wretched wife.

'Now I've found you out. Why didn't I think of it before ? I asked the post-boy. Never a letter, he truly swears, has been delivered to you—never a one. So it is all a lie from the beginning. Very good then. Marry me, or sold up you shall be, and into the cold streets shall you go.'

I bade him begone, and he went, terrified, perhaps, at the fury with which I spoke. Of this I forbear to say more.

When we sought the advice of Mr. Carnaby, we found that he entertained an opinion about law and justice which seemed to differ from that of the Morpeth lawyer.

'Your proofs,' he said, 'though to me they are clear and sufficient to show that Mathew is a surprising rogue, would go for nothing before a court. And I doubt much whether any attorney would be found to undertake, without guarantee of costs, so great a business as a civil action. Justice, my child, in this country, as well as all other countries, may hardly be obtained by any but the rich, and only by them at the cost of vexatious delays, cheats, impositions, evasions, and the outlay of great sums upon a rascally attorney. Beware of the craft. Let the man do his worst, you still have friends, my dear.'

So spoke this kind and benevolent man. I am sure that his

deeds would have proved as good as his words had they been called for.

We told no one in the town, otherwise I am sure there would have been a great storm of indignation against Mathew, and perhaps we did wrong to keep the thing a secret. But my mother was a Londoner, and did not like to have her affairs made more than could be helped the subject of scandal and village gossip.

It was now already the middle of December ; we should therefore be turned out into the street in winter. As for our slender stock of money that was reduced to a few guineas. Yet was I not greatly cast down, because, whatever else might happen, the time was come when I might expect an answer. In eighteen months, or even less, a ship might sail to India and return to port.

Ralph's letter would set all right. I know not, now, what I expected ; I lived in a kind of Fool's Paradise. Ralph was my hope, my anchor. I looked not for money but for protection ; he would be a shield. When the Fugleman came to the cottage we would fall to congratulating ourselves upon the flight of time which brought my letter the nearer. He even made notches on a long pole for the days which might yet remain. Yet, oh, what a slender reed was this on which I leaned ! For my letter to him might have miscarried. Who is to ensure the safety of a letter for so many thousand miles ? Or his reply might be lost on board the ship. A letter is a small thing and easily lost. Or he might be up the country with some native prince ; or he might be fighting ; or he might be too much occupied to write. A slender reed of hope indeed. Yet I had faith. Call it not a Fool's Paradise ; 'twas the Paradise of Love.

Then came the day, the last day, when the money must be paid or we lose our house. That day I can never forget. It was the twenty-third of December. The mummers, I know, were getting ready for the next evening. In the night we were awakened by the waits singing before our house :

'God rest you merry, gentlemen,
Let nothing you dismay,'

and I, who ought to have taken the words for an exhortation to lift my heart to Heaven, lifted it only as high as—my lover. To be sure, he was always a good deal nearer Heaven than his unworthy sweetheart.

In the night there was snow, and when the sun rose the garden was beautiful, and the leafless trees had every little twig painted white ; a clear bright day, such as seldom comes to this county of rain and wind in the month of December. If one has to be thrust into the street, one would wish for a day of sunshine. Is it not a monstrous thing that this injustice should be possible ? Will there ever come a time when justice and equity will be administered, like fresh air and spring water, for nothing ?

So certain was Mathew of his prey that he sent the crier round at nine in the morning to announce the sale for noon. And directly after eleven he came himself with the attorney ; and a man to conduct the auction or sale of the house. We put together, in order to carry with us, our wearing apparel. Mathew was for preventing us from taking anything—even, I believe, the clothes we stood in—out of the house. Even the Family Bible must stay, and the very account-books ; but he was rebuked by his lawyer, who informed him that the mortgage included only the tenement or building, but not its contents. We should keep our beds, then. But where to bestow them ? Whither to go ? My heart began to sink. I could have sat down and cried, had that been of any avail, and if my mother had not set a better example and kept so brave a face.

'The daughter of a substantial London merchant, my dear,' she said, 'must not show signs of distress before such cattle'—she meant the attorney and his honest client. 'Get your things together, and we will see where we can find a shelter. My poor old man shall not feel the pinch of cold and hunger, though we work our fingers to the bone.' Her lip trembled as she spoke.

Meantime my father was giving a hearty welcome to the astonished attorney, whom he considered as a visitor.

'In this poor house, sir,' he said with a lofty air, 'though we have the conveniences which wealth can bestow, we have not the splendour. I trust, sir, that you may give me the pleasure of a visit at my town house, where, I believe, her ladyship will show you rooms worthy of any nobleman's house, not to speak of a plain City Knight, like your humble servant.'

The attorney regarded him with wonder, but answered not. I believe he understood by this one speech how impossible it was that this poor man could have borrowed his client's money.

At stroke of noon the sale was to commence. But as yet there were no buyers. No one was there to bid except Mathew himself, who was impatient to begin.

It wanted five minutes of noon when Mr. Carnaby appeared, bearing his gold-headed stick, and preceded by the Fugleman with his pike, to show that the visit was official. He was followed by a dozen or so of the townsmen, now aware that something out of the common was about to happen.

'Go on with the sale,' cried Mathew impatiently ; 'it is twelve o'clock.'

'Stop !' said his Worship. 'Sir,' he addressed the lawyer, 'you will first satisfy me by what right you enter a private house, and next by what authority you are selling it.'

The attorney replied with submission and outward show of respect that he was within his powers, in proof of which he exhibited papers the nature of which I know not, concluding with a hope that his honour was satisfied.

'Why, sir,' said Mr. Carnaby, 'so far as you are concerned, I may be. I am also satisfied that this business is the conspiracy of a villain against the peace and happiness of an innocent girl.'

Q

'With respect, sir,' said the lawyer, 'the words conspiracy and villain are libellous.'

'I name no names,' but he looked at Mathew, who shifted his feet and endeavoured to seem unconscious. 'I name no names,' he repeated, shaking his forefinger in Mathew's face, 'yet villain is the man who would ruin a helpless family because a virtuous woman refuses to marry him. Villain, I say!'

He banged the floor with his great stick, so that everybody in the room trembled.

'I do not think, sir,' said Mathew, 'that your office entitles you to offer impediment to a just and lawful sale.'

'Prate not to me, Master Kidnapper.'

'If,' continued Mathew, 'Mr. Hetherington disputes my claim, here is my lawyer, who will receive his notice of action. For myself, I want my own and nothing more. Give me justice.'

'I would to Heaven, sir, I could,' said his Worship. 'Go on with your iniquitous sale.'

It appeared at first as if no one would bid at all for the cottage, though by this time the room was full. Then Mathew offered fifty pounds. Mr. Carnaby bid fifty-five pounds. Mathew advanced five pounds. Mr. Carnaby bid sixty-five pounds.

Mr. Carnaby was not rich; yet he had formed the benevolent design of buying the house, so that we might not be turned out, even if the rent would be uncertain. Mathew wanted not only the amount of the (pretended) mortgage, but also the pleasure of turning us out. Ah! where was Ralph now? Where was 'the boy' to whom I was going to write for protection if he dared to move?

'One hundred and ninety!' said Mathew.

'One hundred and ninety-five!' said his Worship.

'Two hundred!' said Mathew.

Mr. Carnaby hesitated. He doubted whether the cottage of six rooms and the two acres of ground in which it stood were worth more. The hammer went up. He thought of us and our helpless situation.

'Two hundred and five!' he said.

'Two hundred and ten!' said Mathew.

Again Mr. Carnaby hesitated; again he saw the hammer in the air; again he advanced.

'Two hundred and ninety-five!' said his Worship, mopping his face.

'Three hundred!' said Mathew.

'Any advance upon three hundred?' asked the auctioneer.

Mr. Carnaby shook his head.

'Villains all,' he said, 'I can afford no more. I cannot afford so much. Poor Drusilla! Thou must go after all.'

'Going! going!' cried the man, looking round.

'FIVE HUNDRED!'

Mathew sprang to his feet with a cry as of sudden pain, for he knew the voice. More than that, in the doorway he saw the man.

He reeled and would have fallen but that someone held him; his cheeks were white, his eyes were staring. The blow he had so long dreaded had fallen at last. His enemy was upon him.

The figure in the doorway was that of a gentleman, tall and stately, still in the bloom and vigour of early manhood, gallantly dressed in scarlet with gold-laced hat, laced ruffles, diamond buckles, and his sword in a crimson sash. Alas! for Mathew. The girl had told no lie.

The Fugleman, being on duty, contemplated things without emotion, even so surprising a thing as the return of the wanderer. But he saluted his superior officer, and then, grounding his pike, looked straight before him.

This was the answer—this was the reply to my letter. Every woman in love is a prophet. I knew, being in love, that my sweetheart would make all well; I knew not how; he would bring peace and protection with him, for those I loved as well as for myself.

Great and marvellous are the ways of Providence. I knew not, nor could I so much as hope that the answer would be such as it was—nothing short of my lover's return, to go abroad no more.

CHAPTER XII.

'GOD REST YOU MERRY, GENTLEMEN.'

WHAT remains to be told?

Ralph was home again. What more could I have prayed for?

While these things went on we were sitting in the kitchen. In my mother's eyes I seemed to read a reproach which was not there, I believe, but in my own heart. I had prophesied smooth things, and promised help from some mysterious quarter which had not come.

'There are five guineas left,' said my mother. 'When these are gone, what shall we do?'

I tried to comfort her, but, alas! I could find no words. Oh, how helpless are women, since they cannot even earn bread enough to live upon. When the bread-winner can work no longer, hapless is our lot. What were we to do when these five guineas were gone? For, if I could find work to keep my fingers going from morn till night, I could not make enough to keep even myself, without counting my father and my mother. What should we do when this money was gone? We must live upon charity, or we must go upon the parish. At the moment of greatest need my faith failed me. I thought no more of the letter I was to receive; I ceased to hope; my Paradise disappeared. I was nothing in the world but a helpless woman, a beggar, the daughter of poor, old, broken-down people, whose father was little better than a helpless lunatic.

We heard from the parlour, where they were holding the auction, a murmur of voices, some high and some low. Suddenly there was a change; from a murmur of words there arose a roar of words —a tumult of words. Strange and wonderful! I should have recognised the voice which most I loved. But I took little heed. The misery of the moment was very great.

'So'—now, indeed, I heard the voice of his Worship, which was a full, deep, and sonorous voice—'so may all traitors and villains be confounded! Kidnapper, where are now thy wiles?'

I heard afterwards how Mathew would have slunk away, but they told him (it was not true) that his wife was without brandishing her cudgel. So he stayed, while his attorney, ignorant of what all this meant, congratulated his client upon the sale of the cottage. Five hundred pounds, he said, would not only suffice to pay his own bill of costs, which now, with expenses of travelling and loss of time, amounted to a considerable sum, but would also repay Mathew's mortgage of two hundred pounds in full, and still leave a small sum for the unfortunate gentleman they had sold up. Mathew made no reply. He looked fearfully into his cousin's face; it was stern and cold. There was no hope to be gleaned from that face, but the certainty of scrutiny and condemnation. What had he done to merit leniency? Conscience—or remorse—told him that he had tried to kidnap his cousin's sweetheart; to drag her down to destitution; while, as regards his own trust and guardianship, none knew better than himself the state in which his accounts would be found.

The words of Mr. Carnaby reached every ear. But yet I heard them not, as I sat looking before me in mere despair. For I knew not what to hope for, what to advise, or what to do.

Then the door was thrown open, and there was a trampling of feet which I regarded not at all, or as only part of this misery. The feet, I supposed, belonged to the man who was coming to turn us out. I buried my face in my hands and burst into violent weeping.

'Is this some fresh misfortune?' It was my mother who sprang to her feet and spoke. 'Are you come, sir, to say that we owe another two hundred pounds? What would you have with us on such a day? We have nothing for you, sir, nothing at all, whoever you are; we are stripped naked.'

'Madam,' this was his Worship's voice, 'you know not who this gentleman is. Look not for more misfortunes, but for joy and happiness.'

Joy and happiness! What joy? What happiness? I began to prick up my ears, but without much hope and with no faith.

'My lord'—this time it was my father, who saw before him a splendid stranger, and concluded in his madness that it was some great nobleman come to visit him. 'My lord, I thank you for the honour of this visit. My lady will call the men and maids. I fear you are fatigued with travel. You shall take, my lord, a single bowl of turtle soup, as a snack, or stay-stomach, the finest ever made even for the Lord Mayor, with a glass or two of Imperial

Tolay, the rarest in any cellar, before your dinner. Not a word, my lord, not a word till you are refreshed ; not a word, I insist.'

At these utterances I raised my head, but before I had time to look around me, a hand was laid upon my shoulder, while a voice whispered in my ear, 'Drusy !'

Oh, we foolish women ! For when the thing we most long for is vouchsafed, instead of prayers and praise upon bended knee, we fall to crying and to laughing, both together.

Why, when I recovered a little, they were all concerning themselves about me, when they ought to have been doing honour to Ralph. The Fugleman had a glass of cold water in his hand ; my mother was bathing my palms ; Sailor Nan was burning a feather ; my sweetheart was holding my head ; and my father was assuring his Worship that nothing less than the King's own physician should attend his daughter, unless she presently recovered. He also whispered with much gravity that he had long since designed his Drusilla for his lordship, just arrived, who, though of reduced fortunes, was a nobleman of excellent qualities, and would make her happy.

We heard, later, that Ralph brought with him an attorney from Newcastle, a gentleman very learned in the law, and the terror of all the rogues on the banks of the Tyne. With this gentleman and a clerk, beside his own servants, he rode first to the mill.

He found Barbara engaged in her usual work of knitting, with the Bible before her open at some chapter of prophetic woe. No change in her, except that she looked thinner, and the crow's-feet lay about her eyes. She recognised him, but showed no emotion.

'You are come home again,' she said. 'I have expected this. Mathew said the girl lied, but he was afraid, and I knew she did not. Girls do not lie about such things. You come at a fine time, when your sweetheart is begging her bread.'

'What ?' asked Ralph.

'I said she was begging her bread. She said you were prosperous. If fine clothes mean aught you may be. Lord grant they were honestly come by.'

'I will now, Colonel Embleton,' said the attorney, 'place my clerk in possession and seal everything.'

'Where is Mathew ?' asked Ralph.

'He is in the town. You will find him selling their cottage— Drusilla's cottage. By this time your dainty girl will be in the road, bag and baggage.'

'What ?'

'Pride is humbled. The girl has begun to repent of her stubbornness. Of course so fine a gentleman as you would scorn a beggar wench.'

With such words did this foolish and spiteful woman inflame the heart of a man whom she should have conciliated with words of welcome.

He left her and rode into the town with such speed as the snow, now two feet deep, would allow.

An hour later, Mathew, pale and trembling, rushed breathless into the mill.

'Has he been here?'

Barbara nodded.

Mathew went hastily to his room. Here he found the attorney with his clerk.

'These are my papers,' he cried, now in desperation. 'Everything is mine. The house is mine, the mill is mine, the farm is mine.'

'Gently, gently,' said the lawyer. 'Let us hear.'

Mathew played his last card.

'A second will was found,' he said ; 'it is in the desk.'

'We will wait,' said the lawyer, 'until the return of Colonel Embleton.'

When Ralph came back, accompanied by Mr. Carnaby, he found Mathew waiting for him.

'Now,' said the lawyer, 'let us see this second will.'

He opened the desk and drew forth the paper which Mathew pointed out. When he had unfolded and looked at it for a moment, he looked curiously at Mathew.

'This,' he said, 'is your second will?'

'It is,' Mathew replied. 'Found five years ago, and——'

'Quite enough,' said the lawyer. 'Friend,' he had by this time compared the signature with that of the first will, 'I make no charge, I only inform you as a fact, that this document is valueless, as bearing neither date nor witnesses, and if it did, it would still be valueless, because the signature is a forgery, plain and palpable. It will hang someone if it is put forward.'

Mathew dropped his hands by his side. This was the fruit of his labours. He had forged the will ; he had made it of no use by neglecting the witnesses ; he had forged it so clumsily that he was at once detected.

'Any well-wisher of yours, sir,' said the lawyer, 'would recommend you to put that paper in the fire.'

Mathew did so without a word.

'Sir,' said the lawyer, 'you have saved your neck. Have you any more to say about the will?'

He had no more to say. The plots and designs of nine years came to this lame and impotent conclusion.

'Then, Mr. Humble,' the attorney continued, 'I have nothing more to say than this: Colonel Embleton expects an accurate statement of accounts and payment to him of all sums due to him without delay.'

Mathew made no reply ; he was defeated. He left the room, and presently, one of them looking through the open door, saw him leave the house with his sister.

Ralph spoke not one single word to him, good or bad. By this time he had heard of Mathew's attempted abduction and all his iniquities. There was no room in his heart for pity.

In the morning Sailor Nan came to draw her pay. She heard that her husband had deserted her. She lamented the fact, because she had intended to be kept in pork, rum, and tobacco so long as he was alive. But she was easily consoled with a jorum of steaming punch.

Thus vanished from amongst us one who had wrought so much evil, for which I hope that we have long since entirely forgiven him (but he was a desperate villain), and we never knew what became of him.

It was ten years later that Barbara came back alone.

We found her in the porch one summer evening. She was worn and thin, and dressed in dreadful rags.

'Oh,' I cried, moved to pity by her misery, 'come in and eat, and let me find some better clothes for you.'

She refused, but she took a cup of milk.

'I want to see the boy,' she replied in her old manner of speech.

When Ralph came home she said what she had to say.

'Mathew ought to have had the mill. If it had been his, he would not have taken to drink and evil courses. You were an interloper, and we both hated the sight of you. When you went away, I used to pray that you might never come back. The waiting for you and the fear of you made him wicked. That is all I have to say.'

'Where is Mathew?'

'Dead. Ask me no more about him. He is dead.'

Ralph led her, unresisting, into the house.

'Wife,' he said to me, 'you have heard Barbara's confession. I, too, have had hard thoughts about her. Let us forgive, as we hope for forgiveness.'

She stayed with us that night—an unwilling and ungracious guest—and the next day Ralph placed her in a cottage, and gave her an allowance of money, which she took without thanks. Perhaps her heart grew less bitter as years fell upon her; but I know not, for she died and made no sign.

On that year Christmas Day fell on a Thursday. Now, Ralph, who, though a grave man and the colonel of his regiment, showed more than the customary impatience of lovers, would be content with nothing short of being married on the very next day after his return. It is almost incredible that he should have had the forethought to bring with him a special license, so that we were not obliged to have the banns read out. Could I refuse him anything? Therefore, on the Wednesday morning, the very next day after he came back, we were married in presence of all the town, I believe, man, woman, and child, while the bells rang out, and our joyful hearts were warm, despite the cold without. I was so poor in worldly goods that I must have gone to the sacred ceremony with nothing better than my plain stuff frock, but for the benevolence of good Mrs. Carnaby, who lent me a most beautiful brocaded silk gown, which, with all kinds of foreign gauds, such as necklaces, bracelets, and jewels for the hair, which my lover—nay, my bridegroom—bestowed upon me, made me so fine that his Worship was so good as to say that never a more beautiful bride had been married, or would hereafter be married, in Warkworth Church.

Thus do fine feathers make fine birds. When the next bride is married in brocaded silk, with a hoop, her hair done by the barber, and her homely person decorated with jewels, people will be found to say the same thing. Yet, since my husband, who is the only person I must consider, was so good as to find his wife beautiful, should I not rejoice and be thankful for this strange power of one's outward figure—women cannot understand it—which bewitches men and robs them of their natural sense until they become used to it.

After the wedding we went home to the mill, where my husband spread a great feast. In the evening came the mummers with Sailor Nan, who drank freely of punch, and wished us joy in language more nautical than polite. His Worship slept at the mill because he was overcome with the abundance and strength of the punch. Even the Fugleman, for the first time in man's memory, had to be carried to bed, preserving his stiffness of back even in the sleep of intoxication. And the next day we had another royal feast, to which all were invited who had known my dear husband in his youth. But to me it was a continual feast to be in the presence of my dear, to have my hand in his and to rejoice in the warmth of his steadfast eyes.

We are all, I hope, Christian folk, wherefore no one will be surprised to hear that on the morning of the day after the marriage, which was Christmas Day, after the singing of the hymn, 'When shepherds watch their flocks by night,' my husband, giving me his hand, led me forth before all the people, and in their presence thanked God solemnly for his safe return, and for other blessings (I knew full well what these meant). Then the Fugleman leading, his pike held at salute, he recited the Lord's Prayer. Thus in seemly and solemn fashion was the long sorrow of nine years turned into a joy which will endure, I doubt not, beyond this earthly pilgrimage.

THEY WERE MARRIED.

PART I.—MON DÉSIR.

CHAPTER I.

A NEW-YEAR'S DAWN.

NEW-YEAR'S DAY, in Palmiste Island, is very nearly the longest in the whole year ; it is also about the hottest, if one may say as much without giving offence to other days. It is on this account that the sun on this day, having so much work to do, gets up as early as six o'clock in the morning, an hour before his July time, after announcing his intention by sending up preliminary fireworks in red and crimson. When the cocks see these rockets in the east they leave off crowing and go to roost. If you ask naturalists why the cocks crow all night in Palmiste, they generally say that it is because the island lies south of the Equator. Those who are not satisfied with this explanation are further told that it is by the laws of development and the natural growth of ideas that the Gallic mind has been brought to prefer coolness for times of crowing. The reasons of things offered by science are, we know, beautifully satisfying, and always make us feel as if we could almost create a world for ourselves if we only had a good big lump of clay and a box of stored electricity and a bucket of water and a pint of compressed air. When the cocks have left off, the white man's dogs, and the Malabar dogs and the Pariah dogs immediately take up the tuneful tale, so that silence shall never be a reproach to the island. The journey performed by the chariot of his Majesty the Sun on that day, a most fatiguing one to his horses, involves a tremendous climb at the start and a breathless descent at the finish ; and is, in fact, nothing less than a vertical semi-circular arc in the heavens. The nature of the curve may be illustrated for unscientific persons by any young lady who will kindly raise her arms above the head, and join the tips of her fingers. At stroke of noon, on that day every man Jack and mother's son in the place becomes another Peter Schlemihl, inasmuch as he has no shadow. Strangers, at such a time, creep round houses and great buildings and precipices looking for the usual shade. They go to the north side, the south, the east, and the west, and find none. Then they think their wits must be gone for good, and sit them down to cry. The woolly-pated sons of Africa, for their part, rejoice in perpendicular rays ; they have taken the roof off their straw hats the better to enjoy them ; they sit in the open, courting their genial warmth ; they acknowledge with a grateful sigh that, after all, there is a little heat sometimes to be got in a generally cold and cheerless world. It is not till after seven in the evening that the sun has finished the journey and is ready to plunge red-hot into the cool waves. For five minutes or so after his header there is a tremendous seething and roaring of the maddened water : it is, of course, too far off to hear the noise, but anyone can see the smoke of it, which is red and fiery, cooling down to sapphire and then becoming grey, after which the stars come out, and it is night.

In this English land of mist and fog we never see the phenomenon of sunrise at all ; for either it is hidden behind cloud, or it rises too early, or it is too cold for us to get up and look at it. There must be, indeed, many men, quite elderly men, among us who have never seen the sun rise at all. Now, in Palmiste most of the people behold this most wonderful of natural phenomena every day. Perhaps the man on the Signal-mountain has the best view, because from his elevated position he can see the leaping of the sun from the sea, and the long furrows of light upon the startled ocean, and the sudden renewal of the unnumbered smiles, and the rolling of the mists about the valleys. But, as the man on the Signal-mountain is too often a mere creature of duty, and must always subordinate sentiment to the watching for ships, it is probable that more joy is got out of the sunrise by the people below, who can give their whole attention to the exhibition provided by Nature.

Certainly, there is plenty to be seen down below. There was a pair, for instance, standing in the verandah of the house belonging to the estate of Mon Désir, who seemed, on this New-Year's dawn, to find a great deal of enjoyment in the hour and the scene before them, though there was nothing that they had not seen before, times out of mind. But then they had one great advantage over the man on the Signal-mountain, that he is one and they were two—Hic et Hæc : Ille cum Illà—which makes a very great difference indeed. And they had other advantages. For, when the sun first appeared to them over the brow of the hill between themselves and the sea he shone on this particular morning straight down an avenue of palms ; he painted every leaf of every tree so that it glowed like red gold ; as for the trunks, the tall green trunks, he painted them in a great variety of colour, such as carmine and golden red, and a dark green inclined to go off into purple, and a most lovely, creamy, rich, soft brown, which did the eyes good to see, all the more because it only lasted a few moments. The two who looked caught their breath and gasped, so beautiful was the scene. To make it the more complete, because a suggestion of life always improves a picture, there suddenly appeared at the end of the avenue an Indian woman : she was dressed rather better than most coolies' wives, and, being a Madrassee and not a common Bombay person, she wore a long skirt or petticoat down to her heels, with a red jacket, and bangles up to her elbows, and, over head, shoulders, and all, a veil of coarse gauze. This is the kind of thing that the rising sun likes : it is good material for a sun to operate upon at his first joyous outset : so he seized upon that woman and turned her into a bride, standing rapt, motionless, waiting for the groom, clothed and veiled, mystic, wonderful, in white lace, and he caused colours inexpressible in words to play about the dress beneath the veil. Only for a moment. Then they raised their heads, this pair of early risers, and saw how, upon the peak of the highest mountain in the island, there lay another bridal veil, but of cloud, and how the sunshine struck it and it flew back as if the bridegroom was come and would gaze upon the face of his bride. And there were smaller things to note, for the lawn at their feet, not quite like an English lawn, because nothing in all the world is so good as a good English thing at its best, but a well-kept and tolerably smooth lawn, glittered as if it was strewn with a million diamonds and was worth the whole of the Cape, with Potosi and Golconda thrown in ; beside the lawn the glorious Flamboyant hung out its flaming blossoms to greet the sun, and the Bougainvilliers proudly showed its purple flowers, and the banana-trees and acacias with their perfumed flowers, and the Elephant creepers, and wonderful things with leaves of crimson and gold and long botanical names, which in England would have had pet and pretty names, welcomed the sun and proclaimed that they had all grown each one twelve inches at least during the night in order to honour the dawn of New-Year's Day.

The house was long and of one story, built with a deep verandah all round it, that on one side forming a kind of general sitting-room, open all day long to all airs that blow, affording almost a quadrangular draught ; grass curtains, now pulled up, protected it from the afternoon sun and the white glare of the moon ; it was laid with grass mats, and there were long cane chairs in it, and small tables with work and books upon them. Evidently a place used for the daily life. Three or four doors opened upon it ; that on the left hand belonged to the private room, or study, or office of Mr. Kemyss, Seigneur of Mon Désir ; that on the right led into the boudoir or schoolroom, or retreat of Virginie when she felt disposed to be alone ; the door in the middle led into the salon, a large room, with a piano, and a few, not many, engravings, and more cane chairs, with books and magazines—a place not in the least like an English drawing-room, yet filled with the atmosphere of home and refinement—the haunt and home of ladies. Such a house in Palmiste is constructed entirely, so to speak, with a view to the salon and the salle à manger. They are the two principal rooms—the only rooms. To the right and left of them on the same floor are the bedrooms ; at the corners and in unexpected places, built out as the family grows, are other smaller bedrooms belonging to the children or the girls. The verandah at the sides is provided with jalousies, so that it may serve for a dressing-room, bath-room, or nursery. The bedrooms are simply furnished each with a pretty little French bedstead in green and gold, protected by a mosquito-curtain and an armoire. There is nothing else, because nobody in Palmiste is expected to use the bedroom for any other purpose than sleep. The salle à manger, papered with one of those French designs—a man on horseback, a girl with a guitar, anything—which repeats the same scene a thousand times, is meant for a feeding or banqueting room, and nothing else. Therefore it contains nothing at all but a table, a sideboard, and chairs. At the back is the kitchen, and one can only say of a Palmiste kitchen that, although many a good dinner is turned out from it, the stranger would do well not to pry into its mysteries, nor to ask of the Indian cook how he does it. Behind the kitchen is a long garden, planted with all kinds of vegetables, European or tropical, according to the season of the year : at the end of the kitchen-garden there is a double row of banana-trees, their leaves blown into ragged ribbons and broken ends, each with its pendent cluster of green fruit and purple bud. And behind the bananas there are the *cases*—the cottages for the servants and their wives ; and here there is quite a colony of little brown babies sprawling about in the sun, with no more clothes than Adam before the Fall, and bright-eyed boys, miracles of intelligence, and already eager to learn the various and multiform tricks, lies, treacheries, and make-believes, by which a crafty Oriental may make his way from small things unto great.

On the right of the great house stands a smaller one, called the Pavilion. The son of the house sleeps here, and all bachelor guests, of whom at the season of the *bonne année* there are always three times as many as there are beds to put them in, so that they toss up for the beds, and those who lose make out as they best can upon mattresses stretched upon the floor. Therefore, the New Year is by this arrangement turned into a most beautiful and festive time for the mosquitoes.

The Pavilion has also its own verandah, but much smaller and narrower, and without any curtains or mats. Yet there are plenty of chairs in it ; chairs with prolonged arms, in which the occupant may put up his feet ; basket-work chairs, with a ledge which may be pulled out for the feet ; low chairs in which one's feet need no support ; rocking-chairs ; and a lovely grass hammock, in which, with a Coringhee cigar, and something with ice in it, and perhaps a book requiring no effort to understand it, and dealing with pleasant subjects, one may while away the hottest afternoon, swinging slowly. There is not much paint left about the old Pavilion, it is true ; the floor of the verandah, which is of concrete, is cracked ; the jalousies of the bedroom windows are out of repair ; but the roof is still weather-proof, and the beds are comfortable, and there are these chairs to sit upon, and the verandah faces the east, so that in the afternoon, when man most inclines to rest and meditation, the sun may be avoided.

To the right of the Pavilion, again, was the sugar-house, a great place, with the mysteries of which we have nothing to do, except that the whirr of the machinery and the wheels, and the loud, well-satisfied breathing of its untiring steam-engine sounded pleasantly on mornings when the crop had commenced. On this day, however —New-Year's Day—the day of the *bonne année*, no man, not even a Malabar, on a sugar estate can be expected to work. Outside the sugar-house lay piles of the white *bagasse*, the refuse of the canes which have been crushed, with their sweet and rather sickly smell ; and here, too, was the great barn-like stable for the mules, with the doors always left wide open, because these sagacious animals know very well which is the best place for them, and are far too wise to go straying from a comfortable shelter where they are well fed and well looked after. Why, as they very well know, mules who have strayed have been known to get lost in the ravines, and to tumble over waterfalls, and be eaten by big eels, or to be captured by Maroons, and made to lead a deuce of a life carrying out their villanies in the forest. Who would be the accomplice of brigands and poachers ? Beyond the mule stable a road leads to the Indian Camp, a village where the coolies of the estate live with their wives, their babies, their brass pots, their dogs, their goats and little kids, their cocks and hens and chickens, and their pigs. It is quite a large and populous village, in which the dreams of the Socialist are realised ; for all the houses are exactly alike, and the people are all on the same social depression, and the way of living is the same for all, and there is a beautiful, monotonous level. There are such villages and communities in England ; but they are rare. One such I remember in the Forest of Dean, which seems to resemble an Indian camp on a sugar estate ; but even there they have a church and two or three chapels, and there are differences of rank and position. The camp is a noisy place, too ; for the babies never cease crying, and the children quarrel continually, and the dogs for ever bark, and the women accuse each other for ever in shrill and ear-piercing voices. What do they accuse each other of ? Matter of cakes, my masters, and ghee, and gungee, and cocoa-nut oil, and nose-rings and silver bangles. What farther, one knoweth not. Every day, after a whole morning spent in invective, retort, accusation and defence, they sally forth, and bring the case before the Sahib, the Seigneur and Lord of the estate, who hears the evidence, and makes an award, and admonishes them to keep the peace. They accept the award as final, but yet they do not keep the peace.

And on all sides of the house there stretch the broad fields of the estate, planted with the sugar-cane ; narrow paths cross them, and sometimes there is a rough-and-ready tramway. All day long the coolies work among them, cleaning and weeding, heedless of the hot sun, because they are anointed, and beautifully shine, with cocoa-nut oil, so that every man's back is a mirror for his friends. Beyond the cane-fields, on all sides but one, is the forest ; for there are yet miles of forest left ; and beyond and among the wild woods stand the everlasting hills.

Now, when the first glimmerings of the dawn were welcomed by the silence of the cocks and the barkings of the dogs, there began in the mule stable an uncertain agitation, as of expectancy, and, each, in his stall, the mules began to open eyes, to kick out in dreams, to whinny, to fidget, to shake a tail, to paw the ground, and to look around. At exactly the moment, and no other, when the sun first touched the topmost leaves and the single spiral shoot of every palm-tree in the Avenue, the oldest and most sagacious mule left his stall, and led the way out of the stable into the bagasse yard, followed by all his friends and lively companions. Then there ensued such a turning over on backs, kicking of legs, rolling about on the soft stuff, champing of the sugary canes, and letting out of heels at each other in pure gamesomeness, that you would have said the mules knew it was New-Year's Day, and had begun at very sunrise to enjoy the holiday. This was not so, however, for mules are a philosophical, albeit a light-hearted race, and know that life is made up of twelve hours' labour and twelve hours' repose. Therefore they do what they can to get through the first half as easily as may be, and go in for unmitigated enjoyment of the second.

After the mules had spread themselves out on the bagasse, and the Indians' dogs were all barking in the camp, and the Indian women all scolding, there was no longer any pretence possible for lying in bed. So that the Chinaman who kept the only shop on the estate rolled off his counter, and opened his door, and let down his shutter, and allowed the escape of the night's accumulated fragrance. A village shop in this our native land presents a rich field for research in the science of smells, particularly on a warm summer morning, when it has just been opened. But what is it compared to a Chinaman's shop in Palmiste? Bacon and cheese form our own staple. One cannot deny that these are good, separately or in combination, for the production of a rich and grateful perfume. But the Chinaman, in a much smaller space, has the fragrant and united product of snook, which was once live cod-fish, half-cured pork, rotten bananas, sardine-boxes lying open for a week, a keg of arrack, cheese, gungee, his own opium-pipe, cocoa-nut oil, blacking, and cigars, all combining together to produce a stench of extraordinary strength. When the doors and windows were open it fell out, a solid though invisible lump of concrete smell, irregularly shaped, which rolled, slowly at first, but afterwards more rapidly, down the hill. On the way it encountered a brood of tender yellow ducklings, who were going along—poor dears—thinking of nothing at all but worms and warm mud. These pretty innocents, when the rolling mass fell upon them, all tumbled over on their backs, opened their beaks, and quacked their last. Then the ball rolled over the side of the road down a steep slope, upon which it met and poisoned a promising family of young tandreks, and so over the edge of the ravine, getting broken into a thousand fragments, and doing no more harm to anybody.

Not far from the Chinaman's stood a little cottage, built of packing-cases and roofed with their tin lining, in which there lived an old, old negress, well advanced in the nineties. She was a witch by profession : she revealed the future, either by cards, or by inspection of the palm, or by interpretation of dreams, or by the reading of omens ; she charmed away sprains, warts, bruises, and internal injuries by the simple application of her own hand ; she cursed people's enemies for them, and made crafty gri-gri, which revengeful persons smarting under a sense of wrong bought and placed under the beds of those who had wrought them that injury, so that these wicked folk presently fell into waste and consumption and slow dying—a joy to behold. She cured all diseases by herbs which she gathered in the forest and under the rocks of the ravine ; and it was whispered that if you wanted such a thing as a safe but elegant preparation of poison, which would kill without leaving a trace behind, this good old lady would make it up for you from plants which she would find in every hedge. She, too, awoke with the dogs and the mules, and perceived that here was another day whose joyful course awaited her running. She found her joints rather stiff at first uprising, a thing which surprised her, because she had not been brought up in her childhood to expect it, and she sat for an hour or two in the warmest and sunniest place, with her grizzled old wool exposed to the rays, and so gradually recovered the use of her limbs and got warm, and felt young again, and set to work upon the finishing of a most beautiful gri-gri, with a cat's skull in it and two dogs' paws and a shark's tooth—a gri-gri which was intended to cause internal pains and burnings not to be allayed, and thirst insatiable, and sleepless rolling about at night, and mental distress, loss of appetite, delirium, convulsions, death and a long black box. And all for five dollars. She is a most useful and admirable creature, and it is sad to think that when she goes—she is not gone yet—she will leave no successor. There used, in the old days, to be plenty of such old women, but emancipation was a cruel blow to them : the new contentment and ease of the negroes discouraged the profession ; there is no longer any demand, to speak of, for gri-gri and vegetable poisons ; the coolies know for themselves where to find stramonium and what it will do in skilful hands : the old slaves are dead, and their sons are not revengeful on account of their fathers' wrongs, and when this old woman goes there will be no one left to carry on her forgotten craft. The reflec-

tion should make the old witch sad ; but she does not reflect : she
thinks she is still in comparative youth ; she takes no heed of time,
and she believes she will live for ever.

The two standing on the verandah were a young man of two-
and-twenty or so and a girl of seventeen. They were always up
first, and they always met here and had their morning talk at sunrise, while the girl poured out the early tea and sent it round to the
. bedrooms. The Indian boy, who had made the tea and brought it
from the kitchen, stood on the steps rubbing his sleepy eyes ; and
lying huddled up, also on the verandah steps, was old Suzette,
the black nurse, in a wonderful blue cotton frock and red cotton
turban and bare feet. Her grandsons, Napoleon de Turenne and
Rohan Auvergne de Turenne, were at the Grand Collége ; and
her youngest son, their father, who had gone into the brokery line
and had been greatly successful, drove about, a splendid personage,
in his own carriage. But Suzette remained a nurse ; and she was too
conscientious a nurse to allow her foster-daughter to get up before
her or to remain talking with Monsieur Tom without her presence.

'Chokra,' said the girl to the Indian boy, 'this great cup for
the burra Sahib, and this little one for the mem Sahib.'

She spoke, only with these two or three Hindustani words, in
the Creole patois, which has been adopted by the Indian and
Chinese coolies, and by the Malays, Singhalese, Portuguese, Malagassy, Somaulis, and all the races who are represented, in this
island of a thousand tongues, as the common medium. But, like
many who have been brought up on a sugar estate, she was a poly-
glot young lady : her father was English and her mother French.
She spoke her father's language perfectly well, with a tendency to
make a soft guttural out of the 'r,' which was not unpleasant ; and
she spoke with perfect fluency her mother's language ; but she
would have been as much lost as any Canadian among the half-
uttered syllables and nods and winks which stand for French in
fashionable Paris ; for, in truth, the French of Palmiste may be
pure, but it is a little old-fashioned. And she could talk Hindustani
of a kind, not the Hindustani of the schools, to be sure, but the
tongue of the people, free and unencumbered by grammar and
syntax, and understanded of all alike, by the gentle Tamulman, or
by him who talks the soft Canarese or the sonorous Pali. . She
could not talk Chinese, because nobody can, and even the Chinamen
out of their native country laugh at their own language ; nor any
of the Madagascar dialects, because the Malagassy are a polite
people, and do not expect it ; nor Malay, because the Malay is quick
to learn for himself any language that may be going about ; nor
any of those African tongues which may yet linger in the memories
of the blacks, because there is nothing the East African negro more
readily forgets than his own tongue, especially when there is such
a beautiful language as Creole lying ready for his use, and because
nobody ever learns any African language who can help it.

'The men,' said the girl, 'are late this morning. I suppose, too, they sat up last night, and drank too much brandy and soda. Did you sit up, Tom ?'

She spoke as if too much brandy and soda was an accident which might happen to anybody ; and, indeed, in this thirsty island there do happen a surprising number of these accidents every year. So that it is a pity steps are not taken to prevent them.

The young man replied that, for his own part, he went to bed when his father left them, which was at half-past ten ; but that some of them sat late, and there certainly were a great many bottles of soda lying on the verandah ; and that they were all fast asleep when he got up, which was before daylight.

He had in his hand a pine-apple, which he had just cut in the garden, and was eating it with a fork. This, if you please, is the true way to eat a pine ; and the best time to eat it is in the morning, when it has been freshly cut.

'Will you have a mango, Virginie ?' he asked. 'They are ready to be gathered.'

'Send some to the Pavilion,' she replied.

'Ayapana tea,' he said, 'would be more to the purpose. Suzette may go round presently and find out if anybody wants it. If I meet old Pierre, I will ask him to take some *cocos tendres* to the Pavilion. Don't forget the letchis, Virginie.'

Ayapana tea is a grateful drink, made by pouring boiling water upon a certain herb so called : its properties are many : it restores tone to the afflicted after a severe night ; it cools coppers ; it drives away headache ; it restores the power of coherent speech ; it revives the sluggish brain ; in fact, it was planted, in the first instance, by the man who made the earliest vineyard, and he placed a root of it between every vine. As for the *coco tendre*, Tom meant the unripe cocoa-nut, which is gathered for the purpose of providing a cool and refreshing morning draught. In cases which do not require the severity of ayapana tea, the *coco tendre* is efficacious, and it brings with it a coolness which mounts to the brain and runs along the veins and gives elasticity to the limbs. And as for man-goes, they are good for all conditions of men ; the temperate, such as Tom. and the eternally thirsty, such as Sandy McAndrew ; they are the sweetest gift of nature to the dweller in the tropics ; they refresh and revive after a hot and sleepless night ; they bring back hope, faith, and courage ; they reconcile one to life even when the rainy season has begun, and the floods of heaven are descending, and a soft and steamy heat lies upon the earth, and a vapour rises like that of a universal washing day, and the mildew grows and spreads visibly on the boots, and the covers drop off the books, and the very cigars go out of curl. These two were too young to know much about shattered nerves and revivers and pick-me-ups. But they had heard of such things. Therefore Virginie received the allusion to ayapana tea with sympathy, and understood what was proposed to be effected by means of the *coco tendre*.

She was seventeen, which is Creole for twenty. And, because

R

she was a Creole, she was of slight and graceful figure ; for the same reason she carried herself well and was *gracieuse*—one would like to add a few more of those delightful adjectives which French poets and novelists have at their command. She was dressed in a simple white frock, with a crimson ribbon round her neck.

Nature, who is always—the dear old lady !—thinking how she can spare something more to set off and adorn a pretty girl, had given her a wealth of lovely light curling hair, as soft as silk, which lay all about her face and clung to her pretty cheeks like tendrils of a vine, as if it loved to be exactly in that place and wanted no other ; her eyes were blue and soft, with long lashes ; her cheek was not ruddy like an English maiden's, but touched with just the tenderest bloom of colour ; for, although she had never left the tropical island, she lived among the mountains—Mon Désir was a thousand feet above the sea, so that the air was sharp. Besides, Virginie rambled and climbed up the slopes of the hills and down the steep sides of the precipitous ravine, and was as sure-footed as a chamois and as steady as an Alpine guide. This it was which lent her cheek its rose. Altogether, a lovely and dainty maiden ; a girl on whom eyes were already bent full of admiration and hope ; but not yet spoiled, though she had been out ever since the last Queen's birthday ball. Her face and her gestures were full of vivacity, because her mother was a French woman ; her eyes were full of truth and loyalty because her father was an English gentleman ; at every turn of her head, at every quick movement of her hand, one was reminded of her descent, because this was French and that was English, and this she caught from her mother and that she inherited from her father.

As for the young man called Tom, he was dressed as only Colonials dare to dress. That is to say, he wore a flannel shirt without any collar and *all* rags, and a pair of flannel trousers, patched and darned in various places, yet almost as ragged as the shirt ; round his waist was tied a belt made of long red silk ; he had on a short coat or jacket of common blue cotton, something like that affected by the British butcher : it is strong, durable, and light, therefore it is greatly in fashion among the people of Palmiste, although it does wear white at the seams : for head-covering he wore an old helmet well battered and bruised. This was his morning dress, the things in which he rode about the fields, looking after weeds and all the evils which assail the sugar-cane. He was his father's manager, and he took this journey every morning, starting at daybreak and returning about ten. He was a well set up youth, not so broad in the shoulder as many Englishmen, with brown hair cropped close, and a small beard and moustache ; not a face betokening great intellect, nor had his shoulders the studious stoop ; nor was he shortsighted ; nor did he concern himself at all about literature or art, or the popular scientific chatter, or the current topics of the day. In fact, very few young men had read fewer books than Tom Kemyss. Yet he was not a fool : he studied machinery so as to understand the engines and works of his mill; he studied agricultural chemistry for practical purposes; he was handy in the carpenter's shop; he was good at all kinds of sports, was cunning of fence, a good shot, and as plucky a lad as ever stepped. And though he had never left his native island, and was seldom absent from his father's estate, he was not at all a rustical person, not a mere *hobereau*, nor a boor. Quite the contrary: his manners and carriage were as good as if he had been brought up in a London square and at Eton and Oxford. And he had been trained by his father in the old-fashioned ideas—which they say, those who know, are rapidly dying out—as to the courtesy, respect, honour, and service due to women.

When he had finished his pine-apple he strode away, and Virginie heard him whistling to his dogs, and then there was a mighty trampling of hoofs, because the daily struggle then began between Tom and his horse. The generous steed, being of high mind and proud of his descent, resolved every morning that this should be the last of obedience, and so attempted to bring about a revolution. When the attempt was quelled he galloped away obedient again.

Virginie poured out another cup of tea more carefully than the rest, placed it on a tray, and carried it away with her own hands. It was her mother's tea, and the girl had done this small service ever since she could carry anything.

When she was gone the chokra was left alone. At least, he thought he was alone. Unluckily, he forgot Suzette, and acted as any solitary boy might be expected to act.

He looked about him for a moment. The sugar-basin was filled with the delightful crystal sugar, as sweet as sugar candy, and as sparkling as so many diamonds. It was made in the mill of Mon Désir, and is the best sugar in the world, a great deal better than the white lumps of which we are so proud. The boy knew this fact, and it made his fingers to curl and his brown eyes to glow.

He had never learned the Church Catechism, this poor child; otherwise, no doubt——

Pring! Prang! Crick! Crack! Four, if you please: two on each ear, so that the report was heard a mile off, and every chokra on the estate jumped clean out of his jacket—because he had no shoes to jump out of—in terror and sympathy.

'Hein! Ha! Thou wilt steal, then, good-for-nothing? Take that—and that—little pig of Malabar!'

The boy fled to the kitchen, where he was received with the jeers of those who had not been recently detected.

And the old woman sat down on the steps again, in the sun, and laughed with her eyes, her lips, her teeth, her head, her hands, her portly person, and her feet. She brimmed over and she shook with laughter.

R 2

CHAPTER II.

THE SQUIRE.

AMONG the many questions which may be put by fools for the discomfiture of those who pretend to be wise, is the question how it is that men can be found to put their money into a sugar estate.

For the dangers and risks are great; the work is hard; the climate is generally trying; and the ultimate results are wrapped in a delightful cloud of uncertainty. As for the capital required at the outset, that is so great that it would maintain a whole family in England. On the mere interest of it they might take a house at Kensington, and give dinner parties, and go every year to the seaside. As for the thing to be grown—the cane—it is surrounded on all sides by innumerable enemies, like everything else which is carefully planted, tended, cockered up, and rendered effeminate. Sometimes it is an insect, which comes from no one knows where, and has no other object in life than just to bore holes right through the cane, and so to destroy it; or it is a worm that appears suddenly in the ground, and refuses to eat anything except root of sugar-cane, and no one knows where *he* comes from either; or it is a kind of rot; or it is a wasting away and a drying up of the sweet juices; or it is some other of the many thousand diseases which affect vegetable life. Sometimes, also, it is a troop of monkeys, who get into the fields by night, and tear up the canes for very wanton mischief. Above all, there are the hurricanes, which lay the canes prostrate, tear them up by the roots, and wash them out of the ground; and they may come any year or every year. So that, unless fortune is more than commonly kind, the end of every planter who has not so large a capital that he can stand up against two, three, or even four bad years in succession is the same—monotonously the same. That end is, in fact, smash; and his estate is sold. And then, because hope goes on springing in that elastic and everlasting way of which we know, there is never wanting a purchaser with a little money to throw away, and the old game begins again, with chinking of glasses and the sparkle of champagne, and the best wishes of friends, and the confidence of the young beginner.

That, however, is only the fate of the small capitalist. If you have got plenty of money to begin with, and want to multiply it by ten, and can afford to wait, and like tropical life and exile, with the things which some weak-kneed brethren call discomforts, such as hot days and vertical suns, and mosquitoes and prickly heat, and insipid beef and tasteless mutton, you can do nothing better than take a sugar estate and manage it yourself. Some day people in England will find out how profitable a thing it is, so long as you need not borrow money to go on with. Then there will be com-

panies started. Owners will sell to promoters for four times the
value of the estate : that will be good for the owners, who will
come to Paris or London, or Monte Carlo, and have a fling so long
as the money lasts : the promoters will sell the estates to the share-
holders for ten times their value : this will be good for the promoters who will make money by one swindle, to lose it in the next :
then the companies will issue shares, publish prospectuses, and
exhibit their sugar in grocers' shops ; and they will appoint
managers of local experience. These managers will be so experienced
that they will sell the sugar, receive the money for the coolies,
put everything in their own pockets, and bolt, working their way
round by New Caledonia and Tahiti to San Francisco, and from
there to New Orleans, enjoying the roses and rapture of gambling
saloons, bars, and billiard-rooms. The company will then 'bust
up,' and the estate will be sold for half its real value to a local person, with no money but what he borrows from the bank, and all
will go on as before, and, if we are all happy, let us not sit down
to ask what odds.

The proprietor of Mon Désir, Captain Kemyss, commonly
called the Squire by his English friends, became a planter through
falling in love. It was in this way.

About five-and-twenty years ago, when people in Palmiste were
beginning to think that they might try to forget the calamity of
their great and terrible cholera year and to leave off telling each
other horrible stories, there arrived in the island an extremely
sprightly regiment, the officers in which were nearly all young,
rich, and disposed to make things cheerful for themselves and all
their friends, so far as lies in the power of the English officer. They
manifested this disposition from the day of landing ; they received
callers with effusion ; they called upon everybody, bought horses,
dog-carts, buggies, pony-traps, American traps, drove about the
country, accepted invitations to all the planters' houses, turned up
uninvited to the Sunday morning breakfasts, held magnificent
guest nights, allowed their band to play as often as they were
asked, and gave balls the like of which had never before been
heard of. Also, they offered prizes and cups at the races, and rode
to win them ; and they had an eleven, and for the first year or so
they played the national game with vigour ; they were always
pleased to see everybody in barracks at all hours and at all meals ;
brandy and soda was continually being produced ; they exhibited
and kept up, to the admiration of philosophers, a real Charles
Lever-like air of solid, substantial enjoyment of life, as if there
were no headaches, as if youth would always last, as if there was
nothing in the world to care for beyond sport— in moderation ;
cricket, billiards, and racquets—always in moderation ; parade and
drill—in strict moderation ; gambling—in tolerable moderation ;
feasting, drinking, and love-making, without stint or stay, moderation, or any restraints beyond those imposed by physical consideration, such as the dimensions of the waist or the absence of

the opposite sex. The colonel looked young, being about forty-eight, but he was tough—besides, the resources of science were called in to maintain the dark glossiness of his hair and moustache ; the majors also looked young, being about six-and-thirty ; the captains were in the early thirties and the late twenties ; the subs. were all under five-and-twenty. It was a thirsty, toss-pot regiment ; a rattling, rollicking, story-telling, song-singing, card-playing, racing, billiard-playing, betting, gambling, drinking, sit-up-late regiment ; a handsome, flirting, dancing, mean-nothing, detrimental regiment ; a regiment, in short, which turned the heads of all the girls with flattery and compliments and dances, and all the things that youth most loves. In this regiment there were a couple of young men—that is, comparatively young, for they had both already got their company—who were close friends, and not, like their companions, wholly given over to sport and amusement ; they had, in fact, the unusual good sense to perceive that life cannot be all champagne and skittles. Wherefore they sometimes went to bed early, did not take soda and brandy as a pick-me-up before breakfast, observed a liberal moderation in strong drink during the day, and did not look upon all pretty girls as made solely for the amusement of the man with the scarlet jacket. In fact, they were the small minority which among every madcap crew are always found to spoil sport by squaretoed temperance. In any other company they would have been considered as rather dashing young fellows ; in this, the comparative soberness of their manners and morals was felt to be a standing reproach to their brother-officers. It is a safe rule that one must not be more virtuous than one's fellows. Therefore the regiment heard with great relief and thankfulness that not only were these two engaged to be married to girls of the island, but that they were going to sell out at once.

They became, in fact, engaged to two cousins, girls of French descent, who had been brought up together and were to each other as two sisters. They were alike in appearance, in tastes, and in accomplishments ; they resembled each other in agreeing to be very much in love each with her own English wooer ; they were both young, both beautiful, and both amiable. They differed, however, in one small point, felt by both young ladies to be of no importance whatever ; namely, that one was rich and the other poor. Captain Ferrier, the grandson of a peer, who married the rich girl, was himself already tolerably well provided ; Captain Kemyss, the son of a bishop, who had only a moderate patrimony, married the one who was poor. Now, if he had stayed in the army, or had gone home and lived quietly upon his modest income, he would have got along very well. But when he found that Ferrier intended to remain in Palmiste and cultivate his wife's sugar estate ; when he learned, further, that his own wife would like nothing in the world so well as to remain all her days in the place where she was born ; when he considered the fertility and goodness of the land ; when the pleasures of a planter's life were pointed out to him, with the chances of a great fortune, he yielded to temptation and bought an estate. Observe the difference at the outset between the two friends. Captain Ferrier married a girl who was the only child of a planter with the largest and most fertile estate in the island ; with his own money and with the money already made out of the estate he would be enabled, whatever happened, to ride out the storm. Therefore, with ordinary care, his prosperity was assured. Captain Kemyss, on the other hand, invested the whole of his own very moderate fortune in purchasing an estate. To complete the purchase he had, like most of his brother-planters, to borrow of the bank a third of the purchase-money at nine per cent. He therefore became, for life, a man encumbered with a hopeless debt. One son was born to him, Tom by name, now his manager, partner, and overseer. His friend Ferrier had several children, but all died except one, a girl—Virginie. When Ferrier died himself, during the great fever year of 1867, Captain Kemyss became the guardian of the child and the executor of the will. Madame Ferrier and her daughter came to live with him, and they formed, Creole fashion, one household.

There are some men to whom the backwoods or colonial life, far from friends, seems to strengthen and deepen their old ideas about the most desirable manner of life. Captain Kemyss—the ' Squire '—carried on in the quiet Palmiste bungalow the kind of life to which he had been himself brought up. He was on his tropical estate an English country gentleman ; he educated his son in his own ideas ; it was through him that Tom showed no rusticity, and Virginie no Creole insularity. He was now a man of sixty ; tall, grey-headed, with a grey moustache ; he had a military bearing still ; he was a member of the Legislative Council, and was, therefore, the Honourable Captain Kemyss, and in the whole colony there was no one who bore so good a name, or was held in such great honour, or was more regarded for integrity and trustworthiness in all his doings as he.

His life would have been perfectly happy, but for a certain grim spectre, which would not be confined in a cupboard, but kept marching about with him wherever he went ; stood behind him at dinner ; sat on his bed at night, and never left him. It was the lean and gaunt ghost of bankruptcy. He first raised this ghost by much calculation and sad foreboding in the hurricane year of 1868 ; two or three good years laid it in the Red Sea ; then bad years followed, and up it sprang again, vivacious and sprightly as Jack-in-the-Box, and more horrible to look at. After that it was never laid again, but came every year nearer to him, looked larger, and shook a more threatening finger. Some men are so thick-skinned that, although they see the danger afar off, and know that they will shipwreck upon it, yet they go about their business in perfect happiness, regardless of the certain future. The Squire, who was as courageous as most men, trembled and shook with shame and terror when he thought of the word bankruptcy. The year 1880 was, for the estate of Mon Désir a bad year ; the yield was poor ; it seemed as if the soil was, perhaps, giving out ; prices were not high ; the crop was short ; the bank was beginning an ominous note of warning. Still, if 1881 was good—if there were no hurricanes and prices improved—the estate would pull through somehow, as it had pulled through so many years before, by being able to meet the interest of the debt ; if not, if anything at all of the many things which might happen went against him, then, then—the blow could no longer be staved off—he must go to the wall. The prospect, to a man turned sixty, of seeing the whole of his life's work destroyed and brought to nought, was a very terrible thing to consider.

There was one way out of the difficulty ; one certain way ; yet it was a way which he would not suffer himself to dwell upon. How if Tom were to marry Virginie ? For then there could be no more troubles about money. The two estates—hers, large and prosperous ; his, small and struggling—adjoined. They could be worked with the same mill and machinery. Tom could manage both. No one knew better than himself, the trustworthy executor and guardian of the child, how, year after year, good and bad together, her estate brought in a clear income of eight thousand pounds at least ; and how this money had been accumulating and piling up during Virginie's minority, until it was now, for a land of small capitalists, an enormous fortune. But to consider the girl, almost his own daughter, as the means of rescuing himself from difficulties was a dreadful thing to him.

Meantime, there were two persons who were as desirous of seeing this result as Captain Kemyss, with the advantage over him, that they did not conceal their wishes.

'Sybille,' Madame Kemyss would whisper when she saw the young people together.

'Lucie,' Madame Ferrier would reply, pressing her friend's hand, silently.

The cousins who were so much alike in youth had grown alike again in middle life. This is a trying time with most women : they have lost the later beauty of womanhood, and have not yet put on that of age. These two ladies, however, were still beautiful, in the soft and graceful Creole way ; only they looked older than they were, which, perhaps, helped them. They were past forty ; and they looked, somehow, though their hair was neither thin nor grey, nor were their faces crows-footed, as if they were past fifty.

'In France,' one would say to the other, 'we should have settled it ourselves by this time.'

'In England,' the other would reply, 'the boy would have settled it with the girl before this time.'

'Tom is a good boy, Sybille. Perhaps he fears your possible displeasure.'

'He is a very good boy, Lucie. That is why I wish he would tell Virginie that he would like her to be his wife.'

The only reason why Tom did not tell her this most undoubted truth was that he was a Creole. Now all Creoles are perfectly happy with the present condition of things, provided that ensures a sufficiency of curry and claret and a roof. It is a land of sweet contentment. Tom was profoundly in love ; but then he had been in love with Virginie ever since she was born ; there was nothing new in that. It was impossible for him to think of life without her. On the other hand, things were so pleasant as they were, that it never occurred to him to desire a change. They tell a story in Palmiste of two Creoles who once lived there ; they were devotedly attached to each other ; they went on year after year enjoying a protracted spring time of love ; their parents died ; they still continued their gentle courtship ; the years passed on ; they became grey and bald ; still they met day by day, and had their little lovers' quarrels and the fond renewings of love, quite in the Horatian style ; when one was seventy and the other sixty-eight— though, to be sure, they still felt like twenty and eighteen—a friend suggested that it might be almost time to complete the long engagement by a wedding. They considered for a few months ; they thought the suggestion reasonable ; they were married ; but they had so long been lovers that they could not bear to give up their old habits, and they presently separated with mutual consent, went back each to his own house, and ' carried on ' as before.

As regards Virginie herself, she was young ; she had never considered or thought of the question at all. She was undoubtedly very fond of Tom ; it seemed as if life without Tom would be impossible. But, as yet she was innocent of any thought of love, just as she was wholly and entirely ignorant of the world, of humanity, of evil, wrong-doing, treachery, and deception. To be sure, the coolies were always in trouble, always suffering or inflicting wrong ; always deceiving, cheating, thieving, and quarrelling. Only, what coolies do, regarded as part of humanity's statistics, is only interesting to those who are able to take a broad and catholic view of mankind, therefore not interesting to those who live among them. In other words, the white residents in Palmiste disclaim the brotherhood of the coloured man. It is difficult to understand the ignorance of such a girl so brought up. She had not only never left the island, but had never slept off the estate, except once, when she went to a Government House ball, and once when she went to a garrison ball, six months before this time. She had been educated by her mother and Madame Kemyss ; her guardian took a share in the teaching, too ; the only friend of her own age was Tom ; he was her companion and confidant. She knew nothing of society, except as she saw it at home when people came to stay. There was no art whatever within her reach, except music, which her mother taught her ; there was no church even within reach, and the Sunday was only marked by the reading of part of the English prayer-book ; there was no talk of literature, because her guardian had but few books, and she had read them over and over

again ; there were no politics.   As regards European events, they
are treated on these estates with about as much concern as if they
were the events recorded in Gibbon.   There were wars and defeats,
and many thousands slain ; treaties made became treaties broken ;
the victor was flushed with conquest, and the enemy rolled sullenly
over the frontier.   Historians never alter their sweet flowing style,
because the events of history are always the same.   To the dwellers
in this far-off land the events of the present are no more real than
the events of the past ; to Virginie, as she heard them summed up
when each mail came in, they were shadows and unmeaning things.
The realities of life were the morning and evening rambles, the
flowers, the water-falls, the hills, the fruits, and Tom.

CHAPTER III.

IN THE BACHELORS' PAVILION.

IN the pavilion the lazy bachelors began, one after the other, to
stir, sit up, curse the mosquitoes, and finally to get up and come
forth, clothed, for the most part, in ragged flannels and rough tweeds
which had known service and were stained and torn.   There
was great diversity as regards hats ; for some had broad Panama
hats, with brims like the spreading amplitude of a family umbrella ;
and some had the ordinary round hat of the period, generously
endowed with flowing puggrey ; and some had solar helmets ; and
one, which was the Padre, wore the ecclesiastical broad-brimmed
felt which we all know and love so much.   He also wore the long
flapping coat which, with the broad felt hat, makes our ecclesiastics
almost as graceful to look upon as their brothers of Spain.   One
only among them appeared as if he was dressed for a battue in an
English preserve, perfectly turned out in garments which made one
or two of the younger men ashamed of their rags.   This was the
Honourable Guy Talbot Ferrier, Virginie's second cousin, only son
and heir of Lord Ferrier, and a captain in the line regiment now
on garrison duty at Palmiste.

Most of the party knew each other as only colonials can know
each other—that is, with a perfect knowledge of all the strong
points, weak points, good qualities, bad qualities, virtues and vices
which distinguish their brethren.   Not the least use for any of
them to pretend to sail under false colours, or to put on side of any
kind.   Of course they did it, but it was no use doing it.   Among
them was Sandy McAndrew, of the great Scotch firm of McMull,
McAndrew, and Company.   The only fault of Sandy, regarded as
a man and a companion, was that he generally fell asleep during
dinner.   In other respects he was perfect.   Then, there was Davy
McLoughlin, his partner, remarkable for the fact that his legs after
dinner had a tendency to tie themselves into knots, which is an

embarrassing thing to witness until you get used to it. There was also the Pink Boy, who was only nineteen, and had but just arrived, and as yet had not had time to display his many admirable qualities. But he was good at laughing; and he was as handsome as Apollo; and he blushed, which, I believe, that god never did. His tweeds were almost as good as those of Captain Ferrier, but they were in different style, because the Boy was not a noble sportsman at all, but an accountant in a bank. And there was the Assistant Colonial Secretary, a person of very great importance in the official world; in private, a great retailer of good things, with a prodigious memory; so that, once started, he would go on, with stories new and old for a livelong day, and very often did. He knew every man, woman, and child in the colony, and had an excellent story to tell about each; a cheerful, even a jovial companion; and he was of the persuasion which allows a curly crisp brown beard to remain upon the chin as a complement to the curly crisp brown hair.

There was also Major Morgan, who came with Captain Ferrier. He was a soldier by profession; but his principal occupation was the playing of cards, which was the reason why he was so frequently the companion of the younger man. Though he was entirely addicted at cards, and found in the changes and chances of the pips the only joy in life, and though he played to win, he was not a gambler. It will never be said of the Major that he was in difficulties by reason of his losses at cards; rather, it may be safely prophesied of him, that in the immediate future, when he has retired from the service, he will begin a long and tranquil career as a morning, afternoon, and evening whist player at his club. But at present he is still young enough to play any game that offers, whether écarté, loo, lansquenet, baccarat, bézique, cribbage, whist, poker, euchre, all-fours, monty, picquet, sechs-und-sechzig, or nap. A cheerful man, who generally won, and therefore regarded the world as a place where justice is accorded to merit.

The Professor—his name was Percival—who had been a resident in the island for four or five years, was always to be found at Mon Désir at the *bonne année*. Perhaps, when he arrived, he had entertained hopes of introducing energy and activity of mind and body into the lazy colony. All such hopes, if any existed, were now gone; he dreamed no more of fostering a love for culture, being quite persuaded that things would go on their old way whatever he said or did. This is, after all, a philosophic line to take; even in quite temperate zones it requires an amazing amount of talk, persuasion, entreaty, tears, expostulation, kicks, shoves, cuffs, boxes on the ear, admonitions of stick, to move the people a small six inches; in tropical countries it wants ten times the energy to produce a far more miserable result, and fever is the almost certain consequence. Therefore, the Professor sat down, and said that uncultured man was probably as happy as he of the æsthetic crowd; and that, for his own part, he should cultivate his garden—which words, like those of Candide, were an allegory. He found himself much happier when he had ceased to make himself unhappy about the downward tendencies, swinishness, and grovelling of the islanders. He was cheerful again ; he recovered his spirits ; began again to tell stories, and regarded life as an optimist. In person he was shorter than most ; he made up for that by being broader than most ; he wore a big brown beard and spectacles ; he had a catholic taste for wine of all kinds, if only it was good, and was almost a Frenchman in his admiration of all pretty women.

There was one other guest whom one should notice among all the rest. It was the Padre.

He was young, quite young, and enthusiastic. When he left Oxford to be ordained a Bishop's Chaplain for Palmiste, he thought he was coming to a place which was crying aloud for the guidance of the Church. He dreamed of an obedient and docile flock, patiently awaiting instruction. He would instruct them ; he would guide them—to be sure, he had only, with great difficulty, secured a humble third in Moderations—he would lead them. And to ecclesiasticism of the Keble College kind he would add, by degrees, æsthetics, athletics, art, and culture. There was not as yet, in the whole island, one single piece of blue china, nor a peacock's feather, nor a picture of the latest school, nor a *ballade* of the prig-poets, nor any old silver, or lace, nor ritual, nor vestments, or incense— all were downright sturdy independent Protestants, Scotch Presbyterians, and so forth. So that a deep depression fell upon the young man's soul. He was so young, too, that he could not bear to see things going on without joining in them ; and so sensitive that he felt the ridicule of his own long skirts ; and so sharp that he saw how his profession was more respected than beloved, and that his presence was too often a *gêne.* Then he was too sincere not to be grieved by the thirstiness of his companions, their random talk, their 'wild words,' their readiness to play cards, and their eagerness to laugh at a good story. He tried to tell a few good stories himself, but perceived with pain that he did not succeed in making his hearers laugh. A tall, thin young man, with the narrow, high forehead and straight features often found in enthusiastic young clergymen ; one of the kind who affect great thirst for knowledge with the air of having known it all beforehand ; who have an exasperating way of saying 'Yes, yes, yes,' to whatever is said ; and a man perfectly sincere, perfectly virtuous, honourable, and religious, whose life is bound to be a failure because he understandeth not his fellow-man.

As they came out upon the verandah of the Pavilion, one by one, they began to disperse. The Assistant Colonial Secretary, observing the remarkable neatness of the Padre's dress, the length of his skirts, and the glossiness of his trousers, proposed to take him for a pleasant walk among the hills ; they set off together. Those who saw them start reported an ominous twinkle in the Secretary's eyes, and a courtesy in his demeanour, not always remarkable in his treatment of the cloth. When they returned, about nine o'clock, the Padre's long coat in ribbons, and his glossy trousers held together by pins and bits of string, they remembered that twinkle, though the Secretary now takes blame to himself, and says that he ought to have taken thought of the Chinese raspberries and other thorny underwoods on that hillside. He may be very sorry, but his impersonation of the Padre in a thorny thicket caught by the skirts is funny, and has been known to make even the Bishop laugh. As for the Professor, he went into the garden and cut a pine-apple, and found a shady place to eat it in. Then he returned to the Pavilion and threw himself into the hammock, there to read a French novel, which the Pink Boy thought was a learned treatise, and therefore would not interrupt. Sandy McAndrew took a gun and went to take pot shots at the bo's'n birds in the ravine. His partner, with an eye to business, borrowed an umbrella, and went to inspect the canes. And the Pink Boy, left alone because no one invited him to join their party, ventured timidly to the verandah of the house in hopes of finding Miss Ferrier alone and getting a talk. She was not there : but the squire was, and they went out for a walk together, which was not quite the same thing.

The Honourable Guy Talbot Ferrier, born, as Debrett tells everybody, in the year 1853, was therefore on New-Year's Day, 1881, in his twenty-eighth year. He was, at first sight, a singularly handsome young man, whose features were regular, figure tall and upright, and eyes of a soft dark blue. His voice was musical and full, and his hands were small. He would have formed, in fact, an excellent model for a sculptor, and, by simply changing his expression—nothing more—a most beautiful and poetical portrait might have been made of him. It was, however, just his expression which spoiled him. He had got, somehow, the wrong one, and so an incongruous and uncomfortable effect was produced. There are a great many young men like him in this respect. Nature intended them for one expression, and they have gone astray, and so got another which does not fit. Later on in life it does not matter ; because the manner of life which gives the expression also changes the features. Now, in the case of this young gentleman, the nobility of purpose, the resolution of virtue, the courage of principle which should have appeared naturally on his face were not there.

Virtuous resolution and high moral principle are not always necessary qualifications for making a young man popular. There were many men much beloved in Ferrier's regiment who were not implacably virtuous ; yet Ferrier himself was a man with no friends ; he was perfectly well bred ; he was not generally insolent ; he was not boisterous, or loud, or contemptuous, or superior, or any of the things which generally make men unpopular. Yet he was not liked. Many reasons might be assigned to explain this fact : one will be quite sufficient—the young man not only thought of no one but himself, but did not pretend, as many quite selfish men do, to think about anybody. He was thoroughly held and possessed by the love of self. He had but one god—the soul within him which continually craved for something new, something which it could devour, something which would keep it in excitement. Now the man who desires, not before all other things, but to the exclusion of all other things, his own personal gratification, is always in the long run, if it comes in his way, mainly attracted by gambling. There is a fierce excitement in it ; there is the rapid acquisition of money—the possession of which means venal pleasure of all kinds ; there is the trampling on other people in order to get it ; there are the alternations of fear and hope ; no one else is benefited by your success ; no one else desires it ; every man is wholly for himself ; there is but one prize, and all desire it; to make one man happy, the rest must be disappointed. Therefore, though there are many pursuits in which the egotist may gratify his favourite passion, there is none so entirely absorbing and so satisfying as gambling.

A man at eight-and-twenty ought, even in colonial garrison life, to have some other pursuits. Ferrier found none which gave him any pleasure. He played continually : he would have played all day ; he was ready to play all night. The pleasing result, so far, was a quagmire of debts and obligations out of which the way would have been dubious even to a rich man. Now the house of Ferrier had never been rich. Lord Ferrier was not rich as a country gentleman ; as a peer he was certainly poor. And at all times there was present to his heir the vision of those debts and the anxiety how they were to be paid.

This morning he awoke raspy in his temper, as often happens when men sit up till two in the morning to play écarté and drink too much soda and brandy. And he remembered that the Major had taken another I O U from him when they parted. And, in addition, he found that his groom had let down his horse and cut his knees. It was small satisfaction, yet some relief, to kick and cuff the fellow ; and when this was done there was still the recollection of that I O U.

'A bad night, Ferrier,' said the Major, looking at the little slip of paper in his pocket-book. 'This makes thirteen hundred and fifty-five, I think.'

Ferrier received the hint in silence.

'If I were you, my boy,' continued the Major, 'I would drop play for a while, just to let luck come round a bit.'

'Luck !' the loser groaned. 'There never was such luck as mine.'

'I don't think, Ferrier, that I ought to play with you ; it isn't fair. I keep my head ; you lose yours. I'm an old hand, and you are a young one. I play for the game ; you play for the stakes.'

'Hang it, man ! You can't mean that you don't play to win ?'

'Of course I play to win. Every man does. But I think of the game, and you think only of the points. See ?'

Ferrier threw himself into one of the long chairs and relapsed into a gloomy silence. The New Year had begun badly, indeed, for him. It was going to finish—but this, as yet, he knew not—worse. The

Major strolled out with an umbrella, and then there were left on the verandah only the Professor and Ferrier. Presently the Professor dropped his French novel, and, lazily swinging in the hammock, contemplated the moody young gentleman with wonder and pity.

'It seems to me,' he said to himself, after a while, 'that here is a young man whose conscience is pegging away at him like the eagle at the man on the rock. I wonder what he has done. To think that Virginie should have a cousin with such a face.'

Indeed, at the moment the face was suffused with such a glow of vindictive wrath, self-reproach, and hatred, that it was quite horrible and terrifying to look upon.

'I wonder who it is, and what he has done : though, perhaps, it is a person of the other sex,' said the Professor. 'But it may be, perchance, that the Honourable Guy is possessed of a devil or two.'

Towards nine o'clock, the sun being high and the heat of the day fairly begun, the men began to come back, and when the Secretary appeared leading the discomfited Padre, with his beautiful skirts cut into ribbons like a banana-leaf after a hurricane, and his black trousers rent in a hundred places, there arose a shout of admiration and joy quite beautiful to hear. And then they all went to bathe.

Tom, who was the last to return, having been the round of the whole estate and made notes of shortcomings, led the way. He knew the pool where water was coolest ; it was half a mile off, where the ravine was the deepest and the narrowest. And he knew the shortest way to it, which was straight down a perpendicular rock about ninety feet deep ; but, as he went down there every morning, it never occurred to him that anybody should think of breaking his neck there, and he was greatly surprised when halfway down to see above him the Padre clinging to the rock like a spread-eagle, unable to move up or down. Presently, the united efforts of the party got him up, and the Professor undertook to lead him to the pool by a safer and more circuitous route.

Oh ! the pools and lashers, and waterfalls and brawling mountain streams of Palmiste ! Oh ! to sit under a little cascade of four or five feet high, to let the cold water flow over the hot and weary limbs, it is a joy which we who shiver in cold latitudes cannot understand or even conceive. It belongs almost to the keen and passionate joys ; it is one which never palls, of which one is never satiated, the desire for which recurs every morning. 'But,' said the Professor, 'I prefer the long way round.'

The bath and the walk home, and the dressing which followed, brought them well on to eleven, which, as everybody knows, is the breakfast hour of the Palmiste planter. Eleven o'clock in the forenoon is, in fact, the proper time, the natural time, for eating. We foolish folk of England have abolished breakfast and substituted luncheon, a meal which spoils the day, depraves the appetite, and ruins the dinner. Nature intended mankind to eat twice in the day, and each time after the fatigue of labour. At eleven, if one gets up at five or thereabouts, the day's work is well-nigh done. After six hours in the saddle among the canes, for instance, which Tom had, one gets home with a hunger almost unintelligible in these climes; a hunger which to a London alderman would make life indeed worth having. With what a cordial will that breakfast was attacked by the guests; how claret flowed without stint or stay down thirsty throats; how, after the simple bourgeoise plenty of *bouillabaisse*, fish fried, fish boiled, chicken and salad, cutlets, grilled turkey, and devilled bones, a stately prawn curry added nobility to the repast; how coffee was followed by a *chasse*; how Tom distinguished himself beyond and above his peers; how the Pink Boy contemplated the thing with rapturous wonder; and how the Padre thought with something like shame of the plain English rasher and the cup of tea—these are things which may be briefly indicated, not dwelt upon. Envy is a hateful passion, and one must always consider the weaker brethren.

After breakfast there was a rest. Most of them went back to the Pavilion for cigars. The Padre, fatigued with the morning's scramble, and perhaps just touched with the unaccustomed wine, fell fast asleep. Only Captain Ferrier remained with the ladies. He had shaken off his moody fit, and was now, having taken a great deal of claret, thoroughly set up and revived. Virginie had a great many questions to ask, and the two ladies sat and listened in their soft and dreamy manner. They talked about England; and the child wanted to know all about her cousins and the noble head of the house; what the castle was like; what they all did when they were at home in it; what the place was like, and what the people. Her cousin tried to describe them all. But what can a girl understand who knows no winter, no fog, no snow, no east winds, no green enclosures, no English villages, and no old English churches standing amid the graves of all the generations, girt with the old trees?

Meantime Tom, who knew not the meaning of fatigue, though he had been six hours in the saddle, and had eaten a more enormous breakfast than any of the rest, was busied with what appeared to be a net. At sight of that net the Professor arose, and softly retired to hide himself in the tool-house with his novel. Tom unrolled his net, examined the meshes, mended one or two places, then rolled it up again. This took half an hour or so. Then he called a boy, and gave it him with a few directions. Then he rubbed his hands, and announced, with a cheerful smile, that everything was ready, and they could start as soon as they pleased.

CHAPTER IV.

'Let us first,' said the Secretary, the only one who had been taking any part in the preparations, 'wake up the Padre. He, too, must go with us.'

He was awakened with some difficulty, and at first exhibited temper, and refused to join the expedition. However, he was young, and not to go might seem like showing a white feather unworthy of an Oxford athlete. Besides, the sport was the gentle and harmless one of angling. Therefore the poor innocent, though with misgiving, put on his broad felt hat and once more adjusted his white muslin puggrey and was ready.

When the Professor had been led forth by the ear from his hiding-place and had been told that he, too, must go, and that resistance would be unavailing, the party was complete, the only man left behind being Ferrier, who had no taste for sport of any kind outside an English preserve. He suggested that the Major should stay behind with him and while away the heat of the day with a little écarté, or vingt-un for two—a very pleasing method of losing money. But the Major refused, and went off with the rest.

First marched Tom, important, because he was the leader or captain of the _chasse aux gouramis_. Next came the Indian boys, carrying the gear; then followed, with a rueful countenance, the captive Professor, grimly remembering fatigues on a certain occasion a year ago, and devoutly wishing that the sport was over; after him the Padre, the long skirts of his only clerical coat left him flapping about his legs, and his white puggrey streaming behind the broad black hat; and then the Assistant Colonial Secretary, with a sweet smile upon him as he contemplated that broad hat and those flapping skirts, and thought of what awaited the owner of those garments. It was the hottest time in the year; in the shade the thermometer would be about ninety; in the sun, anything you please. Yet there was a gentle breeze or stir in the air from the south, whence cometh the breath of the Antarctic, warmed upon its way, yet cool still, and fresh, when it floats across the hot and tropical twenties.

'In the ravine,' said the Professor, in order to encourage the Padre, 'there will be no breeze at all; the rocks catch the heat and hold it till strangers come; then they give it out, and the stranger is as grateful as you will be presently. It will be like the hot room in the Turkish bath—that room, I mean, where, if you want breakfast, you take the materials in raw and hold them in your hand till they are cooked. Last year we brought some tiffin with us—eggs, you know, and bread, and some slices of ham; we put them on a stone just for a few minutes while we went into a pool after the gouramis. When we came back the eggs were hard boiled, the bread was toast, and the rushers of bacon were done to a turn.'

'I wish,' said the Padre, 'that I had left my waistcoat at home.'

'If you had been well advised,' said the Professor, whose only fault was a want of reverence for sacred things, 'you would have come on this expedition in your surplice, and nothing else.'

Presently they came to the break-neck way down the cliff, down which they all scrambled except these two, and they went ignominiously round by a longer and safer way. 'What boots it,' asked the Professor, ' to save ten minutes if you break your neck?'

When they joined the party, the Padre observed, with surprise, that they were all undressing. Further, that the Professor, with a sigh, also began to shed his garments, and that he himself was expected to do the same thing. He realised the meaning of the irreverent suggestion about his surplice when he received a little maillot of coloured cotton, such as Frenchmen use to swim in. And he began almost to wish that he had not joined the expedition. In a few minutes the whole party were arrayed in this primitive dress, in which and their helmets and hats, and nothing else, they began walking along the hot boulders, under and among which the stream was brawling on her way.

The streams of Palmiste are all alike : they rise in the hills and they run into the sea, through ravines beneficently provided by Nature for the purpose. If there were no ravines they would have to tumble, in break-neck fashion, over precipices. As it is, they gracefully roll, run, leap, babble, roar, prattle, fall, hasten, or linger on their way, through most beautiful valleys, sometimes deep, sometimes shallow ; sometimes broad, sometimes narrow ; sometimes with perpendicular faces of rock, and sometimes with sloping sides, clothed with hanging wood. Sometimes the bottom of the ravine consists of great rounded boulders, and one has to get along by jumping from one to the other. At first, this is fatiguing, until you get into the swing of it. Sometimes there is a broad flat bottom, covered over and piled with boulders ; sometimes the ravine closes quite in, and the stream runs noisily between the rocky walls of a narrow way ; sometimes the water dashes over the stones, forming hundreds of tiny cascades ; sometimes it glides under them, and is invisible for half a mile or so, though the dense growth on either hand speaks of the water below ; sometimes it widens out and forms lashers, pools, or basins ; and sometimes it leaps over a cliff and becomes a waterfall, dazzling, feathery, like diamond spray. And everywhere, except on the face of the rock, trees : such trees as one may dream of ; palms of every kind—the date palm, the cocoa, the raphia, the travellers' tree, the aloe with its long mast, the fragrant acacia, the tamarind, and a hundred others, whose names one knows not. In the shade under the trees and hidden behind the rocks are ferns, such as one may not hope to see in any other country, and on the branches of the trees are orchids for those who have eyes to see and knowledge to understand.

The ravine on that hot January day was very silent, winding in and out, growing deeper as it approached the sea. A few bo's'n birds called to each other flying across from rock to rock ; you could hear, perhaps, the chatter of monkeys in the trees. But there was no other sound. The place is so far away from the steps of man that a visitor who should chance to slip and fall might lie there until he died, and long after, without being found. For many miles of its course no one ever goes there, except at rare intervals when Tom brings his friends to fish for gourami, or when he strolls down in the afternoon with a gun on the chance of a shot. The coolies, an incurious folk, have no occasion to go there ; the negroes are afraid of ghosts ; and, of course, no one except an Englishman would venture into those hot and stifling depths at high noon of the New Year, with the sun straight over head glaring into all kinds of nooks and crannies where, save at such seasons of vertical advantage, ray of sun can never enter. The men were barefooted, and presently the Padre began to understand the Professor's allegory of the hard-boiled eggs. He was very hot in spite of his scanty apparel ; he asked himself, with shame, what certain people at home, who thought greatly of his missionary zeal, would say if they saw him now ; he was tired with the early morning walk ; his feet were blistering ; his legs ached with the perpetual leaping from stone to stone ; his shins were bruised with frequent falls.

Said the Professor softly,

'Last year a man came here who was unaccustomed to walking on red-hot stones. We carried him up again after a while, but he has never recovered the use of his feet, and now goes on crutches.'

Then he was silent, and the Padre began to think there might be some truth in it.

But their leader called a halt, and everybody, while the preparations were being made, sat down with their feet in the water.

They were arrived at a most beautiful pool, about forty feet long and twenty broad. Great trees hung over the water, and splendid *lianes*, with stems as thick as the trunk of a good-sized English oak, spread out long arms, octopus fashion, to throttle and destroy the trees which they embraced. They began—those who understood the method—by lowering the net carefully into the water at the upper end. When all was ready the Professor, with a groan, took up his position in the middle, while Tom placed himself at one end and the Secretary at the other. These three were places of honour assigned to those who were most at ease in the water, and presently they were all swimming slowly down the pool, joined by the others. It was a sweet and a beautiful sight to see the spectacles of the Professor glittering under his helmet, as he went through the task, without enthusiasm, yet conscientiously ; and the broad hat of his Reverence shading an anxious face, because

s 2

he was not happy about his feet, and because the proceedings seemed to lack the dignity proper to the cloth ; and the red face of the Major and the delight of the Pink Boy in the coolness of the water. Presently Tom handed over his end of the net to the McAndrew and disappeared. After remaining under the water for about five-and-twenty minutes or so, during which time he was adjusting the net at the bottom, he came up again. At this point the Professor, catching sight of the Padre's nose just out of the water, under the shade of his beautiful broad hat, began to laugh silently, and communicated a shivering to the net, so that Tom thought it was one of the eels, in length from ten to forty feet, for which the rivers of Palmiste are so famous, and went down again to investigate.

By slow degrees and with great care the net was hauled along the whole pool and pulled in at the end. Then Tom's responsibilities began again. For he now had to dive down and bring up the fish, taking only as many as they wanted and picking out the big ones, throwing the young fish back again into the pool. Meantime, those who were not actively employed sat on the edge of the pool with their feet in the water and waited. It was a good haul ; but Tom said that they must have one more cast of the net, and that the next likely pool was not more than a quarter of a mile down the stream. He set off, leading the way, as before. The rest followed meekly, with the exception of the Professor, who beckoned the Padre and made a gesture of silence.

When the procession had disappeared beyond the next bend of the rocks, he rose and asked his Reverence if he wished to play that game any more.

'I—I—certainly think that we have had enough.'

'Then come back with me. We will put on our clothes and we will go cameron-fishing instead.'

'Have we not had enough fishing for one day !' The Padre thought of those awful stones and of his blistered feet, and remembered the cool verandah.

The Professor hastened to explain.

'We shall not take off our clothes for cameron-fishing ; nor shall we jump about on red-hot boulders ; and we shan't walk at all. It is a lazy sport. We shall sit under the shadiest place we can find, higher up, where there is a little air, I will teach you how to fish. I never catch any myself, but I know the way other people catch them ; and perhaps you will be more lucky.'

'All this seems a dreadful waste of time, does it not !' asked the man fresh from Oxford.

'You have only been a month in Palmiste,' said the Professor. 'After a little, you will discover that *you can't* waste time here. There's no such thing as wasting time, unless, indeed, you throw it away on reading. Out here we are irresponsible. Life goes by, I suppose, because there is a cemetery ; but you don't feel as if it was ever going to end. There is no use trying to do any work.

Nobody will ever be improved ; nobody wants to be improved. I*
is warm and sunny—what more can a man want ? '

'If I thought that,' said the Padre, 'I would go straight back
to England and find Work. Why, it was because I thought I
should find my Work here that I came.'

The Professor smiled. 'That is the language of the schools. I
know it.'

'Would you have me,' asked the young clergyman hotly, 'would
you have me take this post in order to sit down in shady places and
catch—what do you call them ? '

'Wise men sit down and meditate,' said the Professor. 'Talk
to the Squire ; he never reads much, yet he is as wise as Solomon.
Restless men buzz about, and shove, and push, and call it work.
Do you know the story in Rabelais about the work of Diogenes ? '

'I do not read Rabelais,' said his Reverence, coldly.

'Poor man ! Never mind. There was a civil chaplain here
until lately who was a miracle of laziness. Yet he always went on
talking about his Work, with a capital W, you know, just as you
do. It is very good to begin with, and the habit remains.'

'I hope the habit will remain.'

'It will. It will. But the thing will vanish. I am going home
myself before long, because I am one of the restless men, and want
to work. It is very foolish of me, and I am sure I ought rather to
stay. Never mind. Let us go catch the cameron. Then we will
find our way home and sit on the verandah till it is time to dress
for dinner, and eat letchees and talk to Virginie. I have known
her ever since I came here, which is now four years ago ; and I am
in love with her, as you will be before long—very likely you are
already—you need not blush, because it does you credit—and I am
deuced sorry she has got that fellow for a cousin.'

'Why ? ' asked the Padre.

'Why ? Because—because I do not like him.'

They had their cameron-fishing. The Professor led the way to
a quiet little stream above the ravine, where there was shade.
Here he cut a long thin branch of a willow-like tree and tied to the
end of it a running noose, made of the thin and strong tendril of
the *liane*. 'Now,' he said, 'you do likewise. Go and sit on that
stone, there, and I will sit there. All you have to do is to keep
quiet. When you see a cameron marching along, pit-a-pat, suspect-
ing nothing, hook your noose over his tail. Then nip him up, and
he is caught. It is quite easy to do it, though I have never been
able, with all my efforts, to catch a single one.'

'What is a cameron like, when you do see him ? '

'He is about six inches long, and he is black, and he looks like
a crayfish, or big prawn. He is good enough to boil a beautiful
red, and he lends himself to curry, or you can eat him boiled. He
isn't proud. Now, go and catch him.'

The Professor was short-sighted, consequently he never saw any
camerons at all. But he sat very patiently, with his noose in the

water and the camerons playing about the harmless trap in dozens ; and he meditated.

'She will be a great heiress'—this was the staple of his reflections—'that cousin of hers will be a Lord, very likely he will want to marry her ; and she ought to marry Tom, because she loves him ; next to Tom, and if I could make up my mind to murder Tom, she ought to marry me, because I love her. And her money would set the Captain's estate on its legs again. Poor old man ! Half a hurricane this year and down he goes ! . . . . . . Hallo ! Padre, old man, wake up. It's half-past five, and instead of catching camerons you've gone to sleep again. I haven't caught any myself, but I've had some splendid misses. Let us go and talk to Virginie.'

CHAPTER V.

HOW THE MAIL CAME IN.

This New-Year's Day was considered by the Mon Désir party as in no way differing from any other New-Year's Day. As usual, there was open house so far as the resources of the establishment allowed : so many beds, so many sofas, so many mattresses, so many guests. They came ; they feasted, talked, sang, and rejoiced ; there was abundance of talk, with the popping of corks innumerable ; there was the prettiest girl in the whole island to court, compliment, and tease. When the brief holiday was over they all went away again to their respective work. That is what happened every New-Year's Day. All things in Palmiste go on as if they were to last for ever, or to recur for ever on the usual day. And certainly no one could have suspected that a time so festive, gay, and irresponsible would bring with it the cause of a revolution—nothing short of a revolution—for the lives of half the people in the party.

When the Professor, after the fruitless hunt for cameron, sought the verandah of the house, he perceived, being with his spectacles nearly as good as other people without, that something had happened or was about to happen.

First of all, the English mail was in, and there was present the Captain of the mail himself, who had just come out, and was sitting in great contentment in one of the easiest of the chairs. The Squire, whose face was troubled, was holding a letter in one hand and the *Home News* in the other. First he read the letter through, then he read a page or two of the newspaper, then he turned to the letter again, and then he went back to the paper ; evidently he was thinking more of the letter than of the printed page. The two elder ladies sat with tears in their eyes, holding each a hand of Virginie, who stood before them, pale and troubled, as if she was going to be offered up in sacrifice. What could be the matter ? Captain Ferrier stood apart, with a small packet of open letters in his hand, occupied with his own thoughts, and they seemed as gloomy as those which had distorted his features in the early morning.

Something was certainly going to happen. As a rule, the excitement of the mail lasts from the first appearance of the signals on the Signal-hill until the issue of the slip into which the news of the whole month is condensed by the Editor of the *Commercial Gazette*. This summary, which is all that anyone wants to see, varies in length from four inches to six inches and a half. Think of getting your news for a whole month condensed into six inches of letterpress! All the great people in the world, the Bismarcks, and the Gladstones, and the Gambettas; all the ministers, states-men, generals, Parliament men, eloquent speakers, persuasive preachers, convincing writers, mischievous demagogues, restless agitators, misleading-article men, poets, prigs, dramatists, his-torians, novelists, actors, artists, Big Rag, Little Tag, and Bobtail —all over the habitable globe toil and moil with the utmost diligence for four weeks in every human tongue, and the result of the whole can be boiled down into a six-inch slip! And even that does not prove that the world has been advanced by one sixth of the length of that slip. The monthly spectacle of a whole world feverishly busy, and doing nothing, is of itself, without considering the climate, sufficient to account for the philosophic calm and resolute inaction of the Palmiste natives. 'Why all this care?' they say. 'Nothing comes of it. Only sometimes knocking of heads together; tumults, broken bones, revolutions, and wars, with loss of property and triumph of the wrong side. Sit down, neighbours, and let us tell each other pleasant stories, and make merry while we may, until the night falls, when we are fain to go to sleep.'

The perusal of the slip finished, the excitement instantly dies away. Everybody reads the same papers, the *Overland Mail*, the *Home News*, and the *Illustrated London News*; some go so far as to read the *Saturday Review* and *Punch*, or the *Spectator*. But they are few; therefore, since no one can boast of any information but that which is open to his neighbours, there is no inducement to talk politics; and since no more information can come for a whole, month, there is no inducement to speculate.

The captain of the mail-steamer arrived, then, about four of the clock, bringing with him the monthly packet of letters and papers for the whole party.

'I heard,' he said, 'who was out here, and I waited for the post to be opened, and so brought all their letters, as well as yours, Captain Kemyss. And how goes it with you and yours, and how is the pretty maid?'

He had been on the line a good many years, and Virginie was still for him his pretty maid, and he was a privileged guest at Mon Désir, to come and go as often as he pleased and was able.

Then he sat down and rested while the letters were read.

There were two for Captain Kemyss—his correspondence with

the mother-country, after so many years of exile, had dropped by degrees, and was now almost reduced to nothing ; one for Madame Ferrier—a very unusual circumstance ; one for Virginie, who had never had a letter from England before ; five or six for Captain Ferrier ; two for the Professor ; half a dozen for the Padre ; a pile for the others ; and a vast quantity of newspapers, *Punches*, monthly magazines, books and pamphlets for everybody.

The first of the two letters which Captain Kemyss opened was from a certain cousin of his, a country gentleman of the Midland counties, and was respecting Tom. 'My advice,' said the writer, 'is to keep the boy where he is. Let him stick to the thing that he knows. As for sugar-planting being precarious, it has kept you for thirty years, and I dare say it will keep him. England is not a good country just now, especially for men like me, who have a dozen farms on their hands ;' and so on—and so on—a letter which does not concern us.

Captain Kemyss laid it down with a sigh. He had hoped that perhaps some chance might have been found for Tom when the crash, so long imminent, should come at last. Then he took up the other letter, which was in a writing strange to him. When, now a dozen years and more agone, his guardianship of Virginie began, there was a second guardian, also one of Captain Ferrier's brother-officers, who had sold out, and was then living at Southsea. It was understood that he was to hold an honorary office, and that the child would continue to live with her mother at Mon Désir, while Captain Kemyss managed her estate. So honorary was the office that the acting guardian had almost forgotten the existence of his coadjutor, and had not even learned that he was dead.

The letter was from his widow, and was as follows :—

'Dear Sir,—

'As the widow of your old friend and brother-officer, one who was associated with you in the office of guardian to Miss Ferrier, I trust I need no introduction or excuse for addressing you.'—'So Jack is dead, is he,' said the reader, stopping to look at the signature. 'Poor Jack ! I had almost forgotten him.'—'Circumstances have not allowed me, until lately, to offer any hospitality to my ward, if I may call her so. I am now, however, I rejoice to say, at last in a position to discharge one at least of the duties accepted for me by my late husband.'—'He married—I heard that he married—I forget who she was,' said the Squire, stopping again at this point to recall things, 'somebody of good family, I know—and she had expectations. Let me see. They were hard up when I heard last—lived in a cottage at Southsea ; that must have been twelve years ago. Then Jack died, I suppose, and she's come into the money at last. I suppose that is what she means.' He went on with the letter—

'I believe that our dear Virginie—or Lucie—forgive me if the name has escaped my memory—must now be seventeen years of age. I hear from the Colonel of the 180th, just returned from your lovely island, that she is perfectly charming and perfectly beautiful. I have also learned, to my great satisfaction, that you have so well nursed her estate that she is now a considerable heiress. Now, my dear sir, do you not think it would be a great pity that this young lady, while she is still young, with her affections free, should not come to England and make acquaintance with her own people ? I have the honour of knowing Miss Ferrier. I was talking on this subject to her on the last occasion of meeting her. I am happy to inform you that she expressed herself in the kindest manner concerning her unknown cousin, and will, I am sure, show her all the attention when she comes home that she can desire or expect. As for me, I do not disguise the fact that I should like to have a young and beautiful girl staying with me, partly because it is pleasant to have young and pretty faces about one, and partly because they make a house attractive and bring people about one. Others may hunt for lions ; it is my principle, my dear Captain Kemyss, that men care more for lionesses. When I get my fair Creole in my drawing-room I shall not let her go in a hurry.

' As regards matrimonial prospects, you may entirely trust me. I will stop the first sign of a flirtation in the very bud, unless the man is thoroughly what you have a right to expect. There are not so many men of the right kind in this town, especially since the terrible blight that has fallen upon landowners ; yet there may be some. Of course, I know there are many dangers which beset a girl of fortune or expectations. London is always abounding in penniless adventurers, literary men, subalterns, younger sons, and even curates, who are longing to marry an heiress and hang up their hats and sit down idle for life. But they shall not get near our Virginie. I will surround her, my dear Captain. I will be like a hollow square with fixed bayonets, until the right man approaches, and then I will be a benevolent Fairy. Of course, a girl of good—almost of noble—birth, who has none but good relatives—I think I have heard that her mother belongs to the House of Desmarets d'Auvergne—who has also a great and productive sugar estate—with, the Colonel said, a hundred and twenty thousand pounds, but perhaps that is too good to be true—should look very high indeed. There is nothing to which she may not aspire, though if we dream of a coronet we should be sober ; our thoughts ought not to run higher than an earl or a viscount. However, I will do my best. Character, of course, as well as position, should be carefully inquired into.

' I have written honestly to you, because if you were really a private friend of my late husband you must be a man of the world. I frankly think that my offer is a good one, and that in the interests of the girl you ought not to refuse it. If her mother lives, my invitation will extend to her ; but, on the whole, I sincerely think it will be better that the child should come alone, and acquire by living entirely among English people, the ideas, the air, and the tone of English society.

'I hope to have a favourable answer by return mail. I am ready to receive my charge to-morrow, if she can come. If a chaperon can be found, the arrival of my ward in person would be the most favourable reply possible.

'I remain, dear Captain Kemyss,
'Yours, very sincerely,
'LAURA HALLOWES.'

The Squire read this frank and plain-spoken letter through twice. The tone of it struck his ears, long unfamiliar with the world of fashion, discordantly. His ward was to go to London, and stand in the matrimonial market with other girls, saying, 'Behold me! I am rich, beautiful, young, of gentle birth. I will take a coronet in exchange for myself.' Yet the letter was honest ; also, the invitation was one which ought not to be lightly refused. It was right that the girl should go to England ; it was part of her education. She ought, as Mrs. Hallowes suggested, to make the acquaintance of her own people ; she ought to go while yet young, with her affections free. And at this point, he said, with a sigh, 'Poor Tom !' and read the letter again. Evidently the letter of a woman of society—of the world ; and probably a woman who would make social capital out of her rich young heiress. Yet, what harm would that do Virginie?

At this point he folded the letter and raised his eyes. A singular pantomime was going on.

First, his own wife took a letter from Madame Ferrier's hands, and read it. Then both ladies and Virginie gazed upon each other in a kind of stupor. Then Madame Ferrier held out her arms, and the girl fell into her maternal embrace.

'Child,' murmured the mother, 'can I let thee go ? So soon ? So soon ?'

'Sybille ?' said her friend, speaking the language of her youth, 'we must let her go. It is for the child's own good ; we are two simple Creole ladies, who have never left the island and never shall. But Virginie has English cousins ; she must visit her father's country, she should learn to love his home. Virginie, child of my heart, what sayest thou ?'

'What can I say ?' she replied. 'Oh ! what can I say ?'

'It was thy father's wish, my dear,' her mother went on. 'He spoke continually of taking thee to England when thou wast *grandie.*'

'It is I,' said her guardian, 'who should have thought of it. My dear, the time has passed so swiftly that I forgot you were grown up. I ought to have remembered that it was due to you that you should go home for a while—for a while'—he repeated. 'We must let you go.' He took her hands and bent over her with his kindly smile. 'We cannot bear to part with you, my dear; but, if your mother consents, we must let you go. May I see those letters ?'

One of them was from Mrs. Hallowes to Madame Ferrier, conveying to her the same invitation as she had made to Captain
Kemyss, but in different terms. For she said nothing about society
or matrimonial projects and ambitions ; but dwelt upon the advantage to the young lady of seeing England, and spoke of her own as
a quiet home among a circle of quiet friends ; and she also dwelt
upon the advantages to be derived in the way of music, art, and so
forth.

'She must be, indeed,' thought the Squire, 'a woman of the
world.'

The other letter was from Virginie's second cousin, Maude,
daughter of Lord Ferrier and sister of the man on the verandah,
who was scowling over his letters. It was a very short letter, but
kindly :—

'Dear cousin,' she wrote, 'I learn from Mrs. Hallowes, the
widow of one of your guardians, that she has invited you to pay
a visit to England next year. I sincerely hope that your mother
may let you come, even if she does not herself accompany you.
Remember that you have cousins who would like to make your
acquaintance.

'Your father was at school with mine, his first cousin. I have
heard a great deal about you and your beautiful country home
already from my brother, and I assure you that I look forward to
making your acquaintance with a very great deal of pleasure. We
spend most of our time at The Towers, but generally have two
months in London. Wherever we are, when you are able to leave
Mrs. Hallowes, come and stay with us, as soon as you can.

'Your affectionate cousin,
MAUDE.'

These were the three letters which fell like so many bombs into
the peaceful verandah on that sunny afternoon. And this it was
which, when the Professor arrived, was making his host read the
Home News with eyes which read indeed but saw not, and turned
again to the letter.

'A Coronet,' he murmured ; 'but why not? Poor Tom ! Yet,
would it have been right—would it have been honest—to take
advantage of her innocence and ignorance before she knows the
world? Let her go. And Tom must take his chance. A poor
chance, indeed ! Rank against rusticity. Fashion against fidelity ;
the lover of the town against the sweetheart of the country.'

Virginie's cousin, meanwhile, had opened two letters. One of
them was from his sister. He read it hurriedly, and crammed it
into his pocket as if it made him angry. What it said was this :—

'Dearest Guy,—I hear from two or three people who know, or
ought to know, that our Creole cousin is rich, young, and beautiful.

Also that she has manners which would fit her for any station
And that she is coming home to stay with a woman who wants her,
I believe, as a help to get on in society. The woman, however, is
very well, and will take the girl to good houses. I have taken
notice of her *for your sake*—mind, *for your sake*—and because such
a woman may, in certain cases, be very useful to you. Now, Guy,
be reasonable. You tell me that you are in desperate straits. It
is now six years, or thereabouts, since these desperate straits began.
I do not reproach you ; but I remind you that you have had, not
only your own allowance, but all my money, and all that I could
persuade my father to add. He does not know of these straits ; if
he did he would ask you how they are caused. *I do know*, Guy.
Again, I do not reproach you. I will even go on trying to help
you, though I know that every ten-pound note we get for you will
only go the same way as its predecessor. Now, consider carefully.
When you were at home last summer I caught an heiress and got
her here on purpose for you to meet her. You remember her.
She was not, I own, in the least degree beautiful, nor was she clever
at all ; and I did not expect that you would fall in love with her ;
but she was rich and she was amiable, and she was ready to fall in
love with you. And men in desperate straits cannot always marry
anybody they please. But you would not have her, although you
were in such straits. Now, here is this other girl. Come home
immediately, on urgent private affairs. Come home, if you can, in
the same steamer with her ; make fierce love to her all the way
home. When she goes to Mrs. Hallowes', let it be with your
engaged ring on her finger. When you get her money you can pay
off your creditors, even if you only begin a fresh course of madness.
There, Guy ; that is all I can do for you at present. I have only
to add that the times are bad for everybody who has got land,
and therefore for us. And it is not the least use expecting any
further assistance from your father, or from your affectionate sister,
Maude.'

'Then,' murmured the young man, 'how the devil is Morgan's
I O U to be taken up?'

The other letter was written in a less clerkly hand, and there
were occasional mis-spellings in it. And it was this letter which
made the young man scowl.

'I told you, Guy,' it began, without any polite or conventional
endearments of speech ; 'I told you that I would let you know
from time to time what I am doing and how I am doing. Very
well, then. I am doing very well. And so is the boy. He is not
like you, I am glad to say, as yet ; in face he takes after me and
his grandfather, the scene-shifter, who was once a very handsome
man ; and I hope he will never become like you in any single
respect. And, as I am not quite a lady myself, though more so
than when you knew me, I have got a girl who *is* a lady to act as
his governess and companion. By the time the child grows up and
can compare, I shall, I dare say, have become more like a lady,

because I do not want him ever to be ashamed of his mother. An actress I am, and shall remain. Ten pounds a week, my gallant Captain, your wife draws. She's got her marriage lines safe ; but nobody knows that she's the Honourable Mrs. Ferrier. Biz is first-rate. We have got a piece good for six hundred nights, and the ghost walks regular. Portraits of your wife are sold wherever she goes—character-portraits, looking in the glass, tying a handkerchief round her head, in a riding habit—all sorts—and she gets letters, offers of marriage, bouquets, and applause, and everything which the heart of an actress can desire. So that she is quite happy. And the boy is so beautiful that she does not so very much repent having fallen in your way. And, as for his rights, why, whatever you do, you can't gamble them away. I do not want ever to see you again, nor to hear from you. The Army List will tell me where you are, which is all I want to know. And, on the least attempt at interference with my boy, we go to The Towers—accompanied by our own people, the respectable scene-shifter—and we see my lord, and we introduce the daughter-in-law and the grandchild. It is a good situation, and I think I should play it rather well. I remain, your wife, not at all affectionate, Violet Lovelace—it is a swell name, and I found it in the Court Guide—but it is not so good as my own real name, which is, as you very well know, Emily Ferrier.'

When Captain Ferrier had got through the whole of this epistle, which did not take long, he fell into a study, in which everything became a nocturne, an arrangement in black. He was roused by the arrival of the Professor, against whom, for some unknown reason, he had conceived a violent and irrational hatred. He glared at him for a moment, and then strode hastily away. First he walked along the avenue of palms, and when he got to the end of it he swore aloud ; then, by way of distraction, he went to the stable to look at his horse, and swore again, and if his syce had been in the place it would have been bad for that poor Indian. But he was not. The man was at the moment with the old witch of Endor bargaining for a charm which would slowly poison a horse, so that no one would suspect what was the matter with him, and an honest groom should not get into trouble. The terms of the transaction were amicably arranged, and the charm, which was to take the form of a little something to pour among the oats, was promised, on condition that this estimable person should pay for it beforehand—because he could write—in forged passes, by means of which the old woman afterwards made much money and helped many of her friends to deceive the police.

We may here observe that, among the many things which once done cannot be recalled, perhaps the most fatal is such a thing as Guy Ferrier did when he was just twenty-one years of age, being then a young gentleman of very headstrong disposition, and fully determined upon having all he wanted, at any cost. He had always from chi'dhood acted upon this principle, and it made him so popular at school, that when he left the boys proposed to have fireworks. In the Army he continued to act on the same settled principle, being now quite certain that he deserved to have all he wanted; and he was so much beloved, therefore, that when it became known, directly after the arrival of this mail, that Ferrier was going home on urgent private affairs—presumably the raising of money to pay his debts of honour—his brother-officers so far sympathised with him as to give thanks unanimously that he was going to enjoy a holiday. It was upon this principle, also, being at the moment consumed and inflamed with passion, that, at the age of twenty-one, he entered secretly into the bonds of holy wedlock with a certain 'young person' named Emily Hicks. She was quite young, extremely pretty, quick, and clever, well able to take care of herself, almost uneducated, the daughter of a scene-shifter or carpenter and 'general service' theatrical man, and she was just commencing a dramatic career, which now promises to be distinctly successful, when this thing happened to her.

The interruption to her professional pursuits lasted rather more than a year. She then returned to Daddy Perigal, and informed him that for the future she should never again speak to her husband, nor take money from him, nor in any way own him; that she should go back to the stage in her first-assumed name; but, for the sake of the child, whom she brought with her, whose rights must be watched, she would assume her legal name when the boy should be grown up. She therefore returned to the stage under her old acting name, and began to work just as hard as if she were still really Emily Hicks, with her future before her, instead of the Hon. Mrs. Ferrier, a woman married and done for.

As for her husband, he went his own way, and contrived, as a rule, to forget her existence, except when he was reminded of it by such a letter as he had just read, or by his sister's well-meant attempts to find him an heiress. Between himself and an heiress there always stood this woman and her boy. At first, he suffered from great apprehensions that she would communicate with his own people. As she did not, he gradually recovered confidence in her word. He could not marry; that was true; but then he did not want to marry. The goddess of Chance was the only bride he cared to worship; some day, most certainly, if Emily lived and the boy lived, there would be a row. Meanwhile, so long as she let him alone, he troubled himself little about her. When his thoughts were turned upon her by such letters as he had just received he realised how bitterly he hated the woman.

'We are going to have a sad change, Professor,' said Captain Kemyss. 'Virginie is to leave us and to go to England.'

'Virginie will go away?' This was, indeed, a change.

'Yes: she had another guardian besides myself, though I had almost forgotten it: she is invited, and we think we ought to let her go: we hope it will not be for long. But who knows? who knows?'

There were letters, too, for the Professor. Among them one which seemed to cause him much agitation.

'Come home at once,' it said, among other things. 'The longer you stay away, the more difficult will it be for you to get what you want. Come, and you shall join the ranks of the penniless adventurers and make a spoon or spoil a horn.'

When they met at dinner, a certain sadness weighed upon their minds. The dinner was silent; for now they all knew what was going to happen, and that the party would be broken up, never, perhaps, all to meet again. Virginie was going to England—the child who had grown up among them. Why, McLoughlin, McAndrew, and the Secretary had seen her every New-Year's Day, and plenty of days between, for seventeen years; they had watched her pass from infancy to childhood; she grew slowly, before their eyes, from a girl, imperfect, bony, angular, to a woman, perfect, rounded, marvellous. She was the joy of the house—the great and chief attraction of Mon Désir. There was no one like her in the island. And now she was to go. What—what would the place be without her?

In Palmiste one is accustomed to seeing people come and go. The officers of the garrison, naturally, are constantly changing; the Governor changes every six years or so; the chiefs of the Civil Service are always changing; and partners and clerks of mercantile houses are perpetually coming out and going home again, to say nothing of those who succumb to the extraordinary thirstiness of the place, and go prematurely to their long home. Therefore, no one was surprised to learn that Captain Ferrier was called home on urgent private affairs.

With the Professor it was different; he was liked by many; he had been in the Colony four or five years, and was regarded, though wrongly, as a permanent resident. He was an eminently cheerful soul; he played a fair hand at whist; he had at times a mordant tongue, and was good at the repression of those who, in Palmiste or elsewhere, endeavour to assert themselves over much; and he had a great fund of information and anecdote, by means of which he could enliven the dinner-tables of the plain, honest Scotch folk who mostly make up the civil society of Palmiste. It was rumoured that he wrote—no one knew what; men who had lived with him knew that he possessed, hidden away in drawers, a quantity of MSS.; that he had been known to extract one, now and then, and to read it for the benefit of his friends; so that, when the news fell upon them that he, too, was going, it was felt that his intention was to go home in order to publish those MSS., or write more.

The dinner languished. The talk was forced. The Pink Boy told about the gourami-fishing; the Padre recounted some of his sufferings on the boulders; and the Professor narrated his fruitless *chasse* of the camerons; but the Squire was dejected, the two elder ladies sad, Virginie anxious and restless, and Tom downcast.

After dinner, the Squire filled his glass and gave his usual New-Year's toast.

'Gentlemen,' he said, 'I drink to all friends at home. Captain Ferrier, I drink the health of his Lordship. Major, Professor, McAndrew'—he bowed to each in turn in his kindly and courtly way—'to you and to yours, here and at home, I wish a Happy New Year.

'It will be a strange New Year to us,' he went on, 'without our child. Virginie will go, I suppose, by this next mail ; we send her to the keeping of good hands ; we trust—that is, we hope—that we shall have her back among us in a year or two, when she has shaken off the rustic ways of Palmiste and learned the talk of Mayfair. But we are not afraid. Our Virginie will not forget her old friends ; and for hostage, we keep Madame Ferrier with us.'

Virginie, who sat on her guardian's left, seized his hand and kissed it with tears.

'As for you, Professor,' went on the old planter, 'it's a disgraceful thing that you can't stay with us. You've got enough to live upon—what does a bookman want more ? You know the foolishness of fighting ; here is a haven of rest ; and you must needs go back to wringle wrangle among the literary men of London. For shame, sir ; for shame ! Haven't we been kind to you ?'

From all voices, except the two officers, there came a chorus.

'Haven't we been kind enough to you, Professor ?'

'Hech, mon !' This was the expostulation of Sandy McAndrew. He felt at the moment that after the many hundreds of sherry-and-bitters, cups of cold tea, brandy-and-sodas, and vermouths taken by the Professor in the room over his office, it was ungrateful in him to go. There needed no words.

'Come with me, Virginie,' said Tom, when he could get speech of her. She went out with him into the night, looking like a white ghost upon the dark lawn.

'I want to say something to you, dear,' said Tom, 'before you go. May I say it to-night ?'

'Yes, Tom. Say what you please and all you please.'

'It is this, Virginie. You are going to leave us. That is quite right. You have rich friends in England whom you ought to see. I always thought that you would go some day. And you are rich yourself. My dear, we have been so much together, all day long together for all these years, that we are almost like brother and sister, are we not ?'

'Go on, Tom,' she said, with a quick perception, almost a pang at her heart, that they were not brother and sister

'I am not clever at books,' he continued. 'The Professor is, but I am not. And I don't know how to talk about things, like your cousin. I am only a Creole, a son of the soil, a sugar-planter. But, Virginie, I want you to believe one thing.'

'I will believe anything, Tom, that you tell me to believe.'

'It is a very simple thing. It is only that I love you——'

'But I know you do, Tom.'

'And that I shall always love you, whatever you do. I mean—because, of course, whatever you do will be right and good, and the best thing that ever any girl did—that even if I hear that you have accepted some man in England, some clever man or some great man, I shall go on loving you all the same. I am what I am, Virginie ; but, whatever happens, good or bad, you will remember, will you not—oh ! my dear—that here, at Mon Désir, there is one man who loves you always.'

'Oh ! Tom,' she said, bursting into tears. 'Why must I go to England at all ? Yes ; you all love me ; you are all too good to me. And I wish it was over, and I was back again, and all was going on just the same as before.'

This can never be. One of the most cruel things that Time, who is always dragging and tearing something from us, does is that he will never let pleasant ways remain or renew themselves. He is always destroying. He tramps on, always a lusty youth, whose companion, as in Watts's picture, is pale Death, and beneath his feet as they go the flowers are trampled down and their grace and perfume lost. There may be—there should be always to the end—other flowers before us, but they are not the same.

And at Mon Désir this is the last of the old New-Year Days when Virginie, the sweet and innocent child, would be there to meet and greet them with her smile and her pretty soft caressing ways.

'She must go, Tom,' said his father that night, ' with her affections free.'

'Yes, sir,' he replied ; 'I have told her to-night that I shall always love her ; I thought I ought to tell her that before she goes. But she will go with her affections quite free, as you say.'

'Humph !' That was all Captain Kemyss said. What he thought was—What will Mrs. Hallowes say if Virginie tells her ?

CHAPTER VI.

HOW THE MAIL WENT OUT.

NEXT morning the party broke up in sadness, and in the early morning they drove or rode away.

The earliest to go was the Professor. He appeared on the verandah with the morning tea. Tom was there in his morning rags, and Virginie in her white frock, always fresh and sweet as a lily. All three were depressed, but the saddest of all was the Professor.

'It is my last visit to Mon Désir,' he sighed. ' In a few days I shall have left the island, never to see it again.'

T

'If I thought,' said Virginie, 'that I should never see it again, I would not leave it.'

'My most pleasant memories,' the Professor went on, lugubriously, 'will be those of the days spent here—and of you,' he added.

'They ought to be,' said Tom, thinking of Virginie, rather than of Mon Désir, though he was narrow-minded enough to think that no place in the world could be more beautiful—which is, indeed, true. Then he got up and went off for his morning ride of inspection. Weeds grow, and coolies are lazy, and Sirdars go to sleep, even though lovely Creoles make all hearts sad by going away.

'You are ambitious,' Virginie said. 'We have always said that you would not make this colony your home. What is an ambitious man to do here? I wonder, though, whether you will be any happier in England than you might be here, if you chose to remain.'

'I dare say not,' he said, with a kind of groan. 'After all, we must not be for ever looking out for happiness. There is no place in the world where one can laze along so happily as here—nor is the claret so good anywhere, I think. But one must work, and after a time one wants to do the work one likes best.'

'Everybody is always going away,' said Virginie. 'It is sad for the people who live here. Directly we get fond of anyone he resigns or gets transferred, and so we lose him. And now I am going too. At all events, we shall go in the same ship.'

'Yes; I shall not have to say farewell until we get to England. Besides, it is a kind of satisfaction to feel that if I am going you are going too. One cannot think with any comfort of Mon Désir without you. It would be too wretched to come here and find no Virginie. To be sure, there are the ladies, and the Squire, and Tom. But, after all, they are not the principal characters in the piece. They come on the stage, you know, to be grouped round the central figure—you.'

'Thank you, Professor,' she said, smiling. 'You have always been kind to me.'

'I have always been in love with you,' he replied, with a frankness which did not displease her. She was accustomed to be loved, and regarded the Professor's assurance in much the same light as if it came from her guardian. 'Not that I presume upon that fact. It is a beautiful thing for a man like me to be in love with a girl like you. I am proud of it, and, I assure you, grateful to Providence for the magnificent privilege of being in love with such a girl as you.'

'Oh! Professor.' This incomprehensible statement confused her.

'I mean exactly what I say, though you do not understand what I mean. So long, however, as you know that I am your faithful servant, that is enough.'

'What have I done,' she asked, 'that you and Tom should both say and think such kind things about me?'

The Professor shook his head.

'You cannot yet understand,' he replied, 'your own power. But you will before long. I do not know what Tom has said, but I hope that he put his case clearly, and that you will not forget anything of what he said. Because, Virginie, sometimes words, when they are first heard, seem to mean little. But, when they are remembered, they get in course of time to acquire their full meaning. Perhaps Tom's words were like these.'

She was very young and she was very innocent. Tom's words had not been understood by her in the sense he intended—that is, not in their fullest sense; not in the sense which we who read them give to them. In other words, this child had no thought whatever of love-making, courtship, and such things.

'I remember perfectly what Tom said,' she replied, considering a little.

'Don't tell me,' he interrupted hastily. 'If you remember them, it is enough. You are going into a strange world; you will get new ideas, and see new people, and learn to think differently in many ways; and you will be far from your old friends. Wherefore, remember Tom always; and if you want counsel think of me, and let me help if I can.'

And then the Squire appeared, and the Professor presently took his leave.

Six days later, the mail steamer, lying in the harbour with her steam up, ready for her start, presented, at five o'clock in the afternoon, an animated and lively appearance. The departure of every mail is attended with plenty of bustle and crowds of visitors; but on this occasion, when, in addition to certain French families, the departures of Virginie Ferrier, her cousin, and the Professor were all to take place together, it seemed as if the whole island were going with them, so crowded were deck, and companion ladders, and saloon. On deck there were gathered little groups of sympathetic friends. French ladies were pressing their infallible nostrums against sea-sickness; there were a hundred words of last parting, of recommendation, and of warning to be given; there was the musical ripple of women's talk; there were the strident voices of Southern Frenchmen. Marseillais especially, and the soft-blurred syllables of Parisians, or those who, by clipping of syllables, would fain pass for Parisians; and there surged up from the saloon the loud laughter of the British officers who had come on board to rejoice with their brother over his departure; and the merchants and civilians who had come to mourn over the farewell of the Professor. Sorrow and joy alike demanded the alleviation or encouragement of brandy-and-soda. Continuous were the poppings of corks : loud was the shouting for the steward; higher and still higher grew the pile of empty soda-water bottles.

On deck a little court surrounded Virginie. Among them were the Pink Boy and the Padre, both desperately in love, though their case was hopeless indeed. His Reverence, for his part

T 2

dreamed of a sympathetic helpmeet, who would admire his ser-
mons, encourage his ambitions, and help him to show the colony
an example of the active Church life. It did not occur to him that
a girl brought up as Virginie had been might become many things ;
but ecclesiasticism was impossible for her. The Pink Boy thought
how delightful a thing it would be to have Virginie with him in
those hot rooms of his over the Bank, in pleasing contiguity to the
guano dépôts, and the port, and the bawling crowd, always engaged in lading and unlading. And, for his part, he did not understand how such a girl could not marry such a boy as himself. They
went on dreaming, however : now, for reasons which will presently
appear, they will dream in this way no more. The girl was flushed
with the excitement and the emotion of leave-taking. She was in
charge of a French lady, who was going all the way to London.
All the farewells had been said but one. There only remained, of
the home circle, her guardian : her cheek was flushed, and her
eyes were bright and tear-stained. She had no heart for the compliments and pretty things which one after the other came to say
to her.

At last there came the time of departure.

A beautiful gradation marks the ceremony of leave-taking on
board the mail. First, the comparative strangers ; next, the
friends ; then the intimate friends ; last, the members of the
household.

Thus, when the officers and the merchants, and those of the
French people who knew her, had offered their hands and wished
Virginie *bon voyage*, and all, even the Padre and the Pink Boy,
were over the side of the ship and in their boats, there remained
the hardest parting of all—that with her fond and faithful
guardian.

He kissed her forehead, cheeks, and lips.

'My dear,' he said, taking her in his arms, 'it is best for you.
It is what your father would have wished. Why should we re-
pine ? Yet, it will be sad, indeed, without you.'

So they parted. Captain Kemyss was the last to leave the ship
before the bell rang ; the whistle shrieked, the screw turned, and
the great ship began once more to drive its long white furrow on
the main. But the old man's eyes were dim, and for a while he
could not see anything.

When they cleared, he became aware that Virginie was standing aft, beside the steersman ; and behind her were the Professor
and her cousin, and she was waving her handkerchief and crying.
At sight of her tears, the Pink Boy's eyes filled, and he choked,
and then he said a wicked word to one of the boatmen, which gave
him relief. And the Padre, who felt a similar inclination to choke,
obtained relief by rebuking the Pink Boy for that wicked word.
So they came ashore, and for many days the light of the sun was
dim to them, and curry, even prawn curry, had no flavour.

It was then six o'clock, and it wanted nearly an hour to sunset.

As for Tom, the reasons why he was not on board were per-feetly well known to everyone, and there was a general feeling that they did him credit. If people are in love, and are soft-hearted and cannot trust themselves to say good-bye in public, then people had better stay ashore, which Tom did. But he had his little plan in his own mind, and this is what he did.

From Mon Désir to the Signal-mountain is a good twelve miles by road. But a man with strong nerves and a steady head can find a much shorter path by way of the mountains, which lie in an amphitheatre round the town. They are rather awful hills to climb about, being provided, more plentifully than falls to the lot of most hills, with bare faces of rock and precipices, and real saddle-backs, along which the rare visitor, who would get along the top, has to drag himself with a leg hanging over each side; but Tom knew the way well, and had too often achieved the feat to think about the danger. Therefore, as he intended to see the last of the girl he loved, he climbed along this break-neck ridge, and made his way to the Signal-mountain.

There is always a man on watch up there; he is provided with a telescope two yards long or so; he has a little hut half buried in the rock, and a mast provided with cross-trees and ropes for signalling the approach of ships; he is up at break of day and re-mains on watch till sunset. And when hurricanes come he is generally blown far away out to sea, hut, telescope, mast, and all.

Tom stood beside the hut with the telescope in his hand, and watched the departure of the steamer. First he saw the crowds on board break up and disappear over the sides, till there were only the passengers and the crew left on deck; then he saw his father, who was the last to leave; and then he saw Virginie standing at the helm waving her handkerchief. At first he could see her face, and he knew that she was weeping. The screw went round. The ship passed out of the quiet harbour waters and began to roll in the waves of the Indian Ocean. Virginie stood there still, after the point was cleared, when she could no longer see her friends, watching the receding shores of the island she had never left be-fore. What thoughts, what memories, were in the girl's mind! Her lover remained motionless, glass in hand, while the ship grew less, and the figure on deck grew smaller, till the white dress, the last he saw of Virginie, vanished altogether. Then he watched the ship itself till the sun went down and the night fell, and ship, and sea, and all dropped out of sight. Then, with heavy heart, he slowly descended the hill. He had seen the last of Virginie. How and when would he see her again?

PART II.—IN THE SEASON.

CHAPTER I.

A ROSE OF JUNE.

On a certain morning in the sweetest month of all the twelve which either adorned, or disgraced, last year, the bright and sunny month of June, when east winds were over and thunderstorms not yet begun, the Row was thronged with those who rode, and the walks with those who did not ride but sat on chairs, or strolled up and down and talked, if they knew anybody, and looked at the crowd, and pretended to know everybody, and to belong to quite the inner circle, and deceived nobody, and came to see, and to be a part of those who were seen. On such a morning Frenchmen in London cease to complain of the endless *brouillard*, and to compare Hyde Park with the Bois; Colonials leave off boasting of their climate—it really is too bad, the way in which Australians, for instance, throw their beautiful climate in our teeth; and good Americans hesitate whether, when they die, they will not ask to go to London rather than to Paris; and financiers thank Heaven that such skies should belong to the city where the money is. As for the leaves on the trees, the golden-rain, and the lilac, the rhododendrons, and the flowers and the grass, everybody knows that they are placed in the Park like the flowers on a dinner-table, the better to set off the guests. They do not belong to nature at all, any more than the cascade at St. Cloud. They are provided by Fortnum and Mason, or some other firm, for a splendid banquet of sunshine and fair weather, to which all are invited alike, but to which none should come who are morose, envious, disappointed, and ill-natured. For these there is Regent's Park, with the daisies and the dandelions of Dame Nature.

Among those who rode was Virginie. With her were her cousins, Guy and Maude Ferrier. Six months of the strong cold English air had taken something from the delicate bloom which lay upon the cheek of the fair Creole beneath her own palms, and had given her a little of the hardy and robust look of her English sisters. Just now, flushed with the exercise and the excitement, the warm air, the soft sunshine and the animated scene about her, the girl had lost for the moment all her Creole languor, and was in very truth become an English girl in appearance. Whether she lost or gained by the difference I do not know. Certainly, of all the young and beautiful women in the Park that morning there was none, English or otherwise, more beautiful than this fair Creole, a fact observed by many of those philosophers who love to lean over the railings and meditate in the midst of youth, beauty, wealth, flowers, gay and careless talk, on the happiness lying ready to hand for virtuous people in the best of all possible worlds. Especially, if virtuous people find their own happiness in witnessing the joy of others. Captain Ferrier was master of several accomplishments, besides the art of card-playing and gambling ; among other things, he could ride well, and looked his best on horseback. Beside him rode his sister, also an accomplished horsewoman. Mounted, she looked handsome, being tall and of graceful figure. When she dismounted you perceived, first, that she was no longer very young, being, in fact, four years older than her brother, and he was twenty-eight ; next, she was thin, and her pale face, with its large and lustrous eyes, wore an anxious look, as if she was continually suffering for the sins of others—which, indeed, was her hapless case. This expression of face is more often found in women than in men, because the manly mind does not set its hopes too much on the achievements of other men ; and when you see it you may be very sure that husbands, sons, or brothers have 'turned out bad.' For the moment, however, she, too, felt happy, because it seemed at last as if a thing on which she had set all her hopes was really likely to take place.

'Make love to her on board.'

That was Maude's injunction to her brother when she wrote to him in Palmiste Island. Captain Ferrier would, perhaps, have obeyed, but for one circumstance : he found on board a young fellow who was as fond of cards as himself ; and he preferred playing écarté or picquet in the smoking-cabin, for'ard, to dangling after his cousin on the after-deck. Besides, he could not present himself, except as a sort of rival—good Heavens ! a rival—to that fellow, Percival. Now Percival, who certainly was not the son of a peer, but had started quite as a second-class passenger in life, and was by no means desirous of passing himself off as anything better, was for some unknown reason peculiarly hateful to this young man ; the more so, because Virginie in his society seemed always more happy than in his own. But, indeed, it is absurd to account for the hatreds and jealousies of selfish men, because they are terribly vain, and brood, and take imaginary offence, and magnify their own importance, and do not see the proportions of things ; so that they become very thorough haters indeed. If their lives were spared long enough, they would end by hating all the world. The disposition of those long-lived Patriarchs Mahaleel and that of his more distinguished great-grandson, are not stated : but if they were as selfish as Guy Ferrier, one perceives clearly how for the last two or three hundred years of their lives they would have regarded the whole of mankind with an unrelenting hatred.

It has been suggested, or dreamed, or told after revelation by some philosophers of the more profound kind, that when this kind of men die they are presently transported to a remarkable island, where there are many beautiful and toothsome things, but not enough to go round. In the general game of grab which is always going on, and on account of its disappointing results, they are said to develop quite astonishing hatreds.

Guy Ferrier learned at school to despise the whole of mankind except a few who need do nothing, but are born to enjoy ; most of the boys in his own set who held those views went out into the world and shook off this narrow view ; he went out into the world and retained it. He despised, for instance, the honest Scotch merchants because they bought, to sell again, cargoes of sugar ; and he despised the Professor because he held a post by which he earned his living. He despised him so heartily, and found it so intolerable to be addressed by him on terms of equality, that he began to hate and despise his cousin for liking him. And his mind was so warped by prejudice, and so narrow, that he found it difficult afterwards to shake off the dislike. He therefore avoided the quarter-deck as much as possible, and spent his time chiefly with his venturous friend, from whom, in the course of his voyage, he won so large a sum that he could afford to send the Major a cheque for five hundred on account. But it is not every day that a man who is a player, but not a fine player, picks up another who is also a player and a more reckless player than himself.

He had one chance. He sat opposite to Virginie at breakfast, luncheon, and dinner, being naturally placed near the Captain, while the obscure Professor had to content himself with a seat at the chief officer's side. It was impossible for any young man to sit opposite to the girl every day for three hours or so—because in this line of steamers meals are considered the chief business of the day, and must not be hurried—without perceiving that she was an extremely attractive young lady. Yet his mind was not open to the sweet influences of love. A lover ought to be light-hearted, and he was heavy-hearted ; a lover ought to look on the world cheerfully ; Captain Ferrier regarded it gloomily, as a place where luck is generally against the player, and where people are wickedly impatient to be paid. So that the innocence and ignorance of the girl, her curiosity about the great world she was going to visit, her vague hopes and little fears, which to most men were charming, irritated him. If Maude wanted him to marry her, he thought sulkily, she might arrange the thing herself—at all events, any kind of marked attention before all these people was out of the question. He paid her no attention at all ; he made no attempt to appear interesting or clever, or profound or remarkable in any way, as is frequently done by men who open the old-fashioned siege in the old-fashioned way, and try to begin by inspiring respect. Virginie thought her cousin a rather morose young man, who never laughed, and smiled only when politeness required the effort. He was, in fact, a morose young man. It is one of the pleasing results of a life devoted to the pursuit of 'pleasure,' that it makes a man, quite prematurely, incapable of mirth, merriment, or joy of heart. It is very odd, but it is so. Sometimes one thinks that those black brethren of Ceylon who never laugh must be one and all engaged in the pursuit of pleasure.

When the voyage was over, and Guy Ferrier met his sister, he was fain to confess that he had made no progress whatever.

She shook her head sadly.

'Things, Guy,' she said, 'can no longer be trifled with. There is absolutely no more money for you.'

'There must be some,' he replied. 'I must get a couple of thousand at least before long.'

'How long can you wait, Guy?'

'I do not know. Perhaps three months; perhaps four or five. I must have money, Maude.'

'Can you not borrow more? You have raised money before or your reversionary interests—can you raise no more?'

'No, not a penny more. They are mortgaged to the hilt.'

She sighed heavily.

'My poor father! If he only knew!' Then she thought of what her brother had done, the futility of helping him; the vain sacrifices she herself had made filled her with wrath which for the moment overcame her affection. 'Oh! Guy—Guy—what a shameful—what a wicked thing it is! All gone the same way, and no use to help, no use to advise.'

'If you have nothing but reproaches, Maude, I will go. I did think that from you I should meet with a little sympathy. But women are all alike.'

'Yes,' she said, bitterly, 'we are all alike: we sit at home and hope and pray, and the Prodigal goes on, and takes everything and throws it away. We are all alike, Guy: we sit and suffer, and can do nothing.'

He made no reply, because there was nothing to say. This thin and anxious woman of thirty had given him everything. He had taken all her own money and all she could get from her father; he had taken her jewels and sold them; he had taken her youth and beauty; he had promised, he had made countless promises, but he broke them all. It would have been better for her—far better—if at the very first mess she had left her brother to flounder out as best he might. Now she had done so much, she was bound to go on; she must stand by him and suffer to the end.

She had sunk into a chair, and sat with clasped hands, and eyes which had no tears in them. She could not cry for the indignation and bitterness in her heart.

'And my father knows nothing,' she said. 'He knows nothing. And some day he must be told, because I can help you no longer.'

'If he must know, he must, I suppose,' her brother replied, carelessly.

'There is your cousin, Guy: can you not even think of her?'

'I have thought about her, Maude. In fact, I think about her every day. Isn't it an infernal shame that a girl like that should have a hundred thousand pounds, and I should be hard up for a trifle of two thousand ? '

'Is that all you think about ? '

'Enough too ; I should say.'

'What is she like ? '

'I believe you would call her pretty. She's a fair girl ; and her manners are good—at least I dare say they are. She doesn't do anything dreadful. But you had better call upon her. She thinks a great deal about the relationship, and you may be civil to her.'

'And won't you think about her, Guy, in the way I want ? Think how it would set you up to marry her. You could buy back all your mortgages. You could start quite fair again. There would be no more debts and worries.'

'I tell you I do think about her.'

'Then why—oh ! Guy—why—— ? '

'Because I do not want to marry any woman. Is that sufficient reason for you ? '

'I shall do what I can for you, Guy. When your difficulties are so great that you can bear them no longer, you will, perhaps, take the step which will relieve you. *It is the only step, remember.* Meantime, I will do my best to prepare the way for you.'

He made no reply, but left her with moody and morose face.

These schemes, these difficulties, were concealed from the head of the house, Lord Ferrier, who, although he found his son difficult to get on with, and taking small interest in the things which interested himself, was yet perfectly satisfied as regards his manner of life. Let the young man do what he pleased up to a certain time : he had, himself, followed the traditions of the House in serving under the colours for a term, before becoming a simple country gentleman. Let his son do the same thing. As for himself, he loved the simple life of his country house. He was a farmer and a landlord before everything else. Things were tight with him, because many of his farms were unlet ; but things would improve. There was no money, because it had all been laid out in unproductive improvements ; and, at the best, Lord Ferrier was poor for a peer. A stately, tall man of sixty odd years, with a Presence, who had gone beautifully grey, which is much better than going bald. He was taller than his son ; his head was larger ; his figure was broader ; his appearance more solid ; and his eyes were better. The eyes are the first of human features to catch the expression which grows out of the life which men lead ; then it goes to the mouth and lips ; and, finally, it is stamped as a seal upon the forehead. The stamp upon the old Lord's forehead was what may be expected in that of a man who preserved those old-fashioned ideas about honour, duty, religion, loyalty, patriotism, property, rank, contentment, thrift, modesty, which formerly stood the old country in good stead, and seem now doomed to decay and disappearance ; a man who was proud of his name and descent, was kind of heart and considerate towards all men ; who was courtly in manner and sincere of speech ; a man who hated Radicals, Republicans, Communists, Socialists, Nihilists, Comtists, Atheists, and persons of 'advanced' views generally, as he hated the DEVIL. As for his estates, he was a tenant for life ; he held them on trust ; it was his duty to hand them on to his successor improved and enlarged. And, as every gentleman ought to have a hobby, it was Lord Ferrier's hobby that he could paint. He had painted steadily for forty years ; and during the whole of the time, according to his friends, his painting had grown steadily worse. Yet every year he sent a picture to the Royal Academy, which was promptly rejected ; and every year he made dozens of studies, landscapes, heads, cattle-pieces, and river-scenes—working as hard at his hobby as any professional man at the calling which gave him daily bread.

Maude called upon her cousin, and was gracious to her and to her guardian. The beauty and the grace of the girl, so soft, so delicate, so ethereal, surprised her. Was her brother a stone, that he should have been blind to this miracle of loveliness? Her manner was a little shy, because she was so inexperienced and so ignorant, but it was the manner of a lady. She invited her, with Mrs. Hallowes, to dinner alone, so that it would be a dinner *en famille,* she said.

To this first entertainment she did not invite her brother—for reasons. Lord Ferrier would interest the girl more. And, in fact, Virginie was greatly moved by the kind and affectionate reception which the venerated head of the house accorded her. He told her how he had been at school with her father, his first cousin, and what a good fellow he had always been, and how she resembled him in face, though her father was never—well—never half so charming ; and he paid her so many compliments and showed her so much kindness that Virginie fell in love with him at once. The compliments and kindness of old men always please girls ; if they are girls of the world they are pleased because men of such wide experience should show such admirable discrimination ; if they are girls new to the world they are pleased because they are not afraid. The worst of young men's flattery is that one never knows what they may say next, and that they may at any moment go on to a proposal.

Maude began at once, so as to lose no time, to acquire that influence over her cousin's mind which would assist her in her designs. She must woo Virginie for her brother. She must make this girl in love with herself, with Lord Ferrier, with the house, with everything belonging to them, before she would try to make her fall in love with Guy. She called nearly every day ; she sent frequent invitations ; she drove with her ; she made her father buy a horse for her, and then she rode with her ; she managed so that if Virginie went anywhere, or saw anything, it should seem as if by her advice or help. She gave her wise counsel in matters of dress.

t

She instructed her in the things which girls *must* know, or seem to know ; and she took her in hand in the matters of art and music, of which Virginie was profoundly ignorant. In all Palmiste there is not such a thing as a picture ; while as to music, they know little or nothing beyond the elementary tune. And always she pleased the girl, who was easily pleased, by a show of affection, sympathy, and interest, as if she had always longed to know her, and had studied carefully how she could be of use to her. At the same time, lest Mrs. Hallowes should be jealous, she treated her as if she was an old and valued friend, instead of a mere acquaintance.

Then Virginie, thus assisted, began to go into society.

From her point of view it was bewildering. All the people seemed to know everybody, and to be able to talk about everything. For herself, she knew nothing, and she knew nobody. She was not able, at first, to talk about anything. After a little, she began to understand something. Maude taught her the way in which pictures, and music, and books are talked about. But the things of real interest, the family histories, the personal gossip, she could not master. She was also greatly astonished, at first, because no one took the smallest interest in the events and politics of Palmiste Island. In her eyes, this place was the most important, in every-body's eyes, of all the British dominions, next to England itself. Small as it was, only a tiny speck in the ocean, it grew such a quantity of sugar, and had so romantic a history, that Australia, New Zealand, Canada, seemed of comparatively small importance. And she could not possibly understand how anybody could fail to be interested in its politics, its fertility, its beauty, or the differences in the social position of the inhabitants. Most astonishing thing of all, she actually once met a coloured man, a native of the island, at a dance, and the English girls were dancing with him ! Happily, the man had not the presumption to ask her for a dance. Then she met a man who had been a Governor there, and nobody called him ‘ Your Excellency,’ or paid him the slightest reverence or respect ; and men talked slightingly of Colonial Bishops ; and gentlemen who were honourable members of the Legislative Council were held as nought. These things were strange to her at first. Maude was worse than anybody. She refused to pretend any interest in Palmiste ; she would talk of nothing but England, and, which Virginie liked, especially of the honour and glory of the Ferrier House. But daily she felt more and more how small a thing was her own sugar estate and simple bungalow compared with the splendid estates and noble houses of the people to whom she now belonged.

‘ Why should you trouble your head about the place ? ’ Maude said. ‘ You will marry and settle in England, and your mother will then, I hope, come home and live with you. You have no other friends there, have you ? ’

‘ Oh ! yes. I have many friends. There is my guardian, Captain Kemys, to begin with ; and Madame, and Tom.’

'Tom ! Who is Tom ? '

'Tom is Captain Kemyss's son, you know. He always told me he loved me.'

'That seems great presumption ; but perhaps he only meant it in a brotherly sense.'

'Of course,' said Virginie. 'Tom was always a brother to me.' Poor Tom !

'And then,' she continued, 'there was the Professor.'

'What was he ? '

'He is in England now. He isn't a Professor any more ; and his name is Percival. He always said he loved me, too.'

'They showed their good taste, my dear Virginie,' said Maude, laughing. 'But I think it was a great impudence to tell you of it. Perhaps they merely wanted to make you understand that they really had good taste. No doubt, however, they have already consoled themselves.'

When the first strangeness had gone off, when Virginie had become an established and constant visitor at the house, when her father became, by his own admiration of the girl, an unwitting accomplice in her schemes, Maude began, but cautiously, to talk about her brother. He seldom went into general society, she explained, because he was too fastidious for general society ; the dreadful want of taste in conversation, dress, and manners irritated him ; he did not, certainly, belong to the dancing set ; it was not to be expected of him that he would go to balls for the sake of the supper, as many men do in this abominable town. Guy was, as no doubt Virginie had already discovered, a man of the most refined and fastidious taste ; he was not a great talker, but his opinions were convictions ; he never tried to show his own superiority, but when he was called upon, Maude said, the true ring of intellect was heard in his every utterance ; what he said was always right ; what he did was always noble. Maude drew the picture of the brother she ought to have had ; the splendid result of generations of careful training ; the perfect knight ; the statesman of the future ; the prop and support of the Conservative cause. Heavens ! if men only understood how women love them to be great and strong ! They know that we want them to be beautiful, and they do their best, all out of the kindness of their hearts, to meet our views. But we, selfish creatures that we are, waste and idle our lives away and do nothing, so that our sisters and wives are fain to be ashamed of us, and to apologise for us instead of being proud and happy because we are so brave, and so industrious. Lay it to heart, my brothers.

One thing astonished Maude ; yet she seemed to understand it. Guy had never fallen in love with any woman. This was not because his nature was cold, for, she said, he was a man of the deepest and warmest feeling, but it arose from his refined taste and the dread which he naturally felt lest he should find something in his wife, when it was too late, to trouble and irritate him. 'Think, my dear Virginie,' she said, clasping her hands, 'if such a man, with nerves so highly strung, should have to live all his days with a person whose very appearance might irritate him hourly.   My dear child, if he could only find a true wife somewhere; if he could only find a woman of your tender heart and sweet temper and sympathetic susceptibilities.   But there,' she sighed, 'men never see what is lying before their very feet.'

'Sometimes I think,' she said, warming to her subject, 'that Guy is like a knight of romance.   There was never any frivolity about him; he could never endure what some young men call fun. Heaven protect us from the funny man?   He never wanted to laugh at foolish jokes and stories.   My dear, did you ever see a whole theatre full of people laughing because a man has tumbled down and hurt himself?   He never wanted to talk, even as a boy, to show his wisdom.   You have observed, probably, his silent moods.   It is by meditation that wisdom comes.   When he is in a silent mood he loves to hear grave music.   I was glad when he came in last night and sat down in a corner, not wanting to talk, that you were playing that sonata.   Your playing, dear child, like your voice, soothes him.   My own voice is too loud for him, and my playing is too—what shall I say?—too brilliant.   I play as I was taught, and I suppose I think too much about execution.

'Guy was saying the other day'—this was during another of Maude's confidential conversations—'that beautiful women are made for beautiful rooms.   Our own rooms, he said, never look properly furnished unless Virginie is in them.   Was it not pretty of him, my dear?'

These and a thousand such sayings could not fail to produce an effect upon a girl so utterly inexperienced as Virginie.   Mrs. Hallowes, who knew perfectly well what they meant, and who perfectly appreciated the value of her ward, fell in with the plot, because she honestly thought the match a highly advantageous one for the girl.   She wrote to that effect indeed to Captain Kemyss. 'I hear nothing very much,' she said, 'against Captain Ferrier's reputation, except that he is a man of very few friends.   His chief fault, in my eyes, is that if he intends to become Virginie's lover, he shows very little ardour.   Indeed, he has not even begun to make love.   But his sister assures me that his affections are very strongly engaged, and that he only hesitates because he thinks that the young lady should at least have time to look round her. This seems honourable, though not what one would expect of a young man, when so beautiful an heiress is in the case.   Indeed, I should prefer a little anxiety lest so great a prize should be carried off by someone else.   As regards our dear girl, she looks upon Maude as her greatest friend; she considers Maude's brother to be all that a fond sister has painted him.   And though I do not suppose that she is at all what we used to call "in love," I do think that she waits but the word.   When that is spoken, there will be no other man in the world for her but Captain Ferrier.

'You must not think that she forgets her Palmiste friends; on the contrary, she is always thinking of you all—and for you, and especially of her brother Tom. But she writes to you so often that I need not assure you any further upon this point.'

'So she will marry her cousin after all,' said Captain Kemyss, laying down the letter with a sigh. 'I do not like him; but I may be wrong. After all, it is satisfactory to think that she will be Lady Ferrier. Her father would have liked it. And as for Tom—her "brother" Tom—as Mrs. Hallowes calls him—clever woman, that!—he must put up with his disappointment. What else could he expect? Perhaps, if things go wrong, he may remain as Virginie's manager. I would rather he had been her husband.'

So things were planned for Virginie. She was to marry her cousin. She had been brought over from Palmiste for that purpose; she had become engaged to him out there, people said: she had been romantically promised to him in infancy, others said. Nobody knew who started these reports, or what foundation of fact they possessed; but everybody believed them, and Maude herself, when she was asked if they were true, did not contradict the statement.

But what a shame, what an extraordinary shame, that so beautiful a girl should have been engaged even before she came out. The soft sweet languor of her manner was roused to animation only when she danced; her limpid eyes; the delicacy of her complexion; her graceful figure; her gentle kindliness to all alike, from peer to Treasury clerk, endeared her to English youth, and made Mrs. Hallowes, who 'ran' this heavenly creature, a Power for the time in the Social world. With an heiress one can always get into good houses; with such an heiress there is no telling to what heights Mrs. Hallowes might have raised herself, but for the events which interrupted her upward flight just when she was beginning to feel herself at her strongest and best. These events were connected intimately with the ride of this particular morning in June.

As these three rode in the Row, there were many who recognised them, and pointed them out to each other. Among these were some—gentlemen dressed with, perhaps, more regard to colour and picturesqueness of effect than is common in society—who seemed to know the Captain professionally, and informed each other that things were looking up with certain pieces of signed paper; for the Hon'ble Captain Ferrier was going to marry a girl; no doubt the fair-haired girl riding alongside him, who had got, it was said, nothing short of a hundred, yes, a hundred thousand at her back. Then they passed by and others followed, and a good many of the men who rode that morning seemed to interest these gentlemen with big cigars and showy garments and diamond rings.

Now where the crowd was thickest, opposite Hyde Park Gate, where the chairs were ranged in a double row and were all filled, there stood a lady, still young, being not more than five or six-and-twenty, accompanied by an old gentleman, and surrounded by a small court of gentlemen. Other ladies as they passed turned their heads and looked at her with curiosity—that is a polite way of saying that they stared their very rudest and hardest at her. She was well dressed—extraordinarily well dressed—and was a most striking and handsome woman, with regular, strongly marked features, a strong mouth and chin, and rather a loud voice. Outside the little circle of her friends stood, or strolled, all looking at her, a noble army of martyrs—young men—who longed to make her acquaintance, but could not because they had no one who would introduce them. For this lady was no other than Violet Lovelace, the new light of the London stage, as clever and sparkling as any who had ever offered their beauty and their wit for the admiration of the public. And this little circle round her consisted of those who could boast of an acquaintance with her, in right of which they became her courtiers. And the old gentleman—he was manifestly old, though his wig was black and curly, because his lips trembled and his eyes were crows-footed—was Paul Perigal, for many years attached to the Princess's Theatre. He was, in fact, in his seventy-fifth year, and he dressed carefully after the fashion of his thirty-fifth summer, which was when her gracious Majesty was still a youthful bride, and when the mode as regards collars, neckties, and hats differed in some important details from the present. Violet Lovelace retained her old friend and tutor in her house as her companion : he kept the house going, paid the bills, was her faithful steward, saw that the 'boy' was looked after when his mother was at rehearsal, and went with her wherever she went. Now as Violet was invited a good deal to supper and breakfast, and liked to accept as many invitations as possible, being a kind-hearted person, glad to bestow a little happiness wherever she could, the old man was more than her companion and friend—he was her chaperon ; and nobody lived who could truthfully boast that Violet Lovelace had accepted an invitation alone.

While they were all talking, the lady half turned her head and looked at the riders. Then she stopped laughing suddenly.

'What is it, Violet?' asked one of her friends—everybody called her by her Christian name. 'You look as if you had seen a ghost.'

'I have, my Lord,' she replied. 'I have seen a ghost whom I hoped never to see again ; and I feel as if buckets of cold water were being poured down my back. So I think I will go home. Come, Daddy !'

'The ghost I saw, Daddy,' she explained, when they were outside the Park, 'was the ghost of my husband. He did not see me. The sight of him made me long to—to say something I should not. A lady must not be violent, must she?'

Paul shook his head doubtfully.

'Violence,' he said, 'sometimes means fire. You ought to rise
to the occasion. Give me a woman who can feel a situation and
rip out the words as if she meant them. But such a woman is hard
to find nowadays. When I was a young man——'

'I do feel the situation, Daddy. I assure you, I feel it very
strongly. And I should like very much to rip out the words. But,
somehow, I don't think the audience would have been pleased.
We must always consider the stalls, you know. In your young
days you only played for the pit. Let us go home. The sunshine
has turned into cloud for us, and the warm air is cold.'

'The "Return of the Husband,"' murmured Paul. 'Adapted
from the French of "Le Mari Repenti." Principal parts by Miss
Violet Lovelace and Mr. ——.' I remember he said his name was
Richard Johnson ; but he looked like Mr. Plantagenet Howard.'

'Never mind his name, Daddy. That was his sister riding with
him—the sallow-faced woman, with black hair and big eyes, and a
thin figure. She looked at me as she passed with the curious contempt which makes us actresses love the real lady so much. Bless
her! I know all about her. My husband takes all her money
from her to pay his debts. Tender, thoughtful brother he is!
Daddy,'—she clasped the old man's arm with both her hands,
though they were in the open, in gay and handsome Piccadilly,
which has a thousand eyes—'Daddy, if I thought the boy was
going to turn out like his father, I would—no—I would ask you to
take him away and kill him.'

'He won't,' said Paul. 'With such a training as I have given
him, and such an example as mine, he can't.'

'Who was the girl with him, I wonder? Not that I care. She
seemed pretty.'

'If he repents, and comes home and asks forgiveness, I suppose
you will take him on again.'

'Never, never! And he knows it. Marriage is always a
lottery. Some men belong to the good lottery ; most to the bad
lottery. My husband, Daddy, is one of the very last and worst ;
he is, indeed, a most disgraceful lottery. But even he won't try
on the repentant dodge. Don't talk about him any more, and let
us buy something to take home to the boy.'

CHAPTER II.

ELSIE'S FRIEND.

'I THINK, Elsie,' said Mr. Percival, formerly called the Professor,
'that this is a chapter which will fire the imagination, and make
the blood boil and the pulses quicken. Don't you find your generous young heart leaping up?'

He was reading from a manuscript, and a girl was sitting at the

U

open window listening. The place was a first-floor in one of these streets of profound respectability—from the lodging-house point of view—about Bloomsbury. A box of mignonette was in the window, which assisted the imagination and helped the listener to follow the reader far away among woods and meadows, streams and hills. The girl was quite young, not more than eighteen or nineteen ; she was listening critically, and she shook her head to express a kind of doubt.   It was a head of a pretty shape, set off by the last fashion of wearing the hair, which reveals the shape of a head, and is therefore fatal to many a girl who might otherwise be counted beautiful.   Her face belonged to a not uncommon type, whose beauty depends chiefly on expression ; it is a good, safe kind of beauty, because when it once takes hold of a man, it grows upon him, and fastens upon him, until he cares for no other kind of face in the world.

Mr. Percival, no longer the Professor, for he had resigned, and was now engaged on making that spoon or spoiling that horn, lived in the house as lodger.   He had lived there before he went abroad, so that he returned to it as an old friend.   Elsie, the daughter of the house, was a school-girl when he went away, and a grown-up girl when he came back.   There was only one other lodger, and he was an old gentleman who gave no trouble ; and on the proceeds and profits derived from her two lodgers, Elsie's mother, who was a widow, paid her rent and taxes and supplemented the family income.   All day long, until half-past seven, Elsie was the governess of a child of five or six ; in the evening, resuming an old custom of her childhood, she became the companion and confidante of Mr. Percival, a pleasant, conversational, good-natured sort of man, who liked companionship, especially of the youthful female kind.   Sometimes she went for walks with him in the quiet squares ; or she sat with him, or she read with him, or even she went to the theatre with him, in a manner which would have been compromising to the last degree in some circles ; but in Elsie's, which can hardly be called a circle, and yet was not a square—perhaps a crescent, an oblong—it didn't matter.   She had no friends who would inquire what were Mr. Percival's intentions, and, indeed, at present he had none, because Elsie seemed to him still the child he remembered when he was last in London, and because he was without an income and was feeling his way along the thorny path of literature, dreaming and devising great things, and meanwhile thinking himself lucky when he had a book tossed to him for review, or got an article accepted, or hit upon an idea which could be afterwards worked up.   As for falling in love with Elsie, that, if you please, no more entered into his mind than into hers.   He was ten years older than herself, which at eighteen seems a frightful difference. She knew, besides, that he was already in love with a young lady as beautiful as a queen, whom he could never marry by reason of one Tom, who somehow stood in the way.   This young lady was in England, having come across the seas in his company, but he did

not go to see her, because, Elsie thought, he felt that it would be
a pity for him to get more entangled in this hopeless labyrinth of
love. Besides, a literary man wants to keep his brain clear, and in
that novel he was writing, from which he read to her sometimes in
the evening, there was a man so madly in love with a young lady
whom both hero and novelist thought was perfect, yet who seemed
to Elsie a whimsical woman, that merely to portray his emotions
it was necessary for the mind of the writer to be quite free from
any troubles of its own ; the largest and fullest sympathy was
required for love of this passionate kind. When the work was
completed it would be time to visit Virginie, whose Christian name
Elsie had heard many hundreds of times.

She shook her head, criticising the chapter.

'I suppose it is a powerful scene,' she said ; 'but, you know,
they wouldn't really go on like that. Nobody possibly could.'

'What would they do, then ?'

'Oh ! I don't know. They would feel angry and disappointed
with each other. Then they would go away and break things off,
I suppose.'

'It is clear to me, my child, that you have not the faintest
conception of the passion of love. How should you ?' he sighed.
'For my own part, I have experience. I portray, with a change of
name, my own feelings towards Virginie.'

'Oh !' She laughed the laugh of the Doubter. 'Your passion,
indeed ! But you have grown desperate, and you—why you go on
as happily as if you had no passion.'

'The sting is concealed,' he said. 'It is like the hair shirt.
Many a lusty knight of old was found after death to have worn a
hair shirt unknown to his friends.'

'Yes,' she said sharply. 'They put on flannel first, I suppose.
Why can't you draw things as they are and people as they talk ?
That is what I like to read about.'

'Profound student of human nature ! Remember that it is the
province of Art not so much to present Nature faithfully as to
present things as they should happen—but don't. Nature is flat.
Situations are wasted. In real life, my child, events do not happen
dramatically ; nor are the right things said at the right moment ;
nor are there surprises—though, to be sure, *il n'y a rien de sûr que
l'imprévu.* Real life, Elsie, is apt to be dull——'

'Horribly dull,' said the philosopher of eighteen. 'Frightfully
dull, sometimes.'

'Yes, and flat, and unhappy ; being made unhappy chiefly by
little things, not big calamities. Temper, I believe, and want of
sympathy, and want of change, and want of society, make up most
of the domestic unhappiness which no he novelist has had the
courage to tackle. It is woman's work, not man's, to write about
the little pin-prickings of the home life. Did you ever have prickly
heat, Elsie ? Of course you have not. Then you can't understand
—but I can—what many of our beautiful English homes are like.

real life? No; I do not think I shall tackle the subject of real life. Romance is what I shall freeze to.'

'Want of change seems to me the worst thing of all,' said Elsie. 'Look at my poor father. He was born in London, he lived in London, and he never went out of London, because he never could afford it. Hampstead he called the country. It was his only idea of country, poor dear. It was mine, too, till you first came and we began to go about together.'

'Yes,' said the great writer, as yet unknown; 'we have made pilgrimages on Sundays, haven't we? We know the pit of the theatre, do we not? We have ventured on the river at Hampton, happy Hampton! we two together. Courage, Elsie, life must not be monotonous for you.'

'Then life ought to be honest,' said the girl passionately. 'Why, I am a common cheat and impostor.'

'Nay, nay,' said her adviser. 'If Miss Violet Lovelace is pleased with your manner and work, surely that is enough.'

'She advertised for a perfect lady for her boy. I answered the advertisement. She was very good to me, and said at the beginning such kind things about my manners, you know, that I did not dare to undeceive her. "My dear," she said, "I want a perfect lady, because my boy will be a gentleman. You may go on calling me Miss Violet Lovelace if you like, because that is my stage name; but I am a married woman, and my husband is a Wretch, although he is a gentleman of good family. I am separated from him. As for myself, I am not quite a lady—off the stage; but I am getting on, and when the boy grows up and can make comparisons, he shall not be ashamed of his mother. Of course, I have few opportunities of knowing real ladies in private life. So now you see what I want, and if you will try, and will be good and patient with the boy, I shall always be more grateful to you than words can tell." That was what she said; and I deceived her, and said I would try.'

'The word lady, Elsie,' said Mr. Percival, putting aside his manuscript, 'covers an area about equal in extent to that claimed for the word gentleman.'

'If I had told her that my father was nothing but a humble clerk in a small house of business, and that my mother took in lodgers, would she have received me as her governess? You know she wouldn't.'

'The question is, rather, if she knew these facts now would she consider you unfit for the post? Because you see, my child, she seems to like you.'

'I am sure she likes me. Nobody could be more affectionate to me, or kinder, which makes the deception worse.'

'Very good then, and you like the boy.'

'Who could help liking the dear child?'

'In that case, Elsie, trouble not your little head about possibilities. For there are many. Enjoy the good fortune that comes in your way. Sunshine is scarce. Kind persons are scarce. If

Miss Violet Lovelace asks you any questions about yourself, tell her what you please. Meanwhile, be as useful as you can to the boy. Now, my child, I am going to put away the Novel. I say, though,' he added, lovingly regarding his manuscript, 'the last is really a most tremendous chapter. I wonder how Thackeray would have treated it. But, poor man, he never could have conceived a situation so dramatic and so terrible ; and I am going to have a quiet pipe. You need not go unless you like. In fact, I would rather you stayed.'

She did stay. Nothing could have been a greater reversal of the manners and customs of the perfect lady, whom Elsie was supposed to present for the ensample of the boy, than for a girl of eighteen to be sitting night after night with a young man of eight-and-twenty—alone, if you please. Yet Elsie liked it. And the young man liked it. And Elsie's mother thought no harm of it, and if she did she was welcome to walk upstairs and put her head in and speak her mind.

'Miss Violet,' said Elsie, 'came home to-day at half-past twelve in a very low way. First, she sat down and sighed as if her heart was breaking. Then she wished she had never been born. After that she kissed the boy, and said that if it was not for him she could wish that she was dead. When they served our dinner, which is her breakfast, you know, because she has to sit up half the night sometimes and gets up late, she would not eat anything.'

'Got a cold ?' asked Percival.

'Oh ! no. She never catches cold, though the theatre is full of draughts. She got up presently and went away to her own room. Then Mr. Perigal, who had been sighing with her, like a pump, whispered to me that she had seen her husband in the Park.'

'This grows mysterious. Is her husband generally invisible ?'

'Mr. Perigal told me all about her marriage. She married a gentleman who was in love with her because she was so beautiful and so clever. Mr. Perigal was at the wedding, with her father, who is a stage carpenter at Drury Lane. Mr. Perigal believes that he was married under a false name. Anyhow, she won't say who or what the man is. But he must be a very bad man, because she left him and came back to Mr. Perigal, and said that nothing would ever induce her to go back to her husband, or to take any kind of help from him. And to-day she saw him riding in the Park, and it gave her a turn.'

'Ah ! Things might be made of this,' said the aspiring novelist.

'Fortunately,' Elsie went on, 'it seems that he did not see her.'

'The Park would be a fine stage for a recognition scene. "It is—it is"—amid the tears of a sympathetic crowd—"it is my long-lost husband ! Behold that scar, inflicted, in our happy, happy days, by your own hand, and with the kitchen poker ! At last you find me"——'

'You forget,' said the young lady without an imagination, 'that he must know where she is and all about her, because her photograph is in all the windows.'

'To be sure. I forgot that. It must be a pleasing thing for a separated married man to be reminded of his bonds by every shop-window. I should walk in the Park—which, it seems, the gentleman was actually doing—so as to get out of the way of the photographs. I suppose Mr. Perigal does not know the cause of the separation?'

'No. She has never told anybody. No one knows her name, or anything about the marriage at all. Her husband, whoever he is, has never sent her any money or help; and at first, before she made a success, I think she was very poor at times. It seems cruel, when she is so beautiful, and so clever, and so much admired, and might marry well if she were free.'

'Yes, it seems cruel. Still, she has the boy.'

'Yes. The boy is to be sent to a public school, she says, because his father was there. And he is to go to Oxford afterwards, if he wishes. And then he is to go into the Army. So that we suppose his father was in the Army, too. As for the stage, it is not to be mentioned in his presence. And yet the child is a born actor, like his mother. But you don't care for this talk. Miss Violet Lovelace is nothing to you.'

'On the contrary, Miss Violet Lovelace is a good deal to everybody who goes to the theatre, if it is only to the pit. You and I have often admired her extremely.'

'You would laugh to see the love-letters and the bouquets she gets. Sometimes she shows them to me; sometimes she tosses them to Mr. Perigal, who puts them in the fire; and sometimes she gets angry with them, and tears them up in a rage. Now your pipe is finished, and perhaps you would like me to go. But if you like to have another, we can talk about Miss Virginie.'

'Woman is a wheedler. You know I should like to have another pipe, and you know I like to talk about Virginie.'

'She lives, does she not, in an enchanted island?'

'Yes; enchanted when she is on it. Formerly it was one of the Fortunate Islands. The shades of heroes used to haunt its woods and sit beside its waterfalls. I saw Ulysses there myself, once; but when I drew nearer, intending to have a talk over a few little things, he changed into an aged nigger with snow-white wool. But there is no doubt that the island was enchanted while Virginie lived there. Now that she has come to England the spell, I dare say, is removed. It cannot be anything more than a commonplace bit of an island, with ups and downs—which they call hills and ravines—and trees and rivers, and it smells all over of guano. I wonder anyone can go on living there. But no doubt they are all packing up to go away as fast as they can.'

'And what sort of a Palace did she have?'

'The Palace was built entirely of jasper, malachite, white marble, and other precious materials, set with sapphires and pearls. It was crowded with works of art, especially in sculpture, and it was hung with rich tapestries and silken curtains ; beautiful flowers stood about, and there were perfumed fountains, and always the sound of dropping music, and wonderful maidens, with lustrous eyes and long floating hair, dressed in amber silk of Greek fashion, to attend the Princess.'

'How delightful ! She was the Queen of the whole island, of course.'

'Why, of course she was. Nothing else was possible. She ruled all hearts, and was, indeed, a most gracious monarch, the fountain of honour, and the dispenser of joy.'

'And you were in love with her.'

'That was not unusual ; in fact, we were all in love with her. But Tom came first. I only came second.'

'That horrid Tom !'

'Yes ; I often regret that I never pushed Tom over the edge of the ravine. It might have been done so very easily, and the consequences to me would have been so delightful. Indeed, I was only restrained from doing so by the consideration that perhaps Virginie might have been annoyed, and one would not vex that divine creature even by a crumpled rose-leaf, to say nothing of a crumpled Tom.'

'I see. Did she like being loved by everybody ? Did it make her vain ?'

'Vain ? Are you aware that you are speaking of Virginie ? Do you know that she is without any fault at all ? My dear Elsie, you must not ask questions which betray ignorance so profound.'

The girl laughed—

'Oh ! it is delicious. And all about a woman !'

'Why—who should it be about, if not a woman ?'

'To think that men can talk such extravagant nonsense, and, I suppose, believe it about any girls !'

'She is a goddess,' said Percival. 'Now, if there were no goddesses we should have to invent some. Do you see ? Which things are an allegory.'

'No, I do not see. Cannot you be content with your Virginie as she is ?'

'"As she is,"' he replied ; 'there is no "*is*." You are to me —what I think you are. You are to yourself—what you think you are. To your mother you are someone else. Virginie is to me—a goddess. What she is to other men doesn't matter.'

'I like it,' said Elsie reflecting ; 'only it must make a girl ashamed of herself to be called a goddess, when she knows very well that she is just like other people, and, I suppose, the best of girls sometimes feel that they ought to be better. Good-night, Mr. Percival. Go to bed and dream of your Enchanted Palace.'

'Now, there is a girl,' said Percival, slowly, as he prepared for going to bed, 'who might make a man, in time, believe that there may be, after all, different kinds and degrees in goddess-ships. May be ? There are—yet—oh ! Virginie !'

CHAPTER III.

AN ACTRESS AT HOME.

NOBODY wanted a Miss or a Mistress to place before that illustrious name of Violet Lovelace ; other people crave for titles ; the more naked his name the better pleased is the actor ; he knows, you see, the difference between real and sham distinction. The young lady arrived at the highest honours of her profession by a single leap. When she began, when Guy Ferrier discovered her, she was only intrusted with those parts which require little speaking, but a good deal of standing about on the stage. In one sense, therefore, she was, from the beginning, one of the brightest ornaments of the British Theatre, and, as one of a group, she helped to form many most delightful pictures.

At the outset, she was quite an ignorant young lady, without very much ambition, and only half conscious of her good looks. If you are born in the neighbourhood of Drury Lane ; if your papa is a 'carpenter,' using the word in its theatrical sense ; if all your friends belong, somehow or other, to the 'House,' so that the children go on with the Pantomime as soon as they can wear a costume, and the grown-up ones are supers, unless they are ticket-takers, carpenters, door-keepers, dressers, and the rest of it ; if the pavement of Russell-court, Duke's-court, and Vinegar-yard is your dancing-school ; if your mother is a dresser at the theatre, and your cousins are ballet-girls, and your brothers also drop naturally into the service, you are also pretty certain to fall in with the stream, and regard the theatre in some form or other as offering you the only means of getting your daily bread.

It was Mr. Paul Perigal—'old' Paul Perigal ; his earliest recollections of the stage are connected with the visit of the allied Sovereigns—who first found out Emily Hicks. Purely in the interest of the drama he kept an eye upon beauty or promise among the humbler children of Thespis. Emily lived close to the theatre. She went on at Christmas till she grew too big to go on any longer. Her mother proposed that she should follow her own line, which is safe, if not lucrative, and become a dresser. But Paul Perigal ordered otherwise. 'Hicks,' he said to the carpenter, 'you've got a girl who may be a flyer. I've observed her, Hicks. She will be, unless my experience deceives me, a beautiful woman. Your own experience of the stage, Hicks, will warrant you in agreeing with me that beauty is half the battle, because a girl can always be taught to stand and turn her eyes about and smile, even if she can't open her mouth to speak. But your girl is as sharp as a needle and as cheeky as a boy. Send her to me, Hicks, and I will do what I can for her.'

Emily Hicks was not slow to recognise the fact that it is ten times more jolly to be dressed and to stand on the stage for the admiration of the world than to be hidden away behind for the purpose of dressing others. She also knew that she was frightfully ignorant of manners as well as of learning, And when she saw—which was every night—the stage ladies with their magnificent stage manners, she wondered whether she, too, would ever have to walk with that air, to sweep back the skirts with gestures so splendid, to wear such frocks as if they belonged naturally to her. Now, in the eyes of such observers as Miss Emily Hicks, it is most true that ' manners maketh the woman.'

Paul Perigal took great pains with her. She was such a sharp, intelligent pupil that he began to conceive the greatest hopes of her. She had a voice of the kind which is good for a song on occasion, though not enough to make her a singer. He had the voice trained ; then he had her taught to dance—perhaps she would become a burlesque actress ; then he taught her to walk and to carry herself ; then he taught her to read aloud, to speak without the use of Drury Lane colloquialisms ; then he persuaded - her father to let her live with him entirely, with the view of separating her from those young friends whose acquaintance in after life might not be desirable. And when all was done, and the sharp-faced, cheeky child of Duke's Court had become in two or three years transformed into an extremely beautiful girl of seventeen, thus trained and drilled, the worthy old actor began to instruct her in the real craft and mystery of the dramatic art.

From such small beginnings sprang the greatness of Violet Lovelace.

She was on the stage in that small way already described for a few months only. Then she left it to marry a man who was madly in love with her : a young man, a handsome man, a man in the army, a man like a hero of romance for dark eyes and dark hair, a man—oh !—who was going some day to have a title. The last fact was her own secret, never revealed to her father or to Paul Perigal.

Paul heard of the intended marriage with a groan of disappointment. He hoped for so much from this girl, who was so clever. Now she was going to marry a swell, and his labour of four years would be lost. Never, never again could he hope to find a pupil so promising. His professional reputation was staked upon her success. He allowed her, he told everybody, to go on in small parts only in order to give her confidence ; but wait—wait a bit—she would make the finest Lady Teazle ever seen on the stage ; as Rosamond she would make an epoch ; as Juliet she would be incomparable. He boasted about her at Rockley's : ' A gem of the first water, gentlemen ; the very first water. I shall be content, for my own part, with the immortality which will be my lot, not as an actor, though, perhaps, memories may survive—I say nothing, but a certain Mercutio of the year 1836 is quoted still—thank you, gentlemen—but I shall not be remembered so much as an actor, but as the happy finder, developer, and instructor of this light in Histrionic Art.' And now this gem was lost, wrested from him, and to be lost to the drama. Pity! pity! a thousand pities!

What, however, Paul Perigal did not foresee, and could not possibly foresee, was the return of the deserter (who looked pale and worn, but resolute), which took place within a year of her marriage, and her announcement that she was ready to take up her old work, and to devote herself with it. She further informed her tutor that no questions were to be asked about her husband, who was a Wretch worthy of the greater condemnation. Then she asked Paul what he thought of the baby, who was wonderful for six weeks old; and then she said that she was ready to begin at once.

'I don't wish to put impertinent questions, my dear,' said Paul, tearfully, because the divided emotions of joy at her return to Art, and of sympathy with her wrecked married life, brought those signs of sympathy to his good old eyes. 'But I should like to ask one, if I might.'

'Can't tell, Daddy,' she replied, in something of her old defiant way. But she looked as if, at touch or word, she, too, might 'go off.' 'Can't tell till I hear it.'

'Only this, my dear,' he said. 'I did my best to make you a lady.'

'You did—bless your dear old heart!'

'But, you know, my experience extended to ladies on the stage, and—and—in point of fact—not those who have played leading parts. I don't think, for instance, that I ever saw a Juliet of the Lane at her own house. And as for Society ladies—ladies in the front—of course I never knew any. Oh! I know it's getting different with the young fellows now. But I'm old, and I understand my position, which is more on the level of the Nurse or Lady Capulet than with Juliet. So that, you see, I've been at times fearful lest, when you went into marble halls and gilded saloons, people might have wondered who you were. Because your manners might not, perhaps, be quite the same as theirs. Don't think me rude, my dear.'

'Don't be afraid, Daddy. I never had any opportunity of showing any manners. Because I have never seen a lady, or a gentleman either, since I went away. Amy Robsart, bless you, was nothing to it. And I believe if my lord and master had been able to make that little trap in the staircase without being found out he would have done it, and I should have gone into it—flop: and there would have been an end of one. Of course I only waited till the boy was born to come away. And, of course, he didn't want the boy at all. I've been locked up since the wedding because he's ashamed of his wife, and he wishes she was dead.

'Never mind asking any more questions, Daddy. I mean to live, not to die; and the boy shall live too. And now that is settled let me get to work. No more standing with one knee bent and a sweet smile—like that—if you please. I must have a country engagement for leading parts ; and then I must come to town. Go to Rockley's, and tell them I've come back. You may gas as much as you like about talent and beauty and such. I'll have my photograph taken again—you don't think I'm going off, do you ?—and with your help, you dear old Daddy, we'll pull 'em in and make some money.'

She went into a country troupe and travelled for three years and more, patient, working hard, studying every morning with Paul, and never neglecting the boy.

Then she came to town and made her first appearance in a new comedy, which would certainly have been a failure but for her acting and her extraordinary beauty. The unforced merriment, the pathos, the ease of the new actress startled and arrested the people. It was a great success, and Violet's fortune was made.

The first thing she did was to advertise for a real lady to take daily care of her boy, now five years old and no longer a baby. Elsie was the real lady. Violet chose her from a good many applicants on account of her quiet manner and trustworthy face. 'Some of them were dressed better,' she explained, 'and some of them pretended to know more, and some of them wanted to teach the boy on a system. Most of them looked as if they would probably beat and pinch the boy when I was out of sight. In that case I should have had to beat them, which they would not like, and there would have been rows. But this girl I am sure won't beat him. I told her I wanted a lady, and she blushed very prettily—Daddy, if only one could blush on the stage !—because, I suppose, nobody had ever doubted that she was a lady ; not a stalls lady, or a private-box lady, but an upper-circle-at-four-shillings-reserved lady, who comes to the theatre by Underground, and is not ashamed to cry and laugh ; father something respectable, I suppose, with a shop somewhere—what does it matter ? She said that she would do her best for the child if I would let her take him ; and she spoke so prettily—don't you think I might find a part for this style of thing ? Look, Daddy'—here she drooped her eyes a little, made her face a little longer, just smoothed her hair, folded her hands and lowered her voice, and became immediately Elsie. 'That kind of thing. I believe it would take, if the people got to understand it at once. But I want an author—oh ! I want an author badly.'

'But about the governess ?'

'Oh ! yes—well—you know she is quite young, and I am four-and-twenty, and I feel ever so old.' Violet was given to mix up things so that it is not always easy to follow her line of thought. What she meant, however, was that she was old enough to read character and to enact the part of a patron. 'So I just kissed her and told her to come every day, and that I was going to be a real lady sometime—in fact, that I am always understudying the part ; but that at present I was a great stage lady, and so on, and so on. And here we are, and here she is, Daddy—and I feel that so respectable a young lady confers dignity upon the house. You are not to bring any more people from Rockley's here, if you please ; the place will have to be as demure as the Foundling Hospital, and if you and I do sometimes have a little supper with a few noble patrons of the drama, we must have it out of the house in future.'

'Very well, Violet,' said Paul. 'Do you think the young lady, at odd moments, would like a little instruction in the——'

'You dear old man !' She threw her arms round his neck and gave him a stage kiss, which everybody knows is done without impressing the lips upon the cheek or brow at all. But she disarranged his wig. 'I believe you would like the whole world to go on the stage.'

'All the world's——'

'Don't, Paul. And let Elsie alone—she is to be my governess, not my rival. I should like,' said the actress, proudly, 'to see the woman who will be my rival, in a year or two. And now, Daddy, one more trial of that scene. Come ! But I *must* find an author.'

It was this assumption of the 'real lady' which preyed upon poor Elsie's mind. Not that it entered Violet's busy head to ask who or what her father was. She was profoundly ignorant of the world outside the stage. Whether she was told that Elsie was the daughter of a Bishop or of a City clerk, she would not have suspected any difference. One sometimes gets glimpses of this ignorance of humanity's cherished social differences. Everything depends on rank, even in the most Radical and Republican countries ; and rank is a thing of so much delicacy, so many shades, that only one born in the middle of it all can truly understand it—can at once feel the true awe for those above him, and the true contempt for those below. This is an advantage possessed by the middle-class man, which has never before been set forth. Violet, you see, was born too low down. In her early days, everybody with a black coat seemed to her a swell, and everybody in kid gloves seemed a lady. This kind of ignorance sticks in a surprising manner, so that you may detect the high-born aristocrat, however he may dissemble, by his not understanding why the solicitor and the general practitioner do not always stand upon the same level, and why the ladies of both decline to call upon the eminent draper's wife.

After a separation of five years the sight of her husband was to Violet the revival of old bitternesses that she had thought forgotten and clean passed away for ever. But you cannot so put things away and lock them up. Nothing is ever really forgotten so that you are quite safe that it will never come back to you. The sight of the man's face brought back to her recollection her foolish belief in him, her trust in his loyalty, her dreadful disappointment in him, the cruel things he had said, his selfishness, his shame of her, so that he kept her a prisoner and would neither let her go anywhere nor bring any of his friends to see her. No one should know, he told her, that he had been such a fool. No one should even guess that he had a wife. When she left him it was with a letter telling him where she was going and what she was going to do. They were to be henceforth as if they had never met ; but, for the sake of the boy, she would preserve her marriage lines.

'Daddy,' she asked, 'could that man take away the boy ? '

'I don't think he could.'

'If he were to try,' she said, with a glitter in her eye, 'I would stab him. Did you see him, yesterday ; how he looked in the face of the girl he was riding with ? That way he used to look at me. Sorrow, and trouble, for any woman who falls in the way of such a man.'

'There are laws about married people,' Paul went on ; 'but I don't know exactly what they are, because I never, somehow, thought about marrying till it was too late. Much better, for an old man like me, to have a young daughter than a young wife about him. No wife could be so pretty, and bright, and clever, as you—and always in good temper——'

'Not always, Daddy ; not when she meets her Wretch of a husband.'

'If I had a wife she would only be disturbing my ease. Well, my dear, I don't know what the laws are. But I believe that whatever you earn, he can take, unless there's been some sort of a legal separation. All that you have is his, you see ; and I suppose that all he has is yours, too.'

'I don't think,' said Violet, laughing rather grimly, 'that he is likely to go to the treasury on Saturday morning ; and he won't want the furniture. Besides, that is yours.'

'We will say so to keep it from him. But it was bought with your money.'

In fact, Violet had displaced all the dingy old sticks and refurnished the house with bright new things of the most modern fashion ; so that the place, though Bloomsbury is not one of the most cheerful and sunny parts of London, was pleasant to look upon.

'It is the boy, Daddy, that I am thinking of. Always the boy. I am sure he hates the boy ; he would do the boy a mischief if he could. Because, you see, the boy is his heir.'

'If he hates the boy, he can leave his money to someone else.'

'It isn't only money, Daddy. It is land, and . . . and other things that he can't leave.'

'He shall only harm the boy,' said Paul, fiercely, 'by passing over my mangled corpse.'

'Thank you, Daddy, dear. I know your fidelity, and I will bring you home a property sabre, one of the sort with a curly blade, you know. But that won't be the way. Oh ! Daddy, I am going to have trouble. He will come to see me.'

'Courage, Violet. He can do nothing.'

'And I can do a great deal. Because he is afraid of me. Patience—patience—Daddy mine.'

CHAPTER IV.

THE ONLY WAY OUT OF IT.

On that night Virginie dined with her cousins. No one was at the dinner except Mrs. Hallowes and Guy, who was for once in a good temper, and actually did something towards promoting the cheerfulness of the evening. For this small mercy Maude was grateful. The reason why he was in a good temper was that he had only that very morning hit upon an idea which seemed to him not only the most excellent way out of his perplexities, but also the only way out. Because he was now perfectly assured that unless he married an heiress there was nothing more that he could do to avert the crash. And because that idea seemed good in his own eyes, he saw a hundred reasons why it should seem good in the eyes of the other person chiefly concerned with it.

The idea was the following :—

On arriving in London he realised, principally through the photograph shops, the truth of his wife's statement that she, the woman whom he regarded with so lively a detestation, had become, almost at one step, one of the most popular actresses of the day. For her face greeted him with smiling eyes from every bookseller's shop, from every photographer's, and from every stationer's. Violet Lovelace was before him everywhere. He could buy her picture showing full face, three-quarter face, side face ; he could buy her looking into a glass, tying a hood round her head, gazing heavenwards, in riding habit, in her favourite character, seated, standing, kneeling. After the first shock he cared very little about it, and ceased to be irritated by the sight of a woman he would fain have forgotten. She had succeeded. Very well ; let her succeed, so long as she kept her secret. It was not until that very morning that he began to think how this very success, instead of being a danger to him, might actually be of the greatest use. It wanted only a little—a little . . . well . . . a little absence of scruple ; and if he found, for his own part, that he could contribute, so to speak, this absence of scruple, why was it to be supposed that she, on the other side, who had as much to gain, would show herself troubled with qualms of conscience ? For the plan which he had formed in his own mind was nothing but this—why not agree with the actress to break off suddenly, and say no more about the bond which tied them together ? All they had to do was to go on as if nothing had ever happened at all. Such simplicity in the idea ! Such a swift and sudden cutting of a Gordian Knot !

He considered the subject dispassionately, as he thought. That is to say, he lay back in his chair, and followed in imagination the various advantages of the plan.

She was still young ; she was—well, perhaps, she still thought
herself beautiful ; how could he have ever been charmed by the
beauty of which men raved? She was clever, they said; certainly in the old times her tongue was free and her temper sharp ;
she had always a little court of admirers about her ; half the men
in London were languishing for her ; a great crowd gathered round
the stage-door every night to see her drive away ; Princes went to
her theatre and applauded ; the men at his club talked about her ;
she was inaccessible ; she was guarded by old Paul Perigal, whom
she called Daddy ; she lived a quiet and blameless life. Why,
such a woman, said Guy, has excellent chances : she may marry
anybody—really, anybody ; she has only to be careful of her reputation. Would it not be best—say as a calm, cold matter of business—to agree together that this business, a most awful nuisance
to both of them, should be terminated? It wanted nothing but
common consent, and silence afterwards.

Best? Why, it was the only thing to be done—the only possible
thing. To go on as they were all their lives : thus to be tied and
yet to be kept apart : could anything be more foolish? If it was a
good thing for himself, it was surely a far better thing for her : so
good a thing was it for her that he hesitated whether he should do
the woman so kind a turn. Certainly, he thought, taking the
mental attitude such a man always assumes, she had behaved in-
fernally badly to himself, and deserved nothing at his hands. Yet,
considering how greatly his own interests were concerned in the
matter, he would go and see her, and make her, by word of mouth,
a definite offer of release. How happy she would be to have her
freedom! How cleverly she had played her cards so that, with
Daddy always at her side, her reputation was blameless ! Yes ; he
would let her marry when and where she pleased. Benevolent
young man ! Most unselfish of young men ! And then, when she
was out of the way, he could marry his cousin—and her *dot.* At
the mere thought of that pile of money his fancy lightly turned to
green meadows, green pastures, green lawns, as large as tables, with
shepherds sitting around, and the click of coin and the voice of him
who held the bank, and the fierce joy of him who won and the
breathless expectations of him who waited the event.

Lord Ferrier sat with Mrs. Hallowes on his right: she told him
stories and amused him ; and with Virginie on his left. It pleased
him, though he hardly knew why, to know that this beautiful
creature regarded him with so much respect: he liked her to ask
him questions, to venture timidly on showing a return of the affection which he bestowed upon her ; he referred things to her, asked
her opinions, proposed plans for her, and gave her presents. He
courted her, as Maude courted her, but unconsciously, for his son.
It was for his sake, not for his own, that Virginie would accept the
offer of her cousin.

Nothing would have been more pleasant than this little dinner
en famille. To Virginie its chief charm was the beauty and fitness

of its setting. Mrs. Hallowes had everything, without doubt, as it ought to be. Her furniture was of the most modern fashion ; her decorations of the most approved type ; the house was spacious and new ; but her rooms lacked something. You cannot make old things ; you cannot add the charm which lies in old furniture old pictures, old bric-à-brac, all belonging to each other. Mrs Hallowes had large rooms, and spacious ; and these were small The things in her house were good, but they were new. Here the plate was old, the furniture was old, the pictures were old ; there was an old-fashioned air about the whole, far more pleasing than anything of the newest fashion. And at his end of the table sat the chief, old himself, yet in the most beautiful and picturesque time of man's life—the time of autumn, the age of stateliness and dignity, not of decrepitude. Maude herself, with her thin, pale cheeks and lustrous eyes, her dress of black velvet, with a diamond cross, looked in her place as doing duty for the Châtelaine. A quiet, easy dinner, in which everyone felt that in a home dinner conversation need not be forced. Maude saw her brother looking at the girl she wanted him to marry with eyes that seemed full ot admiration. At last, she thought, even his cold heart was moved. He was moved—a little—as much as his anxieties allowed him to be moved—as much as any woman could then have moved him. The prospect of release removed a load of those anxieties. The thought that his sister expected him to propose to the girl immedi-ately, and the satisfaction of considering that he might really be free and able to take that step, made him regard her more curiously. Yes, she was certainly a very pretty girl, and of a type not com-mon in these realms. As Maude watched him she thought, but only for a moment—because it was but a wild hope, a hopeless hope—that perhaps his affections might be fixed, and the attrac-tions of the green table be forgotten. But she was too sensible to dwell upon this unhappiness. She knew, from long and patient study of her brother, that his case was really as hopeless as the case of an habitual drunkard. He would have his vicissitudes. With money to spare, he might run on for years ; but, in the long run, the end was certain. All that could be lost would be lost. Yet, with this absolute certainty of knowledge, she would not hesitate for a moment to sacrifice the innocent and truthful girl who believed all she was told, and suspected no motive. If the evil time must come, let it be put off as long as possible ; perhaps it might not come till he who would feel it most would know it and feel it more.

'Guy,' said Lord Ferrier, when they were alone, 'your cousin is a very charming girl.'

'Yes, sir, she is very charming.'

'And very beautiful.'

'She is very beautiful.'

'Is she . . . has she any entanglement ?'

'I believe, sir, she has none.'

Lord Ferrier looked about him, and stroked his chin reflectively.
' Then, Guy,' he said, ' we will go upstairs.'

The three ladies were sitting together. Mrs. Hallowes presently
rose and began talking to Lord Ferrier. Maude went to the piano
and began to play something. Guy sat down beside Virginie.
Perhaps it was the soft atmosphere of the room ; perhaps the wine
he had been drinking ; perhaps the sense of freedom gained by his
newly-conceived idea ; perhaps the words of his father—which
made his heart feel an unwonted glow as he looked upon the girl
whose fortune would make all things right for him.

' You are looking, Mrs. Hallowes,' said his Lordship, ' at one of
my pictures '—it represented a girl in a field ; and Mrs. Hallowes
was wondering, before she burst into admiration, whether it was
meant for a gipsy, or perhaps an Indian woman, or a Nymph, or a
brown fairy. ' My daughter, when at the age of fifteen. Thank
you, yes ; it is admitted to be a speaking likeness. Yet the
Academy refused it. You see,' he added, with a smile, ' they will
not allow a man who has a title to paint. We must not touch
things professional.'

' Is it possible ?' cried Mrs. Hallowes, who knew almost as
much about Art as poor Virginie. ' Is it possible ? The most deli-
cately-painted, the most striking likeness.'

Virginie was sitting in an easy-chair, beside a lamp covered with
a soft, warm shade, whose colour was reflected on her cheek ;
other lamps with soft shades were standing about the room, so that
it glowed with a soft subdued light : she held a fan in her hand :
her eyes were soft and dreamy : she was listening to the soft and
dreamy music.

Maude went on playing, and watched with keen and anxious
eyes. So far all was well : her brother, for the first time in her
experience, seemed attracted : she played more softly — more
dreamily : in the old, old days, when he was a lad fresh from Eton,
and still open to sweet influences, this dreamy music would make
him sit listening as long as she chose to play. The thoughts of a boy
are long, long thoughts ; and now he was a man, with hardened heart,
and the old innocence was gone : but yet the music touched him.

Yet not as it had done formerly, when it roused his mind for a
moment to noble ambitions. Now it fell upon his soul as some
potent drug mounts to the brain, and makes a man see things which
exist not and believe things impossible to be real. His freedom
was already achieved—somehow : he was actually free—in imagination. The ' other one ' had actually accepted her discharge—in
his imagination.

He was able to do—under these happy circumstances—what his
sister wanted him to do. He would make her happy : he would
make his cousin happy : he would make his father happy. Everybody should be happy, till the money was all gone. He put the
thing to himself in this lively benevolent way, as if it was a duty
closely connected with the fifth commandment.

x

'Virginie,' he whispered.

She blushed. It was the first time that her cousin had addressed her by her Christian name.

'Virginie,' he repeated, gently. I have said that he had a low, rich voice.

Maude heard. She saw her brother's bending head and her cousin's blushing cheeks; and she went on playing more softly, more dreamily, as if her very soul were wrapped and lapped in the melody.

'May I see you alone?' he asked. 'Virginie, my happiness is at stake.'

His own happiness, of course. After all, you can't ask a girl to marry you on the ground that it will make her happy. Less selfish men than Guy approach this delicate subject in the same manner.

'My happiness is at stake,' he repeated, feeling quite sure that the magnitude of the interests involved would not fail of moving any woman's heart.

She made no reply. Maude, watching, saw how her colour came and went.

Then Lord Ferrier stepped to her, and interrupted the conversation.

'Will you sing to me, my dear?' he said. 'Will you sing me one of your little French songs?'

'If that will give you any pleasure, my Lord.'

'All that you do, fair cousin, gives me pleasure. You are born under a happy star, to give nothing but pleasure to all who love you, my dear.'

She smiled, and sang her song. Guy stood by her. When she finished, he whispered, again, 'Let me see you alone. Let me call upon you to-morrow. You will see me alone?'

'I will try,' she said, blushing.

Mrs. Hallowes had other engagements for the evening; but when they came away, Virginie requested to be set down at home. She had a headache; she wanted to be alone.

'My dear,' said her guardian. 'Captain Ferrier asked me to-night to allow him to see you to-morrow alone. I told him that I could not possibly make any objection. But your decision is in your own hands, Virginie. Shall I say anything for it—or against it?'

'Oh! no—no!' she replied; 'only . . . it seems so sudden . . . and what will Captain Kemyss say? and my mother? and Tom?'

'If Tom is a good brother,' said Mrs. Hallowes, 'he will be rejoiced. Captain Kemyss is a sensible man. Of course he will be rejoiced. And as for your mother, why, my dear, can it be possible that she would not rejoice at your marriage with the heir, who will some day be the head of the House, the future Lord Ferrier? Ask your heart, my dear, and leave the rest to me.'

'I ask my heart in vain,' said the girl, half laughing, half sighing; 'for I get no reply.'

' You do not dislike him ?'

' Oh ! no—no. How can I dislike a man so good and noble as Guy ?'

Mrs. Hallowes said nothing for a while. She was, in fact, lost in natural admiration of Maude's great cleverness, because she had, for her own part, looked in vain for the least sign of this great nobility; Maude had filled this young person's mind with a romantic and impossible conception of her brother's character. Nevertheless, if the end was good, what matter for the means? Besides is there any romance which lasts beyond the fourth week of the honeymoon?

'If you do not dislike him, my dear child, the way is already paved for love. But, indeed, I would not seek to persuade you. Ask, I say again, your own heart.'

All night long, Virginie lay tossing, disquiet, anxious. If she dropped asleep, dreadful dreams came to her. She was back at Mon Désir. Tom looked at her with reproachful eyes; the Professor held up hands at her and turned away in despair, reminding her that he had always loved her, and expected to be considered, after Tom; even Captain Kemyss, when he saw her coming slowly up the avenue of palms, dropped his face in his hands, as if he were ashamed of her.

But why? For surely a great thing for her, and a thing which her father would have liked ; and Captain Ferrier was the best of men, although of such sensitive and highly strung nature ; and perhaps it would please Lord Ferrier ; and Maude would like it ; and Mrs. Hallowes would like it. And yet—and yet—some fear, some regret, some disappointment in her mind. And when she rose on the morning which was to be that of her betrothal it was with red eyes and a heavy heart.

'Guy,' Maude whispered before they parted. 'What did you say to Virginie to-night ?'

'I could not say much with all of you in the room. What I am to say to-morrow will please you, Maude.'

'I hope it will please her.'

'I suppose it will. Why shouldn't it ?' Most girls like to marry an eldest son. Besides . . . Oh ! of course it will please her.'

'And then . . . Guy . . . Remember a wife is not a sister.' The tears came into her eyes. . . . 'If you make her unhappy—as you have made me unhappy—I shall ne /er forget that, if I had told her the truth, she would rather die than marry you. Yet, if not for you, for my father's sake I would do it again, whatever the consequences. I would rather that Virginie were unhappy than that his last years should be disgraced.'

'Thank you, Maude. You are a kind and loving sister. You always contrive to say such pleasant things when a man has gone out of his way to please you.'

x 2

'I say the truth to you, now and then, because I cannot help it, I suppose. Good-night, Guy! You have got all my little fortune; you have got all the money you can raise on your reversionary interests; you are loaded and crushed with debts; you have gambled everything away. There is this one chance left you—a sweet and true-hearted girl, who will love you for yourself if you show her a grain of sympathy, and who will bring you a fortune that will set you up for life, unless you throw that away as well. But I know —oh! I know—what will be the end of it. It is all I can do for you, Guy; your last chance—your last chance. And God forgive you if . . .' Her voice broke, and she left him.

Guy looked after her angrily.

'What the devil,' he said, 'has come to Maude to-night? As for Virginie——'

Then he thought of the money-bags, and that sweet vision of green cloth floated before his eyes, and he smiled. What mattered Maude's anger or Virginie's happiness, compared with the glorious fight with chance lying almost within his grasp? He went to his club, and drank a brandy-and-soda. Then he remembered the interview which he must have, some time, with his wife. His conscience was pretty well dead within him; but yet he did seem to remember that there was an ugly word in three syllables which stood for a certain unlawful thing, only possible to be committed by men already once married. But, then!—pah!—absurd! Violet would be only too glad to accept her release.

CHAPTER V.

THE ENGAGEMENT.

In the morning Captain Ferrier made a mistake which is common, indeed, but always fatal—that is to say, he put the cart before the horse. In other words, he reckoned his chickens before they were hatched. To be more precise, because he wanted a thing to happen he supposed that it was going to happen, even though rivers would have to run up hills and rain to fall out of cloudless skies. To be intelligible to the meanest comprehension, he neglected to follow an old precept, designed for such as himself, which teaches that it is well to be off with the old love before you are on with the new. Bluebeard owed the greatest successes of his romantic career to remembering this proverb, which Captain Ferrier forgot. To come to facts, he called upon Virginie before he called upon Violet. Now, it was most essential for the successful conduct of his case that the latter should fall in with his views and be a consenting party to that ugly word of six letters and three syllables.

Virginie received him with a conscious blush, because, of course, she knew well what he came to say. She was still actively engaged to following Mrs. Hallowes's advice—namely, in asking her own heart. Nothing is more difficult to do, when you come to try it. For, first, how are you to put your questions? What questions are you to put? And suppose you get no answer—what are you to do next? This was exactly poor Virginie's case. She wanted to find out how she should like to marry her cousin, and she could not get the least glimpse or foreshadowing of what would happen, or how things might be, either towards happiness or repentance in the future. Nor could she understand herself as Guy Ferrier's daily companion. If she had been older, more experienced, a reader of novels or of poetry, she would have understood perfectly well that there was no fluttering of her heart at the prospect before her, and that she cared nothing at all about the man, but only respected an ideal. Also she would have understood that what Mrs. Hallowes and ladies like unto her mean by the phrase of asking one's heart is to be interpreted in the sense of 'consider the establishment and the position.' But this she did not understand, and it would have been incredible to her that her cousin, this soul of honour and fine feeling, could esteem her fortune as of the least importance in asking her to be his wife. She was as yet little more than a child in experience, though eighteen years of age : she knew nothing more of society than she had learned from four months with Mrs. Hallowes, and even that lady knew nothing about the personal character of Captain Ferrier. To be sure, the personal character of the heir to a peerage must be very, very bad to form an obstacle to marriage ; yet there are some vices, of which the inveterate vice of gambling is one, which cannot be overlooked even by women of the world. English girls teach each other and learn from books and the talk of their elders the true meaning, the proportion, the value of things, especially of money and rank, concerning which no 'class of persons' can be said to feel more strongly or to distinguish more correctly. But who was to teach this young colonial that nothing is what it seems to be, and that we build our social structure on make-believe and assumption?

In one of the queer, wild *desréglés* romances of the last century, when the French, like the Russians of the present day, were busy tearing every social institution up by the roots to see whether it would not grow equally well with the roots up and the head down, there was a certain ingenious Abbé, who wrote the history of a young lady brought up in a single room, and introduced to the outside world after she arrived at years of womanhood. Naturally, she took a new, original, and quite unconventional view of the things which she saw. Virginie was in something of the same condition as the young lady brought up in the box. She believed what she was told, and what she saw. Therefore, when Maude told her how great and good and generous a man was her only brother, she naturally accepted the assurance, and wondered where so admirable a man would find a wife worthy of him. That she herself would be asked to occupy that position was, indeed, most amazing. And now he stood before her; he bent over her; he whispered in his low, full voice, which really sounded as if he was full of feeling.

'Virginie! you know why I am here. Will you bid me hope?'
She made no reply, because she did not know what to say.

'It is for my own happiness.' These were the words he had used last night; and it did seem to Virginie, even at that moment, as if, at such a moment, there was more to be considered than her suitor's happiness.

Still she made no reply.

'My sister, Maude, will be pleased, I know. My father will be pleased, I am sure. Virginie, give me your hand.'
He took it. He held it. Then he stooped and kissed her forehead. She had said nothing; not one word; but she was engaged.

Her lover dropped her hand and walked to the window, with a sigh. Why did he sigh? He stayed there for a few minutes without saying anything. Then he came back, and sat beside her.

He spoke slowly, and said little, and that little was strange. It was an arrangement, he repeated, in cold and measured words, that would be satisfactory to all concerned. It was necessary for him to marry; it was pleasant to marry his cousin; they would have an early day fixed; his father would, perhaps, be the best person to write to Captain Kemyss, and she should write to her mother, and perhaps she would tell Mrs. Hallowes, and so they could all go on just the same as before. 'Of course,' he said, 'I shall be delighted to do anything for you that I possibly can. You will, I know, command me. But about balls and evening parties——'

'Oh! I do not want you to go anywhere unless you like.'

'Thank you. I am not fond of these social things. You greatly relieve me. It is very good of you.' He spoke with an approach to feeling, 'I always think that a pair of people who are going to be married look absurd going about together. So glad that you agree with me.'

Then he rose, and said that he believed there was no more to be said, and he kissed her again on the forehead and went away.

Poor Virginie had no experience in love-making, and had read few novels; but she had looked for the display of more feeling. Still, a man of Guy's refinement was not to be expected to make boisterous love, like a common rustic and an ungoverned person. Perhaps, however, he would say more when he recovered from the emotion under which he had been labouring—that sigh!—and when she herself recovered from her fright.

Then Mrs. Hallowes came into the room and asked her, with a smile, if she had seen Captain Ferrier, and then kissed her, and told her that she was a girl greatly to be envied, and that her own fortune, added to her lover's position, ought to enable her to take any place—any place she pleased—in Society. 'And then, my dear,' she said, 'you will remember me, and ask me to your very best parties.'

The happy lover went straight to his sister. He was feeling, in fact, pretty low about the thing he had done. Still, there was no cause for anxiety : not the least. The other person would be rejoiced to meet him half way. But he rather began to wish that he had paid the less pleasant visit first.

'I've done it, Maude,' he said, in deep and sepulchral tones.

'Done it ! You mean that you have actually——'

'Yes. I'm engaged to the Creole girl. That's what I mean.'

'Oh ! Guy. I am so happy and thankful. But why are you looking gloomy over it ? '

'Because I feel gloomy.'

'I suppose I am a fool ; but I confess I cannot sympathise with you, my brother.'

'No. I did not suppose you would.'

'It can't be money at such a moment.'

'It isn't money. It's worse than money. perhaps. Oh ! Maude——' Here he stopped. 'No. Now I'm engaged,' he added, more lightly, ' I shall go round and tell them all to wait.'

'There is no one—is there '—Maude asked suspiciously, 'that you would rather marry ? You are not in love, somewhere else, are you, Guy ? '

'In love ! Women are always thinking of love. No ; there is no one else I would rather marry. Come, Maude, never mind. Be pleased because you've got what you wanted, and I shall have the money—with the wife. Pity I can't borrow it of her, and let her marry someone else.'

'Do you happen to know—but, of course, you could not ask her—how it is settled ? '

'I don't know. I suppose I shall get the spending of it, somehow, whichever way it is settled.'

'I asked Mrs. Hallowes once, but she does not know. Nor does she know how much it is. There is a charge on the estate for the mother for life ; that is all she knows. Well, Guy'—she heaved a great sigh—' you will have it, whatever the amount is ; but I hope, I sincerely hope, that it is all tied up and settled upon her, so that she cannot even sell out.'

'No one loses who can hold on,' said Guy, gravely. 'The devil of it is having to leave off just when your luck is on the turn. Don't be afraid, Maude. I shall do very well. Will you tell my father, or shall I ? '

'Do you tell him, Guy. He will be greatly pleased, I am sure. Go now and tell him ; and, for Heaven's sake, my dear boy, try not to look as if you were going to be hanged.'

'I wonder,' said Maude to herself. 'I wonder what it is—who it is. He says there is nobody he would rather marry. At one

time I was afraid he might have got himself entangled. But it
can't be that. Why has he always set his face against marriage?
And shall—oh! shall I—get my jewels back?'

No; she will never get her jewels back, because now she has
found out why Guy's engagement oppressed him with so profound
a gloom.

Lord Ferrier was, indeed, greatly pleased. Nothing that his
son had done pleased him so much. Indeed, the contemplation of
his successor's career so far gave him little cause for gratification,
although he knew nothing of the quagmire of debts, liabilities,
money raised on reversionary interests and post obits in which Guy
was plunged.

'I congratulate you,' he said, 'on your good taste and good
judgment. Virginie is a most charming girl. I shall go this
afternoon to tell her so, and to thank her for giving you her hand.
Her fortune is considerable, and, properly husbanded, may help to
win back some of our lost acres. You must regard it as a trust for
that purpose, Guy. Think of your successors.'

'I will, sir,' said Guy, with conviction.

'I suppose that there is no need to hurry the wedding. We
must first get the consent of her mother and her guardian, Captain
Kemyss. It is now June. It will take two months or so to get
their reply, which we may understand will be favourable. Let us
hold the wedding in September, if that will do for everybody;
and, considering that Virginie is already a daughter of the house,
I think, Guy, that we should celebrate the event at The Towers.
But all shall be as she wishes; all as she wishes.'

The old man began to make plans for the happiness of the
young pair. They should live at The Towers, if they pleased; he
wanted nothing but bachelor's quarters there: they could have the
town house where they pleased, and so on.

'And, Guy, now that you are engaged, I think you should send
in your papers. You have had nearly ten years' soldiering, which
is five more than my allowance. A country gentleman owes duties
to his country; and, if I were you, I would take up politics. Your
wife, with her wonderful beauty and her manner, which is charming,
is fitted to become a leader of society. She might even become to
the Conservative cause what Lady Palmerston was to the Liberals.
She should be of the greatest help to you, if you care for a political
career. And why not, Guy? Why not? Surely there never was
a time when there was a better opening for a man of ability.
Think it over.'

'I will, sir,' said Guy. 'I will think it over.'

He went away, and his father fell to building castles in the air,
based on the many virtues of his promised daughter-in-law. Then
Maude came, and they talked together about it, and how wonder-
fully things had turned out as they wished, and what a remarkable
Providence it was that a bride and a fortune should be found for
Guy in so forgotten and obscure a place as Palmiste Island.

'Let the fortune be tied up,' said Maude, anxiously, 'so that Guy cannot touch any of it, or dispose of it.'

'By all means,' her father replied. 'Yet I like a wife to show some trust in her husband. All these arrangements should be left to her guardian. We will go and see Mrs. Hallowes this afternoon, Maude. Of course you will be gracious to her. I have observed that you have always been kind to her. Perhaps with a view— Maude, is every woman a match-maker? We will go this afternoon, and we will bring gifts. I shall give her one of my pictures—the Joan of Arc, I think, or the Mary Queen of Scots. And we will find something pretty among the old gimcracks : something belonging to your great-grandmother, who was also her own. That she will value much better than if we bought her some new trinket in Bond Street. Come, Maude, let us go and turn over some of the pretty things.

Thus was Virginie engaged : thus was she welcomed as a daughter by the old Lord and a sister by Maude. They all dined with Mrs. Hallowes that evening. Guy was still silent and pre-occupied, thinking over his great and singular happiness, no doubt. Virginie looked in vain for any words of the deeper heart, because none came at all. And even Mrs. Hallowes thought, though she said nothing, that a little attention was due from the young man to his *fiancée* ; and that Captain Ferrier seemed certainly the coldest lover she had ever heard of. But Lord Ferrier saw nothing of this : he was the lover : he made Virginie sit beside him and held her hand in his, and stroked her hair, and whispered how happy she would make him in becoming his daughter, and what a lucky man was his son.

CHAPTER VI.

HUSBAND AND WIFE.

THE interview with Violet must be held sooner or later, because, from the very nature of the things to be said, they could not possibly be written. One may have no conscience—many men certainly have no conscience ; but few men are destitute of common sense, and there is generally some caution in wickedness. Again, to put down in black and white—which may be read by anybody—an offer to your wife that she may, if she please, go and marry some one else, provided you are allowed the same liberty, would be, besides a very imprudent thing, a thing which might go straight to the head, and lead to repentance before the deed. This kind of repentance is regrettable, because it sometimes ends in preventing the crime altogether. Yet one wonders why it has not been preached up more. Again, if you go and make such an offer in words, you may be able to dress it up in flowers and figures of fancy, so that by persuasive art its great wickedness may be concealed, and its general advantages alone remain in sight. Now the general advantages of a clean slate are obvious to all.

Guy knew his wife's address, because it was the old one. He knew that she still lived with Paul Perigal, as she had done in former days. He called at the house the next morning at twelve. Miss Lovelace was not returned from the theatre : he would wait for her. No ; he would not give his card. Miss Lovelace would see him when she came home.

He walked upstairs with the air of a man who knew his way about the house, and went into the drawing-room.

A young lady—rather a pretty girl—rose as he came in.

'Pardon me,' said Guy, astonished ; 'I am waiting to see Miss Lovelace.'

The girl gathered up some work.

'I will tell her,' she said. 'Perhaps she will not be home for half an hour. But Mr. Perigal will be back immediately.'

'I do not want to see Mr. Perigal at all,' said Guy, rudely. 'May I ask, if you please, who you are ? '

'I am the boy's governess and companion'—it was, in fact, Elsie ; 'and at present he is asleep.'

And then she knew, by the change in her visitor's face and the sudden look of resemblance, to whom she was talking.

'I will go,' she said, hastily ; and fairly ran out of the room.

'A governess ! ' He had forgotten the boy. 'Already a governess. Yes ; he must be in his sixth year. By gad ! And Violet has got on.' He looked about him. The room was hung with bright curtains ; there were flowers in the window ; it was papered and painted in the new style ; on the walls were pictures, some of them good ; there were choice cups and all kinds of pretty things in cabinets. 'She *has* got on. In the old days there was a ragged carpet here, and it was the girl's school-room, where she learned to act ; and a table with marks of beer, and pipes on the mantelshelf ; and an old man in a shabby coat.'

'I think—oh ! Mr. Perigal, don't go upstairs. I think '—cried Elsie, below, in great agitation—' it is her husband come back again. A tall man with dark eyes. When I said I was the governess, he scowled. Shall I go upstairs and watch beside the boy ? Shall I call a policeman ? '

'I will beard him,' said the actor, solemnly.

When the door opened and the old man appeared Guy perceived that he was transformed as well—that is, his coat was no longer shabby. Violet's success meant new coats and new boots for her old friend—it would, also, let us add, have meant honourable retirement to her father the carpenter, and her mother the dresser ; but they would have died out of harness—and new furniture for the house, and newness and brightness generally, with a good deal of champagne, which Paul regarded, just as the young man of the present day, as the drink of the gods. The old man also had a beautiful new wig, curly, well combed, and as black as when he was freshly entering upon the thirties. Also his eyebrows were beautifully pencilled, so that if he could have hidden the crow's-feet and shaken a more jaunty leg he might have passed for forty.

'Oh !' said Paul, recognising him. 'You are the man, are you ? You are—the—man.' He spoke with a hissing breath between every word, which is one way, and very effective too, of expressing contempt.

'What the devil——' began Guy.

'You are my Violet's husband ; and a pretty husband too. You desert her a year after you married her ; you send her back without a penny in her pocket for her baby and herself : you leave her for five years ; and when she makes her mark and begins to command her price you come back to stand in with her. That is the kind of man, sir, you are.'

It was remarkable about Paul Perigal that, even when in deepest earnest, he used old catchwords of the stage. Sometimes they were so very old that they had long since lost their force.

'Good Lord !' said Guy, taken completely aback at this unexpected charge. He expected to be accused of cruelty, and of neglect, and desertion ; but it did not occur to him that his visit would be construed into an attempt to live upon his wife's salary. Yet the suggestion gave him a hint, which he was not slow to act upon. They were afraid that he would claim a husband's rights over her money, were they ? Good.

'We are no longer, however,' Paul Perigal went on, 'without defenders. We have friends. It is no more a question of one old man—nobody but myself—standing between the serpent and his victim-che-yild.' He really was quite desperately in earnest ; but he had personated virtuous indignation so often on the stage that in real emotion he naturally fell back upon the language of melodrama. 'We have but to raise our hands, and all London would rise in defence of its favourite, the fair and accomplished Violet— my pupil—your innocent victim—Mr.—Mr.—Marryer-under-false-names !'

'You are an old fool !' said Guy.

What Paul would have said in reply, one knows not. While he was gathering himself together for the effort of retort, Violet herself burst into the room. She heard downstairs that a gentleman was waiting for her, and she divined who her visitor might be.

'How dare you come to this house ?' she asked, with resolution in her eye.

'I see,' said Guy, slowly. He was sitting in her easiest and most comfortable chair, and did not go through the formality of rising for purposes of greeting or courtesy. 'I see that success has not changed your temper.'

'Daddy,' said Violet, quietly, 'leave us alone. No, I am not in the least afraid of the man, I assure you.' She shut the door after him, and then, standing beside the table, looked her husband in the face, not defiantly, but as one who has the command of the situation.

'I want to talk to you quietly, and without heroics. If you please to listen——'

'Go on,' said Violet. 'The very sight of you fires my blood—but go on—go on—let me hear you.'

'What I have to say shall be brief. When we parted it was on the understanding that we should never at any time trouble one another again.'

'It was. Then why do you come here?'

'You told me to go my way, and you would go yours.'

'I did. I have gone my way. It has been a hard and toilsome way: but I have won what I wanted.'

'Very good, I shall not seek to disturb you in the possession of anything that you may have won if you agree to my proposition. I have gone my way, too. But I have not been so fortunate as you. I have lost what I hoped to win.'

'Oh!' She meant to imply that she cared nothing at all whether he won or lost.

'I am now,' he continued, 'a perfectly ruined man. There is nothing left. I have raised money on my reversionary interests till they are mortgaged to the hilt; I have debts which must be paid—somehow—debts of honour. There is one way by which I can pay those debts.'

'What do your debts concern me?'

'They might concern you very seriously. Of course you know that, as your husband, I have the right to draw all your pay.'

Violet turned pale. That was what Paul had told her.

'Draw my pay? But we are separated.'

'That makes no difference unless we are separated under a bond and agreement, which is not the case. However, the question may not arise. I only mentioned it to show that my creditors might, if they pleased——'

'Go on.'

'There is, I said, one way out of the difficulty. It is nothing for you to consent to—in fact, you will be the greatest gainer by it—which is why I expect you to agree—and yet it is everything for me. Tell me, is there the least chance of any present or future reconciliation between us?'

'Never—never—never.' Her resolute lips were set firm. She meant it. The wounds inflicted on her by this man were still fresh in her memory. She would never forget them.

'Quite so. And what I expected—and hoped. Yes; hoped, by Jove,' he said, in the hard and cruel tones which had formerly maddened her.

'We regard each other,' he went on, 'with profound aversion. We do not wish ever to meet again, not even to hear from each other. Is not that the case?'

'It is.'

'Then, Violet,' he said, springing to his feet, 'make the separation complete. We were married in secret. We will be divorced in secret. I give you your liberty. Go ; marry—if you please—and anyone you please. I am sorry to have stood in your light so long. You are bound no longer—we are divorced.'

He spoke rapidly, gesticulating with his hands.

'You agree ?' he asked.

She was carried way by his impetuous words ; she was on the point of accepting the release offered her, when, fortunately, the old distrust of all he did or said came back to her, and she hesitated.

'You make me free,' she said, 'on condition of my making you free in return. Is that so ?'

'Certainly. It is not a gift which I offer you. I have no gifts for you. The time of making gifts is past and gone long ago. This is a bargain.'

'It is a bargain,' she repeated. 'If I accept it——'

'If you accept it,' he interposed, 'you will be free to make any match you please among your numerous admirers. No one will know anything of the past ; nobody need know. I was married as plain Richard Johnson, you in your own name of Emily Hicks. The only witnesses were your own father and the old actor. They can be squared, I suppose. Who would identify Richard Johnson with me ? Who would find Emily Hicks in Violet Lovelace ?'

'I should be free to marry again. But suppose I do not want to marry again ?'

'Hang it ! you will some day.'

'And you—if I accept—will also marry again.'

'Yes ; I shall marry a woman with money.'

'Do you love her ?'

'What has that got to do with the thing ? She has money ; I want money.'

'Yes,' she was trying to put the matter quite clearly before herself. 'And if I do not accept ?'

'Then—many things will happen to you—and to me—and you will discover that the bond of husband and wife may lead to disagreeable surprises. Come, Violet, do not be revengeful, even if I seem at first to have the best of the bargain. In the long run——'

'And when he grows up—when the boy asks me who was his father—what am I to say ?'

'Richard Johnson, Gentleman, Deceased. Poor Dick ! Wipe your eyes. Call him Johnson. Show the boy your marriage lines. Speak tenderly of his father.'

'And the boy's rights ?'

'What rights ?'

'Your heir's rights—what of them ? No ; when the boy is of age he shall know the truth.'

Guy pondered. When the boy came of age. That would be in

sixteen years' time. Sixteen years. The curate who had married them had long since forgotten the obscure couple who stood before him one cold day in November. The witnesses, Paul Perigal and Hicks, the carpenter, would most certainly be dead in sixteen years. Who was to identify him with Richard Johnson? Who could prove that the Richard Johnson, the undoubted husband of Violet, was himself—Guy Ferrier? And as for letters from him, there was not one—he remembered with infinite satisfaction—not one, because he had never written her a single letter.

'I agree,' he said, softly and persuasively, 'to acknowledging the boy as my heir when he is of age. Till then, you can keep him out of the way. Now, Violet, once more consider my proposal. Let me go free; let me marry without creating any scandal; go and marry yourself, if you like. If you do this, you will have the boy to yourself; you can bring him up anyhow you please. When he is of age, but not before, tell him that he is to be the next Lord Ferrier. Bring him to me, and you will be heartily glad that——'

'What kind of things will happen to me?' she asked.

'First of all, there will be an almighty smash. Then, everybody will know that the beautiful Violet Lovelace is the wife of the man who has smashed, and his creditors will include her money in the estate.'

'And the Boy—oh! the Boy,' she cried.

'A man is always allowed to have the custody of his boy at the age of seven. The boy is now, I suppose, about five. I shall most certainly, if you do not accept my terms, take away the boy as soon as he is seven years old. Understand me quite clearly. I am not at all the man to be moved by your crying and tears. The boy shall be mine as soon as he is seven years of age.'

The mother's cheek grew pale.

'There is no act of cruelty or wickedness,' she said, 'that you would not commit. But have my boy you shall not, so long as there is a house in England where I may hide him. What next will happen?'

'The boy will be the heir to a title, and nothing else.'

'He is that, already. For I suppose you will spend all the money there is.'

Violet had never played in any piece where there had been mention of entail. She therefore knew nothing about the laws of real property. People have different opportunities and privileges of acquiring knowledge. An actress learns the secrets of the outside world by the parts she plays.

Guy was about to explain to her that it might be necessary to cut off the entail by consent of the tenant in possession, his father, and himself, but, as he saw that she knew nothing of the subject, he forbore.

'I will acknowledge him. I daresay we shall find a way out of the row about my second marriage, if there is to be any row. Is not this a fair offer? If you do not accept it, you will have to fight for your money and for your boy ; because I will lay my hands on both.'

' I must consider,' said Violet, presently. ' I do not know what traps you may be laying. I must consider. I will send you a reply.'

'Nonsense,' he said, roughly. ' What is the use of considering ? The thing is perfectly plain. Nothing could be simpler. If you were to consider for a twelvemonth, it could not be plainer.'

' No. I will not decide without consideration. I will send you a reply. Now, if you please, go.'

' If you hate me, as I believe you do, Violet ; if you desire never to see or hear from me again, you will accept.'

' I do, from my very soul, desire never to see you again. I am a most unhappy woman because I ever fell in your way. Yet I will not accept your offer without further consideration. Listen ! Do you hear that voice ? '

It was the boy. He had awakened from his morning nap, and Elsie was bringing him, laughing and prattling, downstairs, to have his dinner.

' That is your son's voice. Would you like to see him ? '

' No.' This evidence of the child's existence startled and alarmed him. ' No. I do not wish to see the boy.'

' I am glad I heard him, for he has made me very certain I can accept nothing at your hands without consideration. He reminds me, too—could I have forgotten it ?—that your offer to me is a mockery. How should I marry, having to tell that boy his secret ? How should I commit this dreadful crime that you propose and dare to look upon the boy and to tell him that secret ? How could I bring upon the innocent child shame for his mother. That shame, at least, he shall never feel. I am an actress ; that I cannot help. Why, if I could help it, I would not, because it is my pride and joy. I do not think the boy will ever be ashamed of his mother's profession. If he is to be ashamed, it shall be of his father. So— I refuse your proposal.'

' Violet, you are a fool ; you do not know what you are doing —you do not consider. . . . Remember . . . I do not use idle threats——'

' Do what you like—what you can. I refuse your offer. Offer ? It is no offer ; it is not in your power to give me back my freedom. What a fool I was not to see that from the first ! No one can. Nothing but death can cut that miserable tie. There is my answer. And now, if you please, go ! '

' One moment, Violet. You can, if you please, set up your back and refuse your consent ; but you had better not. Now I modify my offer. You will do as you like. I care nothing at all whether you marry or whether you do not. All I say is, let me do what I please without molestation or fear of interference. Yes ; yes, I know what you are going to say. Who is there who will tell you that the man you married six years ago has married again ?

Don't interfere with me, and then I will not interfere with you. If
you stand between me and my proposed marriage, then—Miss
Violet Lovelace, or Mrs. Ferrier, or whatever you call yourself—
remember that you have a desperate man to deal with.'

'And yet I will not promise anything. No—I will consider,
before all, the rights of the boy. But I will think it over. If it
were not for him, I would let you commit this crime without a
word. Because of my boy, because I am a mother, I think not
only of him but of the other poor creature whom you are going to
delude and lead into misery. Oh! Guy, if you could see yourself
as those who know you see you! If you could see the miserable,
contemptible figure you cut, when, no doubt, you think you are a
gallant gentleman! Go—you are but a sneak and a coward.'

He made no reply; but he went away. As he opened the
street-door he heard the voice of the boy again shouting and laughing. But this did not soften his heart.

He walked westward, among the squares of Bloomsbury, thinking what he would do. He might break his engagement with
Virginie and let the smash come, and await the consequences. He
might go on with it, and let Violet do what she pleased. That was
the best thing to do. Probably she would do nothing. She would
be too much afraid of his wrath to do anything. He could take
the boy; he could spend her money; he could make himself in-
fernally disagreeable. Yes; he would go on. She would submit.
And as soon as these two witnesses to his marriage were dead he
would snap his fingers at Violet and bid her do her worst.

CHAPTER VII.

LOVE'S YOUNG DREAM.

WHEN the engagement was fairly and happily accomplished,
Maude sat down and breathed more freely. If her brother was
in debt and difficulties, her father knew nothing, and, for the
present, need know nothing, Perhaps a turn might be taken for
the better. Perhaps Guy might be influenced by a wife.

'I shall expect you,' she told him, 'to pay Virginie the attention she deserves. You must pretend to be in love with her, if
you are not. Meantime leave her to me. I have already led her
to believe you are a second King Arthur—Heaven forgive me! I
must manage, somehow, so that the drop from imagination to
reality may prove less than . . . than you have given me reason
to expect.'

'Do you think,' he replied, sulkily, 'that I shall cuff and kick
her? Come, Maude, don't be gloomy. You egged me on. I
didn't want to marry the girl. You ought to be happy about it.'

' So I should bo, Guy, if I could think that any happiness will come to any of us out of it. And it is my doing, whatever comes. Well,' she sighed, ' do not get into any fresh difficulties until your wedding-day. And—oh! Guy; can you—can you keep away from the tables for a little while—only till the autumn ? '

He laughed, but not cheerfully. Because he meant that he was not going even to try to keep away from the tables. It was not in order to abstain from the one thing he loved that he was going to run this frightful risk of marriage. Not at all. Quite the contrary. But, then, women are never reasonable.

When one reads how the most worshipful the Lord Mayor, and with him a following of amiable people, lift up their voices against the wickedness of the French in allowing Monaco to continue, one is reminded of a certain text about a mote and a beam, inasmuch as for every franc which is daily lost and won in that wicked peninsula ten thousand are daily lost and won in the hells of this most virtuous city of West London. Yet my Lord Mayor maketh no sign. If, indeed, hypocrisy be chiefly known in the condemnation of sins to which we are secretly addicted, or to which we feel no attraction, then, indeed, we are a nation of the most gigantic hypocrites—Patagonian hypocrites. We hold indignation meetings about the opium trade—and our people are being ruined, body and brain, by bad drinks worse than any opium ; we hold up our hands at the buying and selling of slaves ; yet we allow women to work twelve hours a day for four shillings a week ; and by this underpayment of women's labour, our long hours of shops, and in a hundred other ways, we keep our white slaves, and grow rich upon their labour. All these things make one long for a Prophet, because, if I understand the Prophetic character aright, his most important function—a very uncomfortable one—was to make people see clearly their own wickedness, and the evil things lying under their very noses. No doubt Ahab, before Elijah came, was often indignant when he thought of the abominable wickedness of his Syrian neighbour, Benhadad.

As my Lord Mayor and his friends have not yet spoken on the subject, there exist, for the convenience of young men like Captain Ferrier, half a dozen clubs, where the noble game of baccarat, not to speak of écarté, picquet, napoleon, pitch and toss, loo, lansquenet, and many other ingenious devices for the exchange of money—the humbling of the mighty for good, and the exalting of the poor for a season—may be enjoyed. They are chiefly maintained by and for the gilded youth and the youth who are believed to be gilded. These young men of the modern time take their fling in a manner not unworthy of their ancestors, save that for punch they substitute champagne ; and for beer, champagne ; and for port, champagne ; and that they do not laugh much, and are generally rather low in their spirits, and therefore need the stimulus of champagne at breakfast and at luncheon, and at dinner, and at the chiming of the midnight bells, and at early matins.

Y

They 'fling' in many directions; but for the present one has only to do with their favourite pastime of the midnight baccarat.

Guy's engagement at first brought him luck. Everybody knows how luck follows luck, just as misfortunes crowd thick upon each other. His tradesmen, whose name was legion, suddenly changed their front, and showed an amount of confidence which was exhilarating, and made him feel like buying everything; the men who held his promissory notes ceased to look anxious; the gentleman who had advanced him money on his reversionary interests began to consider prayerfully the subject of the marriage settlements; and, in addition, he had a steady flow of luck nearly every night. So that he really began to consider the girl who was the cause of all this as a most praiseworthy person, deserving of admiration.

He had to be seen with her a good deal in those early days, though, happily, his father took his place, and was never bored with Virginie's society, as he was himself; and was not wishing constantly to be back again tempting Fortune, as he did. It is not every engaged man who has a father willing to take so much arduous work off one's hands. Then Maude was useful, and between the two, Guy really found that a daily call, or perhaps a dinner at Mrs. Hallowes's house, was quite as much as need be expected of a man.

Love-making, under these conditions, fell very, very far short of what poor Virginie expected. There was nothing in it, after all. She was engaged; her lover came most days to see her, and stayed a quarter of an hour, and seemed anxious to get away again: if nobody was in the room he sometimes kissed her forehead coldly; he communicated nothing about himself, his pursuits, his reading, his ambition; nor was he in the least curious about her own—a humiliating thing for a girl not to be thought worth a little curiosity.

It must be her task, Virginie thought, to make him believe her capable of his confidence. That would, doubtless, come in time. Meanwhile, a little expression of feeling, a little ardour, a little warmth of manner seemed wanting even to this inexperienced girl. In what a different voice had Tom—her 'brother' Tom—as Mrs. Hallowes called him—told her that he loved her! Even the Professor, who owned that he must come after Tom, spoke of his affection for her with warmer voice and greater show of passion. But men are, doubtless, different: this man of reserve kept his deeper feelings in his own heart. Virginie would get at them in time.

'My dear,' said Maude, smiling, though she looked anxious, when the girl confided these thoughts to her, 'do not make an idol or a god of your husband. You know, in a sister's eyes, it is difficult for a brother to do wrong. But a wife is not a sister. You, who will be with him constantly'—Virginie's heart sank at the prospect, though she knew not why—'will find faults in him of which I know nothing. You will have to excuse them.'

'Guy,' she said, passionately, 'have you no heart ?'

'What is the matter now, Maude ?'

'If is your neglect of that poor girl. What do you look for ? A more beautiful woman ? There are no more beautiful women.'

'What am I to do, then ?'

'Pretend that you are in love with her. I have no patience ! Oh ! But for one thing—but for my father's sake—I would break it off even now.'

'Don't do that, Maude. Come, I will go and buy her something. It can't be paid for till after the wedding ; so it does not signify.'

'Oh ! Guy'—his absolute inability to see what was wanted made her laugh—' one hopes you may make a better husband than lover.'

For some reason, he scowled and became moody ; and that something was not bought. He remembered, in fact, that he was already a husband, and not successful in that profession ; also that he had as yet received no letter of submission from Violet—a thing which he confidently looked for. This made him feel ill-used.

Then Maude took Virginie with her to see The Towers, their country house. It was a splendid old place, worth seeing, if only for its age, for the memories of the many generations who had lived there, and for the accumulations of treasures forming part of the family history ; a picturesque old place, many-gabled, built of warm red brick, standing among its gardens and trees ; a stately and proud old place, fit home for an old English family.

'This,' she said, taking her visitor to the rooms, 'will all, some day, be yours, as it was your great-grandmother's. I hope you like this prospect, fair Châtelaine.'

'Oh !' Virginie gasped, 'Maude, it is wonderful !'

It is, indeed, truly wonderful to go over an old house belonging to an old family who have kept themselves and their things together. The family portraits, the books, the arms and armour, the furniture, the plate, the china, the very staircases and landings, the windows, the gables, the roof of the house, are all things that cannot be bought.

'I have never felt before,' Virginie whispered, 'what it meant to possess ancestors. Here one feels what it may mean. All these things speak to us ; they belong to us, but we belong to them. In this old place one seems to hear, day and night, the voices of the dead. They are calling to us to keep up the honour of the House.'

'Yes,' said Maude, 'I feel the same thing every time I come here. It is the place of our ancestors. We are among them all. It cannot be but that their spirits haunt the place which we all of us have loved so well. From generation to generation, from father to son, we have been English gentlefolk ; not great statesmen or great generals ; but we have taken our share and done our work. Not one but has kept the scutcheon spotless ; not one who has disgraced '——. Here she stopped, and her eyes filled with

tears, because she thought of one who had already gone so far as
to bring sorrow and shame upon them, for whose sake she had
done her best to bring sorrow and shame upon the girl with her.

Virginie took her hand, thinking that Maude's tears were due
to her respect and love for her ancestors.

'It is a great thing, Maude,' she said, ' to belong to this House ;
it is a very solemn thing to marry the heir. Forgive me if I seem
to think too little of it.'

'No, dear ; I was not thinking of that. See ! here is a portrait of Guy as a child. Its companion picture is of a former Guy,
Lord Ferrier, taken at the same age, in the time of Charles the
First. Do you see the wonderful likeness in the boys ? Yet there
are two hundred years between them, and one is dust and ashes.
There is another of the same Lord Ferrier, taken later on, after
the Restoration.'

That whole day they spent among the portraits and the family
pictures. Maude knew all their histories, and Virginie, for the
first time, learned the Romance of a great House whose history has
been preserved. It makes one weep to think how our middle-class
people neglect their genealogies, so that they know nothing of their
own people, and have no pride, and learn no lessons from the past.
Cannot something be done, my friends? Can we not write the
annals of our own generation, each for his own family, so that
whatever the fate of our children and grandchildren, they, too,
may feel that they have ancestors who lived, and loved, and hoped,
and made a little success, perhaps, and died and were forgotten,
as they, too, in their turn, shall die?

'Oh !' cried the Creole girl, 'my father told me so little of all
these things.'

'He did not know,' said Maude. 'No one knows except myself.
My father knows something ; Guy, nothing. The women of the
House keep up its memories, not the men. That matters nothing,
if they are true to their name and its ambitions.'

Then they hunted among the old books in the library, and examined the tapestry, the collections, the engravings, and the heaps
of things belonging to their ancestors still preserved in this strange
and wonderful museum. Virginie returned to town strengthened
as to her engagement. Her lover might be cold, but he was the
heir ; it was a great thing to marry the future Master of the Towers.

Guy showed no interest in her visit, and seemed to care little
for the old place of which his father and sister were so proud.
'Could,' asked Virginie, 'could he be one of those who are deaf to
the voice of the dead ?'

Alas ! He was deaf to every voice ; he heard nothing, he saw
nothing ; if all his ancestors had appeared to him—ghostly phan-
toms pointing long fingers of warning, showing him the future that
lay before him—he would have closed his eyes and gone on his
way heedless. Other men, given to vices more repulsive, can listen
to the voice of conscience or the calls of honour and duty. Drun-

kards get hot coppers and see triangles and rats and dogs, and
repent and bang their heads with their fists and call themselves
hard names. Wrathful men, who break the third commandment
and the furniture, are ashamed when the fit is over. Envious men,
backbiters, downcriers, have moments of sorrow when they feel
mean. Even house agents sometimes regret that they must always
play the game so low. The gambler alone never thinks, or heeds.
or feels any emotion for his fellow-creatures. He is concentrated
in himself; he is self-contained; he feels no interest, has no
anxiety, takes no part or share in anything save only the chances
of the cards. The voices of the dead! If the voices of the living
can do nothing for such men what can we expect of the dead?·

CHAPTER VIII.

HER SIMPLE DUTY.

THREE days—four days—a fortnight passed· over during which
Violet sent no message of submission at all, and her husband felt
more ill-used and more indignant.

She was thinking : the longer she thought over the matter the
more difficult it was to act. She had, to be sure, refused his proposal with contempt; but she exaggerated her own helplessness;
she was ignorant and did not know what safeguards may be gained
by claiming protection of the law. She was in the false position
of a wife not owned by her husband's friends. She did not think
of putting herself in a lawyer's hands, still less did she contemplate
the possibility of taking the child to his grandfather, and asking his
protection, for she was firmly convinced that in any contest with
her husband, all his relations would combine to bring the weight of
their united influence against her. The wicked nobleman theory
is not yet quite exploded. Indeed, there are plenty of agitators
who still try to lash their auditors into a rage by depicting the
vices of the bloated Lords.

She was afraid. She might let her husband do what he proposed to do—that is, marry again, just as if she did not exist; or
she might forbid the marriage. In the former case she would be
rewarded by an open acknowledgment of her son's true position
after sixteen years; but how was she to prove after sixteen years
that 'Richard Johnson' was Guy Ferrier? And if she could not
prove that, her boy's rights would have been wilfully and wastefully
thrown away. In the latter case, if she refused her consent, who
would protect her and the boy from her husband's interference?

After a fortnight of anxious consideration she took Paul Perigal
into her counsels and told him for the first time the whole story,
and her husband's true name and the latest proposition he had made.

'You wait,' he said, 'for sixteen years. So much interval between the acts. The boy has grown a man. You take him—yourself closely veiled—to the lordly castle of his ancestors ; you say to him, "Boy, this is yours ! " If his father is living, you bring his son to him. He will be laid up with gout—they always are at five-and-forty. You will say, "My Lord, I restore to you—your son and heir. I am your wife ! " Then " who," cries her Ladyship, clutching her hair with wild gesture and despairing eyes, " who am I ? " It seems a strong part to play, Violet.'

'And who's to prove it, Daddy ? '

'I can prove it, Violet. You forget that you have me—always.'

You can't *tell* an old man of eighty that in all human probability he will be dead in sixteen years.

'If we were to try any other plan, Daddy ? '

He reflected.

'There used to be a situation in . . . what was the name of it ? They played it at the Adelphi . . . The Bridal Party interrupted . . . the appearance of the real wife—" I forbid the ceremony " —Shrieks of the Bride—Impotent Rage of the Villain.'

Violet shook her head.

'I've always got to remind you, Daddy, that we play now for the half-guinea stalls, not for the pit and gallery.'

There was no use in consulting the old man. His views were too narrowly professional. Violet returned to her silent musings, and found no help there.

'What is the matter, Violet ? ' asked Elsie, who had observed with concern the most unusual phenomenon of a failure in her employer's usually robust appetite.

'Elsie, I am truly miserable.'

'I have seen it,' said Elsie, ' for a week and more. Can I help you ? '

'No, child, you cannot ; unless you find me a man to advise with. I want an honest man and a wise man.'

'I think I know the very man ; that is, if you would consult with a friend of mine. He is a gentleman—a University scholar ; and he is going to be a great writer. He lives with us.' Here she remembered her dreadful deception, and she blushed a rosy red and went on, speaking fast :—' And oh ! Violet, I must confess to you. When you said you wanted a real lady I ought not to have come, because my father was only a small clerk and my mother lets lodgings, and if it had not been for Mr. Percival I should never have been educated at all. Now, please, send me away, because I have deceived you.'

'My dear child,' said Violet, ' what a fuss about nothing at all ! Send you away ! Why, what would the boy do without you ? And did you suppose I thought your father was a Viscount ? Goodness me ! he was a Crutch and Toothpick swell compared with mine, who is nothing in the world but a carpenter at Drury Lane—poor old dear ! And what was your father, Daddy ? ' For Paul was standing beside them.

'Hum!' he replied. 'My father—now with the angels . . . was . . . in fact—he was . . . but

'When Fortune means to men most good,
She looks upon them with a threatening eye.'

'You see, Elsie,' said Violet. 'So, there, nothing more need be said. And about this Mr. Percival, I can't ask a stranger here and begin—Once there was a girl. Would he call upon me if you ask him? Most men would like the chance,' she added, with a laugh.

'He admires you very greatly,' said Elsie. 'We often go together to the pit to see you. He isn't rich, you know.'

'Together? Why—Elsie—you, of all people in the world!'

'Oh! no . . . no . . . no,' she cried, blushing. 'It isn't that—of all things. Oh! pray don't think it is that. Why, Mr. Percival has known me for years. He used to lodge with us long ago. And he must be getting on for thirty years of age now.'

'What a great age. But yet . . . Well, Elsie, about this friend of yours. It seems a foolish thing to have no one to ask for advice —to have to ask a stranger. But yet . . . You are sure he is a wise man.'

'Oh! he is very wise.'

'And would he come?'

'He would if I were to ask him, I think.'

'I don't see what I can do. I must ask somebody. Well, Elsie, ask him, please. If he will be so good as to interest himself in a stranger's affairs I will see him if he will come to me. Tell him that I am in trouble, and want the advice of a sensible man with discretion. To think that of all the men I know there is not one to whom I can go and ask for a little real advice. Never be an actress, child; because it is all show and make-believe, and people get to think you have no thoughts, no feelings, no hopes, and no anxieties of your own. You must always look and talk as if there was nothing but laughing in the world.'

Elsie opened upon the subject that very evening, but with little effect; because Mr. Percival was agitated about quite another matter, and could think and talk of nothing else. Yet he promised to see Miss Violet Lovelace. The business Elsie said was connected with her husband, who had come back, and, she supposed, wanted money.

'It will end,' he said, 'in her going to a solicitor, and getting a deed of separation in order to protect her and her child. Well; I will go with you, Elsie, but I do not suppose I can do much. I am not a lawyer nor a solicitor, nor do I know how to apply the screw to gentlemen who wish to live upon the labours of their wives. Three dozen at a cart-tail one might recommend, but the absurd law of the land does not allow it.'

What had happened that day was this—

Percival received a confidential letter from Palmiste—from the Pink Boy, in fact. As the accountant of the bank, where the strictest confidence should be observed, he ought not to have written the letter. But he was young, and anxiety for his friends may be pleaded as an excuse.

'It is all over, I fear,' he wrote, 'with Mon Désir. The poor old Captain has got a most awful bad crop; the estate won't pay working expenses this year, and I know that we can't advance any more money upon it. What he will do I cannot tell, but he will most certainly, unless he can raise any more money, have to become bankrupt. Then the estate will be sold. It seems hard after all these years. Can you go and tell Miss Ferrier? Her mother and Madame Kemyss do not know, I should think, anything about it. And even the Squire himself knows very little. She might be able to raise some money. She will be of age in a year or two; meanwhile the money is wanted at once. It is hard that her thousands should be lying idle, so to speak, without being useful to the man who has been so good a trustee for her. Go and see her at once, and tell her eight thousand or so would pull the old man through this year, and next year one may hope for a better crop. It is very unlucky that the little touch of a cyclone which passed over us in March seems to have picked out Mon Désir, above all others, for damage. Tom looks rather haggard over something, but even he doesn't know the whole danger. Perhaps he is haggard about Virginie. I'm a good deal worn myself—you wouldn't know me again—and the Padre isn't the same man since she went away. I suppose I mustn't send my love, and perhaps if I did you would not be the man to take it. Don't be mean, and try to cut out Tom. But we hear that she is always with her great cousins. If she *should* go and marry that beast of a man——'

Thus far the Pink Boy.

Percival lost no time at all in taking the letter to Virginie. He went that very morning.

'Why,' she asked, 'do you never come to see me?'

'Because it isn't safe. In this country we know our level; I belong to Grub Street; you to Mayfair. Because you are a young lady of fashion, and I am only an obscure person whose fortune for the moment is out at elbows.'

'But we are old friends,' said Virginie. 'You ought to have come here long ago. Sit down and let us talk.'

Then Percival unfolded his tale.

'Oh!' cried Virginie. 'It is dreadful. Something must be done. What can be done? Can't he use my money?'

'You can ask some lawyer here to lend you money, which you must pay to the bank to his account. I can think of no other way. And I am so ignorant of money matters that I do not even know how to advise you; but then any lawyer will know.'

'I will ask Guy,' said Virginie.

'Your cousin, Captain Ferrier? Yes; he would know.'

'I did not tell you, Mr. Percival,' she said, blushing, 'I am engaged to be married to my cousin.'

'Poor Tom !' The intelligence fell upon him so suddenly that he was fain to put his thoughts into words.

She bent her head, and did not reply for a moment. Then she said softly,

'Tom was always my brother.'

Percival rose.

'You will, then,' he said coldly, 'consult Captain Ferrier how best to save this good man—your guardian—and your father's friend—from ruin. I knew that I had only to lay the matter before you. Thank you for your attention.'

He touched her fingers, and left her.

Why had her old friend the Professor treated her in such a manner? What had she done? Alas! she understood, too well. Poor Tom!

As Percival left the house, he met the accepted lover, and saluted him, but without the usual smile of recognition. Guy was in a vile temper that morning; he wanted an answer from Violet, and he was afraid to call upon her again; he was afraid that she might find out his engagement, which was already in the papers; he would have kept away from his *fiancée* altogether but for Maude, who made him go.

His temper got the better of him when he saw a man—one of the many men—whom he hated, actually leaving the house.

'You, sir,' he cried. 'You—what is your name?'

'My name is Percival, as you know very well, Captain Ferrier.'

'What are you doing in this house?'

'You had better,' said the other, 'ask Miss Ferrier.'

'I forbid you the house,' said Guy. 'I will not allow you to call upon Miss Ferrier.'

'Have you anything more to say?' For Virginie's sake Percival kept his temper down. Yet it was hard not to 'go' for that ill-conditioned brute. Poor Virginie!

'No, sir. I have nothing more to say. You have my commands.'

'Then, Captain Ferrier, as I am not in your Company, let me tell you that I do not take commands from you. Good morning.'

Guy found his cousin in tears. He took no notice of her agitation, being still in a towering rage.

'Virginie,' he said, 'that man is never to come to the house again. You must never speak to him if you meet him; you are not to know him. Do you hear?'

'What man?'

'The man who has just been here. Percival is his confounded name.'

'My old friend? Why not?'

'Because I wish it.'

'I have just heard very bad news,' she said, passing over this thing, though she wondered greatly. Then she told her news.

'Going to be bankrupt, is he?' asked Guy. 'That seems a pity. But it isn't your fault.'

'He shall not be bankrupt,' said Virginie firmly, 'if I can help it. Bankrupt! when I have all those thousands, doing no one good. Why, if it cost me all my fortune, he should not be bankrupt.'

He laughed in contempt.

'Give up your whole fortune? Oh! come, Virginie, don't be ridiculous. Your money is not to be made ducks and drakes of in that fashion. These people must help themselves out of the mess.'

'But I *must* save my dear old guardian, Guy, I must. Do you not understand? He was my father's closest friend; his wife is my mother's cousin; he has been everything to me. Cannot you see that I *must* go to their help?'

'No, I can't. Your fortune belongs to yourself—and to your husband.'

'I have no husband—yet.' She looked dangerous; but Guy's temper made him careless of what he said. Of course he meant that her fortune was already promised to himself.

'I shall not allow you to fool your money away,' he went on, in his blundering, stupid, selfish way.

Her colour mounted to her cheek. Was this a way for a girl to be addressed by a lover?

'I do not understand you, this morning, Guy. First you forbid me to keep up the acquaintance of a gentleman for whom I have the greatest regard; next, you refuse to recognise my dearest obligations. As for asking your permission——but you had better leave me.'

It was his cursed temper, he said to Maude, afterwards. What business had the girl to talk of giving away her fortune—his money?

He obeyed; but, still being wrathful, he fired a parting shot.

'I am sorry,' he said, 'that you object to common sense. Perhaps, to-morrow, Virginie, you will have recovered your reason.'

He came away, leaving her bewildered. Was this her gallant and chivalrous lover? Was it possible for a man of such exalted principle and noble feeling to disapprove of the help she wanted to give her oldest and truest friends? Could she have been deceived?

It was the first part of this business which Mr. Percival was still turning over in his mind.

Poor Tom! Poor Virginie!

That was the burden of his song. The coming failure was nothing compared with this loss and throwing away and waste of love. Even the break up of Mon Désir estate was but a small thing compared with the marriage of this sweet and precious girl with a man so churlish, so morose, and so selfish.

'Elsie,' he said 'prate to me no more of Violet Lovelace. I have had to do with worse troubles than hers.'

'Not troubles of your own?' The girl was quick to think for him

'No, not my own. I told you that the spell was removed from the Enchanted Island when Virginie came away.'

'Yes.'

'The palace of jasper and malachite and white marble became a simple bungalow, with elephant creeper and honeysuckle climbing round it, and a compound planted with roses and mignonette and pretty things about it. Now the bungalow itself is to be destroyed and its occupants turned out.'

'Oh !'

'One of them is an old man. And it will probably kill him. One is a young man, and his chances are ruined.'

'Oh ! your poor friends.'

'And Virginie ——' He paused.

'Virginie ?'

'A dreadful dragon has got hold of Virginie. He will first devour and destroy all that she possesses, and after that he will rend her to pieces. Poor Tom !'

'Oh ! is it true ?'

'It wouldn't help me much, now, if I had dropped Tom over the ravine. Yet I wish I had, because it would have saved him this dreadful blow. Going suddenly over the ravine would have hurt less and killed him sooner. I believe it is quite a pleasant way to get rid of life, if it is done unexpectedly. But in these cases, Elsie, everything depends upon the skill of the operator. A clumsy practitioner, now, might make the operation really a painful one. Poor Tom ! I really wish I had.'

CHAPTER IX.

SHALL I TELL HER ?

'It is very good of you to come, Mr. Percival,' said Violet, when he presented himself. 'Elsie told you what I want.'

'She said you want a wise man, Miss Lovelace ; which made it the more remarkable for you to consult me.'

'Elsie says you are wise ; and perhaps, though you may not be wise in your own affairs'—she said this without meaning any reflection on the undoubted shabbiness of the hat—'you may be in other people's. If you will listen to me—if you have the time.'

'At present, Miss Lovelace, I have all the time there is, or nearly all. I will listen like one end of a telephone, if I can be of any use to so charming an actress.'

'Elsie said you were a good fellow,' said Violet. 'Let us be friends, Mr. Percival. You must call me Violet ; it isn't my real name, so it doesn't matter. Besides, lots of men call me Violet who never want to help me at all.'

'Very well, Violet ·you do me very great honour—and if I can be of the least service——'

'Think it is for Elsie's sake,' she interposed, anxious to check the first shadow of a flirtation. 'And then give your attention to an unfortunate married person, whose husband ought to be put in the pillory, and kept there till there wasn't a rotten egg or a bad potato left.'

'For Elsie's sake, then,' he replied, laughing.

Then the actress told her story, anonymously.

'May I call your husband names?' asked Percival.

'If you please.'

'He wants you to stand by and see yourself and your child insulted, while he ignores your existence and marries again; he wants you to be the accomplice in a crime in which you lose all and he gains everything; he wants you to accept his bare promise to acknowledge the boy as soon as he is of age—when the *witnesses who could prove his identity with your husband will perhaps be dead;* and he threatens to follow, rob, and annoy you, to take the boy—to —— Good God! I cannot call him names. There are no names in the English language which I can find strong enough. But I know a little Hindustani, and I will swear at him for a few moments in that tongue.' He did so, which relieved his mind. 'But your course is quite clear. Put yourself into the hands of a lawyer, and have a separation properly drawn up. Is the man—I do not ask out of any impertinent curiosity—but is he a gentleman?'

'Certainly he is.'

'I don't mean—does he wear black cloth instead of corduroy. But is he a man of any position?'

'He is the heir to a Peerage.'

'In that case you are quite safe. There may be one or two bad hats among eldest sons; but there is not one, I am sure—there cannot be one—who would dare to take his wife's salary and deprive her of her son.'

'Not if he were ruined?'

'Not then; because, you see, the heir to a Peerage must—he must—pay some regard to honour. He may drink and gamble: he may do all kinds of bad things; but such a thing as your husband threatens you with he dares not do. No; if he were ten times ruined he could not do it.'

Violet breathed.

'This is a *very* bad man,' she said. 'I think he is the most selfish of all men that ever lived: and the basest. Boys take after their mothers, they say: else I should have no joy in my son for fear he should take after his father.'

'Get your deed of separation drawn up. You have, doubtless, valid reasons for desiring the separation; he would not wish for publicity:—you may rest in perfect safety.'

'But if I refuse my consent, all his family would back him up.'

'Oh! no. What are you thinking of? Do you believe it possible that the family of any English gentleman would back up their son in such abominable wickedness as this?'

Violet had been thinking of the Wicked Duke and the Virtuous Milliner of song and story and melodrama; and now began to suspect that perhaps these picturesque characters might be theatrical, and belong to a melodrama.

'I will tell you all, Mr. Percival, because I am at my wit's end and would do anything—even be an accomplice in bigamy—rather than let my boy's rights be lost. His father is the only son of a Lord; he is about eight-and-twenty; he is completely ruined by gaming; he has mortgaged his reverses—no, his reversions——'

'His reversionary interests——'

'For as much as they will bring; and he is in despair. And he has got hold of a girl with money. If he marries her all will be well, he says. If not, all will be ill. The girl's name I do not know. His name is the Honourable Guy Talbot Ferrier. And I am his —— Gracious, Mr. Percival, what is the matter?'

He sprang from his chair and began dancing round the room, because the wrath which seized him at that moment was too much to be endured.

'The villain! . . . the double-dyed villain! . . . the scoundrel! I knew he was capable of anything from the very first . . . he looks it . . . there is rogue and traitor and liar and common cheat stamped upon his face. Oh! . . . oh! . . . oh!'

Violet looked at him in amazement which partook of amusement. Because she had never before had an opportunity of seeing genuine, unrestrained wrath freely manifested. It is, if you think of it, one of the rarest of things. Afterwards she 'rendered' this portion of the scene to Paul very faithfully, and they made a note of it for future use.

'Do you know him, then, Mr. Percival?'

He stopped in his wild career, in which he had broken two chair legs.

'Yes, I do know him,' he replied fiercely. 'What is more—I know the girl whom he wants to marry. But we shall stop that. Thank Heaven, we shall stop that!'

'Stop it by all means,' said Violet; 'but don't forget my boy's interests.'

'We will not. She is the sweetest girl, the kindest-hearted, prettiest, most noble, most perfect, most lovely of women.'

'But I thought you were in love with Elsie, Mr. Percival. That was why I asked you to help me; and now it seems as if you were in love with . . . no . . . no . . . she can't be my rival, because' . . . Here she stopped abruptly.

'Elsie! Elsie! oh! yes—Elsie. I am in love, first of all, with Virginie. Elsie is a good little thing; but—Virginie!'

'Good little things may have hearts of their own, Mr. Percival. Remember that.'

' As Beatrice was to Dante, as Laura was to Petrarch, so is Virginie to those who love her.' He was so deeply moved with indignation that he said these words in perfect earnestness and solemnity.

' What's the use of loving a woman if you can't marry her ?' asked Violet.

Percival made no reply. The explanation and apology of a man's loves to a perfect stranger was a descent from melodrama to farce. There should always be a funny man in every piece, but Percival had no wish to play the part.

' How shall we act ?' he asked. ' We must think of her as well as of yourself.'

' If you will tell me the girl's name, and where she lives, I will write, or go to see her, and tell her the truth at once. Do you think she is fond of him ?'

' I do not know. Yes ; the sooner the better—not a day should be lost. I cannot think he would dare to marry her without some promise of silence from you. I wondered when I saw him first, last New-Year's Day, what the man had done to make him so morose and black of visage.'

' He had married me,' said Violet, ' and he couldn't get rid of me.'

' That ought not to make a man morose,' replied Percival, gallantly.

Violet laughed.

' If I had married you I think I should have gone dancing and singing,' he said ; yet, with a little hesitation and half a blush, because, perhaps, she would not like this turn of the conversation. But she did.

' I don't mind compliments a bit,' she said. ' Lord ! Everybody pays me compliments. I get them, with bouquets, sent to the stage door ; and letters ; and in poetry and in prose ; and from all sorts of men—prince to potboy. Men are all alike ; they fall in love with a woman made up for the stage with vaseline and rouge and powder ; and they think she is a goddess ; and they think they may " hope," as they call it. But don't get serious, or I must tell Elsie. So you think you would not have been so morose if you had been my husband. I don't think you would, and I wish to Heaven that you were my husband, or any other honest man, instead of the poor creature I have got. Well, . . .' she sighed heavily, ' let us have patience, and spoil his little plot.'

' You may do one of two things—you may tell his father or you may tell Virginie. One of these two things you must do. If you choose the first you can never again be threatened in this way. If the second, she will learn the truth in the most direct way.'

' I cannot tell Lord Ferrier,' said Violet. ' I promised him—my husband—that I would not obtrude myself upon any of his family. Nothing but the interests of the boy would make me break that promise. Let me go to Miss——. What is her name ?'

'Miss Ferrier—she is his second cousin. Perhaps that would be best. But go at once—to-day.'

He sat down and wrote a letter.

'Dear Virginie,—

'I have made a discovery of the highest importance to you. The lady who bears this note will tell you what it is. You may *entirely depend* upon the truth of what she says. I grieve to be the sender—not the cause—of such a tale as she has to tell you.

'Yours always and sincerely,

'PHILIP PERCIVAL.'

'There !' he said. 'The letter is plain and straightforward. You will tell her kindly, will you not ?'

'I will tell her as kindly as I can,' said Violet. 'There cannot be much kindness in telling a girl that the man she—loves—perhaps—I loved him once, or thought I did—is such as my husband.'

'But you will not—oh ! no—I am sure you feel for her. It is not her fault——'

'I will be very kind and gentle,' said Violet, softening. Then she laughed, and said, 'Shall I rehearse the scene to you ? I can be the injured wife—see '—her face became pale, her eyes fixed, her arms dropped to her side, her form rigid—she was a woman in the first despair of a deadly blow. 'Or the raging woman whose lover has been snatched from her. So.' She threw herself back, and became a figure full of life, passion, and wrath, her left arm raised high above her head, her right hand quivering at her bosom. She was Medea. 'Or I will take it crying. See.' She sank upon her knees with a low wail, forced from her by her misery, and buried her despairing head in her hands. 'Or shall I triumph over her sorrow ?'

'You are a wonderful actress. You can represent any passion, and any person. Represent for me, now, the real Violet Lovelace, the woman who has a heart——'

'No.' She took the letter and read it. 'That part is reserved for Miss Ferrier—if there is a woman with a heart at all. But I don't know—sometimes nothing is real but the boy—and Daddy. And the best part of him, poor old man ! is his wig. You can trust me, Mr. Percival. I will be as kind as I can. You know that I have never been taught the gentle ways and soft words that ladies learn—I mean some ladies—not all. Because I have seen them fighting to get out after the performance, and struggling for good places at a sale and a picture show ; and really I think that we behave much better on the stage.'

CHAPTER X.

WIFE AND FIANCÉE.

VIRGINIE had been engaged exactly a fortnight. It is not a long time, but an ardent lover may do a great deal in fourteen days to make himself known to his sweetheart, and to learn her thoughts and her way of looking upon things. The one thing which Guy did to reveal himself was to forbid her to receive the visits of one old friend, and to fly into a rage when she spoke of saving another old friend from ruin. What did this mean? She was astonished and perplexed. Perhaps when Guy came again he would explain how she had misled him. Certainly he would not, he could not, object to her trying to help her guardian. She met Maude in the evening, but said nothing about her trouble. No doubt Guy would come in the morning and explain, and all would be well.

He did not come; he had, in fact, though he knew it not, seen Virginie for the last time; he stayed in his own rooms, morose and savage. Why did Violet make no sign? What did she mean? And if the other girl was going to give away her money—*his* money—it might just as well be broken off at once. Better, in fact, let the smash come.

Virginie waited for him all the morning. As he did not come, she thought of writing to him. Hitherto, no letters had passed between them; none of the little notes meaning nothing, except always, 'Je t'aime—je t'aime,' which are so common among some lovers. Not one note, not one word of endearment—truly a frigid lover and a disappointing engagement. On the other hand, plenty of notes from Lord Ferrier, who was much more in love with her than his son, and was, in fact, the only one of the four concerned who was entirely happy over the engagement. She could not write. He must either come and make rough things smooth, in person, or he must write; she could not.

Early in the afternoon she received a letter, and was informed that the lady who brought it was waiting to see Miss Ferrier. It was Percival's letter. What misfortune could it be? She thought of her guardian, and assumed that it was connected with him. Had the blow really fallen, and so suddenly? But no mail could have come in since yesterday, when her own letters reached her, and spoke about nothing unusual.

It was a young lady, apparently about five-and-twenty, dressed in some plain dark costume. She wore rather a thick veil, for the time of year.

'Oh!' cried Virginie, 'you have come from Mr. Percival to tell me something. What has happened? Is it my guardian?'

'No, Miss Ferrier; it is not your guardian.'

'Will you, please, tell me what it is?'

Violet looked at her for a few moments in silence. She was certainly a very pretty girl, and not the least in her own style.

'Yes,' she said; 'I will tell you. But it is rather a long story.'

'Tell me first whom it concerns.'

'It concerns—yourself.'

'Some misfortune has happened to myself! What can that be?'

'I did not say misfortune. What I am going to tell you will avert the worst misfortune which could happen to any woman.'

'You are mysterious. May I ask your name?'

'I am called, on the stage, Violet Lovelace. I am an actress by profession. You may have seen me at the theatre.'

'Yes, indeed I have,' said Virginie. 'I have seen you several times. But what story can you have that concerns myself?'

'I have a very sad story, and one which concerns you very closely. Tell me, first—do not, pray do not, think me impertinent—do you love Guy Ferrier?'

'I am engaged to him.'

'Yet . . . still . . . do you love him?'

'I cannot answer that question. I ought not to answer it. I do not know how to answer it.'

'You do not know. I am glad of it. Because you would have answered it easily—if . . . You are his cousin, are you not?'

'Yes; I am his cousin.'

'I will ask you no more questions, Miss Ferrier. I will tell you my story.'

Violet is a very clever woman. If she had not been an actress she might have been a great dramatist or a great novelist. She told her own story in the most effective way possible. She did not begin with 'There was once a girl.' She said, 'I was a poor girl, a street child, a gutter child, who played in a court and danced to a barrel organ.'

She struck at once the note of poverty, ignorance, belief in the promises of a gentleman. She told how, after years of training, she came out in small parts at a London house; how a gentleman was introduced to her. 'Very few gentlemen were introduced to me then, because I was a very insignificant little person in those days. This one was young—not more than one or two and twenty —he was one of those young men who must always have what they desire, without waiting for it, and at whatever cost; and he fell in love with me; he fell so much in love that he must needs marry me at once. I was so silly that I thought it a splendid thing to marry a gentleman, and we were married, in a church and before witnesses. He was a handsome man, and, of course, I thought he would be as good as he was handsome; and I was a pretty girl, and he thought he would always love me as much he did then.' So far it was a tale of love; a tale of the Prince and the Beggar Girl.

z

Then her note changed. The second act began with a small lodging, a husband who repented of his act a week after he had done it, and was already weary of his wife ; and then a baby ; and cruel words, with neglect, desertion, and reproaches. And that act closed with the flight of the mother and her child.

Virginie sat listening in wonder. Such a tale, so told, she had never heard or looked to hear. Why, in the gestures, the voice, the look of the actress she saw scene after scene of the sad story as if it was being played by all the actors in it, before her eyes. More than this, out of the words and the voice she constructed the despicable hero of the piece, and she shuddered because she was made, in spite of herself, to think of Guy. As the actress stood when she put hard and cruel words into her husband's mouth, as she held her head, so he stood, so he held his head. But she put the thought behind her. And was it not his very voice that spoke those words ?

Then came the Third Act. But as Virginie listened her heart grew cold, because it seemed to her as if she heard the very footsteps of Guy, drawing nearer and nearer, as if she heard his voice, heard his words. The air was heavy with the presence of her lover.

'Who . . . who . . . is the man ?' she cried.

Before her stood nothing but the thin figure of a woman ; but beside the woman, there seemed to be the ghost of her own lover—no more noble, no more the perfect knight, but downcast, with hanging head, uttering shameful words, a craven, a coward, and a liar.

'Who is the man ?' she cried, passionately.

Violet went on with her drama, heedless of the question.

Then Virginie saw how this ghost, this wretched creature, maddened with debts, sent to the woman he had married, and proposed that they should both go on for the future as if there had been no marriage : how she refused the offer, because the boy should never be ashamed of his mother : how then he asked her—but she refused again—to make no sign if he acted as though he were not already married, because by marrying a certain girl with a large fortune he could put his difficulties straight, and in sixteen years' time, but not till then, when the boy was of age, he would acknowledge him to be his lawful heir.

She stopped : her story was told.

Then she took Virginie by both hands, and said, while natural tears of pity rose to her eyes,

'Poor child ! I hope you do not love him ; because this man, this villain, my husband, is none other than Guy Ferrier.'

'I knew it, from the beginning,' said Virginie, quickly. 'I saw it must be he. I knew his voice, and his gestures. Let me think a little. I do not know what to say, or what to think.'

'Certainly,' thought Violet, 'this is not the way in which a lovesick maid would receive the news. She does not love him.'

'I must ask him,' said Virginie, presently, 'if your story is true. But Mr. Percival says that what you say is true——'

Then they were silent again.

'Shall I show you his son?' asked Violet. 'The boy is not like his father.'

'Oh! No . . . no . . . no. I want to see nothing and no one belonging to him.'

Virginie went to the open window. Outside there were the carriages and the people, and there was the clear bright sunshine of the sweet June day. But she took no note of these things. Presently she returned to the table by which Violet was sitting.

'I know why you asked me if I love him. Tell me—you—do you love him?'

'No.'

'Did you ever love him?'

'I do not know. I was young and foolish. No gentleman had ever spoken of love to me before. I thought I did. Heaven knows, I might have loved him had he chosen. Now I cannot even pity him.'

'Do you think I might have loved him, too—in time?'

'I do not know.'

'To live with him for fifteen years. To be his wife for all that time ; then—suddenly—to learn the dreadful truth. Oh! Guy . . . Guy . . . how *can* men be so wicked?'

This was the part of the wrong which struck her imagination ; the fifteen years of honour and happiness, with the man whom she had learned to love, followed by the rude discovery of his frightful treachery and her own position.

'You look good,' said Virginie, piteously. 'Can you tell me what I should do—I mean—do first? For, of course, I must never see him again. I never could. But there are other people. Lord Ferrier loves me, and will be made unhappy ; Maude, his sister, loves me ; Mrs. Hallowes will want to know why I have broken the engagement ; my guardian will want to know. What am I to say to all of them?'

'I do not know what ladies do, or how they should act. If I were you, I would say nothing. Say that Guy has broken the engagement. Refer them to him for reasons.'

'But—you, will you not, go to Lord Ferrier yourself and tell him?'

'No. I promised him long ago, when he cursed the day that he married me, that I would not be the one to tell the story to his father. I have kept that promise, and I will keep it still, unless I have to break it—for the sake of the boy.'

'Shall I leave you?' Violet asked presently ; 'I think I can do nothing more for you. Can you forgive me?'

'Forgive you?' said Virginie. 'Why, but for you, I might have married him.'

This was a strange speech from a girl who had just been torn from her lover. But it might be taken in more senses than one.

Violet went away.

Left alone, Virginie went over the whole story again, trying to understand it thoroughly. It was, alas! too easy to understand. In place of the perfect gentleman, the Knight without Reproach, the pure Sir Galahad, there stood a Thing with contorted features, hideous, deceitful, a wild beast. Poor Maude! Poor Lord Ferrier! Who was to tell them?

She sat down quickly, and wrote a note.

'I have received a visit from Violet Lovelace, the actress. She has told me a story about you and your marriage with her. If that story is true, do not answer this letter. If it is not true, come and see me. Virginie.'

She sent this letter by a special messenger. If Captain Ferrier was in his chambers he was to wait for an answer. If he was not, the man then was to go to his club and there wait for an answer. He was not to return until he had put the letter into Captain Ferrier's own hands. And, meantime, she was at home to no one.

It was nearly seven o'clock when the man returned.

He had given the letter. Captain Ferrier read it, tore it up into a great many fragments, and said, 'Tell Miss Ferrier that there is no answer at all.'

It was all true, then.

'Where is your ring, my dear?' asked Mrs. Hallowes. 'It is bad luck not to wear an engaged ring.'

'My engagement is broken off,' said Virginie.

'Your engagement broken off? My dearest child, what is the meaning of this?'

'Captain Ferrier has broken it off, dear Mrs. Hallowes. Will you ask him—not me—the reason why? I have sent him back his presents, and there is an end.'

'An end? Virginie, are you dreaming? Yesterday he was with you half the morning—was the engagement broken then?'

'No; not then, it has been broken to-day. You will ask him why, not me.'

'Good Heavens!' said Mrs. Hallowes.

'We are going out to-night,' said Virginie. 'I do not feel very much inclined for dancing, but we will go. And you will tell everybody, please, that the engagement is broken off. I wish particularly that this should be known at once.'

'But—my dear——'

'It is quite true,' Virginie repeated. 'It is broken off so hopelessly that it can never . . . never . . . never be renewed. It is not a quarrel, nor a misunderstanding. It is an *impossible* thing for me to marry him.'

'Have you told Maude?'

'I have written both to her and to Lord Ferrier, telling them

that the engagement is broken. For their sake, I am very, very
sorry. For my own——'
'For your own, dear ? '
'For my own, I can never be sufficiently grateful and happy.'
Mrs. Hallowes said no more. It was clearly no mere lovers'
quarrel. Besides, Captain Ferrier was not in love with Virginie
as she had the sharpness to have perceived very clearly from the
beginning. The man wanted her fortune, and she had learned
something of his character. He had no friends, although he knew
many men ; and he was a gambler. Could Virginie have learned
that he was a gambler ? That would hardly explain her statement
that he himself had broken off the engagement. Could she have
found out entanglements of another kind ? But since he, and not
she, had broken the engagement, that could scarcely be.

She was fairly puzzled.

Their little dinner that evening, usually so full of cheerfulness,
was silent and dull. Presently they went to some party, where
Virginie danced more than was usual with her. Mrs. Hallowes,
obedient to instructions, whispered the news, which was carried
round ; so that by the next morning there was not a single person
interested in the career of the Honourable Guy Ferrier who did not
know that his brilliant match was broken off. Virginie's letters to
Lord Ferrier and to Maude were nearly alike. To the former she
said,

'Dear Lord Ferrier,—Because you wished it, and because you
have been so kind to me—kinder than I could ever have looked for
or hoped—I am very sorry that Guy has broken off our engagement.
He will, perhaps, tell you why,—Your grateful and affectionate
cousin,   'VIRGINIE.'

And to Maude she wrote :—

'My dear Maude,—Guy has broken the engagement. He will,
if he pleases, tell you why ; but do not ask me. For your sake and
your father's sake I am very sorry that it was ever entered upon.
I will write to my guardian by the next mail. Meantime, please
understand that it is *impossible* for us to renew the promise. I
mean impossible in the literal sense of the word. It is not matter
of sentiment at all. IMPOSSIBLE. Thank you most sincerely for
your kindness and your friendship.—Yours affectionately,
                                                          'VIRGINIE.'

They received these letters sitting together after dinner. Lord
Ferrier had been talking of Virginie—of the pleasant times they
would have when she would be with them for good ; making plans
for their residence all together ; Guy settling down to a country
gentleman. He talked constantly of Virginie ; he longed for her
to be married, so as to be at his side every day. While they were
thus discoursing these letters came.

Lord Ferrier dropped the note in consternation.

'What does it mean, Maude? What does it mean?'

'It is some new folly of Guy's—some madness; I do not know what it means.' She sprang to her feet in a kind of despair. 'Oh! Guy . . . . Guy! Then all is useless.'

'What does it mean, Maude?'

'I do not know, sir. Patience a little. We shall know—too soon—whenever the news reaches us; and too much, whatever the reason may be.'

CHAPTER XI.

BROKEN OFF.

VIRGINIE would see Maude; but she refused to give any explanations.

'But, my dear, it is inexplicable. One day you are lovers, and the next you are strangers—and no reasons.'

'There is a very good reason indeed,' said Virginie. 'But yet I cannot tell it you.'

'You say that Guy broke it off. Why? It was his'—she was going to say 'his interest,' but she refrained—'it was his dearest wish——'

Virginie smiled. 'No,' she said, 'it was never his wish at all. Do not think that any longer. He may have told you so; but it was not true. He never wished to marry me: he never loved me. For that matter, he hardly took the trouble to pretend.'

'Oh! Virginie, is it, after all, only a lovers' quarrel?' It seemed, for the moment, as if she might be only piqued or out of temper.

'No: it is far worse than that. It is as I told you, an impossible thing for me ever to see him again. Ask him yourself.'

Maude went to her brother's chambers. He was out: he had left no message: she went to his club, he had not been there at all: then she went home and wrote to him.

'Virginie will tell me nothing. What have you done, Guy? What have you said?'

He answered by letter and briefly.

'Since Virginie will tell you nothing, I do not see why I should: the thing is broken off; it can never be taken up again. I suppose there will be a smash in a day or two. Perhaps you had better tell my father everything.'

Lord Ferrier found no pleasure that day in his studio, though the day was fine and the light good. He was painting a picture for Virginie; he was going to throw into it his very best work; it was to be a picture which even jealous Royal Academicians should not dare to refuse. Yet, if it could not be given to her, what was the use of going on with it? He, too, sought his son, but to no purpose,

because Captain Ferrier was neither at his chambers nor his club.
Then Lord Ferrier took luncheon at his own club, sat uneasily in
the library over the magazines for an hour or two, reading, but
remembering nothing. Then he thought he would try and see
Virginie, and ask her about it himself.

'Virginie,' he said, sadly, taking her hand, 'tell me what it
means. Am I not, in very truth, to call you daughter?'

'No,' she replied, 'I cannot become your daughter. But you
must ask Guy to tell you the reason. He knows that it is impossible I should marry him ; he has known it all along. Oh ! why—
why—did he ever try to persuade himself . . . it is incredible !'

'If you cannot tell me, my dear child,' said Lord Ferrier, 'I
will not insist. It only remains for me to say how truly and deeply
grieved I am at this blow.'

'Oh ! you have always been so kind to me, so very kind '—for
the first time the girl began to cry about her broken engagement—
'but I feel as if I were doing some dreadful ingratitude. Believe
me, it is not my fault ; indeed, indeed, it is not.'

'I am sure it is not. The fault is wholly Guy's. Yet I lose a
daughter ; and it is very hard.'

He took her in his arms and kissed her. Then he left her, and
went home and sat in his study, wondering by what sad fate the
fruits and flowers which had promised to grace his old age were
turning to dust and ashes. The older a man gets the greater
need for him to have always something before him, something full of
light, and sunshine, and warmth. Virginie was to be the source of
light, and joy, and warmth to the old man. Now she was to go.
This was a dreadful thing to think of. He looked very old and
bowed when Maude stole into the room, and sat before him, her
cheek upon her hand, and sorrow and shame written on her face.

'You bring no comfort, Maude,' said her father. 'Poor child !
It is hard for you as well as for me.'

'No, sir ; no comfort, but—more trouble.'

'Go on, my dear. Let me face the trouble—all the trouble that
is in store for us. What fresh trouble ?'

'It is no new trouble to me, sir. The knowledge of it has been
my constant companion for long years. I have done my best to
keep it from you ; but now it can be kept no longer.'

'What is it, Maude ? What is this burden that I am not to
share ?'

'It is concerned with Guy. My dear father '—she threw herself at his feet in tears of pity and of shame—'do you know the
manner of man that your son is ?'

'What is he, Maude?'

'He says I am to tell you all ; well—I will take him at his
word. I will hide nothing from you. He is a hopeless gambler ;
he has lost year after year all the money he could get from you, all
he could get from me ; he has paid none of his tradesmen during
all these years ; he has raised all the money that could be raised by

. . . by . . . the ways in which such money is raised. Do you understand all that I mean ? '

' I believe I understand it all, Maude. What more ? ' His hand, which he laid upon her head, trembled, though his voice was firm.

' He has come to the end of everything. Unless he can raise within a few days some fifteen thousand pounds for immediate wants, including debts of honour, he will be made a bankrupt—and worse.'

' He wants fifteen thousand pounds for immediate necessities.' Lord Ferrier repeated the words slowly. ' How much more will he want ? What is the amount that he must raise ? '

' I do not know.'

' Is there anything more to learn, Maude ? '

' No ; I have told you all. Except the amount of his debts.'

' Is this the reason why Virginie will not marry him ? '

' I suppose so. I know no other reason. I am glad that the engagement is broken. It was my doing. I pressed Guy to clear himself by this rich marriage. I thought that we might save you from knowing anything. Yet I have had no happy moment since, for thinking of the wretched fate I had prepared for that poor girl.'

' Thank you, Maude.' Her father spoke quietly, as if unmoved, as if it was a thing demanding attention, but not disaster.

' Leave me now. I must think over what I ought to do.'

He sat thinking all the summer afternoon. He was never, himself, an ambitious man, but the Ferriers, from father to son, continually looked for the advent of that Ferrier who was going to lead his country to victory and triumph. He thought sadly of the hopes he had formed about his only son, the bright and beautiful boy who was going to be the greatest Ferrier of the line. These hopes had long since been dim, but they had never been altogether quenched ; there was no reason why his son should not leave the Army and enter upon a political career, though as yet he had shown no ambition. He had no tastes : this was a thing which his father had long lamented, but never understood till now. For when the passion for play seizes upon a man it leaves no room for tastes of any kind. You cannot possibly serve God and Mammon. And of all men in the world the player spends most time and most thought over Mammon. He openly worships him. Now, even a buyer and seller of stocks has his Sundays.

As he pondered what would be best to do, a thought grew gradually in his brain, slowly taking shape, like a spectre, that there was only one thing left to do. If all the money was raised that could be raised—of course this meant—on the reversionary interests; if there was no other way—there was still the last resource ; he could, with his son's consent, bar the entail and sell everything—even The Towers. And so an end of all !

He took some action ; he wrote to his son, saying coldly that he had learned from Maude some of his difficulties. He ordered him to go at once to the family lawyers and draw up a complete statement of all his liabilities of every kind : and he added that until this were done, and some order taken with his affairs, Guy need not present himself.

That night Guy made his last appearance at the Green Grass Club, where he generally found the Baccarat he loved so well.

Serious play generally begins about eleven, though there is a little irregular practice—a little duelling, at écarté—before then. It is about midnight that the members drop in from their various haunts, and take their places one after the other. Some of them were little more than mere boys, though their conversation was 'grown-up,' and their knowledge of life—that is, some form of life —was precocious. Guy was one of the older men ; he was so very old that he did not talk their slang. This is, indeed, a kind of tongue, like the purest Parisian of society, which changes every season. Besides, what to the young fellows fired with champagne, and inexperienced in arithmetic, was pure fun and merriment, was to Ferrier and some like him sober and serious business. What were only couters and ponies and monkeys to the lads, mere abstract sums of money, which they might lose or win without any difference, as they fondly thought, to themselves, were to the older men the means of satisfying ravenous creditors, meeting bills, and taking up promissory notes. The lads laughed and chattered about Regie and Freddy and Nellie and Connie and, generally, Jack and Jill ; and told stories, and drank more champagne, and smoked cigarettes, and told more stories, and drank still more champagne ; while the other hands kept cool, and watched the chances.

Guy was at first in bad luck. Before midnight he lost three hundred pounds. Then he began to win again, and won all back, and a hundred and fifty more. This was three o'clock. He thought he had won enough, and would go home.

Now, there is an institution at the Green Grass Club—a very useful little institution to young men who desire to be swiftly and suddenly stripped. It consists of a buffet, where one can find light refreshments, with champagne, or brandy-and-soda. Guy was a little exhausted with the excitement of the game. He drank the greater part of a whole bottle.

Then one of the boys began talking to him.

'Let us go back,' said this youth. 'It's my day out ; and I've lost a thou. But you're in luck, old chappie ; you are not going to desert your luck.'

He went back ; it was as if a rope dragged him to the table ; he sat down and went on with the play.

They left off at seven. The sun had been up for four hours ; the morning was bright and hot ; there were lots of people already in the streets. And Guy had lost fifteen hundred pounds.

He walked home to his chambers in a kind of dream.

There were letters on the table—from Maude, she had told her father all ; from his father—he knew all, and ordered him to make out his list ; from certain gentlemen of the money-lending and bill-discounting business, their language was forcible rather than kind ; from tradesmen ; from 'friends,' who held his I.O.U.s. The smash had come. Well ; it had been coming a long time. It had been deferred by his engagement ; but already everybody knew that it was off.

'As it has come,' said Guy, 'I shall go to bed. Curious ; I wonder what will happen—— What is this ?'

It was only a little packet—with a ring and a bracelet—trifles which he had given Virginie.

He laughed as he put them into his pocket.

'Marrying would have been a deadly bore,' he said. 'I wonder how she took it. Nasty thing facing Violet, if she let herself rip. But perhaps she put her case quietly. One never knows what they will do. Pity, too, for some reasons, that it didn't come off.'

He had had his last fling in that paradise of flinging youth, London. Paris has its points. New York has its corners. But for red-hot continued flinging there is, perhaps, no capital in the world like London. Now, as the first rule among the joyous companies is that he who flings must pay, it may be very well understood that Guy Ferrier was seen no more at his club or among any of his former associates. Nor do they at this moment know what has become of him !

CHAPTER XII.

POOR TOM !

THE Smash was quite as complete as any that has ever been enjoyed by Prodigal Son. The thing is generally very much dreaded before it comes ; yet it has its enjoyable points while it lasts. Nobody is so important *during the conduct of his case* as the bankrupt. It is afterwards, when the eyes of the world are no longer upon him, that the flatness sets in. Guy Ferrier felt, on the whole, happier when the crisis had arrived, though he could no longer go to his clubs, and though he had to spend a part of each day with lawyers, making out a list of liabilities which showed a really sublime contempt for the rules of addition, multiplication, and compound interest. Yet no man can afford to disregard science, and the end of such as do is certain.

It was, indeed, a noble list, regarded only as what a young man with a small allowance and expectations of a moderate kind can achieve in ten years. The contemplation of it raised a kind of rapture in the minds of those who read it. One felt proud of one's

country, since it can produce such heroes in prodigality; and one
marvelled at the man who could calmly see the whole of these
thousands thrown headlong into the sea, getting nothing for them
at all except the usual wage of the spendthrift, now about to be
paid to him.

There is one way, and only one way, in which such a list in
such a case can be met and discharged. It is a complicated way,
and involves all kinds of other things; but in its broad principle it
is simple. The way is for the heir and the tenant in possession to
unite in barring the entail. When this is done, the family acres
may be sold and the debts paid. It is a cruel way, because it
destroys the House. The only way in which a family is kept
together, and kept in the front place won by their ancestors, is by
their lands and by their title. The latter cannot be sold, but the
former can, and a penniless Lord may hide his head, and let the
title die. The longer the line, the older the house, the more cruel
a thing it is; for a man whose ambitions lay not in his own achievements but in those of the future, the thing was most dreadful.

Lord Ferrier accepted the position. His house was ruined.
They could never again lift up their heads; his son was hopeless;
they must save his honour somehow, if that could be done, and
then find some quiet corner where, with his daughter, he could,
sad and sorrowful, wait the end of his days.

' Go, Maude,' he said; 'go to take your last look at The Towers.
I have no heart to go. When the papers are signed we shall be
homeless. Perhaps we may somehow save enough from the wreck
to live upon in some humble way.'

He knew, now, that his daughter's fortune was gone long
before—thrown by his son as a sop to his creditors. They had no
longer any secrets.

' Perhaps, Maude,' he said, with a smile; 'perhaps people may
believe that I *can* paint, after all. We may sell the pictures.'

He uttered no reproaches, and made no complaints. Everything
that he loved the most had come to ruin and wreck; he was going
to lose all that he least looked to lose; through no fault of his. A
hard and cruel case; somehow made worse by the knowledge that
the man who had done the mischief was dead to repentance, and
grieved only for himself.

Once, Maude asked him if he would see Guy. He made no
reply, but he shuddered.

As for Guy, he made no sign of wishing to see anybody. He
vanished. He was no more seen; he could not go to his club
until his debts of honour were paid; he did not appear in any of
his usual haunts. But he had some sense of honour left. He
wrote to all and told them—what they knew already—that he was
in a mess, and that his affairs were in his lawyer's hands. With
that they were fain to be content. But many men, men of small
means and vaulting ambition, who liked to play with those who
could lose without caring much, and who looked for a prompt

settlement of such claims, swore loudly and felt badly about Captain Ferrier.

I think that in those days he went o' nights to a certain obscure corner which exists in Soho. A good many curious and interesting things go on in that *quartier*. One hears stories from time to time ; but it is difficult to get such an introduction to those houses as will allay suspicion, and gentlemen of the press would probably find themselves a hindrance rather than otherwise to the programme of the evening. At the house which Guy found out, a few Russians, Frenchmen, and other foreigners, chiefly of low degree, meet nightly and dally in a small way with the Goddess of Chance Captain Ferrier was not particular about his company, so that he could get the excitement which is to some souls as necessary as ardent drink to others. He was happy if he came away the winner of a sovereign ; he cursed his luck if he lost five shillings ; he came the earliest and left the latest. He had given up his chambers, and lived at a small hotel, whose address was known only to his lawyers, and I think that he was happier in those days, living in this hole-and-corner way, punting for sixpences, than when he was plunging for hundreds and looking forward to the crisis. There was no champagne, but there was brandy-and-water.

In those days Percival plucked up heart of grace and called often upon Virginie ; and they took counsel together. It was well on in July ; the season was nearly over. Mrs. Hallowes, who went in sadness, having lost the most important persons on her visiting-list, was talking of the seaside. But Virginie had other thoughts in her head. She had not yet written to her mother and her guardian about the breaking of the engagement, which lasted but a short fortnight. She was thinking of another and a more excellent way of telling them.

It was concerning the more excellent way that Percival advised her. His arguments were forcible ; and he spoke with plainness, and to no unwilling ears.

'Why stay here ?' he asked her. 'Everything in London will remind you of—of—things you would gladly forget. You have endured a most cruel outrage at the hands of your own people. London will never be a happy place for you again.'

'No : never,' she replied. 'I can never think of London again except with pain. And I shall always remember Lord Ferrier's kindness.'

'Go out yourself,' he went on. 'The mail starts in a fortnight. Carry yourself the news of your freedom.'

She clasped her hands and her eyes sparkled.

'Then there is Tom,' the tempter added softly.

She blushed, but replied not.

'You do not know'—he pleaded the name of the absent Tom as warmly as if it were his own—'you cannot understand the perfect love with which he looks upon you. As for me and the rest of us, of course you know already that we love you just as much ; but Tom of course comes first.'

'Oh ! Mr. Percival,' said Virginie, with a rosy blush upon her cheek and a sweet smile in her eyes, 'you must not say such things to me.' Yet in Palmiste, such things had been said to her without meeting any objections.

'You will let me say such things, Virginie, because I am an old admirer, and you know that I do not presume any farther—while Tom is in the way, for Tom is different : he has watched you grow up beside him : his love is a part of his being : without you he is imperfect : you have been his companion from the time you could run about : you lisped his name almost the first of any : you have felt his affection about you and around you from the beginning. Virginie, is it possible that you could forget him ?'

'I have never forgotten him,' she said. 'How could I ever forget him ?'

'Yet you promised yourself to another.'

'Yes,' she said, humbly. 'But still I had not forgotten him. Can you not understand that he was always my brother ?'

'No, I cannot. Because, you see, he never was. People may call themselves brothers and sisters as much as they please, but they cannot create that relationship by any amount of calling. And if you loved him still, how could you——'

'I never loved my cousin at all,' said Virginie. 'Do not think worse of me than I deserve. I respected the man whose character Maude described ; and they were very kind to me ; and Lord Ferrier loved me ; and it was what my father would have liked.'

'Then, now that you are free, now that you can do so, remember the only man who has the right to ask you for your hand.'

'You forget,' she said, gently, 'that things are not as they were. He has lost his faith in me. If he entertained——those feelings—once—they must have been destroyed——by myself. What respect can he have left for a girl who engaged herself—as I did—to such a man ? I cannot explain to him as I have explained to you.'

'He will know that you were deceived ; he will say to himself that you——'

'Yes, he will make excuses for me ; but can he ever think again —as he did before ?'

'You would not ask that question if you knew and could understand what a man's love is. Virginie, it isn't a question of whether he thinks a little better or a little worse of you. All that is nothing. He *loves you*. Whatever you did, he would love you still. If you were to lose your beauty, he would love you still. If you were to go away and desert him for a hundred and fifty years, he would love you just as much when you came back. It isn't your beauty, or your grace, or your virtue, or your sweetness that he loves ; it is yourself.'

'Has he told you all this ?'

'No ; he never talked about you.'

'How, then, do you know it ?'

'Because, Virginie, I know the man ; and because I judge him by myself. For I love you in just about the same way myself. You are my ideal woman, as you are his.'

The tears came into her eyes.

'What,' she asked, 'can a woman say or do that is worthy of this gift of love ? You, who judge him by yourself, plead for him. Heaven knows it wants little pleading. You are so generous and so loyal to him that I cannot but do your will. It shall be as you desire.'

'Elsie,' he said in the evening—they were taking a stroll in the cool and leafy lanes of Battersea Park ; it was nearly nine o'clock, and the sweet breath of summer was in the air. 'Elsie, I have had an agitated day.'

'Has your novel gone wrong, then ?'

'No ; there are one or two things even more important than the novel, though that will prove an Epoch-maker. What I was engaged upon was more important. You know, of course, Elsie, that I have always been in love with Virginie.'

'Yes, you have told me so a thousand times.'

'Have I really ? So often ? Yet it is a delightful subject to talk about—nothing more so. Being in love, then, and fully acquainted with the various phases of that interesting passion, I judge of Tom's feelings by my own.'

'Yes ; that seems natural—if Tom does feel like you.'

'Of course he does. Now, consider the case. The young lady has suffered a great wrong ; but things might have been much worse, because she might have been in love with the man who did the wrong. That, I am happy to say, is not the case. Not at all. She never really cared a straw about him ; she has been insulted and outraged by the abominable wickedness of the creature, but her deeper feelings are untouched. Now, here is Tom's chance. Therefore I went there this morning to plead his cause.'

'Why not your own, since you love her so much ?'

'You are a foolish child, Elsie. I told you that Tom must come first. And, after a great deal of beating about the bush, because one never quite knows in what light the thing is regarded by the person one is trying to persuade, I succeeded.'

'Yes, Elsie,' he continued triumphantly, 'Virginie will marry Tom. That is the news I have to tell you.'

'And you ?'

'Why, I go on just the same. It has been a great happiness to me to love this sweet and beautiful woman. She will always remain to me the crown of womanhood. Perhaps I should be almost afraid of marrying her. Perhaps it is better to worship at a distance.'

'Perhaps,' said Elsie, a little jealously, 'you might find out that she is not altogether the goddess you think.'

'And what a dreadful thing that would be to discover!' said Percival. 'Now, if I marry a girl whom I know not to be a goddess, that would be better, wouldn't it?'

'I should think so,' said Elsie, blushing—she hardly knew why. But nobody was there to see it, so it didn't matter.

'.Yes ; much better. If, for instance, you and I were to marry.'

'Oh! Mr. Percival.'

'If you would not be jealous, and think that because I have loved Virginie I cannot find any love for you—but I thought you ought to know the whole truth.'

'Oh! Mr. Percival. What will Violet say?'

'You are a very dear and good little Elsie. We will go into that partnership, then. I've got no money ; you've got no money. We will club our resources. And perhaps we needn't move our quarters. And now, my child, as there is nobody in this lane but ourselves, put up your lips and let me kiss you, and tell me that you won't be jealous. Petrarch always made them say that.'

CHAPTER XIII.

FAREWELL.

'I AM come,' said Maude, 'to ask you to forgive me, Virginie, before you go.'

She looked pale and worn ; her thin cheek was thinner ; her eyes more lustrous and more sorrowful. Sad stories in plenty have been written on the wreck of women's lives made by lover and by husband, but few of them which have been ruined by brother or by father ; yet are these the more common. Maude Ferrier gave her brother everything : her thoughts, her work, her money, yet the end was—this.

'I am come to ask your forgiveness,' she repeated.

'Indeed,' said Virginie, 'I have nothing to forgive. You have always been most kind and good to me.'

'My goodness and kindness, Virginie, were assumed, for my brother's sake. I wanted him to marry you for the sake of your money. I wrote to him in Palmiste, urging him to pay court to you. I knew that he was in difficulties, and a gambler ; I knew well that he would only be relieved for a time, and that he would throw away your fortune as he has thrown away his own. You were to be sacrificed to his selfish greed and prodigality, as well as I myself. It was a cruel and a wicked thing to plot.'

'But you told me——'

'All I told you was false. I said Guy was an honourable and a noble gentleman, as the Chief of our House has always been. It was false. He is cold and selfish, cruel and treacherous. This I knew. I was preparing you for the most cruel of disappointments. I deliberately laid my plans for you to become the wife of a reckless gamester. But, remember, my father knew nothing of it. Think ill of me, because I deserve it; but not of him, because he is the soul of honour. I have told him, now. When you found him out what were your thoughts of me ? '

'But, Maude, I have not found him out. This is the first I have heard of his money difficulties or his gaming.'

'Why, then, was the engagement broken off. Is there worse to come ! '

'There is worse to come, but I cannot tell you what it is.'

'To save him even for a year or two ; to keep my father from knowing the reputation and character of his son—I think I would have sacrificed anyone. Yet—Virginie—I am glad that you are saved ; and again I say—forgive me.'

'I forgive you, Maude. Whatever you did, was for your brother. I know already that he is not—the noble character I thought him. But what do you mean by ruin ? '

'His liabilities are enormous ; it is truly wonderful that he should have been trusted so greatly ; to meet them my father has consented to the only course left open ; he will cut off the entail and sell The Towers, and the estates, and the town house and all ; and so there will be an end of us.'

'Sell The Towers ? Sell the estates ? Is it possible ? '

'It is more than possible. The papers are ready, and will be signed to-morrow morning.'

'Oh ! Maude, it must not be. Cannot some of my fortune——'

'Yours, Virginie ? Ask yourself if we could take your money— when we have wronged you so cruelly.'

Virginie was silent. No ; her own money could not be taken.

'To-morrow morning my father will see his son, but only for the signing of the papers, and then . . . then . . . oh ! me . . . there will be no more pride for us, except in the past, and only poverty and shame for the future.'

'Maude ! '

They wept together, and parted.

Now when, an hour later, Percival heard of this intention he fell into a great dubiety. For, first of all, he had no right to interfere ; but, secondly, he had been taken into confidence by a person greatly interested in this barring of entail ; and, thirdly, he thought that if the truth were made known to Lord Ferrier, he might reconsider a decision which would make his grandson a pauper. Finally, he decided on advising Violet to take the boy and go herself to her father-in-law.

'I promised,' said the actress, 'that I would keep his secret— and I have done so. Nobody knows—except that poor child with the pretty face. But for the sake of the boy I would break that promise, or any other that I have ever made.'

'It is for his sake that I advise you to break it. You ought never to have made such a promise at all.'

'What do you say, Daddy?'

'It looks well,' he said, . . . 'a lawyer's office—table with parchments——'

'It won't be parchment,' Percival objected. 'It will be paper.'

'Permit me, Mr. Percival, to know my business. On the stage, wills and agreements and so forth must be on parchment—large, rustling parchment. I will proceed . . .'

He indicated by a sweep of his hand that the scene was set. 'At the table the lawyer, holding a pen—a large goose-quill—the introduction of steel pens has ruined the old goose-quill business—utterly destroyed it. Ah! what business have I seen in the good old farces got out of a simple quill pen! At the end of the table the prodigal, arms folded, brows knit—a prodigal at bay—most effective figure I assure you. Enter the father, bowed with years and grief, supported by his lovely daughter, who gazes reproachfully upon her brother.

' " Will your Lordship sign? "

' " Give me," he says, feebly, " give me the pen. Thus . . . thus . . . I sign away—for ever—the honour of the House."

'He dips the pen into the ink ; he raises his hand. The door flies open—" Do not sign, my Lord ! " Tableau ! Very good indeed, Violet, my dear. It makes up for the loss of that other beautiful situation which you threw away. After all, it would not have taken place for sixteen years, and one does not know where I may be in sixteen years. Starring in the provinces, very likely.'

It did seem a very likely thing indeed, considering that he was already over eighty ; but then Art knows nought of age.

'I think you ought to go, indeed,' said Percival. 'If you will allow me, I will go with you, unless Mr. Perigal would like to go.'

'I would rather go alone,' said Violet. 'And the boy shall go too.'

The papers were to be signed at noon. Guy was instructed to be in the study at that time ; he was also informed that his father refused to speak to him, that he was to go away on the conclusion of the inquiry, and that he would be afterwards informed what provision, if any, would be made for him. The last clause was uncomfortable, because men who are the heirs to great names are not accustomed to consider even the possibility of a failure in the corn and wine, the butter and the oil, and the honey, which go to the daily bread. 'If any !'—but, of course, it could be only a figure of speech.

It was a little after eleven when Violet asked to see Lord Ferrier. She refused to send in her name, but said that she came on business of the utmost importance, and wished to see his Lordship immediately. She was taken to the study, where she waited, and wondered how her communication would be received.

Presently Lord Ferrier appeared. Not quite the man Violet

expected—she somehow thought he would be a fierce, baronial kind
of person, with the air of one who insists on all his rights ; a
French Seigneur of the good old time—though she knew little
about Seigneurs ; a melodramatic Lord, with large, white, fierce
eyebrows.   On the contrary, he seemed quite a mild and gentle old
man, who bowed politely, and apologised for keeping her waiting,
and asked what her business with him might be, and added that he
was himself much engaged at the moment, and would be obliged if
she would come to the point at once.

'Your business, my Lord,' said Violet, 'is connected with
your son ?'

'It is.'

'You are about to sign an agreement which will enable you to
sell your property—all your property—for the purpose of paying off
your son's debts.'

'I am ; though I do not know how you have learned this.'

'Never mind that.   I am thinking, my Lord, how I had best
put into words the things that I have to tell you.   I am here in
hope of inducing you to reconsider that decision.'

Lord Ferrier rose.

'Madam,' he said, 'I cannot discuss this decision, or any other
private concerns of mine, with a stranger.'

'Yet, you will listen to me, directly you know who I am.   It is
only since yesterday that I have understood the meaning of your
Lordship's intention.   Otherwise I should have been here long
ago.'

'I am at a loss to know——'

'You shall know directly.   I have been told that your Lordship
is a . . . a . . . what they call . . . I am told . . . a tenant for
life of the property which you hold.'

'That is so, certainly.'

'And that your son, when he succeeds, is also a tenant for
life.'

'Yes.'

'So that if you agree between you to sell it you will be selling
the property of your grandchildren.'

'If you put it in that way—yes.   But I have no grandchildren.'

Violet had been holding the little boy by the hand ; his back
was turned to the window, so that his face was in shade.   She now
turned him round and pushed him gently forward.

'Does your Lordship,' she asked, 'see any likeness in that boy
to any of your own family ?'

It had been Violet's boast when she wrote to her husband that
the boy was not like him.   That was only true in part.   The boy
was exactly like what his father had been at his age.

'It is Guy himself !' cried Lord Ferrier.   'The boy is like Guy
at six.   What does this mean ?'

'Your Lordship has one grandchild.   That is what it means.   I
am your son's wife.'

'Is it possible?'

'You do not, naturally, accept my statement. Wait. Your son will be here himself in a short time. Let him be witness. I was married to him six years ago, and separated from him five years ago. It was an unlucky day for me when I met your son.'

'Is it possible?'

His eyes were fixed on the child.

'I am an actress. I play under the name of Violet Lovelace.'

'Is it possible?'

He kept repeating these words.

'My Lord, have no doubt that I shall prove what I say. Will you make the future Lord Ferrier a pauper?'

'The future Lord Ferrier. Yes . . . Yes . . . The future Lord Ferrier. Then the house will have another chance. But, if the child is not a pauper, his father will be dishonoured.'

Violet laughed.

'Is he not dishonoured already? Has he not engaged himself to a young lady, hoping that I should keep silence? Did he not come to me and threaten, if I did not keep silence, to take away the boy and rob me of my salary? What constitutes dishonour among gentlemen, if these things do not? I say nothing of the cruel treatment and bitter words that drove me from him as soon as my baby was born. I say nothing of being left to earn my bread as best I might, and keep the child as well. It all forms part of the man. If this is not dishonour, Heaven knows what it is.'

'Let me look at you,' he said.

She raised her veil, and looked up in his face.

'The eyes,' he said, 'are honest eyes. You have a good face.'

She blushed. She had not blushed for years; but now she blushed like an innocent, ignorant school-girl.

'My Lord,' she said, earnestly, 'my child has no cause to be ashamed of his mother, unless he is ashamed that she is an actress.'

'It is well said,' he replied, gravely.

Then he rang the bell, and desired that Miss Ferrier should be asked to come to him.

'Maude,' he said, simply, 'this young lady informs me that she is—your brother's wife—and that this is his son. If this be true— as I have very little doubt——'

'At least, sir, let us first prove it to be true.'

'Let us prove it to be true,' echoed Violet. She was gentle and soft with the man; but with this woman who looked at her with cold distrust she became herself cold and distrustful. She drew the child upon her lap. 'I shall prove that you, Miss Ferrier, are my sister-in-law.'

'Will you, then, take your proofs to the proper persons, our lawyers?' asked Maude.

'No: I will not. I will wait here till my husband comes, he

will prove himself the truth of my statement. Your Lordship will
understand that I am here for no other purpose than to defend my
son's rights.   Your nephew '—she addressed herself to Maude with
some asperity of manner—' may become an actor.   I believe none
of his predecessors have ever followed this profession.'

Maude sighed.   She did not doubt the story.   A foolish
marriage was only one more episode in the history of her brother,
and a most natural episode.

They sat in silence for a few minutes.   Then Lord Ferrier
spoke.

'If it be as you say,' he said, slowly, ' I will respect the boy's
rights at the expense of his father.'

Violet made no reply.   Then there was silence again.

' The clock struck twelve.   And at the moment, true to the
time appointed, the lawyer bearing the paper arrived ; with him,
Guy himself.

He started at the sight of Violet.

'You here ?' he cried.   'You have broken your promise.'

' Who is this lady, sir ? ' asked Lord Ferrier.

.He looked from one to the other.   He remembered the witnesses to the marriage ; further concealment was hopeless ; besides,
it was useless.

' She is my wife,' he said, 'and this, I suppose, is the boy.'

'It is the boy,' said Violet.   'I have the other proofs, but . . .
is your Lordship satisfied ? '

' I am satisfied,' Lord Ferrier replied.

'First, then, you will sign this paper'—Violet addressed her
husband, not Lord Ferrier.   'You acknowledge that you married
me under the assumed name of Richard Johnson.   That is all.
But I wish you to sign it in the presence of your father and your
sister.'

'If that is all,' said Guy, carelessly, ' let us sign.'

He read the paper, signed it, and returned it to her, with a bow.
'I suppose,' he said, 'that we part again.   Quite so.   You have
not kept your promise ; but do not fear ; I shall not interfere with
you.'

' Give me, if you please,' said Lord Ferrier to the lawyer, 'the
agreement which I was to sign.   I have decided, sir,' he said to his
son, ' not to execute this deed.   I will not join you in barring the
entail.   The estates shall be kept—for your son.   I think I have
no more to say to you.   Stay.   You will learn in a few days what
I can do for you.   An allowance of some kind shall be made to you,
on the condition that you leave England and do not return in my
lifetime.   As regards your creditors, I shall see what sum I can set
aside every year, so long as I live, for their use.   Go ; let me forget
that ever I had a son.'

The young man turned and left the room without a word.

'Guy !' cried Maude, catching his hand, but he shook it off with
an angry gesture.   He had not even a single kind word of farewell

for the woman who had given him all she had. She sank into her chair, and buried her face in her hands.

ꞌ 'My dear,' said Lord Ferrier, taking Violet's hand and raising it to his lips, 'you are my daughter-in-law. In this house you will be always welcome.'

'Thank you, my Lord. My secret shall still be kept. I will not take your name to the theatre, and I will go on working for myself. As for the boy, when he is older you shall decide about him. Boy, kiss your grandfather.'

She held up the child to be kissed.

'I will go, now. Do not cry for your brother,' she said to Maude. 'He is not worth a tear. I haven't cried about him for more than five years.'

But Maude made no sign, and Violet walked away, leading the boy with her.

So Guy passed away, and will be seen no more. Nor can one say what will be his end. Where cards and dice and roulette-tables are to be found he will make his home. That is quite certain. It is also certain that he will descend, slowly or rapidly, deeper and deeper, until the outward semblance of a gentleman is lost. As one thinks of him and his future, one remembers stories of Mexican hells and New Orleans gambling saloons, and of shots fired across a table, and a dead body thrown into the street. Or one remembers ghastly things that one has heard : how men have fallen among thieves and swindlers, and cast in their lot with them, owing to the rare possession of a well-bred manner. Or one thinks of the despair that falls upon a man when his last sou is lost, and the cold river is close by.

Soon or late, the end of such men is certain.

CHAPTER XIV.

AN AUSPICIOUS DAY.

THE cold season in Palmiste Island somewhat resembles the summer in the Straits of Belleisle. That is to say, while the latter begins on August the 31st and ends on September the 1st, the former is said to begin on June the 30th and to end on July the 1st. It should be called the 'not-so-hot-as-usual' season. In the very height—or depth—of the season was Virginie married.

Her return to the island was announced by no letters : she arrived alone and unexpected. There were few passengers by the mail, and hardly anyone came on board when the quarantine boat had done its duty. Therefore Virginie, leaving her boxes and things to be forwarded by the trusty purser, landed by herself, and by herself drove to Mon Désir.

It was in the afternoon, about five of the clock, that she arrived
at the dear old Avenue of Palms. All the way out she had been
living over again the tumult and humiliation of the last weeks
in England. When she landed in the old familiar place her
London season vanished, and became like a dream of the past.
The sunshine lay upon the everlasting hills, the fresh breeze of the
afternoon fanned her cheek, the ragged old banana-trees waved a
welcome to her with their torn and disreputable rags of leaves. On
the wharves the dusky coolies shouted as they ran backwards and
forwards with their odorous sacks of guano ; the merchants and the
brokers sat beneath the trees upon the Place ; the drivers slept
upon their boxes ; the mules kicked and bit each other ; once more
she heard the old Creole patois ; once more she felt herself a Creole,
and, as the carriage took her beyond the town, the tears came to
her eyes. What was England to her but a name and a glory?
What was her pride of family worth any more to her? What had
been the vague wonders in her mind before she saw the birthplace
of her father? How was she changed? How little it all meant
now. What were London drawing-rooms—what was the talk of
London society—what were the false friendships and pretences of
English life—what were the nights in crowded ball-rooms—to the
sweet, pure air of the Palmiste table-land ; the rustle and the light,
the colour and the shadow of the waving canes, the wooded hill-
side, the bare, hot rocks; the breadth of sunshine, the deep ravines,
the waterfalls, and mountain streams ; even the ugly wooden huts,
with their tin roofs, of the Chinamen—in her native land?

When the carriage reached the avenue, she stopped it, and,
telling the man to follow very slowly, she went on before with
parted lips and eager eyes, thinking of how she should find them all.

Oh ! Look. In the verandah there sat, as they always had sat,
side by side, her mother with Madame Kemyss. They were not
reading—what real good comes by reading, when you think of it?
Nor were they talking—you do not do any good at all, in general,
by talking. Nor were they working—why should they work, when
they had people to work for them? On a table between them lay a
book or two, and some work, just to look at. They were sitting there
as they sat every afternoon, quite still, silent, and happy, enjoying
the sunshine as it sloped across the lawn and lay golden on the distant
hills, feeling the joy of the cloudless sky, and the breath of the
fragrant air, and the scent of the roses on the lawn. Why talk?
Why argue? Why waste breath in trying to prove the unknowable,
when these things can be enjoyed? Needless work, fuss, prattle,
chatter, fierce argument, and strenuous logic are for temperate
zones. To these ladies there was nothing wanting in their lives but
the return of their Virginie. And she was close at hand, though
they knew it not, looking at them through the branches of an
acacia. The Squire was there, too. But one is ashamed to say
that he was asleep. He had been of late so much troubled and
afflicted about the estate and the hesitation of the Banks that he

often fell asleep of an afternoon. Now he lay back in his long chair and slumbered peacefully.

In a corner of the verandah sat old Suzette, in her cotton frock and red turban, coiled up. In her hands was a piece of work ; but she, too, was half asleep.

A sleepy, peaceful place. As Virginie looked, she thought of the danger hanging over them, and how this peace might be interrupted, this rest disturbed, and these dear old people sent adrift to find such shelter as they might. To be sure, where her mother lived, there would be Madame Kemyss—there, too, the Squire. But—Tom !

And she blushed, because, during all the voyage, Tom had never once been out of her thoughts. What would he say ? What would he say ?

Now, at this juncture, Tom himself came sauntering slowly down the avenue. He was dull because the house was dull, and its silence almost intolerable to him. And in these days he was always dejected, and found no joy in anything nor any brightness in the sunshine. And, behold ! before him stood none other than—— Virginie !

He took her in his arms, and, without a word of question or explanation—perhaps he read her eyes—he kissed her a thousand times, regardless of the driver who sat on his box and grinned approvingly.

'Oh ! Tom,' she cried, 'do you love me still ? '

Did he love her ? Did the sun shine ? Was the sky blue ? Were the flowers growing under their feet ? Did he love her still ?

.   .   .   .

And there were present at the wedding his Excellency the Governor and her Ladyship, his illustrious consort ; also the Right Reverend the Lord Bishop of Palmiste, with the young Padre, his Examining Chaplain—it took the pair of them to read the service —and the Bishopess, and the Bishoplings and the Colonial Secretary, and the Auditor-General and the Treasurer, and all the Heads of Departments—with their wives and daughters ; also all the members of the Legislative Council, with their wives and their sons and their daughters, and their grandchildren ; and the General in command of the Forces, and the Colonel and all the officers of the Regiment in garrison ; and the Assistant Colonial Secretary —he who had taken the Padre for a morning walk—and other assistants in Departments ; and all the French and English merchants, and as many of the planters as were white—you mustn't mix colours in a tropical climate any more than in æsthetic zones ; and among them the McAndrew and the McLoughlin. As for the Pink Boy, he was there, too. His friend the Squire was saved from ruin. His letter had been acted upon ; and, after all, this was the sad and fatal result. Yet he bore up, and acted as best man, looking very pink and young and handsome.

They were married, naturally, at the English Cathedral, which was much fuller than was ever before known in the memory of man, except on St. John's Day, when the Masons go there to solemn service, and hear a sermon full of dark allusion to Masonic rites, and feel reassured about that Greater Excommunication hurled at them by my Lord the Bishop of the Older Branch, whose Palace stands not a hundred yards away. The organ pealed continuously, and the choir boys sang an anthem, and the service was presently under way, and the Pink Boy and all the bridesmaids were in tears.

After the service there was the most generous and noble banquet ever spread, with culinary effects romantically tropical, artistically suggestive of sugar planting, poetically, allegorically beautiful. His Right Reverence proposed the bride : his Excellency proposed Captain Kemyss : the Assistant Colonial Secretary, himself a bachelor, proposed the bridesmaids, and the Pink Boy in reply wandered off to the bride and confessed his passion : and the McAndrew went to sleep in the middle of the feast : and the McLoughlin at the close had to be supported by a friend on either side.

They spent their honeymoon in a little shooting-box hidden in the heart of the woods, where they wandered every day hand in hand. Sometimes they sat beside a sparkling stream, upon some fallen trunk, and watched the flickering of the leaves in the sunlight, or the herds of deer browsing in a lonely glade, in silent happiness. Sometimes they gathered orchids and ferns. Sometimes Virginie would read to Tom, who never read anything for himself. Sometimes she told him of the great world she had seen for a little and left for ever. Once she told him the true story of her engagement, and honest Tom was fain to own that the wickedness of man may be very astonishing. He meant white man— because he knew the coloured varieties pretty well, and had gauged their moral possibilities. Sometimes they came upon little clearings inhabited by settlements of old maroons who had long since forgotten their rancour against the white man, and among whom there was now none living, unless some very old Patriarch, who remembered the lash and the labour. Then the fair white lady sat among them, and talked to the simple people.

A sweet and simple honeymoon ; the prelude to a sweet and simple life. Perhaps Virginie will be happier with her garden and her flowers, her woods and hills, her sunshine and peace, than if she wore the Lady of The Towers, even though her husband were the Bayard that Maude represented him to be.

Another wedding ; it was so obscure that I do not know on what day it was held ; but it was about the same as Virginie's. That of Mr. Percival and Elsie. Nobody was present except Daddy Perigal and Violet and the boy. They have, as they proposed, clubbed their resources. Elsie is to go on governessing, while her husband shapes that spoon. It will never, I think, be a very remarkable spoon; but there will be some neatness and freshness in the design, some taste, with conscientiousness in the execution; and the whole of the man's heart will be thrown into his work, so that, perhaps, there may presently happen to be found a few simple people who will look upon the spoon with a little admiration and a little sympathy.

THE HUMBLING OF THE MEMBLINGS.

It is now forty years since Josiah Membling, clock and watchmaker, retired from Gracechurch Street and the little shop, where he had done extremely well, to his native village in Essex. He was the son of a small farmer and the descendant of sturdy yeomen; the instincts of old family were strong in him; when, therefore, being a good way past sixty, he thought the time had come to sell the business and retire, he was encouraged by the fact that the Hall of his native village was for sale, with the park and grounds. He bought them; took his family into the country with him, and settled down, for the fifteen years of life which remained to him, not as a country gentleman exactly, for the good man had no idea of going into society, but as a mixture of retired tradesman and farmer. He farmed his own land, though he lost money by it; he found life dull after the stir of the city, and he continually yearned after the manufacture of watches and clocks, in which he was no mere seller of other men's work, but himself an ingenious and accomplished workman, who had duly served his seven years' apprenticeship, and was besides a mechanician by native genius.

During the latter years of his life the old man spent most of his time locked up in his own room. It was a very large room on the first floor, having two windows facing the south and four looking west; beside it was a small dressing-room which he occupied as a bedroom; and no one at all was ever allowed to enter the large room, which was always locked; but his grandson knew that it contained a bench, a lathe, and all the tools requisite for mechanical work. Sometimes he worked there till late at night, sometimes he would not come out even for dinner. There was something uncanny about the old fellow working by himself continually, nobody knew at what. He might have made watches, but he brought none out; he might have turned things with his lathe, but none were ever shown; he might have been prosecuting some grand research in the horological mystery, but he said nothing about it.

He kept on working till the day of his death. It happened, one Saturday evening, that his unmarried daughter and his daughter-in-law were in the drawing-room when the old man unexpectedly walked in. He stood before the fire and looked at them, turning from one to the other with a strange smile. It was so seldom that he came out of his own room that the two ladies were perplexed and a little frightened.

'My work,' he said, with another weird and uncanny smile, 'is finished.'

The words were hardly spoken when he suddenly reeled, caught at a chair, and fell heavily to the ground in a fit.

In the morning he became conscious again, and presently began to understand that he was dying, and that he had better give any directions that he had to give at once. They sent for his grandson who was at Cambridge, and it was to him, his heir, that the old man gave the one injunction that he seemed to care about. 'Let no one,' he said, shaking his long and lean forefinger in the most solemn manner, 'let no one presume to enter my room. Let it remain locked, or if any desire to enter'—here he laughed and his hearers shuddered—'let him enter alone and after dark. I shall be there,' he added, while they shuddered again, 'on the watch—a day and night watchman—a watch that always goes—a repeating watch, a keyless watch, with the newest improvements, an everlasting watch'—here his mind wandered a little—'Watches neatly repaired. Established forty years. Clocks kept going.' And then he laughed again and breathed his last. It was dreadful to see an old man die with a laugh upon his lips.

They buried him in the churchyard under a magnificent marble tomb, among a great number of Memblings, including his only son. And it was, as stated above, his grandson who succeeded, being then only one-and-twenty years of age.

His successor shortly afterwards married, and in course of time had a family, like most people, of sons and daughters. The young people knew very little about the watchmaker's shop, but they knew that the churchyard was full of Josiah Memblings, and very easily they grew to believe in a legendary history about the family greatness. They were the ancient holders of the estate, the lords of the manor; they were found on the spot by the Norman Conqueror; they experienced many adventures in the various civil wars; there came a time when their fortunes were quite fallen; even the Hall passed for a while out of their hands; then came the second founder, who amassed wealth in the City and bought back the old house. And they really did not know—the innocent girls who built up this legend—what a collection of fibs they were putting together.

For fifteen years and more the old man's last wishes were faithfully and piously obeyed. No one entered the old man's room at all; the key was in his grandson's possession; it became a matter of common belief that the old man haunted the room. The maids at dusk, and after dark, would hurry past the door; in full daylight they would stop and listen, trembling, if by chance they might hear the sound of a dead man's footfall; and the young members of the family were brought up to feel doubly grateful to an ancestor who had not only restored the fortunes of the house, but had endowed it with a haunted room.

One day, however, when Laura, the eldest daughter, was in her father's study looking for something else, she found hanging up in a cupboard the key of the haunted room. It was a bright sunny morning; there could be no fear of ghosts on such a day; she looked at the key; she remembered the solemn injunction, which of course everybody knew, but the sight of the key filled her with strange and irresistible curiosity and a longing such as she had never before known: she took it down with a trembling hand; she crept like a thief out of the study and up the broad stair to the door; she put the key in the lock and turned it. It was a little rusty, but the bolt flew back and she opened the door. Strange, how hard she had to press that door with her shoulder before it opened; she went in and looked round curiously, yet but for a single moment: a grating noise behind her caused her to turn quickly; to her horror the door was closing of its own accord, and a great bar was slowly rising behind it. She shrieked and fled; there was just time; the door closed as she rushed through, there was a noise as of a falling bar, and Laura fainted away. When she recovered the maids were running up the stairs and about the house, wanting to know who had been ringing bells and who was making such a strange noise in the house.

When Laura told her story, her father put on the semblance of great wrath, but secretly he rejoiced because here was proof positive of the haunting. No family of yesterday ever got a ghost. In fact, it is only the members of an old family who can be got even to believe in ghosts at all. It is a curious thing that in poor and new neighbourhoods, like the East End of London, there seems no place for a ghost. Now, for a thick population of ghosts, give me Northumberland.

The next day, Laura said that she had felt a cold breath upon her cheek.

The day after, she said that a heavy sigh had fallen upon her ear as she fled.

The day after that, she said that the sigh was a faint whisper of the words 'My dear child.'

It was enough. The ghost was established. Henceforth unpleasant things might be said of money made in trade, but the old family tradition would not be attacked. There was the evidence of the supernatural bar, there was the door closed by an invisible hand, there was the voice, there was the ringing of bells, there were the strange noises heard by the maids while Laura was lying supine and unconscious. No ancient Scottish House ever had such a ghost. The Squire, however, put away the key in his strong box, among his valuables. The door, he said, should never again be opened in his lifetime. But Laura used to stand outside like a Peri, listening for another message from the other world, and it became recognised in the family that she was her great-grandfather's favourite. This gave her a kind of rank. Respect was due to one thus singled out by an ancestor who had been such a benefactor as to become not only the restorer of fallen fortunes (which is in itself romantic), but also the family ghost. All the Memblings walked more upright than before ; they stuck out their chins, so to speak ; they believed in their Coat of Arms ; what was better, other people believed in it as well.

They entertained people at the Hall, and when they offered them quarters for the night spoke with reserve of the haunted room ; they laughed, but with affection and reverence, not with scorn, at their ghost ; the girls bade their friends, when they left them after a hair-brushing, have no fear, because their ancestor worked very quietly and disturbed no one outside his own room, though, they added, as might be plainly heard by anyone who listened at the door after dark, he was always at work. It was, in fact, one of Laura's fictions that she could hear the lathe at work, and the Squire, who good-humouredly received the avowed incredulity of his friends, always finished the conversation by saying that the key of the room was in his strong box, where he intended it to remain.

Things might have gone on in this quiet and peaceful manner until now but for a misfortune, the nature and extent of which will become presently apparent. All misfortunes, said the Sage (who married his cook), proceed from love.

Yet, who would have thought that the Humbling of the Memblings would have followed upon so simple and natural a thing as the engagement of young Dalmahoy to Laura ? Certainly not she herself, not her father, nor her sisters and brothers, because Dalmahoy was in every respect a most eligible *parti*, being not only young, tolerably well off, and handsome, a good waltzer, a good rider, a good shot, a good actor, and one of those gallant headlong lovers before whom feminine courage breaks down, but he was also —a point naturally insisted upon by the Memblings—a man of undeniably good family. There was no trace or taint of trade in the long line of Dalmahoys.

When Jack Dalmahoy came to Membling Hall—the girls almost believed that the place had never possessed any other name, so that they could, if they pleased, call themselves the Memblings of Membling—one of the first things they did, after showing him their gardens, stables, and other interesting parts of the establishment, was to tell him of the family ghost. He naturally laughed, and spoke with disrespect of the spectre. Laura rebuked him, letting it be understood quite plainly that she was to be taken with her ghost or not at all. Who would offend his mistress by objecting to such a trifle ? ' I would gladly,' said Jack, ' have the ghost in my room every night if that would give you any pleasure. Invite him, Laura, to visit me.'

Laura gravely shook her head. This was not the proper spirit in which to speak of an ancestor who walked. He might even be listening at that very moment. Indeed, the opportune cracking of a piece of furniture gave some colour of probability to the supposition.

After dinner, when the ladies had gone, Jack asked the Squire to allow him to pass the night in the haunted room. His request was refused, gently but firmly.

'I am not,' said the chief of the Memblings, 'a particularly superstitious man, but the fact that there is undoubtedly something supernatural in the room, and the equally undoubted fact that the appearances and manifestations are connected with my grandfather, make me respect his desire to remain after death unmolested in what was, in his lifetime, his favourite room.'

Laura was angry when she heard of this proposal. Did Jack, she asked, consider her great-grandfather in the light of a common ill-bred ghost, one of those unthinking and vulgar ghosts who break the crockery, throw the furniture about, rattle chains, and are disagreeable in the house? 'For my part,' she said, 'I look upon the tenancy of this room by my dead ancestor as a singular proof of the affection with which he continues to regard us. His spirit remains with us,' she added, clasping her hands and turning her soft eyes, which were as limpid as a pair of opals, up to the heaven, 'because he loves us still. He is our guardian angel, he watches over the house. We are under his special protection, and if we were to lose him, through any act of irreverence or intrusion, farewell the luck of Membling Hall!'

Jack desisted, though loth to relinquish his interview with the ghost. Indeed, when one thinks how seldom one gets the chance of a talk face to face with a ghost, it is not surprising that Jack was sorrowful when it vanished. I have never myself had such a talk, and with the exceptions of a friend who saw the ghost of Joe Morgan, another who was privileged to amuse Lady Kitty, and a third who received Lady Bab, I think I know no one who has actually talked with them. And, without going quite so far as a certain learned counsel of my acquaintance, who ardently desires a half-hour's friendly interview with the devil, I must say that there are many ghosts for whom one would suffer a great deal of inconvenience and loss of time. Doctor Johnson, Emanuel Swedenborg, Cagliostro, Doctor Dee, Cotton Mather, George Psalmanazar, the late Count of Albany, Robespierre, and Cornelius Agrippa, all occur to one in a breath as most interesting ghosts, if they would only come and talk in a friendly way and without frightening one. Two or three days afterwards Jack tried another line. As he could not be allowed to sit up all night and converse with the old watchmaker, he begged permission just to see the room. He would not go in, only open the door and look round. 'It is not, Laura,' he said, 'as if one wanted to go against your ancestor's express rule, simply to pay a kind of—mark of respect—you know—morning call—just to look at the place, not even to go into the room.'

I believe that one of the reasons why the Squire refused permission to spend the night in the room was that he was afraid of revelations. You see, he knew more than his children, he entertained well-founded doubts as to the greatness of the House, he knew all about the shop, and it did occur to him that a conversation between his grandfather and his son-in-law might be awkward. Fancy a poor relation turning up when you have been comfortably established for a generation and a half, to remind your friends that the family crest was only forty years old or so, that the family history was fudge, and that the shop, the good, old, honest, despised shop, was the foundation, and not the restoration at all, of the House; and fancy a Membling asked to turn a guest into a room where he might, and very likely would, be informed by the purchaser of Membling Hall how his money was made. 'We have,' the Squire might have reasoned, 'a highly respectable family ghost. But there are reasons why that ghost should be kept in the family, and if it have disclosures to make or garrulous reminiscences to prattle upon, let these things be conveyed to the ear of a member of the family only. Or, as the ghost shows no inclination to leave his own room, let there be no disclosures at all. There is at least no occasion to invite revelations about the shop.'

The least ghostly time in the whole day, I take it, is the afternoon. No one expects even a medium to have any luck in the afternoon. *Séances* are always conducted after dark; old-fashioned wizards used to conjure up spirits at midnight; if devils, spectres, *lutins,* hobgoblins lasted till the morning, they were gone at all events by dawn. The 'garish light of day' is painful to supernatural eyes; they wink when it begins; they wink horribly if they have to endure it many minutes; long, long before noon they are away and in hiding. Who would have thought, then, that old Membling would have played the tricks he did, actually in the afternoon? You shall hear.

It was an afternoon in January—in the first week of the year. Snow was spread upon the fields, though it had melted on the roads; there was a gentle mist rising from the earth, through which the sun was shining feebly, a blurred circle of pale glory without warmth. But the sun was already sinking, and the pale winter twilight was going to begin, the mist and the white snow making it lighter than usual and yet ghostly, if one can use the word of a four-o'clock appearance—an afternoon-tea-time manifestation. The light was strange.

Jack Dalmahoy and Laura, after luncheon, sat together, talking of the little nothings which please young lovers. Presently the conversation flagged. Then some young and sprightly devil, seeing the chance of doing a little mischief by firing Jack's imagination, which had at the moment nothing to work upon (being tired of pretending imaginary perfections in his Laura), whispered in his ear that it would be something to pay a visit to the haunted room. 'The very thing!' cried Jack with alacrity.

'What is the very thing, Jack?' asked Laura, looking up with surprise.

'My dear girl,' he said, 'let us go this afternoon; go, beg the key, we will pay a visit to the haunted room !'

Laura hesitated.

'You know, dear girl,' said her lover, 'that you are yourself as curious to visit the room as I myself.'

'I have seen it,' she replied, 'and I heard——'

'Yes, Laura.' Jack had heard the story before. 'I perfectly remember. But we shall only open the door and look in. Go, dear, and ask your father for the key.'

The Squire gave his consent with some reluctance. He even returned with his daughter, bearing the key with as much respect as if it were the key of a city's gates, such as that which the citizens of a mediæval town used to bring out when they had eaten up their last rat.

'Here is the key,' he said solemnly; 'if you merely open the door and look in, no harm will be done, I should think. As the sun is setting, you might, even, if you please, go in. The injunction was that no one was to go in except after dark, and alone. But Laura may be considered an exception.'

Jack said that if he went in Laura should go with him, and that, as regards respect, he would look on the room as the family vault. Laura said he meant, she presumed, the church, not the vault.

First he oiled the key, which was rusty; then, accompanied by Laura, he turned it in the lock, and with some difficulty, because, he said, it was like some fellow pushing on the other side. He succeeded in opening it.

Could the 'fellow,' Laura thought, with a shudder, be her revered ancestor ?

When the door was open Jack forgot his promise, and stepped inside, looking about him curiously.

It was a long, low room, lighted by three narrow windows looking west, and reaching from floor to ceiling. It was most curiously furnished. For beside one window there was a table furnished exactly like one of those used by working watch-makers, with glasses in bone frames such as they stick in their eye when they look at a watch, and, observing a piece of dust, which they blow away and thereby release the machinery, declare that the watch requires cleaning, which will be eight-and-six. By such subtleties was the fortune of the Memblings commenced. Lamps, jets for gas, low stools, trays containing portions—dissected bones —of watches, small brushes and dusters, themselves covered with dust, now covered this table. Before the next window stood a lathe with tools, 'chunks,' and wheel. Before the next was another table, larger than the first, and covered with books, papers, mathematical instruments and drawings. 'My great-grandfather,' said Laura, thinking of the mythical and almost disbelieved shop of which even the younger members of the family were somehow conscious, 'was in his day a great mechanician.'

'What did he hang the walls with peacocks' feathers for?' asked Jack.

It was a strange thing : one side of the room was given over to a watchmaker's table, a lathe, and books on mechanics ; the other side was decorated with everything bizarre, as if the old man had resolved on gratifying his own taste without consulting the taste of the age. A Persian carpet lay on the floor ; there was a broad sofa on which he had often s'ept, covered with costly skins, a chair, also covered with skins, stood facing it ; common tobacco pipes and a common tobacco jar stood upon the plain mantelshelf, on which were such trifles as pots of glue and paste, glasses which suggested the 'rummer' of a country public-house, a spirit-case open, a note-book, and and an umbrella. The fireplace itself was a beautiful specimen of costly brass-work and tiles, there were carved cabinets very precious, filled with china, though the old man died before the great china revival was born, and there were pictures worth crying over, so delightful were they. The whole of that side of the room was covered with peacocks' feathers attached one over the other to the wall. The ceiling of the room was of polished oak, dark and deep, relieved with a little gold. The effect of the pale wintry light falling upon their splendours was very strange. Laura clasped her lover by the arm and gasped. Then she looked round and shrieked.

Six years before this, when she stood within the room, she had seen the door closing slowly, *and of its own accord,* before her. Now as she turned she saw that the same thing was happening again, but that it was too late ; for with a heavy, grating noise the door shut closely, while, also of its own accord, there slowly fell behind it a heavy wooden bar.

As the bar fell there was a sound as of a deep sigh. Then all was silent.

The pair, thus strangely made prisoners, looked at each other with pale faces. Even the man, as brave a fellow as may be, saw with a terror which froze his blood this great bar lifted without visible hands, and falling slowly as if guided into its place. He rushed to the door and tried to lift it. Its free end was lying in a strong clamp closed by some spring. He could not lift it out, nor could he by any strength tear it away and open the door.

Another shriek from Laura called him to her side.

'Fingers,' she cried, 'fingers at my throat ! Jack, save me save me !'

Jack took her in his arms and soothed her. 'Nothing,' he said, 'can hurt us. Whatever it is, nothing *shall* hurt you till it first— oh, Lord !'

He stopped, because a breath of ice-cold air blew violently into his face, and again the solemn sigh was heard. Laura sank upon the floor, in a terror the like of which she had never imagined or suspected. Jack lifted her gently and laid her upon the chair beside the fireplace.

B B

What next? Laura held Jack by the hand, imploring him not to leave her—not to leave her alone. He stood beside her, his heart beating, his brain afire with wonder and terror. What next?

A third time they heard the sigh as of one in deep trouble and perhaps anger: again soft fingers touched Laura's throat, and again cold airs vexed their cheeks. Meantime it was growing darker: the sun was quite gone down; the short winter twilight was deepening into gloom, and the snow-fields through the windows stretched white and cold.

Then there began a ringing of bells and a beating of drums. Jack held Laura more tightly and whispered to her to be of good cheer; nothing, he declared with a positiveness which he did not feel, should or could hurt her while he was there.

The bells seemed all round them, as if they were being rung in their ears; they were soft and melodious bells, not harsh and strident, and the drums, like the bells, were soft; their rolling was as that of muffled kettle-drums, and when they stopped for a moment the heavy sigh was heard, as if lamenting the necessity for making all this noise. The bells rang and the drums beat for an hour and a half, as it seemed to the terror-stricken couple, prisoners in the room, who were fain to listen. In truth, they rang and beat for about five minutes, and then they stopped suddenly, and that dreadful, unseen person began to sigh again, heavily. Also Laura shrieked, because the fingers began to play again at her throat.

Of all forms of supernatural visitations, that of fingers at the throat has always seemed to me the least desirable. The apparition of a sheeted ghost, with or without chains, the squeezing of hands left inadvertently outside the sheets, the cold breathing upon the sleeping brow, the groaning behind wainscot walls, the dragging of chains, the sighing or sobbing by the bedside, the shying about of crockery, the shrieking in the garden, the upheaval of heavy furniture, the creaking on the stairs, the lurking in unsuspected places, the unreasonable claim to property in a place after you have become a ghost— all these things are effective, though perhaps overdone. New ghost machinery has to be invented if the popular imagination is to be fired, and I take it that the miserable falling off in ghosts during the last fifty years must be attributed mainly to the weariness of the imagination, which refuses any longer to be stirred by old-fashioned modes of spiritual manifestations. Even rapping has had its day, and one sees no hope for ghosts in the future, unless they are prepared to bring trustworthy information as to the rules and regulations *d'outre-mer*. Then, indeed, there would be so great a run upon ghosts that the good old times would come back again, and many a musty family ghost, long since laughed at, scorned and forgotten, would return, to bloom and blossom again among a curious and credulous posterity.

But to have one's throat felt, touched, and fingered by ghostly fingers! That is, if you please, a thing which in no way attracts the curiosity or stimulates the imagination. Quite the contrary; it simply terrifies.

Laura shrieked and would have fainted, had she thought it would be of the least use. But she was too much terrified for fainting. In real moments of crisis, in supreme moments, as the prigs say, one is too much in earnest to faint. One may faint comfortably when a tooth is pulled out, and feel all the better for it afterwards, but when a more serious operation is performed no one thinks about fainting, and takes chloroform instead.

'N—n—othing,' said Jack, with less heart in his tone than he could have wished, 'c—can hurt you while I am here.'

Yet there were fingers at her throat, and just then Laura would have sacrificed all the honour and glory of the family ghost could she have found herself safe outside that dreadful door with the bar let down to keep them in. Or, suppose her Ancestor had appeared, hungering, ravening for a life, I believe she would have given up her lover in the same spirit of duty as prompted Agamemnon to sacrifice Iphigenia, so as to get out of the mess with as much ease and safety as possible. But all that they had heard and seen were mere trifles, bagatelles, skittles, apple tart, compared to what they were about to see.

Suddenly the bells which had been ringing a melodious peal, and the kettle-drums which had been beating a muffled harmony, clashed and clanged in a horrific discord, at the hearing of which Laura moaned and groaned, while Jack, clutching her hand as if for his own safety, murmured mechanically, 'N—n—n—nothing c—c—c—an h—h—h—hur—' and here his jaws stuck and he said no more.

For at the clang and clash of the bells the curtains fell before the windows, and they were in darkness absolute.

It seemed next as if the end of the room was taken away, and another room opened to their eyes.

There was nothing at all in this room, but it was lighted by a large window at the end, and a long narrow window at the side. The glimmer from the snow without gave sufficient light for the intruding pair to see the things which presented themselves.

The bells stopped, the drums stopped. Then there began a wailing plaintive music, a tune never heard on earth, which seemed, like the bells and the drums, to be played around them, above them, below them. And while this weird and ghostly tune was slowly played, there appeared suddenly, not, said Laura afterwards, as if they sprang from the ground or dropped from the skies, but suddenly, as if they came from nowhere, three skeletons. In the dim light one could discern their shadowy forms, the lean fingers with which they pointed, the long bony legs with which they danced—they actually danced !—the hollow, eyeless sockets and grinning teeth of the skulls. As they came, so they disappeared, as suddenly, as silently.

But the music, the supernatural, weird, and ghostly music, went on, and then—ah ! then—the final manifestion appeared. For, as if he had stepped from the wall, Laura saw her great-grandfather—

the Actual Family Ghost itself—walk slowly, and as if with difficulty, across the room, and as he neared the opposite wall, he
turned, faced his great-granddaughter, and with his white locks
and white beard faintly visible, he seemed to hold up a warning
forefinger and disappeared.

Then the music ceased ; the room of the ghost and skeletons
disappeared ; the curtains which had fallen before the windows
were drawn back, and there was silence.

' Jack !' said Laura.

'G—g—g—ood heavens !' cried Jack.

' Are we living, Jack ?'

'G—g—g—ghosts !' said Jack.

'Do you think it is over, Jack ?' asked Laura.

'N—n—n—othing——' began Jack, when Laura, looking
round, saw to her delight that there was a gleam of artificial light in
the doorway, which showed that the door was open.   She rushed
to the place ; the great bar was gone ; the door was ajar ; Laura
yelled for help, rushed through, and fell headlong in the passage.
The cause of her fall, I am ashamed to say, was no other than Jack
himself, who rushed after her.   Both fell down, like Jack and Jill,
and lay sprawling together.

That evening Laura did not appear at dinner ; her mother sent
for the doctor, and she was ordered to bed,   Somebody sat up all
night with her, and in the morning she was delirious : the system,
said the doctor, had sustained a severe shock.

As for Jack, he ordered his things to be got ready at once, and
drove straight back to Colchester, leaving word that he was ordered
back on regimental duty.   But when he got there he was fain
to drink so much soda-and-brandy that he too, like Laura, was put
to bed.

Thus, for two or three days, the story of the dreadful apparition
at Membling Hall never got about.

When Laura got better she told the story, sitting up in bed, to
her sisters : she was a girl of a fine imagination and an eye to dramatic
situation, therefore the story lost nothing in the telling ; the sighs,
the sobs, the cold breath, the fingers at the throat, the skeletons,
the bells, and the weird music, with the dread vision of her great-
grandfather at the end, were all duly narrated.   The sisters told
their father.   The Squire enjoined secrecy, but left a corner open
in the case of trusted friends ; everyone had a trusted friend.
Therefore, before Jack returned, he was assailed on all sides by
questions about the ghost of Membling Hall, and had to explain,
although with fear of making himself ridiculous, that it was a
real, unmistakable ghost—a devil of a ghost, accompanied by every
kind of row and appearance calculated to shake a fellow's nerves
and make him feel uncomfortable.   Jack was not a man of lively
imagination, but the things he had seen were so extraordinary that
he had only to tell them exactly as he had seen them.   And it
would be wonderful, had we the time, to relate the two forms which

the story took when related by Laura the imaginative, and by Jack the matter-of-fact.

Think, however, of the pride of the Memblings at this proof incontrovertible of their family ghost. Where was there, anywhere in England, a house with such a ghost, so complete in all its parts, so provided with machinery, material gear, and supernatural assistants? Was it not a great honour to them that their ghost did not appear unattended, but was provided with a body-guard, or spirit-ward, of three dancing skeletons? Was there any other ghost at whose bidding bells would ring and drums would beat? It was like a royal progress. Josiah Membling's spirit was welcomed, as he himself would have wished, like a Lord Mayor on Lord Mayor's day. Did ever man hear tell of any other ghost who could command, so to speak, a private orchestra of his own, to play music at his coming!

The mere telling of the story became a fearful joy to Laura and to the faithful Jack. It was a dreadful experience to have undergone; but, like a shipwreck on a desert island, once worried through, it became a grand and splendid distinction. Laura's sisters envied her: Laura's brothers envied her. The Squire was proud of her; the story brought the greatest credit to the family: Laura might have adopted the motto of Queen Elizabeth, *Dux femina facti*.

She became an extremely interesting person, and began to cultivate the sadness which belongs, somehow, to all persons privileged to hold communication with the outer world. She sat in shadowy corners, or in the dim firelight without a lamp, in the long and dark room called the library, where she told her story with clasped hands, while the light of the fire reddened her pale cheek and showed up the luminous depths of her large soft eyes; her audience gathered round her catching breathlessly at her words, and looking over their shoulders on the chance of seeing the spectre behind them. But he never came. 'My great-grandfather,' said Laura, 'will never, I am persuaded, leave the room in which he has chosen to dwell. Let us have no fear. Indeed,' she added, smiling sadly, 'why should we fear? He who restored the fortunes of the House, and is good enough to watch over it after his passing away, can hardly be feared. He may hear, no doubt he does hear, all that is said and done in the Hall, therefore let us always speak of him with the Reverence and Awe which he deserves.'

They came from all parts of the country to hear the story. Laura was obliged to be at home every afternoon. Jack was not allowed to leave her chair, in order to be ready to corroborate any statement. He shone as the lesser light, not being permitted to tell the story himself because he was not a good *raconteur*, and because a certain sterility of imagination forbade those developments of facts which are necessary in a perfect ghost story. But he could put in a word by way of proof, and was immensely useful as the Witness. A ghost, like a miracle, requires the testimony of two or more credible persons.

'I shall never,' said Laura, 'never again bear to hear the least frivolous or scoffing allusion to the appearance of Spirits. The subject will always be associated in my mind, with a Manifestation which was truly Awful.'

'Awfully Awful,' said Jack, behind her chair.

'I cannot understand, now, how I lived through it. Indeed, I must have died with terror, had it not been for the invincible fortitude of Jack, who, I will say in his presence, behaved with perfect courage and reverence throughout. What reassured me first, and convinced me that no harm was intended, was the celestial music which preceded the most awe-inspiring sight, the last scene of all.'

'What was it like, the music?' whispered a young lady.

'Like a waltz tune,' said Jack.

'Not the least like a waltz tune,' said Laura. 'You might as well call a recitative from Handel a waltz tune : better, in fact, because Handel's music is the work of a man, whereas this—oh! this that we heard—whose work was it?' She lifted hands and eyes, and remained silent in ecstatic contemplation of the ceiling. 'My dear,' she continued after an interval, during which the gentlemen thought they were in church and looked into their hats, 'it is impossible to describe that music. It fell upon the soul some utterance of Power : we were awed, not terrified by it——'

'It was something like a musical box,' said Jack.

'It was nothing of the sort, sir,' Laura interrupted. 'The sound was like no earthly music. It was tuneful, but no human voice could reproduce the tune : the harmonies were too subtle and too profound for human art ; the instruments may have been in form like our own, but of a sweetness, of a force, which I could never, never hope to convey to your imagination.'

'Made a devil of a row,' Jack whispered, in corroboration, to a man beside him.

'Was there any singing?' asked another lady. 'Oh! if they had sung a hymn—*what* an addition to our choir it would have been!'

'I heard no words,' Laura sighed. 'That is, I could distinguish none. But it seemed to me as if, far off—oh! far, far away—there was a choir of voices upraised in harmony.'

'One fellow groaning——' Jack began, but was instantly checked as Laura went on——

'The music preceded the Dance of Death '—Laura stopped and trembled—'nothing more terrible could be conceived. As the skeletons danced, pointing their long bony fingers at us, they seemed to warn us of the flight of time. Their aspect was not forbidding, nor were their gestures angry.'

'Grinned at us,' said Jack, 'like the very——'

'Could,' interrupted Laura, hastily, 'could such a pageant, such a spiritual apparition, have suggested the "Danse Macabre" to Holbein and the mediæval painters?'.

'Like a hornpipe,' said Jack. 'Never saw such a lively lot : double-shuffle, heel-and-toe, walk-round, all complete.'

'How long did the dance continue ? ' asked a visitor, shuddering.

'We took no count of time,' replied Laura. 'I do not suppose, that, as the clocks went, we were in the room for ten minutes ; yet what we saw must have taken about a day and a half, at least. How long, Jack, do you think the bells were ringing ? '

Jack shook his head, and said he thought they were never going to stop.

'Then,' continued Laura, 'there were the sighings and the sobbings, the cold winds, the beating of the drums, the playing of the music before the Terrible Dance. Hour after hour passed away : we were ravished out of ourselves : we were lost in wonder and awe : we felt no hunger : our pulses stopped, and the beating of our hearts ! We were without any fear, were we not, Jack ? '

'Quite,' replied Jack. 'I was never more composed in my life.'

'But there was more, was there not ? ' asked another visitor. 'We heard that you saw the spirit of your Ancestor himself.'

Laura sank her voice to a whisper.

'You heard aright,' she said solemnly. 'The manifestations ended with no less an appearance than that of my revered Ancestor himself, the Restorer of the House—even the Second Founder.' She spoke as if Julius Cæsar himself or even King Alfred had been the first of the Memblings.

'How—how did he appear ? ' gasped her audience.

'He was dressed in a long dressing-gown, such as he usually wore in his lifetime.'

'And yet,' murmured a triumphant spiritualist, one of the audience, 'they say that ghosts have no clothes. Absurd ! Matter, as has been proved over and again, can always be represented visibly by spirits. Pray go on, Miss Membling. I have never during all my investigations met with a more interesting experience than this of yours. It will confound every sceptic.'

'Dressed in his long gown,' Laura resumed, 'he moved slowly, almost painfully, across the room. He appeared suffering from the debility of extreme old age——'

'Quite so—quite so ! ' the spiritualist rubbed his hands. 'I have always maintained that they appear as they left the world, no older and no younger. Pray go on.'

'As he moved he turned his face towards us and smiled. You saw him smile, Jack, as plainly as I did ? '

'Well,' said Jack, with hesitation, 'he certainly wagged his head, and I saw his beard wobble, but I can't honestly say that I saw him smile.'

'He would not smile for a stranger,' said the spiritualist.

'The most benignant countenance : the sweetest smile : the kindest look in his eyes : with long silvery locks and a white beard. As he disappeared, he raised his hand as if to bestow his benediction upon us. You saw that, Jack ? '

'Oh, yes ! he lifted his hand.'

'I think, but I am not sure, that I heard him murmur a blessing as he disappeared.'

'Did he, now,'—asked the scientific explorer of Ghostland—'did he sink into the ground, or did he ascend into the air ? '

'He disappeared,' said Laura. 'He seemed to touch the wall and to vanish.'

'He came out of one wall,' said Jack, 'and went into the other wall.'

'And did you,' asked the spiritualist, 'hear the Blessing ? '

'No, I did not,' replied Jack.

'The Blessing,' explained the scientific specialist, 'was for the House alone. You heard nothing, then ? '

'Why,' Jack said, considering, 'he shuffled a bit with his feet as if his slippers were uneasy.'

And so it went on, day after day, Laura receiving the visitors and telling the story over and over again. Jack was neither imaginative, nor was he properly impressed. He had seen things and heard things : that was undeniable. But he drew no conclusions. He was thus a foil to Laura, and by his very downright matter-of-fact doggedness he corroborated her statements. The story, little by little, improved : the heavenly music was, in a few days, provided with a heavenly choir ; the bells were a peal ; the dance of death was a procession of skeletons, who danced as they crossed the room, in number about a hundred and fifty ; the Benediction of the Ancestor was pronounced in a solemn whisper which could not reach the grosser ear of Jack, but was perfectly audible to Laura. The fair narrator herself became daily more penetrated with the greatness and grandeur of her position : she also, to Jack's disgust, became more spiritualised, tried to live on nothing, grew certainly pale and thin, and ceased to take the same interest as of old in the little tendernesses which her lover was willing to lavish upon her.

It was agreed, by the advice of the spiritualist, that the history should be written down—soberly, he said, and with due attention to dates, times, and the corroborative testimony of Jack—and printed, for the good of the world and the solace of mankind. Laura spent, therefore, a fortnight in the production of what was called a 'Plain Statement.' Her intimate friends observed that the written narrative did not quite correspond with her former statements, and Jack owned that he had not heard the choir singing hymns, nor seen the Blessing with both hands. But these things mattered little in the face of so tremendous and undoubted a series of apparitions.

The Squire gave his consent to have the story printed—but, he said, for private circulation only. Let the knowledge of the Ghost be whispered abroad : that could not, he supposed, be avoided : but the actual facts concerned only the immediate friends of the House, and not the general public, whose curiosity he, for one, was not disposed to gratify by relating private events, and the experiences, however singular, of his daughter. The 'Narrative' or 'Plain Statement' was accordingly printed on the finest and creamiest of toned paper, with a portrait of the Ancestor. The date of his death was not stated, but from the mediæval appearance of the face and the cut of the beard, in which the limner improved on the original oil painting (that of Josiah Membling as a Common Councilman), the venerable Ancestor might have belonged to the thirteenth or fourteenth century. All this greatly added to the glory of the family, and tended to confirm their position as belonging to the County. With what face could any one sneer at people as new comers whose ancestors remained in their old rooms, and appeared to give benedictions to the female branches of their posterity? Could the Howards, the Courtenays, the Montmorencies, the Lusignans, expect more?

The 'Narrative' off her hands, Laura began to descend slowly from the higher spiritual levels and to talk of ordinary things in her ordinary manner, so that Jack Dalmahoy plucked up courage and renewed his courtship at the point where the ancestral spirit had broken it off. He was by this time growing weary of the worship or cult of the old ghost, and it bored him to be perpetually recalling the dancing skeletons and the shadowy figure with the long white hair. Then, it was annoying for a plain man to be constantly invited to remember a heavenly chorus, a benediction, a warning look, or a sweet and gracious smile. Therefore he was anxious to get his courtship over and to carry away his bride. When he mentioned the desirability of naming the day, Laura declared at first that nothing should ever persuade her to leave a house possessed of so many and such rare blessings. Jack argued that if a girl gets engaged she means to have her own house. Laura replied that she had not, on entering into the engagement, foreseen that she should receive the benediction of her Ancestor. Jack responded that the benediction did not tell her that she was not to get married, 'unless,' he added, with unusual bitterness, 'you are going to marry your great-grandfather yourself? Don't believe——' He stopped short here, thinking it would be well not to say anything about the heavenly choir or the gracious smile till after his marriage.

Laura reflected, sweetly holding her hands clasped and her head a little on one side in the attitude of reflection. The thought crossed her mind that it would be a pity to give up such a good-natured, good-looking, and well-to-do lover for the sake of a ghost whom, perhaps, she would never see again. And presently she murmured softly, 'Jack, do you think my Ancestor would come with us to our new home and abide with us?'

'Oh, Lord!' cried Jack in a voice of such genuine consternation that Laura forgot her affectation and burst into a hearty laugh, after which Jack found no difficulty in getting her to talk about a day.

They were to be married after Lent, that was agreed upon, and after an infinite amount of discussion it was further covenanted that the day should be the last day of April. This gave them a clear five weeks for preparation, and Jack was ordered back to his garrison work to be out of the way until he should be wanted to take his part in the approaching ceremony.

The excitement of the time that followed kept Laura's thoughts a good deal from her ghost, whose home was not further intruded upon. By some curious current of feeling, assisted, no doubt, by Laura's appropriation of the family ghost to herself, it was generally considered that the ghost might feel offended at the departure of the one member of the family to whom he had condescended to reveal himself, one lady going so far as to prophesy disaster. And when it came, in way and manner as shall be presently set forth, she only said it was what she expected and always said would happen, and that if Laura had not been bent upon going away, no doubt evil spirits would not have been allowed to work their wicked will, and all this shame would not have fallen upon the family.

Among the members of the Dalmahoy family was a first cousin of Jack's, a young fellow of an inquiring mind, who was reading at Cambridge for mathematical honours. He was invited to be best man to his cousin on the joyful occasion, and joined the wedding party at Membling Hall two or three days before the auspicious morning. The house was quite full, and the usual excitement of looking at the wedding presents, flirting with the bridemaids, dancing, and the rest of it, passed the time more agreeably for Mr. George Dalmahoy than if he had been dining in the college hall and spending his evenings in an undergraduate's room. Of course almost the first thing which he heard of was the ghost, and this immediately fired his imagination.

He read the 'Narrative.' Then he cross-examined Jack, and elicited from him that the superstructure, so to speak—the heavenly choir and the rest of it—was an addition made by Laura herself after the event; that is to say, Jack neither saw nor heard any of it. On the other hand, there could be no manner of doubt that the 'Narrative' was substantially true, and that very strange things had happened.

Mr. George Dalmahoy determined that he too would, if possible, witness these things. Why should not the ghost appear to him as well as to his cousin? As for the Benediction, he dismissed it with contempt. Jack had seen an old man's figure, bent, with streaming white hair, 'shuffling,' as he put it, across the floor. That was by itself quite remarkable enough. 'No need,' said George, 'of any benedictions; enough to be able to show himself, lucky old ghost!' He considered himself an expert in the art of investigating stories of ghosts. He was, to begin with, entirely incredulous, and, in the second place, he knew that it is nonsense to deny phenomena. Raps, for instance, are certainly heard, ears are boxed in the dark, noses pulled, heads banged. He had once inflicted unspeakable mortification on a medium by beginning the raps himself before she was ready, and spelling out dreadful messages which she did not understand ; and on another occasion, when a spirit had been good enough to 'incarnate' herself, this untrustworthy person lit a match and disclosed no other than the medium herself dancing about wrapped in a newspaper.　He had also written an article on the subject for a college magazine, and had a shelf full of books treating of spiritualism.　He was thus fully prepared for an encounter with the Ancestor of the Memblings, and ardently longed to begin.

He first approached the subject with Laura, asking her, reverently, if one could be allowed to visit the haunted chamber after dark.　She replied with emotion that no one with her consent should be allowed to open the door of that room at all.　She considered that to disturb its occupant was pardonable only when done by inadvertence and ignorance, as happened to herself and Jack. As for a stranger presuming to do so, that, she said, would most likely draw upon his head the most fatal consequences.　She could only compare the daring of such a deed with the audacity of the ancient king, who drew the lightning down from heaven and was killed by it as a punishment.

Thus rebuffed, George Dalmahoy went to head-quarters and sought the Squire in his library.　Mr. Membling was an easy man, a little touchy about his ancient birth, but now in excellent spirits and on the best of terms with everybody, in consequence of the highly creditable match his daughter was making.　Naturally he was disposed to receive all the bridegroom's people with great civility.

It was after luncheon, and a glass or two of burgundy had disposed the Squire to benevolence towards all mankind.　He was seated before the fire, his legs crossed, his hands folded, prepared for the sleep which sometimes overtakes middle-aged gentlemen after a comfortable midday meal.　To him George stole softly, and taking a chair by the fire, turned the conversation adroitly on ancient families.　Then he began to talk about the peculiarities of families, their ways, their distinctive marks, their little characteristic possessions, how a stutter distinguishes the sons of one house, and a distinctive birth-mark the sons of another ; how in one house no eldest son ever succeeds, and in another ill luck pursues all the daughters ; how a Banshee belongs to one family, a White Lady to another, and a little child to a third.　'As to your own house,' said George, 'we have all heard of your ancient ghost.'　George put it as if the ghost had been established many centuries.

The Squire laughed pleasantly.

'Yes, we have our ghost, and I assure you, Mr. Dalmahoy, that we are rather proud of the distinction, as one may call it.'

'A distinction truly !　Particularly so well authenticated a ghost as it is.　You keep the chamber locked, I believe ?'

'Yes.　You see, we would not have the maids frightened, nor would we—perhaps you think us superstitious—disturb the occupant.'

l

'Quite so—quite so,' said George. 'However, ghosts only walk at night, and as there is no possible fear of disturbing the occupant by daylight, I wish you would lend me the key; I should like just to look round the room, if you have no objection.'

'Well, you see,' replied the Squire, 'the fact is, we have rather a strong objection. The last words of the—the spirit—were that no one was to dare enter the room unless alone and after dark.'

'I respect your feeling,' said George; 'yet I think it would be most injudicious to invade the privacy of the room—after dark. Everything that we know, my dear sir'—here he assumed the character of a believer—'everything that we have learned respecting apparitions, the manners and customs, the preferences, so to speak, of the outer world, shows us that its inhabitants, when they reside among us, are in some way prevented from feeling our intrusion or even our presence in the daytime. They may be sleeping; they may be'—here he dropped his voice and paused—'elsewhere. Their power to be seen and heard is given them for use after dark alone.'

'That seems very true,' said the Squire; 'it was after dark that Laura——'

'So that, in asking you to hand me the key of the room,' his visitor went on, 'I am really doing nothing more than seeking to gratify a curiosity—call it idle, or say it springs from reverence—a desire, in fact, only to see the theatre of these curious and unique manifestations.'

The Squire, moved by these words and by the benevolence of burgundy, and recognising the spirit in which they were uttered, went to his safe and produced the key, adjuring his guest, at the same time, should he see anything, to leave the room immediately.

With a cheerful mien George Dalmahoy proceeded to the haunted chamber.

He experienced the same difficulty in opening the room which had been felt by his cousin. The key turned pretty easily, but the door stuck. And when he pushed it open there was heard a grating noise which did not seem natural to the nature of a door.

We have seen what manner of room was the haunted chamber. But when it was last visited it was in the pale twilight of a January day. Now, at the end of April, the sun was shining brightly through the windows, and the room was cheerful. Certainly not at all the sort of time for a ghost to walk. Spectres shun sunshine, as the copy-books might say. George looked about him with a little disappointment. A curiously furnished room: that was all.

His disappointment did not last long: a creaking sound behind made him turn round. A large bar was slowly descending across the door. The progress was slow, but it finished by dropping into its place: the door was closed. George tried to lift the bar. It was immovable.

'Good!' he said. 'This is how Jack began. Can it be that the Ancestor is going to take an afternoon dander round the room?'

Apparently he was, because the closing of the door was followed by the ringing of bells, beating of drums, sighs, a breath of cold air which had so terrified his cousin.

While he was listening and watching—in some disquietude, it must be owned—he felt something delicate and light touching his cheek ; he turned quickly. Nothing.

'Bells,' he said, 'there certainly are, and drums ; and there is a noise which Tom said was sobbing ; it seems to me like—Hallo!'

Again the gentle touch upon his cheek ; this time he put up his hand as one catches at a troublesome fly, and caught—one of the peacock's feathers. He then observed that several of them were slowly lifting themselves up and down.

'This,' said George Dalmahoy, 'is more curious than the bells.'

Mounting on a chair he examined the place where the feather was attached to the wall. To his great surprise he found that it was fitted into a small brass tube, and that the tube itself was moving slowly up and down, carrying the feather with it.

'Very odd,' said George. 'It was not a ghostly finger at my throat but a feather : and the feather is not lifted by a ghostly hand, but by a brass tube. And what the devil lifts the brass tube ? I suppose,' he added after a pause, 'that the same thing lifts the brass tube which rings the bells and beats the drums. Is it the Ancestor ? Would he come if I called him names ?'

It seemed as if the Ancestor must have heard these irreverent remarks, because at that moment the wall at the end of the room seemed suddenly to disappear ; the bells ceased, and music of some kind was heard.

'All this,' said George, feeling more than a little afraid, 'is most wonderful, and just as Jack reeled it all out. To be sure, I could not make out how he could have invented it. What next ? Oh, Lord !'

For at that moment the skeletons appeared and began to dance.

The young man's knees knocked together for a moment and his cheek turned pale. Then he rallied his courage and 'made for' the skeletons.

They were capering with the most grotesque and extraordinary agility, legs and arms moving all at once, skulls shaking and nodding ; even the backbone twisting, or at least seeming to twist. George presently seized one of the arms.

'Gad,' he cried, 'it's real bones—with wire in the joints—real ribs—and'—here he laughed aloud—'they are all three hanging by strings !'

He contemplated this phenomenon with curiosity, but no terror.

Then the lower panels of the wall beside him opened, and there came out the figure of a man.

'Aha !' said George, 'here is the Ancestor ! How are you, old boy ?'

The figure was dressed in a long dressing-gown, and had on silk stockings and old-fashioned knee-breeches. The knees were bent and the figure stooping, and as it moved slowly and by jerks, it seemed to be on the point of falling to pieces. George stopped in front of it, and began calmly to feel and punch it.

'You're stuffed with sawdust,' he said contemptuously, 'and you are dropping to bits, and the moths have got into your poor old sleeve ; and the white wool is falling off your poor old pate, and your mask is hanging by a thread. You an Ancestor ? You ridiculous old MUG !'

The miserable ghost made no reply, but continued its journey across the room. When he reached the opposite wall the panels opened to admit him, and he disappeared.

'This is the Ancestor !' said George, in great enjoyment. 'Shut up, you with your dancing, you poor old skeletons ! Nobody cares about you. This is the benevolent Ancestor ! This is his Benediction ! This is his sweet and winning smile ! Ho! ho! ho !'

Just then the music ceased : the skeletons disappeared—that is to say, they flew up into the ceiling : there was a sigh as if somebody was tired and glad that the job was over : George observed that what he had taken for a disappearance of part of the wall was really only the folding back of the middle of a wooden partition wall cutting off one end of the room. He also observed that the bar of the door was lifting as slowly as it had fallen.

All was over, therefore.

He had seen the family ghost : it was a big doll, dropping slowly to pieces with age, damp, and the ravages of moths ; he had seen the fearful procession or Dance of Death, 'the gibbering skeletons succeeding one another in swift succession, each playing its antics as it passed, and beckoning to us with lean and bony fingers.' (Extract from the ' Narrative.')

Well, there were three musty skeletons let down from a trap in the ceiling by strings or wires, the lifting and dropping of which produced their contortions and dancings. He had heard the ' celestial orchestra, faint, though complete in all its parts, playing music not to be described, yet ever to be remembered, accompanied by a choir of faint sweet voices, singing what seemed a hymn of praise.' (Extract from ' Narrative.') Yes, he had heard it. ' By Gad,' he said, ' it was a musical-box, and it played an old-fashioned slow *trois-temps* ! As for choir and heavenly voices—fudge !'

He had heard the bells and the drums. Yes ; there were bells and drums ; who could have rung the bells and beaten the drums ?

The bar was up : he could go : the show was over.

Yet, what did it mean ?

George went to one of the windows and looked out, thinking. Beside him stood a table, of which we know. He took up one or two of the things : they were instruments used in making and mending a watch. The table was an old, rough, black bench,

which, in fact, had been the old man's bench during all the years
of his working life. ' I remember,' said George, ' one of them
made his money in trade : he was a watchmaker.' Then he saw
before the next window a lathe with all the appliances, and a carpenter's bench fitted up with tools. Half-made things, rounded
blocks, pulleys, small light chains, lay about the bench. ' Old man
was a carpenter and turner too, I suppose,' said George. Then he
went to the next table. This was covered with books and papers.
' Old man read mechanics,' said George. He took up one of the
sheets covered with drawings. Then he took up another. Then
he looked round him and nodded. Then he laughed. Then he
looked at his watch. Then he went to the carpenter's bench, took
out some tools, and proceeded to work.

It was a quarter of an hour before he finished, and already past
five o'clock. He rubbed his hands with the greatest satisfaction.
' This,' he said, ' is the best day's work I have ever done.'

Then he opened the door and stepped out.

' Holy Moses !' he cried, surprised into an exclamation which
cannot be justified, and yet must be considered pardonable when
one has to tell what he saw.

Now it came to pass that, just as the bells began to ring in the
haunted chamber, Laura herself, accompanied by one of the bridemaids, passed by the door. What was her terror and astonishment
to hear the dread sound, only heard by herself, begin again ! ' He
calls me !' she cried, grasping her friend by the arm. ' He calls
me ; I must go !'

She rushed to the door, but could not open it.

' Can it be,' she gasped, ' that there is some one in the room ?
Is it Jack ? Oh, Katie, run, run to my father—he is in the library
—tell him to bring the key. . . . Ah ! it is in the lock—tell him to
come—to come quickly !'

On being awakened, Mr. Membling acknowledged that he had
lent the key to George Dalmahoy, and followed the bridemaid to
the door. By this time the greater part of the guests were
assembled on the spot, grouped round Laura, who stood gazing at
the door, her hand clasping the faithful Jack's. The bells were
certainly ringing and the drums beating : presently the sound of
music was heard.

' Hush !' said Laura. ' It is the heavenly music ; I hear the
voices of those who sing.'

She sank on her knees ; the other girls followed her example :
kneeling in a semicircle, reverential, but careful that their dresses
lay in becoming folds. An ignorant spectator might have thought
that they were rehearsing the ceremony of the next day. Behind
the kneeling girls stood some of the elder ladies and one or two
gentlemen. As for Jack, he stood, Laura still holding his hand,
visibly disconcerted. He had a round hat, having just come from
a walk, and when Laura implored him to kneel too, he compromised
by putting his head in his hat.

They continued to kneel during the whole time of the noises; when they had ceased, they heard a tapping and a hammering. So they went on kneeling, though all were getting anxious to see what would come of it. And it was into this group that George Dalmahoy plunged when he opened the door and uttered that rude and irreverent interjection.

Laura shrieked; they all sprang to their feet, and shrieked together like a chorus on the stage.

George looked in bewilderment. Then he laughed; he laughed long and loud.

' He is mad,' said Laura, suddenly.

George laughed louder still.

' Jack, this is dreadful,' said Laura.

The others stared in a sort of amazement; what could the man be laughing at? It was like a comic song of which only the singer sees the point. They all looked so bewildered, and Laura so awestruck and terrified, that George speedily ceased laughing. Indeed, the belief in the ghost was now so deep in everybody's heart that they had finally made up their minds that the rash young man, like one who inadvertently looked upon Artemis in the forest, had been slain by the angry Ancestor, or else, like him who chanced to meet great Pan, had been stricken by some madness. And lo! he was before them laughing like an idiot.

' Ladies and gentlemen,' said the young man, ' I have an important announcement to make. The ghost walks by day as well as by night. If you will follow me into the room, you shall see him for yourself. He is a most obliging ghost, and will do no harm to anybody.'

He laid his hand upon the handle of the door as he spoke.

They looked at each other.

' Oh,' cried Laura, 'this is dreadful! Jack, stop him! Mr. Dalmahoy, do not call others after you to their undoing! Oh! What shall we do? what shall we do?'

For now George pushed open the door and the wedding guests crowded after, Jack and Laura following with the rest. Last of all came the Squire, and upon his face there was a look of anxiety. He had a sense of impending evil.

' Spirit of my Ancestor!' cried Laura, sinking upon her knees, ' forgive them! Forgive us all! Let not this intrusion lead thee to revoke thy Benediction.'

Strange to say, this appeal produced no effect upon the young madman, who only laughed scornfully.

' You shall see him directly,' he said: ' you can then ask him yourself.'

At this moment the door shut noisily.

' Look at the bar,' said George; ' that is the first business; now we are shut in.'

They all looked at each other, after observing the descent of the bar.

'The whole secret lies in the bar,' he went on. 'Now look at this wall; you will see the peacock's feathers jumping up and down; if anybody is within reach, they will feel the light touch of ghostly fingers on their cheeks. Very fine business this, for a spectre in a country house.'

In fact this happened as he had foretold.

'Ghostly fingers, Jack,' said George to the joint author of the 'Narrative.' 'Next, bells and drums.'

They began; George pushed aside two panels and showed a bell ringing in each, and a small kettle-drum being beaten in each. The drum-sticks were attached to the frame of the drum by hinges, and were worked by some unknown machinery.

'Very fair business that,' said George. 'These are your church bells, Jack, ringing a regular peal. Two little hand bells, ladies and gentlemen. Next, the sighing and sobbing, with the cold breath.'

He opened another panel and disclosed a great pair of bellows pointed directly to the group of spectators. It began to heave up and down slowly with a noise like a hollow groaning, and the cold air was distinctly felt. 'The sigh of the grave and the breath of the tomb,' said George, again quoting from the 'Narrative.' 'You will next, ladies and gentlemen, observe—ah! there it is'—for then the partition fell back—'now the skeletons.' Here they appeared, and they really seemed to dance as if they had no heart left for the work, and were quite ashamed of themselves. 'Three of them—go and feel them, anybody—simple bones, hanging from the ceiling, out of which they fell, by strings. This is the grand procession where every . . . . eh, Jack?' He did not continue the extract from the 'Narrative,' because Laura was staring straight before her, an angry light in her eyes, and a flush upon her cheek.

'Next,' he went on, 'we have the Ancestor himself.' In fact, at that moment, the poor old doddering figure came out; he looked so palpably a stuffed doll in the machine, his face was so evidently a mask, his hair was so certainly white wool, his knees were so groggy with loss of sawdust, and his whole appearance was so inexpressibly moth-eaten, shabby, and woe-begone, that it was impossible to resist laughing at him. Everybody laughed, including the Squire, though he felt sadly that the laugh was going to turn against himself. There were two exceptions: Laura did not laugh, she looked on in icy wrath and shame; and Jack did not laugh, because he felt that if he laughed at that moment, Laura would most certainly never forgive him. Therefore he preserved great solemnity.

This time it was not George Dalmahoy, but one of the bridemaids who whispered so that all could hear, quoting from the 'Narrative': 'the sweet and gracious smile with which he turned his face towards us, and, uplifting his venerable hands, bestowed his benediction.' She was a pretty girl, who was said to have had designs upon Jack Dalmahoy, and has since married his cousin George. But for some reason or other Laura does not like her.

The poor old Ancestor disappeared in the opposite panel. 'He goes backwards and forwards,' said George ; 'if we do this thing again, he will come out and cross over to the other side. The performance is about to conclude, and, ladies and gentlemen, I am sure that, in retiring from this caravan, you will confess that you have never before witnessed on so grand a scale so ingeniously constructed a piece of——CLOCKWORK.'

Laura, as soon as the door was opened, passed out the first, followed by Jack, whom, however, she pushed away roughly ; then she went to her own room and no one saw her again that day, for, when the second dinner-bell was rung, she sent down a message that she had a headache.

The Squire, too, with abashed countenance, sought solitude for a time. But at dinner he appeared jocund, in high spirits, even forced spirits, and after dinner proposed the health of Mr. George Dalmahoy, who, he said, had rid the house of a very unpleasant occupant—its ghost, and they were all extremely grateful to him. All the members of the family murmured their profound gratitude, and a certain bridemaid, already mentioned, laughed a little laugh which everybody understood to be the equivalent of the immortal 'Fudge ! '

And then George proposed another performance, but the Squire gently remarked that even of mechanical ghosts one might have enough. The irrepressible young man therefore spent the evening, until they began to dance, in explaining how he had discovered the secrets of the machinery, the spring wound by the door, the lubricating oil, and all the rest of the apparatus. All this greatly pleased the family because it brought vividly home to them the mechanical genius of their great-grandfather, and destroyed their ghost and the ancestral glory of the House. It also pleased one of the bridemaids—the one already alluded to.

The next day's wedding was rather a dull affair. Somehow, the romance of the thing was gone. Ghost, indeed ! The impudence of *parvenus* in assuming a ghost when there are already many really old families with no ghost at all, or at best the mere memory and shadow of a ghost. And the honeymoon would have been altogether a time of rebuke, but that Jack put his foot down and would hear no more nonsense about the ghost.

THE MURDER OF NICK VEDDER.

I WAS playing euchre—cut-throat euchre—one night last September, in a certain house at Niagara Falls, with two young ladies, when this story was narrated to us ; but when we had heard it, we played no more.

Cut-throat euchre, if one may be allowed a word of preface, cannot, probably, have its full flavour brought out, and so justify its sponsors, without the melo-dramatic accompaniments of a miner's shanty, a cask for a table, a rock-oil lamp swinging from a beam in the low roof, a whisky bottle for refreshment, and for players, two hawks and a pigeon, or even three hawks. Played in a drawing-room, for love, to the merry music of girls' laughter, it is a bur-lesque rowdy hiding a jovial face behind a ferocious mask, a mere play-acting creature of innocency disguised as a Bandit.

While we played, we talked of the one subject which most interests visitors at Niagara, the rapacity and knavery of the hack-men, the drivers of the hired buggies who infest the cliffs about the Falls, make every walk a battle, and poison the springs of awe and admiration.

They are, indeed, incomparable in their way. They are hack-men in excess ; prigs among drivers, because they overdo their extortions : they exalt their calling : they are superhumanly devoid of conscience. Donkey boys at Cairo may be importunate ; the *cocher* of Paris may be sulky ; the cabby of London may be extor-tionate ; the New York driver may be fond of hurling the luggage at your head as if you were an Aunt Sally, and of charging fifteen dollars for a two-shilling drive ; but the Niagara hack combines in himself the evil qualities of all his brethren ; alone among men and drivers, he hath no bowels ; he would take the last dollar of the orphan, and rob the widow of her mite, on the pretence of 'a dollar and a he'f all the way :' he is a brigand by profession ; he is a blot upon the most glorious spot in all the earth ; it is he who mixes up with the memory of grandeur undreamed of and splendour incon-ceivable the incongruities of a bad dream.

He is, I believe, secretly drilled in a species of chariot charge which I have never seen practised anywhere except at the Falls. Thus it is : When the stranger emerges from the hotel, the hackman waits until his victim is well in the middle of the road, and then, with all his band, two score strong, he charges him from all quarters simultaneously. Thus the visitor suddenly finds himself the centre of a radiating wheel of horses, buggies, and hackmen, and, amid the uproar of a shouting like that of the Homeric way of war, he succumbs generally with a yell of terror, to inevitable fate. There is a cloud of dust, a brief struggle, and in half a minute you will catch your last glimpse of the captive—all that is left of him—hurried off in a buggy to see the whirlpool.

Presently, to us discussing these and kindred topics, there was added a son of the house. A long-limbed pleasant-faced boy of seventeen, with an accent more than a little touched by the infectious nasality of Yankee land, and an affectation of Yankee slang. And he joined in the conversation, which presently assumed the character of a monologue. The future of that youth I consider assured. Such fluency, such richness of digressive power, such ready return to the main topic after episodes which might have led astray altogether a less practised hand, can only meet with a proper sphere of action in an auctioneer's pulpit. Auctioneers, as readers of 'Middlemarch' know, talk wild, but they make money.

'Did you ever,' he began, 'hear the story of the murder of Nick Vedder? Well now, that's a true story for sure. And it's all about those very hackmen you've been talking of. My! ain't they just the worst kind? And all alike, all enough to ruin the morals of an archangel. Not a pin to choose between the lot, only some bigger and some cunninger. Jess Connolly is the biggest, and p'raps Seth Messiter is the cunningest. And I suppose that Dick the guide, who's the politest, has done the most murders. Not that the murdering is anything like what it was, and they do say, now, that a stranger can walk along the cliff of an evening and sometimes get back without being chucked over the edge and then robbed, as used to happen regularly. But I don't think I'd try, if I was a stranger. It might be safe; but for certain, there's a good many bodies do turn up every year in the pool, and not one ever yet found with dollars in his pocket. Now how did those pockets get cleared out? Ask the gang. And if I was you, mister, and I wanted to see the silver spray in the moonlight and that, I'd go with a friend or two, unless Dick was drunk that night. In that case, p'raps you'd be safe, and p'raps you wouldn't. But the real merry time was five years ago when the now judge hadn't come here, and before they murdered Nick Vedder. Then they had it all their own way, robbing around all day and highway plundering at night. Just a chance who they caught. There was old Mr. Scadding, for instance, left this very house at nine o'clock with fifty dollars, and only he had the good luck to hide 'em away in the heels of his boots, he'd have lost every individual dollar. It was a dark night, with snow falling soft, so that you couldn't hear footsteps, and all of a sudden the old gentleman, going along soft and easy, and only wishing he was warm in bed, felt a hand, somebody else's hand, which didn't belong to him, in his coat collar. Naturally he stopped short and began to think fast.

'Then a sheet was thrown over his head, and then a voice told him to hand over what he'd got. Of course he concluded at once to say nothing about his boots, and all he'd got outside of them was a quarter-dollar and a five-cent piece. They pulled his pockets inside out, and they cursed considerable, and then they let him go. He didn't need twice to be told to go straight on and never look behind him; and when he took out those dollars from the heel of his boot, like a brand from the burning, it was, as he always used to say, with a thankful heart.

'As for the day jobs, they used to work in partnership. The most eminent firm was probably that of Jess Connolly and Abb Thomas. Abb is dead now, poor fellow!—died of yellow fever in New Orleans, and his wife went all the way there to see if he really was gone. Seemed to her as if Abb never could die; besides, she wanted to marry another man, and she knew how Abb would carry round if he came home after she'd done it. He was six foot high, and the handsomest coloured man in all America, as he always said himself. On sunny days he used to wax his moustache, and twist it to a point six inches each side, like the Emperor Napoleon. When it rained, he would comb it straight over his mouth and chin, so as to look like a blackleaded poet. And he had such a way with him that he never missed his fare. Nobody rightly knows what that way was : some say he threatened to murder the stranger if he didn't get in and be driven off without more words ; some say he bundled him in, head and heels, before he knew where he was ; but I think he just persuaded him with soft words to the door of his buggy, and then finished him with a gentle shove. Abb always got the pick of the flock, too ; the loneliest of the English travellers —that kind of young feller who comes by himself straight out from Oxford, with a field-glass and knickerbockers, and goes home on the brag after he's been pretty well skinned alive in Niagara and the States ; the tenderest and unprotectedest of the women ; the shakiest of the old men ; that was the kind you would always find in Abb Thomas's buggy. And he generally took 'em that quiet and lonely road which leads to the whirlpool. Why did he take them there ? Because, about half-way back, who would meet him but Jess Connolly ? Jess was the biggest of the gang, and he had a fist like a frying-pan. He's in chokee now for a year, because he made a mistake, thinking the old times were come back again, and tried to bounce an Englishman out of fifty dollars. But the Englishman had a revolver, and he pointed it at Jess's head. "Drive right away to Mr. Hill," he said—Mr. Hill's the judge—"or I'll shoot." But before this misfortune, in the old days, Jess would meet Abb Thomas on the road, and the buggy would stop. Then Abb would turn round : "Place where the fare always pays," he would say. "This is my partner."

'"Twenty dollars," says Jess, holding out his hand.

'"You said a dollar and a half," says the passenger to Abb.

'"Lord forgive you!" says Abb.

'When they'd taken the twenty dollars, they would turn the victim out upon the road, and drive away together. He was sure to be off the next day most likely, and then both of the men were back upon the bank. Another of the gang was Tom Hudson. He's in chokee too, like Jess Connolly, and for seven years, for trying to murder Laurence, the gaoler. He was taken up for something of no great count—forgery, I think—and at the same time Seth Messiter was brought in for a trifle—clearing out a Yankee's pockets. They were both clapped in the same cell. Tom was mad, because he didn't expect to get off; so he proposed to Seth that they should bounce the gaoler, take the keys, and run. Seth agreed, and when Laurence came in with their evening grub, Tom let him have it once on the head with the wooden bench. Down dropped Laurence, but, as bad luck would have it, he had the sense, before he fell, to chuck the keys through the window-bars. Tom was real ugly when he saw the keys fly through the bars, and made at Laurence like a devil. "Let's kill him!" cries Tom. Now what do you think Seth Messiter did? I said he was the cunningest of the hull lot. He remembered that he was in for a little thing, and Tom was in for a big thing, and he saw that Laurence wasn't hurt, not to say considerable. So he set his two legs astride of the gaoler, and when he saw him open his eyes, he struck an attitude like a bold pirate. "Who strikes Laurence, strikes me!" he said, with flashin' eyes and a thump on his breast. There! It was beautiful.

'At the trial, Tom's forgery case broke down, because his brother, who drove on the American side, had hocussed the principal witness. Then they put him up for trying to murder Laurence, the gaoler. When the evidence came to the heroic conduct of Seth Messiter, there wasn't a dry eye in court. Tom got seven years, and the Yankee who was there to prosecute Seth was ashamed to come forward. Said that he felt as if putting forward his fifty-dollar claim on such a credit to Canada was like prosecuting George Washington, when he was President, for cutting down that pear tree. So he walked over the bridge, and he went home. I think he says now that he'd much rather be robbed by a common man next time, and the commoner the better. Doesn't like heroism and thieving to get mixed.

'Gracious! It's one out and the other in, most times. Often the best friends don't get the chance of an evening together for years, and when they do, there's always the chance of interruption. Same as one night when Abb Thomas and Dick the guide were in the bar of Prospect House together, and word came that Dick was wanted.

'"Poor Dick!" says Abb, "we shan't see you for another year." And they didn't meet again till the day before Nick Vedder was murdered.

'Last year, however, there was a case with a Yankee, who was just a little too sharp, and the men got off. Dan Moriarty it was.

He saw a stranger in a store coat and a stove-pipe hat standing by the bridge on the Canadian side, gazing with rapture at the Horseshoe Fall. Moriarty drove up his buggy, so as the stranger was bound to step into that or else to walk over the cliff. Every hackman has his little ways all to himself, and that was Dan Moriarty's. Grantin' that Abb Thomas could lift his passenger in and carry him off, whether he liked it or not, there was no one but Dan who could give him a fair choice between suicide and his buggy.

'But the stranger never moved, and even Dan didn't dare, in broad daylight, to shove him over.

'Presently he extended both his arms in a circular sweep and sung out, just as if he'd sat upon a wasp's nest.

' "Oh !" he says ; "this is too much."

' "What's too much ?" asks Dan ; 'not hef a dollar to Table Rock and back."

' "No, *Sir*," says the stranger, "The prospect is what is too much. It's sublime, Sir. It brings the tears to the stranger's eyes."

' "You bet," said Dan. "Step in and have a drive. Tote yer round for two and a quarter."

' "No," said the stranger, meditatively. "Seems as if I'd rether liquor."

'They went together to the nearest bar, and Dan Moriarty paid.

'It was gettin' on for evening and the sun was low. The stranger returned to the Falls and sat down on the edge of the cliff with the stump of a cigar and his pocket handkerchief. Dan Moriarty sat beside him, and they wept together. When the sun went down, Dan suggested that they should have another drink. So they went off to a crib that Dan knew off, where they found two more of the gang. Here they took drinks around, and Dan proposed a game of euchre. The stranger was through with his weeping, but he hadn't offered to pay for any of the whisky, and he wouldn't play for stakes. All the same, he drank whatever was offered him, and looked as if he could go on drinking for a long time. So when Dan put his hand under the table and pulled out a bottle half emptied, that unsuspicious stranger set it to his lips and didn't take it away till his back teeth were under whisky. Then Dan and his friends looked at each other and smiled cheerful, because the next minute the stranger rolled off his stool like a log. For they'd roped that whisky.

'Next morning the stranger awoke. He was lying on the edge of the cliff ; he was very cold, and he had hot coppers ; and the worst was that his pockets were empty.

'It was easy to identify the three men, and they were all had up before Mr. Hill. Then the stranger told his tale. He narrated how his guileless nature was worked up to drinkin' point by the poetry of the situation and the sympathy of Dan. And then he said how he'd got $500 in his pockets and had lost all the little pile by the hands of that treacherous villain.

'This looked black for Dan. But he whispered his counsel for a few minutes, and the cross-examination began.

'"Where did you carry that pile of notes ? "

'"In my purse," says he.

'"Show the Court your purse."

'He pulled out a purse about big enough to hold a single dime. All the prisoners laughed, and the Court called order.

'"Where did you make your money ? "

'"Working at Buffalo for two months, at two dollars a day."

'"That makes $120. Where did you get the rest ? "

'Well, you see this greedy Yank, he'd been drugged and robbed, and he thought he'd go in for a big claim at once. He'd learned how that dodge pays from the Alabama commission. The subsequents were that Dan got off, and the Court told the witness he was a liar.

'But the most wonderful escape the gang ever had was in the murder of Nick Vedder, that I've been coming to gradually.

'It was five years ago. Nick was a young fellow of twenty-one or so, clerk to a dry goods store in Cliftonville. He was a good-looking chap, and on Sunday afternoons dressed himself up like a Buffalo swell, wore an allround pot with a feather in it, and had a little moustache growing up like a pumpkin in a frame. When he came out o' church you could see by his eyes that he knew all the girls were in love with him, and was only anxious to save one heart from being broken by lettin' on in good time that her love was returned. He parted his hair beautifully right down the middle, so as you might walk straight up if you liked, and finished at the parting with two sweet little curls over his marble brow, so as you could hang on if you slipped.

'It was one Sunday evening in February, while the ice was hanging about the Falls, and there had been toboggining all afternoon down by the ferry. Nick was there, and after it he went to church, just to cheer up the gells, and after church he started to go home. It was a black night, and somehow, through seeing the last of the sweet things go out, Nick was behind all the rest. But he thought nothing of that, and just walked along the planks whistling to himself, till he felt all of a sudden the grip of two arms round his neck and two hands on his lips.

'Nick liked philandering better than fighting, and when he felt that two pair of foreign arms about him, he just stood still where he was, and concluded to let things slide. What inspired Nick with prayerful gratitude was that he hadn't any money in his pocket, not a single dollar, note, nor the chink of one quarter against another. Dry goods store clerks don't have much money as a rule.

'They carried him without a word down the cross-road which leads from Clifton Church to the Drummondville road, and presently they came to a house, and they took him in.

'Just then Nick Vedder fainted. P'raps it was the heat of the store, and p'raps it was the skear, but anyhow he went off, and when he came to himself he was lying on his back upon the floor. They'd set a chair across his legs, and one citizen was sitting in it, a pistol in his hand, ready cocked, pointed straight at Nick Vedder's face. He felt, without being told, that if that pistol went off, he'd lose considerable of his beauty for the balance of his days; so he hoped it wouldn't. But that wasn't all. At his right side there sat another gentleman, with a razor in his hand, and this he was playfully drawin' across Nick Vedder's throat; and at his left there was a third citizen, who held a pair of scissors open, like compasses, across his cheeks.

' "Nick Vedder," said the one in the chair, and he knew it was Chris Dalmage, " Nick Vedder, what the devil do you mean by it ? "

' " Mean by it, Sir ? " asks Nick, as meek as he knew.

' " We see a gentleman going along, on a dark night, easy and quiet over the planks ; we stop that gentleman, and he turns out to be Nick Vedder, clerk in a dry goods store, without a cent. And we've wasted our time. An example must be made, Nick Vedder."

' Then Nick saw that his time was come unless he made an effort, so, because he didn't dare to move, on account of the scissors and the razor, to say nothing of the pistol, he prayed on his back, that they would have pity on a poor dry goods store clerk, who had always, from his humble station, envied the glorious freedom of the hackmen. He had, he said, watched them when the helpless tourist crossed the Suspension Bridge or emerged from the Clifton Hotel. He drew a poetic picture of that tourist, confident as the Gallic cock at starting, and returning like that bird plucked and trussed ready for roasting. Warming with his subject, because Nick was a real clever fellow once put to it, he compared, to the advantage of each in turn, the bold privateering of Abb Thomas, by whom the tourist, surrounded on all sides, was fairly captured and driven whither he did not wish to go ; the suicidal alternative of Dan Moriarty, which presented death or the buggy to the terrified stranger ; the craft of Mr. Seth Messiter, and the admirable politeness of that other excellent citizen, Dick the guide. I think he would have gone on all night, but Abb Thomas told him they didn't want any more chin music, and that his time was up.

' Nick was mighty frightened. When they tied a napkin round his neck he began to cry ; when they sharpened the razor he began to say his prayers ; and when Tom Hudson advanced with the weapon in his hand he began to skreek. But he needn't have been so skeared, because, after all, they weren't going to cut his throat. They only made the beautiful centre-parting in his hair a little wider, and shaved him an inch broad from his forehead to his poll. Then Nick Vedder looked like a clown.

' It was Abb Thomas—he was always rough in his play—who said Nick was a pretty boy, and would look well in earrings if he

only had his ears pierced. So he took the scissors and did the job
for him. After that they let Nick go, and when he got home he
felt real ugly—more ugly he felt, and smaller too, in the morning.
His mother, when he showed up at breakfast, carried on so
shameful, that he was forced to go straight to Mr. Hill and lodge
his complaint.

' They soon caught the men, and though they said it was only
a joke, Mr. Hill bound them over, all but one, against whom there
was no evidence, to appear the following week. No one in the
town knew whether it was burglary, or highway robbery, or plain
assault. If it was highway robbery, the town was likely to be
deprived of its most prominent citizens for a good long spell.

' The next Sunday night, the night before the remand, Nick
did not go to church : he couldn't, because his hair hadn't grown
over the bald place yet. His mother, who was a Primitive Metho-
dist, and strict, did. When she was out of the house and the
bells had done ringing, these four citizens, out on bail, dropped
in in a friendly way, and paid an evening call on poor Nick. They
didn't ask him if he'd like a walk that cold night, but they took it
for granted ; clapped a gag in his mouth, wrapped him up in his
warm great-coat, tied a comforter round his neck, and took him
along of themselves. " Because," said Abb Thomas, " if you so
much as wink, to show that you are not going of your own free
will, when anyone passes, we'll split your skull."

' Nick went very quiet, but he was more frightened this journey
than the last. They walked up the road from Clifton, along the
rapids, where it's dark all the year round, moon or no moon, with
the woods one side and the roaring river, three hundred feet below,
on the other, and they crossed over the suspension bridge, nobody
saying a word. Then they turned to the right, past Prospect Park
till they reached Goat Island Bridge, and they crossed over the
bridge to that lonely and picturesque location.

' It's a very different thing being on Goat Island in the daytime, when you can see as well as hear the rapids above you and
the falls beneath, and you know where you're standing, to being
there on a cold, dark, Sabbath night in winter, in the company of
four virtuous hackmen, uncertain how long you're going to be with
them, the icy spray blowing into your eyes, the leafless branches
dropping their icicles on your head, your feet crunching deep in
the falling snow, and all the time the cataract and rapids about
you, roaring like all the wild creatures of all the Zoological Gardens
in the wide, wide world.

' Nick Vedder was very sorry just then that he wasn't in church;
although his head *was* shaved for an inch all up his precious scalp ;
better to be laughed at by the girls, than be dragged along to
be murdered by the hackmen. I guess his heart was about down
to the heels of his boots as he went along.

' It's a quarter of a mile, I s'pose, across Goat Island, unless you
make it longer by taking in Luna Isle, and this would have been a

waste of time for Nick's enemies, because they were bound straight
for Terrapin Tower. You know Terrapin Tower, mister. They've
taken the tower down long ago, to prevent its tumbling down, but
the shaky wooden footway to it is there still, and then you can
walk clear out to where it stood right over the side of the fall, so
that a man standing at the edge of that ramshackle pier has got his
foot within a few inches of the great flood which rolls over the
edge below him. It is a skeary place on a sunshiny day in summer.
Think what it would be on a moonless night in February, with the
black waters rolling and roaring beneath; above, the clear sky,
and on the rocks around the snow and ice making with their white-
ness a little light, just to show how horrible it would be to go
over.

‘Three of the men dragged poor Nick to the end of the planks.
Then they lifted him up—Nick by this time was long past the
power of praying, or even asking for mercy—and held him right
out over the fall.

‘ “Nick Vedder,” said Abb Thomas, as solemn as a judge, “Air
you proposin’ to give evidence against us to-morrow ? ”

‘There was no answer, because Nick was too paralysed with
terror to say anything.

‘ “One,” said Abb. “If I say *three* before an answer comes—
over you go. And the Lord have mercy on what's left of you, when
you get to the bottom.”

‘There was no answer.

‘ “Two ! ”

‘Next day all the men, leaving their buggies outside, appeared
in the court at ten o'clock looking cheerful. But when the case
was called there was no Nick Vedder.

‘The charge was dismissed, but the judge cautioned the
prisoners. He said he had no doubt that there was an evasion of
justice somehow, and that a serious outrage had been condoned.
Let it be a lesson to them, for it was the last time—and so on.

‘Later on, old Mrs. Vedder came into court screamin’ and
cryin’ that her son must be murdered, that he hadn't come home
all night, and that he was certainly made away with by the blood-
thirsty gang of Abb Thomas and his friends. But there was no
proof.

‘That was Monday. Tuesday, Wednesday, Thursday passed,
and Nick never came home. Everybody thought that he really
must have been made away with. A reward was offered for him.
People began to look more shy of the men on the bank than ever.
Abb Thomas was hooted by the women. Chris Dalmage had a
quarrel with his own wife, who threatened to live no longer with a
murderin’ cut-throat. And even old Mis’ Fuller, who ought to
have known better, through her English high connections, put on
all her six frocks at once, went down to the bank and joined in the
general scream. It was an anxious time. And it was more anxious

1.

still, when, on Friday morning, it was spread abroad that a body was in the whirlpool.

'We all made for the whirlpool. Some walked, some drove : but we all got there. In the pool, goin' round and round, was a body, and no mistake. It went round and round the whole day, while we stood on the bank under the cliff and tried to make out if it was Nick Vedder. But the features were smashed beyond recognition.

'So many people crowded down that all the buggies were hired, and it was noticed afterwards, as a most remarkable thing, that the visitors that day were actually enabled to see the Falls without being robbed. No hackmen on the bank, no photographers, and no dealers in Indian curiosities. The tourists thought it was Sunday, or a keeping of Dominion Day at the wrong time.

'In the night the body left the whirlpool, and was found on the bank in the morning, caught by the trees. They brought it up, and held the inquest.

'Although the face and features were quite smashed and broken, there were two things by which they identified the remains. Old Mrs. Vedder swore to a slipper which was on the foot as belonging to her son ; and Dick the guide, who had reason of his own for wanting to see Abb Thomas in trouble, swore to a tattoo mark on the arm. Said he did it himself one Sabbath afternoon when Nick Vedder and him was alone. And a coloured girl swore that she saw Nick Vedder on Sunday evening with four men, Abb Thomas being one, and going over the suspension bridge.

'The verdict was "wilful murder" against the four who had been bound over to appear for the first charge. They were immediately arrested and locked up. They took the matter quite cheerfully, and were, as the "Drummondville Gazette" said, apparently quite regardless of their awful position.

'Time was required to get up the case for the prosecution, and it was a fortnight afterwards when the real trial came on. It was a solemn sight to see the judge, the counsel, the jury, and the citizens, all got together to hang four hack drivers. Everybody was there, and among them old Mis' Fuller, in the front row, nodding her head at all friends, and every now and then wiping her eyes when she thought of poor dear Nick.

'First the prosecutor opened the case. A man had disappeared; for no reason whatever he vanished from his home : when last seen he was in company with four men ; these men stood before the court in the dock : with them he crossed over the bridge to Goat Island : the gate-keeper, it would be proved, could not remember whether he came back with them : they had an interest in getting him out of the way : a body was found in the whirlpool below the Falls : in height it corresponded to the deceased, Nicholas Vedder : on the foot was a slipper to which the murdered man's mother would swear : on the arm was a tattoo mark which a well-known citizen of Clifton remembered to have himself punctured on the arm of this unfortunate young man so foully made away with.

'He kept pilin' it up about foul play and the murdered man till the folk were ready to lynch the lot if the prisoners had been free. Then he called the evidence. First the coloured girl gave hers. The counsel for the prisoners said he had no questions to ask. Then Mrs. Vedder swore to the slipper, and was quite ready to swear to the foot which had been in it.

'The counsel for the prisoners, to everybody's astonishment, said he had no questions at all to ask her. Was the man going to fool away the case?

'Dick the guide swore to the tattoo mark. When asked if he remembered the date of the tattooing, he burst into tears and said it was when Nick and he were boys together. That was curious, because Dick was forty and Nick was twenty.

'But the counsel for the defence said he had no questions to ask of him neither. And then we began to feel as if the rope was round all four necks.

'When his turn to speak came, however, he rose to his feet, and said that he only had one witness to call. He would call—and here he hesitated, and looked scornful at his brothers in the law : he would call—and here he looked with a smile in the faces of the citizens : he would call—and here he looked full in the eyes of the jury, as if he was going to let them have a facer : he would call —NICK VEDDER himself : and as he spoke the words, the door opened, and in came Nick. His hair was growing again very nicely. But he looked meek and small. There's no denying that the Court was a good deal taken aback : dignity shook out of it, somehow. Mis' Fuller gave a fearful shriek because she thought it was a ghost, and went off into hysterics. It took a few minutes to get rid of her. The people jumped to their feet and began to shout. The jury looked as if they'd been done out of something good. And as for the prisoners, they just stepped over the dock into the court and sat down, Abb Thomas the first, without being invited to.

'We got a little quiet after a while, and the case went on.

'First the counsel told the Court the story about Nick's disappearance. It was this : Chris Dalmage, the only one of the five who wasn't bound over, after they'd frightened Nick at Terrapin Tower, till he was as meek as any two-year-old, kept him on the other side, locked up with a friend or two to take care of him. After the inquest, what with the general excitement, and the impulse to the hack trade, because folk came from Hamilton and Toronto and London to see the place where Nick Vedder's body was found, and what with the pleasure of seeing his friends all locked up together, a thing which no hackman could resist, Chris could not bring himself to produce his prisoner till the day of the trial.

'The counsel only asked two questions.

' "Is that your slipper ?"

' "No," said Nick. "I never had a slipper in my life, and if I had my foot isn't as big as a boat. And who'd go out in slippers in such weather as this ?"

'His mother, who'd been clinging to him and wiping her eyes, let go of his hand, and looked as if she'd like to box his ears there and then.

' "Oh ! you ungrateful boy," she cried.

' "Then," said the counsel, "show the Court your left arm. Turn up the sleeve ; where is the tattoo ?"

' "There is no tattoo," said Nick. "Why should I be tattooed ?"

'Dick the guide stepped out of court. He said it was a curious and disappointing world—and who would have guessed that the boy would round on him in such an ungrateful manner as that after all he'd said and sworn to for his sake ! And catch him ever taking any interest in a murder again. And that night there was some of them at the Falls had a real high time : perhaps as high a time as ever was had. But Dick the guide wasn't invited.'

PRINTED BY
SPOTTISWOODE AND CO., NEW-STREET SQUARE
LONDON

CHATTO AND WINDUS'S
LIST OF CHEAP POPULAR NOVELS
BY THE BEST AUTHORS.
Picture Covers, TWO SHILLINGS each.

BY EDMOND ABOUT.
The Fellah.

BY HAMILTON AIDE.
Carr of Carrlyon.
Confidences.

BY MARY ALBERT.
Brooke Finchley's Daughter.

BY MRS. ALEXANDER.
Maid, Wife, or Widow?
Valerie's Fate.
Blind Fate.

BY GRANT ALLEN.
Strange Stories.
Philistia.
Babylon.
The Beckoning Hand.
In All Shades.
For Maimie's Sake.
The Devil's Die.
This Mortal Coil.
The Tents of Shem.
The Great Taboo.
Dumaresq's Daughter.
The Duchess of Powysland.
Blood Royal.
Ivan Greet's Masterpiece.
The Scallywag.
At Market Value.

BY EDWIN LESTER ARNOLD.
Phra the Phœnician.

BY FRANK BARRETT.
A Recoiling Vengeance.
For Love and Honour.
John Ford; and His Helpmate.
Honest Davie.
A Prodigal's Progress.
Folly Morrison.
Lieutenant Barnabas.
Found Guilty.
Fettered for Life.
Between Life and Death.
The Sin of Olga Zassoulich.
Little Lady Linton.
The Woman of the Iron Bracelets

BY SHELSLEY BEAUCHAMP.
Grantley Grange.

BY BESANT & RICE.
Ready-Money Mortiboy.
With Harp and Crown.
This Son of Vulcan.
My Little Girl.
The Case of Mr. Lucraft.
The Golden Butterfly.
By Celia's Arbour.
The Monks of Thelema.
'Twas in Trafalgar's Bay.
The Seamy Side.
The Ten Years' Tenant.
The Chaplain of the Fleet.

BY WALTER BESANT.
All Sorts and Conditions of Men.
The Captains' Room.
All in a Garden Fair.
Dorothy Forster.
Uncle Jack.
Children of Gibeon.
The World went very well then.
Herr Paulus.
For Faith and Freedom.
To Call her Mine.
The Bell of St. Paul's.
The Holy Rose.
Armorel of Lyonesse.
St. Katherine's by the Tower.
The Ivory Gate.
Verbena Camellia Stephanotis.
The Rebel Queen.
Beyond the Dreams of Avarice.

BY AMBROSE BIERCE.
In the Midst of Life.

BY FREDERICK BOYLE.
Camp Notes.
Savage Life.
Chronicles of No-Man's Land.

BY HAROLD BRYDGES.
Uncle Sam at Home.

London: CHATTO & WINDUS, 111 St. Martin's Lane, W.C.

BY ROBERT BUCHANAN.
The Shadow of the Sword.
A Child of Nature.
God and the Man.
Annan Water.
The New Abelard.
The Martyrdom of Madeline.
Love Me for Ever.
Matt : a Story of a Caravan.
Foxglove Manor.
The Master of the Mine.
The Heir of Linne.
Woman and the Man.
Rachel Dene.

BY BUCHANAN AND MURRAY.
The Charlatan.

BY HALL CAINE.
The Shadow of a Crime.
A Son of Hagar.
The Deemster.

BY COMMANDER CAMERON.
The Cruise of the 'Black Prince.'

BY MRS. LOVETT CAMERON.
Deceivers Ever.
Juliet's Guardian.

BY EX-INSPECTOR CAVANAGH.
Scotland Yard, Past and Present.

BY AUSTIN CLARE.
For the Love of a Lass.

BY MRS. ARCHER CLIVE.
Paul Ferroll.
Why Paul Ferroll Killed his Wife

BY MACLAREN COBBAN.
The Cure of Souls.
The Red Sultan.

BY C. ALLSTON COLLINS.
The Bar Sinister.

BY WILKIE COLLINS.
Armadale.
After Dark.
No Name.
A Rogue's Life.
Antonina. | Basil.
Hide and Seek.
The Dead Secret.
Queen of Hearts.
My Miscellanies.
The Woman in White.
The Moonstone.
Man and Wife.

BY WILKIE COLLINS—*continued.*
Poor Miss Finch.
Miss or Mrs. ?
The New Magdalen.
The Frozen Deep.
The Law and the Lady.
The Two Destinies.
The Haunted Hotel.
The Fallen Leaves.
Jezebel's Daughter.
The Black Robe.
Heart and Science.
' I say No.'
The Evil Genius.
Little Novels.
The Legacy of Cain.
Blind Love.

MORTIMER & FRANCES COLLINS.
Sweet Anne Page.
Transmigration.
From Midnight to Midnight.
A Fight with Fortune.
Sweet and Twenty.
Frances.
The Village Comedy.
You Play Me False.
Blacksmith and Scholar.

BY M. J. COLQUHOUN.
Every Inch a Soldier.

BY DUTTON COOK.
Leo.
Paul Foster's Daughter.

BY C. EGBERT CRADDOCK.
Prophet of the Smoky Mountains.

BY MATT CRIM.
Adventures of a Fair Rebel.

BY B. M. CROKER.
Pretty Miss Neville.
Proper Pride.
A Bird of Passage.
Diana Barrington.
' To Let.'
A Family Likeness.
Village Tales & Jungle Tragedies
Two Masters.
Mr. Jervis.

BY WILLIAM CYPLES.
Hearts of Gold.

BY ALPHONSE DAUDET.
The Evangelist.

London : CHATTO & WINDUS, iii *St. Martin's Lane, W.C.*

BY ERASMUS DAWSON.
The Fountain of Youth.

BY JAMES DE MILLE.
A Castle in Spain.

BY J. LEITH DERWENT.
Our Lady of Tears.
Circe's Lovers.

BY CHARLES DICKENS.
Sketches by Boz.
Oliver Twist.
Nicholas Nickleby.

BY DICK DONOVAN.
The Man-hunter.
Caught at Last!
Tracked and Taken.
Who Poisoned Hetty Duncan?
The Man from Manchester.
A Detective's Triumphs.
In the Grip of the Law.
Wanted!
From Information Received.
Tracked to Doom.
Link by Link.
Suspicion Aroused.
Dark Deeds.
Riddles Read.
The Mystery of Jamaica Terrace.

BY MRS. ANNIE EDWARDES.
A Point of Honour.
Archie Lovell.

BY M. BETHAM-EDWARDS.
Felicia.
Kitty.

BY EDWARD EGGLESTON.
Roxy.

BY G. MANVILLE FENN.
The New Mistress.
Witness to the Deed.
The Tiger Lily.
The White Virgin.

BY PERCY FITZGERALD.
Bella Donna.
Polly.
The Second Mrs. Tillotson.
Seventy-five Brooke Street.
Never Forgotten.
The Lady of Brantome.
Fatal Zero.

BY PERCY FITZGERALD and Others.
Strange Secrets.

BY ALBANY DE FONBLANQUE.
Filthy Lucre.

BY R. E. FRANCILLON.
Olympia.
One by One.
Queen Cophetua.
A Real Queen.
King or Knave.
Romances of the Law.
Ropes of Sand.
A Dog and his Shadow.

BY HAROLD FREDERIC.
Seth's Brother's Wife.
The Lawton Girl.

Prefaced by Sir H. BARTLE FRERE.
Pandurang Hàri.

BY HAIN FRISWELL.
One of Two.

BY EDWARD GARRETT.
The Capel Girls.

BY GILBERT GAUL.
A Strange Manuscript Found.

BY CHARLES GIBBON.
Robin Gray.
For Lack of Gold.
What will the World Say?
In Honour Bound.
In Love and War.
For the King.
Queen of the Meadow.
In Pastures Green.
The Flower of the Forest.
A Heart's Problem.
The Braes of Yarrow.
The Golden Shaft.
Of High Degree.
The Dead Heart.
By Mead and Stream.
Heart's Delight.
Fancy Free.
Loving a Dream.
A Hard Knot.
Blood-Money.

BY WILLIAM GILBERT.
James Duke.
Dr. Austin's Guests.
The Wizard of the Mountain.

London: CHATTO & WINDUS, 111 St. Martin's Lane, W.C.

BY ERNEST GLANVILLE.
The Lost Heiress.
The Fossicker.
A Fair Colonist.

BY REV. S. BARING GOULD.
Eve.
Red Spider.

BY HENRY GREVILLE.
Nikanor.
A Noble Woman.

BY CECIL GRIFFITH.
Corinthia Marazion.

BY SYDNEY GRUNDY.
The Days of his Vanity.

BY JOHN HABBERTON.
Brueton's Bayou.
Country Luck.

BY ANDREW HALLIDAY.
Every-Day Papers.

BY LADY DUFFUS HARDY.
Paul Wynter's Sacrifice.

BY THOMAS HARDY.
Under the Greenwood Tree.

BY BRET HARTE.
An Heiress of Red Dog.
The Luck of Roaring Camp.
Californian Stories.
Gabriel Conroy.
Flip.
Maruja.
A Phyllis of the Sierras.
A Waif of the Plains.
A Ward of the Golden Gate.

BY J. BERWICK HARWOOD.
The Tenth Earl.

BY JULIAN HAWTHORNE.
Garth.
Ellice Quentin.
Sebastian Strome.
Dust.
Fortune's Fool.
Beatrix Randolph.
Miss Cadogna.
Love—or a Name.
Poindexter's Disappearance.
The Spectre of the Camera.

BY SIR ARTHUR HELPS.
Ivan de Biron.

BY G. A. HENTY.
Rujub the Juggler.

BY HENRY HERMAN.
A Leading Lady.

BY HEADON HILL.
Zambra the Detective.

BY JOHN HILL.
Treason-Felony.

BY MRS. CASHEL HOEY.
The Lover's Creed.

BY MRS. GEORGE HOOPER.
The House of Raby.

BY TIGHE HOPKINS.
'Twixt Love and Duty.

BY MRS. HUNGERFORD.
In Durance Vile.
A Maiden all Forlorn.
A Mental Struggle.
Marvel.
A Modern Circe.
Lady Verner's Flight.
The Red-House Mystery.
The Three Graces.
An Unsatisfactory Lover.
Lady Patty.

BY MRS. ALFRED HUNT.
Thornicroft's Model.
The Leaden Casket.
Self-Condemned.
That Other Person.

BY JEAN INGELOW.
Fated to be Free.

BY WILLIAM JAMESON.
My Dead Self.

BY HARRIETT JAY.
The Dark Colleen.
The Queen of Connaught.

BY MARK KERSHAW.
Colonial Facts and Fictions.

BY R. ASHE KING.
A Drawn Game.
'The Wearing of the Green.'
Passion's Slave.
Bell Barry.

London: **CHATTO & WINDUS,** 111 *St. Martin's Lane,* W.C.

BY EDMOND LEPELLETIER.
Madame Sans-Genê.

BY JOHN LEYS.
The Lindsays.

BY E. LYNN LINTON.
Patricia Kemball.
The Atonement of Leam Dundas.
The World Well Lost.
Under which Lord ?
With a Silken Thread.
The Rebel of the Family.
' My Love !'
Ione.
Paston Carew.
Sowing the Wind.
The One too Many.

BY HENRY W. LUCY.
Gideon Fleyce.

BY JUSTIN McCARTHY.
Dear Lady Disdain.
The Waterdale Neighbours.
My Enemy's Daughter.
A Fair Saxon.
Linley Rochford.
Miss Misanthrope.
Donna Quixote.
The Comet of a Season.
Maid of Athens.
Camiola : a Girl with a Fortune.
The Dictator.
Red Diamonds.

BY HUGH MacCOLL.
Mr. Stranger's Sealed Packet.

BY GEORGE MACDONALD.
Heather and Snow.

BY MRS. MACDONELL.
Quaker Cousins.

BY KATHARINE S. MACQUOID.
The Evil Eye.
Lost Rose.

BY W. H. MALLOCK.
The New Republic.
A Romance of the 19th Century.

BY FLORENCE MARRYAT.
Fighting the Air.
Written in Fire.
A Harvest of Wild Oats.
Open ! Sesame !

BY J. MASTERMAN.
Half-a-dozen Daughters.

BY BRANDER MATTHEWS.
A Secret of the Sea.

BY L. T. MEADE.
A Soldier of Fortune.

BY LEONARD MERRICK.
The Man who was Good.

BY JEAN MIDDLEMASS.
Touch and Go.
Mr. Dorillion.

BY MRS. MOLESWORTH.
Hathercourt Rectory.

BY J. E. MUDDOCK.
Stories Weird and Wonderful.
The Dead Man's Secret.
From the Bosom of the Deep.

BY D. CHRISTIE MURRAY.
A Life's Atonement.
Joseph's Coat.
Val Strange.
A Model Father.
Coals of Fire.
Hearts.
By the Gate of the Sea.
The Way of the World.
A Bit of Human Nature.
First Person Singular.
Cynic Fortune.
Old Blazer's Hero.
Bob Martin's Little Girl.
Time's Revenges.
A Wasted Crime.
In Direst Peril.
Mount Despair.

BY MURRAY AND HERMAN.
One Traveller Returns.
Paul Jones's Alias.
The Bishops' Bible.

BY HENRY MURRAY.
A Game of Bluff.
A Song of Sixpence.

BY HUME NISBET.
' Bail Up !'
Dr. Bernard St. Vincent.

BY W. E. NORRIS.
Saint Ann's.

BY ALICE O'HANLON.
The Unforeseen.
Chance ? or Fate ?

London : CHATTO & WINDUS, 111 *St. Martin's Lane, W.C.*

BY GEORGES OHNET.
Doctor Rameau.
A Last Love.
A Weird Gift.

BY MRS. OLIPHANT.
Whiteladies.
The Primrose Path.
The Greatest Heiress in England

BY MRS. ROBERT O'REILLY.
Phœbe's Fortunes.

BY OUIDA.
Held in Bondage.
Strathmore.
Chandos.
Under Two Flags.
Idalia.
Cecil Castlemaine's Gage.
Tricotrin.
Puck.
Folle Farine.
A Dog of Flanders.
Pascarèl.
Signa.
In a Winter City.
Ariadnê.
Moths.
Friendship.
Pipistrello.
Bimbi.
In Maremma.
Wanda.
Frescoes.
Princess Napraxine.
Two Little Wooden Shoes.
A Village Commune.
Othmar.
Guilderoy.
Ruffino.
Syrlin.
Santa Barbara.
Two Offenders.
Wisdom, Wit, and Pathos.

BY MARGARET AGNES PAUL.
Gentle and Simple.

BY JAMES PAYN.
Lost Sir Massingberd.
A Perfect Treasure.
Bentinck's Tutor.
Murphy's Master.
A County Family.

BY JAMES PAYN—*continued.*
At Her Mercy.
A Woman's Vengeance.
Cecil's Tryst.
The Clyffards of Clyffe.
The Family Scapegrace.
The Foster Brothers.
The Best of Husbands.
Found Dead.
Walter's Word.
Halves.
Fallen Fortunes.
What He Cost Her.
Humorous Stories.
Gwendoline's Harvest.
Like Father, Like Son.
A Marine Residence.
Married Beneath Him.
Mirk Abbey.
Not Wooed, but Won.
Two Hundred Pounds Reward.
Less Black than We're Painted.
By Proxy.
High Spirits.
Under One Roof.
Carlyon's Year.
A Confidential Agent.
Some Private Views.
A Grape from a Thorn.
From Exile.
Kit: A Memory.
For Cash Only.
The Canon's Ward.
The Talk of the Town.
Holiday Tasks.
Glow-worm Tales.
The Mystery of Mirbridge.
The Burnt Million.
The Word and the Will.
A Prince of the Blood.
Sunny Stories.
A Trying Patient.

BY C. L. PIRKIS.
Lady Lovelace.

BY EDGAR A. POE.
The Mystery of Marie Roget.

BY MRS. CAMPBELL PRAED.
The Romance of a Station.
The Soul of Countess Adrian.
Outlaw and Lawmaker.
Christina Chard.

London: CHATTO & WINDUS, 111 *St. Martin's Lane, W.C.*

BY E. C. PRICE.
Valentina.
Gerald.
Mrs. Lancaster's Rival.
The Foreigners.

BY RICHARD PRYCE.
Miss Maxwell's Affections.

BY CHARLES READE.
It is Never Too Late to Mend.
Hard Cash.
Peg Woffington.
Christie Johnstone.
Griffith Gaunt.
Put Yourself in His Place.
The Double Marriage.
Love Me Little, Love Me Long.
Foul Play.
The Cloister and the Hearth.
The Course of True Love.
The Autobiography of a Thief.
A Terrible Temptation.
The Wandering Heir.
A Simpleton.
A Woman-Hater.
Singleheart and Doubleface.
Good Stories of Men and other
The Jilt.   [Animals.
A Perilous Secret.
Readiana.

BY MRS. J. H. RIDDELL.
Her Mother's Darling.
The Uninhabited House.
Weird Stories.
Fairy Water.
Prince of Wales's Garden Party.
The Mystery in Palace Gardens.
The Nun's Curse.
Idle Tales.

BY AMÉLIE RIVES.
Barbara Dering.

BY F. W. ROBINSON.
Women are Strange.
The Hands of Justice.

BY JAMES RUNCIMAN.
Skippers and Shellbacks.
Grace Balmaign's Sweetheart.
Schools and Scholars.

BY DORA RUSSELL.
A Country Sweetheart.

BY W. CLARK RUSSELL.
Round the Galley Fire.
On the Fo'k'sle Head.
In the Middle Watch.
A Voyage to the Cape.
A Book for the Hammock.
Mystery of the 'Ocean Star.'
The Romance of Jenny Harlowe.
An Ocean Tragedy.
My Shipmate Louise.
Alone on a Wide Wide Sea.
The Phantom Death.
The Good Ship 'Mohock.'

BY ALAN ST. AUBYN.
A Fellow of Trinity.
The Junior Dean.
The Master of St. Benedict's.
To his Own Master.
Orchard Damerel.
In the Face of the World.

BY GEORGE AUGUSTUS SALA.
Gaslight and Daylight.

BY JOHN SAUNDERS.
Guy Waterman.
The Lion in the Path.
The Two Dreamers.

BY KATHARINE SAUNDERS.
Joan Merryweather.
The High Mills.
Margaret and Elizabeth.
Sebastian.
Heart Salvage.

BY GEORGE R. SIMS.
The Ring o' Bells.
Mary Jane's Memoirs.
Mary Jane Married.
Tales of To-day.
Dramas of Life.
Tinkletop's Crime.
Zeph : a Circus Story.
My Two Wives.
Memoirs of a Landlady.
Scenes from the Show.
The Ten Commandments.
Dagonet Abroad.

BY ARTHUR SKETCHLEY.
A Match in the Dark.

BY HAWLEY SMART.
Without Love or Licence.
The Plunger.
Beatrice and Benedick.

London: CHATTO & WINDUS, 111 *St. Martin's Lane, W.C.*

BY T. W. SPEIGHT.
The Mysteries of Heron Dyke.
The Golden Hoop.
By Devious Ways.
Hoodwinked.
Back to Life.
The Loudwater Tragedy.
Burgo's Romance.
Quittance in Full.
A Husband from the Sea.

BY R. A. STERNDALE.
The Afghan Knife.

BY R. LOUIS STEVENSON.
New Arabian Nights.

BY BERTHA THOMAS.
Proud Maisie.
The Violin-player.
Cressida.

BY WALTER THORNBURY.
Tales for the Marines.
Old Stories Re-told.

BY ANTHONY TROLLOPE.
The Way We Live Now.
Mr. Scarborough's Family.
The Golden Lion of Granpère.
The American Senator.
Frau Frohmann.
Marion Fay.
Kept in the Dark.
The Land-Leaguers.
John Caldigate.

BY FRANCES E. TROLLOPE.
Anne Furness.
Mabel's Progress.
Like Ships upon the Sea.

BY T. ADOLPHUS TROLLOPE.
Diamond Cut Diamond.

BY J. T. TROWBRIDGE.
Farnell's Folly.

BY IVAN TURGENIEFF, etc.
Stories from Foreign Novelists.

BY MARK TWAIN.
Tom Sawyer.
A Tramp Abroad.
The Stolen White Elephant.
Pleasure Trip on the Continent.

BY MARK TWAIN—continued.
The Gilded Age.
Huckleberry Finn.
Life on the Mississippi.
The Prince and the Pauper.
Mark Twain's Sketches.
Yankee at Court of K. Arthur.
The £1,000,000 Bank-note.

BY SARAH TYTLER.
Noblesse Oblige.
Citoyenne Jacqueline.
The Huguenot Family.
What She Came Through.
Beauty and the Beast.
The Bride's Pass.
Saint Mungo's City.
Disappeared.
Lady Bell.
Buried Diamonds.
The Blackhall Ghosts.

BY C. C. FRASER-TYTLER.
Mistress Judith.

BY ALLEN UPWARD.
The Queen against Owen.
The Prince of Balkistan.

BY ARTEMUS WARD.
Artemus Ward Complete.

BY AARON WATSON AND LILLIAS WASSERMANN.
The Marquis of Carabas.

BY WILLIAM WESTALL.
Trust-Money.

BY MRS. F. H. WILLIAMSON.
A Child Widow.

BY J. S. WINTER.
Cavalry Life.
Regimental Legends.

BY H. F. WOOD.
Passenger from Scotland Yard.
Englishman of the Rue Cain.

BY LADY WOOD.
Sabina.

BY CELIA PARKER WOOLLEY.
Rachel Armstrong.

BY EDMUND YATES.
Castaway.
Land at Last.
The Forlorn Hope.

London: CHATTO & WINDUS, 111 St. Martin's Lane, W.C.

[*Feb.* 1897.]

LIST OF BOOKS PUBLISHED BY

CHATTO & WINDUS

111 ST. MARTIN'S LANE, CHARING CROSS, LONDON, W.C.

About (Edmond).—The Fellah: An Egyptian Novel. Translated by
Sir RANDAL ROBERTS. Post 8vo, illustrated boards, 2s.

Adams (W. Davenport), Works by.
A Dictionary of the Drama: being a comprehensive Guide to the Plays, Playwrights, Players
and Playhouses of the United Kingdom and America, from the Earliest Times to the Present
Day. Crown 8vo, half-bound, 12s. 6d. [*Preparing.*
Quips and Quiddities. Selected by W. DAVENPORT ADAMS. Post 8vo, cloth limp, 2s. 6d.

Agony Column (The) of 'The Times,' from 1800 to 1870. Edited,
with an Introduction, by ALICE CLAY. Post 8vo, cloth limp, 2s. 6d.

Aïdé (Hamilton), Novels by. Post 8vo, illustrated boards, 2s. each.
Carr of Carrlyon. | Confidences.

Albert (Mary).—Brooke Finchley's Daughter. Post 8vo, picture
boards, 2s. ; cloth limp, 2s. 6d.

Alden (W. L.).—A Lost Soul: Being the Confession and Defence of
Charles Lindsay. Fcap. 8vo, cloth boards, 1s. 6d.

Alexander (Mrs.), Novels by. Post 8vo, illustrated boards, 2s. each.
Maid, Wife, or Widow? | Valerie's Fate. | Blind Fate.

Crown 8vo, cloth, 3s. 6d. each.
A Life Interest. | Mona's Choice. | By Woman's Wit.

Allen (F. M.).—Green as Grass. With a Frontispiece. Crown 8vo,
cloth, 3s. 6d.

Allen (Grant), Works by.
The Evolutionist at Large. Crown 8vo, cloth extra, 6s.
Post-Prandial Philosophy. Crown 8vo, art linen, 3s. 6d.
Moorland Idylls. Crown 8vo, cloth decorated, 6s.

Crown 8vo, cloth extra, 3s. 6d. each ; post 8vo, illustrated boards, 2s. each.

Babylon. 12 Illustrations.	The Devil's Die.	The Duchess of Powysland.
Strange Stories. Frontis.	This Mortal Coil.	Blood Royal.
The Beckoning Hand.	The Tents of Shem. Frontis.	Ivan Greet's Masterpiece.
For Maimie's Sake.	The Great Taboo.	The Scallywag. 24 Illusts.
Philistia.	In all Shades	Dumaresq's Daughter.	At Market Value.

Under Sealed Orders. Crown 8vo, cloth extra, 3s. 6d.
Dr. Palliser's Patient. Fcap. 8vo, cloth boards, 1s. 6d.

Anderson (Mary).—Othello's Occupation: A Novel. Crown 8vo,
cloth, 3s. 6d.

Arnold (Edwin Lester), Stories by.
The Wonderful Adventures of Phra the Phœnician. Crown 8vo, cloth extra, with 12
Illustrations by H. M. PAGET. 3s. 6d.; post 8vo, illustrated boards, 2s.
The Constable of St. Nicholas. With Frontispiece by S. L. WOOD. Crown 8vo, cloth, 3s. 6d.

Artemus Ward's Works. With Portrait and Facsimile. Crown 8vo,
cloth extra, 7s. 6d.—Also a POPULAR EDITION, post 8vo, picture boards, 2s.

Ashton (John), Works by. Crown 8vo, cloth extra, 7s. 6d. each.
History of the Chap-Books of the 18th Century. With 334 Illustrations.
Social Life in the Reign of Queen Anne. With 85 Illustrations.
Humour, Wit, and Satire of the Seventeenth Century. With 82 Illustrations.
English Caricature and Satire on Napoleon the First. With 115 Illustrations.
Modern Street Ballads. With 57 Illustrations.

Bacteria, Yeast Fungi, and Allied Species, A Synopsis of. By
W. D. GROVE, B A. With 87 Illustrations. Crown 8vo, cloth extra, 3s. 6d.

Bardsley (Rev. C. Wareing, M.A.), Works by.
English Surnames: Their Sources and Significations. Crown 8vo, cloth, 7s. 6d.
Curiosities of Puritan Nomenclature. Crown 8vo, cloth extra, 6s.

Baring Gould (Sabine, Author of 'John Herring,' &c), Novels by.
   Crown 8vo, cloth extra, 3s. 6d. each; post 8vo, illustrated boards, 2s. each.
Red Spider. | Eve.

Barr (Robert: Luke Sharp), Stories by. Cr. 8vo, cl., 3s. 6d. each.
In a Steamer Chair. With Frontispiece and Vignette by DEMAIN HAMMOND.
From Whose Bourne, &c, With 47 Illustrations by HAL HURST and others.
A Woman Intervenes. With 8 Illustrations by HAL HURST. Crown 8vo, cloth extra, 6s.
Revenge! With 12 Illustrations by LANCELOT SPEED, &c. Crown 8vo, cloth, 6s.

Barrett (Frank), Novels by.
    Post 8vo, illustrated boards, 2s. each; cloth, 2s. 6d. each.

Fettered for Life.	A Prodigal's Progress.
The Sin of Olga Zassoulich.	John Ford; and His Helpmate.
Between Life and Death.	A Recoiling Vengeance.
Folly Morrison. | Honest Davie.	Lieut. Barnabas. | Found Guilty.
Little Lady Linton.	For Love and Honour.

The Woman of the Iron Bracelets. Cr. 8vo, cloth, 3s. 6d. ; post 8vo, boards, 2s.; cl. limp, 2s. 6d.
    Crown 8vo, cloth extra, 3s. 6d. each.
The Harding Scandal.   [April.
A Missing Witness. With Eight Illustrations by W. H. MARGETSON.

Barrett (Joan).—Monte Carlo Stories. Fcap. 8vo, cloth, 1s 6d.

Beaconsfield, Lord. By T. P. O'CONNOR, M.P. Cr. 8vo, cloth, 5s.

Beauchamp (Shelsley).—Grantley Grange. Post 8vo, boards, 2s.

Beautiful Pictures by British Artists: A Gathering of Favourites
from the Picture Galleries, engraved on Steel. Imperial 4to, cloth extra, gilt edges, 21s.

Besant (Sir Walter) and James Rice, Novels by.
Crown 8vo, cloth extra, 3s. 6d. each; post 8vo, illustrated boards, 2s. each; cloth limp, 2s. 6d. each.

Ready-Money Mortiboy.	By Celia's Arbour.
My Little Girl.	The Chaplain of the Fleet.
With Harp and Crown.	The Seamy Side.
This Son of Vulcan.	The Case of Mr. Lucraft, &c.
The Golden Butterfly.	'Twas in Trafalgar's Bay, &c.
The Monks of Thelema.	The Ten Years' Tenant, &c.

* There is also a LIBRARY EDITION of the above Twelve Volumes, handsomely set in new type on a
large crown 8vo page, and bound in cloth extra, 6s. each; and a POPULAR EDITION of The Golden
Butterfly, medium 8vo, 6d. ; cloth, 1s.—NEW EDITIONS, printed in large type on crown 8vo laid paper,
bound in figured cloth, 3s. 6d. each, are also in course of publication.

Besant (Sir Walter), Novels by.
Crown 8vo, cloth extra, 3s. 6d. each post 8vo, illustrated boards, 2s. each; cloth limp, 2s. 6d. each.
All Sorts and Conditions of Men. With 12 Illustrations by FRED. BARNARD
The Captains' Room, &c. With Frontispiece by E. J. WHEELER.
All in a Garden Fair. With 6 Illustrations by HARRY FURNISS.
Dorothy Forster. With Frontispiece by CHARLES GREEN.
Uncle Jack, and other Stories.   \| Children of Gibeon.
The World Went Very Well Then. With 12 Illustrations by A. FORESTIER.
Herr Paulus: His Rise, his Greatness, and his Fall \| The Bell of St. Paul's.
For Faith and Freedom. With Illustrations by A. FORESTIER and F. WADDY.
To Call Her Mine, &c. With 9 Illustrations by A. FORESTIER.
The Holy Rose, &c. With Frontispiece by F. BARNARD.
Armorel of Lyonesse: A Romance of To-day With 12 Illustrations by F. BARNARD.
St. Katherine's by the Tower. With 12 Illustrations by C. GREEN.
Verbena Camellia Stephanotis, &c. With a Frontispiece by GORDON BROWNE.
The Ivory Gate.   \| The Rebel Queen.
Beyond the Dreams of Avarice. With 12 Illustrations by W. H. HYDE.
        Crown 8vo, cloth extra, 3s. 6d. each.
In Deacon's Orders, &c. With Frontispiece by A. FORESTIER.
The Revolt of Man.   \| The Master Craftsman.   [May.
The City of Refuge. 3 vols., crown 8vo, 15s. net.
The Charm, and other Drawing-room Plays. By Sir WALTER BESANT and WALTER H. POLLOCK.
    With 50 Illustrations by CHRIS HAMMOND and JULE GOODMAN Crown 8vo, cloth, gilt edges, 6s.
Fifty Years Ago. With 144 Plates and Woodcuts. Crown 8vo, cloth extra, 5s.
The Eulogy of Richard Jefferies. With Portrait. Crown 8vo, cloth extra, 6s.
London. With 125 Illustrations. Demy 8vo, cloth extra, 7s. 6d.
Westminster. With Etched Frontispiece by F. S. WALKER, R.P.E., and 130 Illustrations by.
    WILLIAM PATTEN and others. Demy 8vo, cloth, 18s.
Sir Richard Whittington. With Frontispiece. Crown 8vo, art linen, 3s. 6d.
Gaspard de Coligny. With a Portrait. Crown 8vo, art linen, 3s. 6d.

Bechstein (Ludwig).—As Pretty as Seven, and other German
Stories. With Additional Tales by the Brothers GRIMM, and 98 Illustrations by RICHTER. Square 8vo, cloth extra, 6s. 6d., gilt edges, 7s. 6d.

Bellew (Frank).—The Art of Amusing: A Collection of Graceful
Arts, Games, Tricks, Puzzles, and Charades. With 300 Illustrations. Crown 8vo, cloth extra, 4s. 6d.

Bennett (W. C., LL.D.).—Songs for Sailors. Post 8vo, cl. limp, 2s.

Bewick (Thomas) and his Pupils. By AUSTIN DOBSON. With 95
Illustrations. Square 8vo, cloth extra, 6s.

Bierce (Ambrose).—In the Midst of Life: Tales of Soldiers and
Civilians. Crown 8vo, cloth extra, 6s.; post 8vo, illustrated boards, 2s.

Bill Nye's History of the United States. With 146 Illustrations
by F. OPPER. Crown 8vo, cloth extra, 3s. 6d.

Biré (Edmond).—Diary of a Citizen of Paris during 'The
Terror.' Translated and Edited by JOHN DE VILLIERS. With 2 Photogravure Portraits. Two Vols., demy 8vo, cloth, 21s.

Blackburn's (Henry) Art Handbooks.
Academy Notes, 1875, 1877-88, 1889, 1890, 1892-1899, Illustrated, each 1s.
Academy Notes, 1897. 1s. [May.
Academy Notes, 1875-79. Complete in One Vol., with 600 Illustrations. Cloth, 6s.
Academy Notes, 1880-84. Complete in One Vol., with 700 Illustrations. Cloth, 6s.
Academy Notes, 1890-94. Complete in One Vol., with 800 Illustrations. Cloth, 7s. 6d.
Grosvenor Notes, 1877. 6d.
Grosvenor Notes, separate years from **1878-1890,** each 1s.
Grosvenor Notes, Vol. I., **1877-82.** With 300 Illustrations. Demy 8vo, cloth, 6s.

Grosvenor Notes, Vol. II., **1883-87.** With 300 Illustrations. Demy 8vo, cloth, 6s.
Grosvenor Notes, Vol. III., **1888-90.** With 230 Illustrations. Demy 8vo, cloth, 3s. 6d.
The New Gallery, 1888-1895. With numerous Illustrations, each 1s.
The New Gallery, 1888-1892. With 250 Illustrations. Demy 8vo, cloth, 6s.
English Pictures at the National Gallery. With 114 Illustrations. 1s.
Old Masters at the National Gallery. With 128 Illustrations. 1s. 6d.
Illustrated Catalogue to the National Gallery. With 242 Illusts. Demy 8vo, cloth, 3s.

The Illustrated Catalogue of the Paris Salon, 1897. With 300 Sketches. 3s. [May.

Blind (Mathilde), Poems by.
The Ascent of Man. Crown 8vo, cloth, 5s.
Dramas in Miniature. With a Frontispiece by F. MADOX BROWN. Crown 8vo, cloth, 5s.
Songs and Sonnets. Fcap. 8vo, vellum and gold, 5s.
Birds of Passage: Songs of the Orient and Occident. Second Edition. Crown 8vo, linen, 6s. net.

Bourget (Paul).—A Living Lie. Translated by JOHN DE VILLIERS.
With special Preface for the English Edition. Crown 8vo, cloth, 3s. 6d.

Bourne (H. R. Fox), Books by.
English Merchants: Memoirs in Illustration of the Progress of British Commerce. With numerous Illustrations. Crown 8vo, cloth extra, 7s. 6d.
English Newspapers: Chapters in the History of Journalism. Two Vols., demy 8vo, cloth, 25s.
The Other Side of the Emin Pasha Relief Expedition. Crown 8vo, cloth, 6s.

Bowers (George).—Leaves from a Hunting Journal. Coloured
Plates. Oblong folio, half-bound, 21s.

Boyle (Frederick), Works by. Post 8vo, illustrated bds., 2s. each.
Chronicles of No-Man's Land. | **Camp Notes.** | **Savage Life.**

Brand (John).—Observations on Popular Antiquities; chiefly
Illustrating the Origin of our Vulgar Customs, Ceremonies, and Superstitions. With the Additions of Sir HENRY ELLIS, and numerous Illustrations. Crown 8vo, cloth extra, 7s. 6d.

Brewer (Rev. Dr.), Works by.
The Reader's Handbook of Allusions, References, Plots, and Stories. Eighteenth Thousand. Crown 8vo, cloth extra, 7s. 6d.
Authors and their Works, with the Dates: Being the Appendices to 'The Reader's Handbook,' separately printed. Crown 8vo, cloth limp, 2s.
A Dictionary of Miracles. Crown 8vo, cloth extra, 7s. 6d.

Brewster (Sir David), Works by. Post 8vo, cloth, 4s. 6d. each.
More Worlds than One: Creed of the Philosopher and Hope of the Christian. With Plates.
The Martyrs of Science: GALILEO, TYCHO BRAHE, and KEPLER. With Portraits.
Letters on Natural Magic. With numerous Illustrations.

Brillat-Savarin.—Gastronomy as a Fine Art. Translated by
R. E. ANDERSON, M.A. Post 8vo, half-bound, 2s.

Brydges (Harold).—Uncle Sam at Home. With 91 Illustrations.
Post 8vo, illustrated boards, 2s.; cloth limp, 2s. 6d.

Buchanan (Robert), Novels, &c., by.

Crown 8vo, cloth extra, 3s. 6d. each; pos 8vo, illustrated boards, 2s. each.

The Shadow of the Sword.
A Child of Nature. With Frontispiece.
God and the Man. With 11 Illustrations by FRED. BARNARD.
The Martyrdom of Madeline. With Frontispiece by A. W. COOPER.

Love Me for Ever. With Frontispiece.
Annan Water. | **Foxglove Manor.**
The New Abelard. | **Rachel Dene.**
Matt: A Story of a Caravan. With Frontispiece.
The Master of the Mine. With Frontispiece.
The Heir of Linne. | **Woman and the Man.**

Crown 8vo, cloth extra, 3s. 6d. each.
Red and White Heather. | **Lady Kilpatrick.**

The Wandering Jew: a Christmas Carol. Crown 8vo, cloth, 6s.

The Charlatan. By ROBERT BUCHANAN and HENRY MURRAY. Crown 8vo, cloth, with a Frontispiece by T. H. ROBINSON, 3s. 6d.; post 8vo, picture boards, 2s.

Burton (Richard F.).—The Book of the Sword. With over 400
Illustrations. Demy 4to, cloth extra, 32s.

Burton (Robert).—The Anatomy of Melancholy. With Transla-
tions of the Quotations. Demy 8vo, cloth extra, 7s. 6d.
Melancholy Anatomised: An Abridgment of BURTON'S ANATOMY. Post 8vo, half-bd., 2s. 6d.

Caine (T. Hall), Novels by. Crown 8vo, cloth extra, 3s. 6d. each.;
post 8vo, illustrated boards, 2s. each; cloth limp, 2s. 6d. each.
The Shadow of a Crime. | **A Son of Hagar.** | **The Deemster.**
Also a LIBRARY EDITION of **The Deemster**, set in new type, crown 8vo, cloth decorated, 6s.

Cameron (Commander V. Lovett).—The Cruise of the 'Black
Prince' Privateer. Post 8vo, picture boards, 2s.

Cameron (Mrs. H. Lovett), Novels by. Post 8vo, illust. bds. 2s. ea.
Juliet's Guardian. | **Deceivers Ever.**

Captain Coignet, Soldier of the Empire: An Autobiography.
Edited by LOREDAN LARCHEY. Translated by Mrs. CAREY. With 100 Illustrations. Crown 8vo, cloth, 3s. 6d.

Carlyle (Jane Welsh), Life of. By Mrs. ALEXANDER IRELAND. With
Portrait and Facsimile Letter. Small demy 8vo, cloth extra, 7s. 6d.

Carlyle (Thomas).—On the Choice of Books. Post 8vo, cl., 1s. 6d.
Correspondence of Thomas Carlyle and R. W. Emerson, 1834-1872. Edited by C. E. NORTON. With Portraits. Two Vols., crown 8vo, cloth, 24s.

Carruth (Hayden).—The Adventures of Jones. With 17 Illustra-
tions. Fcap. 8vo, cloth, 2s.

Chambers (Robert W.), Stories of Paris Life by. Long fcap. 8vo,
cloth, 2s. 6d. each.
The King in Yellow. | **In the Quarter.**

Chapman's (George), Works. Vol. I., Plays Complete, including the
Doubtful Ones.—Vol. II., Poems and Minor Translations, with Essay by A. C. SWINBURNE.—Vol. III., Translations of the Iliad and Odyssey. Three Vols., crown 8vo, cloth, 3s. 6d. each.

Chapple (J. Mitchell).—The Minor Chord: The Story of a Prima
Donna. Crown 8vo, cloth, 3s. 6d.

Chatto (W. A.) and J. Jackson.—A Treatise on Wood Engraving,
Historical and Practical. With Chapter by H. G. BOHN, and 450 fine Illusts. Large 4to, half-leather, 28s.

Chaucer for Children: A Golden Key. By Mrs. H. R. HAWEIS. With
8 Coloured Plates and 30 Woodcuts. Crown 4to, cloth extra, 3s. 6d.
Chaucer for Schools. By Mrs. H. R. HAWEIS. Demy 8vo, cloth limp, 2s. 6d.

Chess, The Laws and Practice of. With an Analysis of the Open-
ings. By HOWARD STAUNTON. Edited by R. B. WORMALD. Crown 8vo, cloth, 5s.
The Minor Tactics of Chess: A Treatise on the Deployment of the Forces in obedience to Strategic Principle. By F. K. YOUNG and E. C. HOWELL. Long fcap. 8vo, cloth, 2s. 6d.
The Hastings Chess Tournament. Containing the Authorised Account of the 230 Games played Aug.-Sept., 1895. With Annotations by PILLSBURY, LASKER, TARRASCH, STEINITZ, SCHIFFERS, TEICHMANN, BARDELEBEN, BLACKBURNE, GUNSBERG, TINSLEY, MASON, and ALBIN; Biographical Sketches of the Chess Masters, and 22 Portraits. Edited by H. F. CHESHIRE. Crown 8vo, cloth, 7s. 6d.

Clare (Austin).—For the Love of a Lass. Post 8vo, 2s.; cl., 2s. 6d.

Clive (Mrs. Archer), Novels by. Post 8vo, illust. boards, 2s. each.
Paul Ferroll. | Why Paul Ferroll Killed his Wife.

Clodd (Edward, F.R.A.S.).—Myths and Dreams. Cr. 8vo, 3s. 6d.

Cobban (J. Maclaren), Novels by.
The Cure of Souls. Post 8vo, Illustrated boards, 2s.
The Red Sultan. Crown 8vo, cloth extra, 3s. 6d. ; post 8vo, illustrated boards, 2s.
The Burden of Isabel. Crown 8vo, cloth extra, 3s. 6d.

Coleman (John).—Curly: An Actor's Story. With 21 Illustrations
by J. C. DOLLMAN. Crown 8vo, picture cover, 1s.

Coleridge (M. E.).—The Seven Sleepers of Ephesus. Cloth, 1s. 6d.

Collins (C. Allston).—The Bar Sinister. Post 8vo, boards, 2s.

Collins (John Churton, M.A.), Books by.
Illustrations of Tennyson. Crown 8vo, cloth extra, 6s.
Jonathan Swift : A Biographical and Critical Study. Crown 8vo, cloth extra, 8s.

Collins (Mortimer and Frances), Novels by.
            Crown 8vo, cloth extra, 3s. 6d. each ; post 8vo, illustrated boards, 2s. each.
From Midnight to Midnight. | Blacksmith and Scholar.
Transmigration. | You Play me False. | The Village Comedy.

            Post 8vo, illustrated boards, 2s. each.
Sweet Anne Page. | A Fight with Fortune. | Sweet and Twenty. | Frances.

Collins (Wilkie), Novels by.
            Crown 8vo, cloth extra, many Illustrated, 3s. 6d. each ; post 8vo, picture boards, 2s. each;
                                                cloth limp, 2s. 6d. each.

*Antonina.	Armadale.	Jezebel's Daughter.
*Basil.	Man and Wife.	The Black Robe.
*Hide and Seek.	Poor Miss Finch.	Heart and Science.
*The Woman in White.	Miss or Mrs.?	'I Say No.'
*The Moonstone.	The New Magdalen.	A Rogue's Life.
After Dark.	The Frozen Deep.	The Evil Genius.
The Dead Secret.	The Law and the Lady.	Little Novels.
The Queen of Hearts.	The Two Destinies.	The Legacy of Cain.
No Name.	The Haunted Hotel.	Blind Love.
My Miscellanies.	The Fallen Leaves.	

. *Marked * are the* NEW LIBRARY EDITION *at 3s. 6d., entirely reset and bound in new style.*

            POPULAR EDITIONS. Medium 8vo, 6d. each; cloth, 1s. each.
The Woman in White. | The Moonstone. | Antonina.

The Woman in White and The Moonstone in One Volume, medium 8vo, cloth, 2s.

Colman's (George) Humorous Works: 'Broad Grins,' 'My Night-
gown and Slippers,' &c. With Life and Frontispiece. Crown 8vo, cloth extra, 7s. 6d.

Colquhoun (M. J.).—Every Inch a Soldier. Post 8vo, boards, 2s.

Colt-breaking, Hints on. By W. M. HUTCHISON. Cr. 8vo, cl., 3s. 6d.

Convalescent Cookery. By CATHERINE RYAN. Cr. 8vo, 1s. ; cl., 1s. 6d.

Conway (Moncure D.), Works by.
Demonology and Devil-Lore. With 65 Illustrations. Two Vols., demy 8vo, cloth, 28s.
George Washington's Rules of Civility. Fcap. 8vo, Japanese vellum, 2s. 6d.

Cook (Dutton), Novels by.
            Post 8vo, illustrated boards, 2s. each.
Leo. | Paul Foster's Daughter.

Cooper (Edward H.).—Geoffory Hamilton. Cr. 8vo, cloth, 3s. 6d.

Cornwall.—Popular Romances of the West of England; or, The
Drolls, Traditions, and Superstitions of Old Cornwall. Collected by ROBERT HUNT, F.R.S. With
two Steel Plates by GEORGE CRUIKSHANK. Crown 8vo, cloth, 7s. 6d.

Cotes (V. Cecil).—Two Girls on a Barge. With 44 Illustrations by
F. H. TOWNSEND. Post 8vo, cloth, 2s. 6d.

Craddock (C. Egbert), Stories by.
The Prophet of the Great Smoky Mountains. Post 8vo, illustrated boards, 2s.
His Vanished Star. Crown 8vo, cloth extra, 3s. 6d.

Cram (Ralph Adams).—Black Spirits and White. Fcap. 8vo,
cloth, 1s. 6d.

Crellin (H. N.) Books by.
Romances of the Old Seraglio. With 28 Illustrations by S. L. WOOD. Crown 8vo, cloth, 3s. 6d.
Tales of the Caliph. Crown 8vo, cloth, 2s.
The Nazarenes: A Drama. Crown 8vo, 1s.

Crim (Matt.).—Adventures of a Fair Rebel. Crown 8vo, cloth
extra, with a Frontispiece by DAN. BEARD, 3s. 6d.; post 8vo, illustrated boards, 2s.

Crockett (S. R.) and others.—Tales of Our Coast. By S. R.
CROCKETT, GILBERT PARKER, HAROLD FREDERIC, 'Q.,' and W. CLARK RUSSELL. With 12
Illustrations by FRANK BRANGWYN. Crown 8vo, cloth, 3s. 6d.

Croker (Mrs. B. M.), Novels by. Crown 8vo, cloth extra, 3s. 6d.
each; post 8vo, illustrated boards 2s. each; cloth limp, 2s. 6d. each.
Pretty Miss Neville. | Diana Barrington. | A Family Likeness.
A Bird of Passage. | Proper Pride. | 'To Let.'
Village Tales and Jungle Tragedies. | Two Masters. | Mr. Jervis.

                              Crown 8vo, cloth extra, 3s. 6d. each.
Married or Single? | In the Kingdom of Kerry.
The Real Lady Hilda.

Beyond the Pale. Crown 8vo, buckram, 6s.

Cruikshank's Comic Almanack. Complete in Two SERIES: The
FIRST, from 1835 to 1843; the SECOND, from 1844 to 1853. A Gathering of the Best Humour of
THACKERAY, HOOD, MAYHEW, ALBERT SMITH, A'BECKETT, ROBERT BROUGH, &c. With
numerous Steel Engravings and Woodcuts by GEORGE CRUIKSHANK, HINE, LANDELLS, &c.
Two Vols., crown 8vo, cloth gilt, 7s. 6d. each.
The Life of George Cruikshank. By BLANCHARD JERROLD. With 84 Illustrations and a
Bibliography. Crown 8vo, cloth extra, 6s.

Cumming (C. F. Gordon), Works by. Demy 8vo, cl. ex., 8s. 6d. ea.
In the Hebrides. With an Autotype Frontispiece and 23 Illustrations.
In the Himalayas and on the Indian Plains. With 42 Illustrations.
Two Happy Years in Ceylon. With 28 Illustrations.

Via Cornwall to Egypt. With a Photogravure Frontispiece. Demy 8vo, cloth, 7s. 6d.

Cussans (John E.).—A Handbook of Heraldry; with Instructions
for Tracing Pedigrees and Deciphering Ancient MSS., &c. Fourth Edition, revised, with 408 Woodcuts
and 2 Coloured Plates. Crown 8vo, cloth extra, 6s.

Cyples (W.).—Hearts of Gold. Cr. 8vo, cl., 3s. 6d.; post 8vo, bds., 2s.

Daudet (Alphonse).—The Evangelist; or, Port Salvation. Crown
8vo, cloth extra, 3s. 6d.; post 8vo, illustrated boards, 2s.

Davenant (Francis, M.A.).—Hints for Parents on the Choice of
a Profession for their Sons when Starting in Life Crown 8vo, cloth, 1s. 6d.

Davidson (Hugh Coleman).—Mr. Sadler's Daughters. With a
Frontispiece by STANLEY WOOD. Crown 8vo, cloth extra, 3s. 6d.

Davies (Dr. N. E. Yorke-), Works by. Cr. 8vo, 1s. ea.; cl., 1s. 6d. ea.
One Thousand Medical Maxims and Surgical Hints.
Nursery Hints: A Mother's Guide in Health and Disease.
Foods for the Fat: A Treatise on Corpulency, and a Dietary for its Cure.

Aids to Long Life. Crown 8vo, 2s.; cloth limp, 2s. 6d.

Davies' (Sir John) Complete Poetical Works. Collected and Edited,
with Introduction and Notes, by Rev. A. B. GROSART, D.D. | Two Vols., crown 8vo, cloth, 3s. 6d. each.

Dawson (Erasmus, M.B.).—The Fountain of Youth. Crown 8vo,
cloth extra, with Two Illustrations by HUME NISBET, 3s. 6d.; post 8vo, illustrated boards, 2s.

De Guerin (Maurice), The Journal of. Edited by G. S. TREBUTIEN.
With a Memoir by SAINTE-BEUVE. Translated from the 20th French Edition by JESSIE P. FROTH
INGHAM. Fcap. 8vo, half-bound, 2s. 6d.

De Maistre (Xavier).—A Journey Round my Room. Translated
by Sir HENRY ATTWELL. Post 8vo, cloth limp, 2s. 6d.

De Mille (James).—A Castle in Spain. Crown 8vo, cloth extra, with
a Frontispiece, 3s. 6d.; post 8vo, illustrated boards, 2s.

Derby (The): The Blue Ribbon of the Turf. With Brief Accounts
of THE OAKS. By LOUIS HENRY CURZON. Crown 8vo, cloth limp, 2s. 6d.

Derwent (Leith), Novels by. Cr. 8vo, cl., 3s. 6d. ea. ; post 8vo, 2s. ea.
Our Lady of Tears. | Circe's Lovers.

Dewar (T. R.).—A Ramble Round the Globe. With 220 Illustra-
tions. Crown 8vo, cloth extra, 7s. 6d.

Dickens (Charles).—Sketches by Boz. Post 8vo, illust. boards, 2s.
About England with Dickens. By ALFRED RIMMER. With 57 Illustrations by C. A. VANDER-
HOOF, ALFRED RIMMER, and others. Square 8vo, cloth extra, 7s. 6d.

Dictionaries.
A Dictionary of Miracles: Imitative, Realistic, and Dogmatic. By the Rev. E. C, BREWER,
LL.D. Crown 8vo, cloth extra, 7s. 6d.
The Reader's Handbook of Allusions, References, Plots, and Stories. By the Rev.
E, C. BREWER, LL.D. With an ENGLISH BIBLIOGRAPHY. Crown 8vo, cloth extra, 7s. 6d.
Authors and their Works, with the Dates. Crown 8vo, cloth limp, 2s.
Familiar Short Sayings of Great Men. With Historical and Explanatory Notes by SAMUEL
A. BENT, A.M. Crown 8vo, cloth extra, 7s. 6d.
The Slang Dictionary: Etymological, Historical, and Anecdotal. Crown 8vo, cloth, 6s. 6d.
Words, Facts, and Phrases: A Dictionary of Curious, Quaint, and Out-of-the-Way Matters. By
ELIEZER EDWARDS. Crown 8vo, cloth extra, 7s. 6d.

Diderot.—The Paradox of Acting. Translated, with Notes, by
WALTER HERRIES POLLOCK. With Preface by Sir HENRY IRVING. Crown 8vo, parchment, 4s. 6d.

Dobson (Austin), Works by.
Thomas Bewick and his Pupils. With 95 Illustrations. Square 8vo, cloth, 6s.
Four Frenchwomen. With Four Portraits. Crown 8vo, buckram, gilt top 6s.
Eighteenth Century Vignettes. IN THREE SERIES. Crown 8vo, buckram, 6s. each.

Dobson (W. T.).—Poetical Ingenuities and Eccentricities. Post
8vo, cloth limp, 2s. 6d.

Donovan (Dick), Detective Stories by.
Post 8vo, illustrated boards, 2s. each ; cloth limp, 2s. 6d. each.

The Man-Hunter. | Wanted!
Caught at Last.
Tracked and Taken.
Who Poisoned Hetty Duncan?
Suspicion Aroused.

A Detective's Triumphs.
In the Grip of the Law.
From Information Received.
Link by Link. | Dark Deeds.
Riddles Read.

Crown 8vo, cloth extra, 3s. 6d. each ; post 8vo, illustrated boards, 2s. each ; cloth, 2s. 6d. each.
The Man from Manchester. With 23 Illustrations.
Tracked to Doom. With Six full-page Illustrations by GORDON BROWNE.
The Mystery of Jamaica Terrace.

The Chronicles of Michael Danevitch, of the Russian Secret Service. Crown 8vo,
cloth, 3s. 6d. [Shortly.

Doyle (A. Conan).—The Firm of Girdlestone. Cr. 8vo, cl., 3s. 6d.

Dramatists, The Old. Cr. 8vo, cl. ex., with Portraits, 3s. 6d. per Vol.
Ben Jonson's Works. With Notes, Critical and Explanatory, and a Biographical Memoir by
WILLIAM GIFFORD. Edited by Colonel CUNNINGHAM. Three Vols.
Chapman's Works. Three Vols. Vol. I. contains the Plays complete ; Vol. II., Poems and Minor
Translations, with an Essay by A. C. SWINBURNE ; Vol. III., Translations of the Iliad and Odyssey.
Marlowe's Works. Edited, with Notes, by Colonel CUNNINGHAM. One Vol.
Massinger's Plays. From GIFFORD'S Text. Edited by Colonel CUNNINGHAM. One Vol.

Duncan (Sara Jeannette: Mrs. EVERARD COTES), Works by.
Crown 8vo, cloth extra, 7s. 6d. each.
A Social Departure. With 111 Illustrations by F. H. TOWNSEND.
An American Girl in London. With 80 Illustrations by F. H. TOWNSEND.
The Simple Adventures of a Memsahib. With 37 Illustrations by F. H. TOWNSEN

Crown 8vo, cloth extra, 3s. 6d. each.
A Daughter of To-Day. | Vernon's Aunt. With 47 Illustrations by HAL HURST.

Dyer (T. F. Thiselton).—The Folk-Lore of Plants. Cr. 8vo, cl., 6s.

Early English Poets. Edited, with Introductions and Annotations,
by Rev. A. B. GROSART, D.D. Crown 8vo, cloth boards, 3s. 6d. per Volume.
Fletcher's (Giles) Complete Poems. One Vol.
Davies' (Sir John) Complete Poetical Works. Two Vols.
Herrick's (Robert) Complete Collected Poems. Three Vols.
Sidney's (Sir Philip) Complete Poetical Works. Three Vols.

Edgcumbe (Sir E. R. Pearce).— Zephyrus: A Holiday in Brazil
and on the River Plate. With 41 Illustrations. Crown 8vo, cloth extra, 5s.

Edison, The Life and Inventions of Thomas A. By W. K. L. and
ANTONIA DICKSON. With 200 Illustrations by R. F. OUTCALT, &c. Demy 4to, cloth gilt, 18s.

Edwardes (Mrs. Annie), Novels by.
Post 8vo, illustrated boards, 2s. each.
Archie Lovell. | A Point of Honour.

Edwards (Eliezer).—Words, Facts, and Phrases: A Dictionary
of Curious Quaint, and Out-of-the-Way Matters. Crown 8vo, cloth, 7s. 6d.

Edwards (M. Betham-), Novels by.
Kitty. Post 8vo, boards, 2s.; cloth, 2s. 6d. | Felicia. Post 8vo, illustrated boards, 2s.

Egerton (Rev. J. C., M.A.).— Sussex Folk and Sussex Ways.
With Introduction by Rev. Dr. H. WACE, and Four Illustrations. Crown 8vo, cloth extra, 5s.

Eggleston (Edward).—Roxy: A Novel. Post 8vo, illust. boards, 2s.

Englishman's House, The: A Practical Guide for Selecting or Build-
ing a House. By C. J. RICHARDSON. Coloured Frontispiece and 534 Illusts. Cr. 8vo, cloth, 7s. 6d.

Ewald (Alex. Charles, F.S.A.), Works by.
The Life and Times of Prince Charles Stuart, Count of Albany (THE YOUNG PRETEN-
DER). With a Portrait. Crown 8vo, cloth extra, 7s. 6d.
Stories from the State Papers. With Autotype Frontispiece. Crown 8vo, cloth, 6s.

Eyes, Our : How to Preserve Them. By JOHN BROWNING. Cr. 8vo, 1s.

Familiar Short Sayings of Great Men. By SAMUEL ARTHUR BENT,
A.M. Fifth Edition, Revised and Enlarged. Crown 8vo, cloth extra, 7s. 6d.

Faraday (Michael), Works by. Post 8vo, cloth extra, 4s. 6d. each.
The Chemical History of a Candle: Lectures delivered before a Juvenile Audience. Edited
by WILLIAM CROOKES, F.C.S. With numerous Illustrations.
On the Various Forces of Nature, and their Relations to each other. Edited by
WILLIAM CROOKES, F.C.S. With Illustrations.

Farrer (J. Anson), Works by.
Military Manners and Customs. Crown 8vo, cloth extra, 6s.
War: Three Essays, reprinted from 'Military Manners and Customs.' Crown 8vo, 1s.; cloth, 1s. 6d.

Fenn (G. Manville), Novels by.
Crown 8vo, cloth extra, 3s. 6d. each; post 8vo, illustrated boards, 2s. each.
The New Mistress. | Witness to the Deed. | The Tiger Lily. | The White Virgin.

Fin-Bec.—The Cupboard Papers: Observations on the Art of Living
and Dining. Post 8vo, cloth limp, 2s. 6d.

Fireworks, The Complete Art of Making ; or, The Pyrotechnist's
Treasury. By THOMAS KENTISH. With 267 Illustrations. Crown 8vo, cloth, 5s.

First Book, My. By WALTER BESANT, JAMES PAYN, W. CLARK RUS-
SELL, GRANT ALLEN, HALL CAINE, GEORGE R. SIMS, RUDYARD KIPLING, A. CONAN DOYLE,
M. E. BRADDON, F. W. ROBINSON, H. RIDER HAGGARD, R. M. BALLANTYNE, I. ZANGWILL,
MORLEY ROBERTS, D. CHRISTIE MURRAY, MARY CORELLI, J. K. JEROME, JOHN STRANGE
WINTER, BRET HARTE, 'Q.,' ROBERT BUCHANAN, and R. L. STEVENSON. With a Prefatory Story
by JEROME K. JEROME, and 185 Illustrations. A New Edition. Small demy 8vo, art linen, 3s. 6d.

Fitzgerald (Percy), Works by.
Little Essays: Passages from the Letters of CHARLES LAMB. Post 8vo, cloth, 2s. 6d.
Fatal Zero. Crown 8vo, cloth extra, 3s. 6d.; post 8vo, illustrated boards, 2s.

Pos 8vo, illustrated boards, 2s. each.
Bella Donna. | The Lady of Brantome. | The Second Mrs. Tillotson.
Polly. | Never Forgotten. | Seventy-five Brooke Street.

The Life of James Boswell (of Auchinleck). With Illusts. Two Vols., demy 8vo, cloth, 24s.
The Savoy Opera. With 60 Illustrations and Portraits. Crown 8vo, cloth, 3s. 6d.
Sir Henry Irving: Twenty Years at the Lyceum. With Portrait. Crown 8vo, 1s.; cloth, 1s. 6d.

Flammarion (Camille), Works by.
Popular Astronomy: A General Description of the Heavens. Translated by J. ELLARD GORE,
F.R.A.S. With Three Plates and 283 Illustrations. Medium 8vo, cloth, 16s.
Urania: A Romance. With 87 Illustrations. Crown 8vo, cloth extra, 5s.

Fletcher's (Giles, B.D.) Complete Poems: Christ's Victorie in
Heaven, Christ's Victorie on Earth, Christ's Triumph over Death, and Minor Poems. With Notes by
Rev. A. B. GROSART, D.D. Crown 8vo, cloth boards, 3s. 6d.

Fonblanque (Albany).---Filthy Lucre. Post 8vo, illust. boards, 2s.

Francillon (R. E.), Novels by.
Crown 8vo, cloth extra, 3s. 6d. each; post 8vo, illustrated boards, 2s. each.

One by One. | A Real Queen. | A Dog and his Shadow.
Ropes of Sand. Illustrated.

Post 8vo, illustrated boards, 2s. each.

Queen Cophetua. | Olympia. | Romances of the Law. | King or Knave?

Jack Doyle's Daughter. Crown 8vo, cloth, 3s. 6d.
Esther's Glove. Fcap. 8vo, picture cover, 1s.

Frederic (Harold), Novels by. Post 8vo, illust. boards, 2s. each.
Seth's Brother's Wife. | The Lawton Girl.

French Literature, A History of. By HENRY VAN LAUN. Three
Vols., demy 8vo, cloth boards, 7s. 6d. each.

Friswell (Hain).—One of Two: A Novel. Post 8vo, illust. bds., 2s.

Fry's (Herbert) Royal Guide to the London Charities. Edited
by JOHN LANE. Published Annually. Crown 8vo, cloth, 1s. 6d.

Gardening Books. Post 8vo, 1s. each; cloth limp. 1s. 6d. each.
A Year's Work in Garden and Greenhouse. By GEORGE GLENNY.
Household Horticulture. By TOM and JANE JERROLD. Illustrated.
The Garden that Paid the Rent. By TOM JERROLD.

My Garden Wild. By FRANCIS G. HEATH. Crown 8vo, cloth extra, 6s.

Gardner (Mrs. Alan).—Rifle and Spear with the Rajpoots: Being
the Narrative of a Winter's Travel and Sport in Northern India. With numerous Illustrations by the
Author and F. H. TOWNSEND. Demy 4to, half-bound, 21s.

Garrett (Edward).—The Capel Girls: A Novel. Crown 8vo, cloth
extra, with two Illustrations, 3s. 6d.; post 8vo, illustrated boards, 2s.

Gaulot (Paul).—The Red Shirts: A Story of the Revolution. Trans-
lated by JOHN DE VILLIERS. With a Frontispiece by STANLEY WOOD. Crown 8vo, cloth, 3s. 6d.

Gentleman's Magazine, The. 1s. Monthly. Contains Stories,
Articles upon Literature, Science, Biography, and Art, and 'Table Talk' by SYLVANUS URBAN.
⁎ Bound Volumes for recent years kept in stock, 8s. 6d. each. Cases for binding, 2s. each.

Gentleman's Annual, The. Published Annually in November. 1s.

German Popular Stories. Collected by the Brothers GRIMM and
Translated by EDGAR TAYLOR. With Introduction by JOHN RUSKIN, and 22 Steel Plates after
GEORGE CRUIKSHANK. Square 8vo, cloth, 6s. 6d.; gilt edges, 7s. 6d.

Gibbon (Chas.), Novels by. Cr. 8vo, cl., 3s. 6d. ea.; post 8vo, bds., 2s. ea.
Robin Gray. Frontispiece. | The Golden Shaft. Frontispiece. | Loving a Dream.

Post 8vo, illustrated boards, 2s. each.

The Flower of the Forest. | In Love and War.
The Dead Heart. | A Heart's Problem.
For Lack of Gold. | By Mead and Stream.
What Will the World Say? | The Braes of Yarrow.
For the King. | A Hard Knot. | Fancy Free. | Of High Degree.
Queen of the Meadow. | In Honour Bound.
In Pastures Green. | Heart's Delight. | Blood-Money.

Gilbert (W. S.), Original Plays by. In Three Series, 2s. 6d. each.
The FIRST SERIES contains: The Wicked World—Pygmalion and Galatea—Charity—The Princess—
The Palace of Truth—Trial by Jury.
The SECOND SERIES: Broken Hearts—Engaged—Sweethearts—Gretchen—Dan'l Druce—Tom Cobb
—H.M.S. 'Pinafore'—The Sorcerer—The Pirates of Penzance.
The THIRD SERIES: Comedy and Tragedy—Foggerty's Fairy—Rosencrantz and Guildenstern—
Patience—Princess Ida—The Mikado—Ruddigore—The Yeomen of the Guard—The Gondoliers—
The Mountebanks—Utopia.

Eight Original Comic Operas written by W. S. GILBERT. In Two Series. Demy 8vo, cloth,
2s. 6d. each. The FIRST containing: The Sorcerer—H.M.S. 'Pinafore'—The Pirates of Penzance—
Iolanthe—Patience—Princess Ida—The Mikado—Trial by Jury.
The SECOND SERIES containing: The Gondoliers—The Grand Duke—The Yeomen of the Guard—
His Excellency—Utopia, Limited—Ruddigore—The Mountebanks—Haste to the Wedding.
The Gilbert and Sullivan Birthday Book: Quotations for Every Day n the Year, selected
from Plays by W. S. GILBERT set to Music by Sir A. SULLIVAN. Compiled by ALEX. WATSON.
Royal 16mo, Japanese leather, 2s. 6d.

Gilbert (William), Novels by. Post 8vo, illustrated bds., 2s. each.
Dr. Austin's Guests. | James Duke, Costermonger.
The Wizard of the Mountain.

Glanville (Ernest), Novels by.
Crown 8vo, cloth extra, 3s. 6d. each; post 8vo, illustrated boards, 2s. each.
The Lost Heiress: A Tale of Love, Battle, and Adventure. With Two Illustrations by H. NISBET
The Fossicker: A Romance of Mashonaland. With Two Illustrations by HUME NISBET.
A Fair Colonist. With a Frontispiece by STANLEY WOOD.

The Golden Rock. With a Frontispiece by STANLEY WOOD. Crown 8vo, cloth extra, 3s. 6d.
Kloof Yarns. Crown 8vo, picture cover, 1s.; cloth, 1s. 6d.

Glenny (George).—A Year's Work in Garden and Greenhouse:
Practical Advice as to the Management of the Flower, Fruit, and Frame Garden. Post 8vo, 1s.; cloth, 1s. 6d.

Godwin (William).—Lives of the Necromancers. Post 8vo, cl., 2s.

Golden Treasury of Thought, The: An Encyclopædia of QUOTATIONS. Edited by THEODORE TAYLOR. Crown 8vo, cloth gilt, 7s. 6d.

Gontaut, Memoirs of the Duchesse de (Gouvernante to the Children of France), 1773-1836. With Two Photogravures. Two Vols., demy 8vo, cloth extra, 21s.

Goodman (E. J.).—The Fate of Herbert Wayne. Cr. 8vo, 3s. 6d.

Graham (Leonard).—The Professor's Wife: A Story. Fcp. 8vo, 1s.

Greeks and Romans, The Life of the, described from Antique Monuments. By ERNST GUHL and W. KONER. Edited by Dr. F. HUEFFER. With 545 Illustrations. Large crown 8vo, cloth extra, 7s. 6d.

Greville (Henry), Novels by.
Post 8vo, illustrated boards, 2s. each.
Nikanor. Translated by ELIZA E. CHASE.
A Noble Woman. Translated by ALBERT D. VANDAM.

Griffith (Cecil).—Corinthia Marazion: A Novel. Crown 8vo, cloth extra, 3s. 6d.; post 8vo, illustrated boards, 2s.

Grundy (Sydney).—The Days of his Vanity: A Passage in the Life of a Young Man. Crown 8vo, cloth extra, 3s. 6d.; post 8vo, illustrated boards, 2s.

Habberton (John, Author of ' Helen's Babies '), **Novels by.**
Post 8vo, illustrated boards, 2s. each; cloth limp, 2s. 6d. each.
Brueton's Bayou. | Country Luck.

Hair, The: Its Treatment in Health, Weakness, and Disease. Translated from the German of Dr. J. PINCUS. Crown 8vo, 1s.; cloth, 1s. 6d.

Hake (Dr. Thomas Gordon), Poems by. Cr. 8vo, cl. ex., 6s. each.
New Symbols. | Legends of the Morrow. | The Serpent Play.
Maiden Ecstasy. Small 4to, cloth extra, 8s.

Halifax (C.).—Dr. Rumsey's Patient. By Mrs. L. T. MEADE and CLIFFORD HALIFAX, M.D. Crown 8vo, cloth. 6s.

Hall (Mrs. S. C.).—Sketches of Irish Character. With numerous Illustrations on Steel and Wood by MACLISE, GILBERT, HARVEY, and GEORGE CRUIKSHANK. Small demy 8vo, cloth extra, 7s. 6d.

Hall (Owen).—The Track of a Storm. Crown 8vo, cloth, 6s.

Halliday (Andrew).—Every-day Papers. Post 8vo, boards, 2s.

Handwriting, The Philosophy of. With over 100 Facsimiles and Explanatory Text. By DON FELIX DE SALAMANCA. Post 8vo, cloth limp, 2s. 6d.

Hanky-Panky: Easy and Difficult Tricks, White Magic, Sleight of Hand, &c. Edited by W. H. CREMER. With 200 Illustrations. Crown 8vo, cloth extra, 4s. 6d.

Hardy (Lady Duffus).—Paul Wynter's Sacrifice. Post 8vo, bds., 2s.

Hardy (Thomas).—Under the Greenwood Tree. Crown 8vo, cloth extra, with Portrait and 15 Illustrations, 3s. 6d.; post 8vo, illustrated boards, 2s. cloth limp, 2s. 6d.

Harwood (J. Berwick) —The Tenth Earl. Post 8vo, boards, 2s.

Harte's (Bret) Collected Works. Revised by the Author. LIBRARY
EDITION, in Nine Volumes, crown 8vo, cloth extra, 6s. each.
Vol.   I. COMPLETE POETICAL AND DRAMATIC WORKS. With Steel-plate Portrait.
  "   II. THE LUCK OF ROARING CAMP—BOHEMIAN PAPERS—AMERICAN LEGENDS.
  "   III. TALES OF THE ARGONAUTS—EASTERN SKETCHES.
  "   IV. GABRIEL CONROY. | Vol. V. STORIES—CONDENSED NOVELS, &c.
  "   VI. TALES OF THE PACIFIC SLOPE.
  "   VII. TALES OF THE PACIFIC SLOPE—II. With Portrait by JOHN PETTIE, R.A.
  "   VIII. TALES OF THE PINE AND THE CYPRESS.
  "   IX. BUCKEYE AND CHAPPAREL.
The Select Works of Bret Harte, in Prose and Poetry. With Introductory Essay by J. M. BELLEW, Portrait of the Author, and 50 Illustrations. Crown 8vo, cloth extra, 7s. 6d.
Bret Harte's Poetical Works. Printed on hand-made paper. Crown 8vo, buckram, 4s. 6d.
A New Volume of Poems. Crown 8vo, buckram, 5s.   [*Preparing.*
The Queen of the Pirate Isle. With 28 Original Drawings by KATE GREENAWAY, reproduced in Colours by EDMUND EVANS. Small 4to, cloth, 5s.

Crown 8vo, cloth extra, 3s. 6d. each; post 8vo, picture boards, 2s. each.
A Waif of the Plains. With 60 Illustrations by STANLEY L. WOOD.
A Ward of the Golden Gate. With 59 Illustrations by STANLEY L. WOOD.

Crown 8vo, cloth extra, 3s. 6d. each.
A Sappho of Green Springs, &c. With Two Illustrations by HUME NISBET.
Colonel Starbottle's Client, and Some Other People. With a Frontispiece.
Susy: A Novel. With Frontispiece and Vignette by J. A. CHRISTIE.
Sally Dows, &c. With 47 Illustrations by W. D. ALMOND and others.
A Protegee of Jack Hamlin's, &c. With 26 Illustrations by W. SMALL and others.
The Bell-Ringer of Angel's, &c. With 39 Illustrations by DUDLEY HARDY and others.
Clarence: A Story of the American War. With Eight Illustrations by A. JULE GOODMAN.
Barker's Luck, &c. With 39 Illustrations by A. FORESTIER, PAUL HARDY, &c.
Devil's Ford, &c. With a Frontispiece by W. H. OVEREND.
The Crusade of the "Excelsior." With a Frontispiece by J. BERNARD PARTRIDGE.
Three Partners; or, The Strike on Heavy Tree Hill. With 8 Illustrations by J. GULICH. [*Apr.* 8.

Post 8vo, Illustrated boards, 2s. each.
Gabriel Conroy.	**The Luck of Roaring Camp,** &c.
An Heiress of Red Dog, &c.	**Californian Stories.**

Post 8vo, illustrated boards, 2s. each; cloth, 2s. 6d. each.
Flip.	**A Phyllis of the Sierras.**
Maruja.	

Hawels (Mrs. H. R.), Books by.
The Art of Beauty. With Coloured Frontispiece and 91 Illustrations. Square 8vo, cloth bds., 6s.
The Art of Decoration. With Coloured Frontispiece and 74 Illustrations. Sq. 8vo, cloth bds., 6s.
The Art of Dress. With 32 Illustrations. Post 8vo, 1s.; cloth, 1s. 6d.
Chaucer for Schools. Demy 8vo, cloth limp, 2s. 6d.
Chaucer for Children. With 38 Illustrations (8 Coloured). Crown 4to, cloth extra, 3s. 6d.

Hawels (Rev. H. R., M.A.), Books by.
American Humorists: WASHINGTON IRVING, OLIVER WENDELL HOLMES, JAMES RUSSELL LOWELL, ARTEMUS WARD, MARK TWAIN, and BRET HARTE. Third Edition. Crown 8vo, cloth extra, 6s.
Travel and Talk, 1885-93-95: My Hundred Thousand Miles of Travel through America—Canada —New Zealand—Tasmania—Australia—Ceylon - The Paradises of the Pacific. With Photogravure Frontispieces. A New Edition. Two Vols., crown 8vo, cloth, 12s.

Hawthorne (Julian), Novels by.
Crown 8vo, cloth extra, 3s. 6d. each; post 8vo, illustrated boards, 2s. each.
Garth.	**Ellice Quentin.**	**Beatrix Randolph.** With Four Illusts.
Sebastian Strome.		**David Poindexter's Disappearance.**
Fortune's Fool.	**Dust.** Four Illusts.	**The Spectre of the Camera.**

Post 8vo, illustrated boards, 2s. each.
Miss Cadogna.	**Love—or a Name.**

Mrs. Gainsborough's Diamonds. Fcap. 8vo, illustrated cover, 1s.

Hawthorne (Nathaniel).—Our Old Home. Annotated with Passages from the Author's Note-books, and Illustrated with 31 Photogravures. Two Vols., cr. 8vo, 15s.

Heath (Francis George).—My Garden Wild, and What I Grew There. Crown 8vo, cloth extra, gilt edges, 6s.

Helps (Sir Arthur), Works by. Post 8vo, cloth limp, 2s. 6d. each.
Animals and their Masters. | **Social Pressure.**
Ivan de Biron: A Novel. Crown 8vo, cloth extra, 3s. 6d.; post 8vo, illustrated boards, 2s.

Henderson (Isaac). — Agatha Page: A Novel. Cr. 8vo, cl., 3s. 6d.

Henty (G. A.), Novels by.
Rujub the Juggler. With Eight Illustrations by STANLEY L. WOOD. Crown 8vo, cloth, 3s. 6d.; post 8vo, illustrated boards, 2s.
Dorothy's Double. Crown 8vo, cloth, 3s. 6d.
The Queen's Cup. 3 vols., crown 8vo, 15s. net.

Herman (Henry).—A Leading Lady. Post 8vo, bds., 2s.; cl., 2s. 6d.

Herrick's (Robert) Hesperides, Noble Numbers, and Complete Collected Poems. With Memorial-Introduction and Notes by the Rev. A. B. GROSART, D.D., Steel Portrait, &c. Three Vols., crown 8vo, cloth boards, 3s. 6d. each.

Hertzka (Dr. Theodor).—Freeland: A Social Anticipation. Translated by ARTHUR RANSOM. Crown 8vo, cloth extra, 6s.

Hesse-Wartegg (Chevalier Ernst von).— Tunis: The Land and the People. With 22 Illustrations. Crown 8vo, cloth extra, 3s. 6d.

Hill (Headon).—Zambra the Detective. Post 8vo, bds., 2s.; cl., 2s. 6d.

Hill (John), Works by.
'   Treason-Felony. Post 8vo, boards, 2s. | The Common Ancestor. Cr. 8vo, cloth, 3s. 6d.

Hoey (Mrs. Cashel).—The Lover's Creed. Post 8vo, boards, 2s.

Holiday, Where to go for a. By E. P. SHOLL, Sir H. MAXWELL, Bart., M.P., JOHN WATSON, JANE BARLOW, MARY LOVETT CAMERON, JUSTIN H. MCCARTHY, PAUL LANGE, J. W. GRAHAM, J. H. SALTER, PHŒBE ALLEN, S. J. BECKETT, L. RIVERS VINE, and C. F. GORDON CUMMING. Crown 8vo, 1s.; cloth, 1s. 6d.

Hollingshead (John).—Niagara Spray. Crown 8vo, 1s.

Holmes (Gordon, M.D.)—The Science of Voice Production and Voice Preservation. Crown 8vo, 1s.; cloth, 1s. 6d.

Holmes (Oliver Wendell), Works by.
The Autocrat of the Breakfast-Table. Illustrated by J. GORDON THOMSON. Post 8vo, cloth limp, 2s. 6d.- Another Edition, post 8vo, cloth, 2s.
The Autocrat of the Breakfast-Table and The Professor at the Breakfast-Table. In One Vol. Post 8vo, half-bound, 2s.

Hood's (Thomas) Choice Works in Prose and Verse. With Life of the Author, Portrait, and 200 Illustrations. Crown 8vo, cloth extra, 7s. 6d.
Hood's Whims and Oddities. With 85 Illustrations. Post 8vo, half-bound, 2s.   '   '

Hood (Tom).—From Nowhere to the North Pole: A Noah's Arkæological Narrative. With 25 Illustrations by W. BRUNTON and E. C. BARNES. Cr. 8vo, cloth, 6s.

Hook's (Theodore) Choice Humorous Works; including his Ludicrous Adventures, Bons Mots, Puns, and Hoaxes. With Life of the Author, Portraits, Facsimiles, and Illustrations. Crown 8vo, cloth extra, 7s. 6d.

Hooper (Mrs. Geo.).—The House of Raby. Post 8vo, boards, 2s.

Hopkins (Tighe).—''Twixt Love and Duty.' Post 8vo, boards, 2s.

Horne (R. Hengist). — Orion: An Epic Poem. With Photograph Portrait by SUMMERS. Tenth Edition. Crown 8vo, cloth extra, 7s.

Hungerford (Mrs., Author of ' Molly Bawn '), Novels by.
'.   Post 8vo, illustrated boards, 2s. each : cloth limp, 2s. 6d. each.
A Maiden All Forlorn. | A Modern Circe. | An Unsatisfactory Lover.
Marvel. | A Mental Struggle. | Lady Patty.
In Durance Vile. | The Three Graces.
.Crown 8vo, cloth extra, 3s. 6d. each ; post 8vo, illustrated boards, 2s. each ; cloth limp, 2s. 6d. each.
Lady Verner's Flight. | The Red-House Mystery.
Crown 8vo, cloth extra, 3s. 6d. each.
The Professor's Experiment. With Frontispiece by E. J. WHEELER.
Nora Creina. | April's Lady.
- An Anxious Moment, &c.
A Point of Conscience.   [Shortly.
Lovice. Crown 8vo, cloth, 6s.   [Shortly.

Hunt's (Leigh) Essays: A Tale for a Chimney Corner, &c. Edited by EDMUND OLLIER. Post 8vo, half-bound, 2s.

Hunt (Mrs. Alfred), Novels by.
Crown 8vo, cloth extra, 3s. 6d. each ; post 8vo, illustrated boards, 2s. each.
The Leaden Casket. | Self-Condemned. | That Other Person.
Thornicroft's Model. Post 8vo, boards, 2s. | Mrs. Juliet. Crown 8vo, cloth extra, 3s. 6d.

Hutchison (W. M.).—Hints on Colt-breaking. With 25 Illustrations. Crown 8vo, cloth extra, 3s. 6d.

Hydrophobia: An Account of M. PASTEUR's System ; The Technique of his Method, and Statistics. By RENAUD SUZOR, M.B. Crown 8vo, cloth extra, 6s.

Hyne (C. J. Cutcliffe).— Honour of Thieves. Cr. 8vo, cloth, 3s. 6d.

Idler (The): An Illustrated Monthly Magazine. Edited by J. K. JEROME. Nos. 1 to 48, 6d. each ; No. 49 and following Numbers, 1s. each. The first EIGHT VOLS., cloth, 5s. each. Vol. IX. and after, 7s. 6d. each.—Cases for Binding, 1s. 6d. each.

Impressions (The) of Aureole. Cheaper Edition, with a New Preface. Post 8vo, blush-rose paper and cloth, 2s. 6d.

Indoor Paupers. By ONE OF THEM. Crown 8vo, 1s. ; cloth, 1s. 6d.

Ingelow (Jean).—Fated to be Free. Post 8vo, illustrated bds., 2s.

Innkeeper's Handbook (The) and Licensed Victualler's Manual. By J. TREVOR-DAVIES. Crown 8vo, 1s. ; cloth, 1s. 6d.

Irish Wit and Humour, Songs of. Collected and Edited by A. PERCEVAL GRAVES. Post 8vo, cloth limp, 2s. 6d.

Irving (Sir Henry) : A Record of over Twenty Years at the Lyceum. By PERCY FITZGERALD. With Portrait. Crown 8vo, 1s. ; cloth, 1s. 6d.

James (C. T. C.).— A Romance of the Queen's Hounds. Post 8vo, picture cover, 1s. ; cloth limp, 1s. 6d.

Jameson (William).—My Dead Self. Post 8vo, bds., 2s. ; cl., 2s. 6d.

Japp (Alex. H., LL.D.).—Dramatic Pictures, &c. Cr. 8vo, cloth, 5s.

Jay (Harriett), Novels by. Post 8vo, illustrated boards, 2s. each.
The Dark Colleen. | The Queen of Connaught.

Jefferies (Richard), Works by. Post 8vo, cloth limp, 2s. 6d. each.
Nature near London. | The Life of the Fields. | The Open Air.
*** Also the HAND-MADE PAPER EDITION, crown 8vo, buckram, gilt top, 6s. each.

The Eulogy of Richard Jefferies. By Sir WALTER BESANT. With a Photograph Portrait. Crown 8vo, cloth extra, 6s.

Jennings (Henry J.), Works by.
Curiosities of Criticism. Post 8vo, cloth limp, 2s. 6d.
Lord Tennyson : A Biographical Sketch. With Portrait. Post 8vo, 1s. ; cloth, 1s. 6d.

Jerome (Jerome K.), Books by.
Stageland. With 64 Illustrations by J. BERNARD PARTRIDGE. Fcap. 4to, picture cover, 1s.
John Ingerfield, &c. With 9 Illusts. by A. S. BOYD and JOHN GULICH. Fcap. 8vo, pic. cov. 1s. 6d.
The Prude's Progress : A Comedy by J. K. JEROME and EDEN PHILLPOTTS. Cr. 8vo, 1s. 6d.

Jerrold (Douglas).—The Barber's Chair; and The Hedgehog Letters. Post 8vo, printed on laid paper and half-bound, 2s.

Jerrold (Tom), Works by. Post 8vo, 1s. ea. ; cloth limp, 1s. 6d. each.
The Garden that Paid the Rent.
Household Horticulture : A Gossip about Flowers. Illustrated.

Jesse (Edward).—Scenes and Occupations of a Country Life. Post 8vo, cloth limp, 2s.

Jones (William, F.S.A.), Works by. Cr. 8vo, cl. extra, 7s. 6d. each.
Finger-Ring Lore : Historical, Legendary, and Anecdotal. With nearly 300 Illustrations. Second Edition, Revised and Enlarged.
Credulities, Past and Present. Including the Sea and Seamen, Miners, Talismans, Word and Letter Divination, Exorcising and Blessing of Animals, Birds, Eggs, Luck, &c. With Frontispiece.
Crowns and Coronations : A History of Regalia. With 100 Illustrations.

Jonson's (Ben) Works. With Notes Critical and Explanatory, and a Biographical Memoir by WILLIAM GIFFORD. Edited by Colonel CUNNINGHAM. Three Vols. crown 8vo, cloth extra, 3s. 6d. each.

Josephus, The Complete Works of. Translated by WHISTON. Containing 'The Antiquities of the Jews' and 'The Wars of the Jews.' With 52 Illustrations and Maps. Two Vols., demy 8vo, half-bound, 12s. 6d.

Kempt (Robert).—Pencil and Palette : Chapters on Art and Artists. Post 8vo, cloth limp, 2s. 6d.

Kershaw (Mark). — Colonial Facts and Fictions : Humorous Sketches. Post 8vo, illustrated boards, 2s. ; cloth, 2s. 6d.

King (R. Ashe), Novels by. Cr. 8vo, cl., 3s. 6d. ea.; post 8vo, bds., 2s. ea,
A Drawn Game. | 'The Wearing of the Green.'

Post 8vo, illustrated boards, 2s. each.
Passion's Slave. | Bell Barry.

Knight (William, M.R.C.S., and Edward, L.R.C.P.). — The
Patient's Vade Mecum: How to Get Most Benefit from Medical Advice. Cr. 8vo, 1s.; cl., 1s. 6d.

Knights (The) of the Lion: A Romance of the Thirteenth Century.
Edited, with an Introduction, by the MARQUESS OF LORNE, K.T. Crown 8vo, cloth extra, 6s.

Lamb's (Charles) Complete Works in Prose and Verse, including
'Poetry for Children' and 'Prince Dorus.' Edited, with Notes and Introduction, by R. H. SHEP-
HERD. With Two Portraits and Facsimile of the 'Essay on Roast Pig.' Crown 8vo, half-bd., 7s. 6d.
The Essays of Elia. Post 8vo, printed on laid paper and half-bound, 2s.
Little Essays: Sketches and Characters by CHARLES LAMB, selected from his Letters by PERCY
FITZGERALD. Post 8vo, cloth limp, 2s. 6d.
The Dramatic Essays of Charles Lamb. With Introduction and Notes by BRANDER MAT-
THEWS, and Steel-plate Portrait. Fcap. 8vo, half-bound, 2s. 6d.

Landor (Walter Savage).—Citation and Examination of William
Shakspeare, &c., before Sir Thomas Lucy, touching Deer-stealing, 19th September, 1582. To which
is added, **A Conference of Master Edmund Spenser** with the Earl of Essex, touching the
State of Ireland, 1595. Fcap. 8vo, half-Roxburghe, 2s. 6d.

Lane (Edward William).—The Thousand and One Nights, com-
monly called in England **The Arabian Nights' Entertainments.** Translated from the Arabic,
with Notes. Illustrated with many hundred Engravings from Designs by HARVEY. Edited by EDWARD
STANLEY POOLE. With Preface by STANLEY LANE-POOLE. Three Vols., demy 8vo, cloth, 7s. 6d. ea.

Larwood (Jacob), Works by.
Anecdotes of the Clergy. Post 8vo, laid paper, half-bound, 2s.

Post 8vo, cloth limp, 2s. 6d. each.
Forensic Anecdotes. | **Theatrical Anecdotes.**

Lehmann (R. C.), Works by. Post 8vo, 1s. each; cloth, 1s. 6d. each.
Harry Fludyer at Cambridge.
Conversational Hints for Young Shooters: A Guide to Polite Talk.

Leigh (Henry S.).—Carols of Cockayne. Printed on hand-made
paper, bound in buckram, 5s.

Leland (C. Godfrey). — A Manual of Mending and Repairing.
With Diagrams. Crown 8vo, cloth, 5s.

Lepelletier (Edmond). — Madame Sans-Gêne. Translated from
the French by JOHN DE VILLIERS. Crown 8vo, cloth, 3s. 6d.; post 8vo, picture boards, 2s.

Leys (John).—The Lindsays: A Romance. Post 8vo, illust. bds., 2s.

Lindsay (Harry).—Rhoda Roberts: A Welsh Mining Story. Crown
8vo, cloth, 3s. 6d.

Linton (E. Lynn), Works by.
Crown 8vo, cloth extra, 3s. 6d. each; post 8vo, illustrated boards, 2s. each.
Patricia Kemball. | **Ione.** | **Under which Lord?** With 12 Illustrations.
The Atonement of Leam Dundas. | **'My Love!'** | **Sowing the Wind.**
The World Well Lost. With 12 Illusts. | **Paston Carew,** Millionaire and Miser.
The One Too Many.

Post 8vo, illustrated boards, 2s. each.
The Rebel of the Family. | **With a Silken Thread.**

Post 8vo, cloth limp, 2s. 6d. each.
Witch Stories. | **Ourselves:** Essays on Women.
Freeshooting: Extracts from the Works of Mrs. LYNN LINTON.
Dulcie Everton. Crown 8vo, cloth extra, 3s. 6d.   [Shortly.

Lucy (Henry W.).—Gideon Fleyce: A Novel. Crown 8vo, cloth
extra, 3s. 6d.; post 8vo, illustrated boards, 2s.

Macalpine (Avery), Novels by.
Teresa Itasca. Crown 8vo, cloth extra, 1s.
Broken Wings. With Six Illustrations by W. J. HENNESSY. Crown 8vo, cloth extra, 6s.

MacColl (Hugh), Novels by.
Mr. Stranger's Sealed Packet. Post 8vo, illustrated boards; 2s.
Ednor Whitlock. Crown 8vo, cloth extra, 6s.

Macdonell (Agnes).—Quaker Cousins. Post 8vo, boards, 2s.

MacGregor (Robert).—Pastimes and Players: Notes on Popular
Games. Post 8vo, cloth limp, 2s. 6d.

Mackay (Charles, LL.D.). — Interludes and Undertones; or,
Music at Twilight. Crown 8vo, cloth extra, 6s.

McCarthy (Justin, M.P.), Works by.

A History of Our Own Times, from the Accession of Queen Victoria to the General Election of 1880. Four Vols., demy 8vo, cloth extra, 12s. each.—Also a POPULAR EDITION, in Four Vols., crown 8vo, cloth extra, 6s. each.—And the JUBILEE EDITION, with an Appendix of Events to the end of 1886, in Two Vols., large crown 8vo, cloth extra, 7s. 6d. each.

⁎ Vol. V., bringing the narrative down to the end of the Sixtieth Year of the Queen's Reign, is in preparation. Demy 8vo, cloth, 12s.

A Short History of Our Own Times. One Vol., crown 8vo, cloth extra, 6s.—Also a CHEAP POPULAR EDITION, post 8vo, cloth limp, 2s. 6d.

A History of the Four Georges. Four Vols., demy 8vo, cl. ex., 12s. each.   [Vols. I. & II. *ready.*

Crown 8vo, cloth extra, 3s. 6d. each ; post 8vo, illustrated boards, 2s. each ; cloth limp, 2s. 6d. each.

The Waterdale Neighbours.	**Donna Quixote.** With 12 Illustrations.
My Enemy's Daughter.	**The Comet of a Season.**
A Fair Saxon.	**Maid of Athens.** With 12 Illustrations.
Linley Rochford.	**Camiola :** A Girl with a Fortune.
Dear Lady Disdain.	**The Dictator.**
Miss Misanthrope. With 12 Illustrations.	**Red Diamonds.**

The Riddle Ring. Crown 8vo, cloth, 3s. 6d.   [*May,* 1897.

'The Right Honourable.' By JUSTIN MCCARTHY, M.P., and Mrs. CAMPBELL PRAED. Crown 8vo, cloth extra, 6s.

McCarthy (Justin Huntly), Works by.

The French Revolution. (Constituent Assembly, 1789-91). Four Vols., demy 8vo, cloth extra, 12s. each.   Vols. I. & II. *ready ;* Vols. III. & IV. *in the press.*

An Outline of the History of Ireland. Crown 8vo, 1s. : cloth, 1s. 6d.

Ireland Since the Union : Sketches of Irish History, 1798-1886. Crown 8vo, cloth, 6s.

Hafiz in London : Poems. Small 8vo, gold cloth, 3s. 6d.

Our Sensation Novel. Crown 8vo, picture cover, 1s. ; cloth limp, 1s. 6d.

Doom : An Atlantic Episode. Crown 8vo, picture cover, 1s.

Dolly : A Sketch. Crown 8vo, picture cover, 1s. ; cloth limp, 1s. 6d.

Lily Lass : A Romance. Crown 8vo, picture cover, 1s. ; cloth limp, 1s. 6d.

The Thousand and One Days. With Two Photogravures. Two Vols., crown 8vo, half-bd., 12s.

A London Legend. Crown 8vo, cloth, 3s. 6d.

The Royal Christopher. Crown 8vo, cloth, 3s. 6d.

MacDonald (George, LL.D.), Books by.

Works of Fancy and Imagination. Ten Vols., 16mo, cloth, gilt edges, in cloth case, 21s. ; or the Volumes may be had separately, in Grolier cloth, at 2s. 6d. each.

Vol. I. WITHIN AND WITHOUT.—THE HIDDEN LIFE.

„ II. THE DISCIPLE.—THE GOSPEL WOMEN.—BOOK OF SONNETS.—ORGAN SONGS.

„ III. VIOLIN SONGS.—SONGS OF THE DAYS AND NIGHTS.—A BOOK OF DREAMS.—ROADSIDE POEMS.—POEMS FOR CHILDREN.

„ IV. PARABLES.—BALLADS.—SCOTCH SONGS.

„ V. & VI. PHANTASTES : A Faerie Romance. | Vol. VII. THE PORTENT.

„ VIII. THE LIGHT PRINCESS.—THE GIANT'S HEART.—SHADOWS.

„ IX. CROSS PURPOSES.—THE GOLDEN KEY.—THE CARASOYN.—LITTLE DAYLIGHT.

„ X. THE CRUEL PAINTER.—THE WOW O' RIVVEN.—THE CASTLE.—THE BROKEN SWORDS. —THE GRAY WOLF.—UNCLE CORNELIUS.

Poetical Works of George MacDonald. Collected and Arranged by the Author. Two Vols., crown 8vo, buckram, 12s.

A Threefold Cord. Edited by GEORGE MACDONALD. Post 8vo, cloth, 5s.

Phantastes : A Faerie Romance. With 25 Illustrations by J. BELL. Crown 8vo, cloth extra, 3s. 6d.

Heather and Snow : A Novel. Crown 8vo, cloth extra, 3s. 6d. ; post 8vo, illustrated boards, 2s.

Lilith : A Romance. SECOND EDITION. Crown 8vo, cloth extra, 6s.

Maclise Portrait Gallery (The) of Illustrious Literary Characters : 85 Portraits by DANIEL MACLISE ; with Memoirs—Biographical, Critical, Bibliographical and Anecdotal—illustrative of the Literature of the former half of the Present Century, by WILLIAM BATES, B.A. Crown 8vo, cloth extra, 7s. 6d.

Macquoid (Mrs.), Works by. Square 8vo, cloth extra, 6s. each.

In the Ardennes. With 50 Illustrations by THOMAS R. MACQUOID.

Pictures and Legends from Normandy and Brittany. 34 Illusts. by T. R. MACQUOID.

Through Normandy. With 92 Illustrations by T. R. MACQUOID, and a Map.

Through Brittany. With 35 Illustrations by T. R. MACQUOID, and a Map.

About Yorkshire. With 67 Illustrations by T. R. MACQUOID.

Post 8vo, illustrated boards, 2s. each.

The Evil Eye, and other Stories. | **Lost Rose,** and other Stories.

Magician's Own Book, The : Performances with Eggs, Hats, &c. Edited by W. H. CREMER. With 200 Illustrations. Crown 8vo, cloth extra, 4s. 6d.

Magic Lantern, The, and its Management : Including full Practical Directions. By T. C. HEPWORTH. With 10 Illustrations. Crown 8vo, 1s. ; cloth, 1s. 6d.

Magna Charta : An Exact Facsimile of the Original in the British Museum, 3 feet by 2 feet, with Arms and Seals emblazoned in Gold and Colours, 5s.

Mallory (Sir Thomas). — Mort d'Arthur : The Stories of King Arthur and of the Knights of the Round Table. (A Selection.) Edited by B. MONTGOMERIE RAN-KING. Post 8vo, cloth limp, 2s.

Mallock (W. H.), Works by.
The New Republic. Post 8vo, picture cover, 2s.; cloth limp, 2s. 6d.
The New Paul & Virginia: Positivism on an Island. Post 8vo, cloth, 2s. 6d.
A Romance of the Nineteenth Century. Crown 8vo, cloth 6s.; post 8vo, illust. boards, 2s.
Poems. Small 4to, parchment, 8s.
Is Life Worth Living? Crown 8vo, cloth extra, 6s.

Marks (H. S., R.A.), Pen and Pencil Sketches by. With Four
Photogravures and 126 Illustrations. Two Vols. demy 8vo, cloth, 32s.

Marlowe's Works. Including his Translations. Edited, with Notes
and Introductions, by Colonel CUNNINGHAM. Crown 8vo, cloth extra, 3s. 6d.

Marryat (Florence), Novels by. Post 8vo, illust. boards, 2s. each.
A Harvest of Wild Oats. | Fighting the Air.
Open ! Sesame ! | Written in Fire.

Massinger's Plays. From the Text of WILLIAM GIFFORD. Edited
by Col. CUNNINGHAM. Crown 8vo, cloth extra, 3s. 6d,

Masterman (J.).—Half-a-Dozen Daughters. Post 8vo, boards, 2s.

Matthews (Brander).—A Secret of the Sea, &c. Post 8vo, illustrated boards, 2s.; cloth limp, 2s. 6d.

Meade (L. T.), Novels by.
A Soldier of Fortune. Crown 8vo, cloth, 3s. 6d.; post 8vo, illustrated boards, 2s.
                        Crown 8vo, cloth, 3s. 6d each.
In an Iron Grip. | The Voice of the Charmer. With 8 Illustrations.
Dr. Rumsey's Patient. By L. T. MEADE and CLIFFORD HALIFAX, M.D. Crown 8vo, cl. 6s.

Merrick (Leonard), Stories by.
The Man who was Good. Post 8vo, picture boards, 2s.
This Stage of Fools. Crown 8vo, cloth, 3s. 6d.
Cynthia: A Daughter of the Philistines. 3 vols., crown 8vo, 10s. net.

Mexican Mustang (On a), through Texas to the Rio Grande. By
A. E. SWEET and J. ARMOY KNOX With 265 Illustrations. Crown 8vo, cloth extra, 7s. 6d.

Middlemass (Jean), Novels by. Post 8vo, illust. boards, 2s. each.
Touch and Go. | Mr. Dorillion.

Miller (Mrs. F. Fenwick).—Physiology for the Young; or, The
House of Life. With numerous Illustrations. Post 8vo, cloth limp, 2s. 6d.

Milton (J. L.), Works by. Post 8vo, 1s. each; cloth, 1s. 6d. each.
The Hygiene of the Skin. With Directions for Diet, Soaps, Baths, Wines, &c.
The Bath in Diseases of the Skin.
The Laws of Life, and their Relation to Diseases of the Skin.

Minto (Wm.).—Was She Good or Bad? Cr. 8vo, 1s.; cloth, 1s. 6d.

Mitford (Bertram), Novels by. Crown 8vo, cloth extra, 3s. 6d. each.
The Gun-Runner: A Romance of Zululand. With a Frontispiece by STANLEY L. WOOD.
The Luck of Gerard Ridgeley. With a Frontispiece by STANLEY L. WOOD.
The King's Assegai. With Six full-page Illustrations by STANLEY L. WOOD.
Renshaw Fanning's Quest. With a Frontispiece by STANLEY L. WOOD.

Molesworth (Mrs.), Novels by.
Hathercourt Rectory. Post 8vo, illustrated boards, 2s.
That Girl in Black. Crown 8vo, cloth, 1s. 6d.

Moncrieff (W. D. Scott-).—The Abdication: An Historical Drama.
With Seven Etchings by JOHN PETTIE, W. Q. ORCHARDSON, J. MACWHIRTER, COLIN HUNTER,
R. MACBETH and TOM GRAHAM. Imperial 4to, buckram, 21s.

Moore (Thomas), Works by.
The Epicurean; and Alciphron. Post 8vo, half-bound, 2s.
Prose and Verse; including Suppressed Passages from the MEMOIRS OF LORD BYRON. Edited
by R. H. SHEPHERD. With Portrait. Crown 8vo, cloth extra, 7s. 6d.

Muddock (J. E.) Stories by.
                        Crown 8vo, cloth extra, 3s. 6d. each.
Maid Marian and Robin Hood. With 12 Illustrations by STANLEY WOOD.
Basile the Jester. With Frontispiece by STANLEY WOOD.
Young Lochinvar.
                        Post 8vo, illustrated boards, 2s. each.
The Dead Man's Secret. | From the Bosom of the Deep.
Stories Weird and Wonderful Post 8vo illustrated boards. 2s.; cloth. 2s. 6d

Murray (D. Christie), Novels by.
Crown 8vo, cloth extra, 3s. 6d. each; post 8vo, illustrated boards, 2s. each.

A Life's Atonement.	A Model Father.	Bob Martin's Little Girl.
Joseph's Coat. 12 Illusts.	Old Blazer's Hero.	Time's Revenges.
Coals of Fire. 3 Illusts.	Cynic Fortune. Frontisp.	A Wasted Crime.
Val Strange.	By the Gate of the Sea.	In Direst Peril.
Hearts.	A Bit of Human Nature.	Mount Despair.
The Way of the World.	First Person Singular.	

A Capful o' Nails. Crown 8vo, cloth, 3s. 6d.
The Making of a Novelist: An Experiment in Autobiography. With a Collotype Portrait and Vignette. Crown 8vo, art linen, 6s.

Murray (D. Christie) and Henry Herman, Novels by.
Crown 8vo, cloth extra, 3s. 6d. each; post 8vo, illustrated boards, 2s. each.
One Traveller Returns. | The Bishops' Bible.
Paul Jones's Alias, &c. With Illustrations by A. FORESTIER and G. NICOLET.

Murray (Henry), Novels by.
Post 8vo, illustrated boards, 2s. each; cloth, 2s. 6d. each.
A Game of Bluff. | A Song of Sixpence.

Newbolt (Henry).—Taken from the Enemy. Fcp. 8vo, cloth, 1s. 6d.

Nisbet (Hume), Books by.
'Ball Up.' Crown 8vo, cloth extra, 3s. 6d.; post 8vo, illustrated boards, 2s.
Dr. Bernard St. Vincent. Post 8vo, illustrated boards, 2s.

Lessons in Art. With 21 Illustrations. Crown 8vo, cloth extra, 2s. 6d.
Where Art Begins. With 27 Illustrations. Square 8vo, cloth extra, 7s. 6d.

Norris (W. E.), Novels by.
Saint Ann's. Crown 8vo, cloth, 3s. 6d.; post 8vo, picture boards, 2s.
Billy Bellew. With a Frontispiece by F. H. TOWNSEND. Crown 8vo, cloth, 3s. 6d.

O'Hanlon (Alice), Novels by. Post 8vo, illustrated boards, 2s. each.
The Unforeseen. | Chance? or Fate?

Ohnet (Georges), Novels by. Post 8vo, illustrated boards, 2s. each.
Doctor Rameau. | A Last Love.
A Weird Gift. Crown 8vo, cloth, 3s. 6d.; post 8vo, picture boards, 2s.

Oliphant (Mrs.), Novels by. Post 8vo, illustrated boards, 2s. each.
The Primrose Path. | Whiteladies.
The Greatest Heiress in England.
The Sorceress. Crown 8vo, cloth, 3s. 6d.

O'Reilly (Mrs.).—Phœbe's Fortunes. Post 8vo, illust. boards, 2s.

Ouida, Novels by. Cr. 8vo, cl., 3s. 6d. ea.; post 8vo, illust. bds., 2s. ea.

Held in Bondage.	Folle-Farine.	Moths.	Pipistrello.
Tricotrin.	A Dog of Flanders.	In Maremma.	Wanda.
Strathmore.	Pascarel.	Signa.	Bimbi.	Syrlin.
Chandos.	Two Wooden Shoes.	Frescoes.	Othmar.
Cecil Castlemaine's Gage	In a Winter City.	Princess Napraxine.
Under Two Flags.	Ariadne.	Friendship.	Guilderoy.	Ruffino.
Puck.	Idalia.	A Village Commune.	Two Offenders.

Square 8vo, cloth extra, 5s. each.
Bimbi. With Nine Illustrations by EDMUND H. GARRETT.
A Dog of Flanders, &c. With Six Illustrations by EDMUND H. GARRETT.

Santa Barbara, &c. Square 8vo, cloth, 6s.; crown 8vo, cloth, 3s. 6d.; post 8vo, illustrated boards, 2s.

POPULAR EDITIONS. Medium 8vo, 6d. each; cloth, 1s. each.
Under Two Flags. | Moths.

Wisdom, Wit, and Pathos, selected from the Works of OUIDA by F. SYDNEY MORRIS. Post 8vo, cloth extra, 5s.—CHEAP EDITION, illustrated boards, 2s.

Page (H. A.).—Thoreau: His Life and Aims. With Portrait. Post 8vo, cloth, 2s. 6d.

Pandurang Hari; or, Memoirs of a Hindoo. With Preface by Sir BARTLE FRERE. Crown 8vo, cloth, 3s. 6d.; post 8vo, illustrated boards, 2s.

Parker (Rev. Joseph, D.D.).—Might Have Been: some Life Notes. Crown 8vo, cloth, 6s.

Pascal's Provincial Letters. A New Translation, with Historical Introduction and Notes by T. M'CRIE, D.D. Post 8vo, cloth limp, 2s.

Paul (Margaret A.).—Gentle and Simple. Crown 8vo, cloth, with Frontispiece by HELEN PATERSON, 3s. 6d.; post 8vo, illustrated boards, 2s.

Payn (James), Novels by.

Crown 8vo, cloth extra, 3s. 6d. each   post 8vo, illustrated boards, 2s. each.

Lost Sir Massingberd.
Walter's Word.
Less Black than We're Painted.
By Proxy. | For Cash Only.
High Spirits.
Under One Roof.
A Confidential Agent. With 12 Illusts.
A Grape from a Thorn. With 12 Illusts.

Holiday Tasks.
The Canon's Ward. With Portrait.
The Talk of the Town. With 12 Illusts.
Glow-Worm Tales.
The Mystery of Mirbridge.
The Word and the Will.
The Burnt Million.
Sunny Stories. | A Trying Patient

Post 8vo, illustrated boards, 2s. each.

Humorous Stories. | From Exile.
The Foster Brothers.
The Family Scapegrace.
Married Beneath Him.
Bentinck's Tutor. | A County Family.
A Perfect Treasure.
Like Father, Like Son.
A Woman's Vengeance.
Carlyon's Year. | Cecil's Tryst.
Murphy's Master. | At Her Mercy.

The Clyffards of Clyffe.
Found Dead. | Gwendoline's Harvest.
Mirk Abbey. | A Marine Residence.
Some Private Views.
Not Wooed, But Won.
Two Hundred Pounds Reward.
The Best of Husbands.
Halves. | What He Cost Her.
Fallen Fortunes. | Kit: A Memory.
A Prince of the Blood.

In Peril and Privation. With 17 Illustrations. Crown 8vo, cloth, 3s. 6d.
Notes from the 'News.' Crown 8vo, portrait cover, 1s.; cloth, 1s. 6d.

Payne (Will).—Jerry the Dreamer. Crown 8vo, cloth, 3s. 6d.

Pennell (H. Cholmondeley), Works by. Post 8vo, cloth, 2s. 6d. ea.
Puck on Pegasus. With Illustrations.
Pegasus Re-Saddled. With Ten full-page Illustrations by G. DU MAURIER.
The Muses of Mayfair: Vers de Société. Selected by H. C. PENNELL.

Phelps (E. Stuart), Works by. Post 8vo, 1s. ea. ; cloth, 1s. 6d. ea.
Beyond the Gates. | An Old Maid's Paradise. | Burglars in Paradise.
Jack the Fisherman. Illustrated by C. W. REED. Crown 8vo, 1s.; cloth, 1s. 6d.

Phil May's Sketch-Book. Containing 54 Humorous Cartoons. A
New Edition. Crown folio, cloth, 2s. 6d.

Phipson (Dr. T. L.).—Famous Violinists and Fine Violins:
Historical Notes, Anecdotes, and Reminiscences. Crown 8vo, cloth, 5s.

Pirkis (C. L.), Novels by.
Trooping with Crows. Fcap. 8vo, picture cover, 1s.
Lady Lovelace. Post 8vo, illustrated boards, 2s.

Planche (J. R.), Works by.
The Pursuivant of Arms. With Six Plates and 209 Illustrations. Crown 8vo, cloth, 7s. 6d.
Songs and Poems, 1819-1879. With Introduction by Mrs. MACKARNESS. Crown 8vo, cloth, 6s.

Plutarch's Lives of Illustrious Men. With Notes and a Life of
Plutarch by JOHN and WM. LANGHORNE, and Portraits. Two Vols., demy 8vo, half-bound 10s. 6d.

Poe's (Edgar Allan) Choice Works in Prose and Poetry. With Intro-
duction by CHARLES BAUDELAIRE, Portrait and Facsimiles. Crown 8vo, cloth, 7s. 6d.
The Mystery of Marie Roget, &c. Post 8vo, illustrated boards, 2s.

Pollock (W. H.).—The Charm, and other Drawing-room Plays. By
Sir WALTER BESANT and WALTER H. POLLOCK. With 50 Illustrations. Crown 8vo, cloth gilt, 6s.

Pope's Poetical Works. Post 8vo, cloth limp, 2s.

Porter (John).—Kingsclere. Edited by BYRON WEBBER. With 19
full-page and many smaller Illustrations. Second Edition. Demy 8vo, cloth decorated, 18s.

Praed (Mrs. Campbell), Novels by. Post 8vo, illust. bds., 2s. each.
The Romance of a Station. | The Soul of Countess Adrian.

Crown 8vo, cloth, 3s. 6d. each ; post 8vo, boards, 2s. each.

Outlaw and Lawmaker. | Christina Chard. With Frontispiece by W. PAGET.
Mrs. Tregaskiss. With 8 Illustrations by ROBERT SAUBER. Crown 8vo, cloth extra, 3s. 6d.

Price (E. C.), Novels by.
Crown 8vo, cloth extra, 3s. 6d. each ; post 8vo, illustrated boards, 2s. each.
Valentina. | The Foreigners. | Mrs. Lancaster's Rival.
Gerald. Post 8vo, illustrated boards, 2s.

Princess Olga.—Radna: A Novel. Crown 8vo, cloth extra, 6s.

Proctor (Richard A., B.A.), Works by.
Flowers of the Sky. With 55 Illustrations. Small crown 8vo, cloth extra, 3s. 6d.
Easy Star Lessons. With Star Maps for every Night in the Year. Crown 8vo, cloth, 6s.
Familiar Science Studies. Crown 8vo, cloth extra, 6s.
Saturn and its System. With 13 Steel Plates. Demy 8vo, cloth extra, 10s. 6d.
Mysteries of Time and Space. With numerous Illustrations. Crown 8vo, cloth extra, 6s.
The Universe of Suns, &c. With numerous Illustrations. Crown 8vo, cloth extra, 6s.
Wages and Wants of Science Workers. Crown 8vo, 1s. 6d.

Pryce (Richard).—Miss Maxwell's Affections. Crown 8vo, cloth, with Frontispiece by HAL LUDLOW, 3s. 6d.; post 8vo, illustrated boards, 2s.

Rambosson (J.).—Popular Astronomy. Translated by C. B. PIT-MAN. With Coloured Frontispiece and numerous Illustrations. Crown 8vo, cloth extra, 7s. 6d.

Randolph (Lieut.-Col. George, U.S.A.).—Aunt Abigail Dykes: A Novel. Crown 8vo, cloth extra, 7s. 6d.

Read (General Meredith).—Historic Studies in Vaud, Berne, and Savoy. With 30 full-page Illustrations. Two Vols., demy 8vo, cloth, 28s.   [Shortly.

Reade's (Charles) Novels.
The New Collected LIBRARY EDITION, complete in Seventeen Volumes, set in new long primer type, printed on laid paper, and elegantly bound in cloth, price 3s. 6d. each.

1. Peg Woffington; and Christie Johnstone.
2. Hard Cash.
3. The Cloister and the Hearth. With a Preface by Sir WALTER BESANT.
4. 'It is Never too Late to Mend.'
5. The Course of True Love Never Did Run Smooth; and Singleheart and Doubleface.
6. The Autobiography of a Thief; Jack of all Trades; A Hero and a Martyr; and The Wandering Heir.

7. Love Me Little, Love me Long.
8. The Double Marriage.
9. Griffith Gaunt.
10. Foul Play.
11. Put Yourself in His Place.
12. A Terrible Temptation.
13. A Simpleton.
14. A Woman-Hater.
15. The Jilt, and other Stories; and Good Stories of Man and other Animals.
16. A Perilous Secret.
17. Readiana; and Bible Characters.

In Twenty-one Volumes, post 8vo, illustrated boards, 2s. each.

Peg Woffington. | Christie Johnstone.
'It is Never Too Late to Mend.'
The Course of True Love Never Did Run Smooth.
The Autobiography of a Thief; Jack of all Trades; and James Lambert.
Love Me Little, Love Me Long.
The Double Marriage.
The Cloister and the Hearth.

Hard Cash | Griffith Gaunt.
Foul Play. | Put Yourself in His Place.
A Terrible Temptation.
A Simpleton. | The Wandering Heir
A Woman-Hater.
Singleheart and Doubleface.
Good Stories of Men and other Animals.
The Jilt, and other Stories.
A Perilous Secret. | Readiana.

POPULAR EDITIONS, medium 8vo, 6d. each: cloth, 1s. each.
'It is Never Too Late to Mend.' | The Cloister and the Hearth.
Peg Woffington; and Christie Johnstone.

'It is Never Too Late to Mend' and The Cloister and the Hearth in One Volume, medium 8vo, cloth, 2s.
Christie Johnstone. With Frontispiece. Choicely printed in Elzevir style. Fcap. 8vo, half-Roxb. 2s. 6d.
Peg Woffington. Choicely printed in Elzevir style. Fcap. 8vo, half-Roxburghe, 2s. 6d.
The Cloister and the Hearth. In Four Vols., post 8vo, with an Introduction by Sir WALTER BESANT, and a Frontispiece to each Vol., 14s. the set; and the ILLUSTRATED LIBRARY EDITION, with Illustrations on every page, Two Vols., crown 8vo, cloth gilt, 42s. net.
Bible Characters. Fcap. 8vo, leatherette, 1s.
Selections from the Works of Charles Reade. With an Introduction by Mrs. ALEX. IRELAND. Crown 8vo, buckram, with Portrait, 6s.; CHEAP EDITION, post 8vo, cloth limp, 2s. 6d.

Riddell (Mrs. J. H.), Novels by.
Weird Stories. Crown 8vo, cloth extra, 3s. 6d.; post 8vo, illustrated boards, 2s.
Post 8vo, illustrated boards, 2s. each.
The Uninhabited House. | Fairy Water.
The Prince of Wales's Garden Party. | Her Mother's Darling.
The Mystery in Palace Gardens. | The Nun's Curse. | Idle Tales.

Rimmer (Alfred), Works by. Square 8vo, cloth gilt, 7s. 6d. each.
Our Old Country Towns. With 55 Illustrations by the Author.
Rambles Round Eton and Harrow. With 50 Illustrations by the Author.
About England with Dickens. With 58 Illustrations by C. A. VANDERHOOF and A. RIMMER.

Rives (Amelie).—Barbara Dering. Crown 8vo, cloth extra, 3s. 6d.; post 8vo, illustrated boards, 2s.

Robinson Crusoe. By DANIEL DEFOE. With 37 Illustrations by GEORGE CRUIKSHANK. Post 8vo, half-cloth, 2s.; cloth extra, gilt edges, 2s. 6d.

Robinson (F. W.), Novels by.
Women are Strange. Post 8vo, illustrated boards, 2s.
The Hands of Justice. Crown 8vo, cloth extra, 3s. 6d.; post 8vo, illustrated boards, 2s.
The Woman in the Dark. Crown 8vo, cloth, 3s. 6d.

Robinson (Phil), Works by. Crown 8vo, cloth extra, 6s. each.
The Poets' Birds. | The Poets' Beasts.
The Poets and Nature: Reptiles, Fishes, and Insects.

Rochefoucauld's Maxims and Moral Reflections. With Notes and an Introductory Essay by SAINTE-BEUVE. Post 8vo, cloth limp, 2s.

Roll of Battle Abbey, The: A List of the Principal Warriors who came from Normandy with William the Conqueror, 1066. Printed in Gold and Colours, 5s.

Rosengarten (A.).—A Handbook of Architectural Styles. Translated by W. COLLETT-SANDARS. With 630 Illustrations. Crown 8vo, cloth extra, 7s. 6d.

Rowley (Hon. Hugh), Works by. Post 8vo, cloth, 2s. 6d. each.
Puniana: Riddles and Jokes. With numerous Illustrations.
More Puniana. Profusely Illustrated.

Runciman (James), Stories by. Post 8vo, bds., 2s. ea.; cl., 2s. 6d. ea.
Skippers and Shellbacks. | Grace Balmaign's Sweetheart.
Schools and Scholars.

Russell (Dora), Novels by.
A Country Sweetheart. Crown 8vo, cloth, 3s. 6d.; post 8vo, picture boards, 2s.
The Drift of Fate. Crown 8vo, cloth, 3s. 6d.

Russell (W. Clark), Novels, &c., by.
. Crown 8vo, cloth extra, 3s. 6d. each; post 8vo, illustrated boards, 2s. each; cloth limp, 2s. 6d. each.
Round the Galley-Fire.   An Ocean Tragedy.
In the Middle Watch.   My Shipmate Louise.
A Voyage to the Cape.   Alone on a Wide Wide Sea.
A Book for the Hammock.   The Good Ship 'Mohock.'
The Mystery of the 'Ocean Star.' The Phantom Death
The Romance of Jenny Harlowe.

Crown 8vo, cloth, 3s. 6d. each.

Is He the Man?   The Tale of the Ten. With 12 Illustra-
The Convict Ship.   tions by G. MONTBARD.   [Feb.
. Heart of Oak.   The Last Entry. Frontis.   [Shortly.

On the Fo'k'sle Head. Post 8vo, illustrated boards, 2s.; cloth limp, 2s. 6d.

Saint Aubyn (Alan), Novels by.
Crown 8vo, cloth extra, 3s. 6d. each; post 8vo, illustrated boards, 2s. each.
A Fellow of Trinity. With a Note by OLIVER WENDELL HOLMES and a Frontispiece.
The Junior Dean. | The Master of St. Benedict's. | To His Own Master.
Orchard Damerel. | In the Face of the World.

Fcap. 8vo, cloth boards, 1s. 6d. each.
The Old Maid's Sweetheart. | Modest Little Sara.

The Tremlett Diamonds. Crown 8vo, cloth extra, 3s. 6d.

Sala (George A.).—Gaslight and Daylight. Post 8vo, boards, 2s.

Saunders (John), Novels by.
Crown 8vo, cloth extra, 3s. 6d. each; post 8vo, illustrated boards, 2s. each.
Guy Waterman. | The Lion in the Path. | The Two Dreamers.
Bound to the Wheel. Crown 8vo, cloth extra, 3s. 6d.

Saunders (Katharine), Novels by.
Crown 8vo, cloth extra, 3s. 6d. each; post 8vo, illustrated boards, 2s. each.
Margaret and Elizabeth.   Heart Salvage.
The High Mills.   Sebastian.

Joan Merryweather. Post 8vo, illustrated boards, 2s.
Gideon's Rock. Crown 8vo, cloth extra, 3s. 6d.

Scotland Yard, Past and Present: Experiences of Thirty-seven Years. By Ex-Chief-Inspector CAVANAGH. Post 8vo, illustrated boards, 2s.; cloth, 2s. 6d.

Secret Out, The: One Thousand Tricks with Cards; with Entertaining Experiments in Drawing-room or 'White' Magic. By W. H. CREMER. With 300 Illustrations. Crown 8vo, cloth extra, 4s. 6d.

Seguin (L. G.), Works by.
The Country of the Passion Play (Oberammergau) and the Highlands of Bavaria. With Map and 37 Illustrations. Crown 8vo, cloth extra, 3s. 6d.
Walks in Algiers. With Two Maps and 16 Illustrations. Crown 8vo, cloth extra, 6s.

Senior (Wm.).—By Stream and Sea. Post 8vo, cloth, 2s. 6d.

Sergeant (Adeline).—Dr. Endicott's Experiment. Cr. 8vo, 3s. 6d.

Shakespeare for Children: Lamb's Tales from Shakespeare. With Illustrations, coloured and plain, by J. MOYR SMITH. Crown 4to, cloth gilt, 3s. 6d.

Sharp (William).—Children of To-morrow. Crown 8vo, cloth, 6s.

Shelley's (Percy Bysshe) Complete Works in Verse and Prose.
Edited, Prefaced, and Annotated by R. HERNE SHEPHERD. Five Vols., crown 8vo, cloth, 3s. 6d. each.
Poetical Works, in Three Vols. :
Vol. I. Introduction by the Editor; Posthumous Fragments of Margaret Nicholson; Shelley's Corre-
: spondence with Stockdale; The Wandering Jew; Queen Mab, with the Notes; Alastor,
and other Poems; Rosalind and Helen; Prometheus Unbound; Adonais, &c.
„ II. Laon and Cythna; The Cenci; Julian and Maddalo; Swellfoot the Tyrant; The Witch of
Atlas; Epipsychidion; Hellas.
„ III. Posthumous Poems; The Masque of Anarchy; and other Pieces.
Prose Works, in Two Vols. :
Vol. I. The Two Romances of Zastrozzi and St. Irvyne; the Dublin and Marlow Pamphlets; A Refu-
tation of Deism; Letters to Leigh Hunt, and some Minor Writings and Fragments.
„ II. The Essays; Letters from Abroad; Translations and Fragments, edited by Mrs. SHELLEY.
With a Biography of Shelley, and an Index of the Prose Works.
, Also a few copies of a LARGE-PAPER EDITION, 5 vols., cloth, £2 12s. 6d.

Sheridan (General P. H.), Personal Memoirs of. With Portraits,
- Maps, and Facsimiles. Two Vols., demy 8vo, cloth, 24s.

Sheridan's (Richard Brinsley) Complete Works, with Life and
Anecdotes. Including his Dramatic Writings, his Works in Prose and Poetry, Translations, Speeches,
and Jokes. With 10 Illustrations. Crown 8vo, half-bound, 7s. 6d.
The Rivals, The School for Scandal, and other Plays. Post 8vo, half-bound, 2s.
Sheridan's Comedies: The Rivals and **The School for Scandal.** Edited, with an Intro-
duction and Notes to each Play, and a Biographical Sketch, by BRANDER MATTHEWS. With
Illustrations. Demy 8vo, half-parchment, 12s. 6d.

Sidney's (Sir Philip) Complete Poetical Works, including all
those in 'Arcadia.' With Portrait, Memorial-Introduction, Notes, &c., by the Rev. A. B. GROSART,
D.D. Three Vols., crown 8vo, cloth boards, 3s. 6d. each.

Signboards: Their History, including Anecdotes of Famous Taverns and
Remarkable Characters. By JACOB LARWOOD and JOHN CAMDEN HOTTEN. With Coloured Frontispiece and 94 Illustrations. Crown 8vo, cloth extra, 7s. 6d.

Sims (George R.), Works by.
Post 8vo, illustrated boards, 2s. each; cloth limp, 2s. 6d. each.

The Ring o' Bells.	**Dramas of Life.** With 60 Illustrations.
Mary Jane's Memoirs.	**Memoirs of a Landlady.**
Mary Jane Married.	**My Two Wives.**
Tinkletop's Crime.	**Scenes from the Show.**
Zeph: A Circus Story, &c.	**The Ten Commandments:** Stories.
Tales of To-day.	

Crown 8vo, picture cover, 1s. each; cloth, 1s. 6d. each.
The Dagonet Reciter and Reader: Being Readings and Recitations in Prose and Verse,
selected from his own Works by GEORGE R. SIMS.
The Case of George Candlemas. | **Dagonet Ditties.** (From The Referee.)

Rogues and Vagabonds. A New Edition. Crown 8vo, cloth, 3s. 6d.
How the Poor Live; and **Horrible London.** Crown 8vo, picture cover, 1s.
Dagonet Abroad. Crown 8vo, cloth, 3s. 6d. ; post 8vo, picture boards, 2s.

Sister Dora: A Biography. By MARGARET LONSDALE. With Four
Illustrations. Demy 8vo, picture cover, 4d. ; cloth, 6d.

Sketchley (Arthur).—A Match in the Dark. Post 8vo, boards, 2s.

Slang Dictionary (The) : Etymological, Historical, and Anecdotal.
Crown 8vo, cloth extra, 6s. 6d.

Smart (Hawley), Novels by.
Without Love or Licence. Crown 8vo, cloth, 3s. 6d. ; post 8vo, picture boards, 2s.

Crown 8vo, cloth, 3s. 6d. each.
| **Long Odds.** | **The Master of Rathkelly.** | **The Outsider.** |

Post 8vo, picture boards, 2s. each.
| **The Plunger.** | **Beatrice and Benedick.** |

Smith (J. Moyr), Works by.
The Prince of Argolis. With 130 Illustrations. Post 8vo, cloth extra, 3s. 6d.
The Wooing of the Water Witch. With numerous Illustrations. Post 8vo, cloth, 6s.

Society in London. Crown 8vo, 1s. ; cloth, 1s. 6d.

Society in Paris: The Upper Ten Thousand. A Series of Letters
from Count PAUL VASILI to a Young French Diplomat. Crown 8vo, cloth, 6s.

Somerset (Lord Henry).—Songs of Adieu. Small 4to, Jap. vel., 6s.

Spalding (T. A., LL.B.).— Elizabethan Demonology: An Essay
on the Belief in the Existence of Devils. Crown 8vo, cloth extra, 5s.

Speight (T. W.), Novels by.

Post 8vo, illustrated boards, 2s. each.

The Mysteries of Heron Dyke.
By Devious Ways, &c.
Hoodwinked; & Sandycroft Mystery.
The Golden Hoop.
Back to Life.

The Loudwater Tragedy.
Burgo's Romance.
Quittance in Full.
A Husband from the Sea.

Post 8vo, cloth limp, 1s. 6d. each.

A Barren Title. | Wife or No Wife?

Crown 8vo, cloth extra, 3s. 6d. each.

A Secret of the Sea. | The Grey Monk. | The Master of Trenance.   [March.
A Minion of the Moon; A Romance of the King's Highway.   [Shortly.

Spenser for Children. By M. H. TOWRY. With Coloured Illustrations
by WALTER J. MORGAN. Crown 4to, cloth extra, 3s. 6d.

Stafford (John).—Doris and I, &c. Crown 8vo, cloth, 3s. 6d.

Starry Heavens (The) : A POETICAL BIRTHDAY BOOK. Royal 16mo,
cloth extra, 2s. 6d.

Stedman (E. C.), Works by. Crown 8vo, cloth extra, 9s. each.
Victorian Poets. | The Poets of America.

Stephens (Riccardo, M.B.).—The Cruciform Mark: The Strange
Story of RICHARD TREGENNA, Bachelor of Medicine (Univ. Edinb.) Crown 8vo, cloth, 6s.

Sterndale (R. Armitage).—The Afghan Knife: A Novel. Crown
8vo, cloth extra, 3s. 6d.; post 8vo, illustrated boards, 2s.

Stevenson (R. Louis), Works by. Post 8vo, cloth limp, 2s. 6d, ea.
Travels with a Donkey. With a Frontispiece by WALTER CRANE.
An Inland Voyage. With a Frontispiece by WALTER CRANE.

Crown 8vo, buckram, gilt top, 6s. each.
Familiar Studies of Men and Books.
The Silverado Squatters. With Frontispiece by J. D. STRONG.
The Merry Men. | Underwoods: Poems.
Memories and Portraits.
Virginibus Puerisque, and other Papers. | Ballads. | Prince Otto.
Across the Plains, with other Memories and Essays.
Weir of Hermiston. (R. L. STEVENSON'S LAST WORK.)

Songs of Travel. Crown 8vo, buckram, 5s.
New Arabian Nights. Crown 8vo, buckram, gilt top, 6s. ; post 8vo, illustrated boards, 2s.
The Suicide Club; and The Rajah's Diamond. (From NEW ARABIAN NIGHTS.) With
Eight Illustrations by W. J. HENNESSY. Crown 8vo, cloth, 5s.
The Edinburgh Edition of the Works of Robert Louis Stevenson. Twenty-seven
Vols., demy 8vo. This Edition (which is limited to 1,000 copies) is sold in Sets only, the price of
which may be learned from the Booksellers. The First Volume was published Nov., 1894.

Stories from Foreign Novelists. With Notices by HELEN and
ALICE ZIMMERN. Crown 8vo, cloth extra, 3s. 6d. ; post 8vo, illustrated boards, 2s.

Strange Manuscript (A) Found in a Copper Cylinder. Crown
8vo, cloth extra, with 19 Illustrations by GILBERT GAUL, 5s. ; post 8vo, illustrated boards, 2s.

Strange Secrets. Told by PERCY FITZGERALD, CONAN DOYLE, FLOR-.
ENCE MARRYAT, &c. Post 8vo, illustrated boards, 2s.

Strutt (Joseph). — The Sports and Pastimes of the People of
England; including the Rural and Domestic Recreations, May Games, Mummeries, Shows, &c., from
the Earliest Period to the Present Time. Edited by WILLIAM HONE. With 140 Illustrations. Crown
8vo, cloth extra, 7s. 6d.

Swift's (Dean) Choice Works, in Prose and Verse. With Memoir,
Portrait, and Facsimiles of the Maps in 'Gulliver's Travels.' Crown 8vo, cloth, 7s. 6d.

Gulliver's Travels, and A Tale of a Tub. Post 8vo, half-bound, 2s.
Jonathan Swift: A Study. By J. CHURTON COLLINS. Crown 8vo, cloth extra. 8s.

Swinburne (Algernon C.), Works by.

Selections from the Poetical Works of A. C. Swinburne. Fcap. 8vo, 6s.
Atalanta in Calydon. Crown 8vo, 6s.
Chastelard: A Tragedy. Crown 8vo, 7s.
Poems and Ballads. FIRST SERIES. Crown 8vo, or fcap. 8vo, 9s.
Poems and Ballads. SECOND SERIES. Crown 8vo, 9s.
Poems & Ballads. THIRD SERIES. Cr. 8vo, 7s.
Songs before Sunrise. Crown 8vo, 10s. 6d.
Bothwell: A Tragedy. Crown 8vo, 12s. 6d.
Songs of Two Nations. Crown 8vo, 6s.
George Chapman. (See Vol. II. of G. CHAPMAN'S Works.) Crown 8vo, 3s. 6d.
Essays and Studies. Crown 8vo, 12s.
Erechtheus: A Tragedy. Crown 8vo, 6s.
A Note on Charlotte Bronte. Cr. 8vo, 6s.

A Study of Shakespeare. Crown 8vo, 8s.
Songs of the Springtides. Crown 8vo, 6s.
Studies in Song. Crown 8vo, 7s.
Mary Stuart: A Tragedy. Crown 8vo, 8s.
Tristram of Lyonesse. Crown 8vo, 9s.
A Century of Roundels. Small 4to, 8s.
A Midsummer Holiday. Crown 8vo, 7s.
Marino Faliero: A Tragedy. Crown 8vo, 6s.
A Study of Victor Hugo. Crown 8vo, 6s.
Miscellanies. Crown 8vo, 12s.
Locrine: A Tragedy. Crown 8vo, 6s.
A Study of Ben Jonson. Crown 8vo, 7s.
The Sisters: A Tragedy. Crown 8vo, 6s.
Astrophel, &c. Crown 8vo, 7s.
Studies in Prose and Poetry. Cr. 8vo, 9s.
The Tale of Balen. Crown 8vo, 7s.

Syntax's (Dr.) Three Tours: In Search of the Picturesque, in Search
of Consolation, and in Search of a Wife. With ROWLANDSON'S Coloured Illustrations, and Life of the Author by J. C. HOTTEN. Crown 8vo, cloth extra, 7s. 6d.

Taine's History of English Literature. Translated by HENRY VAN
LAUN. Four Vols., small demy 8vo, cloth boards, 30s.—POPULAR EDITION, Two Vols., large crown 8vo, cloth extra, 15s.

Taylor (Bayard). — Diversions of the Echo Club: Burlesques of
Modern Writers. Post 8vo, cloth limp, 2s.

Taylor (Tom). — Historical Dramas. Containing 'Clancarty,'
'Jeanne Darc,' ''Twixt Axe and Crown,' 'The Fool's Revenge,' 'Arkwright's Wife,' 'Anne Boleyn,' 'Plot and Passion.' Crown 8vo, cloth extra, 7s. 6d.
. The Plays may also be had separately, at 1s. each.

Tennyson (Lord): A Biographical Sketch. By H. J. JENNINGS. Post
8vo, portrait cover, 1s.; cloth, 1s. 6d.

Thackerayana: Notes and Anecdotes. With Coloured Frontispiece and
Hundreds of Sketches by WILLIAM MAKEPEACE THACKERAY. Crown 8vo, cloth extra, 7s. 6d.

Thames, A New Pictorial History of the. By A. S. KRAUSSE.
With 340 Illustrations. Post 8vo, picture cover, 1s.

Thiers (Adolphe). — History of the Consulate and Empire of
France under Napoleon. Translated by D. FORBES CAMPBELL and JOHN STEBBING. With 36 Steel Plates. 12 Vols., demy 8vo, cloth extra, 12s. each.

Thomas (Bertha), Novels by. Cr. 8vo, cl., 3s. 6d. ea.; post 8vo, 2s. ea.
The Violin-Player. | **Proud Maisie.**

Cressida. Post 8vo, illustrated boards, 2s.

Thomson's Seasons, and The Castle of Indolence. With Intro-
duction by ALLAN CUNNINGHAM, and 48 Illustrations. Post 8vo, half-bound, 2s.

Thornbury (Walter), Books by.
The Life and Correspondence of J. M. W. Turner. With Illustrations in Colours. Crown 8vo, cloth extra, 7s. 6d.

Post 8vo, illustrated boards, 2s. each.
Old Stories Re-told. | **Tales for the Marines.**

Timbs (John), Works by. Crown 8vo, cloth extra, 7s. 6d. each.
The History of Clubs and Club Life in London: Anecdotes of its Famous Coffee-houses, Hostelries, and Taverns. With 42 Illustrations.
English Eccentrics and Eccentricities: Stories of Delusions, Impostures, Sporting Scenes, Eccentric Artists, Theatrical Folk, &c. With 48 Illustrations.

Transvaal (The). By JOHN DE VILLIERS. With Map. Crown 8vo, 1s.

Trollope (Anthony), Novels by.
Crown 8vo, cloth extra, 3s. 6d. each; post 8vo, illustrated boards, 2s. each.
The Way We Live Now. | **Mr. Scarborough's Family.**
Frau Frohmann. | **The Land-Leaguers.**

Post 8vo, illustrated boards, 2s. each.
Kept in the Dark. | **The American Senator.**
The Golden Lion of Granpere. | **John Caldigate.** | **Marion Fay.**

Trollope (Frances E.), Novels by.
Crown 8vo, cloth extra, 3s. 6d. each; post 8vo, illustrated boards, 2s. each.
Like Ships Upon the Sea. | **Mabel's Progress.** | **Anne Furness.**

Trollope (T. A.).—Diamond Cut Diamond. Post 8vo, illust. bds., 2s.

Trowbridge (J. T.).—Farnell's Folly. Post 8vo, illust. boards, 2s.

Twain (Mark), Books by.

The Choice Works of Mark Twain. Revised and Corrected throughout by the Author. With Life, Portrait, and numerous Illustrations. Crown 8vo, cloth extra, 7s. 6d.

Crown 8vo, cloth extra (illustrated), 7s. 6d. each ; post 8vo, illustrated boards, 2s. each
The Innocents Abroad ; or, The New Pilgrim s Progress. With 234 Illustrations. (The Two Shilling Edition is entitled **Mark Twain's Pleasure Trip.**)
The Gilded Age. By MARK TWAIN and C. D. WARNER. With 212 Illustrations.
The Adventures of Tom Sawyer. With 111 Illustrations.
The Prince and the Pauper. With 190 Illustrations.
Life on the Mississippi. With 300 Illustrations.
The Adventures of Huckleberry Finn. With 174 Illustrations by E. W. KEMBLE.
A Yankee at the Court of King Arthur. With 220 Illustrations by DAN BEARD.

Crown 8vo, cloth extra, 3s. 6d. each.
Roughing It ; and The Innocents at Home. With 200 Illustrations by F. A. FRASER.
The American Claimant. With 81 Illustrations by HAL HURST and others.
Tom Sawyer Abroad. With 26 Illustrations by DAN. BEARD.
Tom Sawyer, Detective, &c. With Photogravure Portrait.
Pudd'nhead Wilson. With Portrait and Six Illlustrations by LOUIS LOEB.
Mark Twain's Library of Humour. With 197 Illustrations by E. W. KEMBLE.

Crown 8vo, cloth extra, 3s. 6d. each ; post 8vo, picture boards, 2s. each.
The £1,000,000 Bank-Note. | **The Stolen White Elephant.**
A Tramp Abroad.

Mark Twain's Sketches. Post 8vo, illustrated boards, 2s.
Personal Recollections of Joan of Arc. With Twelve Illustrations by F. V. DU MOND. Crown 8vo, cloth, 6s.

Tytler (C. C. Fraser-).—Mistress Judith : A Novel. Crown 8vo, cloth extra, 3s. 6d. ; post 8vo, illustrated boards, 2s.

Tytler (Sarah), Novels by.

Crown 8vo, cloth extra, 3s. 6d. each ; post 8vo, illustrated boards, 2s. each.
Lady Bell. | **Buried Diamonds.** | **The Blackhall Ghosts.**

Post 8vo, illustrated boards, 2s. each.
What She Came Through. · | **The Huguenot Family.**
Citoyenne Jacqueline. | **Noblesse Oblige.**
The Bride's Pass. | **Beauty and the Beast.**
Saint Mungo's City. | **Disappeared.**

The Macdonald Lass. With Frontispiece. Crown 8vo, cloth, 3s. 6d.

Upward (Allen), Novels by.
A Crown of Straw. Crown 8vo, cloth, 6s.

Crown 8vo, cloth, 3s. 6d. each ; post 8vo, picture boards, 2s. each.
The Queen Against Owen. | **The Prince of Balkistan.**

Vashti and Esther. By 'Belle' of *The World.* Cr. 8vo, cloth, 3s. 6d.

Villari (Linda).—A Double Bond : A Story. Fcap. 8vo, 1s.

Vizetelly (Ernest A.).—The Scorpion : A Romance of Spain. With a Frontispiece. Crown 8vo, cloth extra, 3s. 6d.

Walford (Edward, M.A.), Works by.

Walford's County Families of the United Kingdom (1897). Containing the Descent, Birth, Marriage, Education, &c., of 12,000 Heads of Families, their Heirs, Offices, Addresses, Clubs &c. Royal 8vo, cloth gilt, 50s.
Walford's Shilling Peerage (1897). Containing a List of the House of Lords, Scotch and Irish Peers, &c. 32mo, cloth, 1s.
Walford's Shilling Baronetage (1897). Containing a List of the Baronets of the United Kingdom, Biographical Notices, Addresses, &c. 32mo, cloth, 1s.
Walford's Shilling Knightage (1897). Containing a List of the Knights of the United Kingdom, Biographical Notices, Addresses, &c. 32mo, cloth, 1s.
Walford's Shilling House of Commons (1897). Containing a List of all the Members of the New Parliament, their Addresses, Clubs, &c. 32mo, cloth, 1s.
Walford's Complete Peerage, Baronetage, Knightage, and House of Commons (1897). Royal 32mo, cloth, gilt edges, 5s.

Tales of our Great Families. Crown 8vo, cloth extra, 3s. 6d.

Waller (S. E.).—Sebastiani's Secret. With Nine full-page Illustrations by the Author. Crown 8vo, cloth, 6s.

Walton and Cotton's Complete Angler; or, The Contemplative Man's Recreation. by IZAAK WALTON; and Instructions How to Angle, for a Trout or Grayling in a clear Stream. by CHARLES COTTON. With Memoirs and Notes by Sir HARRIS NICOLAS, and 61 Illustrations. Crown 8vo, cloth antique, 7s. 6d.

Walt Whitman, Poems by. Edited, with Introduction, by WILLIAM M. ROSSETTI. With Portrait. Crown 8vo, hand-made paper and buckram, 6s.

Ward (Herbert), Books by.
Five Years with the Congo Cannibals. With 92 Illustrations. Royal 8vo, cloth, 14s.
My Life with Stanley's Rear Guard. With Map. Post 8vo, 1s.; cloth, 1s. 6d.

Warner (Charles Dudley).—A Roundabout Journey. Crown 8vo, cloth extra, 6s.

Warrant to Execute Charles I. A Facsimile, with the 59 Signatures and Seals. Printed on paper 22 in. by 14 in. 2s.
Warrant to Execute Mary Queen of Scots. A Facsimile, including Queen Elizabeth's Signature and the Great Seal. 2s.

Washington's (George) Rules of Civility Traced to their Sources and Restored by MONCURE D. CONWAY. Fcap. 8vo, Japanese vellum, 2s. 6d.

Wassermann (Lillias), Novels by.
The Daffodils. Crown 8vo, 1s.; cloth, 1s. 6d.

The Marquis of Carabas. By AARON WATSON and LILLIAS WASSERMANN. Post 8vo, illustrated boards, 2s.

Weather, How to Foretell the, with the Pocket Spectroscope. By F. W. CORY. With Ten Illustrations. Crown 8vo, 1s.; cloth, 1s. 6d.

Westall (William), Novels by.
Trust-Money. Post 8vo, illustrated boards, 2s.; cloth, 2s. 6d.
Sons of Belial. Crown 8vo, cloth extra, 3s. 6d.
With the Red Eagle: A Romance of the Tyrol. Crown 8vo, cloth, 6s.

Westbury (Atha).—The Shadow of Hilton Fernbrook: A Romance of Maoriland. Crown 8vo, cloth, 3s. 6d.

Whist, How to Play Solo. By ABRAHAM S. WILKS and CHARLES F. PARDON. Post 8vo, cloth limp, 2s.

White (Gilbert).—The Natural History of Selborne. Post 8vo, printed on laid paper and half-bound, 2s.

Williams (W. Mattieu, F.R.A.S.), Works by.
Science in Short Chapters. Crown 8vo, cloth extra, 7s. 6d.
A Simple Treatise on Heat. With Illustrations. Crown 8vo, cloth, 2s. 6d.
The Chemistry of Cookery. Crown 8vo, cloth extra, 6s.
The Chemistry of Iron and Steel Making. Crown 8vo, cloth extra, 9s.
A Vindication of Phrenology. With Portrait and 43 Illusts. Demy 8vo, cloth extra, 12s. 6d.

Williamson (Mrs. F. H.).—A Child Widow. Post 8vo, bds., 2s.

Wills (C. J.).—An Easy-going Fellow. Crown 8vo, cloth, 6s.

Wilson (Dr. Andrew, F.R.S.E.), Works by.
Chapters on Evolution. With 259 Illustrations. Crown 8vo, cloth extra, 7s. 6d.
Leaves from a Naturalist's Note-Book. Post 8vo, cloth limp, 2s. 6d.
Leisure-Time Studies. With Illustrations. Crown 8vo, cloth extra, 6s.
Studies in Life and Sense. With numerous Illustrations. Crown 8vo, cloth extra, 6s.
Common Accidents: How to Treat Them. With Illustrations. Crown 8vo, 1s.; cloth, 1s. 6d.
Glimpses of Nature. With 35 Illustrations. Crown 8vo, cloth extra, 3s. 6d.

Winter (John Strange), Stories by. Post 8vo, illustrated boards, 2s. each; cloth limp, 2s. 6d. each.
Cavalry Life. | **Regimental Legends.**

Cavalry Life and Regimental Legends. LIBRARY EDITION, set in new type and handsomely bound. Crown 8vo, cloth, 3s. 6d. [Shortly.
A Soldier's Children. With 34 Illustrations by E. G. THOMSON and E. STUART HARDY. Crown 8vo, cloth extra, 3s. 6d.

Wissmann (Hermann von). — My Second Journey through Equatorial Africa. With 92 Illustrations. Demy 8vo, cloth, 16s.

Wood (H. F.), Detective Stories by. Post 8vo, boards, 2s. each.
The Passenger from Scotland Yard. | **The Englishman of the Rue Cain.**

Wood (Lady).—Sabina: A Novel. Post 8vo, illustrated boards, 2s.

Woolley (Celia Parker).—Rachel Armstrong; or, Love and Theology. Post 8vo, illustrated boards, 2s.; cloth, 2s. 6d.

Wright (Thomas), Works by. Crown 8vo, cloth extra, 7s. 6d. each.
The Caricature History of the Georges. With 400 Caricatures, Squibs, &c.
History of Caricature and of the Grotesque in Art, Literature, Sculpture, and Painting. Illustrated by F. W. FAIRHOLT, F.S.A.

Wynman (Margaret).—My Flirtations. With 13 Illustrations by J. BERNARD PARTRIDGE. Crown 8vo, cloth, 3s. 6d.; post 8vo, cloth limp, 2s.

Yates (Edmund), Novels by. Post 8vo, illustrated boards, 2s. each.
Land at Last. | The Forlorn Hope. | Castaway.

Zangwill (I.). — Ghetto Tragedies. With Three Illustrations by A. S. BOYD. Fcap. 8vo, cloth, 2s. net.

Zola (Emile), Novels by. Crown 8vo, cloth extra, 3s. 6d. each.
The Fat and the Thin. Translated by ERNEST A. VIZETELLY.
Money. Translated by ERNEST A. VIZETELLY.
The Downfall. Translated by E. A. VIZETELLY.
The Dream. Translated by ELIZA CHASE. With Eight Illustrations by JEANNIOT.
Doctor Pascal. Translated by E. A. VIZETELLY. With Portrait of the Author.
Lourdes. Translated by ERNEST A. VIZETELLY.
Rome. Translated by ERNEST A. VIZETELLY.

SOME BOOKS CLASSIFIED IN SERIES.

₊ For fuller cataloguing, see alphabetical arrangement, pp. 1–26.

The Mayfair Library. Post 8vo, cloth limp, 2s. 6d. per Volume.

A Journey Round My Room. By X. DE MAISTRE. Translated by Sir HENRY ATTWELL.
Quips and Quiddities. By W. D. ADAMS.
The Agony Column of 'The Times.'
Melancholy Anatomised: Abridgment of BURTON.
Poetical Ingenuities. By W. T. DOBSON.
The Cupboard Papers. By FIN-BEC.
W. S. Gilbert's Plays. Three Series.
Songs of Irish Wit and Humour.
Animals and their Masters. By Sir A. HELPS.
Social Pressure. By Sir A. HELPS.
Curiosities of Criticism. By H. J. JENNINGS.
The Autocrat of the Breakfast-Table. By OLIVER WENDELL HOLMES.
Pencil and Palette. By R. KEMPT.
Little Essays: from LAMB'S LETTERS.
Forensic Anecdotes. By JACOB LARWOOD.

Theatrical Anecdotes. By JACOB LARWOOD.
Witch Stories. By E. LYNN LINTON.
Ourselves. By E. LYNN LINTON.
Pastimes and Players. By R. MACCREGOR.
New Paul and Virginia. By W. H. MALLOCK.
The New Republic. By W. H. MALLOCK.
Puck on Pegasus. By H. C. PENNELL.
Pegasus Re-saddled. By H. C. PENNELL.
Muses of Mayfair. Edited by H. C. PENNELL.
Thoreau: His Life and Aims. By H. A. PAGE.
Puniana. By Hon. HUGH ROWLEY.
More Puniana. By Hon. HUGH ROWLEY.
The Philosophy of Handwriting.
By Stream and Sea. By WILLIAM SENIOR.
Leaves from a Naturalist's Note-Book. By Dr ANDREW WILSON.

The Golden Library. Post 8vo, cloth limp, 2s. per Volume.

Diversions of the Echo Club. BAYARD TAYLOR.
Songs for Sailors. By W. C. BENNETT.
Lives of the Necromancers. By W. GODWIN.
The Poetical Works of Alexander Pope.
Scenes of Country Life. By EDWARD JESSE.
Tale for a Chimney Corner. By LEIGH HUNT.

The Autocrat of the Breakfast Table. By OLIVER WENDELL HOLMES.
La Mort d'Arthur: Selections from MALLORY.
Provincial Letters of Blaise Pascal.
Maxims and Reflections of Rochefoucauld.

Handy Novels. Fcap. 8vo, cloth boards, 1s. 6d. each.

The Old Maid's Sweetheart. By A. ST. AUBYN.
Modest Little Sara. By ALAN ST. AUBYN.
Seven Sleepers of Ephesus. M. E. COLERIDGE. -
Taken from the Enemy. By H. NEWBOLT.

A Lost Soul. By W. L. ALDEN.
Dr. Palliser's Patient. By GRANT ALLEN.
Monte Carlo Stories. By JOAN BARRETT.
Black Spirits and White. By R. A. CRAM.

My Library. Printed on laid paper, post 8vo, half-Roxburghe, 2s. 6d. each.

Citation and Examination of William Shakspeare. By W. S. LANDOR.
The Journal of Maurice de Guerin.

Christie Johnstone. By CHARLES READE.
Peg Woffington. By CHARLES READE.
The Dramatic Essays of Charles Lamb.

The Pocket Library. Post 8vo, printed on laid paper and hf.-bd., 2s. each.

The Essays of Elia. By CHARLES LAMB.
Robinson Crusoe. Illustrated by G. CRUIKSHANK.
Whims and Oddities. By THOMAS HOOD.
The Barber's Chair. By DOUGLAS JERROLD.
Gastronomy. By BRILLAT-SAVARIN.
The Epicurean. &c. By THOMAS MOORE.
Leigh Hunt's Essays. Edited by E. OLLIER.

White's Natural History of Selborne.
Gulliver's Travels, &c. By Dean SWIFT.
Plays by RICHARD BRINSLEY SHERIDAN.
Anecdotes of the Clergy. By JACOB LARWOOD.
Thomson's Seasons. Illustrated.
Autocrat of the Breakfast-Table and The Professor at the Breakfast-Table. By O. W. HOLMES.

THE PICCADILLY NOVELS.

LIBRARY EDITIONS OF NOVELS,many Illustrated, crown 8vo, cloth extra, 3s. 6d. each.

By Mrs. ALEXANDER.
A Life Interest. | Mona's Choice.
By Woman's Wit.

By F. M. ALLEN.
Green as Grass.

By GRANT ALLEN.
Philistia. | The Great Taboo.
Strange Stories. | Dumaresq's Daughter.
Babylon. | Duchess of Powysland.
For Malmie's Sake. | Blood Royal.
In all Shades. | Ivan Greet's Master-
The Beckoning Hand. | piece.
The Devil's Die. | The Scallywag.
This Mortal Coil. | At Market Value.
The Tents of Shem. | Under Sealed Orders.

By MARY ANDERSON.
Othello's Occupation.

By EDWIN L. ARNOLD.
Phra the Phœnician. | Constable of St. Nicholas.

By ROBERT BARR.
In a Steamer Chair. | From Whose Bourne.

By FRANK BARRETT.
The Woman of the Iron Bracelets.
The Harding Scandal.
A Missing Witness.

By 'BELLE.'
Vashti and Esther.

By Sir W. BESANT and J. RICE.
Ready-MoneyMortiboy. | By Celia's Arbour.
My Little Girl. | Chaplain of the Fleet.
With Harp and Crown. | The Seamy Side.
This Son of Vulcan. | The Case of Mr. Lucraft.
The Golden Butterfly. | In Trafalgar's Bay.
The Monks of Thelema. | The Ten Years' Tenant.

By Sir WALTER BESANT.
All Sorts and Condi- | The Revolt of Man.
tions of Men. | The Bell of St. Paul's.
The Captains' Room. | The Holy Rose.
All in a Garden Fair. | Armorel of Lyonesse.
Dorothy Forster. | S. Katherine's by Tower
Uncle Jack. | Verbena Camellia Ste-
The World Went Very | phanotis.
Well Then. | The Ivory Gate.
Children of Gibeon. | The Rebel Queen.
Herr Paulus. | Beyond the Dreams of
For Faith and Freedom. | Avarice.
To Call Her Mine. | The Master Craftsman.

By PAUL BOURGET.
A Living Lie.

By ROBERTBUCHANAN.
Shadow of the Sword. | The New Abe·ard.
A Child of Nature. | Matt. | Rachel Dene.
God and the Man. | Master of the Mine.
Martyrdom of Madeline | The H·ir of Linne.
Love Me for Ever. | Woman and the Man.
Annan Water. | Red and White Heather.
Foxglove Manor. | Lady Kilpatrick.

ROB. BUCHANAN & HY. MURRAY.
The Charlatan.

By J. MITCHELL CHAPPLE.
The Minor Chord.

By HALL CAINE.
The Shadow of a Crime. | The Deemster.
A Son of Hagar. |

By MACLAREN COBBAN.
The Red Sultan. | The Burden of Isabel.

By MORT. & FRANCES COLLINS.
Transmigration. | From Midnight to Mid-
Blacksmith & Scholar. | night.
The Village Comedy. | You Play me False.

By WILKIE COLLINS.
Armadale. | AfterDark. | The Frozen Deep.
No Name. | The Two Destinies.
Antonina. | The Law and the Lady.
Basil. | The Haunted Hotel.
Hide and Seek. | The Fallen Leaves.
The Dead Secret. | Jezebel's Daughter.
Queen of Hearts. | The Black Robe.
My Miscellanies. | Heart and Science.
The Woman in White. | 'I Say No.'
The Moonstone. | Little Novels.
Man and Wife. | The Evil Genius.
Poor Miss Finch. | The Legacy of Cain
Miss or Mrs.? | A Rogue's Life.
The New Magdalen. | Blind Love.

By E. H. COOPER.
Geoffory Hamilton.

By V. CECIL COTES.
Two Girls on a Barge.

By C. EGBERT CRADDOCK.
His Vanished Star.

By H. N. CRELLIN.
Romances of the Old Seraglio.

By MATT CRIM.
The Adventures of a Fair Rebel.

By S. R. CROCKETT and others.
Tales of Our Coast.

By B. M. CROKER.
Diana Barrington. | Village Tales & Jungle
Proper Pride. | Tragedies.
A Family Likeness. | The Real Lady Hilda.
Pretty Miss Neville. | Married or Single?
A Bird of Passage. | Two Masters.
'To Let.' | Mr. Jervis. | In the Kingdom of Kerry

By WILLIAM CYPLES.
Hearts of Gold.

By ALPHONSE DAUDET.
The Evangelist; or, Port Salvation.

By H. COLEMAN DAVIDSON.
Mr. Sadler's Daughters.

By ERASMUS DAWSON.
The Fountain of Youth.

By JAMES DE MILLE.
A Castle in Spain.

By. J. LEITH DERWENT.
Our Lady of Tears. | Circe's Lovers.

By DICK DONOVAN.
Tracked to Doom. | The Mystery of Jamaica
Man from Manchester. | Terrace.
The Chronicles of Michael Danevitch.

By A. CONAN DOYLE.
The Firm of Girdlestone.

By S. JEANNETTE DUNCAN.
A Daughter of To-day. | Vernon's Aunt.

By G. MANVILLE FENN.
The New Mistress. | The Tiger Lily.
Witness to the Deed. | The White Virgin.

By PERCY FITZGERALD.
Fatal Zero.

By R. E. FRANCILLON.
One by One. | Ropes of Sand.
A Dog and his Shadow. | Jack Doyle's Daughter.
A Real Queen. |

Prefaced by Sir BARTLE FRERE.
Pandurang Hari.

BY EDWARD GARRETT.
The Capel Girls.

THE PICCADILLY (3/6) NOVELS—*continued*.

By PAUL GAULOT.
The Red Shirts.

By CHARLES GIBBON.
Robin Gray. | The Golden Shaft.
Loving a Dream.

By E. GLANVILLE.
The Lost Heiress. | The Fossicker.
A Fair Colonist. | The Golden Rock.

By E. J. GOODMAN.
The Fate of Herbert Wayne.

By Rev. S. BARING GOULD.
Red Spider. | Eve.

By CECIL GRIFFITH.
Corinthia Marazion.

By SYDNEY GRUNDY.
The Days of his Vanity.

By THOMAS HARDY.
Under the Greenwood Tree.

By BRET HARTE.
A Waif of the Plains. | A Protégée of Jack
A Ward of the Golden | Hamlin's.
　Gate. 　 [Springs. | Clarence.
A Sappho of Green | Barker's Luck.
Col. Starbottle's Client. | Devil's Ford. [celsior.'
Susy. | Sally Dows. | The Crusade of the 'Ex-
Bell-Ringer of Angel's. | Three Partners.

By JULIAN HAWTHORNE.
Garth! | Beatrix Randolph.
Ellice Quentin. | David Poindexter's Dis-
Sebastian Strome. | 　appearance.
Dust. | The Spectre of the
Fortune's Fool. | 　Camera.

By Sir A. HELPS.
Ivan de Biron.

By I. HENDERSON.
Agatha Page.

By G. A. HENTY.
Rujub the Juggler. | Dorothy's Double.

By JOHN HILL.
The Common Ancestor.

By Mrs. HUNGERFORD.
Lady Verner's Flight. | A Point of Conscience.
The Red-House Mystery | Nora Creina.
The Three Graces. | An Anxious Moment.
Professor's Experiment | April's Lady.

By Mrs. ALFRED HUNT.
The Leaden Casket. | Self-Condemned.
That Other Person. | Mrs. Juliet.

By C. J. CUTCLIFFE HYNE.
Honour of Thieves.

By R. ASHE KING.
A Drawn Game. | 'The Wearing of the Green.

By EDMOND LEPELLETIER.
Madame Sans-Gêne.

By HARRY LINDSAY.
Rhoda Roberts.

By HENRY W. LUCY.
Gideon Fleyce.

By E. LYNN LINTON.
Patricia Kemball. | The Atonement of Leam
Under which Lord? | 　Dundas.
' My Love!' | Ione. | The World Well Lost.
Paston Carew. | The One Too Many.
Sowing the Wind. | Dulcie Everton.

By JUSTIN McCARTHY.
A Fair Saxon. | Donna Quixote.
Linley Rochford. | Maid of Athens.
Dear Lady Disdain. | The Comet of a Season.
Camiola. | The Dictator.
Waterdale Neighbours. | Red Diamonds.
My Enemy's Daughter. | The Riddle Ring.
Miss Misanthrope.

By JUSTIN H. McCARTHY.
A London Legend. | The Royal Christopher.

By GEORGE MACDONALD.
Heather and Snow. | Phantastes.

By L. T. MEADE.
A Soldier of Fortune. | The Voice of the
In an Iron Grip. | 　Charmer.

By LEONARD MERRICK.
This Stage of Fools.

By BERTRAM MITFORD.
The Gun-Runner. | The King's Assegai.
The Luck of Gerard | Renshaw Fanning's
Ridgeley. | 　Quest.

By J. E. MUDDOCK.
Maid Marian and Robin Hood.
Basile the Jester. | Young Lochinvar.

By D. CHRISTIE MURRAY.
A Life's Atonement. | Cynic Fortune.
Joseph's Coat. | The Way of the World.
Coals of Fire. | Bob Martin's Little Girl
Old Blazer's Hero. | Time's Revenges.
Val Strange. | Hearts. | A Wasted Crime.
A Model Father. | In Direst Peril.
By the Gate of the Sea. | Mount Despair.
A Bit of Human Nature. | A Capful o' Nails.
First Person Singular.

By MURRAY and HERMAN.
The Bishops' Bible. | Paul Jones's Alias.
One Traveller Returns.

By HUME NISBET.
' Bail Up !'

By W. E. NORRIS.
Saint Ann's. | Billy Bellew.

By G. OHNET.
A Weird Gift.

By Mrs. OLIPHANT.
The Sorceress.

By OUIDA.
Held in Bondage. | Two Little Wooden
Strathmore. | In a Winter City. [Shoes
Chandos. | Friendship.
Under Two Flags. | Moths. | Ruffino.
Idalia. 　　[Gage. | Pipistrello.
Cecil Castlemaine's | A Village Commune.
Tricotrin. | Puck. | Bimbi. | Wanda.
Folle Farine. | Frescoes. | Othmar.
A Dog of Flanders. | In Maremma.
Pascarel. | Signa. | Syrlin. | Guilderoy.
Princess Napraxine. | Santa Barbara.
Ariadne. | Two Offenders.

By MARGARET A. PAUL.
Gentle and Simple.

By JAMES PAYN.
Lost Sir Massingberd. | High Spirits.
Less Black than We're | Under One Roof.
　Painted. | Glow-worm Tales.
A Confidential Agent. | The Talk of the Town
A Grape from a Thorn. | Holiday Tasks.
In Peril and Privation. | For Cash Only.
The Mystery of Mir- | The Burnt Million.
　By Proxy. 　[bridge. | The Word and the Will.
The Canon's Ward. | Sunny Stories.
Walter's Word. | A Trying Patient.

By WILL PAYNE.
Jerry the Dreamer.

By Mrs. CAMPBELL PRAED.
Outlaw and Lawmaker. | Mrs. Tregaskiss.
Christina Chard.

By E. C. PRICE.
Valentina. | Foreigners. | Mrs. Lancaster's Rival.

By RICHARD PRYCE.
Miss Maxwell's Affections.

By CHARLES READE.
Peg Woffington; and | Love Me Little, Love
　Christie Johnstone. | 　Me Long.
Hard Cash. | The Double Marriage.
Cloister & the Hearth. | Foul Play. 　[Place.
Never Too Late to Mend | Put Yourself in His
The Course of True | A Terrible Temptation.
　Love Never Did Run | A Simpleton.
　Smooth ; and Single- | A Woman-Hater.
　heart and Double face. | The Jilt, & other Stories;
Autobiography of a | 　& Good Stories of Men
　Thief; Jack of all | 　and other Animals.
　Trades: A Hero and | A Perilous Secret.
　a Martyr; and The | Readiana: and Bible
　Wandering Heir. | 　Characters.
Griffith Gaunt.

THE PICCADILLY (3/6) NOVELS—*continued.*

By Mrs. J. H. RIDDELL.
Weird Stories.

By AMELIE RIVES.
Barbara Dering.

By F. W. ROBINSON.
The Hands of Justice. | Woman in the Dark.

By DORA RUSSELL.
A Country Sweetheart. | The Drift of Fate.

By W. CLARK RUSSELL.
Round the Galley-Fire. | My Shipmate Louise.
In the Middle Watch. | Alone on Wide Wide Sea
A Voyage to the Cape. | The Phantom Death.
Book for the Hammock. | Is He the Man?
The Mystery of the | The Good Ship 'Mo-
 'Ocean Star.' | hock.'
The Romance of Jenny | The Convict Ship.
Harlowe. | Heart of Oak.
An Ocean Tragedy. | The Tale of the Ten.

By JOHN SAUNDERS.
Guy Waterman. | The Two Dreamers.
Bound to the Wheel. | The Lion in the Path.

By KATHARINE SAUNDERS.
Margaret and Elizabeth | Heart Salvage.
Gideon's Rock. | Sebastian.
The High Mills.

By ADELINE SERGEANT.
Dr. Endicott's Experiment.

By HAWLEY SMART.
Without Love or Licence. | Long Odds.
The Master of Rathkelly. | The Outsider.

By T. W. SPEIGHT.
A Secret of the Sea. | The Master of Trenance.
The Grey Monk. | A Minion of the Moon.

By ALAN ST. AUBYN.
A Fellow of Trinity. | In Face of the World.
The Junior Dean. | Orchard Damerel.
Master of St.Benedict's. | The Tremlett Diamonds.
To his Own Master.

By JOHN STAFFORD.
Doris and I.

By R. A. STERNDALE.
The Afghan Knife.

By BERTHA THOMAS.
Proud Maisie. | The Violin-Player.

By ANTHONY TROLLOPE.
The Way we Live Now. | Scarborough's Family
Frau Frohmann. | The Land-Leaguers.

By FRANCES E. TROLLOPE.
Like Ships upon the | Anne Furness.
Sea. | Mabel's Progress.

By IVAN TURGENIEFF, &c.
Stories from Foreign Novelists.

By MARK TWAIN.
A Tramp Abroad. | Tom Sawyer Abroad.
The American Claimant. | Pudd'nhead Wilson.
The £1,000,000 Bank-note | Tom Sawyer,Detective.

By C. C. FRASER-TYTLER.
Mistress Judith.

By SARAH TYTLER.
Lady Bell. | The Blackhall Ghosts.
Buried Diamonds. | The Macdonald Lass.

By ALLEN UPWARD.
The Queen against Owen | The Prince of Balkistan

By E. A. VIZETELLY.
The Scorpion: A Romance of Spain.

By WILLIAM WESTALL.
Sons of Belial.

By ATHA WESTBURY.
The Shadow of Hilton Fernbrook.

By JOHN STRANGE WINTER.
Cavalry Life and Regimental Legends.
A Soldier's Children.

By MARGARET WYNMAN
My Flirtations.

By E. ZOLA.
The Downfall. | Money. | Lourdes.
The Dream. | The Fat and the Thin.
Dr. Pascal. | Rome.

CHEAP EDITIONS OF POPULAR NOVELS.

Post 8vo, illustrated boards, 2s. each.

By ARTEMUS WARD.
Artemus Ward Complete.

By EDMOND ABOUT.
The Fellah.

By HAMILTON AÏDÉ.
Carr of Carrlyon. | Confidences.

By MARY ALBERT.
Brooke Finchley's Daughter.

By Mrs. ALEXANDER.
Maid, Wife or Widow? | Valerie's Fate.
Blind Fate.

By GRANT ALLEN.
Philistia. | The Great Taboo.
Strange Stories. | Dumaresq's Daughter.
Babylon | Duchess of Powysland.
For Maimie's Sake. | Blood Royal. [piece-
In all Shades. | Ivan Greet's Master.
The Beckoning Hand. | The Scallywag.
The Devil's Die. | This Mortal Coil.
The Tents of Shem. | At Market Value.

By E. LESTER ARNOLD.
Phra the Phœnician.

By SHELSLEY BEAUCHAMP.
Grantley Grange.

BY FRANK BARRETT.
Fettered for Life. | A Prodigal's Progress.
Little Lady Linton. | Found Guilty.
Between Life & Death. | A Recoiling Vengeance.
The Sin of Olga Zassou- | For Love and Honour.
 lich. | John Ford; and His
Folly Morrison. | Helpmate.
Lieut. Barnabas. | The Woman of the Iron
Honest Davie. | Bracelets.

By Sir W. BESANT and J. RICE.
Ready-Money Mortiboy | By Celia's Arbour.
My Little Girl. | Chaplain of the Fleet.
With Harp and Crown. | The Seamy Side.
This Son of Vulcan. | The Case of Mr. Lucraft.
The Golden Butterfly. | In Trafalgar's Bay.
The Monks of Thelema. | The Ten Years' Tenant.

By Sir WALTER BESANT.
All Sorts and Condi- | To Call Her Mine.
tions of Men. | The Bell of St. Paul's.
The Captains' Room. | The Holy Rose.
All in a Garden Fair. | Armorel of Lyonesse.
Dorothy Forster. | S.Katherine's by Tower.
Uncle Jack. | Verbena Camellia Ste-
The World Went Very | phanotis.
 Well Then. | The Ivory Gate.
Children of Gibeon. | The Rebel Queen.
Herr Paulus. | Beyond the Dreams of
For Faith and Freedom. | Avarice.

By AMBROSE BIERCE.
In the Midst of Life.

By FREDERICK BOYLE.
Camp Notes. | Chronicles of No-man's
Savage Life. | Land.

BY BRET HARTE.
Californian Stories. | Flip. | Maruja.
Gabriel Conroy. | A Phyllis of the Sierras.
The Luck of Roaring | A Waif of the Plains.
 Camp. | A Ward of the Golden
An Heiress of Red Dog. | Gate.

By HAROLD BRYDGES.
Uncle Sam at Home.

Two-Shilling Novels—*continued.*

By ROBERT BUCHANAN.
Shadow of the Sword. | The Martyrdom of Ma-
A Child of Nature. | deline.
God and the Man. | The New Abelard.
Love Me for Ever. | Matt.
Foxglove Manor. | The Heir of Linne.
The Master of the Mine. | Woman and the Man.
Annan Water. | Rachel Dene.

By BUCHANAN and MURRAY.
The Charlatan.

By HALL CAINE.
The Shadow of a Crime. | The Deemster.
A Son of Hagar. |

By Commander CAMERON.
The Cruise of the 'Black Prince.'

By Mrs. LOVETT CAMERON.
Deceivers Ever. | Juliet's Guardian.

By HAYDEN CARRUTH.
The Adventures of Jones.

By AUSTIN CLARE.
For the Love of a Lass.

By Mrs. ARCHER CLIVE.
Paul Ferroll.
Why Paul Ferroll Killed his Wife.

By MACLAREN COBBAN.
The Cure of Souls. | The Red Sultan.

By C. ALLSTON COLLINS.
The Bar Sinister.

By MORT. & FRANCES COLLINS.
Sweet Anne Page. | Sweet and Twenty.
Transmigration. | The Village Comedy.
From Midnight to Mid- | You Play me False.
night. | Blacksmith and Scholar
A Fight with Fortune. | Frances.

By WILKIE COLLINS.
Armadale. | AfterDark. | My Miscellanies.
No Name. | The Woman in White.
Antonina. | The Moonstone.
Basil. | Man and Wife.
Hide and Seek. | Poor Miss Finch.
The Dead Secret. | The Fallen Leaves.
Queen of Hearts. | Jezebel's Daughter.
Miss or Mrs.? | The Black Robe.
The New Magdalen. | Heart and Science
The Frozen Deep. | 'I Say No!'
The Law and the Lady | The Evil Genius.
The Two Destinies. | Little Novels.
The Haunted Hotel. | Legacy of Cain.
A Rogue's Life. | Blind Love.

By M. J. COLQUHOUN.
Every Inch a Soldier.

By DUTTON COOK.
Leo. | Paul Foster's Daughter.

By C. EGBERT CRADDOCK.
The Prophet of the Great Smoky Mountains.

By MATT CRIM.
The Adventures of a Fair Rebel.

By B. M. CROKER.
Pretty Miss Neville. | A Family Likeness.
Diana Barrington. | Village Tales and Jungle
'To Let.' | Tragedies.
A Bird of Passage. | Two Masters.
Proper Pride. | Mr. Jervis.

By W. CYPLES.
Hearts of Gold.

By ALPHONSE DAUDET.
The Evangelist; or, Port Salvation.

By ERASMUS DAWSON.
The Fountain of Youth.

By JAMES DE MILLE.
A Castle in Spain.

By J. LEITH DERWENT.
Our Lady of Tears. | Circe's Lovers.

By CHARLES DICKENS.
Sketches by Boz.

By DICK DONOVAN.
The Man-Hunter. | In the Grip of the Law.
Tracked and Taken. | From Information Re-
Caught at Last! | ceived.
Wanted! | Tracked to Doom.
Who Poisoned Hetty | Link by Link
Duncan? | Suspicion Aroused.
Man from Manchester. | Dark Deeds.
A Detective's Triumphs | Riddles Read.
The Mystery of Jamaica Terrace.

By Mrs. ANNIE EDWARDES.
A Point of Honour. | Archie Lovell.

By M. BETHAM-EDWARDES.
Felicia. | Kitty.

By EDWARD EGGLESTON.
Roxy.

By G. MANVILLE FENN.
The New Mistress. | The Tiger Lily.
Witness to the Deed. | The White Virgin.

By PERCY FITZGERALD.
Bella Donna. | Second Mrs. Tillotson.
Never Forgotten. | Seventy-five Brooke
Polly. | Street.
Fatal Zero. | The Lady of Brantome.

By P. FITZGERALD and others.
Strange Secrets.

By ALBANY DE FONBLANQUE.
Filthy Lucre.

By R. E. FRANCILLON.
Olympia. | King or Knave?
One by One. | Romances of the Law.
A Real Queen. | Ropes of Sand.
Queen Cophetua. | A Dog and his Shadow.

By HAROLD FREDERIC.
Seth's Brother's Wife. | The Lawton Girl.

Prefaced by Sir BARTLE FRERE.
Pandurang Hari.

By HAIN FRISWELL.
One of Two.

By EDWARD GARRETT.
The Capel Girls.

By GILBERT GAUL.
A Strange Manuscript.

By CHARLES GIBBON.
Robin Gray. | In Honour Bound.
Fancy Free. | Flower of the Forest.
For Lack of Gold. | The Brass of Yarrow.
What will World Say? | The Golden Shaft.
In Love and War. | Of High Degree.
For the King. | By Mead and Stream.
In Pastures Green. | Loving a Dream.
Queen of the Meadow. | A Hard Knot.
A Heart's Problem. | Heart's Delight.
The Dead Heart. | Blood-Money.

By WILLIAM GILBERT.
Dr. Austin's Guests. | The Wizard of the
James Duke. | Mountain.

By ERNEST GLANVILLE.
The Lost Heiress. | The Fossicker.
A Fair Colonist. |

By Rev. S. BARING GOULD.
Red Spider. | Eve.

By HENRY GREVILLE.
A Noble Woman. | Nikanor.

By CECIL GRIFFITH.
Corinthia Marazion.

By SYDNEY GRUNDY.
The Days of his Vanity.

By JOHN HABBERTON.
Brueton's Bayou. | Country Luck.

By ANDREW HALLIDAY.
Every-day Papers.

By Lady DUFFUS HARDY.
Paul Wynter's Sacrifice.

By THOMAS HARDY.
Under the Greenwood Tree.

By J. BERWICK HARWOOD.
The Tenth Earl.

Two-SHILLING NOVELS—*continued*.

By JULIAN HAWTHORNE.

Garth.	Beatrix Randolph.
Ellice Quentin.	Love—or a Name.
Fortune's Fool.	David Poindexter's Dis-
Miss Cadogna.	appearance.
Sebastian Strome.	The Spectre of the
Dust.	Camera.

By Sir ARTHUR HELPS.
Ivan de Biron.

By G. A. HENTY.
Rujub the Juggler.

By HENRY HERMAN.
A Leading Lady.

By HEADON HILL.
Zambra the Detective.

By JOHN HILL.
Treason Felony.

By Mrs. CASHEL HOEY.
The Lover's Creed.

By Mrs. GEORGE HOOPER.
The House of Raby.

By TIGHE HOPKINS.
'Twixt Love and Duty.

By Mrs. HUNGERFORD.

A Maiden all Forlorn.	Lady Verner's Flight.
In Durance Vile.	The Red House Mystery
Marvel.	The Three Graces.
A Mental Struggle.	Unsatisfactory Lover.
A Modern Circe.	Lady Patty.

By Mrs. ALFRED HUNT.

Thornicroft's Model.	Self-Condemned.
That Other Person.	The Leaden Casket.

By JEAN INGELOW.
Fated to be Free.

By WM. JAMESON.
My Dead Self.

By HARRIETT JAY.
The Dark Colleen. | Queen of Connaught.

By MARK KERSHAW.
Colonial Facts and Fictions.

By R. ASHE KING.

A Drawn Game.	Passion's Slave.
'The Wearing of the	Bell Barry.
Green.'	

By EDMOND LEPELLETIER.
Madame Sans-Gene.

By JOHN LEYS.
The Lindsays.

By E. LYNN LINTON.

Patricia Kemball.	The Atonement of Leam
The World Well Lost.	Dundas.
Under which Lord?	With a Silken Thread.
Paston Carew.	Rebel of the Family.
'My Love!'	Sowing the Wind.
Ione.	The One Too Many.

By HENRY W. LUCY.
Gideon Fleyce.

By JUSTIN McCARTHY.

Dear Lady Disdain.	Camiola.
Waterdale Neighbours.	Donna Quixote.
My Enemy's Daughter.	Maid of Athens.
A Fair Saxon.	The Comet of a Season.
Linley Rochford.	The Dictator.
Miss Misanthrope.	Red Diamonds.

By HUGH MACCOLL.
Mr. Stranger's Sealed Packet.

By GEORGE MACDONALD.
Heather and Snow.

By AGNES MACDONELL.
Quaker Cousins.

By KATHARINE S. MACQUOID.
The Evil Eye. | Lost Rose.

By W. H. MALLOCK.
A Romance of the Nine- | The New Republic.
teenth Century. |

By FLORENCE MARRYAT.

Open ! Sesame !	A Harvest of Wild Oats.
Fighting the Air.	Written in Fire.

By J. MASTERMAN.
Half-a-dozen Daughters.

By BRANDER MATTHEWS.
A Secret of the Sea.

By L. T. MEADE.
A Soldier of Fortune.

By LEONARD MERRICK.
The Man who was Good.

By JEAN MIDDLEMASS.
Touch and Go. | Mr. Dorillion.

By Mrs. MOLESWORTH.
Hathercourt Rectory.

By J. E. MUDDOCK.

Stories Weird and Won-	From the Bosom of the
derful.	Deep.
The Dead Man's Secret.	

By D. CHRISTIE MURRAY.

A Model Father.	By the Gate of the Sea.
Joseph's Coat.	A Bit of Human Nature.
Coals of Fire.	First Person Singular.
Val Strange.	Hearts.	Bob Martin's Little Girl
Old Blazer's Hero.	Time's Revenges.
The Way of the World.	A Wasted Crime.
Cynic Fortune.	In Direst Peril.
A Life's Atonement.	Mount Despair.

By MURRAY and HERMAN.
One Traveller Returns. | The Bishops' Bible.
Paul Jones's Alias. |

By HENRY MURRAY.
A Game of Bluff. | A Song of Sixpence.

By HUME NISBET.
' Bail Up ! ' | Dr.Bernard St.Vincent

By W. E. NORRIS.
Saint Ann's.

By ALICE O'HANLON.
The Unforeseen. | Chance? or Fate?

By GEORGES OHNET.
Dr. Rameau. | A Weird Gift.
A Last Love. |

By Mrs. OLIPHANT.

Whiteladies.	The Greatest Heiress in
The Primrose Path.	England.

By Mrs. ROBERT O'REILLY.
Phœbe's Fortunes.

By OUIDA.

Held in Bondage.	Two Lit.Wooden Shoes.
Strathmore.	Moths.
Chandos.	Bimbi.
Idalia.	Pipistrello.
Under Two Flags.	A Village Commune
Cecil Castlemaine'sGage	Wanda.
Tricotrin.	Othmar.
Puck.	Frescoes.
Folle Farine.	In Maremma.
A Dog of Flanders.	Guilderoy.
Pascarel.	Ruffino.
Signa.	Syrlin.
Princess Napraxine.	Santa Barbara.
In a Winter City.	Two Offenders.
Ariadne.	Ouida's Wisdom, Wit,
Friendship.	and Pathos.

By MARGARET AGNES PAUL
Gentle and Simple.

By C. L. PIRKIS.
Lady Lovelace.

By EDGAR A. POE.
The Mystery of Marie Roget.

By Mrs. CAMPBELL PRAED

The Romance of a Station.
The Soul of Countess Adrian.
Out'aw and Lawmaker.
Christina Chard

By E. C. PRICE.

Valentina.	Mrs. Lancaster's Rival
The Foreigners.	Gerald.

By RICHARD PRYCE.
Miss Maxwell's Affections.

Two-SHILLING NOVELS—*continued*.

By JAMES PAYN.

Sentinck's Tutor.
Murphy's Master.
A County Family.
At Her Mercy.
Cecil's Tryst.
The Clyffards of Clyffe.
The Foster Brothers.
Found Dead.
The Best of Husbands.
Walter's Word.
Halves.
Fallen Fortunes.
Humorous Stories.
£200 Reward.
A Marine Residence.
Mirk Abbey.
By Proxy.
Under One Roof.
High Spirits.
Carlyon's Year.
From Exile.
For Cash Only.
Kit.
The Canon's Ward.

The Talk of the Town.
Holiday Tasks.
A Perfect Treasure.
What He Cost Her.
A Confidential Agent.
Glow-worm Tales.
The Burnt Million.
Sunny Stories.
Lost Sir Massingberd.
A Woman's Vengeance.
The Family Scapegrace.
Gwendoline's Harvest.
Like Father, Like Son.
Married Beneath Him.
Not Wooed, but Won.
Less Black than We're
Painted.
Some Private Views.
A Grape from a Thorn.
The Mystery of Mir-
bridge.
The Word and the Will.
A Prince of the Blood.
A Trying Patient.

By CHARLES READE.

It is Never Too Late to
Mend.
Christie Johnstone.
The Double Marriage.
Put Yourself in His
Place
Love Me Little, Love
Me Long.
The Cloister and the
Hearth.
The Course of True
Love.
The Jilt.
The Autobiography of
a Thief.

A Terrible Temptation.
Foul Play.
The Wandering Heir.
Hard Cash.
Singleheart and Double-
face.
Good Stories of Men and
other Animals.
Peg Woffington.
Griffith Gaunt.
A Perilous Secret.
A Simpleton.
Readiana.
A Woman-Hater.

By Mrs. J. H. RIDDELL.

Weird Stories.
Fairy Water.
Her Mother's Darling.
The Prince of Wales's
Garden Party.

The Uninhabited House.
The Mystery in Palace.
Gardens.
The Nun's Curse.
Idle Tales.

By AMELIE RIVES.

Barbara Dering.

By F. W. ROBINSON.

Women are Strange. | The Hands of Justice.

By JAMES RUNCIMAN.

Skippers and Shellbacks. | Schools and Scholars.
Grace Balmaign's Sweetheart.

By W. CLARK RUSSELL.

Round the Galley Fire.
On the Fo'k'sle Head.
In the Middle Watch.
A Voyage to the Cape.
A Book for the Ham-
mock.
The Mystery of the
'Ocean Star.'

The Romance of Jenny
Harlowe.
An Ocean Tragedy.
My Shipmate Louise.
Alone on Wide Wide Sea.
The Good Ship 'Mo-
hock.'
The Phantom Death.

By DORA RUSSELL.

A Country Sweetheart.

By GEORGE AUGUSTUS SALA.

Gaslight and Daylight.

By JOHN SAUNDERS.

Guy Waterman. | The Lion in the Path.
The Two Dreamers.

By KATHARINE SAUNDERS.

Joan Merryweather.
The High Mills.
Heart Salvage.

Sebastian.
Margaret and Eliza-
beth.

By GEORGE R. SIMS.

The Ring o' Bells.
Mary Jane's Memoirs.
Mary Jane Married.
Tales of To-day.
Dramas of Life.
Tinkletop's Crime.

My Two Wives.
Zeph.
Memoirs of a Landlady.
Scenes from the Show.
The 10 Commandments.
Dagonet Abroad.

By ARTHUR SKETCHLEY.

A Match in the Dark.

By HAWLEY SMART.

Without Love or Licence.
The Plunger.
Beatrice and Benedick.

By T. W. SPEIGHT.

The Mysteries of Heron
Dyke.
The Golden Hoop.
Hoodwinked.
By Devious Ways.

Back to Life.
The Loudwater Tragedy.
Burgo's Romance.
Quittance in Full.
A Husband from the Sea

By ALAN ST. AUBYN.

A Fellow of Trinity.
The Junior Dean.
Master of St. Benedict's

To His Own Master.
Orchard Damerel.
In the Face of the World.

By R. A. STERNDALE.

The Afghan Knife.

By R. LOUIS STEVENSON.

New Arabian Nights.

By BERTHA THOMAS.

Cressida.
Proud Maisie.

The Violin-Player.

By WALTER THORNBURY.

Tales for the Marines. | Old Stories Retold.

By T. ADOLPHUS TROLLOPE.

Diamond Cut Diamond.

By F. ELEANOR TROLLOPE.

Like Ships upon the
Sea.

Anne Furness.
Mabel's Progress.

By ANTHONY TROLLOPE.

Frau Frohmann.
Marion Fay.
Kept in the Dark.
John Caldigate.
The Way We Live Now.

The Land-Leaguers.
The American Senator
Mr. Scarborough's
Family.
Golden Lion of Granpere

By J. T. TROWBRIDGE.

Farnell's Folly.

By IVAN TURGENIEFF, &c.

Stories from Foreign Novelists.

By MARK TWAIN.

A Pleasure Trip on the
Continent.
The Gilded Age.
Huckleberry Finn.
Mark Twain's Sketches.
Tom Sawyer.
A Tramp Abroad.
Stolen White Elephant.

Life on the Mississippi.
The Prince and the
Pauper.
A Yankee at the Court
of King Arthur.
The £1,000,000 Bank-
Note.

By C. C. FRASER-TYTLER.

Mistress Judith.

By SARAH TYTLER.

The Bride's Pass.
Buried Diamonds.
St. Mungo's City.
Lady Bell.
Noblesse Oblige.
Disappeared.

The Huguenot Family.
The Blackhall Ghosts.
What She Came Through
Beauty and the Beast.
Citoyenne Jaqueline.

By ALLEN UPWARD.

The Queen against Owen. | Prince of Balkitan.

**By AARON WATSON and LILLIAS
WASSERMANN.**

The Marquis of Carabas.

By WILLIAM WESTALL.

Trust-Money.

By Mrs. F. H. WILLIAMSON.

A Child Widow.

By J. S. WINTER.

Cavalry Life. | Regimental Legends.

By H. F. WOOD.

The Passenger from Scotland Yard.
The Englishman of the Rue Cain.

By Lady WOOD.

Sabina.

By CELIA PARKER WOOLLEY

Rachel Armstrong; or, Love and Theology.

By EDMUND YATES.

The Forlorn Hope. | Castaway.
Land at Last.

By I. ZANGWILL.

Ghetto Tragedies.